SUPPLICANT

RESONANCE CRYSTAL LEGACY

Petition

Supplicant

JOIN THE RESONANCE GUILD

Get access to the deleted prequel, *The Resonance Guild*, and other exclusives. No spam and no ads; just regular behind-the-scenes updates about what I'm working on and what I've been reading.

Sign up here: https://www.delilahwaan.com/jointheguild

SUPPLICANT

DELILAH WAAN

Supplicant is the second book in the *Resonance Crystal Legacy* series. It is a work of fiction intended for an adult audience.

Content advisory:
https://www.delilahwaan.com/books/supplicant/#content

A summary of the events preceding this book is available at:
https://www.delilahwaan.com/books/supplicant/#storysofar

Report errors and formatting issues:
https://www.delilahwaan.com/errata/

Copyright © 2024 by Delilah Waan.

First edition published 2024 by Paper Tiger Productions (ABN 30 176 535 485) Mailing address: PO Box 175, Leichhardt NSW 2040, Australia.

ISBN (eBook) 978-0-6455100-3-4
ISBN (Hardcover) 978-0-6455100-5-8
ISBN (Paperback) 978-0-6455100-4-1

All rights reserved. No part of this book may be reproduced in any form or by any electronic or mechanical means, including information storage and retrieval systems, without written permission from the author, except for the use of brief quotations in a book review. Any use of this book to "train" generative artificial intelligence (AI) technologies to generate text, audio, and/or imagery, or to develop machine learning language models is expressly prohibited.

Cover design by Damonza.

Map illustration © Charis Loke.

Printed and bound by IngramSpark.
Australia: Ingram Content Group AU Pty Ltd, Melbourne, Victoria. US: Lightning Source LLC, La Vergne, Tennessee / Allentown, Pennsylvania / Jackson, Tennessee, United States. UK: Lightning Source UK Ltd, Milton Keynes, United Kingdom. Europe: Lightning Source UK Ltd, with facilities in Germany, France, and Spain.

The authorized representative in the European Economic Area is Lightning Source France, 1 Av. Johannes Gutenberg, 78310 Maurepas, France. (email: compliance@lightningsource.fr)

*For those
who are still searching
for their why*

[URGENT CONFIDENTIAL AND PRIVILEGED COMMUNICATION]

AUTHENTICATION REQUESTED:

****

RESONANCE SIGNATURE MATCHED:

ELDER ANATHWAN ISSOLM

DECRYPTING MESSAGE...

****

MESSAGE DECRYPTED.

[SENDER: DEDICATE MAKETH IMOS]

*** ENCRYPTED REPLY REQUESTED ***

Duty compels me to bypass the usual channels and bring to your urgent attention the matters I have uncovered in relation to the Issolm Supplicant known as Rahelu.

Born to Hemoru and Jenura of an unnamed fishing village by Lake Elumaje in Chanaz, she arrived in the Dominion on Petition Day in 525 A.F. and passed the Guild's entrance test on the same day. She was unable to pay the registration fee, but was admitted due to intervention by Lhorne Ideth.

She has declared no Conclave training, but is comfortable with the use and deployment of resonance wards in a manner reminiscent of modern Conclave methods.

Despite unremarkable Guild ratings, Keshwar Ideth sponsored her Petition. His seal was not affixed to the original, but a copy—made with assistance from Xyuth of the Tattered Quill, a known forger. (I note the original was destroyed by Nheras Ilyn.)

She made few acquaintances and no friends while studying at the Guild, yet won the challenges in Petitioning decisively, by way of an unexpected alliance with Lhorne Ideth (again) and Dharyas Isca. Her subsequent Ideth audience extended far beyond the standard time allotted.

When informed her Petition was at an end, she proceeded

directly to Stormbane's Rest, stayed, then returned to the Guild. (I note the duration of her visit matches the duration of the fluctuations in Fortune that House Augurs suspect are traces of an unauthorized act of grand Augury.)

I will not rehash the circumstances in which she was caught accessing the Petitioners' assignment board. But Atriarch Ideth's willingness to vouch for her should be examined further, given the departure during her audience.

Most concerning: she seized the opportunity to investigate the ritual murders in the city—prior to House intelligence connecting them to the Belruonian splinter cult's attempts to open the Endless Gate.

Why?

She may not be a Chanazian operative but she is suspect. Attached are the relevant Evocations obtained from the city guard's records, should you wish to review them in detail.

Direct access node: https://www.delilahwaan.com/books/
supplicant/#storysofar

With respect, I recommend her immediate removal from the mission team.

[MESSAGE ENDS]

*** COMMENCING MESSAGE SELF-DESTRUCT ***

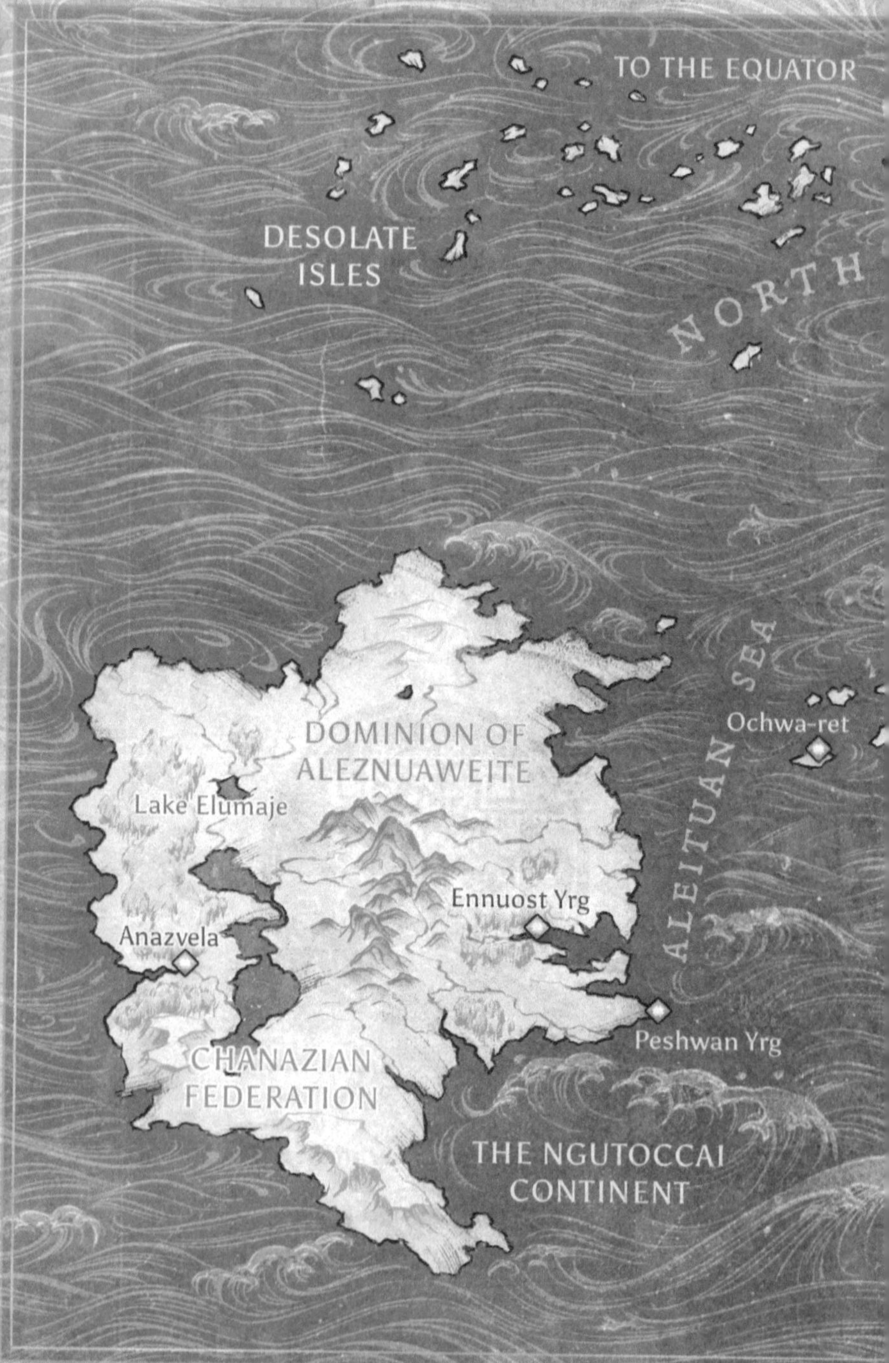

TO THE EQUATOR
DESOLATE ISLES
NORTH
ALEITUAN SEA
Ochwa-ret
DOMINION OF ALEZNUAWEITE
Lake Elumaje
Ennuost Yrg
Anazvela
Peshwan Yrg
CHANAZIAN FEDERATION
THE NGUTOCCAI CONTINENT

DESOLATE ISLES
OCEAN
FREE TERRITORIES OF ABMERDU
DRAGON'S TAIL
DRAGON'S SPINE
Tsorek-fa
ABMERDUAN SEA
DRAGON'S TEETH
DIVINE KINGDOM OF BELRUONIA
TO THE POLE

PROLOGUE: TOLL

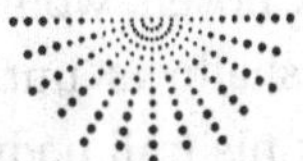

THE 3RD DAY OF TRUESUMMER,
530 A.E./A.F.

Uvesht-mo faltered in the midst of his deepnight prayers.

The stars were ringing.

A chime, a gong, whose round tones were so deep they could not be heard, could not be perceived, except as a thrumming in his bones that shook the very substance of his being until his heart felt like it would burst. Lit sticks of incense fell from his limp fingers to land on the cave floor, their scent smothered by the flurry of damp sand kicked up in his wake.

Outside the sea cave, Uvesht-mo met the Starfather's gaze and wept. Tears of joy and sorrow mingled, pooling in his empty eye sockets before leaking down the wrinkled channels of his face.

Azosh-ek had succeeded.

The Endless Gate was open once more.

Its call was strong, pulling at him until he faced the seat of Enjela's power: the throne between the waves, the door to Fortune's realm, where fate resided. Forged over centuries from the Starfather's blessing with the strength of her will, bound to her blood by eternal bonds of debt, truth, and love.

Then, the heavens had tolled to herald the rise of a new divinity.

Now, the stars would mourn its death.

And Uvesht-mo, who had once been counted amongst the most devout of Enjela's Chosen, would rejoice.

He waded into the shallows until he stood chest-deep, waves drumming against his frail body.

Waited.

And waited.

The tide ebbed and flowed, the sun's warmth rose and fell, but the song of the stars did not cease, as he expected. Neither did it swell, as it would have if Iweth-na had betrayed their cause. Instead, the song went on: melody without counterpoint, legacy without heir, prophecy unfulfilled.

At starrise, Uvesht-mo returned.

He did not gather up the fallen sticks of incense or place freshly lit ones upon the crude stone altar before the driftwood effigy—that he pushed aside, exposing the hollow he had carved into the cave wall behind. Where, long ago, he had buried his faith along with his sacred blade and stargems.

Faith, it seemed, required assistance when it came to dying.

PART I
THE WINGED ARROW

1

DEPARTURE

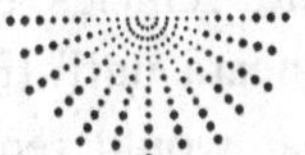

THE 10TH DAY OF TRUESUMMER, 530 A.E./A.F.

RAHELU PELTED THROUGH THE LOWDOCKS.

Though the sun had yet to crest the horizon, the bare stones of the wet market were already slimed with fish guts and seafowl offal (and gods only knew what else) squishing between her toes. A flock of gulls shrilled at her as she tore through their feasting and startled them into flight.

She cursed.

Why were she and Lhorne both such short-sighted, silly, sentimental fools?

Stupid of him to come look for her and then fall into the sea. And stupid of her to linger in the inn room beside him as he slept.

Now she was going to be fucking *late*.

Rahelu berated herself for her lack of good sense and boots and the fierce, resonance-backlash-induced headache that had reasserted itself as soon as she joined the sleep- and hangover-befuddled sailors stumbling out of the dockside taverns. She elbowed and shouldered her way through the press of bodies crowding onto the streets. In turn, the owners of those bodies expressed their appreciation with like endearments: every toe she trod on was answered with blows hard enough to leave glancing bruises, and every shout of "Excuse me!" brought down ill-wishing upon her ancestors and her progeny.

She wanted to scream at all these idiots who couldn't seem to remember the basic traveler's courtesies that required pedestrians and vehicles to keep left and punch every single unnomobunezra until they learned to scramble out of her way. But that would require her to release the hand clutching her coin purse (at which point she might as well toss it to any one of the half dozen pickpockets who had rubbed up against her to check if she had anything worth stealing) or to take her other hand off the heirloom resonance crystal pendant—a priceless focus stone worth a House-born's ransom!—that Lhorne had hung around her neck and called a gift.

Damn his grand gesture of friendship to the fourth hell.

And damn her traitorous heart and its thrilling too.

It's not too late to change your mind, whispered that weak-willed part of her, still echoing his arguments from the previous night. *You could return to the Sable Gull; admit that he spoke wisdom. Go with him before his Atriarch. Hold Mere Ideth to the personal favor she owes you and ask her to match Elder Anathwan's offer.*

She could walk away from her oaths to House Issolm and their contract. Never set foot or sights on the *Winged Arrow*, the ship that Elder Anathwan and her handpicked team had boarded, the ship that Lhorne had said would send her to die on a suicide mission at the other end of the world.

She could even swear to Ideth—without returning House Issolm's signing bonus. Unconditional was unconditional.

But if she did, what would that make her?

The very Issolm kind of lucre-blinded, coin-grasping, mercenary opportunist he so clearly despised.

No; worse.

It would make her like Nheras of Ilyn: a boot-licking, jumped-up, fawning society climber without principles clinging onto the hem of Ideth's robes in hopes of borrowing someone else's wealth and influence to rise higher than she deserved.

Rahelu had calculated what her oaths would cost when she had sworn them.

She had made a good trade.

Doubts newly silenced, Rahelu redoubled her efforts.

She wished the Earthgiver had blessed her with a stouter, taller frame so people would have to dart around her instead of the reverse; wished the Exalted Dominance and his Royal Council cared enough to fix the shitty, unpaved roads on this side of the city; wished that the Isonn live fish haulers didn't use such ungainly heavy handcarts that took up the breadth of the main thoroughfare in and out of the Lowdocks. The thunderous *thud* and *clatter* of wheels and empty barrels juddering down each treacherous step of the north stair made her teeth ache in sympathy.

It was not even full light and the first accident of the day had already occurred. One of the live fish haulers had lost control of his handcart when its wheel pin had shaken loose. Now it lay tipped over on its side at the foot of the stair, its ropes frayed, half its barrels smashed, with its driver desperately trying to right the wreckage while the rest of the Lowdocks ran roughshod over the means of his livelihood, too intent on their own survival to heed his pleas.

On any other day, she would go back and help.

But not today.

Today, she had a ship to catch. Her family's future depended on her getting on the *Winged Arrow*.

Rahelu quashed her internal twinge of guilt as she forced her way up the stair against the flow of traffic by darting through every visible gap no matter how narrow or precarious, and the crowd soon found a new target for their irritation. They seared her ears with their cussing and their collective untrained Projections made the ambient resonance glow bright enough to rival the rising sun.

When she tried to fend them off with a basic Obfuscation barrier, she felt like someone had taken a pickax to her skull.

Eight hells.

The two of them had been so fucking stupid.

"Get out of the way, you lazy Chanazian ghelik!" snarled another live fish hauler, when Rahelu's latest attempt at dodging someone else's mistimed push caused her to collide with his broad back and knocked him into his cart. He threw her off with a vicious shrug. "Are you so slant-eyed that you can't see where you're going?"

Anger seethed at the familiar slurs; urged her to lash out with a nice, demonstrative dose of what a graduated Guild-trained mage could do with a little bit of rage and five years of learning how to shape and wield emotions as weapons. Not only would that shut him up, he and everybody within eyeshot would drop straight to their knees to start kissing the muck at her feet. Then all those stupid handcarts would trundle themselves off the stair and she would have a beautifully clear path.

Gods.

Her first day as a House-sworn Supplicant and she was already fantasizing about using her power to push other people around simply because they inconvenienced her—when the reason for that inconvenience was her own fault for being a damned fool in the first place.

Rahelu swallowed the live fish hauler's insults, her rage, and the crowd's ire at them both for jamming the busiest thoroughfare in all of Ennuost Yrg during the last span before dawn.

"I'm sorry, uncle," she responded in fluent, near-accent-less Aleznuaweithish. "I apologize for my lack of consideration."

She bowed, then pulled out a handful of coins, because the gleam of genuine silver was more eloquent and went farther than any apology.

"Please." She gestured to the fallen cart and its driver. Forty silver kez couldn't cure the world's ills, but it could fix this. "I would be grateful if you and a few of your fellow workers could help him clear the way."

In less than a hundred-count, the cart was up, traffic was flowing, and she was through the Oldgate.

Rahelu turned north onto the wide, elegant boardwalk along the shore and began sprinting in earnest.

Dawn arrived softly in the Highdocks, like the lighting of a candle. Melodic trills—not raucous *keows*—greeted the first golden rays of the Skymother's lamp as they revealed flashes of brilliant blue and deep crimson plumage flitting through the lush green foliage of the parklands to her left. But not for long. The tiny birds were so easily spooked that the rapid drumming of her bare feet against smooth cedar boards abruptly silenced their song. They fled in a frenetic flurry of beating wings, leaving Rahelu alone with the too-loud in-and-out rasping of her breath and a growing sense of dread.

Three hundred strides away, at the very end of the fifth pier, a sleek, sun-gilded courier ship unfurled its brilliant white sails like a gull shaking its wings. Its crew rushed hither and thither, hoisting sails, stowing cargo and luggage, and guiding passengers to the cabins below while a pair of clerks wrestled a large crate of scrolls down the gangplank.

Port officials. The ones who oversaw departure and authenticated the ship's manifests.

Panic jolted through Rahelu; the uncontrolled emotion burst past the thick, spiraling lines of the blood-and-ash resonance ward she had hastily drawn over her heart. Pale orange sparks crackled in her resonance aura as she flew down the pier, feverishly hoping that, somehow, if she willed it hard enough, the extra speed lent by true desperation would also vanish the remaining distance.

Rahelu stopped squinting against the brightening sky.

Ceased measuring her progress in quantities such as the number of planks blurring beneath her feet or the strides that separated her from the three-masted silhouette.

There was only the raw, metallic taste of iron in the back of her windpipe, the burn of thigh and calf muscles stretching, the sharp, stabbing sensation of cracked soles smacking against hard surfaces as her feet began to bleed despite her thick calluses.

Everything hurt.

But if she could still think, she wasn't truly hurting or running fast enough. If her name had already been struck from the passenger lists...

Rahelu put her head down and *ran*.

Heart in her throat, breath shredding her lungs, she cried into the wind: "Wait!"

Her plea went unheard. Drowned out by the crew's steady work chant as they secured the anchor. On the bridge, the captain signaled for his crew to cast off. Mooring lines whistled through the air as the gangplank swiftly retracted and the captain stepped up to the wheel.

Rahelu abandoned ordinary speech to muster the most focused Projection she could:

WAIT!

The captain set his hands to the ship's wheel. Layers upon layers of Obfuscation barriers as thick and solid as the city's walls surrounded the *Winged Arrow*. Her Projection rebounded off the shield with no one aboard the wiser.

True to its namesake, the ship sprang into motion with a *snap* of taut canvas and tensioned ropes.

And one hundred and twenty-five gold kez—coin that would lift Rahelu's family out of their miserable existence in the Lowdocks and let them lead better lives elsewhere—evaporated before her eyes.

No!

The end of the gangplank still dangled out over the water. One—no, two—three strides from the edge of the pier.

She could still make it.

"Hey!" yelped the clerk in House Issolm's white-and-black livery as she barreled straight through the pair of port officials. "What do you think you're doing? That ship is—"

"Wait, please!" she shouted again. A deckhand looked up as Rahelu gathered herself and leapt.

The ship surged.

Her outstretched fingers met nothing but air.

And Rahelu plummeted into the shallows.

BY THE TIME the crew fished her out of the Kuath Bay, the *Winged Arrow* was well underway and Rahelu was half-drowned from being dragged in the ship's wake.

"Easy, lass," murmured the Isonn deckhand who had tossed her the long line. He slapped her on the back repeatedly as she flopped around in a futile effort to control her shaking limbs. "Don't try standing just yet, not after a dive like that." His unguarded resonance aura hummed with amusement that was the same shade and gentle warmth of the newly risen sun. "Y'need to get the seawater out of yer lungs first."

Rahelu coughed. What felt like half the ocean spewed out of her mouth and nose in foam-flecked runnels onto the immaculate deck. She got on all fours and shook her head rapidly to clear stinging eyes and waterlogged ears. While her vision remained clouded and her hearing muffled, her resonance senses had no trouble tracking the concentrated auras of the two senior mages descending from the bridge.

The first must be the captain's: a copper-and-cobalt presence with the deep, abiding stillness of a mountain.

The second was like marble the shade of thunderclouds, with a tracery of ruddy lightning shimmering beneath. And eerily familiar.

Rahelu looked up.

Her eyes were drawn past the captain—a lean, well-muscled Seeker clad in the forest-green tunic and tan trousers of House Isonn—to the swirl of white-and-yellow robes trailing him.

The second mage wore a gleaming golden armband on his left arm with a Guardian's triple peak sigil burned into the leather. His stern face, with its thick eyebrows, looked as though it had been carved out of granite.

Dedicate Maketh of House Imos.

Her insides went cold.

While her rescuer stood to bow, Rahelu immediately flattened herself again—palms down; forehead, nose, and lips pressed into the wood in the best obeisance she could manage—and her mind started frantically rehearsing explanations.

"What do we have here, Kerg?" The Seeker-captain's voice was light; his tone mild but his words were firm. "I thought I had made it quite clear that stowaways will not be tolerated aboard my ship."

Kerg hesitated, then bent even lower. "Captain Csorath, I—"

Since this situation was entirely of Rahelu's making, any

blame should fall on her alone. "Honorable Captain," she said. "I am Rahelu of—"

"Chanaz," Dedicate Maketh cut in as he loomed over her.

Chanaz? Chanaz?!

She had lived in Ennuost Yrg for five fucking years. She was more literate in Aleznuaweithish than her native Chanazian, yet people still assumed otherwise just by the cast of her features.

Rahelu didn't dare straighten her body. Supplicant or not, disrespecting a Dedicate would guarantee her a severe punishment, like a speedy voyage to the bottom of the Aleituan Sea. But she couldn't resist raising her head slightly off the deck as she corrected the record. "Formerly of Chanaz."

All three men stiffened at her presumption.

Shit.

She made an effort to control her emotions and put a proper, respectful tone into her voice.

"Then of Aleznuaweite. From the twenty-second day of early summer in the five hundred and twenty-fifth year after Founding as per the Dominion's migration registry records. Most recently of the Lowdocks, as per the last census undertaken by the Houses, and—effective yesterday—of House Issolm."

The temptation to take her eyes off the two senior mages' polished boots was too great so Rahelu plastered her forehead to the deck again.

"I beg the captain's forgiveness for my lateness. Traffic through Oldgate was blocked due to a handcart accident in the last span before dawn."

"Ah," Csorath said. "Our missing Supplicant."

A gossamer cloud of resonance drifted over from the Isonn captain towards Rahelu. Her skin tingled as his

Seeking swept through her aura, verifying the truth of her account.

"Welcome aboard the *Winged Arrow*, Rahelu of Issolm," Csorath said. "You'll find your fellow Supplicants settling in below. My third mate, Kerg, will direct you to your cabin so you can do likewise. You've a half-span while we get underway before Elder Anathwan expects your attendance at the mission briefing in the great cabin."

Relieved, Rahelu rose on shaky legs. When Kerg bowed to the captain again, she followed suit. Csorath nodded and headed aft but Guardian Maketh stayed where he was, pinning her in place with his scowl.

"This girl was not present for our pre-boarding inspections," Maketh called after the captain's retreating back. "Allowing her to remain goes against mission protocols."

Eight hells.

Just what, exactly, was the Imos Dedicate's problem? He had been curt when forced to induct her as a Petitioner but his subsequent manner as he had overseen the rest of her Petitioning had been professional, if deliberately cold and distant.

Could he be petty enough to hold a grudge against her because he had been overruled?

Rahelu breathed.

Counted to three—slowly—as she visualized the mirror-smooth, blue-gray surface of the Elumaje beneath a clear harvest sky and forced herself to unclench her jaw.

"A technicality," Csorath said while she wrestled her resonance aura into submission. "Supplicant Rahelu was a handful of heartbeats late, delayed by circumstances outside of her control."

"Her presence poses a security risk," Maketh countered, undeterred. "Particularly given the sensitive nature of our joint mission."

Rahelu's mouth went dry as she grasped his unspoken accusation. Though Atriarch Mere Ideth had vouched for her innocence, Maketh remained convinced that she was a Chanazian spy.

Fortunately, Csorath overrode Maketh's objection with a wave of his hand. "Based on my Seeking, I am satisfied she poses no such risk."

"Nevertheless, Dedicate, I strongly advise that we remove her with all haste."

Maketh's choice to address the captain by House rank instead of title—and his ever-so-slight emphasis to stress their equal footing—halted Csorath in his tracks.

"Guardian Maketh, if you question my assessment as a Seeker, I suggest you make your reservations known to Elder Anathwan."

The Dedicates' voices remained pleasant and courteous; their auras undisturbed. No wisp of stray resonance escaped their iron control. Yet the ambient resonance between the two senior mages seemed to crackle with some invisible charge.

"If the Elder deems your arguments to hold merit," the captain continued, "I will remove Supplicant Rahelu with all haste myself. Until then, I have a ship to sail."

Maketh's scowl deepened.

Csorath shifted his attention to Rahelu. "I've not seen anyone dare try for a flight like that in years."

"I—"

Surprise scrambled her reply when she realized the Isonn Dedicate had spoken to her in fluent Chanazian. He must have benefited from an excellent tutor. Csorath rounded off his consonants like someone who hailed from Anazvela, though he spoke her language as an Aleznuaweite would: he had used *'eheli'*—a word that encompassed how birds gifted with the ability to fly belonged in the air—instead of *'ohel'* or '*ahel*', which expressed how earthbound creatures or water dwellers struggled when they dared venture into the Skymother's realm.

Rahelu covered her lapse with another bow, thinking fast.

Courtesy dictated that she answer in Aleznuaweithish.

But Captain Csorath had paid her a great compliment by speaking the language of her heart, and pandering to Maketh's prejudices would not prove him wrong, so courtesy could go to the fifth hell.

One's ancestral homeland and birth language did not determine their loyalties, and she was not ashamed of her heritage.

"Captain, you are very kind to excuse my lateness," Rahelu said in Chanazian. "Next time, I will depart earlier instead of trying to grow wings."

Csorath's lips twitched with a hint of a smile. "Next time," he said, switching back to Aleznuaweithish as if he hadn't purposefully excluded Maketh from their exchange, "mind the motion of the waves when you jump."

"Aye, captain."

Csorath jerked his chin in dismissal.

She backed off with a final bow as the captain turned on his heel and Kerg murmured hasty directions to the Supplicants' cabins before the third mate, too, left to go about his own duties.

Maketh Imos made no further move to stop her as she wobbled over to the starboard rail, though his baleful glare remained glued to her back when she lingered there.

His opinion doesn't matter, Rahelu told herself, trying to ignore his scrutiny.

Let Maketh go and pour his grievances into the Elder's ear. Out of all the successful Petitioners Anathwan could have chosen, she had chosen Rahelu. As long as she drew no further attention to herself and gave Anathwan no reason to be displeased with her, Maketh could not touch her, just as he had not been able to stop her from Petitioning.

She looked steadily westward at the shrinking view of Ennuost Yrg. They were well clear of the harbor, the *Winged Arrow* having sailed past the Isonn fishing fleet and into the Kuath Bay proper. The individual boats were as minuscule as scattered grains of rice. Here, out on the open waters, there was hardly any ambient resonance for few sapient beings lived on the surface and the ship's constant motion meant they never lingered in one spot long enough for resonance to accumulate.

Silly to think she might be able to pick out the patched gray sail and plodding lines of her parents' sloop at this distance. And yet, Rahelu kept straining her eyes. A swift, sharp motion in the eartharc light—a large net being cast—drew her gaze.

A smaller vessel with two figures aboard.

She couldn't be sure, but she thought one looked like her mother, so she waved. It felt right to do so, even if they couldn't see her, and even if they weren't her parents.

Rahelu breathed, filling her lungs with the clean scent of the sea. Wind teased at her hair. Tension thawed from her neck and shoulders, and the racing beat that had been pounding away in her head and heart quieted.

Guardian Maketh had retreated to what must be the senior mages' private cabins at the stern. The cabin adjacent to his contained a powerful presence that radiated warmth like a hearth fire: Elder Anathwan, whose resonance aura shone a green-tinged gold, like the waters stretching towards the fading shoreline.

Nearer to amidships were the smaller auras of her peers. The first and second sat still: tight muffled knots of iceflower-pale frisson clustered so close together Rahelu nearly mistook them for a single presence. The third and fourth—fizzing orange-anticipation lagged by a sullen rain cloud glowing a hot coal-red—sped in her direction.

Great.

You made it!

Rahelu flinched as the shrieking Projection shredded at her hard-won calm. The high-pitched noise emanating from the open hatch rapidly gained in volume and resolved into a piercing squeal.

"Gods in the four heavens!" Elaram of Issolm skidded to a stop to take in her bedraggled appearance, then whistled. "You look like a total disaster."

There was no malice in that greeting, only a giddy exuberance. Rahelu eyed Elaram in return and got the distinct feeling that if she wasn't so thoroughly sea-soaked and the other girl's right arm wasn't still in a sling, she would have been bowled off her feet by a cloyingly enthusiastic hug.

"You should have seen the look on everybody's faces when they realized you were going to jump." Elaram chortled. "I can't believe Isonn had to fish you out of the sea! Now *that's* what I call an entrance."

Another Issolm Supplicant stalked up to them, dressed in a blinding white tunic ironed and pressed so stiff that its collar and folds stood out, sharp as a knife edge.

Rahelu grimaced.

Ghardon of Issolm was not impressed by her entrance; he was livid.

So livid that he bypassed common pleasantries such as 'hello, Rahelu' and his usual compliments of *'you look and smell like a mangy half-starved alleycat that accidentally fell into a pile of dirty dishrags after they've been used to mop up the floor of a fourth-rate tavern'* in favor of yanking her below.

Rahelu went.

She chose not to remark on his seasick pallor and unsteady gait, or the trembling fingers digging into her bicep, because she was ardently grateful that he had not seized her ear.

"Where," Ghardon hissed, "in the eight hells have you been?"

"Brother, dear, that's not the question we should be asking. Whoa!" Elaram said as the next wave caused her to lose her footing on the companionway. She threw out her good arm and twisted to land on her feet, adroit as a cat. Then she sidled forward as if she hadn't almost knocked herself unconscious and hooked Rahelu by the elbow. "The better, more *interesting* question is, what kept you so occupied? Oooooooooooorrrrrrrrr," Elaram's voice dropped into a purr, "should I say, *who*?"

Since her new brother and sister hadn't bothered with any of the time-honored, customary greetings used to welcome a newly sworn Supplicant to a House, Rahelu also dispensed with formalities.

"None of your business."

"Actually, what you do is very much our business." Ghardon paused to make sure he had her full attention before he over-enunciated his next words: "Rahelu of Issolm."

Gods.

Elaram's eager prying was to be expected but she did not need Ghardon adding his misguided sense of House-born responsibility to the mix.

"I don't see how," Rahelu said, as they propelled her towards the Supplicants' cabins. "Nowhere in my oaths of Supplication did I swear to give up my right to privacy."

Ghardon rolled his eyes. "Must I spell it out? You bear our name now. What you do and how you conduct yourself reflects upon all of us."

"Come now, brother," Elaram said. "No need to sound off on the rules and regulations; Anathwan is occupied elsewhere. Besides, I'm sure Rahelu has *excellent* reasons for being late. Reasons completely unrelated to her absence from the Ideth party last night, Lhorne Ideth leaving the celebration early—one that he organized himself, no less—and Nheras Ilyn sniffling to herself in a pavilion." To Rahelu: "You can enlighten us while we help you get cleaned up."

Rahelu had no such reasons, but nothing short of torture would get her to divulge that fact. Nor did she intend to let them discover she now wore Lhorne's pendant around her neck; they would certainly infer all sorts of things from it and she did not need that kind of distraction.

What she needed was an uninterrupted quarter-span to herself inside her cabin. Soon as she could, she would switch the pendant for the standard issue resonance crystal ring House Issolm had included as part of outfitting her for this mission and stash the priceless Ideth heirloom somewhere safe.

"I assure you both that I am fully capable of dressing myself," she retorted. "Besides, we were chosen for our resonance skills, not our looks. I doubt the Elder will weigh our appearances too heavily in our performance evaluations, so what does it matter? I'm here, aren't I?"

"You're here and you stink of Lowdocks filth," Ghardon said. "I refuse to let you dishonor our House further."

That was it.

She might have to bow and scrape before a Dedicate like Maketh, but she was a Supplicant now and sworn to a House herself: she did not have to take this kind of shit from House-born any longer.

Rahelu wrenched at her pinioned arms, but Ghardon and Elaram anticipated her. In one coordinated move, they shoved her to the port side of the passageway. Which should have ended with her shoulders pinned against the bulkhead

—except they weren't prepared for the deck to roll beneath their feet.

Rahelu was.

But she was still dizzy and weak from her involuntary dip in the Kuath Bay, so when the Issolm siblings stumbled, they took her down too, and the three of them half-slid, half-crashed through the door to the first of the Supplicants' cabins.

"Well, this is pleasant," drawled a male voice as they tried to disentangle themselves. "I do so enjoy the sight of admirers desperate enough to throw themselves at my feet that they barge into my bedchamber uninvited."

Everything about the black-haired Supplicant lounging on the lower bunk screamed *so rich that I have no understanding of cost*.

Case in point: his shirt. Golden sigils of power and strength had been woven into—not painted on—the fine white silk, which had then been embroidered until there was more dazzling resonance crystal beadwork than cloth. A masterwork nobody, except for the Atriarchs and the heirs to the four major Houses, could afford.

And he had deliberately cut off the sleeves on that beautiful extravagance to flaunt the ritualistic scars that wound up his arms, around his collarbones, and down his chest.

Ugh.

At least the wasteful display told Rahelu who he was: the strutting ishtrel whose biceps Elaram was so enamored of.

Ylem of Imos. Or was it Ilhaen? Ynan?

Whatever.

No-sleeves would do.

Disgust must have shown in her face if not her resonance aura, because his gaze flicked away from Elaram and skipped over Ghardon to land on her.

"Especially," No-sleeves added as he regarded her with half-lidded eyes, "when they show up this wet."

Coal-black leather boots—polished to a shine that almost eclipsed the gleam of the gaudy, solid gold buckles—swung off the bunk and thudded onto the cabin sole. He sat up and leaned forward, elbows on spread knees, eyes roving up and down her body.

"Hello, love." His suggestive, proprietary smile was infuriating. "I don't believe we've met."

Her suppressed irritation simmered over into a bubbling anger that stained the ambient resonance red. If he wanted an introduction, Rahelu would happily oblige by introducing her belt knife to his foot, just to see if that might wipe the leer off the insufferable prick's face.

At the first twitch of her fingers, Ghardon hauled her back by her collar and Elaram wriggled free to scoot up to No-sleeves.

"That's because Rahelu has had no interest in meeting you." Elaram draped her good arm on No-sleeves's thigh, propped her chin in her hand, and said, "You're just..." She wrinkled her nose and pursed her lips while she gave him back the same scan of appraisal he had inflicted on Rahelu. "I'm sorry, Ylaen—"

Oh, Ylaen. That was his name. Rahelu promptly discarded her knowledge of it; No-sleeves suited him better.

"—but there's really no other way of putting it: you're just not very *memorable*." Elaram patted him on the cheek. "Don't take it personally, dear," she continued breezily. "Rahelu's like that with everyone. But pouting does endow you with a certain—"

"Rahelu is also unwell," Ghardon interjected. "Excuse us."

No-sleeves shrugged and resettled himself against his pillows, the picture of languid ease. "By all means. We are going on a long voyage. There will undoubtedly be many opportunities for us to become…memorable to one another."

That was their cue to leave.

Elaram, however, took it as an invitation and crawled into his bed.

The last thing Rahelu saw as she allowed Ghardon to drag her away was No-sleeves glowering at Elaram, who ignored him entirely in favor of crawling over to someone else Rahelu had overlooked: another Supplicant, sitting with his knees up at the opposite end of the lower bunk scribbling into a notebook. The slight, wiry boy was so quiet and unassuming that he had managed to blend into the shadows despite wearing the bright orange and white colors of House Imrell.

"Jhobon!" Elaram's syrupy coo floated out after Rahelu and Ghardon into the passageway. "What in the four heavens are you doing that's sooooooooooo fascinating it made you forget to say hello? Let me—"

Ghardon hustled Rahelu inside the third cabin (hers, she assumed) and dropped her unceremoniously.

Wonderful.

Rahelu let herself sprawl in a soggy puddle. The panic and anger that had sustained her were gone; only exhaustion and pain—in all their varieties—remained. Aching limbs that refused to stop shaking. Throbbing feet that had left smears of blood over the sole of the otherwise pristine cabin. And the driving, unrelenting pressure behind her eyeballs of severe resonance backlash.

She squeezed her eyes shut.

There was perhaps a quarter-span left before they were due to attend the Elder's briefing and she was going to spend most of it resting. The moment Ghardon dared open his mouth to lecture her further, she would let loose with every curse she had bitten back since waking up and not be sorry for whatever damage she did to his ego in the slightest.

No lecture came.

Ghardon stalked out and didn't even bother to slam the door.

Rahelu rolled over and stuck her head into the passageway. "Aren't you going to—"

"Figure it out for yourself. Elder Anathwan is expecting me."

He disappeared into the second cabin and slammed that door instead. Of course, now that she had encouraged him to speak, he wouldn't shut up. The bulkhead between their cabins muffled his voice, but his words were perfectly decipherable thanks to his crisp diction.

"I trust," he said, with so much sarcasm she could feel it oozing through the gaps in the planking, "that you were not lying when you claimed to be capable of washing and dressing yourself to a degree acceptable to respectable society, historical and current evidence notwithstanding."

When he reemerged in the middle of buttoning a fresh tunic and found she still hadn't moved, he raked her with an ominous look.

"Do you need to be changed, like an infant?"

"Please, Ghardon," she whispered. "Don't. I will get cleaned up. To your standards, I promise. Just..." She closed her eyes again. "Just give me a moment."

It felt so *good* to simply lie here, breathing.

A long pause, followed by a sigh, then the soft *thunk* of the wooden door against its jamb.

Thank you, she sent.

The only reply she got was the sound of his receding footsteps blending into the gentle *slap* of waves washing up against the ship's hull. Rahelu counted them out of habit, letting the monotonous rhythm and the familiar rocking motions of the ship soothe her as she reviewed and reordered her priorities.

Finding a secure hiding place for Lhorne's pendant would have to wait.

Rahelu gave herself another hundred heartbeats, then mustered the necessary will to keep her most recent promise. Groaned. Every muscle protested as she forced herself vertical and tried to loosen gummed-up eyelids. Eventually, she opened them to behold utter luxury.

A polished rosewood desk with four drawers directly opposite the door. Above the desk was a porthole the size of her head, with a round, thick, glass—glass!—window that was currently open to allow the light and fresh sea breeze in and permit a tiny glimpse of the sky.

To her left was the sleeping area: two bunks built into the aft bulkhead with privacy curtains of silk.

To her right was the dressing area: two wooden trunks lined up against the forward bulkhead. The wall niche above held several bookshelves and a small weapons rack. All empty, apart from Rahelu's spear and net, which had been neatly stowed.

The cabin even boasted a private washstand tucked between the desk and the trunks, so she wouldn't have to search out the common wash facilities. The basin of beaten copper was engraved inside and out with swirling waves and lucky carp. The jug next to it stood ready by a little cake of sandalwood soap, filled to the brim with fresh water.

Fresh water! For washing! At sea! The sheer indulgence would have been revolting if it didn't taste so sweet. But it paled in comparison to the chamber pot, which was made of painted porcelain instead of cheap clay.

No wonder House-born were so fucking precious. Who wouldn't be if you were accustomed to *porcelain* kissing your ass whenever you needed to piss or take a shit?

Everywhere she looked, her cabinmate had left markers to stake their claims on the shared space.

A drawn privacy curtain proclaimed the lower bunk taken, relegating her to the upper bunk with its non-existent headroom.

A hand mirror of polished silver, several pots of cosmetics, two makeup brushes, an assortment of perfume vials, a small lacquered jewelry box painted with willows and larks, and a pale jade comb occupied every drawer in the desk, leaving no room for Rahelu's personal possessions.

Not that she owned anything besides the pendant Lhorne had gifted her and the sodden clothes she wore. But the cabin was assigned to two Supplicants, not one, so she was entitled to half of the space, and if she chose to do nothing with all that space, that was her House-given right. She didn't have to cede it to some dainty House-born who packed for a mission like it was a pleasure cruise.

Rahelu stewed as she stripped and left her sea-soaked clothes heaped in the middle of the cabin. She took very little care as she doused her head with what she hadn't drank then lathered up and rinsed over the basin, deriving a great deal of perverse pleasure at leaving the shiny copper surface marred with black flecks of Lowdocks grit and yellow-gray soap scum as she wrung out wet hair.

Her cabinmate could have the lower bunk and the drawers for their frivolities. Rahelu would assert her existence in other ways.

Though her cabinmate had designated everything else in the cabin as *'mine'* or *'yours'*, they had not added any decorative flourishes or other markings to either of the trunks. Both were identical in every respect—made of plain, resin-sealed white oak with House Issolm's sigil burned into the lid.

Rahelu had no way of distinguishing which was hers, so she opened the nearest one.

Formal robes and shirts, silk stockings and ribbons, jeweled hair pins and beaded headdresses (all in some variation of Issolm white-and-black) flew through the air by the handful in her quest to locate a dress tunic, trousers, and polished leather boots that matched Ghardon and Elaram's, and some underclothes that weren't embroidered to a ridiculous degree.

Hurriedly, she pulled on her new clothes (which were a size too big and had too many fucking tiny buttons that took too fucking long to do) over her still-damp skin. Her feet had stopped bleeding but she would have to step carefully in her new boots (and not think about the very expensive pair she had spent ten days breaking in and then abandoned on a boulder by the Lowdocks) so she left them off for now and raided the drawers for her cabinmate's hand mirror and jade comb.

Since the loops and twists of the complicated braids crowning Elaram's head today were beyond her, Rahelu summoned a week-old Evocation. Pushing through the resonance backlash drove her cross-eyed with pain so she had to use Evocation sparingly, which further hampered her efforts. Horror dawned halfway through her attempt to copy the simpler hairstyle Elaram had worn during Petitioning: the collar reflected in the hand mirror did not match the one in her Evocation. There was some sort of cross between an undershirt and an inner robe that was supposed to go under the tunic so its silver-stitched collar would peek out and contrast with the tunic's black trim.

"Fuck!"

Rahelu hurled one of the boots at the door.

Both Evocation and her attempted braid fell apart.

She had to strip and start over.

Just as she threw the jade comb down in a fit and decided nobody other than Ghardon would die if she kept her hair loose since she could not, apparently, apply the same technique she used on rigging to braid hair and expect a result that resembled Elaram's coiffure, she sensed a new, strained green-glass aura wending its way through the passageway that led from Elder Anathwan's quarters to the Supplicants' cabins.

The newcomer's aura was muted, thanks to a partial Obfuscation barrier, but Rahelu was skilled enough at Seeking that she could slip past to detect a resonance signature she would have recognized earlier, had it not been dwarfed by the Elder's formidable presence.

Eight hells.

She hastily shoved everything back where she had found it, then grabbed her boots and took a seat on her trunk. There was no mistaking that combination of steely determination and haughty disdain for anybody else—nor was there any other plausible destination for the sixth Supplicant aboard the *Winged Arrow* besides the cabin she currently occupied.

Nevertheless, Rahelu kept hoping she was mistaken, up until the very moment the door swung open to admit her cabinmate.

Nheras of Ilyn.

2

ACCOMMODATION

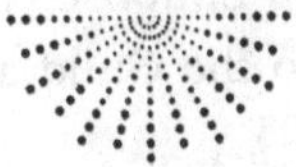

NHERAS SWEPT A COOL GLANCE AROUND THEIR shared cabin.

Surprise spiked through Rahelu's aura at the sight of the Ilyn girl dressed *exactly* alike—in a neatly pressed, tailored uniform of somber Issolm white-and-black.

They had sworn to the same House?

Why would Nheras swear to any House but her grandmother's?

Rahelu repressed the reflexive impulse to duck her head (she had every right to be here) and smooth over the rumpled folds of her stolen uniform (no wonder it didn't fit!) and braced for conflict.

But the other Supplicant simply brushed past Rahelu and stepped over the pile of her wet discarded clothing—without acknowledging either existed—to sit at the desk.

Rahelu waited.

Bright eartharc sun shining through the porthole gilded Nheras's carefully coiffed dark brown curls a soft gold to match her jewelry. She took out her cosmetics and makeup brushes and began to arrange them to her liking.

Nothing? That was strange.

Rahelu studied her cabinmate out of the corner of her eye while she finished lacing her boots.

She and Nheras had never been in such close quarters without one of them initiating verbal hostilities or trying to beat the other into the ground. For five years—ever since the day Rahelu had arrived in Ennuost Yrg—the two of them had fought over her worth to the Guild and her right to Petition the Houses, and now?

Nheras had lost. Rahelu had won.

And everyone knew it.

Perhaps it was not so strange for her cabinmate to say nothing and stare into her hand mirror. Nheras's face was a smooth, doll-like mask; her classically beautiful features strategically highlighted with powder, rouge, and painted lips. Her eyes, though, were reddened and ringed with dark circles, and her resonance aura unsettled: lurking beneath the ever-present disdain and determination were clear traces of caution, envy, and disbelief.

They were equals now. Sisters, in fact.

Perhaps it was time to begin anew.

"Supplicant Nheras." Rahelu paused. What could she say that would ring true without insulting Ilyn pride? "Can we agree that it's past time to let go of our childhood grudge?"

Nheras made no response.

That irked Rahelu, but an enmity that had been as all-consuming as theirs wasn't something that could be erased overnight. If she had lost, she would not have been able to sit here, breathing the same air as her triumphant rival, poise and dignity intact in defeat.

Ignoring her was probably Nheras's way of being graceful.

Fine.

She, too, could be graceful in victory. Rahelu rose and turned to go, but Nheras's words arrested her at the door.

"I should have burned your Petition."

Rahelu counted to ten before she responded. "You had your chance."

"I had many chances," Nheras acknowledged as she reached for her hand mirror. "And each time, I chose restraint, against counsel, thinking that you would eventually see reason."

Possible futures Rahelu had glimpsed but once threatened to manifest in the air between them: *her father a frail, handless beggar; lifeblood draining from her wrists before a shadowed spire; a white-and-black cord that strangled all personal honor and compassion.*

Rahelu suppressed her half-remembered Augury with an effort of will. "You humiliated me in front of half the city as you destroyed my Petition. You extorted a House-born's ransom from me in exchange for my father's wellbeing and my family's livelihood."

The other girl heard the accusations with equanimity; her previously turbulent aura had settled into a soft sheen of quicksilver. "I was trying to do you a kindness."

Rahelu stared.

There had been a few constants in her life. A lack of coin. A lack of time. A lack of friends. A friend would have been nice, but she would have been content spending all five years of her Guild training alone, unremarked and unpersecuted.

But Nheras had made that impossible.

"I don't think you understand what kindness is."

"Think what you like. I don't expect a fish that insists on leaping onto land to know the difference between water and air."

Rahelu frowned.

Had Nheras ever ignored an insult from her, however slight? If there had been such an occurrence, she couldn't recall it. Nheras had always made Rahelu the target of her cutting, pointed reminders: her inherent inferiority; her foreign origins—all designed to make her an object of ridicule to everybody watching.

But right now, nobody was watching.

Nobody except Rahelu and Nheras herself.

The Ilyn girl's eyes were distant as she contemplated her reflection: painted lips drawn and brow slightly wrinkled. She looked troubled, and not by her cabinmate.

Somehow, that was what rekindled her outrage, more than anything Nheras could have said or done.

Rahelu had always taken for granted that they bore each other equal hatred—that, whenever she had gone to sleep, nursing bruises to her body and ego along with revenge fantasies, Nheras had spent the same amount of time delighting in how she had brought her low.

The realization she was but an afterthought to Nheras Ilyn, that none of the blows she'd struck had ever occupied Nheras's thoughts beyond the moment of confrontation, the idea that her best efforts and she herself were insignificant, that the victory she had worked so hard to achieve was irrelevant...

Rahelu's resonance aura flared unevenly, red anger spiking through blue-gray calm.

What had Elaram insinuated earlier? Something about Lhorne leaving and Nheras crying in a pavilion?

"You're jealous," Rahelu said, on nothing more than base instinct and the earlier hints of envy she had detected. "All this time, you've followed him around like a pathetic lost pup." She snorted. "All that primping to dress yourself like a farmer putting gilt paint on a sow being taken to market, all that expense to remove me from contention—"

The corners of Nheras's eyes tightened. Good!

"—and your efforts amounted to naught." Rahelu

laughed; laughed harder as Nheras's perfect mask cracked. "He still spurned you and came to me."

Thin rents shivered through the Ilyn girl's silvery-smooth aura and the bright crimson glow beneath burned hot as a forge fire.

"How many attempts at conversation did you make before you accepted that he only tolerates your company out of courtesy? How long did it last before your subterfuge failed?"

Nheras flinched at each question.

The anger-spikes that riddled Rahelu's own resonance aura shrank to nothing, replaced with the razor-edged vivid yellow ridges of malicious glee. She strode to the desk and leaned over her cabinmate's shoulder. Pressed her advantage and their cheeks together; forced Nheras to confront the sight of Rahelu's face in her mirror.

She punctuated her next remark with the sweetest smile that she could summon: all lips and no teeth and faint amusement in her eyes. "And when the guards told him what you tried to conceal, did he even recall your existence?"

Nheras dropped the mirror with a clatter and shoved Rahelu back as she stood.

That break in Nheras's composure ought to have been enough.

She ought to stop rubbing salt in Nheras's wounded ego before they made themselves late by brawling in their cabin. But Rahelu had spent five years hating Nheras Ilyn—and everything she represented—for being the architect of her daily misery. She'd borne thousands of slights and bruises over the years, insults that any House-born would have dueled over without hesitation, and, last night, when she had formally challenged Nheras on the slopes of the House Ideth estate, Nheras had refused to meet her in the circle like an equal, opting to buy her way out instead.

There was a debt to be paid here.

And now that Rahelu had insulted Nheras in the most personal, most vile, most hurtful manner she could think of?

Nheras was still fucking ignoring her.

Stormbringer. Rahelu was tired of being treated like she was inconsequential.

Let Nheras try and ignore this.

"It must be difficult," Rahelu said, every word drenched with false sympathy as she blocked Nheras from reaching the door, "to accept that his price is one that you can't pay." She dropped her voice, borrowing the conspiratorial tones Tlareth adopted whenever she was about to relate every little intimate detail of her latest conquest. "Would you like to know what it was like?"

Rahelu reached back in time—to a moonlit span in a silver-white bower; to a darkness before dawn; to warm, heavy air caressing bare sweat-drenched skin, fingers on flesh slick with desire and blood coursing through veins, hot as fire.

Passion answered.

Rose-red mist eddied around Nheras's ankles, twining up and up and up around calves, thighs, hips, until it shrouded her form like one of her ridiculous, sheer, formal overrobes. A matching flush crept up her neck and bloomed in her cheeks. White teeth flashed as she bit down on her lower vermillion-painted lip—in vain, for Rahelu was far too close to miss the quick, involuntary inhalation and the uncontrolled flutter of thick eyelashes.

Nheras trembled as her Obfuscation barrier fell away.

Victory was hers, and exquisitely sweet.

"There," Rahelu said, tucking a loose brown curl that had escaped Nheras's silver hairpins behind a delicate ear. "A little taste of what you missed." Silver-and-onyx earrings chimed as Rahelu took her fingers away and released her Evocation-fueled Projection. "Now you know how it feels. As for the rest, imagine whatever you like. If you lack the capacity to do that…" She leaned in and whispered, "Ask me nicely, and I'll Evoke the full experience for you, any time you like, as many times as you like."

"I have no interest in watching the two of you rutting like hogs in heat."

Nheras's control was in tatters; her voice wavered, her breath came in irregular, shallow gasps even as she tried to mask both with a look of disgust.

Rahelu met that look unflinchingly and smiled. "Of course you don't; you'd rather that it had been you in my place instead, but he won't have you, with or without your jewels and silks and perfumes. Allow me to do you a kindness: I won't begrudge you if you wish to pretend otherwise."

She stopped smiling when Nheras's eyes went cold.

"Very well." Her cabinmate smiled back, closing the distance between them until Rahelu was backed against the door. "You have had your turn and said your piece; now I will have mine."

When Nheras next inhaled, she drew everything in the ambient resonance towards herself, and it seemed as though all the color in the world drained away.

Oh, fuck.

Rahelu threw herself forward. Grabbed Nheras by the hair with her left hand; seized Nheras's bared throat with her right. Brawling was her only hope; so long as Nheras was taking punches, she'd be forced to prioritize physical defenses instead of attacking with resonance.

Sure enough, Nheras raked her arms with painted nails in an effort to break her stranglehold. Pain lanced through her. Rahelu welcomed the sensation and how it heightened the eager rush of blood in her veins as she used her momentum to shove Nheras towards the desk. She didn't have the strength to choke Nheras out; what she had to do was stun her, just long enough to get out and get to the briefing, where Nheras would not be able to retaliate.

The ship rocked to port with the next swell; Nheras surged with it and shoved back.

Rahelu fell.

Her skull smacked against the cabin sole; Nheras's full weight landed on her gut an eyeblink later and drove the breath from her lungs. Rahelu lost her grip—on Nheras, on her focus—and that single dazed heartbeat was all it took for the tide to turn. Nheras sat astride her lower rib cage; Nheras's knees pinned her elbows to the deck; Nheras's thighs squeezed her sides like iron bands.

Rahelu found herself immobilized, gasping for air, weak and light-headed. "I—"

Nheras clapped her hand over Rahelu's mouth. "I don't want to hear it. No one wants to hear it."

Slate-gray indifference poured out from Nheras as she reached over Rahelu's head. Unlike her earlier multi-layered attempt at shielding, this was the most basic of Obfuscation barriers, but one constructed with so much concentrated resonance that you could only breach it with a Seeking or Projection of greater strength.

The two of them might as well have been locked in a stone cavern in the depths of the Earthgiver's heart.

The next breath Rahelu managed to pull into her lungs came with a noseful of Nheras's tunic and the scent of jasmine perfume and the sight of the ring Lhorne had bought for her dangling before her eyes from the throat she'd been strangling mere moments ago. The ring she had been forced to sell so Nheras could not hold the title deed of her family's fishing sloop over their heads like an executioner's ax and blackmail her with accusations of theft whenever she pleased.

How dare that jumped-up Ilyn climber flaunt *her* ring in *her* face as if *she* were the one who had lost?

Renewed rage gave her the strength to heave her body upwards.

One casual slap from Nheras's free hand made her vision swim and her head flop back and knock itself against unyielding wood a second time.

When Rahelu's vision cleared, she saw her cabinmate calmly wadding up the sodden piece of linen that had been her loincloth.

"Mmmph!" Rahelu jerked her head from side to side and bucked for all she was worth.

Nheras looked down with clinical detachment and rode out her renewed protests as if she were astride a mildly unruly horse. Strong fingers pinched her nostrils closed with a crab's pincer grip. As soon as Rahelu tried to fill her lungs, Nheras stuffed the improvised gag in her mouth.

"There. Now we can converse sensibly."

It took far more concentration than it should have to gather her scattered thoughts into a Projection.

A conversation, Rahelu sent with some effort, *by definition, requires there to be a dialogue between the parties.*

Nheras sniffed. "The first intelligent words out of you, and yet they prove you're as fish-brained stupid as you look. Clearly, you are capable of engaging in dialogue."

Nheras's voice rang too loud in her ears, whole sentences breaking apart into individual syllables that rattled around her aching skull. She couldn't make any sense of the noises to grasp the wordplay, only the mean-spirited intention behind it.

I...

She was angry, wasn't she? They'd fought without fighting last night, and she'd won, even if she'd lost. For the first time in five years, she'd won—and won decisively—and surely that merited some sort of acknowledgment from Nheras. What was the point of a victory when those you defeated didn't recognize it?

Her resonance aura sparked briefly—then sputtered out. So did her command of Projection. Fatigue was setting in, along with the creeping weight of resonance backlash she had pushed past, far beyond what she ought to.

"I agree, Supplicant Rahelu," Nheras said. "We simply can't continue quarreling like this; such behavior shames our House. How, then, ought we resolve our sisterly differences?"

Nheras flipped open the second trunk and lifted out a thick, black leather-bound tome with silver clasps. She presented its cover, holding it patiently until Rahelu's eyes were able to focus on the large elaborate title script: *'THE ISSOLM SUPPLICANT'S HANDBOOK'*. Printed below in smaller block letters: *'AN ABBREVIATED GUIDE TO HOUSE ISSOLM PHILOSOPHY, POLICIES, AND PROCEDURES'*.

Nheras quickly leafed through the volume until she came to a sub-section titled *'Misconduct'*.

Stormbringer.

Rahelu knew the Guild rules and charter, and the Dominion's basic laws and constitutions; she had assumed that the special exemptions for conflicts between trainees and Petitioners would continue to apply to conflicts between Supplicants (otherwise, the Hall of Adjudicators would surely be inundated with trivial claims) but she wasn't familiar with the policies and procedures of the Houses. When she had gone to swear her Supplicant's oaths, the Issolm headquarters had been frantic with final preparations for Anathwan's voyage. She had been shuffled from one Dedicate to another until someone found an Elder to receive her oaths in Anathwan's stead.

Somehow, she'd expected that once they were underway, Elder Anathwan would give her an official welcome and

House induction and that she would have time to internalize what the Houses now expected of her.

Idiot!

Had she learned nothing from Petitioning?

"It says here," Nheras continued, "that I ought to lodge an Evocation of your unwarranted attack on my person directly with the Elder. Depending on the severity of the attack, the injury suffered by the victim, and the House and Guild standings of the offender in question, disciplinary measures will range from a verbal reprimand to the loss of privileges and/or rank, temporary suspension, exile, or immediate dismissal and banishment."

No, Rahelu tried to say around her gag.

It came out as a muffled whine.

"Having just come from a private audience with Elder Anathwan to discuss my personal goals and her expectations of me as a dutiful Supplicant and a loyal daughter of House Issolm, I'm fairly certain she would take a very dim view of your conduct."

Nheras trailed one painted nail down the side of Rahelu's face; raked away and smoothed out the damp strands of her hair.

"You are a terrible mage with fish shit for brains. But Elder Anathwan would not include you on a mission of such vital importance to the Dominion if there were any other choice.

"So: I will not question her wisdom, and you will learn to be capable of restraint and reason. Here is how things are to proceed."

The way Nheras drew out each word made Rahelu's stomach churn, her palms sweat, and her heart beat faster. Her resonance aura ought to be paling into a chalk-white mist, a bubble of dread whose wispy tendrils smoked in the ambient resonance, but there was only a void.

A void and a tugging sensation, a feeling of her mind being reeled in close by Nheras.

"In public, we shall address each other with a believable—as opposed to a reasonable—degree of courtesy, to make allowances for our past and continuing differences, and to not arouse suspicion from our peers. We shall also comport ourselves with a degree of professional collegiality befitting Supplicants sworn to the same House, meaning that from this moment on, we shall raise neither limb nor resonance against each other, save when we are required to do so by our commanding superiors. In private, you will not—by deed, or word, or inaction—interfere with my life, and I shall suffer the curse of your presence in silence."

That was an accommodation Rahelu could live with. A sensible one that she might have suggested herself if she'd been in a more stable frame of mind. No-sleeves had alluded to a long voyage; it would pass far more pleasantly if she and Nheras had cabins of their own, but as that was an impossibility, this arrangement was the next best thing. After they divided up all the space in the cabin along invisible lines, it would be perfectly possible for both of them to pretend that the other didn't exist.

A good result.

But Nheras never did anything good or sensible.

That sensation of her mind being reeled in intensified as she struggled against her bonds, arms numbed and legs feeble.

"Do not speak to me. Do not touch my belongings without my explicit permission. As far as I am concerned, you are a shade. A leftover memory. An unpleasant echo cursed by the Skymother to wander through time."

Rahelu tried to swallow. The gag was disgustingly salty and wet, soaked through with brine and her own saliva. A moan sounded in her throat as pressure weighed on her mind like a nheshwyr had wrapped the scaly length of its coils around her temples to crush her skull.

Where was her pain? Her fear? The edges of her mind were flaking away like someone had taken a file to them.

Slender hands on her throat. Sharp nails scratching across her skin, idly tracing the veins in her neck from jaw to collarbone. Sudden relief as the weight on top of her slithered down from her ribcage to her hips. Then, the faintest glimmer of panic as she slowly registered the nimble fingers briskly unbuttoning her collar.

Nheras hissed.

She snaked her hand inside Rahelu's tunic and pulled out Lhorne's pendant. The heirloom resonance crystal gleamed in her palm, the mists inside the focus stone swirling slowly in time with the steady pulse of its resonance signature. Inexplicably, she began to laugh. Then she seized the chain; twisted it until there seemed to be no more air left in Rahelu's lungs.

The pendant's clasp popped open. The chain loosened; slithered free of Lhorne's pendant. Rahelu gasped, drawing in as much air as she could through her nose, as the focus stone clattered onto the wood.

"One final thing."

There was a slight wrenching sensation as Nheras removed the hooks in her resonance aura and the restrictions on her mind.

"You may dress and look the part. Someday you may even act the part." The Ilyn girl placed her cool hand on Rahelu's bared chest and leaned in close until all Rahelu could see was her implacable expression; her cruel and beautiful smile. "But a part is all that you can ever play. Because you have no idea what it takes to truly belong to a House."

A stroke of Nheras's silky smooth palm broke the remaining, gritty lines of Rahelu's ash-and-blood resonance ward.

All the anger, pain, and dread that had been leached away from her manifested in a deadly sphere of crackling resonance in Nheras's other upturned hand.

"This is what it feels like," Nheras whispered.

She slammed her left palm into Rahelu's unwarded heart.

WHEN IT WAS OVER, Nheras was all thoughtful, sisterly concern.

She removed Rahelu's gag and kissed her brow. Sniffed. "You still smell like a quarter-span alleyway rut." Sniffed again, then wrinkled her nose. "You've also pissed yourself." Nheras straightened. "My perfumes are inside the third drawer. Use whichever scent you prefer, but no more than a drop, unless you want to be mistaken for an overpriced comfort companion."

With that generous parting advice given, Nheras sauntered out, leaving Rahelu to scrabble after Lhorne's pendant and change her clothes for the third fucking time.

Her sea-soaked clothes, she wrung out and hung up on the weapons rack next to her spear and net.

Nheras's piss-soaked uniform, though, could molder in the middle of their cabin for eternity. This mess was one of Nheras's making, so Nheras could clean it up, especially since it wasn't possible for Rahelu to do so. Nheras had declared her a shade and everyone knew shades had resonance but no substance.

It wasn't enough.

Plagued with a burning need for retaliation, Rahelu decided that since Nheras had freely offered the use of her perfumes, helping herself to the kohl sticks that happened to be in the same lacquered box didn't constitute overstepping their newly defined boundaries, particularly when it was in service of adhering to their 'agreement'. She cherished the vicious little thrills she felt each time a fragile stick went *snap!* during the process of drawing her new resonance ward —one embellished with every elaborate extension she knew because she wasn't otherwise confident she would be able to maintain the requisite veneer of public civility.

She also left the precious vial of perfume unstoppered.

Since Nheras had taken such great pains to save her from the embarrassment of being mistaken for a comfort companion, she ought to return the same favor. As Ghardon had said: it simply wouldn't do for a Supplicant of House Issolm to stink of Lowdocks filth. She assumed the same principle applied to their cabins.

Resonance aura still humming, Rahelu bolted out after Nheras to join the rest of the Supplicants gathering inside the great cabin for Anathwan's briefing, her thoughts filled with a thousand different tiny torments that a shade could inflict on a person without so much as touching them.

3
CHOICE

RAHELU WAS THE LAST TO ARRIVE.

Fortunately—by some miracle of the Starfather—the briefing had not yet begun.

Tall and poised in her white robes, Elder Anathwan Issolm sat in the captain's seat at the head of the massive rosewood table, commanding as an Atriarch upon their throne. She was deep in silent conference with the two Dedicates flanking her: Guardian Maketh Imos and Captain Csorath Isonn. The senior mages' Projections were too tightly focused for Rahelu to pick up on what was being said; even the micro-expressions flitting across their faces came and went too quickly for her to interpret. All three were preoccupied with the large scroll—a map—spread out before them and paid little attention to the chattering Supplicants.

That did not mean Rahelu's entrance went unnoticed.

Guardian Maketh looked up and caught her staring. His eyes tightened at the corners.

Her resonance aura blinked bone-white despite her brand new ward. Somehow, her trembling legs did not give way when she bent at the waist and braced her palms and forearms flat on her thighs. There she stayed, repeating a new mantra to herself while willing her hammering heart to slow from triple to double time: *Work hard, Rahelu. Keep your emotions and resonance aura tightly leashed and your mouth shut. Give Maketh no new reasons to single you out. You can do this.*

She surreptitiously surveyed her peers. Lacking hairstyle aside, she did not look out of place amongst the other Supplicants.

Elder Anathwan briefly acknowledged her with a small smile that waived her lateness and a flick of her long fingers to indicate she ought to go find her seat.

Rahelu hurriedly complied. As the lowest ranked new Supplicant with no birth affiliation to claim, her place was nearest to the door, so that if she were needed to run and fetch or take messages, her coming and going would disrupt no one. But as she was about to get settled on her cushion, she noticed Elaram's cheerful (and frantic) waving.

Not there, Elaram sent. *Here, by me.*

Rahelu halted and scanned the faces seated around the table again.

What convoluted logic was this?

Why would Ghardon, the top-ranked Supplicant, sit furthest from the senior mages? How had Maketh Imos and his still-sleeveless Supplicant ended up on opposite sides, with Jhobon of Imrell and Nheras in between? And what was Nheras doing in the middle of the Imos/Imrell contingent anyway?

(Not that she wanted to sit anywhere near that Ilyn bitch —not now, and not ever.)

Nheras curved her too-red, painted lips into a tight, smug smile just a shade short of her usual smirk, and leaned over to simper in No-sleeves's left ear. As she did, his eyes wandered away from the view outside the great cabin's windows to wander all over Rahelu.

A matching smile broadened his face.

Rahelu was about to clench her hands into fists, so she couldn't give in to the urge to tell them both to go fuck themselves with a crude, two-handed gesture, except all clenched fists would do was confirm they'd gotten under her skin. So she forcibly relaxed her fingers and turned her back on them to edge her way around the great cabin.

A new realization struck her as she reached her seat between Elaram and Ghardon.

Captain Csorath did not sit at the Elder's right hand; that honor was given to Guardian Maketh.

Which made no sense.

Csorath Isonn was the most politically powerful person after Anathwan Issolm. There was no situation Rahelu understood where he, either as a captain aboard his own vessel or as a Dedicate of House Isonn, would not outrank a Dedicate of House Imos, who was a mere passenger.

Yet the way Maketh leaned forward as Csorath's finger sketched a route across the map was as clear as a shout: he did not agree with whatever was being proposed and he had no reservations about expressing his sentiments bluntly.

Anathwan, however, was having none of his objections. Her eyes had taken on the unfocused look of someone in mage trance. One elegant hand cupped her mage pendant, set with a resonance crystal as large as the one Lhorne had given to Rahelu. No; larger. The Elder's focus stone pulsed with glowing light that shifted through the full spectrum from ice-white to night-black as it cast uncertain shadows onto the painted world beneath.

Rahelu craned her neck for a better view—and was utterly mesmerized.

The map was no ordinary simplification of the world rendered down into stark lines that only suggested at land-marks, but a beautifully illuminated work of art drawn in shimmering resonance ink in exacting detail: dark Isonn green for the forests, Issolm white and neutral gray for the mountains, pale Ideth blue lines that snaked their way across the land and emptied into the darker Isca blue of the sea.

For a moment, she experienced the dizzying sensation of wheeling upwards, as if she were a gull being lifted high by warm thermals. She soared along the southern shoreline of the Kuath Bay to hover above a shimmering citadel on the easternmost point of the Ngutoccai continent—Peshwan Yrg —before her wings sent her skimming north and farther east across the ocean. Past the scattered islands that comprised the lawless archipelago officially named the *Free Territories of Abmerdu'* (by cartographers who had been persuaded to do so by way of considerable disincentives) and far beyond the hazy edges of the poorly charted North Ocean.

There was a fog of sorts on the horizon.

She flew into it, straining to reach the hint of new land on the other side. Dark, angular shapes jutting out of that blurring of sky and sea.

A hole in the world.

A void.

There, the resonance echoes that had ensnared her abruptly cut out.

Rahelu flailed as her mind dropped out of the sky. Something was deeply, deeply *wrong* with her. Too ungainly; too unresponsive; too heavy to exist in the Skymother's realm.

Her eyes readjusted first.

Tiny letters in the midst of a blank expanse. A label. In flat black ink, devoid of the telltale shimmer of resonance crystal dust: *'Desolate Isles'*.

Her hearing recovered next—sniggering, to starboard— then it was another heartbeat or two before the rest of her mental faculties caught up and informed her that she'd been flapping her arms, to the great delight and amusement of

Nheras and No-sleeves (and, she realized with a little sting of betrayal, Elaram), and the deep mortification of Ghardon, who had been trying to get her to sit her ass down since the senior mages were now conferring aloud which meant the briefing was about to begin.

Rahelu turned her current arm flap into an exaggerated stretch and roll of her neck and shoulders, then sat her ass down. At least her resonance ward kept searing embarrassment from shading her aura a vivid crimson, even if it did nothing for her burning cheeks.

For the sake of both our sanities, Ghardon sent through the direct skin contact they had via his death grip on her left elbow, *can you please stop being so pigheadedly wilful and refrain from making a public spectacle of yourself within my perceivable vicinity for the duration of this trip so that I can have plausible deniability regarding your actions? Especially since the Elder has decided to make your good behavior my responsibility.*

Anathwan had done what?

Here was the House Issolm guidance she desperately needed; delivered not in the form of the welcome and induction she'd expected, but as the handing off of a bothersome task to somebody whose time was less valuable.

Since when? Rahelu sent as she prised his fingers off her arm.

Ghardon transferred his death grip to her wrist. *Since you boarded. Now stop hunching. We are Issolm; we don't slouch.*

Earlier, he had stuffed Rahelu into her cabin and then left her there, because the Elder had been expecting him; Nheras had also mentioned a private audience with Anathwan.

Had Elaram had one too?

Why, then, did Rahelu not merit the same? Had she not proven herself to be as good as any House-born during Petitioning? Did the preferential treatment that House-born trainees receive continue even after they swore oaths as Supplicants?

Had she already displeased the Elder?

No; she couldn't have.

Anathwan was not angry with her; Anathwan had smiled at her; Anathwan had not allowed Maketh's prejudices to interfere with Rahelu's Petitioning and she would not allow them to poison her judgment now.

But discovering that Ghardon had, effectively, been elevated and given authority over her mere spans into their tenure as Supplicants was a blow to her pride, nonetheless.

Idiot girl, to confuse the courtesy contained in the warm and effusive words in Anathwan's letter of offer for a promise of personal mentoring.

"Supplicants." The Elder held up a beringed hand for silence and the great cabin instantly quieted. "Welcome. My fellow senior mages and I are pleased to have you here. A long journey and many challenges lie before us, in the months and, potentially, seasons ahead."

Across the table, Nheras blinked. Jhobon Imrell bent his head over his notebook, brush pen flying across the page as he diligently took down every word the Elder was saying, while Imos No-sleeves looked bored.

Ghardon's emotions were clear to her through their link, but he was too disciplined for his resonance aura to reflect his despair and too well-bred to slump. *Seasons?!*

Rahelu had not given much thought to how long she would be gone. When her parents had asked when she might be back, she had told them she didn't know, only that she hoped it would be soon.

She'd been thinking in terms of weeks.

Rahelu nearly jumped when Elaram laid a finger on her other wrist.

Oh, come on, Elaram sent, along with a very clear image of her rolling her eyes at them, though her actual face was the definition of rapt attention. *It's too early for you two to be so dour. Just think of all the new places we'll see, new people we'll meet, and new adventures we'll experience!*

Have you not seen the team? Ghardon asked.

A normal person would have left it there, so Rahelu could reply with, 'Yes, Ghardon, we have eyes', then quietly think to herself, *'I don't like them any more than you do'* and *'I wish Lhorne and Dharyas were here instead'*—

Oh.

That thought still hurt; had she not let go of it?

—but no.

Ghardon thought her education deficient (which it was not; what had been deficient was her access to and ability to pay for private tutoring) and woefully ignorant (that, she had to admit, was true, at least with respect to the ways of the Houses).

So, as Anathwan outlined the expectations she had of the Supplicants (all very standard fare: duty to the Dominion; honor to the Houses; submission to the senior mages; adherence to the chain of command; strict separation of personal and professional entanglements; so on and so forth), Ghardon proceeded to give Rahelu the benefit of his unasked-for analysis, and—since his sister found his attitude objectionable—saw fit to subject Elaram to it as well.

Ilyn's a good mage and reasonably versatile, but you can't trust her. Imos is also good, but only for two things—

One thing, Elaram interjected.

—and he's so in love with his own image you'd have trouble getting his attention if you needed his help. Not that he would help. Imrell's skipped every combat class he could; and every single time he couldn't, he's frozen at the first hint of danger. Then there's the two of you.

Together, she and Elaram looked sidelong at him. He gave them an unrepentant look in return.

And me. Why? Why did I have to be dragged out of the city and shoved onto this gods-forsaken glorified wooden bucket for seasons? The point of studying so hard was to avoid shitty jobs like this!

Trust Ghardon to turn his nose up at the idea of honest work. He was probably just upset that their cabins didn't have closets.

Perhaps if you try a little harder, you could Revoke all your Guild medals, Elaram sent, which did provoke a pulse of amusement from Rahelu. *If you hadn't won so many, no doubt you'd be enjoying a leisurely breakfast back home right now.*

Finally, Ghardon plowed on, *to tie all this off with a bow, since the Elder is much too senior to be personally instructing Supplicants and the captain's first duties will be to his ship, that leaves the Guardian as our supervising mage.*

Maketh—usually as impassive as a statue—had pulled his thick brows and thick lips into parallel lines.

He is also far too senior for that duty, and he's pissed.

Ghardon had a point. The team's hierarchy was unusually flat. There really ought to be at least one or two more ranks of junior mages, if not more, between them and the senior mages, in the form of Supplicants who had earned the double or triple ring to go with the Guild's seven-flame sigil on their armbands or newly sworn Dedicates.

This, Ghardon concluded, *is going to be an absolute shitshow.*

You're being uncharitable, Elaram sent. *A man like Maketh has got to have many hidden depths and talents; I'd bet every coin I have on that. Just imagine: how intense would it be to have those stern eyes staring into your soul, pinning you—*

Ela, no.

Gods be thanked Ghardon had cut in before her stomach rebelled. There was no word in any language Rahelu knew adequate to express how vehemently she did not want to suffer through the very experience Elaram was fantasizing about, ever again.

Guys, Rahelu sent, interrupting their bickering. *Our Elder is in the middle of briefing us on a mission of strategic importance to the Dominion; perhaps we should give it our undivided attention.*

Ghardon snorted. *The real briefing hasn't started. This drivel is just to put off the Seekers.*

Ana won't start until she's sure they've stopped spying on us, so we're getting the full spiel. Besides, Elaram added, *the best proof of attention lies in active engagement and we are actively engaged in discussion.* With a sly smile: *If you two don't like Maketh, then what of Csorath? Think of how good things could be with someone who understands—*

Rahelu cut off that inappropriate line of speculation in a bid to satisfy her own curiosity. *Why are we sitting in this arrangement? Did some clerk accidentally transpose all our Guild rankings when they copied out our transcripts?*

We've graduated and Petitioned successfully, Rahelu, Ghardon sent. *Nobody gives a shit about our transcripts, so long as we remain in good standing with the Guild and do our jobs.*

Which explained exactly nothing.

We sit according to our primary resonance discipline now, Elaram helpfully clarified.

Rahelu blinked as her mental map of the seating arrangements reconfigured itself. The possibility should have occurred to her but hadn't, because it was far too early for them to choose specializations.

Which is why, Elaram continued, *you two should be more excited. Three Harbingers—*

Being Elder Anathwan, Nheras, and No-sleeves.

—when we only have two Seekers—

Obviously referring to Csorath and herself.

—two Guardians—

That accounted for Maketh and Jhobon.

—and two Evokers? This is not going to be some run-of-the-mill diplomatic or bureaucratic mission.

Evocation might be Rahelu's best discipline, but she wouldn't have counted herself or Ghardon (regardless of all his Guild medals) as proper Evokers. Nor was she thrilled about the fact that there was no senior Evoker present to supervise them; it implied Evocation was not important to the mission.

There are three mages with Guardian capabilities on this team, Ghardon sent.

Two. Elaram shifted on her cushion as she fiddled with her boot. *You're not as good as you think you are, brother. If you were, you'd be sitting on the other side of this table.*

And you aren't in a position to judge. Discount me, and you'd have to discount Imrell too. Ghardon's lips curled briefly in a half-smirk as he studied Jhobon. *I don't need chalk to work out my formations.*

Without looking up, the wiry, pale-looking youth paused from scribing notes to find a fresh page. In clear, precise, upside-down letters large enough to be legible from across the table, Jhobon wrote: 'Two' before flipping back in his slim, leather-bound notebook.

There was a suspicious pink tinge to his cheeks that hadn't been there a moment ago.

Ela, that is too far, Ghardon sent. *Even for you. You can't just share our private conversation for the sake of proving your point. Especially not if you have to do it by taking off your—*

I didn't share all of it, Elaram retorted, *just the part that pertained to Jhobon. If you're going to disparage someone, you should do it within their hearing and to their face; it's more honest that way.*

"You," Anathwan continued, with the barest lift of her eyebrow, "are part of the next generation of mages who will build on and safeguard the work we have begun in guiding the Dominion towards a new age of prosperity. You represent the future of the Houses."

Rahelu and Ghardon both lowered their eyes, chastened, but Elaram didn't seem to notice.

Oh, I wish Ana would hurry up and get started. Her eyes shone. *She's been so very* mysterious *about what our exact duties will entail. All that talk of security precautions, of a hand-picked team, of danger? The* obscene *amount of gold being paid for our willing participation?*

Five hundred gold kez.

Half of which Rahelu was already entitled to unconditionally—with binding legal assurances that it would be paid out to her parents in the event of her death or demise—and the other half to be paid on completion. More than ten times the annual remuneration she would have earned as a Supplicant to House Ideth employed in more ordinary duties.

Shitshow or mundane mission, Rahelu would happily do whatever Elder Anathwan ordered, without question, chanting grateful prayers to the Starfather for blessing her and her family with such good fortune the whole time.

I'm telling you, this mission is going to be epic. Faint orange sparks fountained from Elaram's resonance aura to fizzle against Rahelu's skin. *It's going to be the stuff of stories!*

Anathwan droned on, empty phrase following empty phrase as she waxed eloquent in obligatory praise of Relk Isilc's wisdom. "Our mission is simple but of paramount importance. The directive comes from the Exalted Dominance himself. House Issolm is greatly honored by his trust in appointing me to lead our endeavors in fulfilling the duty before us..."

I don't like it, Ghardon sent, his Projection shielded this time. *If this mission is so important to Atriarch Isilc, why didn't his House send any of their Dedicates or Supplicants?*

Rahelu sent a mental shrug in reply, also shielded by his efforts. *Seems like a blessing to me.*

Bad enough to be stuck sharing a cabin with Nheras Ilyn; the only thing she could imagine being worse was enduring whole seasons spent with Supplicants from House Isilc like Whiplash and Precious. They held their noses so high that she was always surprised to see one walk in a straight line without falling over backwards.

Elaram scoffed. *Who would House Isilc send anyway? No amount of pride and reminders of their House's former glory can make up for the facts: the best new talent they have are Kyrosh and Myreil. He can't Seek his way out of a palanquin without her to lead him by the nose and she never lifts a finger if she can help it.*

Now who's being uncharitable? Ghardon sent. *And it doesn't explain why our Elder is leading the mission.*

Because Ana has a reputation for getting things done, Elaram sent. *Obviously.*

Explain Maketh then. How is one of Atriarch Hnan Imos's most dependable Dedicates here, free to operate without another Isilc Dedicate or Elder to act as a check on his influence?

Elaram pulled a face. *Relk Isilc's council of Elders is full of decrepit men and his Dedicates are too busy jockeying for position while they concoct opportunities for one of the incumbents to drop dead from their excesses. When was the last time you heard of an Elder of House Isilc doing anything productive other than indulging in wine, dreamleaf, and bedsport? To hear Father tell it, they won't bestir themselves to attend to the Dominion unless something's on fire, and to hear their consorts and comfort companions talk, not even the most potent virility elixirs can get their shriveled cocks to stir.*

Eurgh.

The earlier mental image of Maketh Imos was far more preferable and Rahelu felt a sudden, deep, abiding sympathy for Ghardon.

"...and thus, I would have us dispense with excessive

formality, for we will need to work closely together, more closely than the Houses have ever before." In an abrupt departure from the script so far, Anathwan said: "Captain Csorath, please raise the additional security precautions."

Yeeeeeeeessssssss! Elaram sent. *Here we go!*

The captain touched a small panel of resonance crystal tiles set into the tabletop. The ship responded at once: layers of Obfuscation barriers surrounded the great cabin, so thick that they extended an entire stride inside the cabin walls. Every Supplicant was abruptly forced forward by the immense pressure of the *Winged Arrow's* defenses against their resonance auras—and a collective, involuntary gasp escaped their throats as the edges of the rosewood table dug into their bellies.

She was falling through the sky; she was being smothered by a mountain; she was drowning in the watery embrace of the Kuath Bay once more.

"Captain," someone said. "Allow me to make a minor adjustment."

The pressure eased off and Rahelu could breathe again. She blinked, wondering why none of the books and scrolls were falling out of the shelves around the cabin door since it was now on the ceiling, then blinked again when she realized the coolness against her right cheek was the table.

She peeled her face off the rosewood, gladdened she wasn't alone in having to do so: Elaram, Ylaen, and Nheras all looked as dazed as she was. Only Ghardon and Jhobon had remained upright, despite their pale faces.

"Be at ease." Elder Anathwan waved her hand. Soothing blue-gray resonance washed through the cabin, calming agitated auras. "I will be brief and direct, by necessity, for we cannot maintain these defenses long without drawing undue attention, and they themselves may not be sufficient."

Eight hells, Ghardon sent.

Rahelu counted at least five layers of Obfuscation barriers that, to her resonance senses, seemed nigh impenetrable. They would have been installed by House Isonn's most skilled Guardians in Concordance, the anchors embedded into the wood of the ship itself, the very shape of the formations considered as part of the *Winged Arrow's* design. Raised in addition to the formidable fortress-class Obfuscation barriers that Csorath had activated the moment the *Winged Arrow* had cast off.

And, still, the Elder did not believe these defenses were sufficient.

Eight hells, indeed.

True to her word, Anathwan delivered a barrage of information:

"We are traveling to Peshwan Yrg as direct representatives of the Exalted Dominance, ostensibly to conduct a regular, periodic audit of House affairs in the region, and to investigate the growing number of complaints lodged against the city's port authorities by the local merchants in regards to the imposition and collection of tariffs. This is, of course, a fiction."

Told you! Elaram sent gleefully. We *are going on a* secret mission! *This is going to be so much better than being stuck at home, authenticating documents until my eyes bleed.*

"In truth," Anathwan said as she looked at each of them in turn, "you should not be here. A Dedicate's level of skill and experience—and a Dedicate's oath-sworn assurances to maintain confidentiality and discretion—are what's needed for this mission.

"Reality, however, rarely accommodates our needs." The Elder paused. "There has been a series of unforeseen developments."

Shock arced from Supplicant to Supplicant in a lurid flash of yellow.

How can a whole series of events go unforeseen? Elaram asked. *That's not possible,* Rahelu sent. *Right?*

Dharyas had once told her that Augury, as a discipline, was about being open to the possibilities. Had insisted, in fact, that a person's level of skill in Augury was not predetermined by the amount of in-born talent bestowed by the Earthgiver but depended on the flexibility of their mind—which meant in order to stop someone from Auguring a highly probable event, you had to arrange things so that they couldn't even conceive of the possibility.

No Augury was certain. But if you brought enough Augurs together and they pooled their efforts, given sufficient power and time, they would be able to identify ninety-nine out of a theoretical one hundred possible outcomes and their probabilistic distribution.

It's never happened, Ghardon confirmed. *Ever since Founding, the Houses have kept a strict record of every major event Augured and the Chroniclers have set down the histories. Across five or so centuries, there's been a handful of events the Auguries missed. None were causally linked.*

Something that unlikely could only be attributable to a grand working of Fortunement, on a power scale beyond what even Atriarch Mere Ideth was rumored to be capable of.

Suddenly, Maketh's suspicions of Conclave interference didn't seem so baseless. When Onneja had asked her to act as a focus, could she have—could *Rahelu* have—

No.

She had seen pieces of Onneja's grand Augury for herself. Onneja had warned her not to speak of it and she hadn't, because a request from Onneja was all the reason she needed—and because it made sense. People acted strangely when they had foreknowledge, but no understanding, and, more often than not, chose poorly as a result. (As she and Xyuth had learned.)

Now?

She would be doubly sure to never speak of it.

"As a result," Anathwan said, "the Houses have no Dedicates who can be spared from the critical initiatives they oversee, and our experienced Supplicants have already been assigned to other tasks that cannot be abandoned. Hence"—the Elder swept her hand around the great cabin—"the unusual composition of our team."

The small well of confidence Rahelu had dredged up based on the praise in Anathwan's letter of offer and the assumption she had been chosen due to her skills as a mage evaporated.

Nheras was right, too.

Rahelu was here because Anathwan, quite literally, had no other available mages to choose from.

"There are those who believe that Supplicants are too inexperienced and too untested for this mission," the Elder said. "They argue that, for your own safety and the security of the Dominion, any role you play should be performed under compulsion with your conscious minds bound."

Horrified looks all around.

"They argue that it is better if you retain no recollection of either your involvement or our mission particulars and thus cannot, directly or indirectly, inadvertently or otherwise, betray our mission and place the Dominion in jeopardy."

What Anathwan had just described was worse than being Suborned.

When your will was supplanted by another's and you were forced to act according to their desires, you experienced what your body did, was doing, would do again. You wouldn't get to choose, but you would remain—utterly and unalienably—yourself.

But if awareness itself was taken from you, your body became an empty vessel.

You ceased to exist.

"In light of this mission's strategic importance to the future of the Dominion, their arguments were persuasive."

The ambient resonance paled. Anathwan's tone was flat and her lips were drawn; Maketh and the captain both wore grave expressions to match.

"The Exalted Dominance has authorized the use of these extraordinary measures and we have orders to ensure no Supplicant is exempted."

Silence hung in the air, poised on the knife's edge between disbelief and terror. Rahelu's eyes darted around the cabin for some sort of signal as to which side she ought to land on, and saw the rest of the Supplicants doing the same.

Fuck. Fuck!

Run, idiot—

Nobody moved; her limbs were frozen.

—run *where?*

She was stuck behind a table in a cabin on a ship in the middle of the sea commanded by a Seeker who could guide the Guardian who had orders to obliterate her mind to any hiding place she might find so the Harbinger they both reported to could puppet her body around in the name of the Dominion and—

Oh *gods*, she wished she had fucked up and sat down on the cushion closest to the door after all; she'd rather dive overboard and take her chances in the Stormbringer's realm.

Wait. *Wait.*

Why were the three senior mages just sitting there, watching the Supplicants panic, instead of acting on their orders?

"We have so few mages," Elder Anathwan said quietly. "You were admitted to the Guild for training on the basis of your raw talent. I need not remind you of the long, hard years you spent honing that potential into ability. Ability you amply demonstrated during Petitioning."

Memories Rahelu had locked away behind partial Obfuscation barriers tried to reassert themselves:

Clotted blood pooled on a splintered floor beneath butchered corpses. Cowled black-robed figures, slithering out from the shadows with their gold-flecked, black-bladed serpentine knives, slashing down at—

Rahelu shuddered as she pushed those memories back into the farthest recesses of her mind. Hunting down the cultists behind those gruesome murders had nearly destroyed her.

"You have barely begun your careers, and yet you have already performed at a level above and beyond what is expected of Supplicants." The Elder looked at each of them as she went on: "How much more might you accomplish given the opportunity? Can we be certain that the benefits of enacting these extraordinary measures will outweigh the cost of the sum total of your unrealized accomplishments? For a short mission of a day or a week perhaps we can conclude 'yes' with a reasonable degree of confidence. But for a mission such as ours..."

Anathwan turned to Maketh.

"As any healer will attest, the mind is a complex and individual entity," the Guardian said. "You may recover with minimal adverse effects, such as an awareness of memory gaps. The trauma of undergoing and remaining under extended suppression may gradually destabilize and unravel your consciousness to the point where recovery is impossible." Maketh shook his head. "I cannot say. There have been too few reliable studies on the medium- and long-term effects."

The ambient resonance buzzed with the skittering appre-

hension that leaked from the Supplicants' collective resonance auras.

"And so," Anathwan said, a hint of warmth returning to
her voice, "we shall bend the rules a little.

"Between now and when we arrive in Peshwan Yrg, you
may elect to undertake an accelerated program of intensive
study for a few select resonance skills that, under ordinary
circumstances, you would not learn until you have sworn
your oaths of Dedication. Master these to an acceptable level,
and you may participate in our mission as full members of
the team—then return home, as Dedicates.

"If you cannot, or choose not to participate, you shall
fulfill your duties as Supplicants."

Unease grew in the silence that followed.

That was a false choice.

Not that any of the senior mages seemed inclined to
acknowledge the fact. Anathwan busied herself with pouring
a fresh cup of tea while Maketh and Csorath returned to their
contemplation of the map.

No-sleeves spoke. "What is the true mission?"

No honorific. No request for permission to speak. His
audacity was breathtaking, as was the sheer insolence in his
drawl.

Anathwan regarded the Imos Supplicant with cool eyes
but did not respond, content to sip from her delicate porcelain teacup.

The cloying, dark gray, green-tinged mist swirling through
the ambient resonance began condensing on the great cabin's
bulkheads until they bore an uncanny resemblance to the
slimy, moss-covered outer walls of the Tidelocks.

After some time, during which Rahelu had no idea where
to look and the slight cramp in her left calf grew from a minor
annoyance to a tight pinch, No-sleeves dropped his gaze.

"Supplicant Ylaen." Anathwan set down her teacup. "Do you believe the concerns regarding an inexperienced, untested mage's ability to maintain absolute confidentiality to be without basis?"

"Honorable Elder, I ask only so I may make an informed choice."

Anathwan folded her hands and posed a mild inquiry to the great cabin at large: "Does anyone else feel they lack the requisite understanding to make an informed choice?"

"No, Elder." Ghardon was quick to plaster his palms and face on the glossy rosewood surface in front of him. "I am grateful for the opportunity and I accept. I swear I will not, by word or deed or thought, disclose or discuss the privileged information in this briefing."

"No, Elder," Rahelu echoed and also affirmed: "I am likewise grateful and swear the same."

If there had been room, she would have scooted a full pace back from the table and off her cushion to place both hands and her forehead on the cabin sole. As things were, she simply listened to the others join her and Ghardon in a ragged, subdued chorus and hoped the Elder would deem the obeisance adequate.

"Very good," Anathwan said. "I accept your oaths in good faith and will not require Guardian Maketh to implement precautions to enforce them, for I trust you will be occupied in applying yourselves to your training and studies to the fullest extent and will not waste time by engaging in idle speculation." A lengthy pause to let the full weight of her expectations sink in before she continued. "Now, as a demonstration of my trust, I will tell you this much about our true mission: you may consider it to be a recovery operation of sorts. In terms of more mundane details..."

Anathwan gave them no opportunity to react; she directed

their attention to Maketh with a sweep of her gaze and he immediately rattled off their assignments.

"Report to the main deck each day at the first span after sunrise for instruction. Skyarc will be devoted to approved independent studies. You will take breakfast and lunch with the crew but join us for evening meals to report on your progress."

Apart from the need to formally dine every night with the senior mages, the schedule was not so different to the one she had followed as a fifth-year Guild trainee.

"The remaining spans are yours to do with as you please, so long as you do not disturb the crew or any of the senior mages."

Or didn't care about the threat hanging over your head.

"My thanks, Dedicates," Anathwan said, and kept everyone waiting while she held another silent, Projected conference with Maketh and Csorath.

By the end of it, the two men looked less than pleased. Nevertheless, both gave shallow bows to the Elder before they departed.

"Supplicants."

One quick brush of Anathwan's palm against the resonance crystal panel vanished the great cabin's oppressive Obfuscation barriers—and her frank manner.

"Should you have further questions or concerns, you may come to me privately at any time." Perfunctory, as was the Elder's gesture to the door. "Guardian Maketh awaits you above."

Rahelu stood with the others. Feet shuffled as Supplicants scrambled to bow and file out.

Without warning, Anathwan attacked.

Six whisper-thin darts of ice-white resonance whipped across the table.

The first dart skittered off a shield of dull, slate-gray brick

—Jhobon's—while the second dissolved as it tried to drill through Ghardon's wall of shining gold pride.

The third barrier—a soft, buttery bubble of joy —shattered.

Elaram collapsed.

Two more darts were deflected by a rose-red ribbon from Ylaen and a wave of bright orange curiosity from Nheras.

That was all Rahelu saw before the final dart pierced her blue-gray Obfuscation barrier, swift and deadly as a shear-water in its dive.

Her hands flew up towards the pendant around her neck —it was supposed to protect her, he'd said that it would protect her—no, no; she'd decided that she couldn't use it— and fell away before her fingers could touch the focus stone. Panic gripped her with icy claws, the weight of it growing with every heartbeat until it seemed as though her heart had turned to lead.

Chill surged through her veins as her knees buckled and she joined Elaram on the cabin sole.

The Elder attacked me; she attacked me, a sworn Supplicant of her own House!

The small sparks of her anger fizzled out, no match for the Elder's Projection. It was so cold that she felt like she burned from the inside out. Everywhere the sensation spread, Rahelu lost her ability to control that part of her body —she would freeze, she was freezing—as if she had been encased in truewinter ice from the heart of the Unomelaje.

Lhorne, she thought and squeezed her eyes shut.

But the rose-red mist that she had summoned so easily a span ago refused to come now. The cabin floor was too distant from a bed of soft grass; the precise lines of sunlight bleeding through the shuttered windows and the guttering oil lamps were too far removed from the moon's lambent glow of yellow-blue; and though it was dark and the air warm and still and damp with sweat, the scent was rank with fear instead of passion, and her rigid limbs were frozen she was still frozen her thoughts were—

RISE.

She rose stiffly, pulled to her feet by another's direction, dimly aware of five other puppets rising in synchronous motion.

REMEMBER.

There had been a challenge.

A test.

She thought she had passed, but perhaps not. Perhaps she had failed. Yes, she had failed. The Elder had expected something of her, and she had failed. She must do better. She would do better. She did not want to disappoint the Elder.

RETURN.

Rahelu found herself leaning against the windows beside Elaram, both of them rattling the shutters with their trembling. The rest of the Supplicants were standing through their own efforts but were shaking no less.

Anathwan sighed. Lamplight glinted on her golden curls as she shook her head. "You all have much to learn. However, since you each performed in an exemplary manner as Petitioners, I expect you will work hard to rectify your deficiencies. It would be a great pity if such promising careers were cut tragically short."

The Elder's warm manner was at odds with the ice-white shards that lingered in the ambient resonance.

"Go." Anathwan waved her hand once more in dismissal. "I will test you again, in Peshwan Yrg. When I do, I trust you will not disappoint me."

4

LIMITS

THE WAY MAKETH IMOS PACED UP AND DOWN THE line of Supplicants assembled on the main deck reminded Rahelu of a stymied wyrhound who had sniffed out his quarry but was unable to give chase.

"Six graduated mages," he said. Each word dropped into the midst of their cowed silence like stones. "And none of you are capable of defending yourselves the moment you're put to the test outside of a training yard."

Rahelu shivered despite the sun's growing warmth, unable to shake the aftereffects of Anathwan's attack. It did not help that the captain had set the *Winged Arrow* on a direct course down the middle of the Aleituan Sea and the south-westerly breeze filling the sails felt like a blown kiss from the Unomelaje, where winter reigned eternal.

"You are unworthy of your Houses." Maketh alternated between raking them with hard stares and shaking his head while looking away over the afterdeck. "Your performance makes me question the accuracy of your Guild ratings—"

A faint *creak* to her left as Jhobon shifted his weight.

White-and-yellow robes snapped as Maketh spun sharply.

"Apathy to counter panic! What a waste of resonance. Simple calm should have been your first response."

Jhobon wilted. On the other side of their line, Ghardon preened, but his satisfaction didn't last long.

"And you." Maketh scowled. "Don't mistake luck for skill. Pride only worked because this was a test. In a true attack, any intelligent foe would have incorporated secondary Projections into their assault and you would last no longer than a handful of heartbeats."

Rahelu quailed inwardly as Maketh turned his scrutiny on her. The back of her shirt felt cold and damp where it stuck to her spine. She stood straighter, stiffened her knees, clasped her hands behind, and locked her fingers together.

She wasn't trembling. Not at all.

"You lack versatility," he said.

That was fair. She had enough trouble summoning the one Obfuscation barrier she was comfortable with that she had never tried experimenting with another.

"And instead of improving your sloppy technique, you are content to wallow in mediocrity—"

That was unfair. She'd worked hard over the last few weeks to improve her Obfuscation skills. It was unreasonable to expect a newly graduated mage who hadn't even pursued electives in Obfuscation studies to be able to withstand an assault by an experienced Harbinger—and an Elder at that!

"—and rely on crutches to shore up your laziness."

Lazy?!

Rahelu would bet her entire signing bonus that she, aside from the crew, was the only person aboard who spent her daylight spans doing honest work—she had the callused fingers and scarred palms to prove it—and then the spans between dusk and dawn studying resonance theorems by the dim light of a fish oil lamp until it guttered out.

Rahelu concentrated on breathing, only breathing, as

Maketh directed a look of such disgust at her that she was sure he would spit.

I control my emotions; they do not control me.

Thankfully, the Imos Guardian was quick to move on to Nheras and No-sleeves, the Supplicant from his own House. Both of the would-be Harbingers held their heads high and met the Guardian's gaze without flinching.

"I will defer to Elder Anathwan's assessment of your skills in Projection," Maketh said in neutral tones. "As for your instincts…" Heavy disapproval returned. "Leave your showy strategies for duels, where rulesets place limits on what your opponents may do and crowd-pleasing tactics can sway sentiments in your favor. Outside of the sparring circle, they will only get you killed."

Finally, the Guardian swiveled around to Elaram.

She met his silence—a condemnation louder than any scolding—with the woebegone expression of a half-drowned cat that looked foreign on her face.

After ten heartbeats that felt more like a quarter-span, the coiled tension in Maketh's stance drained away.

He sighed. "Your lack of skill in Obfuscation is a liability to everyone on this mission, and your command of Projection is hardly better than a second-year trainee's."

Unlike his previous scathing critiques, his tone now was matter-of-fact, and all the crueler for it. Blue-black fog stole into Elaram's resonance aura, and her lower lip wobbled.

The Guardian's forehead creased as he stared off into the horizon. "Two weeks is insufficient for me to teach and you to internalize two years' worth of grounding in elementary principles; we must find some alternative solution."

Just then, the sun dipped behind a band of cloud cover and threw the deck into temporary shadow.

A very bad omen.

Stormbringer, I beg your patience. In her haste to reach the

Winged Arrow, Rahelu had neglected to make a blood offering at the Seaspire. She would have to ask Kerg where she could find the ship's shrine during their lunch break.

The squawk of a questryl circling overhead put an end to Maketh's contemplation. He shook off his abstraction and strode over to a large crate lashed to the main deck.

"At least, we may assume your familiarity with basic Obfuscation barriers," the senior mage said, only half of his attention on his charges as he rummaged through the crate. "Now, what about resonance wards?"

Tentative nods up and down the line.

Maketh heaved a clinking canvas bag out of the crate. He undid the leather ties and tossed the bag onto the deck before them. It landed with a glassy *thud*, gaping open to reveal an assortment of warding supplies: brush pens, corked jars (containing mixtures of salt, ash, sand, and clay), and a large collection of smooth river stones.

"How many of you have mastered the fifth principle of construction or above?" Maketh asked as he retrieved a second, smaller sack.

Rahelu didn't count herself an expert, but the more elaborate variation of her resonance ward did make use of the fifth and sixth principles. Should she speak up?

The glance Maketh gave Jhobon was expectant. When Jhobon shook his head, Maketh turned to Ghardon.

Reluctantly, Ghardon also shook his head.

That decided it.

If the two Supplicants who showed the greatest potential to be Guardians didn't know, then as far as Dedicate Maketh Imos was concerned, Rahelu was also ignorant.

Maketh had hauled her into an interrogation chamber for simply looking through the Petitioners' assignment board on suspicions that she had tampered with the records. (Which she had; but not for the reasons he thought, and he hadn't caught her while she'd been doing the tampering.) He had tried to have her removed from the *Winged Arrow* because he still suspected her of being a Chanazian spy. What would he do if he discovered Rahelu had a working knowledge of resonance wards far beyond her peers—and that a Conclave journeymage had been the one to teach her the very basics so she could hide the emotions she struggled to control?

She didn't want to find out.

The Dedicate's scowl returned as he saw only blank faces. "Not one of you?"

"It wasn't part of the Guild curriculum," Ghardon said.

"Elementary warding should have been part of your second-year studies."

This time, they all shook their heads.

Maketh took a deep breath. "What did you cover instead?"

No-sleeves rattled off the subjects: "Beginner Seeking, Elementary Obfuscation, Beginner Projection, Beginner Evocation, Introductory Augury, Introductory Fortunement."

Maketh threw a beseeching look to the heavens. "Earthgiver grant me patience and sense to the idiotic fools on the Guild's academic council. What are a bunch of Supplicants going to do with Augury and Fortunement?"

"But they're the most valuable resonance disciplines!" Elaram said. "All the Houses want Augurs."

Jhobon nodded, piping up for the first time. "Any graduate showing the slightest ability always Petitions successfully regardless of how they perform in the challenges..."

He trailed off as Maketh's attention swung back to him.

"It's true," Jhobon mumbled. His fingers rubbed at the pink, slightly puckered lines on his left forearm peeking through the gap between the leather of his Imrell armband and his rolled-up sleeve, as if his scar itched or it was some sort of good luck charm. "They do."

Dharyas. Rahelu's heart contracted. The last time she had seen Dharyas, the Isca girl had added a scar just like that one to her left arm too.

The Guardian's scowl deepened. "And not one of them will have the experience needed to make heads nor tails of any significant Augury they might be able to perform, nor the wisdom to know which probability to choose. Even Atriarch Ideth does not meddle lightly with the future."

Guilt that Rahelu thought she had reconciled with pricked away at her. She had taken advantage of Xyuth's fears and twisted the scrivener's future to suit her own purposes. Had she followed the platitudes she had spouted instead of meddling, Xyuth might yet be alive.

Dharyas might yet be alive.

What folly! What incredible arrogance! To think that she knew better than the Starfather. What business did the Guild have teaching something as dangerous as Augury and Fortunement to its trainees?

Maketh rubbed his forehead, as though he had been thinking the same thoughts and they gave him a headache. "You could go your whole life without needing either Augury or Fortunement. The same can't be said for Obfuscation and resonance wards."

He didn't need to emphasize the point further—at least, not for Rahelu. Obfuscation barriers were ubiquitous and required constant upkeep: every House building incorporated at least one in its design, and their relay networks were encrypted with many more. And life in Chanaz and in the Lowdocks would have been a lot better if she'd known how to construct resonance wards as a child.

"I don't see why knowing resonance wards would be necessary if you can Obfuscate," Nheras said.

Typical. Always going for the obvious, brute-force solution.

Nheras continued, "They both do the same thing—"

Sure, in the same way that nets and traps both catch fish.

"—but Obfuscation barriers are far more effective. Particularly when there is limited time for preparation."

Rahelu's snort slipped out before she could help it.

All eyes turned to her.

So much for not drawing attention to herself.

"Supplicant Rahelu," Maketh said, "You seem to be the only one who thinks Supplicant Nheras's assessment is incorrect. Why might that be?"

"I—"

Stormbringer strike her down for being an idiot with poor self-control. Maketh might not be a Seeker, but if Rahelu denied that she disagreed—and she did disagree; vehemently so—he would know she lied.

"It's not incorrect," she said. "Merely incomplete."

"And how does a mage who never progressed beyond third-year Obfuscation studies arrive at that conclusion, when the Guild's first-year curriculum confers only a passing knowledge of resonance wards?"

What would be an obvious rebuttal to Nheras's argument? Something that didn't reveal she knew more about wards than Maketh thought she ought to?

Her eyes caught on the small sack he carried; its contents chimed softly with each step as he advanced on her.

Rahelu resisted the urge to fall back. "Obfuscation barriers can be more effective—but only if you do not consider the cost and power involved in their construction. Once you equalize for these factors..." She shrugged. "I'd guess a less capable mage with limited resources would do far better with a ward than a barrier."

"Very well," Maketh said. "Let us put your hypotheses to the test."

DESPITE HIS EARLIER DISDAIN FOR dueling, Guardian Maketh nevertheless decided a contest of abilities—with modified parameters—would provide an appropriate and swift demonstration of his point.

"Resonance skills only; no weapons, no hand-to-hand combat," Maketh said as he finished drawing the chalk circle around Rahelu and the bag of warding materials.

Two strides away, caged inside an identical circle on the starboard side of the deck, was Nheras and the smaller sack. The *Winged Arrow* was built for speed rather than hauling cargo or carrying passengers, so space on the main deck was limited. Both circles were barely three strides across, smaller than they should be according to the tournament ruleset.

Maketh dusted his hands and faced the four Supplicants outside the circles. "Stay on this side of the chalk lines. Disturb the crew and you forfeit. Siege ruleset: break through their defenses and you win; if those two can outlast your attacks for more than a half-span, they win."

"But Guardian," Elaram protested as she pointed to Nheras, "you gave *her* a whole sack of resonance crystals, and *she*"—that accusatory finger jabbed at the scroll in Rahelu's hand—"got a schematic for an advanced resonance ward of your design. Shouldn't we get some help too?"

"No," Maketh said. "You don't get to pick and choose your enemies' resources or the circumstances in which you encounter them. They might be better equipped but you outnumber them. I'd call it fair."

Elaram made a face at the Imos Dedicate's back as he addressed Nheras and Rahelu.

"No attacking or counter-attacking and no leaving your circle. The purpose of this exercise is to discover the limits of your defenses. Use everything at your disposal. You have half a span to prepare."

With that, Maketh strode away—presumably to inform the captain, warn the crew, and confer with the Elder. Or to criticize the questryl soaring overhead that it was wasting energy by flapping its wings instead of riding the thermals.

Their four opponents gathered in a close huddle, strategizing. Nheras was already deep in meditation.

Rahelu laid out her scroll, weighing its corners down with river stones to keep it unrolled as she studied the schematic.

Multi-layered in construction. Maketh's specifications called for four different warding materials, some of them blended together. Dual-purpose foundation lines. The outer set was designed to deflect resonance around the warded location while the inner set shared more than a few commonalities with the suppression ward she wore over her heart—they would contain any stray resonance that escaped her control and prevent it from leaking outside her circle.

A siege ward?

She hadn't studied those in detail, having no practical use for something that elaborate, but she did recall a thing or two. Siege wards were designed to work in tandem with other fortifications. Which she did not have, because Maketh had put her circle in the most exposed place possible. And since he hadn't explicitly forbidden the others from moving, they could attack from any direction. A minuscule notation in the lower right-hand corner indicated she was to repeat the design four times to create an enclosed ward.

Rahelu squinted as she rooted through her bag of supplies for the jar of sand. It would be more efficient to construct all four sections at once, so why hadn't Maketh drawn the whole thing? With a ward this complicated, you never wanted to leave room for ambiguity in its construction. Now she had to visualize how those repeating sections were supposed to be linked together, because if that wasn't clear in her mind before she began...

Rahelu glanced up to check the sun's position.

Shit.

Half her allotted time was gone.

Nheras had already Imbued a dozen or so resonance crystals. They pulsed erratically to Rahelu's resonance senses, their link not yet completed. As she watched, Nheras added another crystal, then another, until she held twenty pulsing crystals, humming discordantly in her hand.

Far, far more than Rahelu could have managed.

Nheras drew on the bright sky-blue glow of contentment and warm yellow camaraderie that rose from the combined resonance auras of the off-duty crew members in their hammocks below and pushed that gathered resonance into all twenty crystals simultaneously. Their conflicting signals blended, smoothed over into a joyous chord that echoed softly through the ambient resonance.

The four attacking Supplicants had split up from their unified huddle: Elaram and Ghardon's chestnut heads close together by the mainmast, conferring; Jhobon, aft of her circle, shuffling on his knees with a handful of resonance crystals he'd pulled out of his own pockets, sticking individual stones to the deck with glutinous rice paste in a formation she didn't recognize; and as for No-sleeves...

A tingling between her shoulder blades, like a very light scratch down her spine.

Rahelu spun.

He prowled between the perimeter of her circle and the portside rail on a meticulous circuit around the main deck. As she tried taking his measure, he began taking off his ridiculously expensive shirt. The exaggerated way he undid each button wouldn't have looked out of place in one of the Wanton Warrior's lavish evening entertainments. The intricate, jagged scars covering his chest and abdomen didn't fit the picture—though there was something familiar about the overall design that she should know but couldn't quite place —but the skin on his back was smooth and unbroken.

A faint whiff of green-brown resonance wafted past as No-sleeves gave her a slow, knowing smile.

Over by the mainmast, Ghardon caught her glance, her answering eye roll, and mouthed back 'ridiculous' as Ylaen discarded his poor, wrongfully butchered shirt.

She smirked, on the verge of telling Ghardon he was a hypocrite since he'd more or less done the same thing to squeeze through a gap in an alleyway until she remembered what had waited for them inside the Tattered Quill.

Her grin faded.

Focus, idiot. You don't have time for anything else.

She slowly poured out the jar of sand, following the precise lines Maketh had inked on the scroll. The further she got, the less certain she became. The ward she was copying didn't make sense. Some of the proportions were...off and several lines extended further than she felt they ought to. Wouldn't those create intersections where resonance would accumulate? If so, the sheer accretion of resonance would eventually overwhelm the inner lines of enclosure and—

Rahelu paused.

A test within a test. Devised to put her in an impossible bind:

Construct the ward as it should be and she would reveal the full extent of her knowledge.

Construct the ward as given and she would lose the contest. That seemed like it might undermine the Imos Dedicate's message about the value of warding as a skill, but he could simply blame her flawed execution, using facts to shade his lie with truth. Who would know the difference? He was a Dedicate and she a Supplicant; she couldn't defend herself by blurting out, *'But I copied the design you gave me exactly!'* One didn't just go around accusing senior mages of incompetence or sabotage—especially if one's Elder had placed that senior mage in charge of one's instruction.

Maketh had set her up.

Could she afford to lose?

Another glance around told her Elaram, Ghardon, and No-sleeves had settled into meditation trances with their own focus stones. Rings and smaller crystals on necklaces; none big enough to anchor a Concordance. Across from her, Nheras finished arranging her anchors in a formation that looked like an inversion of Elerynn's Gambit. Aft of them both, Jhobon was putting the finishing touches on whatever formation he was attempting: a branching, twisting, construction of angled lines that sprouted outwards from one anchor point a stride forward of the mizzenmast.

So what if she lost?

This was just a training exercise. It wouldn't be the first— or even the hundredth—time Rahelu ranked dead last in a contest. She had no standing amongst the other Supplicants to protect. Undoubtedly, Nheras would crow—silly fish guts, how could you possibly think you might win, go jump back in the ocean and drown yourself before you dishonor our House again—but that sting was nothing new.

No. Not again. She had sworn to begin anew.

Idiot girl! Self-preservation, in the form of her mother's voice, shouted down her surge of stubborn pride. *When caught in a net, would you surrender your knife too?*

"Two hundred heartbeats!" Maketh called as he returned from below and paused to inspect Jhobon's odd creation. The Guardian pointed as he barked rapid, half-questions at the Imrell Supplicant, who hovered, mumbling and twisting his hands and nodding jerkily at each remark.

A myriad of emotions poured out into the ambient resonance as Nheras cycled through everything from golden joy to black despair. Her Obfuscation barrier—a rainbow sphere of resonance noise that obscured her physical form entirely—sprang into being, fueled by the power in her anchors. Finally, the red anger over green jealousy in Nheras's aura bled away, replaced with the dull slate-gray blankness of a basic Obfuscation barrier.

Though Ghardon and Elaram remained seated in meditation, No-sleeves had moved. Still forward of her circle, limbering up through a series of stretches with his eyes closed, his bare feet skimming over the polished planks. His stretches took him sternwards, toes and heels unerring in evading the edges of her ward. His aura was colorless, as if he had none, yet there was a hint of shimmering around his limbs like heat rising off sun-baked sand. Ambient resonance shivered against her wards as he passed by.

Same dance-like movements. Same confident carriage.

But he no longer looked like a preening, pampered House-born discovering a mirror for the first time or a pouting, pretty player in costume strutting about on stage, soliciting bids from the wealthier patrons in his audience to see who would play Enjela to his Symezosh (in scenes that Tlareth delighted in but which, as far as Rahelu could ascertain, had never appeared in any Chronicler's historical record).

Imos looked like Symezosh himself on the eve of the first battle in the War of the Five Dominions.

Rahelu's earlier unease returned tenfold.

None of her opponents planned to hold back. She didn't like the gleam in Elaram's eyes or the arrogant tilt to Ghardon's head or the strain Ylaen was putting on the ambient resonance from…whatever he was doing. As to what Jhobon planned—she couldn't begin to guess.

She felt like a bluegill stuck swimming around inside a basket trap, waiting to be speared.

Think, Rahelu.

Assume Maketh discovers your knowledge of wards.

Knowledge that, according to him, should never have been removed from the Guild's curriculum, and that, according to Elder Anathwan's direction, he is supposed to teach you anyway.

Knowledge that, if you prove to be deficient in, will give him an ironclad justification to obliterate your mind under the Exalted Dominance's orders. And the Elder would be bound—by her word and those same orders—to support him.

Therefore: hiding what she knew was pointless.

Counterproductive, even.

Maketh had said the exercise's purpose was to discover their limits, and Rahelu wasn't quite at her limits yet.

She turned her back on Ylaen's prancing. Swept the flawed lines of sand onto the scroll, then removed the river stones. Maketh's parchment obligingly re-rolled itself so she could tip the loose sand back into the jar.

Now...*now* she could begin anew.

She poured a thick, unbroken line of sand that hugged her white chalk border; added whorls of it on the half-circle facing the stern. Curling waves the size of one or two hands —none overlapping and each oriented in a slightly different direction—then used her fingers to draw each wave's mirror image in golden grains on the circle's inside. The jar was empty when she finished the half-arc facing her opponents.

Next, she laid down four more overlapping wards—salt, then ash, then clay, then stone—wishing as she shaped them that she had thought to bring her canteen up with her. Casting the sand and ash wards with water would make them less fragile. Some grains were already blowing away. She checked the bag again for oil. Found none. Not surprising, since the wards only needed to last for a half-span.

It didn't matter. She had another resource at her disposal.

Rahelu sat cross-legged in the center of her five concentric wards, facing east: into the past and the cool sea breeze, letting the sun's rays warm her face and soak into her skin.

Sloppy, lazy, and mediocre, was she? Perhaps she was. She'd hated second- and third-year Obfuscation studies—the Guild's insistence on rigid formations had never been appealing. Memorize them all, their relative strengths and weaknesses, the standard decision chart on their deployment, until it was second nature.

The Guild method was effective; of course it was; hundreds of mages had spent thousands upon thousands of hours developing, testing, and refining endless variants.

But Onneja had shown her a different approach.

Rahelu breathed in time with the waves caressing the *Winged Arrow's* sides as it cut its swift path through the water —in the slow eight-count of the Conclave, instead of the double-count taught by the Guild—and stretched her resonance senses outwards, scanning the ship.

Most of the free resonance was flowing into Nheras's Obfuscation barriers. She couldn't reach Nheras herself and the auras of the other Supplicants were full of skittering anticipation and pulsing eagerness—both useless to her. Beyond them, the open waters carried no resonance.

So rather than drawing on the ambient resonance and conjuring her usual visualization of blank stone or blue-gray waters, Rahelu reached inside, throwing herself fourteen spans back in time, to the moment between day and night when she had jumped into the waves after Lhorne into the still depths of the ocean's embrace. She visualized a shadowy ring of submerged rocks that cradled her on all sides: smooth water-worn forms, black on black, rooted to the seabed and immovable, deflecting the incessant push and pull of the rising tide as it sought to drag her out to sea.

Rahelu held the crashing waves in her mind as she stole a

final glance at the others. Nobody saw her slip the hand wearing her Issolm-issued resonance crystal ring inside her tunic.

She laid her palm over Lhorne's pendant, letting the gentle swish of the pendant's resonance signature wash over the smaller crystal in the ring until the two aligned. Fed the relentless rhythm of the waves into both focus stones until all three of them thrummed to the heartbeat of the sea. Imagined the swirling haze inside the pendant expanding into a whirlpool; an impenetrable vortex centered on her that could swallow the world.

Unlike the last time she had used the pendant, its resonance signature changed instantly, blending its innate signature with the beat of crashing waves into an Obfuscation barrier. Her ring, now linked to Lhorne's pendant by sympathetic resonance, did the same.

Vision blurring, Rahelu released her focus and braced her pounding head in her hands, letting the two crystals fuel her Obfuscation barrier as the resonance backlash she had repeatedly pushed through overwhelmed her. If the other Supplicants breached her defenses, there was nothing more she could do, so she concentrated on not falling over instead.

Maketh, from somewhere far aft of her: "Begin!"

5

SIEGE

R AHELU TENSED FOR A BARRAGE OF PROJECTIONS.

That was what Nheras would have done. Nheras would have used every aggressive emotion in her repertoire, relying on sheer power to overwhelm Rahelu's wards, putting more and more resonance into every Projection until each one struck with the force of a battering ram.

None came.

Rahelu looked up.

No-sleeves waited at the point of Jhobon's formation. Behind him, on the other side of the crystalline divide, Jhobon touched a hand to the anchor. Jagged lines of resonance crystal fragments flared in the sunlight, arcing from root to branched tips like lightning.

Inside that conflagration, No-sleeves began to dance.

The rose-pink mist he summoned was the nuanced work of a songhouse artisan, not the crude onslaught Rahelu had wielded against Nheras. He conjured wisps of desire from nothing, letting each one build; plied them in an ebb and flow of resonance like the pull of the undertow; layered one crescendo after another so the effect of the whole was an unceasing yearning for release.

As his movements changed, so did the mix of emotions: undercurrents of lust and curiosity and recklessness joined desire, filling the ambient resonance with an orange-rose-red haze that called to some primal part of her soul.

Ylaen's Projections rolled over the two chalk circles like enveloping fog; seeped through sand, through salt, through ash. Rahelu felt his siren call as it washed up against clay and stone, a net that spread itself over the Obfuscation barrier she had anchored to Lhorne's pendant. Tendrils of rose-red mist twined themselves around her limbs.

She looked to the sky.

Saw stars in place of sails; sunlight changed to moonglow.

She closed her eyes to the heavens; felt the whisper of the breeze as warm breath against her cheek. Remembered a low voice whispering a promise of a different future.

Rahelu...

The faint voice was so hard to hear. The waves were too loud; she willed them to be quieter so she could listen.

Rahelu...

Young. Male. Husky with longing and hurt.

Come with me...

Why had she raised these wards and barriers against him?

He loved her.

He had come to find her.

He had found her but the sea had taken him. He couldn't swim; she needed to go to him.

Come to me, Rahelu.

This time it was a command, and her heart leapt to obey.

I...

That wasn't right.

He had been patient; he had been angry; he had pleaded

his case; but he had never, and would never, try to command her in this when she had sworn an oath.

An oath that led to the *Winged Arrow* and a course that took her far away from the future that could have been.

But you could not reach another shore if you kept turning back, and when your ship sailed before the wind it was far easier to stay the course.

Rahelu opened her eyes and found herself standing at the very edge of her circle, toes touching the inner line of river stones, her shadowy Obfuscation barrier greatly diminished —it would have vanished entirely if it hadn't been anchored. The rose-red ribbons of resonance Ylaen had bound around her shoulders, waist, and limbs were dull, their lustre gone. She seized them; wrapped the lengths around her forearms like bloody bandages, and pulled.

They snapped.

Pain stabbed through her eyes at the recoil. Broken streamers fluttered to the deck around her, edges smoking. Unless she maintained control of them, the resonance would quickly expand and lose form as it evaporated.

Outside her circle, No-sleeves gathered his half of the severed ribbons. They flowed like water as he coiled them like an eight-stranded whip. He met her eyes and she tensed; started reshaping rose-red ribbons into a crimson spear before she remembered counter-attacks were forbidden.

A corner of his mouth quirked up in a half-smile—the first self-deprecating expression she'd seen from him—then he turned and sent his remaining ribbons against Nheras.

Rahelu let go of her partially formed spear and her stance, and sat, nursing her headache. How much longer did she have to last? She glanced at the sun; whimpered into her knees with relief when she saw the half-span was almost up.

Even Jhobon had left her alone. While Nheras was preoc-cupied fending off attacks from the other three, Jhobon had been crawling around, chalk in hand, studying her barriers. Nheras hadn't secured her crystals because Maketh hadn't provided her with binding agents, and over the course of the contest, the ship's motions had shifted her anchors until they were no longer perfectly aligned.

Rahelu watched with exhausted detachment as Jhobon drew several swift strokes—lines of incidence and reflection? —then scrawled something else she couldn't read from this perspective. The *tap-scrape tap-scrape tap-tap-scrape* of chalk on wood fitted the rhythm of someone figuring an equation. Calculations for angles of incidence, perhaps?

Why that would be useful, Rahelu had no idea. Nobody took out *chalk* once the sparring circle had been drawn. You went first for focus stones, then for weapons, then fists and feet if you had nothing else.

One of Nheras's anchors glowed brighter than the others as her barrier sought to repel the combined onslaught. Nheras paid it no attention; she was busy reinforcing an anchor on the opposite side. Even lacking a sizable focus stone, Ghardon and Elaram had managed a Concordance, and now they brought their combined power against her defenses, probing every finger-width for weakness.

Drained as she was, prejudiced as she was, Rahelu shivered at the sight of Nheras holding off a coordinated assault from multiple fully trained mages. Alone. Without a greater focus stone or an advanced barrier formation.

Bright blue sparkles leapt out from her wrung-out resonance aura. This was not the first time that Rahelu had admired Nheras. But it was the first time she had felt this way, without being compelled to by Nheras herself.

Perhaps Nheras *had* worked for and earned her place, as much as Rahelu had.

Perhaps if you took away her House-born privileges of

wealth and power, Nheras would still best Rahelu seven times out of ten in a fair fight.

Perhaps there was reason for House Ilyn to hold Nheras as their brightest hope, beyond the fact that she was their Atriarch's granddaughter.

The frantic *tap-tap-tap-scrape* stopped. Jhobon tossed what was left of his chalk at one particular crystal in Nheras's network of anchors, closed his fist as he pulled on a handful of awe in the ambient resonance, then flicked his fingers. Sapphire stars soared after the chalk and collided with crystal —like the edge of a blade scraped across cut glass.

Rahelu's resonance senses screamed.

Nheras's outer barrier collapsed.

No-sleeves raised his arms. Eight rose-red ribbons reared back like nheshwyr preparing to strike. He lunged, sweeping his arms towards the deck, and his ribbons lashed down onto Nheras's second Obfuscation barrier. A larger crystal placed close to where she sat—the central anchor to her outer defenses and the lynchpin to her formation—exploded.

Nheras reeled, clutching her temples as No-sleeves struck again. Three more crystals exploded. Rainbow light stretched, the Obfuscation barrier thinning to compensate for the holes that riddled its foundation. His unrelenting attacks overloaded Nheras's remaining anchors.

Crystals keened; a chorus of death knells choking the air.

The rainbow sphere collapsed.

Nheras cried out; whether that was from resonance back-lash or the flying shards of overheated resonance crystal, Rahelu couldn't tell. Ylaen's remaining Projections crashed into Nheras's inner Obfuscation barrier at full strength.

Slate-gray indifference crumbled before rose-red passion.

Shit.

Elaram—gossip-hungry, eternally nosy, mischief-loving Elaram—must have gone Seeking the moment she noticed

Nheras had joined Rahelu inside their cabin. Stupid! Stupid to forget to guard against eavesdropping; Rahelu had been so caught up in their confrontation that Elaram's subtle surveillance had gone unnoticed.

Stop, Rahelu wanted to cry out, but she knew it would be useless. She recognized the look on Elaram's face; she'd seen it at point-blank range on the wrong end of Elaram's crossbow: a relentless desire for winning matched with a wide, beaming smile that held no malice but gave no quarter.

Wars are won first in the mind and then upon the battlefield.

All Rahelu could do was bear witness.

Though she was watching for the transition of control, when it happened, it happened so seamlessly she missed it.

One moment, Elaram was deftly threading the Issolm Concordance through the turmoil No-sleeves had roused in Nheras's aura, digging out the writhing jealousy she had tried to keep buried. Then, between that heartbeat and the next, they'd switched and Ghardon had control.

He seized upon that jealousy and traced its strands back through time. Found a moment that vibrated in sympathetic resonance with the waves of unfulfilled longing No-sleeves Projected—and Evoked Nheras's memory for all to see:

She has been careful, so careful, to lead him gently down the path that courtesy sets before him. Sensitive to his mood, she diverts him with conversation and small entertainments. By now, she has memorized his preferences: tales of the common folk and coarse humor cause him to forget formality; games of strategy bring out his wit; news of a mechanical device that keeps time with the annoying whirring of wound gears provokes his curiosity. Coaxing and cajoling by turns, she entices him out of his melancholy; precisely timed sympathy elicits a hand clasp in thanks, and for once, he does not excuse himself when she draws him away from the main gathering.

This new turn of events is precious—a hard-won battle in a years-long siege. She knows what must come next; steels herself to see her orders through. The fine gravel path is treacherous for her sandals and prevails upon him to offer his arm. A feigned stumble—caused by treading on her hems as he helps her across the stepping stones of the pond to the secluded pavilion—results in a solicitous examination of her turned ankle and a loan of his silver-trimmed robe to replace hers.

She sits up; lets sheer cloth-of-gold and folds of cream fabric—now torn, dirtied, and damp with pond water—slide off her shoulders in a fall of silk. A subtle tilt of her head emphasizes the bare, unblemished expanse of her throat and the swell of her breathing.

His green eyes are dark as he leans forward to wrap her in silver-trimmed, sky-blue brocade. A slight Projection encourages the rose-pink undertone in his resonance aura to come to the fore.

He is not thinking of her but she does not need him to think of her.

Her House does not need him to think of her.

Her House does not think of her.

His hands on her bare shoulders. His breath on her cheeks. She should soften her jaw, allow a slight parting of her lips, deftly stoke the unfulfilled passion suffusing his aura entirely. For she is here and she is not, and if that fact makes any difference to him, well, he will not care so long as her Projection holds and her own wants are irrelevant as long as she gets results.

Her body trembles.

She has to act. Now.

Now!

The opportune moment comes and goes; the whole time she is as stone. New weight settles upon her shoulders. The robe is still warm from his body; she shivers; resists the urge to push it away. Servants in sky-blue-and-pale-green livery arrive to light the sheltered pavilion's braziers: one carries word from the estate guards.

He abandons her with the barest word of farewell.

She is relieved; she is distraught; she is trapped here, for the rest of the night, for her grandmother bade her not to return home in failure.

The last vestiges of Nheras's control shattered. Intense shame—hot, crimson as blood—spilled out from her resonance aura as she curled up inside her circle and wept.

"Time!" Maketh called.

The Evocation faded as the others let go of their resonance techniques. The wind soon whisked the remnants of Ylaen's Projections away, leaving Nheras's humiliation as the only ongoing ripples in the ambient resonance.

Rahelu had wished many times for revenge; had prayed that Nheras would know the same depths of despair and shame that she had suffered at the Ilyn girl's hands; had tried to inflict that pain herself just a few spans ago.

Watching Nheras's entire body shake with heart-wrenching sobs should have brought her joy.

What she felt was ill.

"We won!" Elaram whooped as she hugged Ghardon around his neck, gloating without any regard for Nheras's feelings, her earlier misery forgotten.

"You have not," Maketh said, as he descended from the afterdeck. "Supplicant Rahelu's defenses are still active. She wins." He leaned over her to inspect her work and frowned. "This ward has not been constructed in accordance with the design you were given. Many of the extension lines have been omitted and the overall proportions have been modified."

"Apologies, Guardian." Rahelu bowed. "I could not reproduce a design so complex in the allotted time without error." Because he had made it fucking impossible. "I had to improvise something simpler." Something that would actually work. "I did my best to follow its general shape."

All true enough.

The Guardian's resonance aura hummed but he didn't press her for further answers. Instead, he crossed into the other circle and handed Nheras a handkerchief.

"Supplicant Nheras did very well, all things considered.

With more preparation and a better choice of formation, like Syne's Defense or Kergann's Wall, she could have held for another span or two. But Obfuscation barriers must draw power from somewhere—either from the ambient resonance, a focus stone, or from the mage—in order to remain active."

He nudged the crystal fragments littering the deck with the toe of his boot. "They are powerful but inflexible. A flaw in an anchor, the wrong choice of barrier, and your defenses will collapse. A good way to waste expensive materials. Wards, though, don't require resonance to function. They are cheap to construct, easy to repair, and easy to adapt."

"If they're so superior, why don't more mages use them?" Ghardon asked.

Maketh turned to Rahelu, eyebrows raised. "Well?"

"They aren't perfect defenses," she answered. "Resonance wards work by disrupting the flow of resonance. Their effectiveness is limited by the materials used in their construction. Sustained Projections"—she nodded at No-sleeves—"will get through most wards, eventually. And temporary wards are easy to disrupt." She stood and swept one foot through her wards. "If there had been more wind, or if the sea was less calm, I would have been in trouble."

Elaram stared. "All we had to do was to run over there and mess up those lines?"

"Yes," Rahelu said, then shut up when she realized she had spoken at the same time as Maketh.

He continued, unperturbed: "But there are ways to discourage such attempts, hence why you were forbidden from doing so. On that note"—Maketh cast a stern look at Jhobon—"I ought to disqualify your team for tampering with Nheras's anchor." He held up a hand to forestall Elaram's protest. "I won't, as you did strictly abide by the rules. The lesson, however, remains. In a real siege, resonance wards would be permanent, tied to natural landmarks and other features of the battlefield. Supposing you managed to dismantle them, you'd still have to contend with her Obfuscation barrier." The shadowy ring surged and ebbed with the waves. "By the time you take that down, Supplicant Rahelu would have called for reinforcements and—"

"In a real siege," Imos No-sleeves said, "I would not rely on a frontal assault to win the war."

"Explain."

Unlike he had done with Anathwan earlier, No-sleeves did not back down from Maketh's stare. He stepped clear of the mainsail's shadow until he stood in the sunlight, muscled arms crossed over his bare chest and his wind-tousled hair streaming behind him like a banner, and quoted: "There is no greater weakness than that which lies in the heart."

Great gods.

How the melodramatic ishtrel managed to keep a straight face while spouting bad poetry from the most overwrought version of Symezosh's speech like it contained great wisdom was an incredible feat because she sure couldn't keep herself from dissolving into a fit of snorting.

She wasn't alone either; she could hear Ghardon chuckling to himself. Even Elaram groaned softly at the awful line.

Maketh was obviously made of sterner stuff.

"If you have the ability to commit entire ballads to memory," the Guardian said without the slightest change in his inflection, "then doing the same for four years of missing curriculum should pose no great difficulty."

He let that sink in, then clapped his hands. "Take a break for a half-span, then report to the ship's study. We've a lot to cover if you're going to learn how to ward yourselves properly."

6

QUESTIONS

MAKETH HAD LIED.

The knowledge he deemed missing from their education did not amount to four years of curriculum—it was more like fourteen. The Guardian blazed through a condensed explanation of the first five principles of ward construction so fast that Ghardon and Jhobon, who had both nodded along initially, rapidly descended into panic and bewilderment.

Neither were helped by Elaram, who kept pestering one or the other, asking them to repeat and summarize everything Maketh said. While the Imrell Supplicant was too polite to tell Elaram to stop distracting him, her brother was not. Eventually, Elaram devoted all her energy and attention to deciphering the messy scrawl of Jhobon's hurriedly dashed notes once his mumbled replies started petering out in the middle of his sentences. Soon after, Ghardon stopped trying to understand anything altogether. One look at his pinched expression told Rahelu that his plan was to absorb the entirety of skyarc and Evoke it for study later, when he could slow down Maketh's delivery to a manageable speed and pause it as often as he needed.

Meanwhile, Rahelu sat quietly at the back, trying to gauge how she ought to position herself within the group.

How much understanding should she demonstrate, and how much confusion ought she pretend? She had to admit some knowledge—she could not otherwise believably pass off what she had done with the flawed ward to win—but too much would inflame Maketh's suspicions. Only the spectacular manner of Nheras's defeat had kept him from questioning her further at the time.

Rahelu snuck another glance at the Ilyn girl.

Post-duel, Nheras had slunk off to their cabin, face dripping with kohl and snot and tears, Maketh's pristine white handkerchief balled up in her fist. Precisely half a span later, she had rejoined them in the ship's study, clad in fresh Issolm whites and blacks, still face repainted so heavily it could have passed for a songhouse mask. She had not said a word to anyone since, not even to No-sleeves, who had leaned over to murmur something in her ear as she sat down next to him. Instead, she had chosen to stare fixedly at the Guardian with steel stiffening her resonance aura and spine, as if she could simply manifest mastery of a skill she disdained through strength of will alone.

Not only did Nheras seem well recovered, she had evidently also deemed the rest of her fellow Supplicants shades one and all, along with Rahelu.

Amusing as it was to watch No-sleeves's increasing consternation (which seemed to stem more from being snubbed for the third time that day than Maketh's teaching, which he was only paying cursory attention to), Rahelu also had to start fully concentrating once Maketh dove into the sixth and seventh principles of construction.

Three spans later, the other Supplicants' eyes had glazed over but the Guardian had only just finished warming up to his subject. Dissatisfied with the rate at which they were absorbing his instruction, Maketh ordered lunch trays brought to the ship's study so they could continue with a minimum of disruption from human weaknesses, such as the need for sustenance. At one point during skyarc when they were all fighting yawns, Jhobon tried to sneak out while the Dedicate expounded upon the properties of various warding materials and their relative advantages and disadvantages. He got as far as two strides from the passageway before Maketh pinned him to the spot with a glare.

Apparently, the need to piss wasn't acceptable either. Offered the alternative of a jar, Jhobon meekly shook his head and resumed his seat without argument.

Unreasonable expectations aside, Maketh turned out to be a patient and thorough instructor—possibly the best instructor Rahelu had ever had, barring Onneja. He had a knack for simplifying complex topics into easily digestible chunks. Most were already familiar to her through her years of self-study, but the way Maketh framed them helped her draw connections between seemingly disparate concepts until they formed a larger, unified whole. He encouraged all of the Supplicants to ask questions—even Rahelu—and though sometimes their questions strayed beyond what they were supposed to be learning, he always answered them in full before bringing the discussion back to the topic at hand.

If the memory of him hauling her through the Guild's hallways to an interrogation chamber like a bharost dragging a fresh kill hadn't been imprinted so vividly in her mind, Rahelu might have enjoyed herself.

Despite her fears, Maketh didn't single her out again.

Skymother be thanked.

Relief kept her buoyed through the stilted banquet-style dinner (twelve courses of tiny plates and Rahelu had hated them all equally) and their first round of progress reports.

Instead of allowing them to report individually, Maketh

summed up their collective performance as "lacking" and devoted the remainder of the quarter-span timeslot to laying out an even more intensive program of study.

To which Elder Anathwan said, "Commendable work, Dedicate. I see great potential in your proposal and will raise it to the Guild Council at their next meeting. However, it is neither practical nor desirable for our purposes. We must have something more focused on immediate application." She added, "Supplicants, you are dismissed," before turning her attention back to Maketh, who seemed to rally with another round of silent, Projected objections.

Rahelu stood with the others and masked the yawn she could no longer hold back with a deep bow. Her mind was so wearied and muddled it automatically reduced the senior mages' back-and-forth and the Supplicants' chattering to a soothing burble that nearly made her forget to get up again.

Shrine first, she decided as she doddered from the table. It was bad to keep the Stormbringer waiting for his due. *Then sleep.*

"Rahelu."

The coolness in Anathwan's voice—and the omission of her rank—cut through her stupor and halted her escape. Only her resonance ward prevented anxiety from shading her aura a jittery orange.

"Remain here and bolt the door."

She did so with trembling hands.

"Dedicate Maketh has made a number of interesting observations concerning you."

Nervous energy flooded her, urging her to move—move! Yank that door back open and flee, or scurry beneath the massive rosewood table, where she might be safe from the penetrating gazes that kept her riveted in place.

Rahelu did neither. Instead, her legs folded under her of their own accord and she sank down in the eighth—ninth—

she didn't know the exact number; she had lost count of her many bows.

"Captain Csorath and I would verify these observations for ourselves."

She was about two heartbeats away from falling into full-fledged panic. It took several swallows to wet her papery tongue enough to say, "Whatever my Elder requi—"

Before she could get another syllable out, Csorath slapped his palm on the resonance crystal panel in front of him and the great cabin's Obfuscation barriers flattened her.

She whimpered. Curled up like a spooked sea slug, forehead to knees, fists in her mouth while she waited and waited for one of the senior mages to modulate the barriers.

The tremendous pressure did not abate; only increased.

Maketh said, "Get up."

Rahelu bit down on her knuckles until the taste of salt and iron flooded her mouth. The sharp pain of her new self-inflicted wound pierced through the crushing sensation of the barriers and the dull ache of resonance backlash and lent her the strength to stand.

"Show them your ward."

"...my...ward?"

"Yes. Your ward."

Slowly, deliberately, she summoned Evocation.

Got no further than the first pale shimmer of a golden, wave-ornamented circle before the Guardian smothered it with a single gesture and clasped his hands before him as if by restraining them he also restrained the thunderous aspects building in his resonance aura.

"Your other ward."

Blood rushed from her cheeks. "What?"

"Do not take us for fools."

"I—" Rahelu stumbled, suddenly lightheaded, and caught herself on the edge of the table. Kept her hands braced there, so they couldn't betray her with their twitching. "I don't understand."

Maketh leaned forward, easily looming over her though she was standing and he was seated. "The ward you wear over your heart. Now."

Oh, Stormbringer.

What had she drawn such an elaborate ward for? Why was she such an intemperate idiot? The short-lived glee she'd felt from exercising her petty revenge had not been worth putting Onneja's secret and her family at risk.

How could she salvage this?

Her fingers shook as she struggled with her buttons. The slower she went to compensate for their unsteadiness, the stormier the Guardian's expression, which made her fingers shake all the more beneath the senior mages' combined ominous, silent regard until she could bear it no longer. She gripped the wonderfully soft cotton of her tunic, the roughened skin of her fingertips snagging on the impossibly smooth black silk trim; tore at it until those stupid tiny buttons popped off their threads to bounce, scatter, and disappear against the dark grain of the great cabin's polished planks like a palmful of shells offered to the Elumaje.

Rahelu removed her tunic and set the ruined garment on the table. The rest of her layers followed swiftly—including the troublesome one she had no name for, easily distinguishable in the heap thanks to the stark black kohl smudged across the beautiful silver stitches on its collar. Finally, she gathered her hair up and out of the way and stood barechested for judgment before the three senior mages, heart hammering so hard she was sure it would burst.

The Elder said, "Approach."

She complied.

Outside, the glow of the Skymother's lamp had dimmed. The evening had grown cold enough that the few land breezes wafting through the great cabin's open windows raised gooseflesh on her skin. The *Winged Arrow* had dropped anchor for the night in one of the many coves along the forested coastline and the woody scent of fresh pine was a welcome change from the stuffiness of the ship's study. Several white shapes cut through that glimpse of dusky sky. Questryls, by their large wingspans and gliding flight.

Rahelu longed to climb out, soar after those birds.

Csorath's voice drew her back.

"...ploying unorthodox methodology is not a crime," the Isonn Dedicate was saying.

"That is not merely unorthodox. That"—Maketh jabbed a finger at the tracery of kohl on her skin—"is an advanced suppression ward of Conclave design."

"And not an uncommon sight in the Dominion," Csorath said. "Particularly among the lesser trained in Obfuscation. The advantages of such a suppression ward are well known."

"And are reflected in the licensing fees charged by the Conclave for their use and thus beyond the means of a common-born fisher girl of unremarkable talent!"

"Indeed?" The Isonn Seeker-captain tapped the resonance crystal panel a second time and it obligingly spat out an Evocation of a parchment stamped with an elaborate seal in glittering green-and-blue resonance ink. "Keshwar Ideth found her sufficiently talented to sponsor her Petition."

"In a highly irregular manner!"

Maketh's finger stabbed through the circular scrap glued beside Keshwar's seal. The parchment had clearly been torn to pieces but the Guild's shimmering violet seal was intact.

"Yet it seems that Atriarch Ideth approves." Csorath's gaze flicked to the pendant she wore and her breath came faster. "Did you not say that she won your little challenge by improvising an intermediate-level repulsion ward?"

Maketh ignored the barb in favor of inspecting her handiwork with the kind of intense, thorough scrutiny that she assumed he usually applied to enemy barrier formations.

"Her Guild admission records state that she declared no Conclave training. This is patently not the case," the Guardian said. "Perhaps I do not have the evidence to conclusively prove she is a Chanazian operative. However—" Maketh broke off from restating his list of grievances to address Anathwan. "Our mission is fraught with enough difficulties as it is. We cannot afford to imperil it further. She should be neutralized."

The deadly undertone to his words left no doubt as to their meaning: *bind her, scour her mind for Conclave secrets until it breaks, then sink what remains.*

"Please, no!" Rahelu blurted out. "I am no Chanazian operative." She was so afraid that she actually rushed forward and stretched her hands out across the great expanse of the rosewood table towards the Elder in a desperate appeal.

Anathwan's impassive expression recalled her to her senses and she fell back, into the lowest of all the obeisances.

One defense left.

"Upon my lineage and my parents' honor, I am a loyal daughter of the Dominion. And Atriarch Ideth," Rahelu rushed on before Maketh could deny her innocence again, "Atriarch Ideth has verified the truth of this!"

Csorath tensed.

Rahelu hastily elaborated, lest she be accused further. "During Petitioning, at the end of my audience, the Atriarch requested I submit to a direct Seeking. I agreed. Later, while I was detained in the, the—"

Terror had not diminished with time; she had to force the rest of her defense out in a dry, squeaky rasp.

"—the Guild's interrogation chamber—"

Do you recall it? Rahelu thought furiously as Anathwan creased her elegant brow. *Please say you recall it.*

"—Atriarch Ideth vouched for me personally!"

Into the ringing silence, the Isonn Seeker-captain said, "She speaks the truth as she knows it."

There, done.

An Atriarch's given word was an incontrovertible defense and, in the absence of that Atriarch's presence, a Seeker had accepted her statement. Let Maketh Imos try to imply that Csorath Isonn—that Atriarch Mere Ideth—was mistaken, or incompetent, or lying. Rahelu didn't know much about House politics, but she was fairly certain House Isonn would not let House Ideth be insulted by House Imos.

Of course, Maketh did not dare. But that didn't mean he gave up. "In that case..."

Something landed in front of her with a *splat*. A fine white cotton handkerchief turned dun from being dipped into tea.

"Supplicant Rahelu," Maketh said, drawing out the vowels of her name so much that he briefly sounded like No-sleeves, "surely you have no objection to submitting to another direct Seeking?"

Fuck!

He'd trapped her. Again.

The only true answer Rahelu could give was to repeat herself: "I am a loyal daughter of the Dominion."

She snatched up his dripping handkerchief. Put the wet cloth to her left shoulder, squeezing as she dragged it over her heart, down her sternum, and across her belly to her right hip bone. Kohl-blackened trickles of cold tea wept from the severed lines of her resonance ward to soak into the waistband of her white Issolm trousers.

"Ennuost Yrg is my home," Rahelu said as she tossed Maketh's dirtied handkerchief onto the table before him.

Absolute stillness. The heavy kind that preceded a storm.

Anathwan spoke at last. "Seeker Csorath, you have my authorization to proceed."

All traces of resonance in Rahelu's immediate vicinity vanished, leaving her stranded in a bubble of uncanny blankness two strides wide in the ambient resonance. For the second time that day, Csorath's mind touched hers. If the Seeker's first mental contact had been the light brush of a summer breeze, this was the shock of falling into icemelt from the Unomelaje's heart.

Maketh's questions came thick and fast.

"Who trained you?"

"The Resonance Guild."

"How did you gain your mastery of wards?"

"From a book."

"Which book?"

"Venazelunaje's Codex."

"Who gave it to you?"

"No one." He was so certain of her guilt that he was using questions with a limited range of answers to pin her down. Her thoughts raced ahead along his inevitable line of questioning; somehow, she had to cut it off before she was forced to mention Onneja by name or implication. "It came in the bundle of third-year texts I got from an Echo Alley merchant's liquidation sale."

Csorath said, "That's an evasion."

She gulped and tried again. "I went looking for it."

Next would be, '*Why were you looking for that specific title?*' and that she couldn't answer with anything other than, '*A Conclave journeymage told me to*', so she had to preempt Maketh by giving a different answer to a broader version of the question on his lips. A narrative so intertwined with the truth of her life that none of the senior mages would think to question it further, because it played to the ideals underpinning the Founding of Aleznuaweite itself and the preconceived notions that House-born held of the few common-born who were able to join their ranks.

Was the Dominion not a land of opportunity? Where anyone, regardless of birth or station, could rise to the greatest heights, if they were willing to do whatever it takes? Rahelu thought of every disadvantage she had had to overcome and gave them the recitation they expected:

"I was doing badly in Obfuscation studies." She focused on the misery and the all-encompassing guilt and self-hatred she had felt when she'd come close to failing the Elementary level examinations. "I'd gotten through first-year on Evocation-aided rote memorization alone; I couldn't read any Aleznuaweithish. But there was so much to cover in second-year that the instructors assigned all the theory as prescribed readings and devoted class time to practicum. Everybody else had the texts and the supplementary materials and the private tutoring so they did just fine."

Bitterness at those entrenched disparities came easily. She patterned her mind after the ice that formed on the upper lakes of Anuvelomaz in truewinter: at least a stride thick and so clear that, when you brushed the accumulated snowdrifts away, the sunlight glinting off the jewel-toned scales of the carp moving in sluggish circles fathoms below fooled you into thinking that you saw straight into the depths.

"My family went without rice and firewood for a month so I could take the three silver kez we had scraped together to every secondhand book merchant in the city in hopes of finding an older edition or another book on resonance defenses." It had been a long, exhausting search that had filled her with discouragement. "Venazelunaje's Codex was the only book I could afford. It took me a week of sounding out the letters to realize it had nothing to do with Obfuscation techniques. But when I brought it back, the merchant refused to return my money. 'You asked for a book on resonance defenses,' he'd said, 'and you hold one in your hands.' He had been trying to get rid of the thing for years."

No one else had wanted to bother with such a poorly translated volume of abstract, philosophical meditations on the nature of resonance when it contained no schematics or diagrams. Four years on and the hurt and betrayal she'd felt at being so roundly cheated was still as fresh as the blood seeping from her bitten knuckles, without Evocation.

She had cried twice that day.

Once outside that coin-grubbing cheater's shop before returning to their miserable hovel so her face and aura could not betray how badly she had squandered her family's hard-earned coin as soon as her parents laid eyes on her.

And once, much later during deepnight, after her parents' snores reassured her they were fast asleep.

"After that, I was determined to learn everything I could from the book; I couldn't let my family's sacrifices go to waste." When Rahelu raised her eyes from the cabin's deck to meet Maketh's gaze defiantly, her cheeks were wet. "I learned well."

That put an end to his questions, for the Guardian could find nothing objectionable in her answer.

Then Csorath spoke: "A moving tale." The Seeker-captain seized on the glimpse of buried guilt behind the frozen memories she had presented. Just as Elaram and Ghardon had done earlier to Nheras, so Csorath hunted the erratic pulsing of the blue-black resonance through the murky churning of Rahelu's aura. "What secret are you protecting?"

Memory stirred:

The warmth of the skyarc sun. Gull cries upon the wind. Wave song blending with muffled sobs as she mourns the end of her parents' hopes. Instead of going to Market Square to admit her failure, she goes to sit cross-legged upon the clifftop heights of Stormbane's Rest in meditation, across from—

Panic rose as Onneja's parting warning reverberated in her soul: *Let no one discover what you have seen.* She had to suppress it before Csorath managed to fully draw out the image of her sitting with the silver-haired Conclave journey-mage at the center of a spinning vortex of futures—

No. The only reason she was being questioned gently was because Maketh had not managed to fully convince Csorath and Anathwan she was guilty. Any hint of resistance would doom her and her family.

What other truth would stand up to a Seeker's scrutiny? What narrative would the Houses find believable?

There!

Her eyes caught on the fading Evocation of the Guild seal she had reconstructed two days prior to meeting Onneja. When she had meditated in that same spot at a similar span, felt the same wretched shame and crushing despair as she attempted a desperate, equally ambitious working.

Rahelu folded chronology.

Prayed that, in the absence of a fully trained Evoker, no one would notice how she melded the later event's beginning to the earlier event's middle so instead of witnessing her traditional gesture of apprentice to master as she sat across from Onneja, the scene Csorath uncovered showed:

—the troubled scrivener's gifts laid out before her: brush pen, ink stone, violet resonance dust, and three sheets of new parchment that she has to weigh down with the glittering black gem—

HOLD.

Rahelu, her past, her thoughts froze at Anathwan's Command. Even Maketh and Csorath were caught in the ripples; the Guardian half-risen from his cushion and the Seeker-captain's deeper probe into her mind arrested as the Elder plucked the black gem from the vision. The rest of the clifftop puffed away as Anathwan turned the fragment of Rahelu's memory in her hands, examining how the gold-flecked facets of the black rock drank in the sunlight. And—for the first time—Rahelu noticed the strange shadows that the gem scattered across the parchment. They defied reality; their shapes did not match the spherical form of the stone.

Anathwan set the illusory gem on the table and time restarted in the cabin.

"How did you obtain this artifact?" the Elder asked.

"I found it in a scrivener's shop in Blackforge. The Tattered Quill. The scrivener—" Rahelu moistened her lips. "He got it from another mage. A veiled stranger in a pale robe with a powerful talent for Augury who came to him, offering a glimpse of his fate for a favor. A woman, I think; I didn't see her, except through a brief Seeking. She had a woman's figure and a woman's voice, but spoke a tongue I do not know. I heard them arguing and I thought—I feared—"

The impatient drumming of Anathwan's fingers cut her nervous rambling short.

"The scrivener did not like the futures he saw. I helped him avert them with a minor Fortunement. In return, he gifted me the writing materials I needed for my Petition along with the stone, which he believed to be cursed."

Xyuth had been right. He and Dharyas had died for it. Hzin had died for it. Her own mother had nearly died for it.

The Elder's fingers stilled. "This Augur. Did she aid you in performing the Fortunement?"

Rahelu shook her head. "By the time I arrived, she had fled but her Augury remained active. All I had to do was sway the probabilities towards the outcome he preferred."

"Interesting. Was it difficult?"

She blinked. Now that she thought about it...

"Easy as slipping into a current," she said.

"Where is this artifact now?"

"I—"

Oh, how desperately she wished that she could simply reach into her pocket and set the real gem before Anathwan in place of its memory! But no, she had been a short-sighted fool and, in her haste to catch the *Winged Arrow*—

"I left it behind in the city."

Lying on the floor on her side of the pallet, near-invisible in the pre-dawn dark. Perhaps it was still there. Lhorne might have overlooked it (though, in that case, Tlareth had likely found and sold it to some curio merchant by now). Or he might have had the good sense she hadn't and thrown it in the Aleituan Sea, as Xyuth had urged her to do.

But in her heart, she knew he hadn't.

Lhorne had given her a gift.

She had not offered one in return—and he hadn't expected her to. That had been clear in how he had turned away; had remained so, even in sleep, even in his dreaming, until the very moment of her leaving, when that single unconscious surge of longing had made his hopes plain.

Idiots, the both of them.

"Where?" Anathwan pressed.

"At the Sable Gull, an inn owned by a woman called Tlareth in the Lowdocks. I'd meant to take it to the Seaspire as an offering to the Stormbringer but—"

Alarmed by the sharp rise of the Elder's eyebrows and the severe line of her lips, the last shreds of Rahelu's composure fled and she abandoned all attempts at justifying her actions. Words poured from her mouth as bone-white mist flooded from her unguarded resonance aura.

"Forgiveness, Elder! I didn't know it was an artifact; I—"

CRACK!

Resonance erupted from Csorath. Black lightning sundered the ambient resonance and rent her aura in two.

"You lie."

Csorath's Seeking stripped away every self-deception she had ever indulged in and laid bare the unpalatable, unshakeable conviction at the very core of her being:

Not good enough.

There was a limit to how far you could sink into the depths of the sea, but no limit to the heights of heaven. No matter what she learned or how accomplished she became, she would never be good enough.

Never.

The Seeker said, very softly, "Do not lie again."

Spirit thoroughly tested, beaten, and cowed, Rahelu meekly yielded up the answers she had, which were not the answers they wanted. Yes, she had known the stone was unusual; no, she had no idea what a stargem was, save that it was an object that those black-robed cultists—the ones she and her team of Petitioners had failed to stop from murdering two more citizens—had been hunting. Yes, she—they—had eventually realized that the black crystal-that-was-no-resonance-crystal must be the stargem the cultists had spoken of since its substance was a match for their strange serpentine knives; it was why Elaram had suggested that—no, she hadn't ever thought of turning in the stargem to the Houses because…because…

Her thoughts swam around and around in circles.

"I don't know," she confessed. "It was pretty. It was nice having something in my pocket to fiddle with and I liked the solid feel of it in my palm. It didn't seem important."

Gods. Her reasons sounded so childish and stupid. Rahelu cringed, but the three senior mages had moved on to greater concerns.

Anathwan laid one hand on the resonance crystal panel, the other on her pendant, and sank into mage trance.

Csorath went to the shelves and retrieved a large scroll.

Maketh swept aside the remnants of their dinner banquet

—carelessly stacking cups of cold tea, congealed bowls of sweet red bean soup, and plates of crumbling almond cakes and wobbling slices of thousand-layer rice pudding in teetering piles on top of fruit platters that still held slices of citrus fruits and melon—to make room for Csorath's map.

Rahelu held still; she had not been dismissed. But since Csorath had released his Seeking and no more questions were being directed at her...

Tentatively, she eased herself into a sitting position. No rebuke came, so she tried standing. Only when that, too, went unpunished, did she dare reach for her clothes.

Starfather be thanked; her ploy had worked.

"So far, the Free Territory fleets remain preoccupied with their summer raiding," Csorath said as he tapped the stretch of open ocean between the eastern part of the Ngutoccai continent and the western isles of Abmerdu. Faint, dotted white lines of resonance ink shimmered as he traced over the main sea routes, conjuring a ghostly flock of tiny vessels that swarmed in midair like mosquitoes. "If their sages have also been impacted by the recent perturbances in resonance, it has not affected their movements." Csorath turned his attention to the southwestern part of the Ngutoccai continent. "However, House Isca agents have reported an unusually high number of Chanazian merchant ships setting sail from their home ports."

Rahelu froze with one arm partway through a sleeve.

A detailed tactical discussion? Involving confidential reports from House intelligence? In front of a Supplicant?

Ah, *shit.*

She darted another glance at the two Dedicates huddled to the entranced Elder's left, their heads bent over the map, then gauged the distance to the door.

She had to leave—right now—before she overheard more of what she wasn't supposed to, and got mind-wiped for it.

But leaving meant unbolting the door, which would disrupt the closed circuit of the great cabin's barriers, which would expose the senior mages' discussions to any Conclave Seekers monitoring the *Winged Arrow* (just as House Seekers were monitoring all those Chanazian ships), which would compromise the security of the Dominion, which only a traitor would do, which would prove Maketh's point, and then he would erase her mind so thoroughly you would never know she had ever possessed any thoughts.

Fuck!

Why couldn't they just have dismissed her once Csorath's direct Seeking had given them sufficient proof of her loyalty? What was so important about that stupid stargem that news of the artifact overshadowed everything else?

Best get dressed and make herself part of the furniture, and hope they would remain so preoccupied that they would continue to overlook her existence.

"What of the Divine Kingdom?" Maketh asked.

"No sign."

"Their agents must be embedded more deeply within our ranks than we anticipated." Maketh's frown deepened. "Or we simply do not have the skill or the means to detect them."

Csorath sighed. "Let your theory go; I know for a fact that neither the mage-priests nor the Conclave are behind this."

"Both stand to gain much from occluding our Auguries. Just three seasons of muddying our short- to medium-term forecasts has wreaked havoc on the allocation of resources across the Dominion, severely curtailing both our expansion initiatives and defensive capabilities." The Guardian's tone took a turn to the sarcastic. "Yet, somehow, someone was able to perform an act of grand Augury—undetected—in the middle of our capital, despite these difficulties."

On and on, the two Dedicates debated. Their arguments

were so sharpened, so polished that the discussion quickly became too truncated and technical for her to follow.

Looking down, she saw that she'd managed to put her underrobe on with the seams facing out. The fledgling sense of House-born propriety that Ghardon had tried to instill in her despaired, but she quashed it. Since no one had reprimanded No-sleeves for going about with half his attire missing, Rahelu loosely belted her underrobe with a simple overhand knot of her sash and decided she, too, was now sufficiently dressed. She made herself and her aura as small and as near-invisible a presence as possible, without doing something even more suspicious, like drawing on resonance or slithering under the table.

Tried to shut her ears and distract herself with the task of locating every single one of her tunic's missing buttons.

Unsuccessfully.

"While you have spent your time composing political tracts and babying Petitioners, I—and every other Seeker that could be spared—have ridden and sailed the length and breadth of the continent. There's no evidence to support your conjectures but the Evokers have discovered plenty of records in the Chroniclers' less well-maintained histories going back several centuries that point to similar recurrences every—"

"There is nothing natural about these perturbances in resonance," Maketh snapped. "They are patterned! Some intelligence is behind them."

Curiosity overwhelmed fear. She crept closer, on the pretense of retrieving those stupid buttons, and listened avidly to every unguarded word.

"...suspect the artifact is untraceable," the Isonn Seeker was saying. "Pity the other two are dead; Ideth has had very limited success with only one source of information. Has Alozei found the origins of—"

Maketh snorted. "Only rumors and wild fancies. In a few

more days, perhaps." He rubbed the back of his neck as he cast another disgruntled look at the map. "I wish the Atriarchs had not backed this plan," the Imos Guardian muttered as he rested his head in his hands. "We have become so reliant on Augury that we are blind without it."

"Perhaps," Anathwan said as she surfaced from mage trance. "And perhaps not." The Issolm Elder smiled. "Peace, Maketh. The Houses already have, or will soon have, secured this artifact, thanks to your timely insights, Captain Csorath's perceptiveness, and Supplicant Rahelu's..."

Every muscle went rigid as that beautiful smile—and the Dedicates' renewed attention—alighted on her.

"...initiative."

Rahelu nearly melted into a boneless puddle of relief as the Elder's smile widened to include her.

"I expect confirmation of our target in the coming days. Captain, how soon can we reach Peshwan Yrg?"

"Eight days. Assuming fair winds and no complications."

"That will not do. Per the latest viable Augury, we must make landfall before the summer solstice."

That was less than six days away.

A long pause as both Dedicates digested that statement.

Eventually, Csorath offered a curt bow and said, "Honored Elder, excuse me while I make the necessary adjustments to our course."

Anathwan nodded, eyes drawn to the Evocation of the stargem once more.

Csorath deactivated the great cabin's Obfuscation barriers and strode out, clutching the map in his fist and shouting for his officers. Ambient resonance rippled and whooshed in his wake as the pressure within and without equalized.

Maketh said, "A week is not enough for the Supplicants to acquire the necessary understanding, let alone mastery."

"The Exalted Dominance requires neither mastery nor understanding, only results. You have three days."

The impossible deadline rendered him speechless.

When Maketh made no move to leave, Anathwan added, "Do whatever you must."

He bowed.

Rahelu held her breath and remained perfectly still, praying that he—like the captain—would be too preoccupied with the enormity of his challenge to recall her presence.

The hem of his robes tickled her feet as he passed by on his way to the door.

Maketh glanced down absently. Blinked once, twice, at the disheveled sight of Rahelu: kneeling, partly shadowed by the overhang of the rosewood table, half of her Supplicant's uniform squashed into a bundle under one arm and a palmful of buttons cupped in her hands. He shook his head, clearly chagrined by his near oversight. Bright light flared as he drew on his pendant. Power rapidly coalesced into a yellow-hued mist, dulled by blue-gray undertones. Contentment, blended with calm. For docility and forgetfulness.

Oh, *gods*.

Her hands shook, spilling the buttons she had gathered in a soft *clatter*.

Maketh ignored her. "Honored Elder?"

"Hm?"

"Your permission?" Maketh prompted, raising his voice to be heard over the groggy work-chants of the crew Csorath had roused from their hammocks.

Anathwan stirred. "For?"

"To conclude the interrogation." He gestured. Four glowing tendrils of mist streamed through the air to settle across Rahelu's shoulders. Dizziness returned as they slithered around to coil tightly about her neck like smoking scarves.

Or nheshwyr.

Or nooses.

Rahelu squeezed her eyes shut. *Please*, she begged, even as drowsiness stole over her body. She slumped, not quite sure whether she had meant to Project the thought or utter it aloud in prayer. Maybe she ought to do both?

"Please…" she croaked.

There were more words that ought to follow that one; she knew that much but not the words. Those eluded her, shrouded by billowing mist.

Please, she repeated.

The mist answered with, *peace-peace-peace*, and she was so physically, mentally, emotionally, spiritually, and magically wrung out and weary that all she wanted to do was lie down, let its blissful touch roll over her, and not think because thinking hurt. Easier to simply breathe and watch, mesmerized, as darkness encroached upon her mind.

Somewhere, dimly, she heard a firm, "No."

Blazing ice-white clarity burned away the darkness.

Rahelu came to with a gasp, heart racing.

"Leave her memories intact," Elder Anathwan said as she released her Projection.

"Our security protocols—"

"May bend a little without breaking. I see no point in tampering with a promising mind, particularly when Supplicant Rahelu's unexpected skill with resonance wards will be sorely needed for this mission. Given the constraints, I would have thought you'd agree."

Maketh's face darkened. "She has not proven—"

"I am aware of your concerns, Dedicate. You have discharged your duty by expressing them, and you have had your chance to prove your case. I do not, however, accept your conclusions. That said, I am always receptive to revising my assessment should further evidence come to light."

Anathwan tapped the resonance crystal panel, vanishing the last echoes of the stargem and Rahelu's Petition.

"So," the Elder said lightly, "let this be an additional, specific test for Supplicant Rahelu. Dedicate Maketh, if you discover any intelligence leaks pertaining to the matters we have just discussed whose origins are traceable to her, you have my full authorization to immediately strip her of rank and memory.

"And, Supplicant Rahelu, for avoidance of doubt, the topics under embargo include, but are not limited to, the nature and existence of this additional test. We spoke of resonance wards and your commendable skill with them; nothing more." Anathwan stood, blue eyes cool and unreadable as she studied her two remaining subordinates. "Is this satisfactory?"

Rahelu instantly prostrated herself. "Yes, Elder."

Maketh said nothing; only bowed.

Anathwan departed for her cabin without a backward glance, leaving Rahelu alone with the Imos Dedicate. He stared at her for another heartbeat, which seemed to last an eternity, before retreating to his own cabin.

Safe! She was safe!

Giddy exhilaration possessed her. Made her want to toss the garments in her hands into the air as if they were ribbons and dance and shout. A wild sob-laugh ripped free; she smothered it with a mouthful of cotton, shuddering as she forced herself to breathe—slowly!—through her tunic and recall Onneja's advice as a sweet, light, floral scent filled her nose:

Relax. And simply be.

Gull cries.

Wavesong.

Breathe.

Only after the *Winged Arrow* had exchanged the still

waters of the sheltered cove for the restless waves of the open sea, did her resonance aura recover a semblance of composure.

She fled to the ship's shrine to make good on her vow.

Ten times she bowed to the Stormbringer's driftwood effigy. Drew her knife from her belt and kez after kez from her purse until what she clutched added up to a full fifth of her wealth. Threw the coins overboard in a glittering rain of gold and silver because parting with kez hurt more than parting with blood and if she didn't do it all at once, she feared she never would.

A rope-laden Kerg came across her stalled at the top of the companionway. Too far gone to negotiate the ladder without clinging to the handrail but unable to muster the strength in her feeble fingers to do so. And furiously embarrassed by both shortcomings.

The third mate eyed her self-inflicted wound and her makeshift bandage—a strip torn from that stupid decorative underlayer, made useful at last—but asked her no questions.

"Here, kit." He sat down and handed her a rope.

Her hands moved automatically.

Kerg watched. Satisfied she knew what she was doing, he took up his own rope. "Heard y'was a fisher from th' fishing fleet proper, not one of them House-born whelps who've ne'er seen more water in one place than their bath nor them trouble-making Free Territory ship clan flotsam."

She nodded. "My parents have sailed with the fleet for five years. But I grew up on the Elumaje."

Her voice caught.

His kindness, the cool caress of the breeze in her hair, the seeming nearness of the incomprehensibly distant stars in the Skymother's vast cloak, the soothing, familiar action of straightening snarled rope—

All of it prodded at some tender place inside her and Evocation unspooled:

She is eight; all skinny, tanned limbs with a wild black sheaf of tangled hair, the golden glow of her resonance aura bright enough to compete with the sun for the late summer day's glory.

'Anenje! Anenje!' she shrieks from her rickety raft, loud enough to startle the lakebirds nesting along the reed-covered banks of the Elumaje into flight. The force of her springing leap to soar across the two-stride gap between raft edge and silty shallows sends the little watercraft spinning. 'Come, look! I did it, just like you showed me!'

There is no answering cry from the third thatched hut along the eastern bank. She searches the village with eyes and ears and resonance senses.

'Venaz?'

Anenje is not here. Her clever eel traps, her fishing spear, the large reed baskets she uses to transport her catch to market—all gone.

Only a snarled mass of rope remains.

Anenje had left the village and traveled to the Dominion, where she had taken a new name and made a new life for herself. Not long after, Rahelu's family had done the same. When she and her venaz had last spoken after finding each other again, years later, Tsenjhe had seemed...if not happy, then content.

Kerg regarded the moonlit lake of her memory. "Beautiful."

"It is," Rahelu said, then abruptly cut off the involuntary Evocation. She did not want to relive the subsequent tantrum that her stupid, ungrateful, manipulative eight-year-old self had thrown.

Things had seemed so simple back then. Anenje had left to be a mage; why couldn't she do the same?

Now she was one.

Why did she still feel so trapped?

When Kerg stood with an armful of neatly coiled ropes, she stood with him, grimly contemplating the companionway.

"If y'd like t' bunk up here where y'cin feel the wind and look at the stars 'stead of being cooped up below inna box, I'll get you a hammock," he offered.

"Thank you," she said, touched. "But I should bunk with the other Supplicants."

She could not afford to stand out any more than she already did.

Kerg bowed and did her the favor of not hanging around to watch her descend the companionway on her ass like a toddler and half-stumble, half-crawl through the darkened passageway.

To her surprise, the other Supplicants weren't around to witness and make fun of her clumsiness either. Nor were they clustered together, drinking and whiling the night away with whatever frivolous amusements House-born liked to pursue when there weren't any dinner parties to attend. A quick Seeking confirmed her peers were quiet in their cabins: Jhobon hunched over his notebook at the desk; No-sleeves slouched against the open port, tossing knives at a knot in the wood on the back of their door; Ghardon and Elaram seated on their trunks with their hands joined in Concordance, watching a ghostly Maketh scribe foundation lines at half speed.

Nheras, however, had brought a lantern and an incense holder with her to the ship's study. Wisps of fragrant smoke rose from the stick she had lit. She sat in Rahelu's earlier seat, brow knitted in ferocious concentration as she tried to puzzle out the disjointed notes on minimizing interference when combining component wards into a greater ward that

Rahelu had not bothered to erase when the ship's gong had summoned them to the great cabin for dinner.

Good.

More than anything, Rahelu wanted—needed—to be alone and *sleep*.

The unmistakable smell of urine hit her as soon as she opened the door to their cabin; the reconfiguration of the cabin a heartbeat later.

Nheras must have switched their bunks during the break. And emptied the full chamber pot onto Rahelu's new bed.

Rahelu burst out laughing.

Nheras's use of physical space and symbolism to reassert superiority was just so *blatant*. But you had to award credit where credit was due. She hadn't thought her House-born cabinmate capable of any stratagem other than ones that involved overwhelming people with bluntly wielded power or a mountain of coin.

Alas, the stench and the supposed indignity did not have the desired effect on Rahelu. If anything, it actually reminded her of the Lowdocks.

Poor Nheras, miscalculating two nights in a row.

Rahelu piled the soiled bedding on top of the festering uniform in the middle of their cabin but left the Ilyn girl's sheets and things alone. 'Keep your silks,' that would say to Nheras; 'I'm no soft, pampered House-born in need of coddling.' She grinned as she bedded down in what had formerly been Nheras's bunk and made herself comfortable by stretching out on the bare wood platform.

She did not bother staying awake to catch Nheras's reaction. If Nheras couldn't stomach studying here when the offense to her nostrils was so minor, there was no way she would be able to abide sleeping in their cabin.

Rahelu had, unquestionably, won again.

7

OPTIONS

THE 11TH DAY OF TRUESUMMER,
530 A.E./A.F.

ON THEIR SECOND DAY, GUARDIAN MAKETH IMOS announced there would be no more lectures in the ship's study. Instead, he commandeered the great cabin, distributed chalk and slates and Supplicants evenly throughout the larger space, and spent eartharc putting them through a series of impromptu practical examinations.

Clearly, the Elder's remarks had stung deeply.

Maketh did not bother to hide his disillusionment with his orders, the Guild's decisions with regard to curriculum, the bleary-eyed Supplicants he was charged with teaching—and the fact that Rahelu had been permitted to remain amongst them. Glowing lines sprang into existence above the table as he tapped the resonance crystal panel in front of him.

"Begin from foundation lines. Raise your hand when you have completed each variant." A chorus of soft *scrapes* and *taps* rose as everyone bent their heads to the task. "You will not progress further until I am satisfied that you are capable of producing something that bears a passable resemblance to work from a mage's hand instead of a child's scribbles."

With that ringing vote of confidence in their abilities, the

Guardian took to prowling, pouncing as soon as any Supplicant twitched a hand upwards to issue rapid-fire critiques. He berated Elaram for drawing lines that were too loose and Ghardon for lines that were too rigid; harangued Jhobon for taking too long to begin and excoriated Nheras for confusing an extension line with a foundation line.

Harsh, but fair. If he didn't correct those mistakes now, they would have no hope of constructing functional wards.

Maketh cast a dour glance at her slate, found nothing objectionable, and motioned for her to proceed to the last of the eight basic wards. He then reached over the next Supplicant's shoulder and rapped his knuckles sharply on the slate. "Eyes on your own work, Ylaen."

No-sleeves put his chalk down, leaving his fifth basic ward unfinished. "I beg my Dedicate's pardon, but...is all this"—he gestured languidly—"really necessary?"

All eyes swung to him at last.

Maketh's answer was stiff. "You are free to withdraw your choice." The Guardian jerked his chin at the door. "I cannot force you to learn if you do not wish to."

"Begging my Dedicate's pardon again, but that's not true; I am always eager to learn. What I am not eager to do is waste my limited time in pursuing the impossible."

Translation: *'I'm too fucking lazy to apply myself.'*

"As I recall, we were allotted the time it takes to sail from Ennuost Yrg to Peshwan Yrg to devote ourselves to learning the basics of two or more higher-level resonance skills. But the captain's been keeping a straight course through deeper waters, instead of following established routes close to the shoreline, and doubled the dark watches after weighing anchor last night. Word from the crew is we'll make Peshwan Yrg in five days—not eleven—unless the Stormbringer summons a tempest. Even then, they've orders to sail through it."

Jhobon Imrell looked unsurprised, but the rest of the Supplicants started as if the possibility that they might have less time than they'd anticipated had not occurred to them.

It probably hadn't.

Shit. She should've told them.

"Besides"—No-sleeves leaned forward, heedless of smudging his work—"the Elder requested we take an applied approach to our study. These days, we have more efficient and direct means of effecting knowledge transfer."

Rahelu stared. Where was he going with this? Did he think the Houses had established the Guild with all its expensive instructors and forced their trainees to suffer through five years of classes just for fun?

You couldn't just shove information into someone's head with Evocation (or steal it with Seeking) and expect it to be retained. The mind was porous as a sieve and whatever immediate recall was gained would be lost just as quickly as the knowledge decayed. No, you needed to preserve it in a more permanent form, like books and scrolls and resonance crystal matrices, or personal experience, or—

"Shades," No-sleeves said.

To her right, Ghardon made a choked noise, which sounded suspiciously like barely withheld laughter, and she had to suppress her own disbelieving snort.

Oh, both of them knew—theoretically—how to do something like that. Shade summoning wasn't taught by the Guild, but anyone paying attention could extrapolate from the principles that were covered in Intermediate and Advanced Evocation, and piece the technique together from first principles. Except it was nigh impossible to execute—unless you were an Evoker with power on the level of an archmage and you had the soul you wanted to summon as a shade, alive and consenting, acting as your focus. Which she doubted Maketh Imos was willing to do. Few were comfortable with the notion of reproducing themselves in simulacra. The technique was an expensive, last-resort preservation attempt by those who did not, for one reason or another, expect to be able to pass on their irreplaceable knowledge to a living heir during their allotted lifespan.

Just when she was starting to think that No-sleeves might have an inkling of substance to back up his flashy looks, too.

"Resonance crystal legacies," he continued, despite the growing titters.

Which required the soul with the knowledge you wanted to be a highly trained mage in the first place. And die.

Both Elaram and Nheras joined her and Ghardon in casting dubious glances at No-sleeves.

He ignored them but returned her look of ridicule with a long, implication-laden look of his own. "Spirit essences."

Rahelu's response was immediate. "No."

She barely withheld the rest: *'The heavens will fall and set the sea afire before I let any of you inside my head to dissect and distill my life down to the few memories that you think are worth ingesting.'*

But, to her alarm, both Elaram and Ghardon acquired a sudden, almost avaricious gleam in their eyes, and the Imos Dedicate did not dismiss the idea out of hand.

She did, however, gain some unexpected support.

"That's cheating," Nheras said, her aura tinged with green-brown disgust.

"It's sharing, love," No-sleeves corrected her. "And I'll take survival by any means. One of us has already done the work; I don't see the need for the rest of us to suffer in duplicating the effort at the risk of not meeting the Elder's expectations in other areas. Especially when Issolm here"—he smiled lazily at Ghardon—"has already been cheating his way through the test."

Ghardon gave him a flat stare. "Evocation-aided recall is *not* cheating."

No-sleeves shrugged and turned his smile on Elaram. "Seeking certainly is."

Elaram didn't bat an eyelid at the accusation. "Guardian Maketh only said we had to draw the lines ourselves; he didn't place any limitations on how we obtained the knowledge of producing them."

Rahelu couldn't bear to hold her tongue any longer. "Because the whole point is for you to do the work yourself!"

Why, in the eight hells and under the four heavens, did she have to explain the basic facts of life obvious to anyone except these oblivious, entitled, sheltered House-born brats?

"Suppose I agree," she said to No-sleeves. "I Evoke the sum total of my experience with resonance wards."

Every self-taught morsel bitterly won through the painstaking process of trial and error.

It had taken her a year to sound out the abstruse passages of Venazelunaje's Codex by lamplight, one letter at a time; two more before she began to truly grasp the meaning behind what she read; and countless spans upon spans upon spans drawing the same line ten thousand times with cramping hands until the motions became second nature.

"I distill years of my memories to their essence, Imbue that know-how into crystal, and I hand it to you."

Just speaking the notion aloud offended her so much she could feel her anger bubbling through her resonance ward.

A corner of his mouth curled up, as if the glow in her aura was a delight to him, and set her blood boiling.

"Good luck absorbing the essence before it erodes! And good luck harnessing the instinctive responses it grants without the context of my experience to inform you!"

Her tirade washed over him and left no impression behind, the way water ran off a gull's back.

"One," No-sleeves said.

"One *what?*"

He held up his hand, palm out towards her. Gold gleamed between his fingers. The red in her aura briefly dimmed at the glimpse of coin and he smirked.

Rahelu hardened her resolve. "The answer's still no, Imos."

No-sleeves put on a hurt look, as if she were the one who had wronged him, and terribly so, like stabbing him in the heart instead of reasonably and politely refusing his crass, cheap offer. "One for each year, love."

She wished he would stop waving that coin around; it kept catching the sunlight in the most distracting way.

"Or," No-sleeves drawled, "one for each of us if you'd prefer to count things that way."

"Enough!" Dedicate Maketh glowered. "This is not an auction house. Supplicant Rahelu has the right of it. Replicating someone else's knowledge does not translate to understanding, and the exercise of skill without understanding does not unlock the true mastery required for swearing the oaths of Dedication. Furthermore, none of you will obtain the barest modicum of knowledge if you do not stop looking for shortcuts and start applying yourselves."

The Guardian looked like he had further thoughts on their collective incompetence that he wanted to impart, but all he ended up saying was, "Back to your lines, Supplicants. And if I hear so much as a squeak that isn't coming from your chalk, you will be drawing until your fingers bleed and then you can practice drawing your lines with mixed mediums."

They turned back to their slates with alacrity.

Rahelu's slate, though, Maketh snatched from under her nose. Ten heartbeats passed as he inspected her work before he erased it, then handed back her slate and issued her with her own set of specialized questions.

"Standard amplification ward, third variant."

She hesitated.

"I'm waiting, Supplicant." Somehow, Maketh conveyed a whole conversation in three words: *'Drop the farce; I know you know I know you are capable of much more than what you've shown.'*

Fine.

As soon as she completed what he had asked for, he erased her slate again and demanded something else.

"Intermediate diffusion ward, fifth variant."

Easy.

"Advanced repulsion ward, first variant."

That took longer. But—as with every other ward she had drawn to date—he found no fault to point out in her work.

The Guardian took up her chalk.

When Rahelu got her slate back, it was covered with a design of interlocking diamonds joined with twisting lines that looped back on themselves in convoluted whorls.

"Deconstruct this ward."

"Fifteen components," she said slowly. "No—sixteen. These eight first. To dampen and then attenuate uncontrolled resonance. The rest..."

She'd never come across anything quite like it. But those components did (somewhat) resemble a linked series of deflection wards.

"They rebuff direct Projections." She squinted at the ward's perimeter. "The design is flexible; modular, even, so the ward can be extended to any circumference at need."

"And the ward's purpose?"

"I don't know."

"Guess."

She balked.

He raised an eyebrow.

"Protection."

"Against?"

"I don't know."

This was as far as her theoretical knowledge extended.

Maketh frowned, clearly unwilling to take her at her word though her resonance aura was transparent as glass.

"I'm not lying!" Rahelu snapped.

But she was tired of having to continually justify her existence to him.

He abruptly changed his line of questioning. "What methods would you use to mask the presence of a small party from Seekers?"

"In what kind of terrain?"

"Variable. Assume they are traveling."

"Active or passive Seeking?"

"Account for both."

"Do I have any limitations on my available materials?"

"Answer the question, Supplicant." The Guardian's expression was carefully neutral. "This is just a thought exercise."

Sure, in the same way that the *Winged Arrow* was just a courier vessel.

"I need more information to be certain that I've accounted for all the relevant factors."

She snuck another glance at the rest of the Supplicants.

Ghardon and Nheras were still struggling through the eight basic resonance wards with Elaram far behind—they'd finally gotten the foundation lines correct. Their extension lines were mostly in the right place but the remaining mistakes stretched their wards out of proportion.

No-sleeves and Jhobon, though, had finished and were listening in—with great interest—on her increasingly tense exchange with Maketh.

"Perfect information exists only in the classroom."

She bit the inside of her cheek before her budding irritation got the better of her and made her point out that they were, in fact, in a classroom.

Steady, Rahelu. Breathe. And exhale.

"Then I would wait until House intelligence provides me with more information."

"Unacceptable."

Gods. Why did he have to be such an—

"You will make do with the parameters I have given. Now, answer the question."

Rahelu swallowed her ire. "One general suppression ward, embedded into their method of conveyance, assuming they are not mounted on horses. Three layers of general suppression wards—stone, wood, and salt—around the party's camp each night. Individual diffusion wards, in copper thread, sewn into the lining of their clothing. Individual suppression wards drawn on the skin, over the heart, in resonance ink mixed with blood."

The Guardian moved on without giving any indication of what he thought of her response. "Assume you're in hostile territory and have run low on warding supplies during a mission. How would you allocate the remainder and what are the best options for replenishment?"

"Ward the individuals who are the least capable with Obfuscation during the day and the individuals who are most vital to the success of the mission at all times. Make camp in heavily wooded areas, caves, or close to a water source—as large as possible, ideally with running water. Minimize the size and number of general wards, using wood or stone or dirt, depending on their availability given the terrain. Build cookfires during the day and collect the ash before nightfall. Or, if fire poses too great a detection risk, rely on blood."

"Which is the best ward to defend against assault from hostile forces while in retreat?"

"It depends. What are the disposition of the—"

Maketh scowled and she scowled right back.

"That's impossible to answer without more information."

The Guardian didn't bother to repeat himself; he simply stood and out-waited her.

She chose the most ridiculous, destructive option there was. "A set of deflection wards, one for each pursuing force, oriented away from our escape vector. Assuming the wind is in our favor, done in flame."

"That would send up multiple beacons visible for at least twenty to thirty kual."

She shrugged. "We would not be in retreat if they did not already know where we were."

"What about the resultant damage to the surrounds?"

"Presumably not our problem, if we are in hostile territory and our primary objective is escape."

"And if the weather conditions are unfavorable?"

"Then I suppose the question of which ward to use would be the least of our problems. The time that would be required to construct anything sufficiently mobile would be better spent fleeing."

That ought to be the end of it.

She had proved, beyond all doubt, that she possessed the requisite skill in wards Elder Anathwan demanded. They had been at this for a full span now—during which Elaram had, at last, completed sketching the eighth basic resonance ward— and Rahelu had had enough.

Maketh, however, did not agree.

"Suppose your objective is to infiltrate a high-security facility in a remote, unknown location. How would you accomplish this task without the use of resonance skills?"

This time, Rahelu didn't even get to open her mouth before he cut off her protest.

"Let us say that you have been rendered incapable. By whatever means are available to the enemy, whether it be heartbane poisoning or an offensive Obfuscation that has cut you off from your resonance abilities."

"I would wait until I—"

"Time is of the essence, Supplicant. The Dominion is not the only power in the world and you are not the only one tasked with this objective."

But she was the only one he seemed bent on driving right over the edge of insanity.

"I would still wait."

Her tone was borderline combative, but 'combative' was arguably a mere hair's breadth from 'assertive'. Since she'd said the words at the same volume, the Imos Dedicate couldn't accuse her of disrespecting him by raising her voice. Furthermore, her ward was doing its job; her resonance aura remained a polite neutral gray.

"Proceeding without," she said, "would be suicide."

"Very good, Supplicant. Your ineptitude has allowed Conclave journeymages to storm the facility—"

That was just absurd.

"—and they have now seized the unique weapon within. How," Maketh drawled, "do you propose to seize the asset back, and thereby prevent Chanaz from discovering a method of mass replicating the weapon's capabilities?"

They had ventured well beyond the bounds of resonance theorems applicable to wards and the small squad combat strategies covered in Guild training into the ludicrous.

"I don't," Rahelu said.

To the eight hells with answering his questions seriously; she responded with an equally implausible scenario.

"I commandeer our fastest ship, take the contents of the House treasury to Tsorek-fa, and hire a bonded team of Belruonian mage-priests in exile to assassinate the Conclave's researchers."

"Word of the wealth you're transporting spreads through the relay networks and your ship is intercepted by raiders."

"I attack."

"You have no cannons and they sink your ship."

"I flee."

"Your navigator is unfamiliar with the waters and your vessel is no match for theirs in speed."

"I offer bribes."

"They accept. They also take every soul aboard as captives. You arrive in Tsorek-fa in time for the next slave auction. In the interim, the Conclave successfully develops a working prototype of a commercial version of the weapon. Within five years, relations between the Dominion and the Federation deteriorate into open war. Within a decade, the Houses of Aleznuaweite are subsumed into Chanaz as another collection of provinces. The Archmages of the Conclave declare an end to the Era of Exile and mandate the adoption of a new calendar to commemorate the so-called reunification of Aleznua under Federation rule."

Rahelu stared. Was he fucking kidding?

Dedicate Maketh said, "Attempt the scenario again, Supplicant. How will you infiltrate this facility and secure the weapon without the use of resonance skills?"

"I wouldn't!" she finally exploded. "If I were in command of such a situation, I would take precautions to ensure the enemy could not sabotage my resonance capabilities so I could send Seekers and Evokers out under diffusion wards to observe the facility so I have reasonably accurate intelligence to form the basis of an infiltration plan that effectively utilizes the Guardians and Harbingers at my disposal!"

"Your continued inability to adapt to given constraints suggests your lack of versatility extends beyond your resonance skills." Maketh's voice hardened. "For the last time, Supplicant, you do not have the opt—"

Rahelu cut him off with a wild gesture; her palpable frustration was clogging up the great cabin in gusts of reddish smoke.

"Then I suppose I would order all the wine casks opened, have everyone write out whatever comes to mind on the walls, no matter how insane, and invite them to vote by throwing their knives at those options while blindfolded and well past their third cup."

Out of the corner of her eye, she saw Ghardon giving her a tiny headshake. But she'd been answering these stupid fucking hypotheticals for nearly two spans now and she was sick of trying to guess at what Maketh wanted from her.

"We would have the same probability of landing on an appropriate course of action, but at least we'd have some fun while we're at it..."

Stop it, you need to stop and shut the fuck up, she thought, but the anger seething inside her had been given an outlet and the words just kept rolling off her tongue.

"...and in the highly likely event that I've made the wrong decision, at least we'd be happily drunk while we're getting our throats cut—all because you didn't give me any other means of accomplishing the fucking impossible!"

The bleached-bone hush that descended upon the great cabin in the wake of her ringing words weighed as heavy as a mountain.

Shit. *Shit!*

What had she just said? And why, in the Stormbringer's name, had she said it? She'd lost her temper before, but never like this. How had she allowed herself to get so caught up in the argument that she'd forgotten who she was talking to—especially after the events of the previous day?

Elaram and Ghardon closed their eyes; even Nheras paled. And Maketh's stony regard was as pitiless as the sea.

Rahelu dropped to her knees and pressed her forehead against the cabin sole. Ambient resonance gathered directly above her head, an ominous, crackling cloud that grew darker with each passing heartbeat.

"For a House that has few allies, Issolm grows presumptuous indeed."

The Guardian's voice was calm, in the same way the world was calm during that eerie, soundless tranquility of the earth holding still before the Stormbringer's judgment.

"Honored Dedicate, I beg you: the dishonor is mine alone."

She dared not look up.

She dared not touch her fingers to Lhorne's pendant.

She dared not listen to the instincts screaming at her to raise an Obfuscation barrier; that would only make her punishment worse.

"How," Maketh asked, "would you ward against direct mental incursion?"

An incredibly dense knot of gathered resonance pressed against the back of her head. A narrow Projection, its width no bigger than her smallest fingernail, blunted and oppressive as a warhammer.

"I..." She tried speaking again from within a bubble of dread. "I..." Her tongue felt like it was made from dust; what little moisture left in her mouth was being stripped away. "I know of no resonance ward that can prevent a direct mental incursion."

The next breath she took was like breathing in molten steel turned to steam. Resonance boiled in through her nose, her throat, her lungs to converge behind her eyes. Blood rushed to her head, a continuous roar that drowned out the ever-present song of the waves.

His next words reverberated in her skull. *Then your understanding of the principles is more well-rounded than I had hoped—*

It was too much; the pain was too much. She choked, coughed, spat; tried to retch up all of the foreign resonance invading her body; sweep it out of her aura and seal the entrances to her mind by flooding it with the blue-gray calm of deep lakewaters.

The depths of the Elumaje were peaceful...

—but you are less capable than you should be.

Scores of smoky barriers flew through the corridors of her mind, unimpeded by the defense she had summoned. She batted at delicate, half-translucent jellyfish-like swarms—

The depths of the Elumaje were safe...

—that melted away like smoke then reformed again, obscuring surface memories like a layer of cobwebs. She couldn't go back. More barriers, formidable as fortress walls, were bricking themselves in, cutting off entire pathways to skills, knowledge, and central memories.

She pushed at them. They didn't belong here. The depths of the Elumaje had no walls.

Those walls grew like sea moss; a rush of soft oblivion encircling her inner self, diminishing the slim thread of awareness that told her someone was sifting through her past for—

A vortex of light burning high above the sea—

A dark head weighed down by a dark crown—

A towering gilded throne soaked in blood—

She flew towards the last, shrinking gap.

The depths of the...the...

8

TRUST

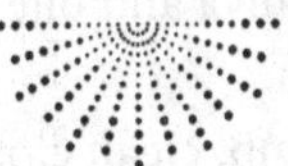

Was she?

"Rahelu?" The girl sounded worried.

Odd.

"Can you hear me?"

Why was that odd? Should she know that voice?

Something pushed—pulled?—her up. Or was it down? She slumped sideways—left, or right, she couldn't tell which was which—and landed against a warm, slight body.

"If you can hear me, drink this."

Something cool and smooth and hard against her lips. Gentle steam wafted into her face. She inhaled; smelled home: plain fish broth, made from fish bones that were fried until golden, then boiled until the liquid turned as white as rice water. The rich flavor of salt and spotted cod and kelp trickling onto her swollen tongue was exquisite.

She opened her mouth wider and pushed down.

"Careful!"

Broth slopped over the edge of the wooden bowl, spilled down her chin, and dribbled onto her neck. She spluttered.

There was a soft *clack*, then someone helped her fold herself over and pounded her on the back.

She wheezed; heaved up a thin splatter of liquid. Spat.

Darkness resolved into wooden planks, waxed to a high shine beneath the flickering of a lantern, striped with weak beams of moonlight diffused through a clouded sky. Now wet with vomit. Strands of saliva and bile dripped from her lips to join the pool.

Someone thrust a damp, clean cloth under her nose.

"Thanks," she croaked. Her voice came out at least half a register lower than usual, a hoarse thing that she didn't recognize as her own.

Her mind, though—

She squeezed her eyes shut. Experimentally quested out with her resonance senses to catalog her mental condition. A warm rush of relief chased away the lingering chill of apprehension when her senses responded and her visualization of her inner mind showed tranquil blue-gray waters beneath a cloudless sky.

Rahelu dove in. Plumbed the depths for foreign trails of inky smoke. Saw none. Hunted for submerged fortress stones. Found only silty sand. Swaying lakegrass, moss-covered rocks, shimmering shoals—even the currents—everything seemed unchanged.

She had come out of the ordeal with her memories more or less intact and her mind was still her own.

As far as she could tell.

Thoroughly perplexed, she surfaced and summoned Evocation. She held her most recent memories at arm's length so she could focus on the chain of events that had led to her downfall: how Maketh's overbearing manner had driven the others to frustration, how No-sleeves had flung fuel on that fire with his suggestion, the uncharacteristic way that the Guardian had stood back to let his charges debate the issue among themselves until she had given in to her temper, and then the subsequent interplay between Maketh's questions and the changes in her resonance aura. Her rage had felt like such a natural progression from her irritation at the time, such a reasonable response to being singled out and asked to solve his impossible scenarios that she hadn't thought twice about her reaction until it was too late. Hindsight illuminated the obvious: she'd been a fish-brained idiot to assume her emotions had been hers alone, just because no one had been actively wielding Projection in the moment.

So this was what it felt like, to fall victim to someone else's Fortunement.

Sickened, she lapsed into a coughing fit as she retched again and again, expelling nothing. The sudden, desperate urge to conjure the strongest Obfuscation barrier she was capable of took her. She reached blindly with her hand and resonance senses for the steadying influence of Lhorne's pendant, intent on surrounding herself with an impenetrable bubble of calm.

Oh gods.

The pendant was gone.

"Hey, hey! Stop, Rahelu, stop. You're safe."

The helpful hand that had held broth to her lips, rubbed her back, held her hair, now betrayed her—kept her firmly mashed against the soft cotton-padded bamboo sleeping mat with the slight pressure of its fingers against the nerve at the base of her neck.

"Take it slow," Elaram said, then released her once she stopped struggling. "You've been out for almost three days."

Rahelu snapped her head up, reeling as much from the discovery as from the dizzying effect of the rapid motion and the rolling of the ship.

"Three days!" she yelped.

The door opened to admit a wan-looking Ghardon. He

staggered in with a bucket in his right hand, a jug in his left hand, and what looked like a clean set of a House Issolm Supplicant's uniform bundled under his arm.

"Three days," he confirmed as he kicked the door shut. The ship surged and he belatedly braced himself, cursing as water spilled from the jug.

Elaram prised the rag out of her clenched fist. "Drink your broth," she said, offering the bowl again.

Rahelu's stomach rumbled as she fought to sit upright in the silken nest of blankets she'd been wrapped in. Joints cracked and tendons protested as she stretched out shaking hands. She sucked the whole bowl down in four noisy slurps that made Ghardon curl his lip.

He didn't remark on her terrible manners though, only sighed as he handed the jug to Elaram and dumped her clothes on the bed next to her. The bucket he upended over her lap. A stack of cleaning rags and a cake of perfumed soybean soap cascaded out. Half fell onto the cabin sole. He irritably cleared a spot and set the bucket down. By the time he had wobbled over to fetch the wash basin and wobbled back, the bucket had skittered away.

Another sigh, much louder.

Eventually, when Ghardon had assembled her impromptu wash stand to his satisfaction despite the sea's best efforts to interfere, he nudged everything towards her with the toe of his boot and only the slightest wrinkle of his nose.

She didn't even scowl at him for it as she wrestled free of her blankets; she was so grateful that he and Elaram cared enough to bother.

They could have left her to rot. But they had carried her to their cabin and laid her on one of their beds, instead of dumping her on the bare wooden platform inside the urine-soaked cabin she shared with Nheras. And while she needed the bath badly, she didn't stink as much as she should have:

she was wearing the same tunic and breastband but she didn't have any trousers on and her loincloth had been recently changed.

She ducked her head as she stripped and scrubbed herself with soap and water furiously, trying not to cry.

Three days.

They had been sleeping on the hard planks of the cabin sole and watching over her in shifts, keeping her clean like an infant, not knowing how long she would be insensate, for three days.

She didn't deserve that kindness.

Ghardon picked his way across the cabin, through the detritus of crumpled pages and broken bits of charcoal and the incongruous lone pillow—a silk-covered, soft-looking thing resting atop a folded pile of more sensible woolen blankets—to perch on the edge of the cluttered desk beside a stack of books.

He waited until she was done, then said, "Maketh Imos isn't normally one for those kinds of theatrics. I haven't seen or heard of him making an example of someone like that since..."

"Since ever," Elaram supplied when Ghardon failed to come up with a citation.

"I'd've put eight gold kez on him making you the Elder's problem. That's more his usual style."

The Imos Dedicate must have accepted her plea to punish her alone, even though he would have been well within his rights to punish the other Issolm Supplicants for her insolence too. At least, she assumed so, since Elaram and Ghardon's resonance auras were equal parts of relief and exasperation floating over the top of burning curiosity instead of red-spiked anger.

Even then, Maketh had refrained from exercising his full rights as a Dedicate.

He could have ordered her beaten. He could have beaten her himself. He could have made her insolence a matter of House honor, and thereby demanded recompense from Anathwan, neatly circumventing the conditions the Elder had set for the special test of Rahelu's loyalties.

But he hadn't so much as revoked her cabin privileges.

Why? What had he seen in her mind that had made him change his?

"Maketh is about as tolerant and even-tempered as the Earthgiver makes anyone Imos-blooded; I didn't think he would stoop to this level of vindictiveness. Yet somehow, sister dear," Elaram's tone turned very dry as she handed Rahelu her clothes, "you've managed to provoke him, and Ana doesn't seem overly concerned by his handling of you. Would you care to enlighten us?"

"And while you're at it," Ghardon added as he fished something out of his pocket, "would you care to explain what you're doing with Ideth's legacy?"

Her heart stuck in her throat as he dangled Lhorne's pendant in front of her.

Rahelu swallowed, weighing her next words carefully as she dressed.

She owed them an honest answer—personal honor, as well as House honor, demanded it—but did she owe them a full answer? If she gave them one, would it turn them against her? More to the point: could she even give them a full answer without failing the test Anathwan had set for her?

She couldn't.

Yet neither was there any partial answer she could give that would satisfy Elaram. She could feel the other girl holding herself back from unleashing a full Seeking out of politeness. But there was a lot of room for interpretation between keeping your resonance senses to yourself and simply being mindful of the shifts in someone's aura without it ever verging into Seeking, and she had just dismantled her resonance ward. If she wanted to maintain any form of emotional privacy, she would have to put up an Obfuscation barrier, and the way Ghardon's eyes narrowed as he watched her avoid Elaram's penetrating gaze suggested he might find that suspicious enough to go beyond asking nicely and help Elaram dig through her mind for the answers.

Rahelu looked from one calculating face to another, then said: "The honorable Guardian Maketh has become enamored of the notion that I'm a Chanazian spy." Two sets of eyebrows shot up into chestnut hairlines and she added: "The pendant was a friendship gift, according to Lowdocks custom."

They stared at her for five heartbeats straight, without blinking an eye, stunned disbelief pouring out of their resonance auras.

And then a blade-like Projection shaped out of that dazzling yellow-white river snapped into Ghardon's hand as he asked, "Are you?" while Elaram put her left hand to her forehead and said, "It was a what?"

"No!" she said to Ghardon, then she repeated, "A gift," to Elaram, and then there was no peace to be had for the next span as they peppered her with questions.

It didn't take long before she ran out of viable answers.

"You really don't trust us." Blue-black hurt seeped into Elaram's resonance aura, dulling her lively orange-curiosity to a muddy brown. Quietly: "We're Issolm, Rahelu; we look after our own." She exhaled slowly as she huddled into herself, knees tucked to her chin on the end of the bunk. "Ana brought you into our House. But you swore our oaths and took our name and still don't consider yourself one of us. You're just here for the coin."

"That's—"

Rahelu couldn't pretend otherwise; not when pierced by Elaram's overly round, overly bright eyes.

"—true," she admitted, and hated herself for it; hated Elaram, too, for laying out her mercenary motives so baldly. "But I swear—*I swear*—that's not the reason why I can't answer your questions. I want to tell you, I do; it's just..."

Half a dozen defenses sprang to mind: *'I didn't want to drag you into my mess'* (weak); *'I was planning to tell you, that night, but never got the chance'* (even weaker); *'This is another test; Anathwan forbade me from telling you'* (but the Elder had forbidden that disclosure too).

"It's juuuuuuust...?" Ghardon prompted.

The excuses died on her tongue.

"Come, sister mine: speak. Because I'd like to know why *we* had to learn just how little time we really had from Ylaen fucking *Imos* when you knew all along—and had the means to easily overcome the problem in your head."

When she remained silent, he began openly mocking her.

"Were you so hungry that you swallowed your own tongue? Or did you sell it?" He idly tossed the pendant in his hand; smirked as her eyes tracked its glittering arc. "If a pathetic dinner with you cost Ideth a ring, what did a resonance crystal legacy buy him?"

Slowly, evenly, teeth gritted tight against her stirring anger, Rahelu reiterated: "It was a friendship gift."

"Is that what we're calling it? Well, I hope he got more than a single night of fucking from you." Ghardon raised his eyebrows. "Or perhaps he simply sat there, staring at you, with those lovesick pup's eyes." Laughed as she fisted the blankets in an obvious effort to not rise to the bait. "Didn't even lay a finger on you, did he? Congratulations, little sister. You might have set a new record for the most expensive—"

"Think what you like," she snapped. "But give me back my pendant."

"I'll give it back when you start giving out some answers."

"I've given you all the answers I can!"

Ghardon shot her a look of complete loathing. "And I don't trust any of them."

She should have been able to weather that look. (She had had plenty of practice doing so, courtesy of Nheras.) Should have been able to take the bitter sting of the lurid green mist smoking off his aura and tainting the ambient resonance, and transmute that caustic resonance into a perverse thrill (born of thwarting a House-born's will) wherever it brushed against her.

But seeing that look come from him...

"I'm sorry," she rasped, cheeks and aura burning.

Ghardon put the pendant down on top of the book. "Me too."

Her throat grew tight. There was a finality to the way he crossed his arms over his chest and moved his stare from her to the door...and she was getting nothing from Elaram at all.

Now there were three people aboard this ship who refused to acknowledge her existence.

That was a good thing; it made it easier for her to keep Anathwan's confidence—and Onneja's too.

Stay focused. Don't disappoint the Elder. If she worked hard, she would be rewarded. The sooner they finished the job, the sooner they could all go home—as Dedicates. Maketh could never pull rank and use his position to threaten her again.

Her family would never want for anything again.

"I'll go."

No reactions as Rahelu scooped up the pendant and looped it around her neck once more.

The only thing that tried to stop her was the stupid pillow she nearly tripped over as she shuffled towards the exit. She was about to stomp on it, kick it out of her way so she could deflect some of her pent-up anguish onto a justifiable target because she couldn't bear this, this *coldness*. From Nheras, yes; it would be—was—a blessing, but not from *them*; not Ghardon, who ought to have clobbered her senseless for her countless moments of idiocy on their first day as Supplicants, but who still kept trying regardless, no matter how resistant she was to his coaching; not Elaram, whose irrepressible verve and smile could coax laughter out of her no matter how inappropriate the occasion; Elaram, who had invited a common-born fisher brat to dinner with her family at her home simply because she enjoyed her company before any of them had successfully Petitioned.

They were right to be angry with her.

Lhorne had been angry with her too.

His impassioned words echoed in her mind. Not the ones she had refuted (even if she was beginning to realize that there might have also been a seed pearl of truth buried in his wrong-headed arguments) but the fierce rebuke she had earned, the last time she had tried doing things alone.

We're a team, remember? We're supposed to do this together!

What was a House, but a much larger team?

Rahelu picked up the pillow. Hugged it to her chest as she sat back down on the bunk. "I can't tell you everything," she said, "but I can show you some things."

She drew on Lhorne's pendant.

Power answered, in the form of an Obfuscation barrier far superior to anything she could manage on her own. She anchored it, then overlaid the inside of that protective measure with another precaution: a looping Evocation of Ghardon and Elaram pursuing independent study two days ago—he at the desk and she sprawled belly down atop the woolen blankets—both glancing over at the lower bunk occasionally whenever her body disturbed the silence with a faint rustle of silks.

Only then did Rahelu share her full, unredacted memories.

The origins of Dedicate Maketh's suspicions, from the moment he had caught her tampering with the Petitioners' assignment board to her narrowly won escape from a Guild interrogation chamber.

The entirety of her argument with Lhorne about the wisdom of accepting Anathwan's offer.

Over and over, she relived that moment as they dissected and debated every possible nuance behind Lhorne's outburst—

> *I refuse to believe that the point of the past two weeks was for you to sell yourself for pocket change so Issolm can send you to die on a suicide mission at the other end of the world!*

—his phrasing, his word choices, the way his clear green irises had contracted as he pleaded with her, how his pupils had dilated until all she could see was her reflection, her stupid face, contorted with righteous rage.

Fish-brained fool.

Rahelu shut her eyes, listening to Ghardon and Elaram chew over possible theories, each one wilder than the last, then opened them again to inspect her surroundings.

She remembered the cabin as a trim and tidy space. In her Seeking, the desk's surface had been clear of clutter and objects, other than a copy of *The Issolm Supplicant's Handbook*. In addition to Elaram's crossbow, Ghardon's shortbow, and their quivers, there had also been three silk paintings hanging from the weapons rack and padded cushions placed atop their (very non-standard) trunks—personal touches of color and warmth that were noticeably absent from the other Supplicants' cabins.

Now?

The Issolm Supplicant's Handbook was nowhere in sight. The desk groaned beneath a mountain of books, scrolls, slates, and loose chalk that were jumbled up with used tea cups and empty glass vials. More than a few had cracked or chipped after being knocked off due to an errant elbow or rolling away from not being secured.

The silk paintings had been taken down and replaced with a collection of pages that looked suspiciously close in size to the handbook's, their edges stuck together in a large sheet that sported the same complex ward Maketh had drawn on her slate, made four times larger. Done in the Guardian's style, but not drawn by his hand. Where Maketh's lines flowed and were full of artistry, the jerky charcoal strokes on the oversized schematic and the faint grid beneath them suggested the ward had been traced or copied by an uncertain hand in conflict with the mind guiding it.

Elaram had unwound her sling and was methodically prodding at the length of her right collarbone with her left hand. Her eyes were closed; her normally rosy skin pallid, with a gray cast.

Ghardon still sat on the desk, his forehead creased in furious thought as he stared at the schematic hanging from the weapons rack. The book next to him lay open to a page with a cramped illumination of the hanging ward annotated with his neat letters.

Rahelu craned her head to read his writing, then blinked in surprise.

A dreamward.

Nobody used dreamwards.

The average person didn't need them; only the strongest of nightmares or the most pleasant of dreams could move them enough for unconscious Projections to become disruptive.

Guild-trained mages didn't need them most of the time either: you couldn't pass first year without developing the emotional control necessary to curb the instinctive urge to lash out with Projection when you were asleep. By the time you had trade secrets to protect, you were either sworn to a House and slept in the lodgings provided to you, under permanent Obfuscation barriers, or you spent half your income (or time) on maintaining your own barriers or hiring a residence that came with one. They were less complicated to construct, far more secure, and lasted for seasons instead of spans. Most inns, even the ones in the Lowdocks, had cursory Obfuscation barriers surrounding each room for privacy. It was part of the reason why Tlareth had always been so generous; without Rahelu's help to recharge those anchors, she would have spent most of the Sable Gull's seasonal turnover on replacement crystals.

No wonder she hadn't recognized Maketh's ward for what it was; dreamwards had fallen so far out of common usage that she had never wasted any time trying to construct one based on the vague and perplexing instructions in Venazelunaje's Codex. There was no reason to use dreamwards. Not unless you knew yourself to be under close surveillance or planned to be sleeping in hostile territory for a prolonged period of time where even the weakest Obfuscation barrier against Seeking would draw unwanted attention and you could not afford intelligence leaks.

Presumably, though, one had already happened because Lhorne had known something and, in the heat of their argument, he had let that slip.

Rahelu decided to ask a few questions of her own, more to break the silence than anything else. "Did either of you ask for this assignment? Or did the Elder request you, specifically?"

Elaram stirred. "We were meant to stay in Ennuost Yrg. Mother had called in a few favors to make sure of it. But I...I wanted to go away. Out of the city. Just for a little while. So I asked Ana if I could go with her and she said yes." She looked sidelong at her brother. "He got orders."

Ghardon glared down at his book. "I chose Evocation specifically"—*thump!* went the heavy tome as he snapped it shut—"so I wouldn't have to leave the city."

Upset as he was, he still slid his copy of *The Study of Resonance Wards: A Modern Guardian's Encyclopedic Reference (Third Edition)* inside a drawer carefully with *The Issolm Supplicant's Handbook* and what looked like an advanced Obfuscation text, borrowed from the ship's study.

"Issolm Evokers don't get field assignments. We just don't."

He looked around the cabin—at the cramped nest of blankets that took up all of the narrow space bounded by the trunks, the desk, the sleeping area, and the door; at the dried bits of flattened rice and fish slivers that had stuck to the rough fibers and wooden planks; at the dark drips and stains from spilled sauces and stray ink marring every visible surface—then flopped face down atop the pile of folded blankets.

"I want to go home," Ghardon moaned into the rumpled wool, seemingly intent on suffocating himself. "I'm not cut out for this!"

She and Elaram both tactfully refrained from pointing out the obvious.

After a short, muffled cry of despair, Ghardon sat up and amended his lamenting to the slightly more viable, "I want to undertake that routine House audit we're supposedly carrying out instead."

Doubtless, Anathwan would entertain the notion for no more than an eyeblink.

"I'd rather spend every waking span plying each self-important merchant in Peshwan Yrg with wine and platitudes about how much the Exalted Dominance cares and redoing all their accounts without an abacus for the next two years by myself."

"At least now you know why House Ideth has been deliberately withholding support," Rahelu pointed out.

The thought did not cheer him. "For a mission this important, they shouldn't have the option to. You'd think House Isilc would have pressured Ideth into sending an Augur along to smooth—or at least, scry—the probabilities."

Rahelu ventured a guess. "Dedicate Keshwar is the Ideth heir; he's far too important to send."

"Anathwan is a first-ranked Elder, and our House is sending four Supplicants," Ghardon countered. "A major House like Ideth can afford to commit one of their newly sworn Supplicants with Augur potential, like Cseryl, at the very least, without straining their ranks."

"You're both overthinking this," Elaram said. "Ana's our Augur and Csorath's here on House Ideth's behalf." Ghardon slowly nodded, as if that made perfect sense, and left it up to Elaram to elaborate for Rahelu's benefit: "Csorath's Ideth-born; he swore his Supplicant's oaths to Atriarch Mere Ideth."

How was that relevant? "He wears Isonn colors now."

"Nheras wears Issolm colors now," Ghardon said. "But she's still Ilyn to the bone."

"*I* wear Issolm colors."

He eyed her. "Poorly."

"My argument stands."

"So does Ela's. Nheras Ilyn is a painted doll who has never had a thought in her head that wasn't placed there by

Lynath Ilyn. If she's sworn to House Issolm, it's because she was ordered to."

"Forget Nheras," Elaram interrupted. "House Ilyn is too minor to matter. Consider the team as a whole: two Seekers, two Guardians, two Evokers, and *three* Harbingers." She sat up very straight as she ticked off her count on her fingers. "Maybe Anathwan had limited choices, but she still selected a team for stealth first, combat ability second, and flexibility third." She flashed him a cheeky grin. "Brother, dear, I concede: you'd do a fair job doubling as a Guardian, and Rahelu here"—that grin again—"isn't half bad as a Seeker. You don't send a team with this much combat capability on a recovery mission for missing persons, sunken cargo, or stolen merchandise—"

"You might, if you were after trade secrets," Ghardon said. "Some of those are better defended than most House vaults."

Elaram shook her head. "If it were something as mundane as trade secrets, we would have brought more Evokers along for extraction. Just look at how much trouble you had crafting a set of spirit essences from Maketh's memories— and not only did he willingly hand them to you, he was *helping* you."

"The Guardian did what?" Rahelu blurted out. Then, before she could help herself: "Do I get one?"

"Cheated!" Elaram cried gleefully. "He told Ana that we're done with our study of resonance wards at dinner—finally!"

At the same time, Ghardon deflated her hopes with a blunt, "No," then preemptively headed her off with, "And before you complain, it's because he said you don't need it."

Accurate—but still unfair. Worse, she couldn't even be angry about it; at least, not with Ghardon. Crafting spirit essences was no minor conjury. He mightn't have done the work, but he had done work.

"Maketh only gave us the bare minimum we needed to draw that monstrosity"—a jerk of his chin at the hanging dreamward—"and even after three fucking days of doing nothing but that, it's still all Belruonian gibberish to me. I haven't the foggiest idea how any of these lines work or why they seem to stop working if I draw them holding the charcoal the way I prefer instead of the way he prefers. Gods." He massaged his palms. "It's worse than my archery drills."

Elaram slipped off the bunk to join him on the blankets and slung her arm around his shoulders. "But it's for a much better cause!" Her eyes and aura sparkled with enough wonder to light up the ambient resonance with the blue-gold wash of a warm skyarc in summer even though it was well into stormarc now, with a squall rising. "I'll bet ten gold kez that we're playing 'Break and Enter' instead of 'Seek and Retrieve', or maybe even 'Search and Destroy'!"

Neither Rahelu nor Ghardon took the bet.

Elaram didn't seem disappointed, though she did ask, quite bluntly: "Rahelu, are you hiding any other secrets?"

Rahelu met Elaram's eyes squarely and said, "Yes." And then, because she had learned her lesson: *Please don't ask me anything more about that*, she sent. *I can't say. I swear on my mother's life that my silence poses no harm to the Houses or the Dominion that I know of.* She extended her hands. *You can check that—just that—if you like.*

She sat still and did not resist when Elaram and Ghardon joined hands and she felt their Concordance questing at the edges of her mind.

They stayed just long enough for Elaram to ascertain the truth of what she had said, and for Ghardon to verify that there wasn't anything left of Maketh's barriers, and then they withdrew.

Ghardon was still frowning. *That you know of,* he sent. Aloud, he said: "Everyone thought you would choose Ideth," then glanced at the pendant around her neck. "Not that I'm complaining," he said. "It's been very profitable."

"What?"

"You idiot." Elaram smacked him in the arm, then explained: "He was the only one who didn't change his bet. The rest of us thought it was a foregone conclusion when you and Lhorne went for your little moonlight stroll by the pier." She pouted at her brother. "I still think everyone should have gotten what they'd staked back once Nheras showed up. The original parameters didn't account for outside interference."

"What?" Rahelu felt the blood drain from her face as she stupidly repeated out loud: "What?"

Ghardon shrugged. "It wasn't my fault that you all overlooked the possibility. Nobody from Ideth or Ilyn knew about the bet—and no one who knew told them about our dinner party."

Rahelu was still catching up to the realization that what she had believed to be a private moment between her and Lhorne had been broadcast at an Issolm dinner party. Whose idea had that been, to make her life into their entertainment and exploit her raw emotions for their benefit? What had those depraved voyeurs been betting on? A kiss? A live show? Had odds been given on all the possible aspects of their performance together? Who would initiate and who would respond and which positions they might favor, for how long, and—

Her temples throbbed, her fists clenched, savage words boiled up in her throat and fought a war between themselves to be the first to leave her mouth.

What ended up coming out was an inarticulate cry, followed by:

"What in the eight hells is *wrong* with you people?" she yelled at the two oblivious House-born who were still sniping at each other about the terms and conditions of the most inappropriate, stupidest fucking bet she'd ever heard of.

For a wild moment, she considered reaching out to Nheras with Projection, to ask her if she would like to join her in obliterating these two unnomobunezra. Nheras wasn't all that far away—one deck up and a brief jog down the passageway above, in the ship's study—and for once, Rahelu was pretty sure that she was not at the top of Nheras's list of most hated people. (If their last conversation had been anything to go by, perhaps she never had been.)

But no, this was no insult to Nheras; this was an insult to her, and to Lhorne, and she needed no help to exact revenge. New disgust and rage overwhelmed her recent gratitude; she growled and picked up the closest hard object, ready to smash it in their faces, looking through a rust-colored haze as she swung.

Elaram had raised her good arm in defense, while Ghardon had thrown himself over his sister, even as he called up a hasty Obfuscation barrier. Both of them had the grace to look ashamed and the guts to remain where they were. Their eyes were closed, heads partially turned away to shield their faces as they waited for her blow to land.

Her improvised weapon happened to be the meal tray with the empty bowl that had held her fish broth.

At the last possible moment, Rahelu changed the trajectory of her swing and let go. The tray hurtled across the cabin. Delicate lacquered wood smashed against the bulkhead and splintered. She breathed heavily, trying to impose some semblance of calm on top of her seething resonance aura.

"Why," she spoke in as neutral a tone as she could manage, "would you do that? Whatever ancient feud House Issolm has with House Ideth aside, what did Lhorne and I ever do to deserve that?"

"Nothing," Elaram said in a very small voice. "It was just a bit of fun."

"And you had the nerve to take me to task about not trusting you, just because we wear the same clothes now." Rahelu laughed; it was all so absurd. "I think I was right not to. Why should I, when you have such a clear disregard for privacy? How can I trust you not to share my secrets if you're so ready to air my most intimate moments to the world and—"

"You chose," Ghardon cut in, "to have those moments in a public place."

"We were alone." How dare he try to place the blame on her for this transgression? "You weren't invited."

"Oh? Then why didn't either of you raise a barrier?"

"I didn't think that—"

"That's right; you didn't." He made a show of slapping his forehead. "You've got these charming, common-born notions that you can act however you want whenever you want, as if nobody is ever watching you and be damned to the consequences. But Ideth should have known better and now"—he raised his voice over her furious spluttering as he gestured towards her still-active Obfuscation barrier and the looping Evocation inside of it—"you do too. Don't you?"

Rahelu challenged him right back: "Tell me you would have done the same to anyone else." To any House-born. To the sister who had crawled out of the same womb, not the 'sister' he'd been saddled with by his Elder. "Tell me that you would have turned their lives into a diversionary amusement for others simply because it would net you a 'very profitable' result."

"I have," came the brazen reply, and—Stormbringer, he wasn't lying. "Everyone has. Did you think we all had access to Ideth's bottomless bank account?"

She had. And now—

Now she didn't know how to feel.

Rahelu let her barrier and her Evocation go as she thought of Nheras, sobbing on the main deck, her innermost emotions on display. How not a single House-born had stepped forward to show her any sympathy, save for Maketh. How the Ilyn girl had said: *'I was trying to do you a kindness'* and *'I don't expect a fish that insists on leaping out onto land to know the difference between water and air'* and *'you have no idea what it takes to truly belong to a House'*.

Gods. It was true; she really didn't.

"You were in public," Elaram added. "Anyone is fair game if you're in public. And we bet on all sorts of things. This kind of bet isn't unusual."

"Really." Several more vomit-colored puddles started forming on the cabin sole from the ambient resonance. "How many gold kez were staked on whether you could finally convince Imos No-sleeves to go without his trousers and take him for a ride?"

She had expected to be met with anger similar to her own, or a sheepish kind of silence in acknowledgment of her point.

Instead, Elaram said, "Well," and before she could launch into the rest, Ghardon said, "Thirty," then threw a piece of broken chalk at his sister's head. "And if she could have been less picky for just one night, I wouldn't be out four gold."

A handful of orange-red sparks crackled in Elaram's aura. "I was not being *picky*."

Rahelu stared.

Ghardon was being serious. *Elaram* was being serious. Both of them were out of their fucking minds, treating this like it was a serious topic of conversation instead of the incredibly intrusive and reductive irrelevancy it was.

House-born really did bet on anything and everything.

"I have standards," Elaram continued, "and he wasn't

meeting them. Just because he's so very pretty to look at doesn't excuse his lack of trying: leaning on Projection instead of learning actual techniques is simply lazy."

"Right, whatever." Ghardon got up. He sighed as he saw the bits of crushed charcoal and chalk dust stuck to his trousers. "I don't need to hear this a second time so I'm going to go inform Elder Anathwan and the ship's healer of your recovery." He cast another mournful look around the cabin and frowned when his gaze came back to Rahelu and her disheveled uniform. To Elaram, he said: "When I get back, you'd better have her ready to go."

"Go where?" Rahelu asked, but Ghardon had already left. Elaram took advantage of his departure to scoot closer to Rahelu, on the bunk.

"Half a span!" she declaimed indignantly. "Can you imagine?"

"Uh, no." Rahelu started edging after Ghardon immediately; she recognized that gleam in Elaram's eyes. "I don't think I will."

Unfortunately, leaving the bunk required climbing over Elaram, who was getting so worked up that the brief pops of orange-red in her aura were spreading out and clumping together in the ambient resonance. Then she spoke the dreaded words: "There I was, on my knees, for half a span— an entire half-span!—on that stupid gravel Ideth's got spread out everywhere in their gardens…"

"Yes, yes, it was very uncomfortable, far from an ideal location for an assignation, and the pleasure of the experience did not live up to the expectations you built up in your head based on his biceps," Rahelu said. "Got it, Elaram. I don't want to—I don't need to know any further details."

Elaram giggled. "You do if you want to get out of here."

Her hand instinctively went to her belt…which had no belt knife sheathed in it. "Move, or be moved," Rahelu said anyway, in a threat so unconvincing that an untrained applicant would have known how half-hearted it was.

Gratitude could go to the fifth hell.

"Or, if you really hate that option, I'll give you a different one," Elaram said, in a much smirkier voice that made Rahelu's palms sweat. "How about you share some more details of your night with Lhorne? I bet he wasn't like Ylaen, was he? I've always wondered if—"

"No."

Elaram pouted again. "You'll happily Evoke the experience for Nheras but not for me? After all we've been through together?" She waved her sling around at their surroundings.

Rahelu was about to say, *'Yes, because Nheras didn't want to know and you do,'* only that didn't reflect well on her at all. Not to mention that the thought of sharing such an intimate memory—even with mere words—made her feel ill. Even though nothing had happened, not even a kiss, so it wasn't like Elaram would get any of the salacious details she was hoping to experience secondhand.

Yet everyone else had evidently assumed otherwise—an assumption that she had deliberately encouraged because she had lost her temper—and was operating accordingly. Too late now to correct the record...and she wasn't sure that she ought to. She didn't know enough about House politics to understand what the ramifications might be.

"Nothing out of the ordinary happened."

No matter how much she wished otherwise.

She cursed her regrettable phrasing and her lack of a resonance ward as soon as she uttered the words because Elaram's eyes grew huge in her face.

"Wait, so you mean to say that Ghardon was right and Lhorne was—"

"No!"

"It's alright if that's what happened. Not everyone is able to—"

"Elaram, that is not what I said."

To her horror, Elaram reached out with a hug. "I understand. You don't have to say anything more. It's too bad that it wasn't—"

Gods. The next sentence left her mouth before she quite knew what she was saying. "I assure you that he was entirely well prepared."

"Oh," Elaram said. Then: "Oh!" and Rahelu did not like the sound of whatever conclusion Elaram had just drawn either.

"No. I swear to the Stormbringer—"

Sure enough, Elaram's hand had gone from patting her shoulder solicitously in consolation to stroking her lower back.

"—if you do not take your hand off me and stop talking about this, I will get violent."

"The first time can be scary, but—"

"That is not a problem."

"—it doesn't have to hurt as long as you know your own body and—"

"That is not a problem either."

"—I can help you if—"

"We are not having this conversation."

But in the absence of an Evocation—which she was most definitely not willing to share—Elaram would not be dissuaded.

Rahelu resorted to the only option she had left: she gritted her teeth and asked, in the tones of the condemned, "...what happened between you and Imos?"

9

GAMES

RAHELU WAS UNPREPARED FOR HOW LONG ELARAM could drag out her narration of events. It was impressive, considering that her encounter with Ylaen Imos had lasted—at most—no longer than the time it took to cook rice.

(As far as Rahelu had been able to determine, based on Evocations that Elaram insisted were necessary for her to share so her point of view could be properly appreciated. The most interesting part had been when Ylaen's companions, Jhobon and Csinyrg, had been distracted by news from House Imrell...or it would have been, had Elaram paid any attention to it. Unfortunately, the specifics of *that* conversation were an inaudible blur; front and center in Elaram's memories were thoughts of how thoroughly disappointed she was with the way reality failed to measure up to rumor in every respect.)

In very short order, Rahelu became certain of a few things.

First, being insensate was preferable to suffering through the torture Elaram was inflicting on her. She was now more thoroughly acquainted with both Elaram and Ylaen's most intimate parts than she ever wanted to be.

Second, Elaram was right. Ylaen was a terribly selfish lover.

Third, she owed Nheras an apology—a truly sincere one.

When Rahelu heard Ghardon's returning footsteps, she was so profoundly relieved by the prospect of his intervention that she rushed over to open the door for him and overlooked his wounded exasperation when he saw that not only was she nowhere near presentable, she had also broken several teeth on one of his ivory combs.

Meekly, she held it out, doing her best to copy Elaram's most contrite expression whilst ignoring the other girl's unending monologue. "Help?"

He sighed—for the third time—and pocketed the broken comb.

(Behind them, Elaram ranted on: "It's not the inadequacy of his performance that upsets me, it's his total lack of consideration. I can work with inexperience or incompetence, but what am I supposed to do with *indifference*? A statue would've been a more obliging partner.")

"Sit," Ghardon said, gesturing to his trunk.

He pulled out a different comb—wide-toothed, made from tortoiseshell, with wickedly sharp points. Rahelu gulped as he sighted down its spine with deadly intent, the same way he lined up his shots on the archery range, but did not cry out or flinch when he repeatedly stabbed her in the head with what felt like five thousand needles and dragged them across her scalp so hard she was sure he'd cut through to her skull—because the pain was far, far preferable to listening to more of what Elaram had to say, not that Elaram seemed to care whether anyone was still listening.

"You're a mess," Ghardon pronounced as he stepped back to look at his handiwork, "but we haven't the time to do better. Ela, come on." He steered Rahelu to the door by her arm. "Leave off disemboweling that pillow and let's go. Tiles was your idea in the first place."

Tiles? Elaram's idea?

Rahelu planted her feet in the cabin's entrance and said, "I'm not feeling so great after all." One bowl of fish broth did not miraculously undo the effects of three days lying abed, unconscious. "I'd better go get some more rest."

Tiles was a long, drawn-out game requiring skill and luck. Lacking either meant you'd end up with empty pockets, naked, or owing favors, and she had spent far too much of her whole life mired in poverty, shame, and debt to risk it.

Her refusal to join in on—or become—the evening's entertainment was, apparently, what it took to get Elaram to switch topics.

"Oh no. None of your excuses. This is the first chance we've had to use our leisure time for actual leisure and we"—said very emphatically, as she peeled Rahelu's fingers off the door frame—"are making the most of it. You are off duty. Your parents are not expecting you. You do not have plans."

"And it is not a party, though only the Skymother understands why you're so opposed to those when there's free food to be had," Ghardon said. "Nor will it involve anything more physically strenuous than sitting up and moving your arms. So you are going to come and socialize with your peers, like a normal person."

Like any real person could afford to idle away half the night when there was still work left undone and more of it to be done before dawn the next day.

"And maybe, just maaaaaaaaaaaybe," Elaram sang, "you might discover that having fun is not the crime that you seem to think it is. If you don't know how to play—"

The jibe—and the presumption of her ignorance—stung.

"I know how to play tiles, Elaram." She had learned from Tlareth on a set whittled out of driftwood, and they had played for shells and polished pebbles. "I'm just tired." Of guarding her thoughts. Of House-born company. "So thank you both, but no. I," Rahelu announced as she tried to extricate herself, "am choosing sleep. Good night."

"No, you're not!" Elaram said brightly, snaking an arm around her waist. "Sleeping is for babies, old people, and—"

"Irritating, insubordinate idiots." Ghardon tightened his grip on her bicep and wheeled her around. "You are a Supplicant of House Issolm now; you don't get to shirk your duties to do whatever you want."

"Funny. I was under the impression that *leisure time* meant exactly that."

"Not while I'm in charge."

Eight hells; the Elder *had* put him in charge.

"Rahelu, sister dear; relax," Elaram said as Ghardon smirked at her crestfallen expression. "I promise you that this is not going to be the chore our brother is making it out to be, nor the horror that you dread. All we're going to do is have a few drinks, play some games, and have a good time."

"Besides…" Ghardon arched his eyebrows suggestively at her. "Wouldn't you like to try your chances at parting a rich House-born or two from their coin?"

It would be a nice change.

"Imos rarely plays, Imrell doesn't know how, and Ilyn is notoriously inflexible; she always goes big, no matter her hand, and never concedes if she thinks she can still win, regardless of her odds."

That did sound more promising than she initially thought.

"The buy-in's only four hundred silver."

Only? Only?! Rahelu opened her mouth to tell Ghardon exactly what she thought of the idea of placing two-thirds of her family's annual income at risk, only for the intrusive, logical part of her mind to point out several inconvenient facts: that four hundred silver kez was but a fraction of what she had in her purse, and that but a fraction of the wealth held in her name per the House Issolm ledgers; that she had already given more than that to the Stormbringer, and—

Shit; she could lose her whole purse and still count herself richer than any single person had the right to be just by the value of the clothes on her back.

Also: who said she would lose, anyway?

"What about you two?" Rahelu asked as she fingered the fine cotton weave of her sleeve.

They exchanged glances; laughed. Then Ghardon said, in a perfect imitation of Elaram's earlier hurt tone with his long-lashed eyes wide and bottom lip jutting out: "We're Issolm, sister."

Meaning, *'I won't sabotage your chances'*. Possibly even, *'I'll help you so long as you help me'*, with the addendum of, *'until it suits me not to'*, which was always a given in the late stages of any hand. Her thoughts raced ahead. If she stuck to lower-ranked hands, if she didn't let herself get caught up in what-ever posturing might happen once they all sat down around the table, if she was careful and avoided being the one to discard tiles that might be claimed for a win—

She could make back what she had given to the Storm-bringer, and then some.

Ghardon saw her wavering and offhandedly added, "I'll lend you an edge if you like." Evocation glimmered in his upturned palm. "Call it insurance."

Rahelu hesitated, then extended a tentative Seeking. Tantalizing snatches of foreign understanding and skill bloomed in her mind as she trailed through the surface reso-nances—then faded to nothing as Ghardon snatched his hand away and flashed her a shark-toothed grin.

"How much," he asked, "would you like to win?"

CONTRARY TO WHAT ELARAM BELIEVED, Rahelu was not opposed to fun.

Fun was sleeping in until the second span after dawn in the Sable Gull's hayloft on the last Sixthday of every month, then sitting on its thatched roof to recharge the handful of resonance crystals that kept the inn rooms shielded while listening to Tlareth's off-key humming as she scrubbed and hung the bed linens in the yard below.

Fun was digging for clams and roasting them in their shells on the beach in the early summer while watching questryls soar on the thermals and shearwaters dive for sweet- and spotted cod and shrimp, and the antics of their newly fledged young trying their wings for the first time.

Fun was a skyarc with Tsenjhe in her Blackforge workshop, swapping stories in jumbled Aleznuaweithish and Chanazian while stuffing their faces with fried dumplings and drinking freshly pressed sugarcane juice.

Sitting on silk cushions with her hair pulled back into a tail so tight that the skin at the corners of her eyes and hairline protested every time she blinked, pushing little carved bone-and-bamboo tiles around while being forced to swallow Ylaen's horrid spiced wine as he looked her over with a jhalyx's half-lidded eyes from where he lounged on his bunk was not what she was inclined to term 'fun'.

Ordinarily, she would've deeply regretted capitulating—or at least deeply regretted not resisting to the point where Elaram and Ghardon would've resorted to employing actual combat techniques.

While Ylaen and Jhobon had the largest of the three cabins assigned to the Supplicants, it was uncomfortably cramped with all six of them inside, crowded around a game table improvised out of four folding lap desks pilfered from the ship's study, draped with somebody's white silk overrobe turned inside out to create a smoothish playing surface.

Rahelu had picked her seat partly to benefit from Ghardon's discards, partly because Jhobon was too busy trying to grasp the rules to make much sense of the tactics Elaram fed him so he couldn't take advantage of her discards, but mostly so she could sit as far away as possible from Nheras (who had acknowledged her arrival with the barest of double takes: red painted lips briefly parting in a mildly surprised 'O' while blinking in a *'I'd-forgotten-you-existed'* kind of way) and not think about the apology she owed her cabinmate. That choice had come with the downside of placing her directly opposite Ylaen—No-sleeves, Rahelu mentally corrected herself; she was not going to let Elaram's views influence how she regarded him. Ever since she had walked in, he'd been using his eyes to caress her body the way Elaram's hand had stroked her back. The brazen way he smiled every time she looked up from her tiles and caught him deliberately running his gaze over her slightly reddened face, down past the patches of her resonance-ward-marked skin that were visible through the uncombed strands of her still-damp hair and open collar— and even lower—was practically begging for her to launch her fist at his nose.

On any other night, she would've done so two spans ago.

But *tonight*—

Tonight, she ignored the gradual unraveling of her own composure, the quickening of her pulse, the unevenness in each intake of breath, the heat that rose and rose in her wine-flushed cheeks, and forewent glaring at him in return.

Tonight, No-sleeves could stare at her all he wanted while she and Ghardon won hand after hand after hand and he put in more and more coin to ensure he and Jhobon remained in the game. Sooner or later (and she, personally, was betting on sooner) the Imos and Imrell Supplicants would be down to forfeiting their clothes—or owing favors.

Tonight, she was *having fun.*

Rahelu rubbed the tile she had drawn with her thumb. Eight or nine lines, at the least. Sparse, angled. Stalks? Maybe a four or five tile, from the house of blossoms.

She relaxed her mind into an almost meditative state.

No, whispered the deep inner certainty that had guided her all night. *An honor tile. One of the three legacies.*

She slapped the tile down in front of her, face up, without peeking first. (Exactly as Tlareth would've done, exactly as she had always wanted to be able to do but never had because trying to learn how to tell tiles by touch had been too hard with the callused pads of her fingers; thank you, Ghardon, thank you.) Took her hand away to reveal…

Crystal.

Rahelu chuckled. "Pay up." She flipped over the rest of her tiles to a long, low whistle from Elaram and a deep frown from Nheras. "Two hundred and fifty-six silver kez each."

Just like that, she had added another seven hundred and sixty-eight silver—nearly eight gold kez—to her bulging purse. Half would go to Ghardon later, as per their agreement. (She did not begrudge him his hefty cut; the temporary loan of his jaw-droppingly extensive experience at tile tables was well worth it.) The other half—minus the fifth she had promised to the Stormbringer—was hers.

Hers.

Rahelu tried not to gloat too much as the others took turns drinking from the silver chalice; tried very hard not to picture herself walking away with all of that beautiful wealth as she relished the sweet, head-spinning, toe-tingling thrill of victory surging in her veins; as each cheerful *clink* of gold on silver on bamboo sang in her ears; as Jhobon half-rose on his cushion to puzzle over her winning hand; as Ghardon counted out a stack of silver, looking almost proud as he slid them over to her along with the dice and the calendar token; as Ylaen No-sleeves carelessly tossed six, sun-bright coins into the center to pay for Jhobon's loss in addition to his own (Jhobon had run out three hands ago, having had to cover everyone's losses when Ghardon's hand had proven stronger than he thought); as she scooped up her winnings and tucked them away. The *clackclack-clack-clackity-clickclack* of tiles being shuffled and stacked and drawn was a pleasant accompaniment to her humming.

She could get used to this.

Do not get used to this, she cautioned herself as she flipped over the die embedded in the calendar token indicating the prevailing season and the next hand began. That, in all likelihood, was her final big win for the night. Her fingers moved, automatically grouping her tiles. Honors to the left, houses to the right; all ranked in descending order of dominance. The instincts she had borrowed from Ghardon considered her hand—

(Five honors, none paired. Nine scattered tiles equally distributed across the houses of feathers, blossoms, and scales, with only four close in sequence forming two partial melds. No auspicious blessings to ameliorate her draw.)

—went '*ugh*' in unison with her own internal cursing, then faded.

No more speculative plays, Rahelu decided as she regretfully rearranged her tiles and discarded. She needed to stick to the most basic of strategies: develop a legal hand as quickly as possible, in whatever manner possible, and to the seventh hell with that too, if she so happened to draw enough auspicious blessings to elevate an unranked hand that would otherwise be illegal to the three rank table minimum.

Twelve turns in, her resolve was tested as Ylaen picked

out a tile from the center of his raggedy line and flicked it across the silk. It spun to a stop before Rahelu.

Two scales.

"Fuck." He gave her another of his knowing, siren smiles.

Her fingers twitched as Ghardon's instincts urged her to call—

(*Forget this low-ranked jumble,* they shouted at her. *We're only twelve turns in! Bide your time, wait and see which tiles turn up; watch the pattern of play to see what everyone else is doing. Call, idiot; start discarding those redundant blossoms and feathers and building your hand up into a minor house of scales.*)

—but calling meant deviating from her plan and there was no good reason to deviate from her plan because she was two melds away from winning and any hand she won would fuck up those of her opponents. Putting thirty-two silver into her pocket was better than putting gold into theirs.

Rahelu flicked the two scales tile back into the center of the discards pile where it belonged, next to its twin. "Pass."

"Are you sure?"

"She passed, Imos." Ghardon drew and tossed his tile without looking at it. "Consort."

Four scales. Damn. She had a sudden, vivid flash of (fear; *not* Augury) sitting here, watching the others discard scale after scale, turn after turn, when she could've collected them into tidy relays and Concordances worth at least a gold at face value, maybe more. She should've called; she should've kept on eking out those instincts of his; she should—

Rahelu drew: eight blossoms. The Starfather's luck was not with her.

Ylaen's smile widened as if he had picked up on her inner turmoil. "Looks like a clear-cut case of regret to me."

Gods. Everything about him was insufferable. Nothing and no one aboard seemed to faze him.

"Don't worry, love. I'll give you plenty more chances."

Ordinarily, she would've kept the shitty eight blossoms tile (which didn't fit with the rest of her hand) and broken up her pair of two scales (which did) by slapping one down on the wall in front of him just to prove how very much she did not need his stupid fucking tile.

But *now*—

Rahelu discarded the eight blossoms tile and smiled right back. "Kill."

She also released the remnants of the Evocation Ghardon had shared with her. They—she—had won enough and, as this turn had demonstrated, she didn't need the distraction posed by the clash between his instincts and hers.

Two seasons left. Eight hands, so long as they didn't have to repeat any due to a draw or someone (technically anybody, but really, Ghardon) found a winning streak while holding the Harbinger's seat. So long as she and Ghardon stuck to their tacit agreement to not claim wins from each other's discards, the stockpile of coin she had amassed should sustain her until the end, even if she won no more hands.

She could do this on her own.

Jhobon reached for her discard. As he did, he darted an uncertain glance over his shoulder at his coach—Elaram, who batted her eyelashes at him—and opted to draw instead. Then he dithered, cross-eyed, as he moved the new tile from spot to spot in his hand, which had been broken up into assorted groupings: a pair, two triples, and a row of five.

"You're overthinking again." Elaram tapped the tile on the end of the largest grouping. "What about this one?"

"I–I don't know. It seems reasonable, but I've got an equal amount of—" Jhobon clammed up before he revealed any more specifics about his hand which had to be a confusion of houses and honors because there was no discernable strategy behind his discards.

"Earthgiver grant me patience," Ghardon said. "Stop stalling, Imrell. Just close your eyes and pick one at random."

"If the objective is to maximize winnings, then play should be governed by probabilities—"

"No Augury," Nheras reminded Jhobon, from her place by Ylaen's elbow. "Else you forfeit."

"...Obviously." Jhobon looked about as comfortable talking back to Nheras as a rabbit facing down a nheshwyr but he had warmed to his subject and so he continued: "But mathematically speaking, it should be possible to prove the existence of an optimal solution—if you would all just shut up long enough to let me work it out."

"It's alright, Jhobon. This is the answer." Elaram leaned across him to discard one of the pair: kez. "Fuck, by the way."

"Hold on; how do you know that's the best option?"

Bereft of his journal and bewildered by the speed of play, Jhobon had somehow forgotten Ylaen had discarded another kez tile earlier. Ghardon had called it five turns ago and the three matching tiles were neatly tucked away, face up in a tidy Concordance in front of him.

"Fucking," Elaram said as she scooted closer to Jhobon, "is always the best option."

"Th-that's not—"

"Because killing and consorting are so final." Elaram put her good hand and her chin on Jhobon's shoulder and fluttered her eyelashes again. "It's better to keep your options open. Don't you agree?"

"Read the room, not the tiles," Nheras said, without pointing out his mistake. "You're missing half the game."

What in the eight hells? When had Ilyn ever overlooked the chance to kick someone so obviously struggling?

"I thought no resonance skills were allowed?"

Elaram patted his knee. "Why don't I give you a hand?"

"Uh," was as far as Jhobon got before Elaram practically

crawled into his lap. "Sure!" he squeaked and retreated from the table, his face and resonance aura a mottled red.

With Elaram taking over for Jhobon, the pace picked up until the steady, rapid *click-clack-click-click* rhythm of tiles being drawn and discarded underscored the conversation.

"Take all the time you need to think over the move and if you haven't worked it out by tomorrow, you can come find me in my cabin—"

"Do not show up to our cabin, Imrell," Ghardon said, "unless you want to spend the rest of this trip reliving your days as a drooling babe. I've set up an active Obfuscation barrier that's specifically attuned against you."

The active Seeking Elaram had set up and anchored to her ring for their other, concurrent game flared orange at Ghardon's outright lie.

He amended his statement: "I will have it set up by the end of tonight," and the orange glow winked out.

"Come find me later anyway—I'll be happy to explain at length." Elaram poked Jhobon in his side. "You're not off the hook for your other answer, though."

Jhobon looked even less enthused than before, which Rahelu had not thought possible. "Who was it again?"

"Kyrosh of Isilc." Nheras inspected her nails. "And I agree with fish guts: kill."

"Kill?" Jhobon shook his head as he shuffled back on his cushion and retreated to the corner. "He's not even the Isilc heir; Myreil is. Why would you kill him?"

"Why wouldn't you?" Rahelu countered. "Not only is he spoiled and arrogant, he's also useless."

The Isilc scion had been so confused and angry during Petitioning when the hidden tokens he'd been Seeking hadn't simply fallen into his lap, and when Nheras and her Ilyn lapdogs hadn't been able to recapture the tokens Rahelu and Lhorne and Dharyas had stolen from under their noses.

"But killing him? Wouldn't it be better to—"

Jhobon apparently needed a reminder, so Rahelu summoned Evocation. Besides, the expression on Isilc's face as all of House Imrell's applicants had laughed when she told him to go fuck himself with a clear, unambiguous Free Territory hand sign was worth revisiting.

"This?" she asked Jhobon while Elaram sniggered and Nheras stiffened as they watched the sulky Isilc brat stomp off without a word for his Ilyn allies. "Is this sore loser someone you'd want to fuck, let alone choose as consort?"

Ghardon gave Rahelu a look that she knew all too well from their Evocation classes, the one that questioned her ability to perform basic functions like breathing. "Kill Kyrosh and you piss off Myreil. She's fond of her second cousin."

"Pass, then." Jhobon had huddled up against the spare cushions piled behind him with his legs drawn to his chest. He stared at his knees as though there was something fascinating written across them.

"Nuh-uh," Elaram said. "That's not an option."

"Why not?"

Rahelu squinted in the dim lantern light and was impressed: the Imrell Supplicant had, in fact, managed to pull out a book and was now doing his best to bury his nose in it and pretend he wasn't in the same cabin as the rest of them.

"Because it's against the ruuuuuuuuuules," Elaram sang as she leaned back and confiscated Jhobon's reading material in between turns. "Break the rules, pay the penalty." She pointed to the silver chalice of spiced wine. "Who's next?"

Jhobon sighed and drank. "Can I have my book back?"

Elaram dangled the thin volume by one of its covers. "Not until you tell us who we're considering neeeeeext."

"Don't! Oh don't!" Jhobon cried. "It's one of the only five remaining copies of Reshwim's works!"

"Hey!" Ghardon narrowed his eyes. "That's from Elder Ana—"

Elaram read the title aloud: "'*An Annotated Oral History of the Nine Great Voyages and Explorations of Silcarez Isilc the First: Volume I*'," and immediately perked up. "This is a banned text!"

Both games ground to a halt as Elaram leapt to her feet and everyone was obliged to put their tiles face down while she scampered around the table with Jhobon in pursuit.

"Elaram! Elaram, stop! You need to be careful of—"

"Skies, Jhobon," Nheras said. "Don't you have better things to waste your time on?"

"Evidently not," Ghardon said, then yelped as his sister trod on his ankle. His hand shot out to grab Jhobon's sleeve. "The better question: how did you get this?"

"Elder Anathwan let me borrow it," Jhobon said, shaking him off and darting after Elaram. "Please, give it back!"

The most important question: what was Elder Anathwan doing with a copy of this in her personal library?

Chroniclers on both sides of the Aleznuaweite/Chanaz border generally agreed that Silcarez had been a rogue arch-mage without scruples, who had blackmailed and bribed his way into power until Aleznua had fractured itself. (House Isilc, of course, maintained a different history.)

In the last decades of his life, Silcarez had become so obsessed with the mystery of Enjela's fate that he had emptied most of his House treasury to construct the greatest fleet in the history of the Ngutoccai continent so he might sail in search of answers. Along the way, he had made a great many maps of the previously uncharted waters in the North Ocean and been the first to set foot on the then-unknown Belruonian continent.

The maps and the trade and diplomatic relations gained from Silcarez's voyages were still prized.

No serious scholar, however, gave any significant weight to his wild, unsupported conjectures on the inner workings of the Divine Kingdom. Those had been set down by Reshwim, his most trusted deputy—and she had an infamous reputation of her own for forgeries.

"Wooooow, what kind of dreamleaf was Silcarez smoking? He's asserting that their proclaimed Divine Holiness was actually Enjela herself, made immortal when she was crowned by the Starfather's blessing."

"Eh." Ylaen shrugged. "That's not ludicrous enough for the text to be banned. Half the temples used to believe the gods would take human avatars."

"Gods in the four heavens!" Elaram's eyes lit up as she scanned the page. "I didn't know academic texts could be fun."

"Elaram!" Jhobon tried changing directions to catch her but only succeeded in catching his shins on a corner of his trunk. "You'll damage the pages. Elaram, I'm serious!"

"I'm serious too—seriously upset with you for keeping this all to yourself. It's too glorious not to share."

The way Elaram managed to keep rifling through the pages one-handed for further choice excerpts while navigating the obstacles in the cabin was an impressive display of acrobatics, considering the cramped confines.

"Silcarez claims that Enjela's Chosen have a different rite to govern and bless every aspect of life and the"—a giggle—"the one they hold the most"—more giggling—"s-s-s"—the giggles turned into a low, half-purr—"sacred"—said with a long, drawn-out vowel—"is the—"

Whatever name the Belruonian mage-priests had given to the rite was lost in Elaram's shrieking, snorting laughter.

"The xuuqoshtalog-te?"

"Yes! That. The sacred ritual of—" Elaram composed

herself into a prayer pose common to the Earthgiver's disciples. Intoned, very solemnly: "Suck cocks a lot."

"*NO!*"

Huh. So that was what it took to get a forceful remark out of Jhobon. Then again, Elaram had a special talent for riling people up. Perhaps Jhobon had the right idea; Rahelu ought to take notes, so the next time Nheras did something to piss her off, she could piss her off right back, Elaram style.

"That's not what it is—did you even read the footnote?—it says the rite involves—"

"'I saw that which remained covered and chaste laid bare'," Elaram read aloud, "'upon the sacred altar where he made offerings of silk and salt, incense and perfumed oils, flesh and wine. By burning blade he opens the hidden gate, hard steel sheathed in hot blood, the proof of his devotion writ in resonance. By the stars' grace, he enters; the price of admission: his heart. Into the void, that place between souls where time ceases to exist, the everywhen and nowhere. And from those darkest depths rises heaven's song. Holy hymn; delight divine, ecstasy without end...'"

Eight hells.

Was Reshwim writing a biography or attempting erotic poetry?

"Why are you all laughing?" Jhobon asked. "Death rituals aren't funny!"

Nheras arched one eyebrow at Ylaen. "Do you want to tell him, or shall I?"

Ylaen never got the chance to respond because Elaram shouted, "Here's the footnote to the footnote!" and read out a lurid passage so detailed and descriptive it left no doubt as to its subject matter and so explicit that it would make Tlareth blush—and then ask for it to be read again.

"That can't be the right translation!" Jhobon spluttered. "We know from other historical and contemporary records that a mage-priest binds no fewer and no more than three protectors, and the original text is making use of verse from Belruonian scripture so you're misapplying the wrong frame of reference. Not everything is about fucking as many people as you can in as many orifices as they possess with as many appendages and instruments as you own!"

That was a string of words Rahelu never thought she'd hear from Jhobon in the same sentence.

Elaram widened her eyes at him. "Well," she purred, "what other method would you use to discover the most mathematically optimal position?"

Jhobon's ears went bright red, as did his resonance aura. When Ylaen threw his head back and gave a full-throated laugh, Nheras joined in.

Ghardon, meanwhile, looked every bit as pained as if someone had told him that he could only wear rough home-spun cotton for the rest of his life.

Despite herself, Rahelu had to crack a smile. "Shouldn't you be doing something?" she asked Ghardon. "To uphold and defend Issolm dignity or some such nonsense?"

He shook his head. "I don't waste my time on lost causes." He eyed the cavorting Elaram and said, in a bleak tone, "Con-gratulations, Rahelu. You are now officially my favorite sister."

"I'm not sure I want to be considered a relation right now."

Elaram had found the section of illuminated pages where Reshwim had done a series of sketches of tiny, human figures enacting the scandalous steps in the Belruonians' supposed sacred rites, all helpfully labeled with exacting detail.

"Aren't you the least bit curious, Jhobon?" She jumped on top of Ylaen's trunk and held the book up so they could all appreciate the artistic rendition of a double-page spread featuring two people doing something that looked anatomically impossible for anyone who wasn't employed full-time by an exotic pleasure den catering to a very specific clientele. "Don't you want to try these?"

"No!"

Elaram's active Seeking flashed orange, and the cabin erupted with mirth.

Nheras's whistles, Elaram's squeals, and Ylaen's dead-on impression of Jhobon trying to take notes during such an encounter made even Ghardon give up on staying serious and Rahelu laughed so hard that her sides ached worse than her resonance-backlash-induced headache.

Jhobon did the impossible: his face flushed redder than Nheras's lip paint and Ylaen's spiced wine. "Not like that!"

"Oh, you have improvements?" Elaram asked. She waggled her fingers at him. "Why don't you come over here then, and we can conduct some hands-on experiments?"

"Because I—the average person isn't that flexible and your—their legs aren't—" Jhobon stopped at the fresh roar of raucous laughter. "I am leaving!"

He fled, leaving a cobalt trail of hurt in the ambient resonance.

"Jhobon…" Elaram hopped off the trunk and left the book lying open, illuminated pages down, on the lid, and ran after him, heedless of who she trod on and what she knocked over. "Jhobon, wait! I was only teasing!"

Snap!

Two of the flimsy lap desks folded and set off a horrendous clangor as an avalanche of tiles struck the silver chalice. Crimson liquid sloshed out, vivid as fresh blood against the white silk. Yelling—from Ghardon, from Nheras, from her own throat—as they scrabbled back to avoid the red runnels snaking across the other unsteady half of the table. Wine splattered their faces and forearms, splashed shirt sleeves and hems, dribbled onto their trousers, and soaked into the cushions and cabin sole.

Awkward, awkward silence descended as the four of them regarded the wreckage Elaram had left in her wake.

Nheras stood, pinching a dripping cushion by its corner, as if she had a diseased wharf rat by the tail.

"Well." Ylaen peeled off his butchered, sopping-wet shirt. Dropped it on the broken table with a limp *splat*, then picked up the silver chalice. He squinted at what little remained of its contents before draining it dry. "I could use more wine," he said, to nobody in particular, and strolled out.

Ghardon said, "I am so, so, so sorry about—"

"Your sister," Nheras said, making no effort to curtail her acid tone or the green-brown disgust wafting from her aura as she flung the cushion at him, "is a damnable menace."

A completely fair descriptor of Elaram.

Ghardon took the sodden cushion and Ylaen's shirt to the washstand without saying a word in defense.

Nheras went on: "You owe us damages."

That, though, was completely unfair to Ghardon.

"Damages? For what? Getting a little wet?" Rahelu scoffed as she mopped up what she could of the spill with the overrobe. "Don't be absurd."

"I'm not being absurd; I'm asserting my House-given rights. And perhaps it's you who ought to be paying for the damages, considering what you're doing to my overrobe."

Oh.

Most of the garment was now streaked with a pinkish-orange that vaguely reminded her of Ilyn coral. Or the sunrise, peeking through bands of wispy clouds.

Rahelu bit back the instinctive retorts on the tip of her tongue (*'I'm not paying you a single copper kez'* went without saying, and pointing out that *'It's wine, not blood, and even blood will wash out'* would certainly come across as too flippant, no matter how factually true the statement was), and tried—earnestly so, for once—to make peace instead of a spectacle, for Ghardon's sake.

"I'm sorry," she told Nheras and meant it.

There. Not as difficult an endeavor as she'd thought, though she had to follow up with something else lest Nheras construe her sympathetic acknowledgment of her cabin-mate's feelings as some kind of concession and agreement to pay the damages demanded.

Perhaps a joke?

Rahelu held out the overrobe. "I thought you were fond of this hue."

As soon as the words left her mouth, she knew she had made a mistake.

Nheras's eyes flashed at the unintended slight. "You think many things, all of them embarrassingly wrong." She ignored the offered overrobe and slid into the seat Elaram had vacated. "Perhaps it's time to correct your misconceptions."

A small wave of those perfectly manicured nails mani-fested a ghostly trail of fallen tiles and collapsed desks that flew up and righted themselves in a perfect reconstruction of their interrupted game, where Rahelu had been one tile away from winning.

Guided by her Evocation, Nheras reached over and unerringly plucked a tile out of the pile in front of Rahelu—a Seeker from her hand, a lone tile awaiting its match—then retrieved three more that had been in Jhobon's hand.

All Seekers, in a complete Concordance.

How the fuck had she missed it, and how had Nheras known? There had been no active Seekings other than Elaram's and she had had that tile from the very start.

Rahelu turned her jaw drop into a yawn—it was almost deepnight—and feigned indifference. "I would have discarded that on the next turn. Still my hand to win."

That was the beauty of a common hand of Concordances —she didn't have to limit herself to honors or a single house. Her winning tile could be anything, anything at all.

Nheras smirked. "No, it wasn't."

She flipped over the next tile Rahelu would have drawn— that stupid eight of blossoms again; her win, right there, if she hadn't thrown the first one away—and kept scrounging around until she had reassembled Ghardon's hand.

The major house of blossoms, with four completed relays and three possible paths to victory, one of which was...the eight of fucking blossoms.

His turn came before hers.

Fuck. She'd been so dead set on winning, so sure her strategy was the right one, that she had lost all perspective.

"Allow me to summarize." Nheras leaned forward, elbows framing the superimposed hypothetical of how the game ought to have ended, hands demurely folded underneath her chin. Her voice was sweet and gentle with false concern. "There is no scenario where you win, fish guts."

Rahelu tamped down her surging annoyance before it could cross her resonance ward and tossed the wine-soaked overrobe aside. "Evoke what you want, but that doesn't change the present: nobody won, so nobody lost. But if you insist on trying to determine a winner..."

She upended her heavy purse. Coins poured out across the table in a melodic cascade, a river of gold and silver that obscured the traces of red spill and her past mistakes to quickly overflow its tile banks as it sung all of her victories in a lovely lilting metallic melody.

"I think," Rahelu said, as she mirrored Nheras's pose, "that the results speak for themselves."

"Oh, Skymother." Nheras laughed. "You've played only two rounds, every win you've scored but the last has been off Jhobon's discards, and you never would've built that hand up into a major house if Ghardon hadn't kept tossing you crumbs." She scooped up a double palmful of Rahelu's coins and let them trail through her fingers. "None of this was earned in your own right. Was it?"

The restraint Rahelu had kept on her temper snapped. "Are you making an accusation?"

"Should I be?"

"If you've got something to prove, Ilyn, then prove it, instead of dancing around the point with snide insinuations."

"What insinuations? I'm simply making observations." A delicate pause as they locked stares. "Like how coincidentally similar your playing style is to Ghardon's. You've both got this odd quirk of clinging on to your Evoker tiles no matter which seat you're holding or what hand you're developing."

...shit.

"You know what?" Rahelu straightened and started shoveling coins back in her purse, fully aware that retreating was tantamount to admitting guilt, but unable to devise a more graceful exit. "I'm done."

She headed for the door—all too conscious of Nheras's self-satisfied smirk burning between her shoulder blades and the slow, methodical, *clack, clack, clack,* taunt of tiles being picked up and put back on the table—only to come nose to nose with Ylaen: scarred and shirtless, new flagon in hand, already drinking straight from the spout.

He licked his lips. "Leaving so soon?"

"Of course she is," Nheras jeered. "The silly fish finally figured out that the deep dark sea is nothing like her quiet little pond, so now she's lost and afraid."

"I'm bored, Ilyn," Rahelu retorted, "because these ridiculous House-born games of yours are both inane and uninteresting. Some mage you are, if you can't tell the difference."

"Bored?" Ylaen repeated. "If only you'd said something

earlier." That siren smile again as he appraised her. "Stay, Issolm, and let's change the rules to be more entertaining."

"No thanks."

"Why not?" he drawled.

"I'd rather jump overboard and swim with razorfangs."

Something—a shadowed expression?—flitted across his face, and he said, in a serious tone she'd never heard him use before, "You don't mean that. It's a terrible way to die." His seriousness vanished, as suddenly as it had appeared, and insufferableness returned: "But if getting wet and bitten is what excites you, I'd be happy to oblige, love."

"Call me 'love' again and I will cut out your tongue with your own damned knife and feed it back to you in pieces."

"That's enough, Rahelu," Ghardon said, from right behind her. He laid a firm hand on her shoulder and squeezed. Hard. A clear *'stop blabbing threats at a scion of a major House while we're guests in his cabin'* warning. "Thank you, Imos, for the invitation and the wine, but I think it's best if my sister and I retire."

Ylaen made no move to dislodge himself from the doorway. "I think not. What kind of host would I be if I permitted your evening to end on such an unmemorable note?"

"A prudent one," Ghardon said. "I'm sure none of us wish to come so close to failing the expectations placed upon us by the senior mages a second time and jeopardize our prospects of being recognized as Dedicates in due course."

An excellent point no one could argue with.

If only it had occurred to her earlier.

"One last hand," Ylaen proposed as he slowly drew his knife, the one she'd threatened him with, a serpentine blade of polished steel nearly as long as his forearm. Quick as lightning, he threw. It whistled over her shoulder to bury itself in the center of the table before Nheras with a loud *thunk*, its golden hilt quivering from the impact. "Personal stakes," he

said, that smile of his morphing until it was a jhalyx's laugh:
all lolling tongue and flashing white teeth. "Drink on every
turn. No limit."

Ghardon, whose winnings had been capped by the table
limit at least five different times tonight, relented immediately. He countered with, "Six rank minimum," as he
resumed his seat opposite a still-smirking Nheras and set
about restoring order to the tiles. "I stake my bow."

Nheras reached inside her collar and pulled out a very
familiar resonance crystal ring.

Rahelu could not look away as Nheras unthreaded it from
her silver necklace and flipped it into the air. Just the sight of
the bright arc scribed by the spinning ring made her heart
skip faster, and the soft crystalline *plink-plink-plinkplinkplink* of
the focus stone as it struck tile and settled beside Ylaen's
knife reverberated in her ears.

"Concealed hands only," Nheras said, with a clear challenge in her eyes: *'Let's see what you can do when you can't rely on
anybody else.'*

In all the years of her existence, Rahelu had never once
backed down from a direct challenge. Every time she had
come home, sniveling and beaten, her mother would berate
her for her foolishness and stubborn pride, but her father
would kiss away her tears and tend her bruises and scrapes.

*'Jenura, avela. We prayed that our daughter would find the sky,
and so the Earthgiver blessed her with an indomitable spirit. It is
not in her nature to concede. Do not scold her for trying to grow
wings.'*

'I know, Hemoru, I know. But it is so very far if she falls.'

'Better to fly and fall, than to never soar.'

Rahelu stalked back to her cushion. Plonked down her
entire purse and instantly regretted it; all she could see was

thirty-eight gold and seven hundred and forty-two silver kez evaporating before her eyes.

Idiot. Idiot!

Ten days ago, if someone had put twenty copper kez down for her to take, she would have laid both hands on the coins and run off faster than anyone could blink. And now she wanted to risk what was still an inconceivable amount of wealth? Of all the stupid, senseless, blind—

Rahelu visualized the cool waters of the Elumaje and forced herself to breathe normally.

Done was done.

Nheras shot her purse a disdainful look. "We agreed on personal stakes, fish guts."

"Coin is as personal as it gets in the Lowdocks. But if that's not personal enough for your House-born sensibilities, then I'll willingly pay in blood and let you cut me."

"What is a fish's blood worth to anyone? It's the first thing to be discarded."

Fucking House-born word games.

Before she could tell Nheras where she could stick her glib tongue, Ylaen uncoiled himself from the doorway and said, "Lifeblood, freely given, honors the gods." He sauntered to his bunk and quelled any remaining objections by adding, "I will offer the same."

So Rahelu sat when he did and issued a further stipulation as they shuffled the tiles: "Winner takes all."

She was not going to let Nheras get the better of her. And if she was risking everything, then she wanted the chance to win everything.

"But of course," Ylaen said as he poured.

It wasn't good enough, though, not when Nheras had staked something that wasn't even really hers to begin with.

Rahelu narrowed her eyes.

What kind of loss, what kind of humiliation would truly

hurt the Ilyn girl, as much as the loss of every kez would hurt her? A girl who wore powder and lip paint, silk and satin, haughtiness and hair ornaments like armor?

Oh, it was obvious, wasn't it?

Rahelu borrowed Ghardon's shark-toothed smile and Ylaen's wandering stare and said, "Clothing included."

Ylaen raised the refilled chalice. "I like how you think."

Nheras's reply caught her completely off guard. "Why stop at clothing when that's not all you've got to wager?"

Focus on the tiles you're stacking, Rahelu. Try not to let them slip and crash because your fingers are sweating and your palms are shaking from your rushing pulse and you're trickling blood from the back of your knuckles where you scraped them against Ylaen's knife because you were in too much of a hurry to mind the edge.

Clack. Clack. Clack. Clack. Four walls of tiles rose up and enclosed the prizes at the center.

She rolled the dice. "I don't know what you're talking about."

Honors to the left, houses to the right; in descending order of dominance. An overwhelming wash of red. Tiles of blood and crimson feathers and bold Harbingers drowning the blue-green dragon, the pale yellow-white starblooms, the smattering of other honors, bamboo-backed ivory sticking to each other with wine.

Rahelu discarded the first tile: crystal.

Here, Nheras. For you. Go on. Look all you like. Did the heavens endow your hand with a pair just like it? Does it torment you to see this one slip away from you, to know you can't lay a finger on it unless you want to forfeit?

I hope it does. I hope it burns you, slow and bitter, the way this wine burns my throat.

Nheras drew. Discarded a Guardian. Sipped from the chalice and said, "I'm talking about Ideth's pendant."

That got everyone's attention, though the only one who looked surprised was Ylaen. "Lhorne Ideth?" he asked while staring at the tile he had just drawn. He drank and discarded a dragon, smiling no longer. "Kill."

Ghardon's turn to draw. "Fuck." He drank, then added: "The pendant is not hers to wager."

Good, she thought as he passed the wine and discarded a phoenix. He wouldn't be competing with her. Time to declare her intent. Rahelu discarded a second dragon, took another swig, then shoved the horrid wine at Nheras. "Fuck."

"Oh?" Nheras drew. "I heard the pendant was a gift."

It was, but: "Gift or not, it's irrelevant because instead of fucking him you froze," Rahelu said. "And since I have it on good authority that House Ideth only wants Supplicants who are capable of acting instead of freezing…" She tapped her cheek in mock thoughtfulness. "The only real option you have is 'kill', but maybe you can't do that either." She folded her arms. "You want my pendant? You can challenge me for it, separately, once we're done here."

Go on; renege on our agreement. Meet me, mage to mage, in a contest of abilities again—here, now, before witnesses— and let's see who wins when we begin on equal footing.

"But you won't, will you? You keep refusing to meet me in the circle."

Nheras sent her tile careening into the discards. *Clack!* Blood.

"Why," Nheras asked, "would I exert any effort when you're so capable of sabotaging yourself?" Her resonance aura darkened to a deep coral, edges sharp and shimmering with a malicious light as she swirled the chalice. "Do you know how to count, fish guts?"

Rahelu's eyes flicked down to her row of tiles: three, six, nine, twel—oh, shit. *Shit.* Shit! *SHIT!* Thirteen, there ought to be thirteen tiles, so why—how the fuck had she—

Cold sweat slicked her palms as an ugly flush crept up her neck and red-and-white swirls of mortifying horror invaded her aura. She'd forgotten to draw before discarding and there was no way to Revoke that mistake once her turn had passed.

Stormbringer's mercy. She couldn't win.

She was going to have to destroy her own Earthgiver-blessed hand.

She was so utterly, utterly *fucked*.

Rahelu sent her Harbingers to die first. She tore down her greater relay, starting with her nine feathers and working her way down to her phoenix. The more feathers she discarded, the more replacements she drew—a glut of the Starfather's luck that, had she not fucked everything up, would've seen her win twice already—until it seemed as though every feather tile in the set had passed through her hand and the table was soaked in red again.

The remaining stacks dwindled.

She watched the others draw and drink their way closer to victory, choking on every mouthful of bitter wine as she frantically extrapolated from their discards, searching for a way, any way, to thwart them.

If no one won, then no one lost.

But Nheras had accounted for that by mandating concealed hands. No one could call, except to declare a win, so Rahelu could do nothing to interrupt the order of play. Her only recourse was to kill off the tiles she suspected they needed as quickly as possible or hoard them in her hand.

She scattered dead honors into the sea of discards.

Fifteen stacks to go.

The game was Ylaen's for the taking. Halfway through the hand, he had put all of his tiles face down like he was ready to declare a win, but his discards since then had been as defeatist as hers—three Concordances of scales over nine successive turns, which made no sense. Only Nheras and

Ghardon had any possibility of victory remaining, and both seemed resigned to a draw. Probably deadlocked in their bids to control the house of blossoms.

Finally, Ylaen drew the last live tile. Snorted. Placed it face up in front of him as he gulped his wine, alongside his three other blessings: earth, sky, and stars.

Storm.

He'd drawn all four celestials.

"The Four Heavens." Ghardon groaned. "You have got to be joking." He picked up the odd tile stacked atop the dead wall—the last eight stacks that, under the stupid Aleznu-aweithish ruleset they were using, were to remain undrawn —and handed the tile to Ylaen. "If you end up scooping the moon's fucking reflection from the seabed..."

Ylaen glanced at his tile and barked in laughter. He selected a different tile from his concealed hand and slapped the final discard on top of the pile.

Dragon.

Oh, thank you, wonderful, merciful, *glorious* gods for stalemate!

"Fun game." Rahelu snatched up her purse. She'd gotten halfway to her feet before Nheras caught her wrist.

"Put the purse back, fish guts. A stalemate means we repeat the hand."

She broke Nheras's grip with a sharp twist of her arm. "One last hand was what we agreed, and now it's over. Sorry you didn't win. Move on." Rahelu jerked her chin at Ylaen, who had reclaimed his knife but abandoned the empty chalice in favor of the mostly empty flagon, and Ghardon, who had crashed his incomplete hand into the dead wall. "The rest of us have."

"More wine, Issolm?" Ylaen slurred. "Nheras?"

Ghardon eyed the door, then closed his eyes for a brief

Seeking. It took all of a heartbeat before he visibly cringed and reached for the flagon. "Sure. Why not?"

Cold silence from Nheras.

"Pass." Rahelu stood, swayed into the table, and sent Ylaen's tiles skittering; had to put her hand out to stop herself from falling. "Good night all," she mumbled as she staggered over to the door, then threw a glance over her shoulder to fire one last parting shot at her cabinmate. "And you...you..."

She stared at Nheras holding and staring and frowning at one of the tiles she had knocked over—something blue and green from Ylaen's hand—but couldn't think of anything to say.

Leave it, Rahelu, just leave it. You got what you wanted, and Nheras is busy shaking with rage. Now go, before she decides to—

CRACK!

Nheras slammed the tile against the table. "Ylaen Imos," she hissed, "you are a *coward*."

Ylaen said nothing in response because Ylaen had slumped over on his mattress, eyes slightly unfocused like he was in mage trance (he was way too drunk to hold mage trance), his body sluggishly responsive to Ghardon's none-too-gentle prodding for him to move over so Ghardon could steal his pillow and pass out, since he was apparently either too inebriated to attempt climbing into Jhobon's bunk, or had gained a newfound appreciation for sleeping on the firm surface of the cabin sole.

Not that Nheras was waiting around for a reply. She shoved past Rahelu and stormed out in a flurry of flouncing hair and sharp elbows, resonance crystal ring clutched in her white-knuckled fist.

Rahelu wobbled down the passageway on her heels and—

BANG!

"OW!" Rahelu tasted copper as she gingerly felt at her nose; Nheras had closed their cabin door right on her fucking face. "What in the eight hells, Ilyn?"

The metallic *scraaaape-click* of an iron deadbolt being drawn.

Oh, come the fuck *on.*

Rahelu smacked, then pounded, then rammed the door repeatedly as she cursed Nheras, her petty-minded actions, and eight generations of her ancestors. But no matter what kind of hell she raised, the door to their cabin did not open, and Rahelu was forced to seek out the hammock Kerg had offered.

She bedded down in the crew's empty quarters, listening to the *shrieks* and *creaks* of the rigging and the shouts and cries of the captain and his crew holding the *Winged Arrow* to its course against the Stormbringer's breath. Lay in the dark and tried, in the deafening pauses between each thunderous shock of the Stormbringer's strikes, to imagine a world where gifts came without chains, where a win for someone else did not automatically translate into a loss for her, where she did not have to fight—tooth and nail, every moment of every span—just to survive.

But all she dreamed of was blades and blood and crystal shackles.

10
PROJECTION

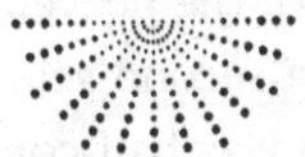

THE 14TH DAY OF TRUESUMMER, 530 A.E./A.F.

RAHELU AWOKE IN DARKNESS, IMPRISONED BY THE tangle of her sweat-dampened hair. Her throat was hoarse; her tongue thick and swollen; her jawbones ached as if they'd been locked in place all night.

She pulled on her wine-soured uniform, taking care not to disturb Kerg and the other crew slumbering in the hammocks next to her, then went in search of food.

The mess deck was mostly full, with those of the Isonn crew not on dawnwatch swinging from the beams overhead like great oversized bats. But the fire hearth was lit and the cook was at work, kneading dough for a second batch of flatbread as the first lot cooled. His assistants were close by, chopping root vegetables. They nodded in greeting as she helped herself to breakfast: yesterday's rewarmed stew, ladled into a rolled cone of fresh flatbread. The meat had a strong, earthy flavor she'd never tasted before, the thick sauce oozing and rich with spices. The first few bites went down easily to sit heavy in her stomach.

She devoured the whole thing on her way up to the main deck.

Fog blurred the boundary between sky and sea, the waves so still the water looked almost flat. The sun was yet to rise though the moon had already retired, and all that could be seen was the Skymother's infinite star-studded cloak spread across the horizon. Here, away from city watchfires, the stars were bright and endless. If she leaned against the rigging and tipped her head back until the heavens were all she could see, it was like looking into a second sea. In her imagination, she reversed them, until she was half-convinced that if she let go of the ropes, she could dive into the depths of the sky.

The *Winged Arrow* had flown along the Aleituan coastline, violently propelled eastward by the Stormbringer's breath. In just four days, they had passed the Gulf of Alostim. Soon, perhaps as soon as the sunrise, they would sail through the narrow channel into the greater Aleituan Sea and change course, heading southeast until they reached Peshwan Yrg in another day or two, when the Elder would test them again.

Rahelu wasn't sure she would pass.

She spurned the horizon in favor of heading aft to find somewhere to stretch without tripping over coiled ropes and hatches. Someone had chalked out a sparring circle on the upper deck; its thick white line was scuffed in a dozen places.

Her muscles were stiff and cold; her body slow to obey her. She stumbled through the first exercise and had to repeat it five times before she got through it without erring. The second went better; she made only one mistake and got it right on the next attempt. By the the third, her body had finally reacquainted itself with the routine. She breathed, drawing in comfort and strength from the clean air and open space and burgeoning light that surrounded her as she settled into the rhythm, her heartbeat joined to the steady chorus of the waves slapping against the ship's hull.

This—this was what it was to be alive.

She began the fourth exercise with her eyes closed, trusting to her extended resonance senses. Her mind flew free with the circling questryl as she moved seamlessly from one spear form to another, flowing from offense to defense in the prescribed steps as she danced with the wind.

She wished she had her spear.

The forms felt off balance without its heft, but Nheras—but there wasn't enough room to swing the weapon without getting it caught in the shrouds and ratlines. So Rahelu looked deep within herself instead, summoning the anger and fear she had wrestled with all night and buried, channeled it through her palms until it took on the familiar shape of her spear: a bone-white shaft nine-and-a-half hands long, tipped with a shark-sleek, wedged blade that extended her reach by another two hands. Red lightning crackled as she swung; resonance and heat arcing from her aura and along the shaft to set the spearhead aflame.

It wasn't the same—there was no physical weight to her Projection, only an illusion of one where it met the edges of her resonance aura—but it helped. She spun it in her hands, shifted forward in a high block, and twisted left to avoid the counterstrike of her imaginary opponent. The *Winged Arrow* crested another swell and sea spray speckled her skin as she brought the exercise to a conclusion: she surged forward and struck the featureless shadow-opponent in her mind's eye with a two-handed thrust to the heart.

Her Projection slammed into an Obfuscation barrier. Hot anger met cool amusement and the resultant reverberations sheared through the ambient resonance with a raw screech.

Ylaen—No-sleeves—of Imos stood before her, just inside the sparring circle, looking none the worse for wear. (The same could not be said for his shirt, a fresh one, which—like every other shirt she'd seen him wear—also had no sleeves.)

He dropped his left arm; with it went his partial Obfuscation barrier. In his right hand, he carried his long, serpentine steel knife; at his waist, a second, more ordinary knife and a pouch of chalk.

He swept his gaze over her; she returned it in kind.

"I'm sorry." She eyed him warily. He reminded her of a mountain bharyx: all lean, corded muscle and sharp, angular planes in a compact body. "I didn't realize you were here."

"You dance with the swiftness of the questryl and the grace of the fan-tailed kite."

"Thank you." Rahelu gave him a slight bow and stepped out of the circle. If Ylaen was awake, the others might be too. If she arrived bearing a hot breakfast, Ghardon and Elaram would probably let her borrow their washstand and another change of clothes one more time.

"Please, stay." Another slow smile as he tossed the pouch of chalk to one side and stepped back with a wide sweep of his knife. "Would you leave me unpartnered?"

'Yes, actually,' she wanted to say, 'because you seem to lack the consideration necessary to being an equal partner' for Elaram's indignation and complaints were all too fresh in her memory.

But, thanks to Elaram, she was indifferent no longer. He stood there—no, he *posed* there, like he was readying himself to be immortalized in some Chronicler's account, with full awareness of how the light of the rising sun burnished his skin to gold and made the jagged lines of the ritual scars that decorated his bare arms and torso seem to glow.

"My knife is in my cabin. Perhaps some other time."

"Ah, love." That smile widened as he flipped his knife around to hold it by the blade. "Did you not say that you would use mine?"

Gods, his arrogance and self-satisfaction were irritating.

She stepped back over the scuffed white line and wrapped her fingers around the golden hilt. "No resonance skills."

"No resonance skills," he acknowledged, drawing his second knife.

They both fell into stance.

"To the first touch?" she asked.

"To the first touch." He brought his knife to his heart, rapping his right fist against his left breast in a ceremonial gesture she didn't recognize. "Achwa-te, Rahelu."

She lunged.

Their first exchange was a series of feints. She had the longer knife, but it was heavier than she was used to, and he had greater reach. Also, Ylaen could and did wield his knife with both hands—twice, he switched his weapon from one hand to the other—though he favored one side: his left-handed strikes were cleaner and carried greater force. His footwork was light and effortless; his sense of physical aware-ness keen—he had no trouble distinguishing her feints from her true attacks, and turned each one aside unerringly.

He anticipated her perfectly as if he'd Augured each move.

She narrowed her eyes and changed tactics.

Instead of pressing her attack, she hung back and waited.

And so their second exchange was a chase—full of long, drawn-out stretches where his bare feet stalked hers as they circumscribed the edges of their sparring circle; followed by quick, irregular bursts of motion where he tested her guard. He had just enough reach to make things difficult; the circle was just big enough that she was able to elude him.

Until she answered one downward slash at her left shoulder by sliding away to her right, instead of deflecting it. The bright, rising eartharc sun dazzled her; she flinched and shut her eyes against its light instinctively.

She knew she had lost, even as she ducked the strike that she knew would follow. He had her off balance; her footing was wrong, the weapon in her hand all but useless while she was blinded and prohibited from using resonance skills. She dropped his knife with a clatter and, with a quick prayer to the Stormbringer, threw herself forward.

They tumbled to the deck. He wheezed—by sheer chance, she'd judged correctly and had driven her shoulder into his midsection—and she scrambled to press her advantage. She was too slow though, and he had the advantage of weight, so five heartbeats later, she found herself pinned to the deck, his knife kissing her throat, breathing heavily.

"Your match," she said, blinking away the white spots in her vision.

"My match." Ylaen's teeth gleamed in another lazy smile. He did not climb off her. "Shall we dance again?"

The wind carried the sound of voices—voices that belonged to the other Supplicants. She looked past him, through his mane of wavy black hair that shielded their faces like a curtain to the main deck, where Guardian Maketh waited for his charges to assemble.

And where four pairs of speculative eyes were busy taking note of Ylaen pressing the length of his body against hers.

"No," she said. "Get off me now, or we'll be late."

He did as she asked—and also reclaimed the knife he had loaned her. "Another time, then. I'd like to try you with a different weapon. Perhaps a spear." He offered her his hand.

She ignored it.

"Perhaps." She levered herself up with one hand and left him to follow as she all but ran down the stairs towards the gathered circle of Supplicants on the main deck, her cheeks and body flushed with heat from sparring.

Guardian Maketh wasted no time.

As soon as Rahelu and Ylaen were within earshot, he

said, "Today, we will review your command of Projection."
The Imos Dedicate did not spare either of them a glance;
indeed, he seemed not to notice nor care that Rahelu was
free to walk the decks. "Elder Anathwan will join us later, as
her schedule permits."

Rahelu glanced up sharply. She'd been under the impression that any instruction they required in Projection would
come directly from the Elder. Not that Maketh wasn't competent at Projection, but senior mages didn't typically give
instruction in a specialization not their own, particularly with
an expert present.

Clearly, Anathwan had other priorities.

That was fine with Rahelu, because being on the receiving
end of a Projection from a senior Harbinger was not an experience she had any desire to repeat. Having her will
supplanted like that...it was too close to being Suborned. Far
better for them to be lobbing Projections at each other, even
if it was disruptive to the crew. This far out to sea, they
would have to really work at gathering enough resonance.

Perhaps Maketh was uncomfortable with the idea. Instead
of his usual direct approach, he paced along the main deck
before them, hands clasped behind his back.

He stopped in front of Ghardon, still frowning in thought.
"Supplicant Ghardon, what is Projection?"

"The opposite of Obfuscation," Ghardon said immediately. "Projection is the outward manifestation of resonance,
instead of an inward one."

"A simplistic answer," Maketh said. "Let me ask the question in a different way. What is Obfuscation?"

"Obfuscation is..."

Hiding was how Rahelu would have answered. The question ought to have been an easy one for Ghardon, but Maketh
had put him off balance. He started to speak, then stopped

himself half a dozen times, before he went with: "It's the controlled suppression of resonance, which generally takes the form of a constructed barrier against unwanted resonance."

The Guardian made a disappointed noise in his throat. "I did not ask for a technical explanation of what Obfuscation can do; I asked what it *is*."

Nobody knew how to answer that—this was an oddly philosophical turn in Maketh's teaching methods.

Eventually, with the timidity of a mouse venturing out of its burrow when it can scent a cat nearby, Jhobon said, "It's a veil," and flinched as Maketh spun around in a swirl of yellow-and-white robes.

"Yes!" the Guardian said, stabbing his finger in Jhobon's direction. "Exactly. It is a veil. What, then, can you tell me about the nature of Projection?"

By now, Rahelu was thoroughly lost. Of all the resonance disciplines, Projection was the most aggressive. When you used Projection, you amplified an existing source of resonance. How was that related to veils?

"Projection is asserting one emotional reality upon another," Nheras said.

The Guardian nodded. "Which means…?"

"It is also a veil," Ylaen said softly.

"Indeed."

The Guardian paused, his gaze roving from face to face expectantly. Rahelu waited for his next question, his next instructions—to arrange themselves in teams or sparring pairs, perhaps—a demonstration of first principles, or even a lecture that would simultaneously cover second-year basics and topics from fifth-year electives.

But Maketh said nothing and did nothing, except continue to stand there, a mountain of a man, for the next half-span while they all did their best not to fidget.

What kind of instruction was this? She almost wished she was back inside a sparring circle, facing down four opponents —at least she had learned something from that exercise.

Her peers were equally puzzled. To her left, Jhobon was staring at his feet again; on his left, Ylaen and Nheras had their eyes closed in meditation. To her right, both Issolm siblings stood attentively: Ghardon looked dreadful—he kept rubbing at his temples—but Elaram was her usual perky self and considered the Guardian with narrowed eyes.

What had Elaram noticed?

Rahelu closed her own eyes and stretched out her resonance senses:

Seven vibrant auras pulse on the main deck. Six in a slightly curved row. The seventh—the strongest—faces them, two strides from the center of their line, its strict, stately rhythm as unchanging as marble.

She held onto her visualization as she opened her eyes.

Maketh looked much as he always did: thick eyebrows, deep-set eyes, large nose over stern lips set in an impassive visage, with a resonance aura as sturdy as city walls. If she stuck some horns on his head, painted him gray, and draped a few vines and wreaths around his neck, you could stash him in a niche at the Earthgiver's temple and he'd fit right in.

Except they'd been standing here for nearly a span and he hadn't said a single disparaging word about the Guild's curriculum or their theoretical knowledge of Projection.

Rahelu frowned, comparing what she saw to what she remembered. The longer she stared at Guardian Maketh, the fuzzier the details became, like her eyes were having trouble focusing. Characteristics she hadn't paid particular attention to seemed to shift before her. Did he keep his face clean-shaven? Had the patches of darkness along his jaw that she recalled from that terrifying night in the great cabin been stubble or had it simply been faint shadows cast by the flickering lantern flame? As she studied Maketh's chin with an intensity she never imagined she would apply, she could have sworn that physical detail flowed from one possibility to the other in response to her thoughts—yet that was absurd; as absurd as the nagging insistence that something was off about his resonance signature; a faint warping a little too regular to be random fluctuations in the ambient resonance.

It had to be a trick of the sunlight filtering through the sails or the aftereffects of wine-dulled wits; she wasn't seeing clearly, and without the benefit of an Evocation, she couldn't trust the accuracy of her memory. But summoning Maketh's likeness right next to him, the way criminal investigators would match physical appearances and resonance signatures to recorded eyewitness accounts to pick out the culprit from a lineup of potential suspects, probably constituted another insult he could use to justify punishing her again.

And yet...

Something didn't seem right.

To the eight hells with it. Rahelu straightened, leaned forward, and half-raised her hand to summon the past.

Elaram beat her to the accusation. "You're not Guardian Maketh," she said, certain as the tides. She stretched out a hand and the outer layers of resonance in their instructor's aura parted like curtains before Elaram's Seeking.

"No." The face of Guardian Maketh smiled, wavered, then dissolved. "I am not."

Stern, masculine features softened and remolded themselves, like clay in an invisible sculptor's hands, into blue eyes the color of heartleaf tea, with a thin, elegant nose, and bow-curved lips. Straight, dark brown hair lengthened and kinked into golden curls that fell past shoulders; even the timbre of the voice had lightened from a man's deep baritone to a woman's honeyed lilt. The yellow trim on the Dedicate's robes bleached to white; the golden chain of his resonance pendant turned to silver; and the triple peak sigil of a Guardian embossed on the gilded leather armband of House Imos blurred into the black flame engraved into the white armband of a House Issolm Harbinger.

"Well done, Elaram," Elder Anathwan said, gifting the Issolm Supplicant with one of her warm smiles.

No longer hidden behind seemingly impenetrable walls, Anathwan's resonance aura swelled. Golden radiance enveloped them like the rays of a second summer sun.

"Projection is a veil; in this regard, Projection and Obfuscation are the same. But where Obfuscation seeks to negate the existence of an emotional reality, Projection seeks to assert the existence of an emotional ideal."

Anathwan's gaze roamed over the line of Supplicants. "Most mages apply this principle in only the crudest of manners—they rely on exercising pure, brute strength to attain their purpose."

Summer vanished. The ambient resonance froze, solid as the Unomelaje's heart. Gasps sounded down the line; Rahelu half-expected to see their breaths as puffs of frost; she felt a bone-chilling fear so deep that it bled the strength from her limbs until she folded to the deck.

"What is a deadly hail of arrows compared to terror that pierces the soul and turns bowels to water?"

Her pulse raced erratically; every thump of her heart an agonizing hammerblow against her ribs; tears ran unchecked down her face as she drowned in a sea of dead faces. Welm. Hzin. Xyuth. Dharyas, oh *Dharyas*, and—anma, *anma*—

"How could a sword thrust to the heart wound more deeply than love lost or betrayed?"

Tears fled before anger. Sweet, familiar anger, a burning tide that overwhelmed sense and urged her to move, to act, to sweep away all obstacles until her desires were attained.

"Why bombard a fortified position when the defenders would easily abandon them if goaded into righteous rage?"

She rushed forward, gripped by a crimson haze, outstretched hands ready to seize and strangle that slender throat, to choke the life out of that falsity, silence its gods-cursed words—

Her fingers closed upon soft flesh.

All fury extinguished.

Leaving six gasping Supplicants throttling their own necks.

"Such is the mind of one who believes Harbingers are so named for their ability to bend others to their will by coercion."

As one, they spun on their heels to face the Elder. She stood with her back to them, leaning on the bulwark on the port side as she contemplated the eastern horizon.

"It is true that in a duel, a battle, a contest of force, there is nothing so demonstrative as a Harbinger unleashed. But such contests are destructive by nature and the Dominion does not profit from destruction. True success—self-sustaining success that forms the foundations of a House and feeds future generations—cannot be achieved in this way."

The Elder indicated the horizon with an elegant sweep of one white-robed arm. Out of the clouds, the sea spray, the blurred, shadowy forms of the Aleituan coastline, and the circling gulls and questryls weaving through the golden rays that spanned the expanse of the solid deck beneath their feet to the distant heavens, rose an impossibility:

The great city of Ennuost Yrg hangs in midair, its form half-realized, thick walls and tall spires translucent as glass. There: the palace, a white marble crown that topped the hill at the center of the Sunset gardens; there, beside it, the peaked rooftops of its smaller twin, the Issolm headquarters; there, squatting on its other flank, the Imos and Imrell complexes, like dark reflections or shadows taken form.

"In the hands of a master, Projection allows you to manifest the realities you desire."

Right before Rahelu's eyes, the city *changed.*

Tenements sprout around the outer walls, homes and humanity bursting through them like stubborn spring weeds. They disappear, encircled by the safety of a second, newer, thicker wall. Behind the inner walls, buildings shoot up and proliferate like bamboo, until the palace no longer dominates the skyline, the distinctive ridges of its rooftops and scrying towers lost in a forest of even taller structures.

The surreality of it left her breathless. Yet the more she looked, the more substantial the altered city became until she was half-convinced that the Issolm scrying tower truly did stand taller than the palace's; that the road through the Westwoods was paved with gleaming stone; that Ennuost Yrg was so large that it spanned the sky from one horizon to the other, without end, until the world was the city, or the city the world, and every soul lived and loved and lost within its walls.

The tiny, white-robed figure standing before the city's massive gates snapped its fingers.

The city vanished.

The only evidence that it had ever existed lay in the awe shrouding the *Winged Arrow.* Brilliant blue sparks drifted skyward upon the wind, shed as glittering dust from the sails, while sapphire resonance streamed from the ship's decks and railings into the sea.

"What is possible is only limited by the strength of your desire, the scope of your imagination, and the number of people you can persuade to share your vision."

Elder Anathwan faced them once more.

"A true Harbinger does not merely command the hearts of others. Guardians may preserve the present; Seekers and Evokers may know the truth of all things; and Augurs may see the farthest. But Harbingers..." Anathwan smiled her warm, confiding smile; a smile full of conviction and the promise of change. "Harbingers bring forth the future."

11

TEST

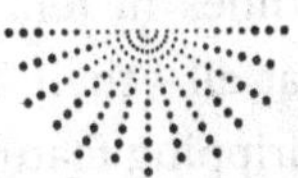

SUMMER SOLSTICE
THE 15TH DAY OF TRUESUMMER,
530 A.E./A.F.

THEY SPENT THE REST OF THE VOYAGE TRYING TO conjure illusions.

Unlike Guardian Maketh, whose insistence on methodically testing everyone beginning from first principles had irritated Rahelu with its pedantry, Elder Anathwan's instruction was so limited that it bordered on nonexistent. Apparently, she considered her spectacular display a sufficient demonstration of the principles involved and left them to waste the better part of six spans getting on each others' nerves as they worked out the limitations of Seeming.

The Elder's speech had made it sound simple: begin with the vision you want, lock onto the dominant emotion that vision inspires, then pour resonance into the Seeming until it takes form.

The reality was nowhere as straightforward.

For one, Seemings were bound by the same principle of plausibility that underpinned successful Auguries. You could visualize whatever you wanted, but the more implausible the vision, the lower the likelihood of success—and plausibility wasn't just dependent on causality, but on the perception of the casting mage *and* everyone within their range. Thus, while Elaram and Ghardon could create Seemings to pass themselves off as each other nine times in ten (an achievement that pleased Elaram no end and a fact that made Ghardon sulk for the rest of skyarc), Ylaen and Jhobon only managed the same six times in ten. Nheras and Rahelu, of course, had no success at all—their attempts either resulted in twisted visages with dripping features like half-melted wax or both of them curled up on the deck, gritting their teeth through resonance backlash.

For another, it was possible to selectively direct a Seeming so it affected a smaller number of people. But doing so required both incredible control and unwavering focus because instead of maintaining a single, sustained Projection in all directions, you had to divide your attention.

The upside: your Seeming was more likely to succeed. Rahelu had so little trouble persuading only Nheras to see her as Tsenjhe that she had to repeatedly resort to Seeking to ensure the Ilyn girl wasn't lying about it.

The downside: Ylaen immediately took advantage of their discovery. Thanks to his preferred combat style, he had no problem splitting his focus five ways and sustaining that effort all day. Worse, he had somehow worked out how to link his direct Seemings at a conceptual level so that everyone he targeted saw him differently.

Running into Lhorne aboard the *Winged Arrow* made her heart soar and plummet over and over again, despite her repeated reminders to herself that it was not him. No matter where she went on the ship, Ylaen would inevitably find her, whether she was down in the hold or up in the rigging. She would be meditating in the sparring circle at the stern, or reading in the ship's study, or lost in thought at the railing, wondering whether her parents had remembered to eat, whether they had received her instructions on how to access the coin House Issolm had transferred to her account so they could move out of the Lowdocks at last—and then he would appear with a touch on her shoulder and a soft, "Hey," that sent her resonance aura churning in a mess of pale violet and black-blue.

"Quit it," she snarled at Ylaen after he'd snuck up on her for the tenth time. She'd been prepared—she had heard him coming, thanks to the faint creak of his weight on the third step of the ladder—and the moment she felt the tap of his hand on her shoulder, she had turned around, slammed her Seeking and open palm against his chest, and *shoved*, tearing apart the confusing lie of Lhorne's clear green eyes and open smile. "Test me again and I'll gut you for fish bait and use your intestines as my line."

"There is so much anger in you," he said with a shake of his head. "Tell you what, since I'm already here—you can try and gut me now." He jerked his chin towards the sparring circle. "I could use the exercise. Unless..."

Ylaen smiled at her again—and this time it belonged to him: full of unassailable self-assurance and knowledge of his own desirability. "Captain Csorath says we won't make port until high sun, and Jhobon's absorbed in a musty old scroll. I can think of several pointers I could give you that would improve your Seeming." His mane of wavy black hair started straightening into copper locks as he stepped back within arm's reach. "We could do a little private studying in my cabin if you prefer."

"Shut up and get in the circle, Imos." Rahelu stalked into the sparring circle herself with murder in her heart.

Half a span and three losses later, she fled, leaving her pride and dignity behind, desperate to find some place of refuge to seclude herself for the rest of eartharc in meditation, where she could sort through all that confusion in her resonance aura and try to forget.

Her feet led her below, to a part of the ship she had not set foot in for days.

Rahelu breathed. And breathed. Several thousand counts and a litany of self-directed insults later, she still stood there, breathing, unable to make herself knock on the door to the third Supplicants' cabin.

Gods. She beat her forehead against the jamb. Why was it so fucking hard to begin anew?

The door opened a crack.

She fell back, startled. Nheras's gold-ringed eyes were flat, unfriendly, and full of suspicion (which she deserved) at the sight of her showing up here, now, after their dispute over cabin territory had been so conclusively decided.

"What do you want?"

Rahelu licked dry lips and swallowed, but the words *'I'm sorry'* remained stuck in her throat like a fishbone, no matter how much she moved her mouth.

How could she meet those eyes and say those words again without inadvertently triggering the sympathetic resonance of her last disastrous attempt at an apology three nights ago?

How could they begin anew?

It was impossible.

There was too much history for any verbal apology to overcome, no matter how sincere Seeking declared it to be. No matter what she tried—and she *had* tried, twice in one week!—they could not break their vicious cycle: watching for the slight in each look, each word; trading insults until one of them said something unforgivable to the other and the exchange escalated beyond wisdom; waiting for the inevitable stab in the heart that would fling fresh fuel on the fire of their hatred.

Rahelu nearly turned away, right then and there, until she realized that Nheras had not immediately closed the door, and not only had Nheras spoken to her, she had also refrained from calling her 'fish guts'.

Nheras was still looking at her through the door.

The Elder's words rose in her mind: *What is possible is only limited by the strength of your desire, the scope of your imagination, and the number of people you can persuade to share your vision.*

Was her desire so weak, her imagination so limited, that she could not even persuade herself?

She put her discomfort aside and tried to consider their past without her own feelings coloring her understanding of events.

What had it been like for Nheras?

From the first moment Rahelu had laid eyes on the Ilyn girl, it seemed to her that she had had everything: an abundance of resonance talent and a family who could afford to train it; a life behind the curtains of a palanquin that would carry her in safety to anywhere she desired; the bliss of being preoccupied with lesser worries—like who would be her dinner partner, rather than whether there would be dinner at all; with power and wealth and influence accorded to her simply because she was the granddaughter of an Atriarch.

But the past week aboard the *Winged Arrow* had shown her just how wrong her assumptions were. The burden of expectations that Nheras bore, as the pride and hope of House Ilyn, was no less than hers. Withstanding Atriarch Mere Ideth's scrutiny had been the second-most nerve-wracking quarter-span of her life; what would it have been like to grow up under Atriarch Lynath Ilyn's calculating eyes?

Start over, she thought. *And this time, really mean it.*

"I have been a poor sister to you," Rahelu said abruptly. "I will do better."

Such a short admission seemed insufficient, but what else was there to say? If she were Nheras, she wouldn't trust a sudden change of heart regardless of Seeking, so a long list of itemized apologies ordered by degree of offense would be a waste of breath.

She got down on her hands and knees instead. Touched her forehead to the sole of the passageway, in the same obeisance she had offered to Guardian Maketh after she had gravely disrespected him, and said: "Nheras Ilyn Issolm, I beg your forgiveness."

A long, long silence before she dared look up.

Nheras wore a carefully masked expression that betrayed neither surprise nor anger nor forgiveness. Exactly like the painted doll Ghardon had named her.

Cautiously, Rahelu sat back on her heels. "And I thought perhaps—if you're not already busy with something else—if it wouldn't be a huge imposition and waste of your time—perhaps we could try practicing Seeming again until we make port. Since Elder Anathwan will be testing us, again, soon."

Staring from Nheras.

"If you want. Might be useful. Practicing, that is. We don't have to practice together. But we should, I mean, could. Not that you weren't already. And I think we might learn—I might—I would learn something. Ylaen isn't the only talented Harbinger around."

More staring.

"Or I won't! I mean, not! As in, I won't if you're not willing, not that you've nothing to teach me, or that I won't learn from you. And if you're not willing, well, I-I understand why—"

Shut up, Rahelu, shut up! You've said what you had to say, so now you should keep your word and go and stop making this more uncomfortable.

"—so, um, let's forget that, it was a fish-brained stupid idea. I'll go and practice somewhere else instead of disturbing you here."

Nheras disappeared from view...

...but left the door ajar for Rahelu to step inside.

THEY PASSED span after eartharc span peaceably, melting each other's faces, until they were interrupted by a loud shout from above—

"Land!" the lookout cried. "Land two points aft of the starboard beam!"

—and a summons.

Supplicants, Elder Anathwan sent. *Report to the great cabin for briefing immediately.*

THEY HAD BARELY FINISHED their bows when Guardian Maketh shut the door and the Elder promptly squashed them by raising the great cabin's barriers.

Rahelu had been ready; had arrived with her focus-stone-fueled personal Obfuscation barrier in place; had braced herself to take that incredible pressure for the third time—and it had still hurt no less.

While the Supplicants crawled to their cushions, Maketh laid down another barrier of his own inside the great cabin's defenses: a thin, translucent bubble that Rahelu wouldn't have noticed if she hadn't seen him raise it. Its oil-slick iridescence was only detectable thanks to the eddies in the ambient resonance. The Guardian did not join them around the rosewood table with the Elder; he stood sentinel in front of the door so that no one might come in or go out, except through him.

Captain Csorath was notably absent. Elder Anathwan sat in his seat, elegant hands folded. In front of her was a large slate, twice the size of those the Supplicants had been using in their study of resonance wards. In place of chalk, there was a medium-sized brush pen resting on a copper inkstone.

Without any preamble, Anathwan said: "Two weeks ago, the Houses captured the killers responsible for taking the lives of five Ennuost Yrg citizens in their attempts to enact an ancient ritual using strange artifacts of power. These appear to be linked in some sort of relay."

No mention of the fact that the Houses' involvement had been strictly limited to the 'capturing' part, after they had left the hard work of hunting down and stopping those cultists to mere Petitioners—Rahelu, Lhorne, Ghardon, and Elaram, specifically. The omission would have rankled if Anathwan hadn't bestowed the three of them who were present with a very slight smile of acknowledgment.

"As of last night, joint efforts between the Houses have confirmed the facts: this ritual is connected with the recent... blockages that Augurs across the Houses have sensed in the resonance when attempting short- to medium-term Auguries. Interrogation by Seekers has revealed these killers to be exiles from the Divine Kingdom, a splinter cult that worships the Starfather to the exclusion of the other gods. One of their number—a mage-priest, likely the very same Augur responsible for the unsanctioned act of grand Augury three weeks ago—remains at large. Using the artifacts we have captured, Evokers were able to narrow down the probable locations of two more artifacts. One is here, in Peshwan Yrg."

Rahelu caught a whiff of a salt-and-metal tang—seawater? —as the Elder filled the inkstone with a small teapot, then dipped her brush into the clear liquid. She drew four straight lines forming an elongated box that didn't match the shape of any landmarks in the few maps of Peshwan Yrg that Rahelu had seen.

"The Bronze Turtle is a workshop located in the Outer-market owned by an artificer named Ruarem, a Guild graduate who established himself as an independent mage after being unsuccessful in his Petition. He has a known habit of acquiring rare and curious objects for study or resale. Just now, we have received word from Imrell agents, confirming Ruarem's plans to hold a black market auction next week, with the main item of interest being his latest acquisition: a so-called 'legacy of the heavens' that the artificer claims has been blessed by the Starfather to grant anyone, trained or not, the gift of Augury and any mage the power of Fortunement."

The ambient resonance blazed with sapphire awe as the Supplicants hissed collectively.

Lhorne's pendant, the distilled power of one of his Ideth ancestors, was attuned to Obfuscation. Capable of boosting her average skill in that discipline to a respectable level. Capable of augmenting his talent to a degree far beyond his years of experience. But priceless as the Ideth legacy around Rahelu's neck was, it was nothing in comparison to an artifact on the level Anathwan had just described.

HOLY—

Rahelu winced at Elaram's mental shriek.

—FUCK!

"This is the best mission ever!" Elaram squealed, an outburst that clearly contradicted the expectations of dignified decorum that Anathwan had set out at their first briefing, while Ghardon said: "Impossible. There has never been a legacy attuned to Fortunement."

"Fortunement as a discipline did not exist until a few decades ago." Anathwan gave a light shrug of her shoulders as she dipped her brush again. "The same was once said of Augury until the passing of the archmage Dethiram."

Oh. *Oh.*

Dethiram had been the founder of House Ideth. By all accounts, his legacy had weakened over the centuries, but

Mere Ideth, who wielded it, was an archmage with a peerless command of Augury herself. That was how she had re-established House Ideth at the forefront of the major Houses after generations of decline.

Mere Ideth was also the first mage to truly master Fortunement since Conclave researchers proved it was mathematically possible to coax future possibilities to collapse in favor of a specific outcome. Elder Anathwan's oblique statement was a reference to the common speculation that, upon Mere Ideth's passing, Keshwar Ideth would inherit the first archmage legacy attuned to Fortunement to wield along with his own incredible gifts.

What could Keshwar do with that kind of power?

No, no; more like, what *couldn't* he do with that kind of power?

Holy. Fuck.

Suddenly, the political alliances—and House Ideth's less than enthusiastic support of the mission—made much more sense.

"We suspect these artifacts are sacred Belruonian relics, stolen from the Divine Kingdom by the cultists." The Elder's drawing was practiced, her style bold and sparse. The tendons that stood out in Anathwan's wrists were the only sign of the iron strength in her fingers. "Their scriptures proclaim the Divine Holiness to be an avatar of the Starfather, and Silcarez's accounts attest that the mage-priests had practical knowledge of Augury and had long mastered the discipline."

Ghardon looked troubled. "If this artifact is real, and Ruarem truly has something so powerful in his possession, why would he auction it off? Why not keep its existence a secret and use it for himself?"

Anathwan made no response other than to dip her brush pen again, so it was Maketh who answered instead:

"That is beyond the scope of this mission and academic at this juncture. Our orders are to locate and seize the asset, using speed and stealth to our advantage, before it can fall into Conclave hands." The Guardian grimaced. "House intelligence warns us to expect at least one Chanazian operative, perhaps more."

There was no undercurrent of suspicion in his voice, though his frown lingered on Rahelu just a fraction longer than it had on the others and she could feel the strain in the ambient resonance as both Ghardon and Elaram fought the urge to look at her.

"They, however, will be our concern," Maketh said. "You have a different task."

Anathwan laid down her brush pen, done with her beautiful rendering of what looked like a jewelry case. (Nheras had half a dozen of them, all far more gaudily decorated with precious inlays and carvings.) The lid and sides of the box were plain and so were its clasps; there was no distinguishable mark about it at all.

"Ruarem's vault holds a wooden box. The artifact, we believe, is inside it," the Elder said. "Your task is to obtain entry to the Bronze Turtle, secure the box, and deliver it to me, at the citadel."

That was it? That was the mission? Rahelu glanced from the fading water drawing—the lines were evaporating so quickly—to the other Supplicants, who all looked just as perplexed as she was.

"You may not use any means other than resonance skills to do so. That includes coin or force or any other methods that may be traceable to the Houses."

Anathwan's expression was bland, as though she were asking them to go fetch and carry instead of committing theft.

"You have one span inside these barriers where you may

safely discuss and agree upon your plan. After that, further discussion will be at your own risk. Are there any questions?"

They had dozens.

Nheras got hers in first. "Are we being evaluated individually or collectively?"

"As a team, for we owe our duty first and foremost to the Dominion. However, your individual contributions will be taken into consideration in accordance with your House's policies on performance evaluation."

Ghardon was next. "How long do we have?"

"Until starrise."

"Does the box do anything?" Jhobon wondered.

"It is an Imbued object." A pause, then a serious look. "Do not open the box."

Elaram, eagerly: "What happens if we do?"

"Do not open the box under any circumstances."

That set the other Supplicants a-buzz with curiosity. They fired question after question at the Elder about the artifact, the box, the vault, the workshop, and the artificer. Anathwan turned most of the questions away with smooth, not-answers.

Not a single one of them was thinking about the most important question.

"What constitutes failure?" Rahelu asked, raising her voice to cut across the hubbub of speculation.

"A good question." Anathwan smiled. "Anything other than a successful retrieval of the box by starrise—without its disappearance being remarked upon and connected to any potential House involvement—will be considered a failure."

Excitement fizzled, like dying coals in a flooded hearth.

"And if your actions raise any questions for either the Hall of Judgment or the city guard that will require intervention from either Guardian Maketh, Captain Csorath, or myself to resolve, that will be considered a failure of not only your task but also of our overall mission."

"What are the consequences of failure?" Ylaen's voice was strangely quiet and meek, as stripped of affectations as she had ever heard.

"If you are caught by the city guard, they will apply the usual penalties for theft." All of them involuntarily curled their fingers around their thumbs. "And should you disclose the slightest detail regarding the nature of this task or our mission to anyone outside of the mission team, inadvertently or otherwise, you will be stripped of rank and memory, and bound to serve elsewhere."

Apprehension rose like mist in the ambient resonance, adding sickly yellow shadows to the ones thrown by the flickering lantern light.

"On that subject…" Anathwan turned to Maketh. "I think it may be best if we implement the mission precautions we discussed now."

The Guardian nodded and stepped away from the door. The resonance pendant on his chest bloomed, coming to life with a steady, blue glow.

"Surrender your armbands," Anathwan said.

No one moved.

"Now." The Elder calmly undid the leather straps on her armband and laid it upon the rosewood table, sigil side down. "Where we are going, these will prove to be a liability, not an asset. From now until our mission has been concluded, we are all mere ordinary citizens of the Dominion. You may reclaim them upon our return."

If we return, but Rahelu did not voice that thought. She tugged at the silver buckles on her armband with fingers that felt weak and clumsy. The precautions made perfect sense. Still, she suppressed a shiver as she laid her white-and-black armband face down. Even in the lantern light, the pale band of skin on her left forearm was clearly visible.

It was wrong. She didn't want to look at it.

She tugged at the rolled-up sleeves of her shirt until they covered her wrists. That helped a little, but not enough—her arm felt too light, too cold, without that leather band wrapped around it.

She wasn't the only one. Across the table, Ghardon and Elaram were doing the same; and Nheras even moved half of her bangles over in a short burst of metallic chimes. The remaining two Supplicants didn't—Ylaen couldn't, thanks to his choice of attire, and Jhobon was the only one who seemed unbothered.

Guardian Maketh was the last to remove his armband and place it on top of the pile.

"Your clothes, too."

They stared.

Rahelu must have heard wrong. Anathwan couldn't possibly be asking what she thought she'd heard her asking.

Ghardon found his tongue first. "Pardon, Elder, did you say our clothes? But surely, we need those for—"

He faltered at the steely glint in Anathwan's eyes. "Your clothes mark you out as Supplicants of the Houses. You will find more appropriate clothing, similar to the shirts and trousers that Dedicate Maketh and I are wearing, waiting for you at the House citadel."

What? Rahelu blinked as the two senior mages' figures fuzzed. Coarse shirts and patched trousers briefly popped into existence, replacing formal robes—

Maketh looked like an unkempt version of himself, if he had joined up with the city guard instead of Petitioning the Houses, but Anathwan was nearly unrecognizable in scruffy undyed linen instead of white brocade with her golden curls shorn to her shoulders. Her mind protested the evidence before her eyes loudly: '*No, no! The Elder looks like* this; *the Guardian looks like* that.'

—and then their clothing and visages firmly resettled back into what she knew and expected as Maketh and Anathwan's Seemings reasserted themselves.

Try as she might, Rahelu couldn't pierce the illusions again, unaided.

"Once the *Winged Arrow* docks, the Guardian, the captain, and I must be about our own tasks. While we will be monitoring your progress, we will not be at liberty to assist you with yours. I trust that all of you, capable potential Dedicates that you are, will have no trouble gaining entrance to the House citadel and managing your assignment."

The implication was clear.

Ghardon swallowed. "Yes, Elder." He bowed his head, closed his eyes, and drew in a deep breath as he began to disrobe.

Rahelu quickly followed suit with the others.

She shut down her sense of sight, hoping that would make it easier to overcome the disjunction between the image she had to maintain and what her body knew to be real: limbs free to move, unconstrained by tailored sleeves and trouser legs; the air warm against her exposed back because she'd tied her hair up while she and Nheras had been practicing earlier, thinking it might help her feel more like her cabinmate; the sensation of bare thigh brushing against bare thigh as she moved to deposit her bundled uniform on top of the discarded armbands, her body as a whole lighter now without all those outer layers of fine cotton to weigh it down.

Then, she visualized herself the way she had been reflected in Nheras's hand mirror—neat, at last, in House Issolm whites and blacks, hair tidily combed smooth, Supplicant's sigil prominent on the white leather armband hugging her left forearm—then breathed out, letting go of the blue-gray resonance she had formed into her Obfuscation barrier so it coalesced against her aura in a Seeming, calm flowing over her like a second skin.

Issolm, she thought as she opened her eyes. *I am Supplicant Rahelu of House Issolm.*

She held firm to that idea—that truth—as the Elder studied each of them in turn, her dark blue eyes unreadable.

At last, Anathwan nodded.

Rahelu exhaled.

The first test passed. The second, too, if you counted the additional test of her ability to hold her tongue. Only the third remained.

But the Elder was not finished. "One final matter: Guardian Maketh will be placing a deep mind block on each of you. It will only activate in the event of your capture and only if you are unable to withstand interrogation under Seeking."

That wasn't ominous at all.

Rahelu cast a furtive glance around; the others all looked as uneasy as she felt. "What happens if it activates?" she asked.

"It will erase your memories of the Houses," Maketh said.

That was awfully vague. Would it erase all knowledge of the Houses or just her personal experiences with the Houses? What about her resonance skills?

"What about the gaps?" Ghardon asked. "Won't those impair our ability to function?"

There was a very long pause as both senior mages simply looked at him. Eventually, Maketh spoke. "Assuming no tampering occurs, the mind block will dissipate on its own in two seasons."

"If you have reservations, you may elect to forgo this opportunity and serve the Houses on this mission in your original capacity as a Supplicant, as the Exalted Dominance has decreed," Anathwan said. "But if you wish to serve as a full member of the team, you will consent to the mind block."

Still, they hesitated.

Maketh added: "This is standard procedure for a mission of this nature. Know that we senior mages are not exempt from this precaution. Each of us received our mind blocks from our Atriarchs before we departed."

One by one, they reluctantly nodded.

"Very good. Guardian, I leave the matter of implementation in your capable hands." The Elder swept up the accouterments they had shed and stood. The air shimmered and suddenly, all Anathwan appeared to hold in her arms were a bundle of scrolls. "Supplicants, do your Houses honor. Once you have completed your task, you may have whatever spans remain of the solstice to pursue your own amusements. Tomorrow, we shall depart from Peshwan Yrg's Sunport at dawn."

The door swung shut behind Anathwan with a dull *thud*.

Maketh tapped into his focus stone. Yellow-blue mists coiled around him, eel-like, their ghostly luminescence coruscating around the great cabin. Dread crawled down Rahelu's spine as the Guardian's implacable gaze roamed across their faces.

He raised one mist-gloved hand and asked, "Who wants to be first?"

12

SOLACE

THE *WINGED ARROW* THRUMMED EAGERLY WITH THE anticipation of every soul on board as the ship glided into harbor, its keel skimming the great underwater meadows of varicolored eelgrass blanketing the shallows.

"Peshwan Yrg, the pearl of the east," Elaram breathed, as she regarded the pale-walled, silver-topped structures sprawling over the verdant peninsula. "Oh, it's so beautiful! Doesn't it look just like a white jade dragon coiled around a pearl?"

More like clumps of rice spilling from a porcelain bowl someone had overfilled out of greed. Rahelu had seen many places during the two-year overland journey from Chanaz to Ennuost Yrg—idyllic villages, bustling towns, lush stretches of forest, and endless plains. She had spent the whole time building up a shining image of the Dominion's capital based on the utopian tales: a golden city of wealth and opportunity.

None of those tales had mentioned the sewer muck running beneath Ennuost Yrg's glorious facade. Undoubtedly, the tales of Peshwan Yrg's beauty were also greatly exaggerated.

The sharp lines and pure whites of her Issolm uniform and armband blurred; faded to a dirty gray.

Focus, Rahelu. Breathe.

Pungent scents of tilled earth and fresh vegetation. The distinctive odor of hundreds and thousands of toiling bodies. Fragrant temple incense. Burning charcoal from forge fires. Mouthwatering smoke from the hearths of taverns and inns and homes and the carts of street vendors.

Enjoy the new sights, like the others. Remember the story: you're a Supplicant of the Houses, with gold in your pocket and all of skyarc to spend it and tonight is the summer solstice.

Her Seeming steadied; the glory of House Issolm restored to blinding white.

"They say that on a clear day, it's possible to see all the way to the shores of the Divine Kingdom from the top of the citadel's scrying tower," Elaram continued. "And there are stories about heavenly treasures washing up on shore, just waiting for someone to find them in the sand."

Tiny figures picked away at the thick, dark lines that ran along the beach, stark against the white-gold sand like a warding line inscribed by some celestial hand.

Here is where the Stormbringer's domain ends; here is where the Earthgiver's domain begins. Here is where you'll rise to Anathwan's expectations—

Or fail.

"Oh, there are treasures alright." The corners of Nheras's lips twitched downwards. "Seaweed, seaweed, and more seaweed. They even build their houses out of that stuff."

Jhobon stirred. "Just the roofs." The Imrell Supplicant was fidgeting again, picking at and peeling tiny splinters from the ship's rail with his fingernails. He only stopped when Ylaen covered one of his hands with his own. "The walls are sea stone and granite. And they're white because of the dried salt and powdered shells in the plaster."

"That's a half-step removed from living in grass-and-mud huts."

Rahelu's fingers tightened on the toprail and she had to make a deliberate effort to relax them and bite her tongue. That barb had not been aimed at her; Nheras was just on edge, nervous. (They all were. The single span allotted to them for planning had been used up far, far 'too quickly.) She did her best to tune out the others, wishing she had some menial task to keep her occupied—it was so *odd* to stand idle while the Isonn crew hastened about, watching them furl sails and uncoil mooring lines, drumming her nails in impatient *da-da-da-das* against polished wood, counting the heartbeats until she could get off this ship, find the citadel, and get her hands on some real fucking clothes.

But that, too, went against what was expected of her, so she remained where she was and made a study of the kelp boats instead. The little vessels were little more than dinghies, laden so high with piles and piles of the thick, frilly fronds that it was hard to pick out the fishers from their harvest.

Oh, how Nheras's silk scarves must envy those intense greens and deep purples and vivid corals!

Oh, how easily the kelp fishers scooped up their catch— they didn't even have to dive! Just stick anything in the water, be it hand or oar or pole, and it would come back out with a basket-sized tangle of eelgrass attached.

One span, two at most, Rahelu decided, for a single-handed boat to go from empty to full. At least forty baskets per trip; four or five trips per day. One basket of dried kelp fetched up to sixty copper kez at Market Square. Convert that to barrels, adjust for the cost of transportation from Peshwan

Yrg to Ennuost Yrg, deduct the merchant's margin, estimate the yield after drying, and—

Great gods!

Each boat must bring in anywhere from five to ten silver kez per *day*. She squinted at the vast quantities of kelp spread out across the fields surrounding the city; quickly gave up guessing the precise value of Peshwan Yrg's annual seaweed production in favor of concluding aban and anma should have brought them here to fish for kelp because it was 'a lot'.

Finally, just after high sun, they tied up at the dock.

Captain Csorath was the first to disembark. He strode down the gangplank in full House Isonn formal robes, instead of the tunic and trousers he preferred when at sea, with Kerg at his side. Port officials immediately swarmed him. ("Most honorable captain, I'm afraid you must wait until—captain! Captain!") He dismissed them with a curt wave to his first and second mates, who stood ready to receive them and supervise the inspections of the *Winged Arrow*, and disappeared inside the forest-green shrouded palanquin that awaited him.

Anathwan and Maketh went next. Neither the Elder nor the Dedicate broke off from their hushed conference as they crossed the deck and descended to the pier, though they both dismissed their Supplicants—a smile from Anathwan; a slight nod from Maketh—before separate palanquins bore them away too.

The Supplicants followed, Elaram skipping ahead of their ragged clump. Ghardon stumbled over his own feet no less than four times while trying to negotiate the descent. After the fifth time—when he would have fallen off the gangplank into the harbor and taken Nheras and Jhobon with him, save for Ylaen's quick intervention—Rahelu had had enough. She hauled him past the horde of carpenters, shipwrights, and porters, and over to the public palanquins like a drunkard or a feeble, infirm old man, swearing under her breath the whole way.

Ghardon didn't notice. His eyes still had the same glazed, inward-gazing look he'd worn from the moment Maketh had laid the mind block on him. Nobody had been happy about getting their mind block, but Ghardon—Ghardon had needed...convincing. When Jhobon's logic, Elaram's encouragement, Rahelu's sarcasm, Nheras's disdain, and Ylaen's jibes all failed to move him, Maketh had taken matters into his own hands.

Rahelu had had to look away.

It took almost a full span for two palanquins to convey them from Stormport on the southeast side of Peshwan Yrg, through the bustling Innermarket, and up to the carved gates of the citadel.

No separate dominions for the Houses in this city—they shared a single complex built like a ghuonnik's shell: eight small towers clustered around a larger ninth spire. Long, silk banners trailed down the sides of each tower; their brilliant House sigils, stitched with resonance crystal fragments and threads of precious metals, sparkled in the skyarc sun. The central spire had no banner; it needed none, for its entire outer surface was tiled with millions of cut shells that gave off an ever-changing pearlescent glow far more mesmerizing than the shining white marble of the Ennuost Yrg palace.

The palanquin bearers had to make several attempts before Rahelu's ears registered their timid, repeated inquiries about the matter of their fee. She paid them out of her own purse, then lightly kicked her speechless, staring companions in the ankles.

"Starrise," she reminded them pointedly, as they shook off their awe.

In they strutted through the main doors. Backs straight, heads high, chattering voices raised in speculative gossip as befitted a rowdy bunch of off-duty Supplicants newly arrived from the glorious capital, their Seemings so solidly rooted in the power of the Houses surrounding them that not a single one of the many guards noticed that, if Nheras had truly been dressed in her formal wear, Ghardon really ought to have trod on the hem of her overrobe and tripped them all by now.

"Stop it!" Elaram leaned forward to hiss at her brother when he stumbled again as the six of them slunk out of the service gate a quarter-span later, attired once more, but in the plain, roughspun cotton shirts and trousers of common-born citizens. "You keep prodding away at it and eventually you'll set it off." She jabbed him in the side.

That jolted Ghardon out of his trance. He scowled but did start walking under his own power instead of relying on Rahelu to prop him up like a dummy. "How can you wear this stuff?" He yanked at the collar of his shirt and then at the waistband of his trousers. "It's giving me rashes."

"Get used to it," Nheras said from behind them. Without the constant jangle of her earrings and dozens of bangles, Rahelu kept forgetting she was there. "Do you hear the rest of us complaining? It is what it is."

"You're all taking this far too seriously," Ylaen said, looking strange in his sleeved shirt.

Their clothes had been provided by House Isca—meticulously stained to appear dirt-worn and aged, raggedly patched on the outside, and lined with a thin layer of cotton stitched with suppression wards on the inside in scratchy, resonance-crystal-dust infused copper threads. The Imos Supplicant seemed resentful of the fact that he couldn't continue his personal vendetta against sleeves, since tearing them off would have destroyed the embroidered wards, so he'd left all his buttons undone instead.

Which still rendered the wards useless. Idiot.

The two scarred Supplicants walked in front—they were

the only ones familiar with the streets of Peshwan Yrg. Jhobon was actually leading for a change; his normally distant eyes watchful as a wyrhound's as he scanned the low, eelgrass-thatched sea-stone buildings and teeming streets on their way through the busy Innermarket. Ylaen, in contrast, sauntered down the West Road with his hands in his trouser pockets as if he were on an aimless jaunt.

"It's summer solstice; we should have some fun," Ylaen said, returning every interested leer he received from House-born, merchant, and common-born men and women alike. In Ennuost Yrg, the ritualistic scars he displayed would have been remarked upon; in Peshwan Yrg, they simply helped him to blend in. As the easternmost port on the Ngutoccai continent, half the people in the city carried some sort of ritual scarring—from single cuts on their fore-arms to elaborate designs that covered their entire body— and displayed their scarring with pride. "Especially while we're here."

"You want to partake in the common-born celebrations?" Nheras sniffed. "Why don't you just hand over your valu-ables, swallow some adder's milk, then go lie down in the gutter and let the beggars piss on you?"

"Nheras, Nheras," he said, rolling the syllables of her name around his mouth like a sweet. He looked over his shoulder and gave all of them his slow, lazy smile. "If I did that, I would miss out on the best part of the festival: the Night of Solace."

That piqued Elaram's interest. "Ooooh! I've always wanted to go but Mother wouldn't hear of it. Have you been?"

"Once," Ylaen said, then his smile widened. "Best night of my life."

"Worst night of my life," Jhobon muttered as he dodged two porters pulling handcarts loaded with bolts of silk and baskets of ginger across the road. "I was happy to pray at the temple."

"Ah, tsol-ek, you'll thank me for it someday." Ylaen's voice grew wistful as they passed through the Lesser Gate into the Outermarket. "Peshwan Yrg keeps ship clan traditions."

Picky or not, Elaram slipped past Rahelu and Ghardon to fall in beside Ylaen. "I've heard it said that the Skymother will grant all those who seek a different path their desires," she said. "Is that true?"

"It is. The day of the summer solstice is for remembrance. At dusk, when the sky embraces the sea, we light the fires to farewell those regrets. And the night"—Ylaen put an arm around Elaram's waist and drew her close—"the night is when we find solace."

And right in the middle of the crowded intersection, with wagons trundling and palanquins floating and porters and washerfolk and liveried servants jostling them about, Ylaen lifted Elaram high into the air and spun her about. She kicked up her heels and threw her head back, and the clear peal of laughter coming from her throat drew stares.

"Are you two done with prancing around like ishtrels?" Nheras said. She stalked forward and held her hand out imperiously to Ylaen. "I believe we have an appointment with a certain artificer?"

Ylaen carefully set Elaram on the ground; she, in turn, landed lightly on her feet with a great deal of unnecessary sliding down his front.

"All business and no pleasure makes for a dull mage," Elaram said as Ylaen took Nheras's hand. "Lean upon him a little more, sister dear; we all know you're capable of it."

Nheras's face, already puckered up in what appeared to be a permanent look of distaste, twisted further.

Elaram smirked and grabbed Jhobon by his elbow to

demonstrate. "Smile, flutter your eyelashes, and try not to act like you've just bitten into a lemon." She proceeded to drape herself all over Jhobon like she was a cloak and he a coat rack; Rahelu nearly burst out laughing at the sight of the sheer panic that stole over his face. "No consort-to-be would wear such a sour expression and stand so woodenly while in the arms of their beloved."

To her credit, Nheras's resonance aura only flickered once with a light green-brown. Then, like flame racing over oil-soaked cloth, the Ilyn girl's entire bearing transformed. "Let's go, darling," she said to Ylaen, in a sickening coo that somehow managed to sound entirely genuine. "I simply can't wait to go shop for some lock charms."

With that, the two Harbingers-in-training wandered over to the next block and disappeared into the Bronze Turtle.

"That was cruel," Rahelu said to Elaram.

"Don't you lecture me on that subject," Elaram said airily. "Since when do you care about her feelings?"

Since five days ago, Rahelu thought, but what she said was, "Since she became one of us."

Elaram ignored her. She hadn't taken her eyes off Jhobon for so much as an eyeblink because the Imrell Supplicant was in the process of turning redder than a New Year lantern. "Say, Jhobon, why don't you take me with you instead of my brother? I think we'd have more fun that way."

Ghardon let out a weary breath. "Stop mauling Im—" All three of them shot him alarmed looks and he hurriedly corrected himself. "Him. Stop mauling him, sister, before he dies of embarrassment. There's plenty of other prey around for you." He looked down at his sandal-clad, dust-covered feet and sighed. "Let's go. The faster we do this, the faster I can go drown myself in the nearest bathhouse."

He trudged off towards a narrow laneway filled with the sounds of tapping hammers and rasping files without waiting to see if Jhobon followed. By the time Jhobon had extricated himself from Elaram, Ghardon had already begun negotiations with one of the woodcarvers.

"Jhobon's sweet," Elaram said, as she and Rahelu skirted around a stonecarver and her apprentices wrestling a massive granite statue of the Earthgiver onto a cart to slip into the laneway behind the Bronze Turtle. "I had no idea."

"Can we please focus?" Rahelu asked, eyeing the worn crates stacked against the wall of the neighboring shop. She tested the first crate with one foot; when it proved reassuringly sturdy, she clambered on top of it. "Once we've done our part, you can terrorize him all you want."

WHEN THE SIX of them regrouped two spans later at an alleyway food stall three streets over, they were all in agreement: Ruarem was a paranoid man.

"No exits other than the main shop door." Rahelu kept the partial Evocations she summoned in the middle of their table as small and insubstantial as she could without compromising visibility. "Not a single window; only narrow slits spaced out close to the roofline for ventilation, too tight for even a cat to slip through. Might be that I could find some other way in if I Evoked the building's construction, but I'd need a good excuse to get closer to do that without looking suspicious."

She let her Evocation go and waved at Elaram to continue with their findings so she could eat. Anathwan might have forbidden them to use coin to complete her test but lunch was a different story. If she'd been on her own, she would have stuck to ordering a single grilled skewer. But, as things were, when Ghardon called for an entire platter along with seaweed soup, deep-fried sweet buns, and a pitcher of iced fruit juice, she hadn't objected. She wasn't a kezless common-born anymore; even if she wasn't in House colors, even if she had deposited her gold with the House treasury at the citadel, she had plenty of silver in her purse. Enough that she didn't need to fret over every copper kez—if she ran out, she could always go back and get more.

Anywhere she cared to go in the Dominion (and in every major trading center in the Chanazian Federation as well as the two biggest Free Cities in Abmerdu), so long as she was in a population center big enough to warrant a regional House branch, she would never be more than a half-span away from the gold kez in her Issolm account.

Rahelu picked up a skewer and sank her teeth into the cubes of pork. It was deliciously sweet—sheer decadence on her tongue (even though Nheras picked at the food and Ylaen gnawed it disdainfully as if it had been scooped out of the gutter)—and she couldn't have said whether it was the meat or the headiness of having coin to spend guiltlessly that made it so.

"Ruarem keeps two guards on premises at all times," Elaram said. "They're from the Jade Eye Company; one of the most reputable independent security companies around. Very reliable, better trained, better equipped, and better paid than your average back alley thug—the best you can buy without going to the Houses. Most of their enlistees are third- and fourth-borns of trade families, many with a decent knack for the resonance skills but who, for one reason or another, never made it past the Guild's admission tests. The watch changes every four spans, except for starwatch, and they actually have a rudimentary watch reporting system in place, as well as a system for authenticating orders. Any forgeries we introduce will be discovered pretty quickly unless we falsify at least a season's worth of documents."

"That's not workable," Ghardon said. He looked over at

Nheras and Ylaen. "We'll have to go with the secondary plan."

That plan was based on the assumption that it would be far easier to bypass the guards and the doors to steal the wooden box in daylight.

Unfortunately, both of their Harbingers were shaking their heads.

"Customers are only allowed inside one group at a time," Nheras said. "There are no displays or shelves inside, just you, and Ruarem's apprentice, and a table, discussing your answers to a standard list of questions so long that some Evoker must have designed it for him." She picked away at the fried bun on her plate—the last one—ripping it to shreds with her unadorned fingernails. "The apprentice has been there two seasons. Long enough to be trusted with keys and he's well-trained. The moment Ylaen tried to have a look around, he'd already moved to block him. And short of a direct Command, I couldn't make him leave for any reason."

"Not even to fetch goods for sale?" Elaram asked.

"Not even then," Ylaen said, reaching for his eighth skewer. "He took what we brought and passed it through a small window. The ready-made wares are kept in the vault too—which is the entire back room, sealed off with a set of walls twice as thick as the ones outside—and Ruarem never leaves it, except to sleep and to pray."

Nheras added, "His wares don't leave it either, not unless and until you've paid for them in full." She pulled out a small lacquered square box and put it in the middle of the table, between the platter and the empty pitcher.

Rahelu grabbed the box. It was the jewelry case Nheras kept her earrings in—Rahelu recognized its design of willows and larks, but not the shiny new resonance lock fitted to its latch. There was no visible keyhole. Instead, there were three wheeled mechanisms shaped like gears with pronged teeth, each tooth gripping a resonance crystal fragment. She ran her fingers over them, feeling faint whispers of joy, melancholy, and ambition as she turned the dials until pride, envy, and disdain lined up in a row.

She pressed on the latch.

Nothing happened.

"Give me that," Ghardon said. He snatched it from her and proceeded to rattle it like an overexcited Chronicler with a new set of bells.

"And people will buy his work, sight unseen?" Rahelu asked. "I wouldn't buy a sack of turnips without inspecting it first."

Elaram patted her on the shoulder. "Not all of us are as cynical and untrusting as you, sister dear."

"It's not cynicism," Rahelu said. "It's due diligence."

Nheras snorted. "It's shortsighted. Ruarem has a reputation for trustworthiness; his entire business rests on that foundation. He would not risk cheating customers with inferior work for a handful of gold; and if he did, no one, least of all you, would know the difference."

"Merchants come from as far as Anazvela to commission work from Ruarem's hands," Jhobon said. "He does run a legitimate business in addition to the illegitimate one. Nobody else besides the Houses could afford resonance-enabled security before he started selling his new style of resonance locks. The Bronze Turtle provides its customers with a guarantee against theft, you know."

This Ruarem sure was confident in what he peddled for someone whose training in the resonance disciplines had ended after his time at the Guild.

"Fat lot of good that guarantee will do," Rahelu said. "It makes no sense to attack the strongest point of defense. Why should I bother with the lock when I could smash the box?"

Nheras scoffed. "Do you need me to spell it out for you, fish-brains? Or did you forget your own findings?"

"No," Rahelu said. She helped herself to another pork skewer from the platter and stole a piece of fried bun off Nheras's plate for good measure. "I—"

"Please, stop!" Jhobon said. "This isn't helping." He shot Ylaen a pleading look as he fiddled with the knotted fabric in front of him. "Did you get a glimpse?" The object he toyed with was roughly the size of a slim volume, wrapped inside shimmering, black silk. Whenever she tried to look at it directly, her eyes wanted to slide right off it.

Ylaen reached out across the table to clasp Jhobon's hand. After a moment, Jhobon said, "It won't fool Ruarem if he does more than look at it in passing, but it's the best we can do on short notice."

"Great," Ghardon said. "So our decoy will work. Still doesn't solve the problem of getting in."

Five pairs of eyes swiveled to Rahelu.

Elaram asked, "Could you just pick the lock?" as if that were a skill she ought to have.

"Why, in the four heavens, would I be able to?"

That seemed to be news to the others, who were taken aback by her rejoinder, which set her resonance aura buzzing.

That was so...so...typical that Rahelu wanted to grab a fistful of used bamboo skewers and hurl them across the table like throwing darts. "Could any of you pick the lock?"

"Of course not," Elaram said. "But that's because we don't have your..." She fluttered a hand in the air. "...background."

"And what, exactly, do you mean by that?"

Elaram hesitated but Nheras had no such qualms. "Don't be dense. You can't honestly sit there and expect me to believe that you paid your way through Guild training by selling fish." The Ilyn girl's voice dripped with impatience.

"Can we skip over the part where you pretend righteous anger? If it's hairpins you lack, you can help yourself to as many of mine as you need."

Hairpins. These sheltered House-born thought all it would take was some fucking hairpins.

Rahelu gripped her mug of fruit juice and took a long draught from it to steady herself before she said something she would regret.

"First: I know it's hard to tell the difference between songhouse fiction and reality from your rarified gilded palanquins, but for your information, no real shroud would use hairpins. That's like asking a mage to use a glass paperweight to anchor a working instead of resonance crystal.

"Second: lockpicking is one specialty in a field as technical and wide-ranging as resonance skills. The best crews, like the Breakers or the Yellow Fangs in Ennuost Yrg, have multiple shrouds on their payroll. And if you don't believe me on that count, then you should ask Jhobon here to arrange a few discreet meetings with the local crews."

The Imrell Supplicant shifted uncomfortably in his seat and mumbled, "We're not supposed to go through those channels for this assignment," but didn't deny that he could arrange those meetings if he wanted to.

"Third: that door is made of brass, treated teak, and banded steel; five men wielding axes couldn't get through it in less than eight spans and it won't burn. The lock is one of Ruarem's own making; not even Nhiz"—she named the most notorious shroud in the Lowdocks—"could pick it, if she tried. And she wouldn't do something so stupid as to try picking the lock; she'd go for the hinges instead."

Rahelu pointed at the air above the mostly finished platter of skewers and summoned a tiny Evocation to illustrate her point in fine detail.

"But Ruarem's no fool; he designed them to span the

height of the whole door, not just two points at head and knee height. He also crafted them from steel; they're anchored and mortared into the walls with long pins, and riveted to the door with at least twelve bolts, each as thick as a measuring rod."

Rahelu drained the rest of her clay mug and set it down on the table with a hollow *clunk*. "So, no. I cannot 'just pick the lock'. We need the physical key. And I would bet Ruarem has an Obfuscation barrier on the perimeter too. One that would set off an alarm if anyone who's not keyed to the matrix tries unlocking the door."

While they were all busy processing that, Rahelu pulled the platter towards herself and polished off the rest of the skewers.

"Alright, new plan," Elaram said. "We steal the key from either Ruarem himself or his apprentice and go in after dark. When does the Bronze Turtle close up shop?"

"Two spans before sunset," Nheras said. The pile of shredded fried bun on her plate now resembled pork floss. "The entire city is closing up early for the festival. Ruarem will be down at the Earthgiver's temple, making offerings."

"What about his apprentice?" Elaram asked.

"Probably down at the fields, indulging in the festivities." Ylaen gave her a slow, expectant smile. "This is his first solstice; he couldn't stop asking about the Night of Solace."

"Perfect." Elaram perked up immediately. "Here's what we're going to do."

13

MISTAKE

Towards the end of the tenth span, every artisan, merchant, and street vendor began closing up awnings, shutters, and doors like soldiers preparing for battle. The two Jade Eye guards shifted restlessly from one foot to the other, eyes following the throng swarming westward to the fields where you could see the beginnings of the faint lines of smoke rising from the newly lit festival fires. Ruarem's apprentice was similarly distracted—he fumbled with the latches and bolts securing the workshop's great front door, his hands shaking with eagerness.

"Like a companion-starved ship rat running for the first pleasure den they clap eyes on," Rahelu muttered. She and the others had wedged themselves between a stone relief of the Stormbringer and an empty handcart parked in a shadowed niche opposite the Bronze Turtle. "If he takes any longer to lock up, the relief guards will get here first."

Elaram must have thought the same. She tottered out of the alleyway ahead of schedule, hair loosened from its usual braids, holding an uncorked flask of spiced wine in one hand. She wove her way through the street on a zigzag course that had her stumbling into a well-dressed clerk, then nearly tripping over a pair of common-born Guild trainees clutching paper prayers. Each swaying step brought her closer to the front of the Bronze Turtle.

The guards and the apprentice straightened up.

Elaram missed her next stride over an uneven rut left by a wagon wheel and tumbled forward.

The apprentice instinctively reached out to steady her and Elaram had no hesitation in taking advantage of the opportunity: she wrapped her arms around him with a grasping fluidity an octopus would envy and said a breathy, "Hello!" with a hefty fluttering of her eyelids.

"There is no way anyone is stupid enough to fall for that," Nheras said. "It's so disgustingly obvious."

Meanwhile, Elaram had persuaded one of the guards to hold on to her flask—"Go on," Elaram urged her, "have a drink on me, I've another," whereupon she produced a second flask from her pocket and took an enormous swig. Half the wine spilled out of her mouth and soaked through the front of her thin cotton shirt. The apprentice went as still as a startled deer, transfixed by his new view. Elaram giggled and said, "Oops!" She hiccupped. To the second guard, she said, "I think you'd best hold this too," and he took the flask she pressed into his hands with very little hesitation.

"Two gold kez says the apprentice is," Ghardon said. "And I bet she won't have to use Projection at all."

"I'll take that bet," Nheras said. "But not for kez. Servant's duties: loser has to do the winner's bidding for a day and a night."

Ghardon laughed. "Deal."

"Oh dear," Elaram said as she surveyed the state of her

attire. She gave the apprentice a coquettish glance through her eyelashes and asked, "I don't suppose you've a handkerchief or a cloth I could borrow?" to which he blushed redder than the sky and began searching through his pockets.

Jhobon stirred from his Seeking trance. "She'd better hurry. The relief guards are ten blocks away, coming down through the Lesser Gate."

"I can do something about that," Ylaen said. He braced himself against the stone relief and closed his eyes.

The gentle thrum of anticipation wafting through the streets thickened; rose with the evening land breeze that carried the scents of sizzling meats and the low, insistent sound of drumbeats from the western fields. Its caress was enough to make the two dozen or so people who remained in the street hasten.

Go away, Rahelu willed at the guards, wishing there was some way she could aid Ylaen with his Projection, knowing that she'd ruin it all if she tried because she didn't have his deft subtlety at surfacing subconscious desires. *Go away, get nice and drunk, and let that poor farm boy enjoy his first Night of Solace, so we can grab that key off him, get in, get out, then hand the key back to the real relief guards while wearing your faces, and go celebrate the solstice ourselves.*

Shutters slammed into sills and doors quickly pulled shut as every last proprietor and lingering customer rushed down the West Road without a backward glance. Most of the street was shadowed now and the two guards were growing increasingly impatient with waiting.

"Hey kit," said the first guard. "It's past the end of our shift and the boss don't pay us extra for sticking around. You gon' be a'right on your own?"

"Um," the apprentice said. He had managed to find a dusting cloth in one of his pockets at last.

"Oh, you're a treasure!" Elaram gushed. She helpfully undid four more buttons on her shirt and thrust her chest forward at him.

The apprentice's eyes bulged; so did his trousers. "Yeah. You two go on," he mumbled. "I can take it from here."

"You most certainly can," Elaram purred with a shamelessness you had to admire, though not, apparently, if you were Nheras: "If I watch any more of this disgusting display I'll puke. I'm going to do a final check of the perimeter, and she'd better be done by the time I get back."

Dab, dab, dab, went the apprentice's inadequate cotton cloth. "It's alright," he said to the guards. "My master's already gone to the temple and Shualm and Pir will be here any moment."

That seemed to decide things for the two guards; they strolled off with a clink of their flasks and didn't give the shop a single backward glance.

Rahelu took a quick look with a Seeking of her own:

Two men in the green tunics of the Jade Eye Company struggle against the press of the crowd. One curses his employer and his fortune under his breath. What rotten luck to draw starwatch on the night of the summer solstice! Ridiculous of that paranoid mage-tinkerer to insist on full security tonight—if his locks are truly the miracles that his customers claim them to be, then they ought to be fit to do the damned job of guarding themselves, and what thief is dumb enough to steal some fucking locks anyway, especially on the summer solstice? The whole city is out in the fields, where disciples sworn to the Earthgiver's temple have brought their offerings, making free with seaweed wine and liquor and each other—but the boss likes the artificer's coin and the artificer has been very free with it of late so here he is, with Shualm, on the summer solstice, as he has so often dreamed but never dared to ask. He glances sidelong at his partner; notes his slowing steps. That handsome, clean-cut profile belongs on a coin, or a stone carving, or pillowed against—oh. He swallows as that sly-eyed glance slides down his face, his throat in return. Looks ahead, down the West Road, choked with all those damned lucky fools. Perhaps they can light a fire of their own. There is a little shadowed niche by the mason's workshop; it has an unobstructed view of the Bronze Turtle and privacy enough for observing the Night of Solace...

"Crowd won't keep them away much longer," Rahelu said. "I'd say we've got another three hundred heartbeats at most."

Ghardon cursed. "We need more time than that."

"Five hundred for the door," Jhobon added. "Twice that for the vault—"

"—then double everything, just in case," Ghardon said. "And to make sure we can remove any and all Evokable traces." He looked at the orange haze clouding the Outermarkets. "You'd better dial up the anticipation."

"Can't," Ylaen said. "Not unless you want a lust-crazed mob trampling people in the streets. Most of them are well into their second or third cups and the ambient resonance is starting to churn. It wouldn't take much to whip them into a frenzy."

Drumbeats thudded in the distance. The great, ponderous *da-dum dum-da da-da-dums* reverberated across the city from the Earthgiver's temple, so loud that they seemed to shake the ground, like the heartbeat of the earth itself. The upper heavens dimmed and the lower heavens burned orange-red as the sun touched the horizon, its fire merging with the ruddy glow rising from the fields to the city's west.

Hmmm.

Rahelu considered Ylaen—his range, his control, his ability to craft varied, layered Projections that affected multiple targets in different ways all at once—then sent him the impressions she had gathered from the relief guards.

"What do you think?" she asked.

"Ah, sweet summer solstice," he said, without opening his eyes. "The perfect time to confess secret affections."

Ylaen didn't have to look far to locate an appropriate source of resonance: rose-red mist streamed off the apprentice like a fountain.

In the time it had taken Rahelu to run her Seeking, Elaram had moved on to the next stage of the plan. A coy smile coaxed the apprentice away from the shop's door towards its corner and the mouth of the alleyway. A light shrug of her shoulders sent her shirt fluttering to her waist. One (rather forceful) pull on the back of his neck with her hands overcame his hesitation and disbelief at the turn of events.

"You know what, I think I agree with Nheras," Rahelu said. "I don't understand how anybody can possibly be this stupid."

The apprentice was drooling—literally drooling, ugh!—slobbering enthusiastically all over Elaram on his way down her torso, the dusting cloth and related pretense forgotten as she twisted her fingers in his hair.

"I don't understand either," Jhobon said. "This is illogical behavior." He looked completely bewildered, then completely panicked as Elaram looked straight at him while she urged the apprentice's head to go lower still.

She blew Jhobon a kiss.

He flushed.

Ghardon smirked. "Don't let her hear you say that, or you'll—"

"Be eaten alive," Rahelu said. "Focus, guys. You're up next."

Sure enough, when the apprentice reached the waistband

of Elaram's trousers, she quirked one finger—it had a lock of his hair wrapped around it—and tugged. Obediently, he went with her, a panting dog on a chain, and they disappeared down the alleyway.

Leaving the key behind in the lock of the unguarded workshop door.

"Let's go," Ghardon said.

He and Jhobon burst out from their cover and sprinted across the road to study the door.

Rahelu nudged Ylaen with her knee. "Status on the relief?"

"Busy having a heart-to-heart. In a quarter-span or two, they'll probably have a very nice head start on finding solace."

"Great," she said, ignoring the languid smile he aimed at her. "Put our faces on; it's our turn."

He concentrated; one heartbeat passed, then another, and another, and then she felt a slight warping of the ambient resonance—like mist billowing across her skin. Green bled through her undyed cotton tunic and thin, raised scars patterned like coral decorated the back of her hands.

An older man with an aquiline nose and copper skin looked her over from head to toe, then nodded. "Stay close to me," Ylaen said, in a much deeper voice. "Or you'll break the Seeming."

They marched over to the workshop door—where Ghardon, Jhobon, and Nheras were *still* milling around, hissing and gesticulating at each other like spooked cats.

"Why aren't you three inside already?" Rahelu asked. She eyed the entrance: up this close, you could see shimmers of red, blue, and green resonance radiating from the rough gray stone. "Can't you get past the authentication protocols?"

Ghardon grimaced. "I can," he said. "Elaram sent me the apprentice's resonance signature."

"The problem is, it's rigged," Jhobon said. "Ruarem used Kan's Defence—that's a permanent, active barrier—which means whoever unlocks the door also has to keep spoofing the resonance signature in order to keep the alarms deactivated."

Rahelu exchanged blank looks with Ylaen.

"What does that mean, in non-Guardian speak?" he asked.

"It means," Nheras drawled, "one of these two will be more or less incapacitated, and like two bharosts butting horns, they can't agree on who should tackle the vault."

"His approach to barrier-breaking lacks rigorous methodology…" Jhobon began.

"And we'll all die of old age while he's busy mapping the matrices," Ghardon snapped. "We don't have time for that."

"I still think the problem is best solved by getting the apprentice back here," Nheras said. "A little tap on his head, two of us drag him inside, and he can sleep it off in a corner while we work."

"Right." Ghardon snorted. "So one moment he's having the time of his life; the next, he's waking up after someone's knocked him out in an alleyway, with no memory of how he got back inside the workshop. That's not suspicious at all!"

"So we'll dump him back in the alleyway." The orange glow of Nheras's aura was enough to make anyone paying attention to their resonance senses think another bonfire had been lit right here. "With the key back in his pocket."

"Why yes, that'll solve the problem," Ghardon said. "He surely won't have any reason to remember the girl who lured him into said alleyway to be ambushed, or recall that she did so before he finished locking up the shop. And surely his master wouldn't have any cause to call in the city guard or contract an independent Evoker to investigate exactly what happened here, discover this exact conversation, and then trace this all the way back to you-know-where."

"Well, if one of you doesn't do it soon, we're going to have a different problem," Ylaen said, voice strained. "The longer there's five of us out front instead of two, the further I have to stretch the bounds of plausibility, and I'd like to spend some of the summer solstice finding solace myself instead of whimpering alone in my bed with resonance backlash."

"Fine," Ghardon said. "I will stay out here and play 'yes, I'm really the apprentice' with the security protocols while you"—he glared at Jhobon—"go inside and take care of the vault. But I want it noted for the record that I disagreed because this is going to go badly."

He took hold of the key, pressed his other hand to the door, then yanked on the orange thicket of impatience sprouting out of Nheras's aura.

Three layers of Obfuscation barriers shuddered as Ghardon picked and poked away at them with the resonance he had gathered—then the part of the barrier over the entrance split. Severed edges retracted from the door, wavering like a slice of rice pudding that hadn't set properly, leaving irregular patches that evaporated back into the ambient resonance now that they were no longer connected to the rest of the barrier.

Click! Ghardon swung the door open and sagged against its frame. "Go," he said, all the while keeping his palm flat against the steel-banded teak.

Nheras and Jhobon slipped through the narrow gap into the dark.

Rahelu wrested her eyes away and turned her attention to the street. She stood parade-straight, ears alert, half-poised on the edge of Seeking with her right hand resting on the hilt of her belt knife.

Behind her, a whispered, "Ow, careful, careful!" from Jhobon, along with the scratch of a match head on stone. It had grown dark enough that the spark that briefly fizzled into existence was visible without turning her head; thank the Starfather that it fizzled out just as quickly. "Never mind that"—Nheras, in a hiss—as candleglow blossomed inside, then Ylaen said, through gritted teeth as his features shifted before her eyes, "Shut the door, shut the door, they wouldn't have it open during starwatch," to which Ghardon said, "Don't! I need to be in contact with—" but Rahelu had already grabbed it by its black iron handle and heaved it shut.

Nheras's muffled cursing cut off.

Ghardon's eyes rolled up inside his head. His knees buckled; he fell against the door, cheek first; his hand slid down polished wood and across shining steel, and the wavering edges of the slice he had made in the barrier surged across the expanse of wood and stone that he no longer controlled.

"Fuck." Rahelu lunged forward.

Not a moment too soon: she caught him just before he—and more importantly, the palm that he had somehow kept in contact with the door—hit the ground. His fingers started to curl. That wouldn't do at all. She grabbed his hand, pinned it flat against the wood with hers, and struggled to lift him back up on his feet.

Two muscled, heavily scarred arms joined her efforts. Together, she and Ylaen tried to wedge Ghardon's slumped body into a position that might pass for standing if you were drunk and half-blind, without breaking the contact between their hands and the door.

Handspan by handspan, the slice in the three-layered barrier reluctantly reopened itself.

A low groan sounded from Ghardon's throat.

"He can't hold the barrier open like this," she said as Ylaen helped her sling Ghardon's other arm over her shoulders. "I'm going to try a Concordance. Can you keep watch until Elaram returns?"

"I'll manage. Here, lean against the wall a bit more, so if anyone walking past glances over, it looks like there's just one of you."

Rahelu did as suggested, then left Ylaen to split his attention between maintaining the Seeming and a light short-range Seeking.

She slid her free hand inside Ghardon's collar:

—need to restore open connection—the breach—temporary; need it to hold until he's done—should've been me—

His thoughts raced so frantically that she heard them through their direct skin contact, without any need for Projection.

—wrong about the lynchpin—Imrell's too slow, he won't realize —barrier's layout doesn't match the configur—gods! Circuit is unstable, if I—fuck this hurts—I can't—sister, where are you—

Ghardon, she sent as she drew on the power in her pendant. *Ghardon, I'm—*

Sister!

—I'm—

'I'm here, I'm ready' was what she was going to tell him, but when his mind latched onto hers she was not, in fact, ready. He seized control of their Concordance; sent their focus down through their overlapping hands and inside the chamber of the door's lock where three resonance crystals the size of apples pulsed in shifting shades of yellows, violets, and grays.

Ghardon, what—and then she knew; she'd given him the bloody idea herself. *Switch,* she sent, *I've done this before.*

No time, he sent. The barrier shuddered, its sliced edges shaking like wet curtains. Hairline fractures appeared at its edges, bits of resonance crumbling off the barrier. *We've got about a hundred heartbeats before the whole system collapses.*

More fragments of the barrier fell away. The stray resonance battered at their Concordance and it wavered. He was juggling too much: Projecting the apprentice's resonance signature, holding the gap in the barrier, and trying to find the heart of the door's matrix.

Just...just anchor, alright? As long as you keep things stable...

Alr—

Ghardon slipped his hand out from under hers; she staggered as the full weight of the barrier slammed into her mind. Pain reverberated through her skull in a horrible irregular throbbing, like the iron-shod hooves of a runaway horse on stone.

Rough hands clamped over her mouth and a new voice cut in. *Stop making that noise!* Ylaen sent. *I can't sustain this—*

Shit.

They had miscalculated badly. Ghardon was meant to be inside with Jhobon and Nheras (what in the eight hells was taking them so long, anyway? If they would just *fucking hurry up* she could let go of this gods-cursed barrier and they could all leave) but he wasn't, he was out here, with her and Ylaen, straining the plausibility of the Seeming that was supposed to make the three of them look like the two relief guards, and he was barreling through the first crystal's matrix without any regard for its integrity—

—if you two—

Skymother! Go easy, or you'll break it and then we'll be—

Shut up and let me—

—and she was here straining her mind against this stupid fucking barrier to hold the breach open. It was about as effective as standing in the shallows, trying to hold back the waves with her bare hands instead of a breakwater. The barrier's resonance crashed into her; its pressure squeezed the air out of her lungs; she had to draw deeply on the pendant around her neck to resist drowning (it was so warm it had to be glowing now and she had to hope it was sufficiently hidden).

Like waves washing up against a promontory jutting out into the sea, resonance surged around and behind her to meet itself, cutting off the arched opening Ghardon had made in the barrier.

The result was inevitable.

Ghardon, she sent urgently. *Ghardon, it's collapsing—*

Frustration, then: *twenty more heartbeats!* but between the direct skin contact of her palm against his heart and their Concordance, he couldn't lie.

Leave it! she insisted.

He reluctantly pulled away from the lock to take over anchoring their Concordance so she could send their combined focus through the rapidly shrinking gap in the barrier in a Seeking for Nheras.

Within the workshop, smaller barriers interwoven amongst permanent resonance wards thwarted their progress. She sensed Nheras's resonance signature (a prickly, staccato beat) in fractional glimpses, followed it to its source—

> *She frantically prowls the cramped aisles between the cluttered shelves of Ruarem's vault—step, step, step, turn, step, step, step, turn—as Jhobon sits in a mage trance before an iron safe, a cloth-wrapped package in his lap.*

—only to discover the signal was coming from a directional resonance ward, one with a concave construction that combined a dozen different fractured reflections into jumbled images:

> *—swings open at last: sacks of coins; ledgers; schematics; more lock charms; where was the fucking box—*

—perhaps the others are already gone: captured by the city guard and locked up in the mage cells, awaiting trial before the Hall of Judgment at the next session—this was such a stupid, overly complicated plan—

—'Got it!' Jhobon says. He turns a hand crank on the safe's iron door—

"Rahelu!" A hand shaking her by her shoulder. "I need you to come out of there. Someone's coming."

She couldn't; that would leave Ghardon bearing the weight of the barrier alone and his mind was buckling under the pressure.

—looks at Jhobon for what feels like the hundredth time. She rubs her hands over her bare forearms; being adrift in the dark is worse than she thought; she can't hear anything inside this cursed vault, except for her own shallow breathing; she can't hear his breathing, she glances at him again just to reassure herself that he is still breathing—

They needed to know if Jhobon and Nheras had succeeded; she needed to get through to Nheras with the apprentice's resonance signature; Nheras needed to—

—how much time has passed? A span? More? Less? It's so dark; she hates the dark, the dark is—

"I'm sorry." That stupid voice; she was going to lose herself in the refractive ward maze if it kept interrupting her. And again, "I'm sorry," but the voice had changed, it had changed—

—and there, tucked away in the corner, is the box. He unwraps the bundle in his lap; reaches in to swap their decoy for the real thing. A slight shimmer of resonance across the front of the open safe. 'Stop!'

*she says, but his fingers have already triggered the hidden Projection.
Surprise spikes through his aura before his face catches up and less
than a heartbeat later, both his aura and his face smooth out to utter
blankness—*

Warmth blooms against her heart suffuses her veins in a
rush of heat as rose-red ribbons stir in the ambient resonance
and wrap themselves around her pulling her back from the
ward maze and the Concordance and—

*—a fucking stupid plan and Issolm could go fuck him and fuck
herself—*

She was hot she was cold she was being dragged through
corridors of unstable resonance that broke apart and recom-
bined in surreal combinations of bone-white flashes, red-hot
fountains, and ice-blue fractals, and somewhere through that
tangle of real and not-real and then and now was Nheras but
the force reeling her back was so much stronger that all she
could do was hurl every last bit of strength she had into a
shrieking Projection—

NHERAS!

—that carried the apprentice's resonance signature. It
bounced around the ward maze, creating a cascading
cacophony as each reverberation multiplied with a vengeance;
a million fragmented signals shredding her mind like knives.

She opened her mouth to scream.

The thread anchoring her Concordance with Ghardon
snapped.

Without support from the stored power in her pendant,
he gave way beneath the pressure of the barrier. Resonance
backlash set in so quickly that he slipped from her arms
without a sound.

And Rahelu abruptly surfaced out of the resonance storm

she'd created to find herself inside Ylaen's embrace with her shirt hanging open and he was kissing her and running his hands up and down her bare back and—

WHAT THE FUCK?!

She hammered him with a direct Projection so hard it should have thrown him three strides back and off her the way she wanted to hammer him with her fists and shove him away from her, but he'd tightened his embrace and pinned her arms to her sides and her body against the door and—

Get the fuck off me, Imos, before I—

A low whistle and the sound of clapping broke through her rage and Ylaen's unwanted attention.

The Imos Supplicant drew back. She could barely make out his shadowed face; it was stormarc and full dark now. A bank of gray clouds had rolled in from the southeast. They hung low in the heavens; heavy, rounded, undersides glowing orange. She saw the aquiline profile of his nose silhouetted against the bonfire-lit sky and knew it was not his.

His eyes were full of warning.

Ylaen didn't turn to face the newcomer. "Kindly go fuck off," he said in that too-deep voice, to a distant rumble of thunder. He was tracing a pattern of triangular scars across her very naked, very flat, very male chest. "We're busy."

"I can see that." The woman who spoke was also dressed in a jade-green tunic. A half-shuttered storm lantern hung from her belt, casting a thin beam of light across the cobblestones, the only source of illumination in the street besides the yellow-blue crescent of the waxing moon. "Boss got a fright when the alarm went off a quarter-span ago. You got anything to report?"

"We might've rattled the door a few times," Rahelu said, and the timbre of her voice was altered too. She hoped the shaky way her words came out made her sound like she was half-dazed with passion, the way someone right on the edge of losing themselves to carnal pleasure would sound. "False alarm. Sorry."

"You're sure that was all?" the woman asked as she unhooked the lantern and held it up. Her clumsy Seeking slid around their resonance auras like an eel nosing basket traps, but she'd get nothing from Rahelu and Ylaen except what she expected: a tumultuous mix of shock, desperation, and unfulfilled desire.

Ghardon, on the other hand…

The woman frowned. "What's this?"

Ghardon lay crumpled at their feet, unmoving. A dark line of blood trickled from his left nostril, to drip from his upper lip onto his tunic.

"Some drunkard," Rahelu said. Her voice was still unsteady; she made an effort to speak more calmly. "Poor bastard was already here when we arrived, mumbling to himself."

Clouds rumbled.

The woman's frown deepened. "Dhirne and Csolim didn't mention him in their report."

"They wasn't here." Ylaen scowled, took his hand off her thigh to run it through his hair—his auburn hair—and trained a fierce glare on the woman at last. "We was held up by the crowds; by the time we got here, those two and the 'prentice had already buggered off. This sod had planted hisself in the doorway and wouldn't be budged; what else were we s'posed to do? Boss don't pay us to move things."

"True," the woman said.

"Now, if you don't mind?" Ylaen said. "I just got done convincing Pir here that he ought to light a solstice fire with me." His resonance aura went from a prickly, red-brown irritation back to a deep rose-red as he dismissed the woman and smiled his slow, knowing smile at Rahelu.

Heat spread through her lower body as his fingers trailed

down her belly, past a tapered waist and narrow hips, towards a visibly stiff portion of human anatomy protruding from her trousers that definitely did not belong to her.

"About time, if you ask me." The woman winked at Rahelu. "Enjoy the Night of Solace, boys. Mind you don't set off any more false alarms or the boss'll send me to interrupt you again."

"Aye," they said and watched her walk off into the shadows.

Ylaen tried to let go of her; his eyebrows rose when Rahelu gripped his wrists to keep them where they were.

She's still there, Rahelu sent. *Around that corner. Hiding.*

The woman had put up a passable Obfuscation barrier and shuttered her lantern so no light would betray her, but her presence was clear to Rahelu's Guild-trained Seeking.

Somehow, the woman knew they were imposters. Not consciously, perhaps, but something must have roused her suspicions. They'd barely managed the minimum research needed on the Jade Eye Company's handover procedures; they hadn't had the chance to do a thorough study of the four guards assigned to stormwatch and starwatch as well. It had been pure coincidence that one of the guards claimed ship clan ties and Ylaen had managed to figure out how (through a very convoluted deconstruction and reconstruction of the conceptual relationship between Supplicants and their Houses, the Houses within the Dominion, and his own ship clan ties that nobody other than Jhobon had been able to follow) he could pass Rahelu and himself off as Pir and Shualm. But their accents, their mannerisms, the way they held themselves were bound to be different from the real Pir and Shualm—that was why they had needed Elaram to get rid of the two guards so they could pick up the key from the apprentice at changeover instead since Dhirne and Csolim would have known them for imposters immediately.

And now that woman was waiting and listening to see what they would do when they thought no one was watching.

Shit.

Another murmur of thunder punctuated the silence; this time, accompanied by a brief flash of lightning.

Eight hells.

She couldn't do this. She wasn't Elaram. She couldn't pretend that—

I'll handle this, Ylaen sent. *Just don't fight me.*

He leaned down and kissed her again.

She went rigid in his arms.

Don't fight me, he repeated. *Close your eyes.*

She wanted to push back anyway; carve out a bubble of cool, blue-gray calm within the molten rose-red mist wrapping around her limbs—but he was right, she couldn't fight him, because no desperate lover in the height of newly confessed passion would do that, so she squeezed her eyes shut and restrained the instincts that urged her to knee him in the groin—

Relax.

He tasted like peppermint and cardamom and star anise; she hated star anise—it reminded her of Anathwan's bitter, herbal teas—and she jerked her mouth away.

Her eyes flew open.

Pretend I'm him.

Rahelu hurriedly shut her eyes again and did her best. Too many ridged scars crisscrossed his chest; she had to slide her hands around his ribs to the smooth, unblemished skin of his back instead. The rose-red mist he had summoned helped; and the kisses that he rained down the length of her neck, past her collarbones, and over the curves of her breasts weren't unwelcome either.

A small gasp escaped her lips; he was paying far more attention to her pleasure than he'd given to Elaram's because, like Elaram, he was putting on a show, and if it was going to be a show convincing enough to make their unwanted spectator go away so they could finish Anathwan's stupid test, she would have to do her part too.

So she forced her worries about Ghardon and Nheras and Jhobon away into the back of her mind, where it could stew away with her resentment at Elaram for not being here. She concentrated on stoking the heat of the rose-red mist in the ambient resonance; drew Ylaen closer so his resonance aura wrapped around hers.

His mouth blazed a hot trail down her navel that was immediately chilled by the sea breeze; deft fingers loosened the ties on her trousers and hooked underneath the waistband. A gentle tug. Roughspun cotton slid down over her hipbones, just a finger-width or two, enough for him to graze her skin with his lips and his tongue in that sensitive crease just above the top of her thigh.

She shivered, and this time, the pleasure wasn't feigned; it was real, it was remembered, he had ducked his head underneath Elaram's formal dress robes and done exactly the same thing in the Ideth gardens and Elaram had made her live it, so her body remembered how it felt and craved what came next and it was easy, so easy to forget about how they were going to lift the barrier and unlock the door without Ghardon or Jhobon because they couldn't do that while that woman was still watching them, so fuck her.

Rahelu threaded her left hand through his hair—*red* hair; she could see the orange-red glints in his hair from the firelight—drew his face up to hers and kissed him back.

From somewhere around the corner: the rhythmic tread of boots on cobblestones as the woman's footfalls gradually faded into the distance.

Here, now: the patter of warm summer rain. Small droplets beaded on her forehead, her eyelids, her nose; so light that she barely felt them until their sheer number combined into rivulets that ran down the sides of her face and neck to soak her skin.

They could stop. The woman was gone. Certainly he assumed that was what she wanted because he broke off their kiss, breathing heavily. But all that rose-red passion he had summoned still hung heavy around them in the ambient resonance; the night was warm; she was warm; he was warm; and he clearly wanted *someone*. Maybe not her, but she was here and her body wanted—*she* wanted...not him; *him*, but she couldn't have him; she could've had him, and she'd wanted him, still wanted him, but he wasn't here and *he* was right here, with his arms around her, still looking at her— with his own eyes now and it was dark, so dark, she couldn't tell what color they were—his bare skin still pressed against hers, his hands still cradling her hips as she straddled his thigh, and he'd just told her to pretend, hadn't he, so clearly he didn't care if she didn't, so she leaned forward and kissed him again because she could think of and do whatever she wanted with whomever she pleased, and if anybody dared judge her for wanting a quick fuck on the summer solstice, well they could go fuck themselves.

(Nheras did, Nheras would, Nheras was still trapped in the dark with an insensate Jhobon behind a barrier she couldn't lift and the door she couldn't unlock from the inside, but Nheras could damn well wait another hundred heartbeats.)

He sensed her intentions—by the downward motion of her hands; by the wild surge of desire in her resonance aura —and he shifted his hips slightly to accommodate her. Her fingers landed on the brass buckle of his belt and trembled as she took a deep breath.

It was a mistake.

The scent of cedar and sandalwood flooded into her lungs.

It's not him, her mind protested, and she froze halfway through unbuckling his trousers.

What in the eight hells was she doing?

"Fuck," she swore and pushed Ylaen away.

"Fuck," he agreed and leaned the back of his head against the wall.

And right at that moment, Elaram emerged from the alleyway. She turned the corner, alone and full of good cheer, sharp eyes and resonance senses picking out Rahelu hitching her trousers up and Ylaen doing up his belt.

"Well, well, well." Elaram chortled as she walked up to the doorway with a spring in her step. "Did you two just"— all mischievous amusement drained from her as she spotted Ghardon's crumpled form—"fuck!" She threw herself down beside her brother, pressing her hands to his temples, his neck, his heart. "What happened?"

"The barrier," Rahelu said. She finished buttoning her shirt and still felt naked: Ylaen had made a mess of her resonance ward so it no longer functioned, and confusion and yearning rampaged freely through her aura. Her fingers itched to redo it, but there was no point: it was raining, she had neither charcoal nor resonance ink, and they had other priorities. "Where's the apprentice?"

"Frolicking in the fields with six disciples from the Earthgiver's temple," Elaram said, promptly quashing the possibility of using Nheras's suggestion as a backup plan. "Where're the other two?" A pause as she read the shifts in their auras. "Great. Just great. I say we take my brother and leave." She rested her head on Ghardon's chest and closed her eyes, clasping his hands in a white-knuckled grip. "Maybe we can get as far as the next town before we're caught. Do you think they'll bother with a trial before an Adjudicator or go straight to slicing off our thumbs?"

There was no point in hoping for a trial. If they managed

to survive the city guard's interrogation, there was still the direct Seeking before the Hall of Judgment, and at the first sign of trouble, the Adjudicator would call upon House Seekers.

Anathwan, under authorization from the Exalted Dominance himself, would take steps to ensure nothing of their mission became a matter of public record.

And once their mind blocks were triggered…

Ylaen laughed. It was short and bitter and full of sharp edges. "I hear there's always a demand for new indentures in the Suborned dens."

The three of them looked grimly at the door. Ruarem's barrier swirled across its surface in a mesmerizing taunt.

"We'll just have to lift it," Elaram said. "Will the three of us be enough?"

"Maybe." Rahelu glanced at the comatose Ghardon. "Maybe not."

"What did you do with the relief guards?" Elaram asked.

Shit.

Delaying the guards had seemed like a good idea when they'd been confident that they could get in and get out within a half-span. The guards would have arrived to find the door locked, the barrier intact, and the previous guards and the apprentice long gone, with every incentive to cover up anything odd.

But now…

Elaram sighed. "Alright. You take our brother back to the citadel while Ylaen and I go and take care of those guards properly. Then we'll meet back here to try and figure a way out of this mess. At least the rain will help cover our tracks."

The rain.

They'd been standing here, by the door, underneath the lip of the roof's narrow overhang this whole time. The leading edge of the storm had passed some time ago and the rain now fell in heavier sheets that puddled in between cobblestones.

The only rain that splashed down on them came from the sky.

Not the roof.

The roof sloped back, away from the street.

"Wait!"

Elaram and Ylaen stopped in their tracks, halfway to the turnoff to the Lesser Gate.

Rahelu jerked her head at the roof. "I want to try something." She pulled the key out of the lock and tossed it to Elaram. "Take this"—she kicked off her sandals—"and these and Ghardon too. You go hide and keep watch from the alleyway, while you"—she looked at Ylaen—"take care of the relief guards. I don't care what you do, so long as you keep them away from here until well after deepnight."

He nodded, then bent to help Elaram pick up Ghardon while Rahelu jogged over to the laneway behind the Bronze Turtle.

The stack of crates by the neighboring shop was still there; even better, a few more had been added so the top of the stack loomed as high as the windows on the second storey. They wobbled precariously as she leapt up, layer by layer, to grasp the edge of the roof and swing herself over the lip. The unglazed terracotta tiles and her bare feet made it easy to scamper to the very top of the peaked roof.

There, she squatted on her haunches to peer through the rain at Ruarem's workshop and recover her breath, heart pounding in her chest.

The sturdy single-storey building stood on the opposite side of the laneway. Its stone walls were square and topped with a slate roof. From this angle, she could see scores of narrow air vents cut into the top row of stones, just beneath the overhang of the roof. The four-sided roof itself consisted of eight sections, all angled inwards. Rainwater rushed over the slate tiles and sloshed into the four central channels, feeding into a pool that must drain into a system of pipes that ended in a water reservoir somewhere inside.

She laughed and she cursed—she was right and yet not right enough.

Ruarem was so fucking paranoid that he had stuck a great, big, barbed steel spike on top of the drain on his roof. She would have called it a lightning rod, but the grate and the tip of the spike was a good five hands lower than the highest part of the roof so the only purpose it could have was to stab any would-be thieves.

Rahelu stood.

She flexed her ankles and steadied her breath as she balanced on the balls of her feet on the angled tile that capped the ridgeline, feeling cool, rough terracotta beneath her feet. Not so different to the planks of her family's sloop. The distance between the edge of this roof and the next was only a little farther than the gap she had to jump from deck to pier to tie up their boat.

She had leapt that distance hundreds of times, rain or shine, from a much shorter, flatter run-up.

A quick, silent prayer to the Starfather was all the hesitation she allowed before she pelted down the steep pitch of the roof, eyes fixed on the landing point four strides away: the middle of the closest side of the Bronze Turtle's roof.

Ten strides—eight—five—two, then she curled the toes of her right foot over the round lip of the roof, swung her arms forward, extended her left leg, and launched herself into the air. Landed a half-stride short. Her feet slipped and she fell, hands and elbows and feet scrabbling frantically on the wet slate tiles for purchase. Her fingers snagged on the chipped edge of a tile and she stifled a cry of pain as three of the fingertips on her left hand bore the full force of her uncontrolled slide for a heartbeat. She splayed her limbs out like a seastar, trying to generate friction by maximizing the total surface area of her body in contact with the roof before she spiked herself on the drain.

It worked. Kind of.

The spike pierced her leg—she bit down hard on the inside of her cheek and stifled a scream. Once tears had stopped leaking from her eyes, she twisted around to assess her wound. The razor-sharp tip had stabbed into the back of her right thigh, a handspan above her knee. It had only penetrated the fleshy part by a finger-width or two, stopping shy of its barbed fangs, and had missed slicing any important tendons.

Lucky. Starfather blessedly lucky.

Rahelu gritted her teeth, gingerly wedged her left foot against the angled join between two sections of the roof, braced her left elbow against the tile and her right hand underneath her hip, and tried to pull herself off the spike. Slipped. For one agonizing moment, the weight her fingers had taken shoved her thigh further onto the spike.

A low cry of pain escaped her—there was no holding that back. She tasted blood as she shifted the bulk of her weight over to her left foot, stuffed her left forearm between her teeth, and screamed into her sodden sleeve as she freed her right leg from the spike.

Blood welled up from her wound and dripped into the draining water, a dark twisting line spiraling round and round the base of the spike until it disappeared. Down the tiny circular grate—no bigger than her fist; welded to the eight steel bolts driven through the slate tiles into the gray wall stones—in a spiteful gurgle.

The Starfather must be laughing.

There would be no getting in or out that way.

She hurriedly bit into her sleeve, tore away strips of

wet cotton as she cursed through her teeth, mixing graphic descriptions of pestilence in Free Territories speech with maledictions upon Ruarem's loins in Chanazian as she bound up her leg, then wiped off the remaining stains from the spike with the hem of her shirt.

Halfway through her calls in Aleznuaweithish for the horrors of the seventh hell to descend upon Ruarem, she got an answer that echoed out of the drain.

"Fish guts?"

Anger flared. She'd risked life and limb to come rescue Nheras; they were sisters in the eyes of the Houses; their fates were bound together in success and failure of this mission, and still Nheras wouldn't give her the courtesy of using her damned name.

"Fish guts!" The rasped words came from a hoarse voice caught halfway between a whisper and a scream. "Is that you?"

That voice sounded nothing like Nheras; those high-pitched, trembling tones belonged to a terrified girl who had been left alone with her worst fears for far too long.

Rahelu bit back the retort on the tip of her tongue.

"It's me," she said. "What's your status?"

"We're...we're..." There was a faint sound that might have been a sob but it was lost to the rain. Then Nheras's voice steadied: "I got your warning. The inside of the safe was trapped, not the vault. A buried Projection, a—" Another pause. "I switched the boxes and I reset the trap, but I...I can't rouse him."

Rahelu had known, had pieced it together from her fragmentary Seeking. Her heart sank anyway. "Are you still in the vault?"

"No," came the reply. "It was too—" *Too dark* was how Rahelu filled in the silence but what Nheras ended up saying was, "—risky to stay there. We're back by the door. Is it safe?"

There was such hope, such pleading in Nheras's voice that Rahelu felt like a traitor for her next words.

"Ghardon's unconscious too; the door's not an option."

A very definite sob.

Rahelu rushed on; she had to prioritize the box. "It's almost starrise. There's an air vent on the south side of the shop, right by the roof. Do you see it?"

She crouched down over the drain, clutching onto the length of the spike with rain-numbed hands, listening for a shuffle, a rustle, the scuffling of sandals on tile—any sound that would indicate Nheras had managed to pull herself together and wasn't sobbing on the floor the way she'd been sobbing on the *Winged Arrow's* deck five days ago.

"Do you see it?" she repeated, louder.

A dead, flat, "Yes."

"Meet me there in ten heartbeats. That's as long as I need to climb over; ten heartbeats, and not a moment longer," Rahelu promised. "Can you do that?"

"Just go."

She went.

The rain and the wet slate and her throbbing leg and aching arms made a liar of her; by the time she had slither-crawled over to where the air vent should be, she'd counted to ten at least a dozen times. She hauled herself up with both hands, belly dragging across stone tiles, and wrapped the length of her left forearm over the edge.

Rahelu looked into the air vent and met Nheras's eyes through a black steel mesh so fine that she hadn't been able to see it from further away.

Another fucking grate.

"Stormwinds!" she swore and pulled out her belt knife. She jabbed at the mesh furiously, probing for weak spots in the center of the screen, jamming the blade at the junctures where steel mesh sank into gray stone, and when that didn't work, she growled, reversed her grip and simply started bashing the hilt into the mesh over and over again.

The sight of her knife driving down at Nheras's eyes was surreal; familiar, yet strange; she had always imagined it happening when they'd finally pissed each other off enough to skip past street brawls and clawing at each other's faces like alleycats to drawing weapons with the intent to make a permanent end of their years-long feud. Screams and sobs, yes—in pain, in rage, in long-frustrated purpose—but not from her own knife slipping in her own hand and slicing into her own fingers.

"Get back," Nheras said.

Rahelu barely had time to jerk out of the way before an iron poker smashed through the screen, into the air where her head had been. She grabbed its other end; together, they prised the grate's loosened edge away from the wall until Nheras could thrust a cloth-wrapped package through the newly unencumbered opening.

"Go."

"I'll come back," Rahelu said.

"Don't." Long-nailed fingers reached out to yank the grate back into place, a determined summons that the grate easily refused. "I don't need your help. I can take care of myself."

That was it.

She was tired, she was confused, she was angry, and Nheras being her usual, unreasonable, ungrateful self brought out the worst in her.

"Fuck you."

Rahelu threw herself off the roof without another word— a stupid, reckless move that left her dazed in pain on landing, but which had the benefit of summoning Ylaen from the alleyway.

"Take it." She shoved the cloth-wrapped box at him. It now bore a bloody handprint from her. "And get Elaram and Ghardon out of here."

His face twisted as he glanced at the box, at the barrier, at the sky, at the blood that stained the makeshift bandage on her thigh, but he did not argue as she placed the shaking, uninjured fingers of her left hand against the door and clutched her pendant with her bleeding right hand.

Ylaen drew the key out of his pocket, set its teeth into the lock, and left her to it.

14

PROMISE

SHE DID NOT KNOW HOW LONG SHE STOOD THERE, thoughts moving as sluggishly as lakefish under truewinter ice, trying to muster up the courage to pit her will against the barrier again.

Even with a focus-stone-anchored Concordance, she and Ghardon hadn't been able to hold out for more than a hundred heartbeats. It was too strong and too well-crafted; ludicrous to think mere Supplicants could defeat it.

But Elder Anathwan seemed to think them capable. Rahelu had to believe that—the alternative spoke of a ruthlessness too terrible to contemplate.

What had they not tried?

What prevented her from opening that door and walking through it?

Not its mechanical or physical attributes, however impressive, for she had the key. The door was subject to the laws of physics that commanded its material composition, its hinges, and the geared mechanisms of its lock.

No. The real defense against unauthorized entry was Ruarem's three-layered barrier. The first layer was a gray, maze-like fog of confusion, designed to negate entry by force. The second was a smooth, steel-shine mirror of unyielding calm, designed to negate entry by malicious intent. The final layer was a bristling spear-forest of sharp, orange-black suspicion, designed to negate entry by deception.

The barrier had fought Ghardon because he had picked a hole in it by force, intent on theft, but it had not entirely resisted because he'd been successful in forging the apprentice's resonance signature. The alarm had gone off in that brief moment—between when they'd lost control of the breach and when Nheras had received her warning—because they'd stopped spoofing it.

Obfuscation negated the existence of an emotional reality.

Projection asserted one emotional reality upon another.

They had misunderstood Anathwan's lesson entirely.

Rahelu let go of Lhorne's pendant. She took off her sodden shirt, wrung it out, and used it to wipe off the smudged remains of her resonance ward. The new ward she drew was a variation on the dreamward Maketh had made them learn: a single, spiraling line of blood that formed a labyrinthine pattern over her heart. It glistened in the moonlight; a glimmer that seemed to pulse in time with her heartbeat to her resonance senses.

Finally, she turned her pendant over so its bloodied face touched the end of the ward. She couldn't see it through the silver backing, but she could feel the change as the ward channeled her resonance signature into the crystal.

She closed her eyes and reached out with a Seeking:

A girl leans upon the shop door, her forehead resting against the hand upon its lock. She is barefoot, half-naked, and shrouded in glowing mist. The active pendant around her neck is a star; the brightest point of concentrated resonance inside a five-block radius.

Reality: now. But not as it was then. She followed the ripples of resonance through time, the Evocation unspooling in her mind, until she found another summer night:

He has spent the better part of three seasons constructing his workshop: mixing his blood into the mortar that bound the stone walls together, laying hundreds of anchoring crystals for the protective formations, carving the door from heartwood, and forging the lock himself. There is but one final task: he places his hand on the door and gives it its commands. Triple barriers of gray fog, shining steel, and orange-tipped black spears materialize. He departs, pleased that all is in good order and confident in what he has wrought. Tomorrow, he will bring his wares and his guards— but tonight, the door can stand watch over the empty street on its own.

Rahelu wrenched the closing portion of that Evocation forward, using it to lend weight to her visualization of her absence from the world.

Hide me, she instructed the pendant. *I am not here; I was never here; I am not.*

The mist-filled crystal shimmered in response, and she could no longer sense her own resonance signature. She breathed deeply, drawing in the clean scent of fresh-fallen rain. Instead of using the single-count meditation the Guild taught for Projection, some instinct prompted her to fall into the five-count pattern Onneja had used for her Augury:

The apprentice lies sprawled in a tangle of limbs, hidden deep within the vegetable field. He is deliriously content, deliciously sated, and delightedly drunk. Warmth from the still-smoking embers of the bonfire and the sweat-soaked, naked bodies around him urges him to sleep, yet something keeps him from slipping into peaceful dreams.

There is something that he has forgotten, something vitally important, something that he must do without fail.

The thought nags at him, a worming worry he can't ignore, and suddenly, all the minor sensations he has blocked out surge forth in a wave of irritation. The gritty, dry dirt chafes his skin; his left leg is going numb; a fallen branch digs into his back; further away, the rhythmic moans of a disciple, who had wandered off when this circle's dance had concluded, grated on his nerves. Someone's elbow is digging into his side; someone's hair is itching at his neck. He shifts over, reclaims one hand from where it has been trapped underneath some-one's ribs, and digs his fingers underneath the thin, knotted string he wears to scratch at his collarbone.

His master's key is not on the string.

He has left it in the lock.

Now: reality. As it *could* be.

Rahelu wove the apprentice's resonance signature through her aura with bits and pieces of other plausibilities; where she wielded a set of pliers instead of a spear in Tsen-jhe's workshop; where she stood behind an ink-stained counter and sold seashell brooches instead of fish; cobbled it all together and donned it like a patched storm cloak.

Her Seeming snapped into place and she reached out to the barrier, the door, the lock as she gripped its key.

Here I am: to enter by my master's consent.

Fog receded. A *click* as the key loosened the lock.

Here I am: my purpose to retrieve that which is in my care. Here I am: one that you know. I am the one who bids you to open and close each day at my master's command.

Steel mirror and spear blades rippled like water, then parted.

Rahelu pushed the door open and entered with the moonlight.

Two huddled forms in the corner, behind the table. Nheras jerked upright with a soft cry. Faster than thought, the bone-white terror in her aura drained into her upflung hand as a shining bolt.

Before Rahelu could say a word, Nheras's Projection lashed forward and slammed straight into her skull. Her limbs froze—so strong and potent was the fear Nheras had conjured that she couldn't get her arms up at all. She barely managed to turn her head as she toppled forward, stiff as a board, and took the full impact of the fall on her face.

And then, to her utter embarrassment, she also pissed herself.

Her Seeming wobbled—

No! she thought, *nonono, that is me, this is me, this is where I am meant to be.*

—then steadied as the terror passed.

Rahelu glared at Nheras as they both trembled. "You stupid, short-sighted, chicken-hearted shadow of a mage!"

"It's…" Nheras took a deep, shuddering breath. "It's you. It's really you."

"Yes, of course it's me. I said I'd be back!" She'd landed on her cheek, not her nose, thank the Starfather, but it hurt like she'd taken a fist to her face and she wondered if she'd fractured something.

Nheras looked uncertainly at the door. "You opened it."

"Yes, I opened it." Rahelu put a hand to her forehead and closed her eyes; the floor was making her dizzy with all its shaking. "Got any other useless observations to contribute?"

"I was going to wait until eartharc," Nheras said. "We would've stayed hidden until the apprentice came in to open shop, and then I would've slipped us out."

Getting up seemed like a difficult proposition so Rahelu dragged herself over to Jhobon on all fours and plucked at his limp form until she got him onto her shoulders.

"Stay here if you want," she said to Nheras, "but the two

of us"—she hefted Jhobon up a little higher so his weight was more evenly distributed—"are going."

They were going, they would be going, as soon as she got her legs to take their combined weight. Slight and wiry though he was, his extra weight was too much for her injured leg—she staggered and fell onto her knees, then saw the dark tracks her urine-soaked trousers and dripping shirt and bleeding fingers had left on the shop's polished floor. "Shit."

The splotchy trail taunted her all the way to the door.

She needed to clean that up; in all honesty, she ought to scour the place thoroughly with Projection, to remove any Evokable trace resonance. That was supposed to have been Ghardon's job, but Ghardon wasn't here and she couldn't do that and maintain her Seeming and carry Jhobon outside.

(She didn't even want to think about the long walk back to the citadel; she might not even make it to the Lesser Gate with him but that was a knot to be undone later.)

Rahelu did the next best thing: put Jhobon back on the floor, then roll and drag him by turns. Afterward, when Maketh put him to rights (assuming Maketh could put him to rights), he'd feel every bump and bruise. She would apologize for her means once they were safe and sailing far, far away.

That plan lasted for the twelve heartbeats it took for them to tumble over the threshold, down two small steps, and into the street. Jhobon landed mostly facedown, arms twisted awkwardly. Rahelu fared better—she landed on him.

In the distance, she could see the panicked figure of the apprentice pelting towards them, shouting in alarm.

Gods. *Gods.*

After all that, they had still failed.

Her Seeming dissolved to nothing. She wanted to break down and weep. And why shouldn't she? Anathwan had made no allowances for failure; had told them as such from the beginning. She had known that; Lhorne had known that, and in her pride and arrogance, she had given no serious consideration as to what that meant.

She was bleeding; she was half-dazed from resonance backlash; she was weaponless and barefoot once more (she'd lost her belt knife somewhere and Elaram had her sandals) and everyone, everyone who could help her, she had sent away, and now the Starfather's luck had abandoned her.

Time seemed to slow as she watched her doom approach, lending an unnatural clarity to her sight. The wet cobblestones that flew out from underneath the apprentice's feet gleamed with iridescence, almost pearl-like, in the bright starlight. The buttons on his tunic were done up badly in mismatched pairings that gave him a lopsided look as every row became a diagonal, with the top two buttons at his collar and the bottom two button holes at his hem at loose ends. His bootlaces were undone; the trousers he clutched in his right hand weren't the same pair he'd worn earlier; the way his skinny legs flailed around as he ran reminded her of the Sable Gull's scrawny old rooster being chased through the yard whenever it had been caught nipping at the ducks.

The apprentice arrived in a panting, flustered flurry. "Shit," he said, staring at Rahelu and Jhobon with wide-eyed terror. "Is that a—"

"Thief? Yes, and no thanks to you," snapped a peevish male voice behind her.

Nheras stalked out from the shop to snatch the apprentice by the front of his shirt, lifting him until his sand-and-grime-caked toes barely touched the cobblestones.

"This was s'posed to be a nice, quiet starwatch an' now it ain't, a'cos you couldn't keep your trousers buttoned!"

For once in her life, Rahelu found herself thankful for Nheras's quick thinking. She sat up and put on a scowl, doing her best to play her part.

She let Nheras do the talking.

"Leavin' the key in the door? That's temptin' the Starfa-ther, that is, an' here's the thief to prove it." Nheras shook the apprentice like a ragdoll, with enough force to rattle his teeth, all the while drawing on the bone-white mists in his resonance aura to fuel her Seeming. "None of youse was here for the changeover, so me an' Pir here arrived all unsus-pecting like, an' if the rotten light-fingered guttersnipe hadn't knocked over one of your master's hammers, we wouldn't've caught 'im."

"We waited…" he protested weakly. "You were late!"

"A'course we was late; it's the summer solstice, nitwit. The streets was full-packed from here to the Lesser Gate an' all the alleyways too. Boss'll want reports now"—Nheras hocked up a wad of phlegm and spat it in his face—"to s'plain to your master, which means we gots to do the s'plaining."

"Did the thief take anything?" the apprentice choked out. His face was starting to darken and if Nheras didn't put him down soon, he was going to pass out.

"You think I'm gonna go stick my fingers in places they don't belong?"

If their situation wasn't so dire, Rahelu would have laughed. Sticking her fingers in places where they didn't belong ranked somewhere up the top on the list of *'things Nheras likes to do'*, between *'making fish-related insults'* and *'slathering her face with cosmetics'*.

"I—"

"We saw 'im here in the front. He pissed hisself then got lucky enough to stick a knife into Pir while tryin' ta s'cape. Well, Pir took care of that—we searched him an' he ain't got nothing on him. An' now that you're here, we don't need to break our backs on cleaning up in there—we gots a thief to take to the city guard's mage cells an' a report to write."

With that, Nheras hauled the apprentice up the shop's front steps and tossed him through the door, and he slid bare-assed backwards across the damp, bloodied floor.

"The mage cells?" The apprentice blanched. "He's a mage?"

"Yes, 'course he's got to be a mage," Nheras said. "Your master's alarm ain't going off, is it?"

"We need to report him to the Resonance Guild and the Houses!"

"What are you, blind as well as half-cocked?" Nheras snorted. "He ain't one of theirs—no armband, see? Just a handful of scars along the forearms. Probably a Free Territories cast-off, looking to make some gold kez to join a crew. But the way I sees it, none of this would've happened 'cept for you so that's how we'll be writin' up our account of things, an' you can go s'plain to your master how you was so eager to get your dick wet that you let a thief break into his precious shop an' leave the boss an' me an' Pir out of it."

"No! Please, no! He'll whip me and send me to the work gangs," the apprentice said. "If he isn't Guild or House and he hasn't taken anything, then no real harm done, right? So what good would putting all that detail down in ink do, except put you to a whole lot of trouble you don't need?"

Nheras folded her arms. "You want us to lie for you."

"No, no!" The apprentice wilted beneath Nheras's hard stare. "I just don't see the point in upsetting everyone. As long as nobody talks, nobody will have a problem."

"That's very fine for you and your master and the boss, but Pir and me, we're dead men the moment this one wakes up in the mage cells and starts to squeal to the city guard. Boss don't keep liars around; it's bad for business."

"So don't take him to the city guard. Can't you just leave him in a tavern or an alley somewhere, or..." He gulped. "You know."

"Ain't nothing come for free in this world, kit," Nheras said. "I hate doing reports as much as anybody else 'cept a scribbler, but I like being gainfully employed an' all my bits attached to me. What'll you give us in return?"

The apprentice hesitated, then disappeared behind the counter. He came back with two gold coins.

Nheras held out her hand. The apprentice dropped them into her open palm with a *clink* and she smiled.

Rahelu recognized that smile—she had been on the other end of it many times, usually when Nheras was about to make a very blunt point of her total victory.

"Pir an' me, we'll be going presently," Nheras said, pocketing the coins. Then she stepped forward to loom over the apprentice, leaning down until she was nose to nose with him. "But we'll be back after that, to see the end of our starwatch through an' to make sure you've done your part setting things to rights in here. If you find a single thing out of place, it's your lookout; we ain't helping you no more. An' as the Skymother is our witness, you will never, ever speak of this to us or to anyone, an' if you do, we'll swear before Seekers that we don't know a thing. You understand that?"

The apprentice nodded his head so hard that Rahelu was sure that any moment it would spontaneously detach itself from his shoulders.

"Good," Nheras said. "Now get on with it."

The apprentice scurried off obediently, presumably to fetch a broom and cleaning rags.

Turning swiftly on her heel, Nheras strode out of the shop with an authoritative *clack-clack-clack-clack* of her sandals. She disappeared around the corner, then returned a moment later with Rahelu's bloodied knife.

Rahelu expected her to wipe it off and stick it in her own belt, perhaps, or hurl it at her feet. Instead, Nheras offered her the weapon hilt first, then crouched next to her.

"Can you stand?" Nheras asked as she draped Jhobon's right arm over her shoulders.

"Yes," Rahelu said and put her belt knife away. Gritting her teeth, she hauled on Jhobon's left arm until it rested on her shoulders. With Nheras taking half of his deadweight, she managed to force herself up onto her feet.

"Can you walk?"

"I'm fine. Let's go."

Slowly, with Jhobon slung between them like a carcass, they staggered off into the night together.

WHEN THE FIERY pain that ruled her began to recede, Rahelu found herself propped up in an elegantly appointed bed by a mountain of pillows.

Someone else climbed onto the silk-covered quilt and sat on it, cross-legged, with her.

Elaram, she thought in her delirium as the white-robed figure placed a lacquered tray between them, in the middle of the bed, but that was not quite right. The unfamiliar, backlit silhouette was too tall, too poised and graceful to be Elaram.

Nheras, then?

No; there was something not right about the hair. Curled, yes, but cropped—too short—to the shoulders.

Rahelu strained, trying to remember how she had gotten here, but Evocation refused to answer. The effort made her head ring—too much resonance backlash—as if someone was currently using her skull as a mortar to pound her brains into a fine paste. A series of maze-like streets, then that long, agonizing trek up the sloping hill to the citadel, its pearlescent tower aglow beneath the bright yellow-blue moon and silvery stars. Somehow, they had gotten past the guards to the stairs; all those fucking stairs, spiraling round and round and round up the central spire to a landing that led to a corridor full of doors. One had opened for them. A jumble of noises in many voices, rushing syllables that she didn't bother stringing into words and sentences, for she couldn't think of anything other than the pain, the burning ache in her thigh, throbbing against the ragged, too-tight strip of cotton bound around the hot flesh—

She gasped as someone bathed her in ice-cold clarity.

"Elder Anathwan!" Yellow-white sparks crackled through her aura as she struggled to swing her legs out of bed so she could fall onto the rug-covered floor and bow. "I—"

The Elder laid a hand on her knee. "Be at ease."

Anathwan's voice was lullaby-gentle; her resonance aura warm and comforting, like a cheery hearth fire, but the Projection coursing through Rahelu's body was so cold it burned, inside and out. The emanations from the crystal-infused silk scroll hanging above her head—a dull drone, like a bronze gong whose dying echoes never quite faded—set her teeth on edge, chattering, as tremor after uncontrollable tremor shook her. She tucked her knees to her chest and hugged her shins in an effort to stop the shaking; whimpered as the movement tore at her wound. Her fingers came away from the makeshift bandage damp and slippery, smelling of iron and something sour. Closed her eyes and listened desperately for the soothing sound of the waves to steady the irregular cadence of her thumping heart.

The musical trickling of tea being poured. Fragrant steam rising from the cup held to her nose.

"Breathe."

Rahelu breathed. Steadied.

"Drink."

Bitter liquid touched her lips.

She spat it back into the cup. The medicinal brew was hot enough to scald and its scent reminded her of heartroot.

"Drink," Anathwan urged.

Underneath the Elder's watchful eyes, aided by the Elder's steady hands, Rahelu sipped and sipped again, until heat spread through her chest and belly. The red haze clouding her mind and vision gradually dimmed as her pain settled into a more bearable, muffled soreness.

"Good," Anathwan said when she had swallowed every last drop and could think again. The Elder took the cup away, but her eyes—intent, searching—never left Rahelu's face. At last, she asked, "Are you well, Rahelu?"

Words clamored in her throat; the flippant *'What do you think?'* and whining *'What do you care, you left me to rot for three days after a Dedicate of House Imos snuffed out every thought in my mind like a candle!'* (that had not been the Elder's fault; it was hers—hers and Maketh's, but really hers) and the bleeding obvious *'I've been stabbed through the leg, trying to steal that stupid box for you, and we very nearly didn't make it back to the citadel; of course I'm not bloody well'* shoved at each other to leap off the tip of her tongue.

As all of them skirted the same pitfall that had earned her Maketh's ire four days ago, Rahelu swallowed them and said: "Yes, Elder."

In a way, that was true.

She was alive. Her mind was intact. Her body less so, but she still had all her limbs and fingers.

Most importantly, they had successfully completed the task they had been set: no Supplicant left behind; false trails laid, pointing away from the Houses to Ruarem's apprentice and the Jade Eye Company; the box they had stolen secured —unopened—sitting on Anathwan's desk, next to a glass bowl filled with four wooden spheres.

The Elder had seemed pleased when she and Nheras had turned up with Jhobon. So why had Anathwan granted

Nheras leave to go and enjoy what remained of the summer solstice, but not released Rahelu?

Why was she being kept in the Elder's chambers, where the thick sea-stone walls were deeply carved with twisting, interwoven lines (a triple ward against any unintentional leakage of resonance) and cocooned by a permanent Obfuscation barrier anchored to the crystal lamps, one that made the barrier defending the *Winged Arrow's* great cabin look like a trainee's attempt?

Rahelu's skin prickled. Her unease grew, twisting around and around upon itself like a particularly recalcitrant vine, its grayish tendrils escaping into her aura.

What had she done now?

"This will not do," Anathwan said, and shifted the lacquered tray so it no longer lay between them. Steady, blue calm flowed from the Elder until her dread was just a faint murmur. "Look at me, Rahelu."

Rahelu dragged her gaze from the floor to meet the Elder's unblinking eyes: they were the same dark blue as the freshly poured tea in the blue-and-white cup that Anathwan held out to her.

"You are a daughter of Issolm now," the Elder said, pressing the steaming cup into Rahelu's hands, "and may speak freely with me." Anathwan poured herself another cup and patted the space next to her as though summoning a favorite pet. "Come. Sit beside me."

"Yes, Elder." Rahelu shuffled closer obediently.

"Let us take advantage of this rare opportunity to get to know each other better"—Anathwan leaned back against the pillows as she sipped—"for there may not be another."

Rahelu copied the Elder and took her own wary sip. "The most honorable Elder is very kind to take an interest in me."

"Please, Rahelu; let us dispense with such excessive formality in private. You may call me Ana."

"Yes, Ana."

"You are afraid." A pause. "What is it that you fear?"

Oh, nothing in particular, just the usual, petty concerns you'd expect of someone common-born: empty baskets and nets and sloops; missing thumbs; fists; the crunch of shattering bone and its ugly thrill; life seeping from her veins, a second-rate offering; dreamleaf haze and crystalline bites; the balancing act of exchanging dignity for coin and debt.

And dreams of blades and blood and crystal shackles.

Rahelu shrugged. "Death. Dishonor."

Both true; both insufficient.

"A very proper answer, one in keeping with Aleznuaweithish ideals." Anathwan seemed almost...disappointed. "Yet thrice now, you have chosen to pursue the most dangerous course before you. Some would call that bravery. Arrogance. Perhaps even ambition."

Some had preferred the term 'stupidity'.

But Anathwan's words were a statement, not a question, and thus Rahelu was well within the bounds of propriety to sit and sip at her awful-tasting tea and listen like a respectful little Supplicant instead of volunteering a response.

All the same, she stopped short of nodding along. Hubris was not an attribute she wanted listed alongside her name in whatever dossiers Anathwan kept on her Supplicants. She kept her eyes lowered, tracing the embroidery of silver thread on the Elder's silk coverlet; the decorative floral patterns hid carefully stitched resonance wards.

"They would be wrong. Those are the actions of someone left with no other alternative."

That jerked her head up.

How many of her secrets did Anathwan know?

"So you leveraged a scrivener's fears and an unsupervised Fortunement into assistance for forging your Petition"—she had; she had done it for the sake of her family, and she would do it all over again, still, even though she now knew what it would cost—"gained unauthorized access to the Petitioners' board"—which was an offense only punishable by warning—"and tampered with the House authenticated list of Petitioner identities."

Shit.

But that meant Anathwan had known the truth all along; had known and had decided to intervene, to cover for her; had *lied* for her—

(Had it been a lie? She tried to remember Anathwan's exact words without the benefit of Evocation; failed; and anyway, did it matter when and how she had convinced Anathwan to support her Petition? The result was the same.)

—and then made her a Supplicant.

Breathe.

Sip. Swallow.

Put the teacup—still nearly three-quarters full—down on the tray without a rattle, like you're not trying to stop your shaking hands from spontaneously shattering the whole thing into smithereens, like there isn't an extraordinarily speculative smile playing over the Elder's lips exactly like a gambler who had put a few careless coppers on dead-end odds and walked away only to come back and discover the dice roll had paid her dividends in gold.

"There," Anathwan said, putting down her empty cup. "Let there be no more secrets between us. No need to tremble so, Rahelu, for I am impressed." The Elder refilled both their cups to the brim. "It's remarkable—quite remarkable, really; improbably remarkable, as Guardian Maketh would put it—for a common-born fisher girl to manage all that on her own."

She would have called that a veiled accusation except for the conspiratorial laughter in Anathwan's eyes, and the curious lack of reference to Onneja's Augury.

"Of course, House Imos are traditionalists; they cleave to hierarchy and status as strongly as Ideth cleaves to their pretty ideals. But Issolm...."

Anathwan's smile grew wider; a subtler, more mature version of Elaram's coy invitation that snagged in the part of her that missed Anenje's comfort, reeling her in as surely as a fisher's line.

"We do what needs to be done. And we recognize potential when we see it." Another sip of that bitter brew. "Have no regrets, Rahelu. You made the right choice."

Tension she didn't realize she'd been holding in her neck and shoulders melted.

"And I believe, given the right direction, given the appropriate incentive, you will continue to do remarkable things." Anathwan leaned forward. "I see great promise in your future."

Visions danced in the air between them:

Rahelu, receiving a Dedicate's armband from Anathwan's hand.

Rahelu, at Anathwan's right shoulder, entering a grand hall with sixteen fluted pillars.

Rahelu, tall and proud with a bloodied spear in her hand, standing guard as Anathwan, crowned with gold-flecked obsidian, mounts an ebon throne and summons glory in all its blinding brilliance.

She looked up; counted thirty brushstrokes in the calligraphic scroll hanging above her head as she stretched her eyes wide, wide, wider so the tears welling up wouldn't spill over on the next eyeblink. Aleznuaweithish in style; the elegant sweeps of resonance ink and ornate flourishes recognizably Anathwan's brushstrokes but the subject—a single Chanazian character—was an incongruent choice.

"Do you recognize it?"

No.

"Anaz?"

Strange to speak the word without its matched gesture; stranger still to speak it to anyone but Onneja.

"Velaz."

A word that came up frequently when discussing the subject of her future with her parents—particularly her mother. Which meant either *'the master's sight'* or *'the sight that masters'* or even *'the sight mastery requires,'* depending on the context of its usage.

Usually, her mother meant the first.

"It is beautiful."

"Yet it is flawed. Do you see it?"

Rahelu shook her head.

"Ah," Anathwan said. Another sip of tea, a graceful shrug that sent the shorn golden curls skimming over her shoulders; a woman at perfect ease with the world and the world at ease with her command. "Perhaps in time you will. It took me years and some days it eludes me, too." The Elder's gaze flitted over her full tea cup. "My dear, is the tea not to your taste?"

"Forgive me." Rahelu took a hurried sip. "I am unused to such delicacies." Still too hot and too bitter; she would blow on it—she would've, at home—but Anathwan wasn't doing any such thing, which probably meant it would be rude.

And ruder still if she asked to be excused. Yet that was all she wanted to do with every passing moment.

How could she get out of here?

Her thoughts must be as transparent as glass for the Elder sighed again and said, "Very well. These things cannot be forced. I hope in time you'll come to trust me, as my Ela and Ghardon do. But there is one thing I must be absolutely certain of. Tell me, Rahelu: what did you agree to barter for one of Ideth's legacies?"

"I..." The room was very warm. "Nothing," she said.

"Nothing?"

"It was a gift." Anathwan raised an eyebrow at that, and Rahelu hastened to clarify. "A gift of friendship."

"You swore no oaths?"

"No." Not to him.

"Shared no blood?"

"None." Only a pallet, divided in two.

"And you are certain"—the polite, neutral tone belied the intensity of Anathwan's regard—"you gave no gift in return?"

Part of her longed to confess; longed to hear Anathwan speak those words of absolution again: *'Have no regrets, Rahelu; you made the right choice; you did what needed to be done'*, and yet—

"I'm certain," she said.

She hadn't.

The stargem didn't belong to her; it belonged to that woman, that mage-priest whose Augury she had exploited to twist Xyuth's future to her own purposes. And even if it did —even if Lhorne had wanted to keep the stargem, thinking she had left it behind for him—once the Houses had learned of the stargem's nature as a Belruonian relic, once the senior mages had dug its existence and location out of her mind, the artifact would have been taken from him.

The Elder held out a hand expectantly. "May I see your gift?"

'No', Rahelu wanted to say, but she had no grounds for refusal. Reluctantly, she complied and chewed on the inside of her cheek as the Elder prodded at the clouded resonance crystal legacy with her fingers and her resonance senses.

Anathwan frowned. "This is most unexpected." Her left hand closed upon the pendant as she seized Rahelu by the wrist with her right. Then, before Rahelu could brace herself, the Elder unleashed her Seeking:

A smear of light-splattered black-gray on purplish-blue on blue-black —clouded skies; open sea; meandering coastline—an enormous stone serpent coiled around its torch-lit hoard; gilded edifices of marble sprawls and painted white cedar towers piled between the cliff-jaws of a generous, tree-lined bay—Ennuost Yrg! How small the city seemed when viewed from the vantage of a questryl a-wing, yet still a world unto itself—*wide, terraced streets bustling; buildings bedecked with lanterns; flame-light flickering on rain-slicked cobblestones—Northpoint—a red-headed youth—Lhorne; oh, Lhorne!—in a plain, undyed tunic entering a utilitarian, gray stone complex—*

Anathwan's Seeking shuddered; the vision lost in a spinning, eye-stinging blur as some force *wrenched* the Elder's sharpening focus away from her target; an arrow arrested mid-flight and redirected:

A woman in shadow, wielding a mage-staff topped with an enormous crystal. Her gaze is as cold and implacable as a glacier.

Anathwan Issolm. Atriarch Mere Ideth's Projection caught Rahelu unprepared; the strength of it, as it tore through her skull, made her cry out—and it was not even directed at her. *I trust there is a good reason for this unscheduled conference. Have there been difficulties?*

None that are insurmountable, given time, the Elder replied. *Distance poses a problem, but the theory remains sound. Though the early signs are faint, they show promise. We should proceed with the safeguard.*

A long silence from the Atriarch. Then: *Very well.*

Something grazed the edges of Rahelu's resonance senses.

A deep, slow rumble, a tone oscillating at such low frequencies that she would have dismissed the hairs rising on the back of her arms and neck as her body's natural reaction to overextension if she had not felt a slight tightening of the Elder's fingers around her wrist.

But Anathwan continued as if nothing had happened. *I also wish to express my overdue thanks on behalf of House Issolm. House Ideth's generosity is unparalleled; I confess some difficulty in reciprocating this gift under current circumstances.*

The mission with which you have been entrusted is vital to the stability of the Dominion, Atriarch Ideth sent. I will consider the friendship between our Houses fully affirmed by your exacting efforts.

For the sake of the Dominion, I can do nothing less. The greatest of futures can only become reality when many share in the same vision.

Mere Ideth smiles, and her mage-staff flares with bright white light—

A searing sensation lanced through Rahelu's mind, like forked lightning. Warm liquid leaked from her eyes and nose —tears and snot, she assumed, until she opened her mouth to draw breath and tasted copper.

She almost wiped her face on her sleeve by instinct, then stopped herself. Instead, she rubbed at her eyes with her fingers until she heard Anathwan say: "Here," and felt a soft towel brush against her face.

Rahelu took it and looked up through bloodied eyelashes.

Elder Anathwan was still the very image of composure: her young face was unlined, her much-shortened golden curls artfully tumbling to her white-robed shoulders, her hands steady as she raised her cold teacup to her lips. Lhorne's pendant lay in her lap, its silver chain pooled around the hazy focus stone.

Rahelu's fingers twitched; she wanted to snatch it back,

feel its comforting weight around her neck and its stately pulse in sync with her heartbeats once more.

"Elder?" she asked. *'Are you done?'* sounded impertinent and *'May I have my pendant back?'* was far too direct. "Can I assist you any further with your examination?"

"No." Anathwan scooped up the pendant and let it fall into Rahelu's outstretched hand with a metallic slither. "That will be all."

Rahelu yanked the door open with trembling fingers and escaped into the receiving chamber, where she could bow properly. "Good night, Elder."

The Elder dismissed her with an absentminded wave. Golden curls fell forward in a curtain as she reached forward for the wooden box, hiding her face and the front of her robes from view.

But not before Rahelu saw the crimson droplet on the otherwise spotless white robe.

INTERLUDE I: MEDDLING

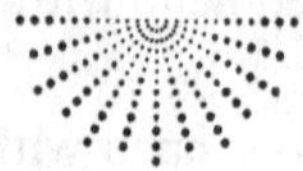

THE FUTURE WAS NOT AS UVESHT-MO HAD LEFT IT.

He squinted at ghostly visions that existed only in his mind. (Starfather, it had been too long since he'd last done this if he was *squinting*.) There was a slight chip in the stargem in his left eye that chafed against his socket. (*Careless*, he chided himself.) An irritating distraction. (The *itch*. The *pressure*. He'd forgotten.)

Threads of fate once entwined were frayed. Souls set on particular paths had strayed. Careful convergences—the product of many, many probabilities, chained in meticulous sequence—had twisted, the shape of them gone awry from what the Starfather had intended.

Why did Iweth-na wander alone, crownless, without their starbound, stargems, and sacred blade? How had Azosh-ek allowed himself to be caged and parted from his anchor? Of Egiss-te and Ogoch-em he could find no trace, as if their destinies had been snuffed out.

Was this divine punishment for their transgressions?

No, no.

Someone had been meddling.

A lesser adept would not have seen the telltale signs but they were obvious to Uvesht-mo: here, a nudge so that a heathen priest takes more than a passing interest in Iweth-na's prayers; there, a pull so a beggar's belligerence enflames Azosh-ek's erratic compulsions to new heights.

The elegant handiwork of an adept both talented and skilled. Practiced as any of his lesser once-brethren in manipulating the Starfather's grand design to their own purpose. Able to sustain the effort of Fortunement over the course of several weeks to ensure outlier probability after outlier probability eventuated.

How had the Tower known to watch for Enjela's return?

Fool. The years mired in solitude on this island, bereft of the Starfather's blessings, had rotted his brain. Those heathens would have sensed the disturbances in Fortune. As he had. As his once-brethren had.

Uvesht-mo paused to weigh the result of the meddler's work.

The gains: a fruitful alliance he had not anticipated. Sacrifices located, made, accepted. The Endless Gate opened before his once-brethren were prepared. Their cause, a half-completed ritual away from victory.

The setbacks: Iweth-na—lost—and the Divine Kingdom's most sacred instruments in the hands of heathens. The blade Azosh-ek had surrendered. The crown Iweth-na had sold. The stargems...

One still remained with Iweth-na, both guard and guide. They eluded pursuit only by virtue of its dwindling power.

The other...

The other Iweth-na had been forced to leave behind, anchoring a lesser Augury for one of the fallen children in a dingy workroom redolent with fear and pain.

So: Iweth-na had chosen to abandon their cause, as they had abandoned their sacred duties. (As Uvesht-mo had abandoned his. Well, may they both find forgiveness in the endless eyes of the Starfather.)

He pressed on, mapping unruly probabilities back through time, and discovered a second set of deviations that bore none of the same, elegant hallmarks. The original point of divergence was a heavy-handed wrenching of a scrivener's Fortune, anchored in—

Ah.

Uvesht-mo watched as a barely-trained apprentice smashed a master's grand work in ignorance:

The little black-haired meddler picks up the stargem, despite the scrivener's urging; carries it with her as she climbs the altar of old and sits, entranced, in what was once Symezosh's seat. Blood trickles from her nose; she wipes it away with her fingers; smears it across the gold-flecked, glittering surface as she bundles the stargem into her dirty tunic along with her parchments, inks, and brushes. She caresses the stargem often, unthinkingly, over the days that follow as she pursues a future that should not exist, collecting tokens and new friendships and spheres.

Then: an offhand remark from a girl with scarred hands provokes a moment of unguarded honesty. Fate diverges. The girl with the scarred hands abandons her path to collect her own promises of gold and patronage; returns to the scrivener's dingy shop to make it her own. Iweth-na's starbound dispatch both girl and scrivener with ease but do not find the stargem. They do not linger to see the little meddler rush in and kneel beside the bodies.

The sun sets; rises; sets again as her spear and her arrow make Egiss-te and Ogoch-em into sacrifices.

The Endless Gate opens.

And high upon the clifftops, at the moment of transcendence, Azosh-ek drops the sacred blade.

There was no grand act of betrayal at work. Just a senior

adept, painstakingly reassembling the leftover, shattered pieces of a masterwork, and wayward souls pursuing their most selfish desires by wielding power that was best lost and forgotten.

This, then, proved the worthiness of their cause.

All the sorrows of the world had come from Enjela's meddling; mortals ought not interfere with what the Starfather ordained.

So: the heathens, their apprentices, and the little star-touched meddler would fly across the ocean on the wings of a wooden gull, following the deeper echoes of resonance to the throne between the waves.

So: his once-brethren would choose a new heir to inherit the seat of Enjela's power, to consecrate the Endless Gate and shape the Fortune of Divine Kingdom.

So: Uvesht-mo would meet them at the door to Fortune's realm and break the eternal bonds Enjela had forged from debt and truth and love.

Let the Divine Heir Ascendant bring their Chosen; let the Tower and the Dominion bring their adepts. Let the sages of the fallen people come and make war among themselves over their leavings.

Let the very stars be heard by every soul as they herald the coming death.

The age of meddling was past.

PART II
THE SOOTY GULL

15
SUNRISE

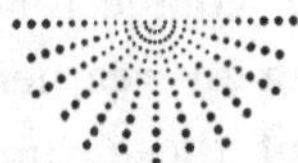

THE 16TH DAY OF TRUESUMMER,
530 A.E./A.F.

NHERAS WISHED THE SUN WOULD RISE.

Unlike Ennuost Yrg—which had been built, razed, rebuilt, re-razed, and re-rebuilt again as different Houses waxed and waned in ascendancy and newly Exalted Dominances sought to make their mark on the city felt by undertaking great public works—Peshwan Yrg adhered to no master's grand design. Districts and streets had sprung up according to the fleeting whims and transient lives of its inhabitants, which meant navigating this rat's nest of smugglers was an exercise in mazewalking.

Shivers plagued her as she followed the senior mages out of the citadel's side gate. So did the muck, no matter how carefully she placed her feet, for the excesses of the solstice festivities had glutted the clay drain pipes and, thanks to last night's rainstorm, that which belonged in the gutters could not be contained. Streams of discarded filth brimmed in the deserted streets to lap at buildings and defile their white sea stone walls.

Silence swaddled the comatose city; even the sea breeze dared not disturb the hush. They slipped down side streets and darkened alleyways, the way she used to creep through the halls of her grandmother's house on silk-stockinged feet. She had to concentrate to prevent herself from flinching at every sound. No matter how lightly she treaded, each disgusting footstep was marked by an equally disgusting *squelch* and the thick soles of her too-loud boots seemed to ring upon meeting the cobblestones. Her heavy canvas seabag, too, liked catching on weathered stone as she negotiated the tight corners of these cursed warrens; its *bump-scraaape-thuds* a steady beacon broadcasting her exact location.

Without meaning to, Nheras found herself holding her breath and listening.

Listening to the sounds behind her for angry shouts, the *crash* of thrown glass and hurled porcelain, the heavy thunder of tromping feet closing in on her position to signal that she should run as far and fast as she can.

Nothing.

Just Elaram's muffled cursing whenever Ghardon's weight unbalanced them and the occasional low murmur from Ylaen to Jhobon in that barbaric mongrel speech of theirs. And the uneven hobbling gait of Fishguts limping along on the crutch the healers had given her, right at the very back of their dismal group.

Of course there was nothing; of course they passed through the Lesser Gate unchallenged. She was letting her feelings get in the way of deliberate, rational thought. Why, the whole city had scarcely passed out from its solstice revelry in a drunken stupor before Csorath had shaken them out of their beds and into the costumes Anathwan had ordered them to wear as part of their adopted guise as smugglers.

There was no reason to think that anybody would be after them. She had scoured the insides of the Bronze Turtle with the most intense Projections she could muster before Ruarem's apprentice had returned. She had done everything possible to ensure that any blame once Ruarem discovered the switched boxes would fall upon his apprentice—and had suitably impressed that fact upon him before they had left.

But the events of the previous night kept replaying themselves in her mind. Like a waking nightmare she could not shake, or an Evocation gone wrong.

It is two spans past deepnight by the time they return to Anathwan's apartments at the citadel.

The Elder welcomes them with a smile. She has nothing but good things to say as they lay Jhobon down on the rug next to the equally unconscious Ghardon.

She is pleased to inform them that they have passed her test.

She is effusive with praise for Rahelu's tenacity, her inventiveness, her determination to leave no one behind.

'A show of loyalty worthy of a true daughter of Issolm,' says the Elder to the glassy-eyed fisher girl. 'House Issolm has great need of such unwavering loyalty.'

She concludes her review with a simple remark for Nheras: 'A fine display of strength.'

During her private audience, when Nheras had intimated her (well-received) goals, the Elder had seeded expectations of her own and Nheras had taken note.

'Strength' was not among Anathwan's most desired attributes for her handpicked Supplicants; 'loyalty' was what topped the list.

'The Elder is kind and gracious beyond words,' they chorus.

Nheras had seethed inwardly as she bowed. So sharp was the contrast in the Elder's appraisal of her two Supplicants that even the slow-witted upstart Lowdocks brat understood the implications.

Fishguts had actually been *gloating* as she mimicked Nheras, badly—all of the forms, with none of the humility.

Anathwan waves away their bows and their Elder-you-honor-me's. 'Worry not for your brother or for young Jhobon here; Guardian Maketh has things in hand.'

The mage-tranced Imos Dedicate looks like he is one working away from collapse. Maketh has stuffed the corners of two small handkerchiefs in his nostrils to stem what must be the mother of all nosebleeds. Twin droplets form at the dangling ends of the saturated cotton as he bends over the two unconscious Supplicants.

'Go,' the Elder instructs Nheras, and Nheras alone, for her former cabinmate has not risen from her obeisance. 'The rest of the night is yours to enjoy as you please. Supplicant Elaram is in her apartments and Supplicant Ylaen departed for the solstice festivities a little while before your return.'

Neither option appeals. 'Elder, Supplicant Rahelu—'

'Will remain here with me a little longer.' Anathwan makes a little shooing motion at her—the kind reserved for stray cats and small children—then bears Fishguts away in her arms.

The door to the Elder's bedchamber shuts.

Nheras had passed, but she had been bested—which effectively equated to failure.

By definition, there could only be one favorite.

Dazed by the summary dismissal, she had remained where she was, thoughts and resonance aura a-whirl until Dedicate Csorath arrived with two men in tow.

One was the Winged Arrow's third mate. Like his captain, Kerg had adopted the guise of a tavern tough.

The other terrified-looking man—the artificer, Ruarem—had shuffled in with the stiff gait of someone being propelled by a heavy-handed Projection, his reluctance manifest in his white-knuckled grip on his necklace of prayer beads.

Csorath's Seeking precedes him into the room: a black, blade-edged whirlwind that tears through Anathwan's apartments, slicing through the active barriers and flaying the resonance auras of every soul present until the ambient resonance bleeds with their memories. The Seeking rouses Maketh from his mage-trance (his aura no more intact than any of the Supplicants') and knocks her to her hands and knees.

While she gasps and struggles to reconstruct the shattered layers of the identity her grandmother has carefully crafted for her, the Guardian says to the Seeker:

'Are we secure?'

'For now. Your target?'

'Fled.'

Csorath grunts. 'Our transport?'

'Compromised.'

'The crew?'

'Also compromised.'

Heavy silence.

'I have enacted countermeasures. Alozei has supplied an alternative.'

An even heavier silence as Csorath confirms the new arrangements with another Seeking.

'Kerg.' Csorath's voice is devoid of inflection. 'Find Captain Alozei and thank her for providing us with House Imrell's best. Supply her volunteers with tokens of our appreciation and conduct them to the nearest solstice festivities to spend them. Then go to the Winged Arrow—you and two deckhands of your choosing will not be continuing on to Anazvela after all.'

A flagrant (but understandable) violation of security protocols on the Isonn Dedicate's part; she wouldn't want to step aboard an Imrell vessel without somebody she could rely on unreservedly either.

Not for the first time, Nheras bitterly resented the fact that Rahelu had Petitioned successfully and Bhemol and Kiran had not. She didn't want two new sisters and a brother who conspired to keep her out of their confidences and insisted on referring to her by her grandmother's name instead of the one they all shared; she wanted the cousins who understood her.

Maketh's retort is swift. 'They have not been cleared for this mission.'

'Nor have Alozei's rabble. I want them—and Alozei's ill-gotten goods—off my ship.'

'You do not have the authority to—'

'Neither do you. Will you reacquaint Alozei of the strict need to adhere to mission procedures or shall I spare you the strain?'

A pause. Maketh reluctantly concedes the point. 'I will remind her that only those who have been vetted by the Atriarchs may sail with us, as I need not remind you that House Imrell's best—ill-gotten or not—is what enables us to continue. Now: will you recall the guise we are to adopt and countermand your orders?'

'The crossing can be treacherous. I'll not attempt such a passage with an unfamiliar crew.'

'Anathwan kept those concerns in mind when she chose our Supplicants. Ylaen, Jhobon, and Rahelu are accustomed to sailing.'

'Your nephew will be drunk; his sly shadow is comatose; and the foolhardy fisher girl has heart but has never sailed beyond sight of the shoreline.'

Maketh grimaces. 'They are what we have.'

'They will not suffice. Even if your current undertaking succeeds.'

Maketh has no rebuttal to that.

'My mate sails with us. Kerg, go make your farewells, then see to the loading of that Imrell sloop. None of Alozei's ruffians are to stow so much as a single parcel before it passes your inspection.'

'Aye, captain!' the mate says and leaves.

The door to Anathwan's bedchamber reopens. Out stumbles Fishguts, backing away in a clumsy bow, fingers shaking as she tucks the Ideth pendant back inside her shirt.

Elder Anathwan herself emerges shortly after, stolen box in hand. 'Ah, Dedicate Csorath. Thank you for your safe escort of our guest. Welcome, artificer. Your arrival is most timely. Dedicate, you may leave the artificer in my care, for I wish to consult him on a matter of some minor importance, and you'—Nheras's stomach plummets as a slight crease appears between the Elder's brows at the sight of her, still present, contrary to orders—'are required elsewhere.'

Fearful of jeopardizing her diminished standing with Anathwan and House Issolm even further, she scuttles out after a hasty bow of her own.

Nheras had kept pace with Rahelu as she headed for the House stores. More out of habit than conscious thought, for she detested walking about alone.

She had also grown accustomed to the fisher girl's presence. The first night aboard the *Winged Arrow* had been almost unbearable; she'd spent it lying awake in her bunk, eyes squeezed shut against the dark, counting the heartbeats until sunrise, the sound of her cabinmate's breathing and restless tossing about her only reassurance that the night was not eternal. Then the next day Fishguts had to flap her tongue in some ill-considered backtalk, like she always did, and the second night with its tomb-like silence was the worst night Nheras had spent in a long, long time. When the third day had dawned without her cabinmate reporting to the main deck, she'd almost approached Ghardon and Elaram about taking a turn in their vigil.

She hadn't, because that would have required her to speak to them, and also because they wouldn't have let her since they thought she would try to steal the Ideth legacy that Rahelu didn't deserve. (Which she would not. There were other legacies; other paths to power. Especially if the rumors about the artifact they had stolen were true.) So she'd spent the rest of the voyage to Peshwan Yrg exploring the library in the ship's study and becoming thoroughly acquainted with her copy of the Issolm *Supplicant's Handbook*.

At any rate, they'd gotten no further than fifty strides from the Elder's door before Fishguts said—

'Your apartments are down the other hallway.'

The apartments assigned to her at the citadel are dark and windowless.

She glances from Rahelu's wobbly trajectory through the hallway to the filthy makeshift bandage around her right leg and the still-bleeding slices on her fingers and tells the dense, resonance-mazed girl in no uncertain terms: 'Don't be fish-brained stupid. You need to see a healer.'

Instead of taking her statement as the sensible, correct advice that it is, Fishguts glares back, aura ruffled red and leaking through her short-lived resonance ward. 'I'll be fine. More than fine, after I pack it with enough numbweed and get some private, undisturbed rest.'

Seeing how Elaram had run off and Ghardon had been in no state to look out for House Issolm interests, it had fallen to Nheras to explain.

She patiently points out how Rahelu is not remotely qualified to make that assessment on account of her failing the second-year prerequisites for healing and her impaired judgment, and that self-administering back-alley cure-alls is not an appropriate act for a daughter of House Issolm to engage in when they are about to embark on the next stage of a critical mission, Elaram's usual conduct notwithstanding.

That had unleashed a slew of insults ("What would you

know about taking care of injuries? You've never so much as stubbed your toe on a cobblestone!") that were below both Nheras's dignity and her pay grade to respond to.

'Suit yourself,' she says. 'We all must do our duty to the Dominion and our Houses, however we can. The rest of us will serve as the combat-capable Supplicants the Elder requires. I suppose you'll still be of some use, even as a cripple with a clawed hand. As you were so quick to remind me, you've had a lifetime of practice at hauling and gutting fish. Best that you stick to your area of expertise; we wouldn't want you to overexert yourself.'

And while Rahelu works her jaw in a perfect imitation of a gasping goldfish that had stranded itself on a decorative rock lining its pond, she pulls out one of the two gold coins in her pocket.

'Here.' She tosses the gold kez at the fisher girl, knowing full well she won't have the reflexes or the hand-eye coordination to catch it through her resonance backlash, and says: 'Your share of the spoils,' before striding off in the direction of the House stores herself in order to lay her hands on as many oil lamps as possible.

Nheras had not looked back to watch Rahelu fumble the coin and listen to her mangle whatever unoriginal, tedious response her fish brain managed to squeeze out.

Nheras did not look back now, as their stealthy procession snaked through side streets to steer well clear of the Bronze Turtle then turned south towards the narrow piers of Sunport. Rahelu's irregular footsteps had gradually grown fainter, as though she had fallen further behind, but the Chanazian curses she was muttering to herself carried well enough on the early breeze so Nheras felt justified in her decision to walk in the uncertain gap behind the senior mages and ahead of the other Supplicants.

Thanks to her, Fishguts was doing just fine.

No need to shame them both by offering an arm.

When Rahelu tripped and fell over for the sixth time at the junction where the rough-hewn stone of the city met the weathered wood of the docks jutting out into the sea, Nheras had the unwelcome twinges of guilt in her stomach under control.

Ahead of her, the senior mages slowed their steps and stopped.

Dedicate Csorath held up one hand, his shoulders tensed. "Kerg?"

Elder Anathwan, in a low voice pitched to carry no further than a stride or two: "What is it?"

The Isonn Seeker-captain stared at the rickety sloop tied up in front of them with the pointed regard of someone contemplating arson. Understandably so. The only thing the *Sooty Gull* had in common with the *Winged Arrow* was that their namesakes both possessed feathers. If you squinted very hard, you could be persuaded of a vague similarity in the shape of the *Gull's* narrow hull and the first eartharc rays brightening the sky did reveal the sails to be more or less whiteish underneath heavy patches of scrap canvas. Nails and planking creaked as it bobbed up and down at anchor.

This was the best Alozei Imrell had to offer?

What was House Imrell playing at by giving them such a rundown boat? Nobody expected them to be happy about turning over one of their ships to be sailed under Isonn command, but this mission's success was in House Imrell's interests as well as those of every other House.

"The *Gull* sits too low in the water and is listing to port." Without further preamble, Csorath braced his feet wide and sank into mage trance.

There was no change in Anathwan's bearing or posture, but the ambient resonance around her seemed to thicken and quiver even as Maketh turned towards the sloop's waiting gangplank.

Nheras backed up five strides and dropped her seabag to hiss, "Ssshhh!" over her shoulder at the other Supplicants.

Jhobon made no complaint as Ylaen eased him down into a sitting position on the dock but Ghardon raised a brief flurry of protests in the form of flailing arms that required a more pointed, poorly shielded Projection of, *Sit down, stay put, and don't try to be a hero,* from Elaram to quell.

Fishguts remained prone, bruised cheek resting against the sea-damp granite, numbweed-dilated pupils swimming in and out of focus.

Probably for the best.

Nheras loosened her baton from its leather tie on her belt; Ylaen and Elaram followed suit with throwing knives and crossbow. They held their stances and readied Projections while Csorath's Seeking raked the sloop from prow to stern and topmast to rudder before spiraling out to sweep every boat in every berth in the Sunport and probably a good part of the Outermarket district.

The Isonn Dedicate surfaced from his Seeking trance just as the Skymother's lamp cleared the horizon. "Kerg is below, dealing with an uninvited guest."

An impression flashed between the senior mages. Slippery and quicksilver, too fast for Nheras to catch more than a glimpse:

> —a vivid, too-real sensation of being squeezed through a cracked door into a lightless space that is already full. The resisting force inside pressing back. Air, from her lungs, and the very essence of herself streaming out to join the bone-white mists drowning her resonance aura as—

"I can find no traces of any others," Csorath added as the Elder and the Guardian examined the sloop for themselves.

Anathwan pursed her lips. "There are no active Seemings."

"And I sense no barriers," Maketh said.

Csorath nodded and strode towards the gangplank with Maketh close behind.

"Hold," the Elder said.

The two Dedicates stopped.

Anathwan beckoned Nheras, Elaram, and Ylaen forward.

The Guardian objected immediately. "I do not think that—"

"They are here to learn."

Maketh Imos looked past the Elder to the end of the pier, where the other three Supplicants had slumped together, then back at the three of them.

Elaram, whom he had named a liability.

Ylaen, who idly spun his knives, then ruined the image by nearly dropping one in an uncharacteristic fumble, the product of the night of overindulgence Csorath had predicted.

And Nheras herself.

She lifted her chin in response to the Guardian's scrutiny. *Here I am.* The only Supplicant fit for the job at hand. *And I am ready.*

"Perhaps a supervised Concordance—" Maketh began.

The Supplicants on either side of her shifted restlessly; Elaram was practically hopping from foot to foot. While Nheras didn't do anything so undignified, she agreed with the sentiment: she had not left her grandmother's House just to be a passive source of power for a senior mage's workings some of the time and a glorified servant for the rest.

"They will learn nothing if you shield them from all risk," Anathwan said.

"We will learn nothing if they fail."

"Even so."

Maketh pressed his lips into a thin line. Would he argue further?

Nheras hoped not.

"Do not underestimate their capabilities," the Elder continued. "Their results thus far are proof enough. Let them investigate what is amiss."

A fine display of strength.

The memory rankled.

May the gods show mercy to whoever had tried to interfere with their mission because Nheras would show none, just as soon as Anathwan gave the order. She gauged the distance to the sloop, the tentative way its gangplank bridged the gangway and the dock as if whoever had lowered it had both been in a great hurry and didn't care much if it fell into the sea, for the bottom edge was precariously balanced on the very lip of the dock and the sloop's up-and-down motion had pulled half of it into midair.

She had a reputation to repair.

After another brief hesitation, Maketh stepped aside, but Anathwan gave no orders herself; instead, she turned to Csorath.

The Isonn Dedicate looked from Elaram to Nheras to Ylaen. "Exercise vigilance. Expect resistance. Capture them alive for questioning," he said. "Do not damage any part of the ship."

Nheras sprang into action. A straight sprint down to the end of the pier, followed by a strategic, bounding leap across the gangplank that knocked its base loose from the dock and sent it splashing into the water.

How unfortunate.

For the others.

Nheras smiled as her boots were first to land on the *Sooty Gull's* deck with a satisfying *thump*. She duly sent her resonance senses racing over the sloop in a precautionary Seeking. Of course, nobody else was on deck from bowsprit to sternpost, nor hiding in the rigging or behind a Seeming.

Lynath Ilyn, though, had a favorite saying: *Trust, but verify.*

It was always worth the effort to confirm what she'd been told for herself.

Nheras stopped smiling as two more pairs of boots thudded behind her and an orange ribbon of resonance snaked its way around her, down through the cargo hatch.

Oh no. Ylaen could have his way in any number of things —certainly, she'd been very accommodating of his whims thus far—but this wasn't one of them. She threw open the hatch, snapping his ribbon in two, and steeled herself for the next jump.

In that fraction of a heartbeat, Elaram ducked past and scurried down the companionway.

"Hellooooooo!" the Issolm Supplicant sang. "We know you're in here! Come on out and let's talk."

Damnable, excitable Elaram.

Nheras gripped the edges of her fear, pulled every bit of it out of her aura, compacted the resonance into a crackling, bone-white sphere.

Down into the darkness.

"Move," she said to Elaram, trusting more to her resonance senses than her eyes to pinpoint the Seeker-in-training on the stern side of the hold.

Then, to herself: *move!*

Her feet stayed rooted to the spot directly beneath the hatch, inside the faint square of dim, grayish light.

It didn't matter.

Muffled pulsing behind the aft bulkhead. The resonance signature was too regular and too simple to belong to Kerg. Some sort of partially Obfuscated beacon, then. Either containing embedded Projections to be broadcasted at preset intervals and intensities through an encrypted relay, or a prepared node that would allow a Seeker to bypass any resonance wards or Obfuscation barriers around the vessel.

Or both.

Whatever it was, it had not been fully keyed yet, which meant whoever had planted it was still nearby. But before she could flee back up the ladder and rush over to the aftercabin, Ylaen made his presence felt.

Cool amusement swelled on the other side of the bulkhead and snuffed out the beacon.

Bested *again*.

Nheras wanted to scream.

Clearly, she had spent too long around Fishguts because that was the sort of perfectly undignified reaction Rahelu loved to indulge in.

But something was not quite right.

Elaram had stopped pressing her ear against the aft bulkhead; Elaram was wriggling across the cargo deck on her belly and elbows like a worm; Elaram was so preoccupied with her Seeking that she crawled between Nheras's shaking, planted feet and underneath the bottommost rung of the ladder, past row after row of water casks and crates, deeper and deeper, into the guts of the cargo hold, towards the gaping black maw at the ship's fore.

Footsteps overhead announced Ylaen's exit from the aftercabin.

I foooooooouuund them! Elaram sent, without bothering to shield her Projection at all.

Which was as good as a broadcast to anyone on board—and anybody listening. Had the Issolm Supplicant lost her senses, assuming she had had any to begin with?

Elaram met Nheras's glare with a wide, merry smile, waving frantically. *You two have got to look at this. It's the strangest thing ever.*

Was this a truce? Or a trap?

Probably neither; she was simply Elaram's only available audience at present. Also, Elaram was a coward who always tried to keep at least two other people between herself and any possibility of melee combat so she could pick off her targets from a distance.

As soon as she gripped Elaram's grimy, cobwebbed-strewn hand, the crisp details of a Seeking bloomed in her mind:

Two bodies in a chalk circle, drawn in the tight space between a disordered stack of waxed-canvas-wrapped silk bolts and bales of fine cotton.

The first body sprawls face down, half-buried by fallen sacks of humming resonance crystal fragments. No detectable resonance signature.

Dead, then; or close to it, though the fresh wound spanning the right arm from wrist to elbow did not seem deep enough to be the cause. Matted hair hid the face and clothes hid most of the skin, but the fraying cotton could not hide what the body was: a dirty, gangly girl who was mostly bone and couldn't have been much older than twelve or thirteen summers. Her left arm bore a deeper scar that mirrored her new wound.

Not the Conclave spy they'd been led to expect.

The second body—Kerg's—bleeds freely from a matching gash down his left arm. The third mate's eyes are wild; his chest heaving in erratic, shallow gasps as he struggles with himself, jaw working soundlessly as though he is trying to scream while holding his tongue.

One hand drives a bloodstained blade towards his throat—

Unease prickled her at the sight of the serpentine steel dagger.

Every Free Territories ship clan member carried a ritual knife once they were blooded, but how many of those knives had golden hilts?

And Kerg had no scars.

—as the other hand clamps its fingers tight around the wayward wrist and tries to wrench the weapon away. His resonance signature is disjointed; the calm, placid beat that had held steady before the Stormbringer's breath clashing with a second syncopated rhythm.

Nheras frowned. *What is that?* she sent. *It's like his resonance signature has been corrupted.*

"No idea," Elaram whispered back. "It's strange, right? But he's no Seeming. That's Kerg, in the flesh."

Nheras stood and craned her head over water casks to get a direct line of sight.

"Why are you dithering? Hurry up and hit him with a heavy dose of calm or something already, so we can get to the fun part!"

Nheras snorted. *Not how this works, Issolm.*

You couldn't just throw Projections around without regard for how their frequencies might interact with the prevailing resonances, especially if you wanted your target to be capable of coherent speech afterwards. Kerg's emotional state was too volatile. His fear had naturally thickened into a rudimentary Obfuscation barrier and the ambient resonance surrounding him was rank with uncontrolled emanations. And of all the primal emotions, fear was the strongest and reacted in the most unpredictable ways.

Too little calm and she wouldn't be able to get through. A failed Projection was just as liable to freeze him in place as to incite a mad, frenzied attack, and the last thing they needed was a disadvantaged fight in unfamiliar, cramped quarters with close to zero visibility.

Too much calm, too suddenly, and his mind would snap.

No, the current situation required the more controlled approach of a true Harbinger in the making. Let Elder Anathwan see that she was capable of subtlety as well as strength.

Nheras drew on the percolating bone-white mists and forged it into a thick, gleaming chain that bound the mate's will to hers. Envisioned the action she desired from him: dagger relinquished; weaponless hands to his head; four slow, measured steps to bring him into the weak shaft of light shining through the open hatch.

Intent rippled down their connection.

Kerg stiffened.

She felt resistance—his untrained mind instinctively rejecting her intrusion before his body could act on the sudden compulsion—and pushed harder.

His will was divided; hers was not. His innate desire for autonomy was strong, but her desire for dominance was stronger; backed by the power in the resonance crystals she wielded, and the absolute conviction that what she wanted him to do was also the *right* thing for him to do.

COME OUT.

Kerg stood, blade wavering.

Put the knife down. She sweetened her subliminal Projection with another visualization. Added a touch of reassurance. *The intruder is dead. Put the knife down. Reinforcements have arrived. Put the knife down. Your captain awaits you. Put the knife down. The danger is past.*

The mate shuffled out of the darkness. Slow, measured steps, just as she'd intended, with his arms hanging loose and relaxed at his sides.

But he still held the knife.

"Uh, Nheras?"

Kerg's eyes locked onto the two of them, pupils shrinking as they focused.

Up went Elaram's loaded crossbow as she scurried back. "You *do* have him under control, don't you?"

"Of course I do." The brief resistance she'd felt before was gone. Kerg was hers, mind and body, and so her will was his. He walked forward to meet them because he wanted to, because she wanted him to, because there was no longer a distinction between what he wanted and what she wanted.

Nevertheless, Nheras began moving too. "Put that crossbow away before you ruin everything."

"Not if you're retreating."

"I'm not retreating; we're relocating to somewhere more appropriate for an interrogation."

Somewhere more conducive to monitoring physical reactions so those could be corroborated with what they gathered through Seeking. Like the sunny main deck.

"If that's what you want to call it." Elaram darted past the companionway to take cover behind the ship's unlit fire hearth. "But if *you* can't make him drop the knife—"

Nheras ground her teeth. Some nerve, from a nosy little nuisance who had barely passed second-year Projection studies, whose shoddy Obfuscation barriers meant the average third-year trainee taking Harbinger electives could flatten her at will.

Commands weren't wishes; they were substitute decisions.

Just because she was currently in charge of how Kerg's decisions were made didn't mean he wasn't aware of what he was doing. If she wanted to retain control, she needed to feed him rationale that he would accept, and right now, she was contending with a layer of his mind that was unnaturally attached to that golden-hilted knife.

"—*I'll* make him."

Oh no. Nobody was going to steal further credit away from her. Nheras braced her body against the nearest supportive surface—a wooden post—and poured more of herself into the next Command:

SURRENDER.

Her awareness split. For one disorientating moment, she confronted herself twice: the power-wreathed form of she-who-was-Nheras pulling on the wounded, resonance-enchained body of he-who-was-Kerg. Resolute, she shut her eyes, tightened her grip on their forced connection, and hurtled through.

The solidity of the post against her back and the coolness of the shadow someone had cast across her face fell away.

They gasped.

How that gash in his arm burned!

Focus on the pain, and only the pain.

The pain. The pain!

Doesn't it hurt?

Oh, it hurts so much.

Don't you want that pain to go away?

Yes, yes; anything to make it go away.

Then drop the knife.

The knife?

Yes, the knife. Let go of it.

Let go. The knife.

Let go, Kerg, and—

Who do I see, descending from the sky?

Ah, *there* you are.

Who is he who brings the sunrise as his shadow?

Hello, little cub.

The *thud* of Ylaen's sudden arrival—of course he would choose that exact, most inconvenient moment; of course he had to make his entrance stupidly dramatic—upset their delicate stand-off.

Kerg raised the knife.

Elaram took aim.

And Nheras could not afford to lean on subtlety any longer. She called to every focus stone she wore as Ylaen busied himself with gawking at the wound in Kerg's arm, the golden-hilted ritual knife that had made it, and the trail of blood that led deeper into the hold, face pale and waxen like he'd seen a vengeful shade.

Power flowed down the chain-bond as she unleashed everything she had:

SURRENDER—

Her Command went awry. Somebody—not Ylaen—snatched control away from her. The connection she had forged out of their mutual fear snapped; her claim on Kerg's body superseded by an inexplicably greater one.

—*TO ME.*

Panic surged as the usurper robbed her of all physical senses. She couldn't see; couldn't hear; couldn't taste or smell or touch. She dangled over the void—an absolute, all-consuming darkness that threatened to swallow her soul— from the end of a disintegrating chain anchored to a pinprick of light.

Her body.

The faintest strain of music. A cascade of sparkling notes plucked from a zither, in a bright and beautiful memory.

Nheras grasped at those notes, those flickering links of resonance, begged them to *hold, please hold, just stay together for* —*for*—what had she been promised?—*ten heartbeats.*

Ten heartbeats; that was all she needed to find her way back from the void; that was all she had before the thin wisps of the anchoring connection completely dissolved, subsumed into whatever battle must surely be taking place between Ylaen and Elaram and the usurper who had Suborned Kerg somehow.

Ten—eight—five—two—one—

Pain. *Pain.*

Left side numbed from the blunt impact of her fall; right side spasming, body curling in upon itself. Throbbing in the back of her skull. Eyes boiling in their sockets. The smell of scorched wood and singed hair and smoldering cotton. Hot liquid running from earlobe to collarbone; hotter, searing shards of resonance crystal and glowing globules of molten metal spraying across cheek and jaw.

My earring. Her heart lurched. The little songbird of polished jet in its tin wire cage; the shimmering resonance crystal bead in its open beak had shattered. At that realization, an even more useless part of her wailed: *My earring, my earring, my—*

Shut up, shut up, shut up!

So her father's cheap little gift was gone; the granddaughter of Lynath Ilyn (or the favored Supplicant—Dedicate —of Anathwan Issolm) could easily afford another. Of real onyx and silver, or perhaps even black opal or jade.

She forced the silly voice and its stupid fixation to the back of her mind and turned her attention to the garbled sounds coming into focus.

"—your last chance!"

Elaram's high-pitched warning floated over the guttural phrases Ylaen and he-who-was-no-longer-Kerg flung at each other, quickly and viciously, with the same kind of force that Ylaen might use to hurl knives.

"I don't want to hurt anyone but I will shoot if I have to."

Do not *shoot, you trigger-happy little imbecile!* Nheras wanted to scream at Elaram but her lungs wouldn't inflate and her mouth wouldn't stop retching and reaching for Projection felt like shoving a hairpiece made from a string of firecrackers wrapped around barbed wire onto her head while someone lit the fuse: *pop-poppop-pop-POP-POP-POP-POP!*

"Soul eck na." Kerg's mouth moved, spewing Free Territories gibberish: "Uh chwaar te geesh nor."

Soul—or sole?—*eck*—deck?—*na*—no?—*uh chwaar te geesh nor.* Spoken emphatically, with grave importance. Had she heard wrong? Had he perhaps named 'Ochwa-ret,' the westernmost port in the Free Territories?

Long answers in the same nonsensical shit from Ylaen. He and Kerg growled at each other like circling dogs, desperate urgency distorting everything they said.

"I mean it!" Elaram cried.

Nheras flailed around for her baton, the post, any free sources of resonance and something to support herself with, so she could get up and Command them all to speak a civilized tongue she understood but nothing and no one obeyed her, least of all her own damned, resonance-wracked body.

The only thing her ringing ears could pick out of the noise

filling the hold were the last few syllables Ylaen spat: "—xov resh e soareck far, zaiya!"

Soar wreck far? Tsorek-fa!

The pirate-infested stronghold on the largest island in the Free Territories of Abmerdu, which the ship clans loftily called the city of sails.

Elaram shouted, "Three!"

Orange flared in the other girl's resonance aura as Kerg charged Ylaen.

Oh no; no, gods, *no*.

That wasn't Elaram's panic; that was hers, *hers*; hers that had spilled outwards from her uncontrolled resonance aura in that fractional heartbeat when she had lost her senses and overwhelmed the other girl's laughable Obfuscation barrier to infect her.

Steel blades *clanged*.

A shriek: "Two!"

The older, bigger mate forced the Imos Supplicant back, and back again—

(Ylaen wasn't fighting; he was still *talking*; why, in the four heavens, wasn't he fighting, or using Projection, or doing anything remotely useful?)

—until they slammed into the water casks. Their blades, locked hilt to hilt, crept closer and closer to Ylaen's throat. Waved edge ground against tapered edge in a shrill metallic *screeeeeeech* that drowned out Elaram.

Who mouthed, *One*—

Nheras screwed her eyes shut.

"Kerg," Ylaen gasped.

All technique, all clever tactics, all control exhausted. The only resource available to exploit: her own raw emotions. She attempted visualization anyway—sunrise, to vanquish the darkness—as she surrendered to pure panic.

One, yes, one; one; one unending scream to slash

through wall after wall curtain after curtain night after night of smothering stone and silk and darkness, until there is nothing left no veil no hiding no hindering that scream as it rings and rings across the room through the halls the house the cold, cold city and the wide, wide world until the skies and the very heavens must ring with it.

A fiery orange conflagration exploded from her aura, setting the ambient resonance in the ship's hold ablaze and knocking everyone inside akilter.

Elaram jerked.

Click-THUNK! as her crossbow bolt slammed into something wooden.

Then finally, *finally*, that shrinking coward started acting like the Imos-blooded mage he was supposed to be instead of the drunken ship lout he'd been playing at.

Ylaen reached, but not for Command; for fucking useless *Seeking*:

Kerg.

The mate's resonance signature rippled through the hold. It cut across the wake of her uncontrolled release of emotion to reach Elaram on the opposite side; Elaram who picked up the pulse and returned it, doubled, until the ambient resonance and the surrounding timbers thrummed with the steadfast beat:

Kerg. Kerg. KERG. KERG. KERG!

Recognition sparked.

The wild look in Kerg's eyes receded (as shadows recede before the sun).

The knife he still held receded (its shining steel edge

came away from Ylaen's bobbing throat crimsoned from the thin line it had nicked alongside his windpipe).

The mate's aura sputtered as the foreign, jagged rhythms tried—and failed to reestablish themselves as the steady pulsing that was Kerg's true resonance signature swelled and tripled.

Gods, oh gods be praised; they had attained their purpose after all.

Well done, Nheras. You can stop screaming in panic any time you like now. As Grandmother says, the daughters of House Ilyn do not scream.

Imagine the sunrise shrinking, shrinking, shrinking until it becomes a lantern, a candle, a single burning coal you can snuff out, leaving only its residual traces to fade and haunt the dark.

"Thank fuck that worked," Elaram said, while she lowered her spent crossbow, while Ylaen sagged to the deck, while Nheras finally managed to locate her dropped baton and roll onto her hands and knees, while those very last residual traces of panic sank into Kerg's untrained, unshielded person, unsettling the hard-won control he had wrested back from whoever had seized his body.

Steel flashed in the third mate's hand.

No, no!

She was up, she was moving; Elaram scrambling to reload; Ylaen, the closest, had raised his knife—

Disasters, Maketh Imos had called them. Graduated mages incapable of protecting themselves the moment they were put to the test. Unworthy of their Houses.

The Guardian was right.

They were too slow, too sloppy, too late to stop Kerg from slashing his own throat.

16

GULL

Rahelu panted as she heaved the last sack of resonance crystals out of the concealed compartment Elaram had discovered in the forepeak and shoved it overhead through the hidden hatch.

How she had ended up being the one crawling in here when she was also the only one sporting a leg injury as well as the world's biggest resonance-induced headache, she didn't quite recall. In point of fact, most of the walk from the citadel to Sunport and then boarding the sloop that had awaited them was a long blur lost to the lovely, floating sensation that had settled over her after being dosed up on numbweed and an assortment of other potions by the House healers. She had a vague recollection of being escorted from the healers' level to unfamiliar apartments to the citadel's side gate, skipping through wonderfully silent streets, followed by a restful time of lying down on soothing, cool rock that alleviated the feverish flush in her face while she marveled at the play of light and shadow as the Skymother lit her lamp over the sea, then being picked up and carried like a ragdoll by somebody who was all willowy curves over a strong, sturdy frame. At some point, when the fog had mostly receded (though the floating sensation remained), she found herself leaning against the inside curve of the prow and Nheras's nasally voice demanding would she please hurry up and start passing her those sacks before Captain Csorath berated them for their lack of visible progress. Between the residual haze and the numbweed and the shock of Nheras actually including the word *'please'* in anything she said, Rahelu had sat there blinking to herself in the cozy little space before a second, ruder, more normal remark from Nheras prodded her into action.

As the sack disappeared from view, Rahelu wondered whether anyone would come to pull her out, too.

The Isonn Dedicate had set the Supplicants to work: searching every nook and cranny aboard for other tracking beacons and embedded Seeking nodes masked by the presence of more obvious resonance crystals and planted inside hidden compartments that might be secreted in the hull, the keel, the bulkheads, the decks; inspecting the contents and seams of every sack and cask and barrel for evidence of tampering; airing out every piece of fabric aboard, from the bales of cotton and bolts of silk to the spare sails and hammocks, examining every finger-width of rope to ensure all were in good condition; and ten thousand other tasks that would have been at least a solid day's work for a full complement of twelve crew. Once all chores had been assigned, the captain had marched off to join the Elder and Dedicate Maketh, who had barricaded themselves inside the aftercabin at the stern.

A soft *thud* overhead as Nheras dropped the sack next to the rest of the cargo they had dragged out of the *Sooty Gull's* hold.

Rahelu folded her arms across her drawn-up knees and rested her head for a little while longer. The numbweed and the potions had done their job; she felt no pain at present, only a muted throbbing in her thigh and stiffness to her gait.

Nheras did not come back.

Not that Rahelu expected her to. Nheras hadn't shown her any sympathy or solidarity last night; hadn't offered an arm earlier so she could lean on her for support the way Jhobon had leaned on Ylaen; hadn't even bothered to walk silently in step with her the way Elaram had stuck to Ghardon's side.

But she had thought that—given their truce; given that she had apologized, properly, and meant it; given everything they had gone through, together, to pass Anathwan's test— she and Nheras might have transcended their history to arrive at a new understanding.

Nothing so ludicrous as friendship (that was the kind of tale songhouse storytellers loved to spin but Rahelu knew better) or sisterly concern, but surely some sort of vague periodic check on her condition in a professional (collegial, even) manner indicating that *'yes, I, Nheras Ilyn Issolm, do, in fact, acknowledge that you, Rahelu Fishguts Issolm, exist and are worthy of being considered my equal'* was warranted.

Huh. Was that...?

No. She didn't—couldn't—care.

Whatever elixirs the healers had dosed her with must have included resonance-crystal-dust-infused soporifics in addition to numbweed, because everything felt fleeting and flat, like rippling reflections glimpsed in a puddle.

Anyway, even if Nheras had offered her arm, Rahelu would not have accepted because she was doing absolutely, totally fine on her own.

If she wanted to, she could get up and climb out, right now, without any help.

"Rahelu?" Ylaen called. "Nheras says you're done with clearing the forepeak. You're supposed to come help us take down all of the sails so we can rerig the sloop with the spares your brother's finished fussing over. Captain wants every line replaced with new rope."

All the sails? *Every* line?

Rahelu groaned. The sloop was old and worn but not that old or worn. Could she be bothered thinking up an inventive curse for Csorath? Plead her injuries to get out of the duty without being taken to task for laying about?

Probably not.

Forced to helm a vessel vastly inferior to his beloved *Winged Arrow*, with Kerg dead, their security compromised by the beacon Ylaen had discovered, no Imrell representative in sight to explain how they had allowed some Free Territories outcast to stow away on the sloop they had supplied and to Suborn his mate, unable to unearth the truth of what had transpired since Rahelu and Ghardon were still suffering the aftermaths of severe resonance backlash, with Maketh in his ear and Anathwan in his face, both steadfastly refusing to let him go and recruit another experienced deckhand to act as mate, Csorath's normally serene demeanor was nowhere in sight.

She prodded at her dulled sense of sympathy—come on, Rahelu; Csorath and Kerg both showed you kindness when you deserved none; surely you feel something?—prodded it again when it failed to quicken into empathy.

Nothing.

Try to mourn Kerg later, she decided. All she could do now was not add to Csorath's burdens.

Still…

"My leg," she said. "Can't Jhobon do it?"

Ylaen said nothing as he descended into the hold. When he next spoke, he sounded a lot closer. "It'll go faster with three."

It would go far faster with four, but Csorath was the only

other person besides Ylaen, Jhobon, and herself who knew how to sail and the task was far beneath a captain, who really ought to be doing things like setting their course and generally overseeing departure.

House matters, however, currently precluded Csorath from going about said captain's duties.

A sloop this small granted no privacy, so though Rahelu was ensconced in the forepeak, she—and likely every Supplicant on board, Jhobon included, even if he was already aloft —heard every word that passed between the senior mages in the aftercabin:

Maketh was adamant. No, he would not countenance subjecting each and every person aboard to a direct Seeking. For one, the Supplicants had been under their supervision the entire time; for another, Csorath had already verified there were no imposters among them, last night, in what Maketh could have construed as an attack upon his person but which he had not (seeing as he had shared the same concerns regarding the possibility of infiltration by a Conclave impersonator), and which Elder Anathwan had not (seeing as she had prepared contingencies for such an outcome). There was no way to know whether Kerg had died by his own hand through his own volition, to prevent whoever had Suborned him from turning him into an unwilling spy, or whether his puppeteer had chosen to silence him, to prevent them from gleaning any secrets from his mind—not an unreasonable assumption, given that the stowaway urchin Elaram discovered had no personal effects to examine and no mind to interrogate and therefore had yielded no secrets before bleeding to death. In either case, dead was dead. The breach of their security protocols—which Csorath's overstepping of his House-given authority had introduced; which Maketh had opposed from the beginning— had now been resolved. No more unauthorized persons remained. More importantly, since Csorath believed the Aleituan crossing treacherous and the Supplicants unequal to the challenge when they were in full possession of their mental faculties, Maketh wished to know how the situation would be improved by what Csorath proposed, for it wasn't unheard of for an Isonn Seeker with blood in his sights to press too hard during an interrogation, which—in the current circumstance—would, in all probability, make simpletons of their inexperienced Supplicants by activating their mind blocks. And if Csorath thought he could sidestep Dominion laws with his tenuous arguments and demand that Maketh and Anathwan submit to his direct Seeking and so obtain access to their Houses' secrets, then House Isonn could—

Anathwan intruded.

Peace, Maketh, peace; Csorath intended no offense. Oh, the Elder was deeply grieved that Csorath had lost such a trusted deputy. The Elder also wished to see justice for Kerg's death, but Peshwan Yrg's port authorities were so very bureaucratic and slow to act. If Dedicate Maketh's suspicions were correct—if Kerg's Subornation had been the work of mage-priests from the Divine Kingdom or similarly knowledgeable intermediaries (many of whom might be found in several ports in the Free Territories and whom might also be acting on behalf of half a dozen different ship clans or as free agents on mercenary contracts)—then was it not possible that publicizing the incident would alert the Dominion's enemies that their gambit had nearly succeeded? Of course the Elder would never question the good captain's judgment in matters under his jurisdiction or while aboard his ship, however, did Csorath not perhaps agree that it might be best if he took Kerg back to the citadel and left his body in the care of those whom he trusted to discreetly organize his funeral rites and the return of Kerg's legacy and ashes to his family? For had Csorath not been the one to conclude last night that it was vital they sailed with all speed while the tide was setting out and the weather Augured to be favorable, while the Conclave's operative licked wounds in defeat and waited for reinforcements, while they possessed the advantage?

Rahelu didn't bother to listen in on Csorath's reply. No one could resist Anathwan's arguments; the Issolm Elder had a way of talking people around until 'yes' became 'no' and 'no' became 'yes' and they left with the impression that they had gotten the answer they needed even though it was the exact opposite of the one they had sought.

A scarred hand reached in through the gap above her head.

"Do you need help?" Ylaen asked.

"No," she said. "Get out of my way."

She tried to stand. Succeeded. Tried to pull herself out through the concealed hatch, roll herself sideways, and swing her legs out of the cramped berth and onto the deck of the hold.

The muscles in her arms, her torso, and her left leg obeyed.

Her traitorous right leg rebelled and collapsed.

And Imos fucking No-sleeves, that smarmy, self-absorbed, self-satisfied bastard, swooped in to catch her right before she hit the cargo deck like she was some fainting stageflower and they were in a songhouse play.

White teeth flashed briefly in that lazy smile of his. "'By what stars, strange and fair, do we meet, my lo—'"

"If you do not stop spouting that nonsense and let go of me at once, I will ask every gull in the harbor to shit on you."

Ylaen put her down and chuckled as he followed her out of the hold. "I'd like to see you try."

Rahelu held up the gold kez she'd gotten off Nheras. "I bet I can get them to mob you."

"And I," Ylaen said as he pulled a matching gold coin out of his pocket, "I bet I can convince them to take you flying."

SHORTLY AFTER THEY had joined Jhobon aloft, Csorath Isonn flung the aft hatch open and stalked out with Maketh Imos close behind.

"Leave those sails!" the captain bellowed as he knelt beside his dead mate. Somebody had laid Kerg's body out on top of what looked like an old jib. (The other dead body, Rahelu had gathered, had been disposed of, somewhere dockside.) Csorath rolled up the mate's corpse inside the patched canvas, the tenderness of that gesture at odds with his strident tone. "Jhobon, Ghardon—with Maketh. I want this sloop painted up and locked down with so many wards and Obfuscation barriers that I wouldn't be able to Seek a scrap of resonance if I were knocking my head against its sides."

Firm *aye-captain's* in answer. Ghardon immediately abandoned his cataloging of their food supplies to snatch up two sacks of resonance crystals. Jhobon, however, was taking his sweet time climbing down.

Csorath, in any case, had moved on.

"Ylaen!" The captain kicked at a coil of rope that someone had dumped haphazardly right in the middle of the space around the tiller. "Clear this trash and the rest of the cargo from my deck and show Nheras how to stow it in the hold, then hoist the jib and staysail."

"Aye, captain."

Ylaen did not bother waiting for Rahelu to descend first; he swung himself off, over, and neatly caught himself on the shrouds next to Jhobon, who yelped. Ylaen clapped the Imrell Supplicant on the shoulder and murmured something in Free Territories speech. In the time it took Jhobon to move down another handspan, Ylaen had jumped, crossed over from midship to prow, and joined a pale-faced Nheras in wrestling the wine barrels over to the cargo hatch.

Rahelu gritted her teeth and clambered down after Jhobon, stiff leg first. They alighted on deck at the same time, she with a grunt and he with a whuffed sigh of relief.

"Elaram! You're on Seeking duty. Nobody save our team sets a foot on deck. If you sense so much as a rat trying to sneak on board, shoot it."

"Aye, aye, captain!"

Elaram smacked her right fist into her left palm, jerked her upper body down and up over her wrapped fist in the most truncated observance of deference Rahelu had ever seen a House-born give, and enthusiastically scrambled into the rigging with her crossbow. Shrouds and ratlines shook vigorously with the force of her passage up to the crosstree.

"Rahelu!" Csorath leaned over the *Gull's* starboard toprail and scowled. "Get over the side. Swell's fouled up the harbor with eel-grass. I want every strand of that stuff off my keel, rudder, and anchor in the next span."

"Aye, captain!"

Rahelu hobbled over to the starboard side and began shedding clothes as fast as she could. She stole a glance at the captain as she piled her boots on top of her heaped shirt and trousers and drew her belt knife.

The Seeker stared at the sky.

Dozens of gulls hovered, white bellies near invisible against a thick blanket of white clouds, tracing slow, lazy loops from foreshore to harbor and back. Loud *keows* filled the air, broken by the occasional *splish-splash* as birds swooped, snatching up half-eaten bamboo skewers in their beaks.

"Maketh," Csorath called, his tone as sharp as the grief in his blackened aura. "A word."

Rahelu clenched the steel blade of her belt knife between her teeth. Footsteps sounded behind her as she boosted herself up and swung her legs over the toprail.

She looked down and wished she hadn't.

The harbor was fouled with more than just eel-grass. So much torn silk and tattered talismans and soggy paper prayers and broken lanterns and other detritus bumped against the hull that she couldn't see a single clear spot to slip into the water—and that was murky with runoff from the city's streets and sewers. Effluent slicked the sea's surface and greased the *Gull's* sides; something blobby drifted past her dangling toes in a tangle of loose, stringy limbs that could have been a nest of ribbons, somebody's knotted loincloth, or hanks of human hair.

Her gorge rose.

Csorath wanted her to swim around in that filth?

Last night, while Elaram had had her fun; while Ghardon had fainted; while Ylaen had stood around looking pretty and stealing kisses; while Jhobon had been snug inside, enjoying his impromptu nap; while Nheras had sat on her hands and waited to be rescued, Rahelu had: successfully deflected suspicion from the Jade Eye Company; secured the box Anathwan wanted; and single-handedly bested Ruarem's defenses and opened his door.

The Elder herself had praised her performance four times as much as she had praised Nheras's. By Rahelu's reckoning, if she applied House-born logic, she was entitled to claim at least eight-tenths of the credit for passing Anathwan's test so one of the others could pick up the slack for a change. If Csorath had assigned her because Ghardon and Elaram and Nheras didn't know how to swim, well, Ylaen and Jhobon did, and she was better with wards than Jhobon and Ylaen hadn't been stabbed through the leg, and besides, if physical fitness was a problem when it came to stowing the cargo,

Nheras was strong enough to move most things on her own and somebody had to tell her what to put where and how to lash it down properly and Rahelu had become very well-acquainted with the hold thanks to all the dust and mold and grime and cobwebs she'd choked on when she'd been grubbing around in that hidden compartment earlier.

She was not going to jump into water that was filthier than the stuff that flowed through the Lowdocks gutters.

Not for a hundred gold kez.

Rahelu was about to swing her legs back onto the deck and propose a new assignment for herself when her ears caught Csorath's last order.

"Tell Alozei I hold her responsible."

Not a name she recognized and not something she could ask about without flouting the Elder's rule of silence: from the moment they had left the citadel, they were to act as if they were Houseless.

Maketh's reply was a low rumble. "It will be your word against hers."

"It would not be, had our little Evokers not been used up so early." The Isonn Dedicate slung his dead mate over his shoulder. "Tell her to expect a full accounting of our loss."

"Why not tell her yourself?"

"I will," Csorath said.

Four of the gulls broke from the flock to wing their way north and west.

"But I want to be sure she pays attention." Csorath's gaze snapped back to the Imos Dedicate. "For I will not repeat myself when the time of reckoning comes."

Three more gulls wheeled around to fly straight for the citadel as Csorath strode down the gangplank and stepped off onto the dock.

Maketh closed his eyes. He sucked in a long breath, then pinched the bridge of his nose and exhaled for a slow count of five. When he opened his eyes again, his bloodshot, black-ringed gaze immediately found Rahelu.

He frowned.

Before the Guardian could say a word, she launched herself off the side.

———

EEL-GRASS DEALT WITH, Rahelu joined Ylaen and Nheras in clearing the main deck.

It was slow going. There was at least a season's worth of provisions, plus cotton, silks, spices, resonance crystal, and weapons there to lend veracity to their supposed identities as smugglers. She didn't know what kind of arrangement the senior mages had come to regarding their accommodations in the aftercabin but the Supplicants would be sleeping like trussed corpses in the hold.

They also had to work around Maketh and Jhobon and Ghardon as those three painstakingly embedded resonance crystals and painted thick lines of resonance ink all along the inside and outside of the ship's toprail and the edges of the main deck. Eventually, they formed a sort of production line: Ylaen ferrying goods to Rahelu, at the top of the cargo hatch, to be handed down to Nheras, below.

Rahelu had never seen so much food in her life. Out of habit, she tried estimating their combined market value.

Water, water, water, water, water, wine, wine, wine, and oil, and more water, so much water, a hundred and ten large casks in all, which was water enough to fill all the baths at the Tidepool twice—no; thrice over. Forty sacks of rice, barley, wheat, beans. Twenty-two crates of cabbages, turnips, taro, bamboo shoots, braided ropes of onions and garlic. Small stoppered jars of dried herbs; medium stoppered jars containing pickled cabbage and plums, and—Earthgiver's bountiful treasures!—there were *luxuries*: a large clay urn of salted duck eggs, packed in lime and ash; packets of dried beef jerky, made sticky and fragrant with honey and sprinkled sesame; bundles of fatty sausages—

Her belly growled and growled and growled. Its refusal to be silent made her lose track of her count (and thus any reasonable basis for an estimation) long before they finished cramming supplies back into every last square stride of usable space in the hold.

When Nheras next disappeared from view and everybody else had their back turned, Rahelu took advantage of Csorath's absence to remedy the situation. But the edge of her belt knife had dulled from sawing away at all that stupid eel-grass so instead of being able to sneak a savory-sweet slice or two of that delicious preserved pork, she had to take a whole stick or not at all.

Ylaen caught her with her mouth full of sausage.

Before he could venture any innuendo, she smiled—with all her teeth showing—and took another very large bite.

Chewed. Vigorously.

He got the message and obligingly kept his mouth shut as he passed her a log of neatly rolled waxed canvas. Nheras still being absent, Rahelu took the storm trysail down into the hold herself.

Partly because she didn't care to stick around to be mocked by the low hum of amusement in his resonance aura and the ribald tune he whistled as he rerolled the rest of the spare sails that Ghardon had left piled in a heap.

Partly because she didn't trust Nheras to string up the hammocks properly.

Mostly, though, it was because her jaws ached. She had bitten off far more than she could chew and really needed to spit out that mouthful of pork before she choked.

NOBODY WOULD HAVE CALLED the *Sooty Gull* impressive but it was no simple fishing sloop. It had five sails to manage instead of two, and the mainsail was gaff-rigged instead of square-rigged, resulting in an exponential number of additional lines to decipher.

So when Dedicate Csorath returned from the citadel (alone, grim-faced, bridled grief blanked behind a solid Obfuscation barrier), he found Ylaen and Rahelu scratching their heads over the snarled mess they had made of the halyards.

Rahelu braced herself for recriminations—a lengthy tirade on their incompetence, as Maketh was inclined to give, or perhaps the quiet, understated disappointment Anathwan would likely have wielded.

Csorath voiced none, embracing the situation with taciturn resignation. The Isonn Dedicate patiently demonstrated each thing they did not know, then spun dozens of direct Auguries on their clumsy attempts. He did them the courtesy of correcting their mistakes preemptively and silently, via shielded Projection, before those mistakes could be realized in reality and delayed departure further.

Yet this made Rahelu feel even stupider than if he had simply yelled at her. Her mother's voice filled in the silences between Csorath's corrections—idiot girl, so slow to learn, stop and think before you act, don't do it that way, can't you see how it will go wrong, waste of time and effort—and the more he corrected her, the more flustered she got.

It should have been easy to tell the ghostly visions monitoring her future progress apart from the ones monitoring Ylaen's just by the hands doing the work but Csorath's Auguries flickered in and out of existence so fast she couldn't grasp any details, let alone catch her own mistakes before she made them.

Her! Getting her lines mixed and messing up basic knots like she was some pampered House-born who couldn't do the ties on her own robes without some simpering servant on hand to assist her.

Orange-red frustration crackled through her unwarded resonance aura; she gritted her teeth and tried to tamp it down, mindful of Ylaen's sidelong glances. While her vision had cleared, her temples still throbbed so she couldn't resort to Evocation, which meant she was stuck making stupid mistakes—six for every one of his—and if she was keeping score, surely the captain and Ylaen were too.

"You look tense," Ylaen said when Csorath left them to check on Maketh's progress and to see to the tiller.

"I'm fine." She jerked her current knot tight and resisted the temptation to massage her neck.

"You can admit it." He rolled his head from one side to the other, joints shifting in faint, audible pops. Made a long, drawn-out "Mmmn..." so low in his throat that he sounded like a purring jhalyx, then rolled and flexed his shoulders for good measure. "If it helps, I feel rather sore, too. That leg of yours must be stiff by now. Did the healers recommend any particular treatment?"

As a matter of fact, they had. She was to keep as much weight off her leg as much as possible to avoid aggravating the wound, change the numbweed poultice daily, apply warm compresses twice a day, and—

"Massages, perhaps?" Ylaen picked up the last line lying loose—the main halyard—and dared a suggestive smirk as he coiled it. "I have excellent hands, I'm told."

Resonance backlash be damned.

Rahelu looked for the nearest gull—there was one

perched on the hawser tying the ship to the slip—and Projected a very clear suggestion.

The effort cost her a brief stabbing pain that robbed her of vision for two heartbeats but the warm glow of golden victory as her ears registered the gull's flapping wings and a faint *blaaat!* was worth it.

She blinked open watering eyes to the sight of grinning teeth.

The gull had missed him by a good two strides.

Ylaen fastened the coiled halyard to the cleat. "My offer of private coaching still stands."

"I'm afraid I have to decline. Conflict of interest, you understand, given our current wager."

She hobbled away before he could make another move.

Maketh gave her that frown again when she volunteered herself to help with the ship's wards but sat her down at his makeshift workstation: a wooden crate that held a small mortar and pestle, three thick-bristled brushes, and a pouchful of resonance crystal fragments shimmering a serene blue-gray.

"Grind these to a fine powder." The Guardian eyed her erratic aura—an undertone of green-brown disgust had joined the orange-red crackles of frustration. "Make sure you do not contaminate the product by introducing incompatible resonance." After considering the depleted pendant around her neck and her unmarked skin, he added: "No Obfuscation. You've already pushed through more resonance backlash than you should have; keep that up and you might do yourself permanent harm."

Rahelu stared.

Did he…did he just show concern? For her?

Maketh looked away. "There's charcoal in the crate."

Not an order, but an offer. Diffident, like they were just two common-born people instead of Dedicate and Supplicant sworn to different Houses in an uneasy temporary alliance. They were dressed in identical shirts and trousers, after all.

He hovered.

She kept staring.

Did he intend to say more? Or was he waiting for her acknowledgment?

From the stern, Jhobon called out, "Guar—um, M-Maketh? We're done, we think."

Maketh shook his head, glanced once more at Rahelu, then strode off to inspect Jhobon and Ghardon's work without waiting the twenty heartbeats it took her to wrestle the yellow shock radiating through her aura into submission.

She found the charcoal.

Barely paid attention to it, trusting her fingers to draw the resonance ward by rote, as she struggled to reconcile his dogged accusations of her disloyalty to House and Dominion, her recollection of being interrogated, then rendered insensate for three fucking days, and then ignored, with this new, unexpected show of concern for her well-being.

Her *long-term* well-being.

What was going on with Maketh Imos? She grabbed palmful after palmful of resonance crystal fragments and pounded them into dust as she pondered theory after theory.

Theory one: Maketh is the real spy. The best way to deflect suspicion is to point it at someone else—repeatedly and loudly.

Theory two: Maketh no longer believes her to be a spy. But as a Dedicate of House Imos, he can't possibly admit to being wrong, so being nice to her is his way of saying sorry without actually saying sorry.

Theory three: Maketh is not a spy and still suspects Rahelu. Being nice to her is his way of putting her off her guard so she'll betray herself.

Theory four: Rahelu had imagined the whole thing.

To her exhaustion-addled, resonance-backlashed brain, each seemed equally plausible. So she gave up trying to solve the conundrum, put her aching head down, and concentrated on grinding crystal fragments into dust for resonance ink as they weighed anchor and fought the tide, the wind, and the incoming fishing boats on their way out of the Sunport.

In the middle of the Aleituan Sea proper, living in the *Sooty Gull's* close quarters, there would be no place to hide, nowhere to turn for privacy, no reprieve from the company of your shipmates, and no avenue for escape.

If Maketh was wrong and Csorath was right, there would be time aplenty to sniff out the traitor.

17
SONG

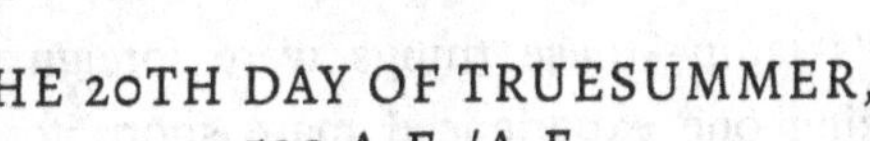

THE 20TH DAY OF TRUESUMMER, 530 A.E./A.F.

THE FIRST FEW DAYS PASSED IN A BLUR.

While Rahelu had never worked a vessel so large—had never ventured so far beyond the sight of land—she counted herself an experienced deckhand.

She had spent more of her life on water than not and had swum before she could walk. The earliest memory she had ever Evoked was of her as a babe, playing in the sunlit shallows of the Elumaje, paddling after brilliant, jewel-toned lakefish. She knew the moods of her childhood lake as well as her own; knew how its surface liked to shift from placid calm to choppy wavelets when the south wind rose; knew how the waters could go from a serene crystal blue so clear you could see straight through to the depths of the lake bed to a muddy brown when icemelt from the Unomelaje transformed the calm inlets into a torrent of glacial floodwaters that could snatch the strongest swimmer off the sturdiest raft and dash them to pieces on the rocky banks. The Stormbringer was an exacting god—he kept all that he embraced but balanced the scales with bounty for those who respected his domain—so Rahelu had learned how to recognize the first signs of his displeasure before she had learned to talk. By her sixth summer, her parents and Tsenjhe had taught her to read the wind and the stars, steer a safe course to shore if she had to, and how to weather a storm if she couldn't.

Sailing the Aleituan Sea was another matter entirely.

The currents, the winds, the four-spans-on-eight-spans-off watch system, rising and retiring from a swinging hammock according to Captain Csorath's regular end-of-watch Projections instead of the lighting and dousing of the Skymother's lamp—these things were foreign to her. The captain, being one experienced mate short, forced to rush their departure from Peshwan Yrg, and highly distrustful of the seaworthiness of the ship provided by House Imrell, ran them ragged. One mage was on active Seeking duty at all times—even Elder Anathwan and Dedicate Maketh were not exempted, though Csorath did not require the other two senior mages to climb aloft with the spyglass as he demanded of the Supplicants. Every finger-width of the standing rigging, the running rigging, the sails, the deck had to be constantly inspected for evidence of wear and tear, then sealed against rot with paint or wax or tung oil. The salt air and sea spray thrown up by the *Gull's* breakneck speed (for the captain had laid on every scrap of canvas the ship could bear to make up for lost time) steadily eroded the suppression wards painted along the outside of the ship's toprail and they had to be renewed every second watch. The anchors of Maketh's triple-nested barrier formation were more durable; still, Maketh ordered the thousands of tiny resonance crystal stones inspected every other watch when they weren't attending to the frailer resonance wards—to recharge depleted stones and repair gaps left behind by stones that had been shaken loose or that had fractured due to their flawed matrices. The barriers themselves were never activated save for their twice-daily testing at the end of the inspection or in emergencies.

In theory, the suppression ward ought to minimize the detectability of the Obfuscation barriers; in practice, the barriers were treated as a defense of the last resort: to conserve resonance and to avoid drawing undue attention from Seekers of other ships that might be in range.

Many, many other ships were often in range.

Truesummer was the height of the trading season and a small flock of gulls and ships had followed them out of Peshwan Yrg. Not a span passed without the shout of, "Sails! Sails on the horizon," from whoever was serving as lookout, and then the games would commence.

Sometimes, those ships would hail the *Sooty Gull* with flags or polite pulses of Projected curiosity, and Csorath would give answer accordingly.

Other times, the captain would order them to tack or gybe so the *Gull* flitted away before they were spotted in turn.

Once, they were pursued.

Another sloop—bigger, sleeker, and outfitted with several cannon and crimson sails—flirted with the *Gull* for several days, chasing them off the main trade route and through the stretches of contested waters and islets that lay between Ochwa-ret and the main island of Tsorek-fa.

Every night, Csorath would try to slip the *Gull* away, under the cover of darkness and Maketh's active defenses.

Every day, without fail, they would spot the coming of the raider, its crimson sails cresting the horizon with the sun, and Csorath would set the Supplicants to scouring the ship with Seeking as they beat every finger-width of the *Gull's* insides with mallets in search of hidden beacons or stowaways or smuggling compartments they might have missed while Maketh glowered, trusting no one with the task of going over each ward line and every resonance crystal anchoring the ship's Obfuscation barriers.

At dawn on the fourth such day, a grim-faced, thin-lipped

Anathwan came out of her seclusion in the aftercabin, stolen wooden box in hand, and ordered Csorath to take the *Gull* east.

To which the Seeker-captain said, "We will find no aid there," but, resigned, beaten, he did take the *Gull* east—into the open sea, as the Elder demanded—and at dusk, they came upon a floundering merchant vessel.

The Free Territories raider immediately veered towards the easier, richer prey and allowed the *Sooty Gull* to escape.

Only Rahelu looked back as they left those poor, doomed merchants to their fate. Everybody else seemed to accept the sacrifice as an awful—but necessary—cost of fulfilling their mission.

"How long?" the Elder asked the captain over their cold evening meal: fresh seaweed salad, pickled vegetables, and beef jerky.

Csorath scanned the sky.

Rahelu craned her neck along with the others. Through the gaps in the billowing sails of the *Sooty Gull,* she glimpsed the sign of the bell. A bright array of five blue stars had risen in a fuzzy gray-white patch of night sky to the east: three in a straight line bisecting the celestial cloud—handle, neck, and bell mouth apex; two more forming the endpoints of the bell mouth's curve.

The captain said, "In another two or three days, we shall pass through the true heart of the Aleituan Sea and cross into Abmerduan waters. Then, who knows?" He kneaded the back of his neck as he worked out the kinks in his shoulder. "Few ships have ever sailed past the edges of the North Ocean, for the waters beyond are said to be inimical to life." Csorath fell silent, thinking. "A month," he said at last. "Perhaps longer. A vessel like ours ought to be too small a prize for the larger ship clans, but—"

The silence filled itself with the almost-accusation

Csorath had not voiced: '—*but that raider ship found us, despite our defenses.*'

Nobody dared glance at Maketh.

Csorath shook his head as if recollecting himself. "We've provisions enough to go two months without putting into port, so I will take the *Gull* as far from the main sea routes as possible. It would be best not to offer the ship clans a tempting target."

"I'd like to see a Free Territories ship up close," Elaram said wistfully, as though they hadn't just spent the better part of a week trying to avoid being captured by one. "I've heard it said that the Crimson Storm's flagship is a grand five-masted warship with a thunderhead of sails and triple-banks of oars that flies swifter than a questryl. Is it true that its decks are stained red by the blood of a thousand fallen foes?"

"You've been listening to too many fireside tales," Csorath said. Pale moonlight, diffused by the cloud cover, deepened the shadowy crags of his face until he looked more like a brittle wood carving than a man. The Isonn Dedicate had to be exhausted; as far as Rahelu knew, he didn't so much as slumber on the quieter watches as snatch sleep, one eyeblink at a time. "The *Stormbringer's Judgment* does have five masts but only one bank of oars. It's an ugly, deep-hulled monstrosity with half the firepower of our own *Csonnyrg's Hammer* and triple the complement you'd expect for a ship of that size. Every deckhand and officer is a blooded cutthroat and a slaver besides—and they adhere to no code of honor. They'd sooner sell you into Suborned indenture for a quick pittance than hold out for a fortune in ransom. You'd best pray we don't glimpse its sails."

"That's so boring," Elaram grumbled in Rahelu's ear as they scrubbed bowls and rinsed up. "What's the point of going on a secret mission without having a good adventure?"

The silly complaint made Rahelu shake her head; the

whole point was to survive and to ensure everyone you cared about survived—anything beyond that was folly.

The next day, Anathwan instituted a change in their shipboard routine.

All six Supplicants were now required to join the Elder in a Concordance before the evening meal as she performed Augury after Augury, a task that seemed to be part weather watch, part navigation, part risk assessment—and part placation.

For, despite having met every single one of Anathwan's expectations to the last requirement, they were still yet to be briefed on vital details like *'where are we going?'* and *'what are we doing when we get there?'* but no one, not even Ylaen Imos No-sleeves, was so brash or foolish as to demand aloud, *'When? When will you treat us as full members of the team, as you promised?'*

'Soon' was all Anathwan intimated, but not by word. What they got from the Elder whenever an opportune moment for their enlightenment arose were coy, sidelong glances, conspiratorial looks, and clever, ambiguous, layered allusions that Rahelu would have called *'provocative'*, had she gotten their ilk from Elaram or No-sleeves.

Perhaps the answers were obvious.

Lhorne had said House Issolm would send her to the other side of the world. Csorath had sketched a route that led them past the scattered islands of the Abmerduan archipelago and beyond. Into the North Ocean, where even the ship clans did not venture, where Silcarez had turned back after mapping but a fraction of its vastness, where legends whispered of the thousand glittering jewels that the Starfather had scattered into stillness and the thousand more raised by the Earthgiver from the firemounts beneath the Stormbringer's waters.

The Desolate Isles.

Did it matter that Anathwan hadn't told Rahelu which of the several hundred isles that hadn't crumbled into the sea (or had been newly born during the centuries since) they were sailing to?

Of course it didn't, because the answers *were* obvious—

(They were Seeking the last remaining artifact that the cultists had used in their ritual. And—if the box they had retrieved in Peshwan Yrg was anything to go by—they were to figure out if the artifact could be exploited. If so, they would bring it home to the Dominion; if not, they would destroy it, so that it could not be used against the Houses.)

—so Rahelu was not going to ruin the Elder's hard-won estimation of her as someone who had *potential* and *great promise* in her future—and, therefore, was not a fish-brained idiot—by opening her mouth to prove otherwise.

Still, the follow-up questions fairly shouted themselves through the impatience permeating what little ambient resonance the wind and the Guardian allowed to accumulate on board:

Have we not achieved all that you asked?

Have we not proven ourselves as more than mere Supplicants?

Have we not earned the right to call ourselves—and be recognized as—soon-to-be-Dedicates?

Those questions Anathwan did not deign to acknowledge.

Though they all forwent their House names, ranks, and titles, and both the Elder and the Guardian had given the Supplicants permission to address them with familiarity (Csorath had not done the same; then again, Csorath alone possessed the sole remaining title of 'captain'), Rahelu and the others were still barred from the senior mages' nightly Projected conferences in the highly secured aftercabin. Maketh still treated them as the raw mage graduates they technically were, their success in Peshwan Yrg notwithstanding, and Csorath—

Csorath had grown taciturn to the point of terseness in the wake of Kerg's death, rebuffing company from all save the ship's cat. (He had, however, accepted the lantern Rahelu had woven out of dried eel-grass and that, too, was no longer with them, though she had not seen him light it and set it upon the water.) Even Elaram watched her tongue and walked softly around the grieving Isonn Seeker.

Thus they bided, trusting that Anathwan had good reasons for delaying, content with the priceless opportunity to work with—and directly learn from—an Elder at Augury. Initially, they were excited. Augury was, after all, the most sought-after and difficult-to-master resonance discipline next to Fortunement. But creeping forward into the future, moving one quarter-span at a time along a single thread of probability just to see themselves performing the same tasks over and over, then repeating the exercise for a dozen more probabilities brought new meaning to the definition of 'mind-numbing eternity'.

By the end of every Concordance, Rahelu of Elumaje did not exist. Nor did Rahelu of the Lowdocks or Rahelu of Issolm. There was only Rahelu of Aleznuaweite, daughter of common-born fisherfolk, a junior deckhand aboard the *Sooty Gull*, serving under Captain Csorath as he smuggled weapons and resonance crystal and silks and renegade Guild mages exiled from the Dominion looking for extralegal mercenary work with the predatory ship clans laying claim to the Free Territories of Abmerdu.

Soon, not even that much-rehearsed fiction remained.

Deep and deeper into the Abmerduan they sailed, encountering few and fewer ships. Anathwan gradually stepped up the number and length of Concordances she led until the captain's end-of-watch Projections also heralded yet another combined Augury—and they had the dubious privilege of experiencing, firsthand, the blockages the Elder had mentioned in passing during their last briefing aboard the *Winged Arrow*.

Rahelu had not given much thought to the problem plaguing the Houses. Her Auguries failed more often than not, and she was too unskilled an Augur to blame that on anything other than her own lack of competence, so she had learned to live her life (for the most part) without relying on that discipline. (Guilt pricked her then, and she quashed it with a firm, *I have no regrets*.) As for the unguarded argument she had once overheard between Csorath and Maketh, what little curiosity it had piqued had been extinguished by the all-consuming business of surviving then and since. Exhaustion had left her indifferent to the academic question of whether the perturbances in the temporal flow of resonance were some sort of naturally recurring phenomena, as Csorath had argued, or if they were attributable to nefarious intent, as Maketh had insisted.

Now, though, the Concordances forced her to wrestle with those perturbances seven times a day, and they weren't anything like what she'd expected. They didn't manifest themselves as the blankness you got when you tried Seeking a resonance signature that didn't exist or that wasn't in range. Their Concordances didn't slam into the same unyielding resistance she'd felt during Petitioning when she had been fixated on seeing a specific outcome in her attempts at Augury. And, according to Ghardon, they didn't feel like the kind of Obfuscation you'd sense from a specialized barrier, designed to shield a person or place from being the unwitting subject of an Augury.

No, Maketh was right about some things. The perturbances were patterned. Dissonances—or distortions—in resonance that almost felt like an alien music.

That was as far as she ever got in her musings. The Elder needed to wring so much power from them to push through those blockages that she also claimed every last shred of will. By the time Rahelu got to hand off the spyglass to the next person on Seeking duty, she was a bone-weary, soul-worn mess on the verge of resonance backlash.

Sleep brought no rest, only dirge-filled dreams of blades and blood.

Yet she was content, for the days were still long and leisurely paced, the seas bountiful with goldtrout and silver-bream and striped mackerel and shrimp and kelp, and the nights were warm and peaceful and filled with song.

Not only was Csorath adept at playing the flute and the lute, Elaram had a lovely, lilting voice—high and clear and sweet; a good complement to the lower, darker tones of her own—and Jhobon turned out to possess a fine tenor, and Ylaen had improvised a hand drum from a piece of scrap canvas stretched over a cracked gourd and tied with a spare bit of fishing line. Between the five of them, they formed a passable ensemble. Csorath taught them at least a dozen different Isonn sea shanties and hunt songs; Jhobon shyly contributed a rather rousing oar chant in Free Territories speech; and while everyone knew both the Aleznuaweithish and Abmerduan tellings of Enjela's ballad, they were pleased to learn the Chanazian version from Rahelu—though this led to heated debates.

"Enjela lived," Jhobon said, as animated as she'd ever seen him. "After the Battle for the Dawn, her soulsworn renounced their stations, settled their worldly affairs upon their heirs, and bore her away across the Aleituan Sea in search of a cure for her wandering spirit. In the memoirs documenting his first voyage, Silcarez discovered many shrines built in her memory, on various islets scattered between the Abmerduan archipelago and the northwest coast of the Belruonian continent."

"That's ludicrous," Ghardon said. "We have no credible maritime records from that century, but every Evocation study to pinpoint the exact location of that battle turned up a handful of possibilities. And three of those sites are located in the heart of the Ngutoccai continent, at least a hundred kual from the nearest coastline."

"Both of you are missing the point," Elaram said. "It doesn't matter whether she lived or died; she saved her city. I think it's deeply romantic."

"Enjela was a heartless manipulator, without mercy or honor," Ylaen insisted from his perch on the boom, where he looked far more comfortable than he ought to be. "She betrayed her people, enslaved her allies, deceived Symezosh, and assassinated him in his sleep."

"She was not!" Elaram cried. "Symezosh refused to open his heart to her; he was a prideful, cruel killer who desired absolute rule above all things. After he refused her entreaties, Enjela had no choice but to do as she did."

That triggered a point-by-point rebuttal from Ylaen, which in turn elicited counter arguments from Elaram so vociferous that when Ghardon started trying to shove his sister out of the circle, Rahelu lent him a hand. Between the two of them, they wrestled Elaram over to the mast so she and Ylaen could yell at each other face to face instead of over everybody's heads.

"The last line you sang in the final stanza of Enjela's victory," Csorath said as Rahelu and Ghardon rejoined the huddle around the fire hearth's chimney. "I've not heard it sung that way before. And to an alternate harmony?" He repeated the phrase in his booming bass, a drone to anchor the tonal center as he strummed several chords in quick succession on his lute. "It takes an otherwise joyful melody and puts a melancholic twist on it—a tension that is left suspended and unresolved."

Rahelu shrugged. "That is how my father sings it," she said. "In my village on the shores of the Elumaje, we know that part of the ballad as Enjela's Lament. I've always liked the tragedy of it. The Aleznuaweithish version is…". She teased out a length of cotton from the skein in her lap, winding it around the fraying fibers of the net in her hands until she had repaired the damage Ghardon had caused when he'd botched his cast earlier. "…incomplete," she finished. "It extolls the glory of her sacrifice without expressing the pain of it."

"An interesting interpretation," Csorath said, then smiled. "I like it too."

"I have heard that melody before," Maketh said, "but not as part of Enjela's tale." He hummed it again, transposed a full fifth below and slightly off-key, and when he reached the end of the phrase, he did not stop but continued on with three more: variations that stepped through eight, hauntingly beautiful changes of rising tonal centers until the final note ended a full octave above the first.

And now that she had heard them, it seemed incredible that Enjela's Lament had stopped at the end of the phrase she knew.

"Where did you hear it?" Rahelu asked.

"In the refrain of a lay," Maketh said, "from my"—there was a pause so slight that she nearly missed it—"a songhouse. I do not know the name."

Anathwan stirred from her meditative trance. "That is a favorite of Enilm's, is it not?" Maketh made no response and Anathwan gave no sign that she expected one. "Sung to the melody of a hymn from the Divine Kingdom: 'Stars divine, heir of mine, blood to bind, heart to mind…'"

Jhobon sat up very straight. "Is that a passage from the scripture of the soul?"

Anathwan nodded.

"The—" Jhobon hesitated, his resonance aura caught between a lurid orange excitement and the nausea-inducing yellow-green of extreme nervousness. His eyes darted astern, where Elaram and Ylaen remained occupied in their debate, then he seemed to gather up all his courage to utter, "The xuuqoshtalog-te?" before his cheeks flushed and crimson washed over his resonance aura.

Rahelu bit her lip to keep herself from snickering—Jhobon had mumbled the Belruonian phrase so quickly that it really did sound like 'suck cocks a lot' in Aleznuaweithish—and inadvertently exchanged glances with the other Supplicants.

Ghardon smirked.

The expression instantly mirrored itself on Nheras's face; Rahelu's too. Ylaen and Elaran's faces were too shadowed to make out their expressions but Elaram's peal of laughter rang out, like a chord struck on a zither's strings.

Jhobon ducked his head, resonance aura paling to the silvery-purple of regret.

Anathwan, however, did not laugh; Csorath was in no mood for laughter; and as for Maketh, Rahelu did not believe that the Earthgiver had made him capable of ever laughing.

When no rebuke came from the Elder—and since Elaram's laugh had not incited the other Supplicants to open ridicule—Jhobon ventured another question.

"Silcarez's accounting of the ceremonial preparations involved seems to imply that the xuuqoshtalog-te is some sort of death ritual, akin to the Earthgiver's final rites, but"—his hesitance vanished even as the blush spread from his cheeks to the tips of his ears and extended down his neck—"Reshwim's annotations translate the old Belruonian phrase as something rather like a consummation ritual, and her illustrations go further to suggest a number of prescribed forms for the consummation to follow. Which is it?"

"Both," Anathwan answered. "And yet, neither. The xuuqoshtalog-te is the holiest of the Divine Kingdom's rituals. It is how the mage-priests mark the transference of the Starfather's Eternal Gaze from one earthly vessel to the next."

"An accession ceremony for the Divine Holiness? As when a new Atriarch takes their throne?"

"The form of Belruonian used in the scriptures is better translated as 'ascension', and much of what we know about the ascension ceremony is couched in religious metaphor. Nevertheless, some things can be inferred or deduced. The Eternal Gaze, for instance, refers to the act of grand Augury undertaken by the Divine Holiness at the commencement of their reign, in Concordance with a full assembly of mage-priests."

"Fanatics," Ghardon muttered to Rahelu under his breath. "Why go to the trouble of inventing a name? They could have simply said 'we choose the most powerful Augur among us to rule and make them prove it'."

She muttered back, "Wouldn't sound half so mysterious or poetic and, therefore, important," and he snorted.

"What about this passage then?" Jhobon asked, flipping through his ever-present notebook. "'She'," he read aloud, then interrupted himself by interjecting—"and the Divine Holiness is always referred to in the feminine in their scriptures, even though all diplomatic correspondence from the Divine Kingdom consistently applies the neuter regardless of the actual sex or gender of whoever holds office—why?"

Shrugs all around the circle, save from the senior mages.

Jhobon continued: "'She will ascend to the heavens; and from the heavens, she will return, enthroned with the blessing of infinite sight'. That directly precedes the verse you quoted earlier—'Stars divine, heir of mine,' and so on—which itself precedes another passage:

> *'Mortal once, with mortal woes.*
> *The battle she lost, but the war she won.*
> *To death, she consigned herself, with her foes.*
> *In death, alone; by devotion, the doing undone.*
> *Drink, and rejoice in your soul,*
> *As the stars sing and the heavens toll,*
> *For with the coming of the sun,*
> *She arose.'"*

Jhobon leaned forward, all earlier reticence gone. "Our sages weren't wrong in their telling of the ballad; Enjela lived! She lived, and became the first Divine Holiness, the one whose bones Silcarez found at that island shrine, in the Desolate Isles." The Imrell Supplicant's normally mild eyes were alight with fervor. "'The doing undone'—that's an allusion to Revocation, isn't it?"

Then Anathwan did laugh. A warm, throaty, golden laugh that ought to have crushed Jhobon, only her laugh was so light and so beautiful that it drew Elaram back and drew Ylaen in, and all of them in the circle, Supplicants *and* Dedicates, were transfixed by the music of her laugh and never gave thought to joining in.

They only remembered to breathe once the Elder had trailed off.

"No," Anathwan said, composed once more, but elaborated upon seeing Jhobon slump and his crestfallen look. "Some have argued so. Chroniclers in the Dominion and Conclave researchers have debated for centuries over differing interpretations of the translations from ancient Belruonian. On the whole, though, they agree: that particular hymn is a clear allusion to the Evocation and binding of shades."

Quietly, Jhobon shut his notebook.

"That's awfulness!" Elaram shuddered. "I'm as sentimental as the next person and I don't mind my life being celebrated with Evocations at my funeral but the dead ought to stay dead instead of haunting the living. Please; let's talk of something else, or I'm going to have nightmares." She lifted the dozing ship's cat into her lap; the cat yowled and swiped a forepaw at her cheek in protest as she snuggled it tight to her chin. "Maybe a story of a grand adventure and dashing deeds?" Elaram glanced around their circle. "What about you, Nheras? What's your favorite story?"

Nheras shrugged. "I don't have one."

Ghardon scoffed. "Everyone has one."

"Not me."

"Come now, don't be embarrassed," he said. "Ela's favorite is the story about the Skymother's mirror—"

"That children's tale?" Ylaen snickered; Elaram stuck her tongue out at his back but didn't deny it.

"—and I'm partial to Solmoram's legend myself."

In a theatrical whisper, Elaram said, "I caught him reciting Solmoram's lines to his own reflection in our pond when we were seven; he had borrowed a tray from the kitchens for a shield, Mother's best silk wrap to wear as a cloak, and Father's knife as a sword. He sliced through half the hangings in the pavilion before someone put an end to it."

"I saved the pavilion," Ghardon said. "Those hangings clashed terribly with the garden."

"How very good for you both." Nheras stood abruptly. "Wake me when it's my watch," she said and proceeded to lift the hatch to the hold.

The *Sooty Gull* surged as it topped the next wave and Nheras dropped the hatch squarely on Ghardon's foot.

"Ow!" Ghardon glared at Nheras's back as she descended the companionway. "Watch it!"

No apology came forth from below.

"Nheras is wise," Anathwan said. She stifled a yawn. "I, too, believe I shall retire. Tomorrow, the true test begins. We must not allow anything to delay us further, for the future of the Dominion—no, the world itself—turns upon our success."

If those words had come from anyone else, Rahelu would have dismissed them as exaggeration. But Elder Anathwan's face was drawn and she had a far-off look in her eyes as she paused to let the enormity of their task sink in, and so...

Rahelu swallowed.

Eight hells. The Houses were betting a lot on a couple of senior mages and a bunch of inexperienced Supplicants. Suddenly, Maketh's training regime seemed too lenient in retrospect.

"Fortunately"—the Elder smiled as she also stood—"we have an advantage that the Conclave does not."

Anathwan went to the aftercabin.

As if her departure was a cue, Maketh touched his mage pendant and activated his newest set of barriers.

Three walls of resonance sprang up around the ship—all varying shades of gray: the mild gray-white of disinterest, the familiar blue-gray of calmness, and the stiff slate-gray of apathy. The burgeoning excitement in their resonance auras rose into the air and evaporated as it brushed against the innermost layer, like stray droplets sizzling on heated hearthstone.

Anathwan soon returned with the plain, wooden box they had stolen from Ruarem's workshop in her hands. They all leaned in, ambient resonance sparking with bright orange anticipation, as she undid its latch.

Nestled inside the velvet-lined case was a glassy black circlet.

Rahelu's breath caught in her throat. Where had she seen this before?

"That's it?" Elaram asked as she dislodged the ship's cat from her lap to scoot forward on her knees for a closer look. "That's the supposed legacy of the heavens?" She wrinkled her nose. "I can't believe we went to all that trouble to steal an unfashionable hair accessory."

The disgruntled cat emitted an unhappy *mrow!* and stalked in front of Elaram, blocking her view. It stopped at the center of their circle to sniff once at the circlet before making a straight line to the other side.

The Elder's reply was serene: "Fashion is but one representation of power. It changes with the moon as fortunes wax and wane."

Unexpectedly, Maketh spoke. "It is a key."

Rahelu looked up to find the Guardian's gaze resting on her, even as the shameless cat *mrowed* and butted its head insistently against his hand.

"To what?" Ghardon asked. "A barrier? It's no resonance crystal."

"A door," Jhobon guessed. "Or a gate."

Ghardon's retort came swiftly. "That implies a contiguous circuit. This is…"

Though the Elder did not smile again, she did not forbid the Supplicants their speculation—not even when Maketh deactivated his barriers and Csorath cautioned them to keep their voices low as he headed to the tiller—before she retired to the aftercabin.

"Please, Maketh." Elaram widened her eyes, batting long eyelashes and jutting her lower lip forward. "Won't you tell us what it unlocks?"

Maketh said no more. While he was immune to laughter

and Elaram's pretty pouting, he was not, apparently, entirely immune to human weaknesses—the purring cat in his lap luxuriating in head scratches was testament to that—but that didn't make being the subject of his regard any easier, even if his previous hostility had been displaced with...with...

Rahelu debated *'curiosity'*, *'perplexity'*, and *'pity'* before finally landing on *'indecision'*. It was the look of someone who had discovered a contradictory data point, torn between dismissing it as an anomaly and clinging to their worldview or embracing it in search of a new theory.

"Power," Imos No-sleeves said and looked to his Dedicate for confirmation.

Maketh stood, his expression impassive as ever. "It is late," he said—a world of disapproval packed into those three little words—and retired himself.

Ylaen nodded and said, "Power."

"No prizes for you; that's too general an answer," Elaram said. "I bet it's a beacon."

"It's a literal crown, Elaram. What is a crown but power, distilled into a symbolic, physical form?" Ylaen turned his head and raised his chin to strike a familiar pose that was stamped on the back of every gold kez in circulation. Bright moonlight etched his face in profile but threw his features into darkness.

"Wouldn't suit you," Ghardon said. "Black on black is a terrible look."

The senior mages' collective equanimity was suspicious. Either they believed themselves safe now in this empty vastness of the ocean—or this was a calculated revelation to flush out the supposed spy. Who would...

...do what? There was no sending off intelligence reports from the middle of the ocean. If there truly was a spy hidden amongst them, one who had somehow evaded all their searching, they would have to wait until the *Sooty Gull* put into port—or find some way of making contact with another agent on a nearby ship.

"What are you betting, Rahelu?"

Ghardon's question drew her attention back. The others were crowded around Jhobon, who scribbled furiously in his notebook and said, "The buy-in is fifty silver kez."

Rahelu stared.

Even Jhobon? She'd thought him too sensible to get involved with frivolity like this but apparently not. Was this all just a game to them? Had they forgotten how close they'd come to losing their thumbs and minds? The terrible expression on Csorath's face as he rolled Kerg's dead body in a sheet of canvas? The distant cries of the passengers and crew of the twice-doomed merchant vessel that Anathwan had sacrificed so they might escape?

Did they not realize that their Houses were betting their very lives on finding this artifact?

Nheras had left early at the first signs of their nonsense; Rahelu wished she had too.

"Come on." Elaram poked her in the ribs. "It's two hundred and fifty silver if you win."

Two hundred, actually; she wasn't going to count the return of her initial wager as part of the profits.

Out loud, Rahelu said, "I'm going to sleep. I only bet when the prize is worth my while," and went to join Nheras in the hold.

The other girl said nothing as Rahelu climbed into her hammock. Sweat dampened the chilled forearms she rested on her burning forehead and aching eyes. She lay in the dark, listening: to the chatter of the other four above; the gentle rhythm of waves washing against the sides of the ship's hull; the sounds of Nheras's shallow, labored breathing; her own beating heart; the nagging sensation of a memory struggling to surface, an ebb and swell that tugged at her frayed resonance senses.

Above them, Ghardon said, "You're not seriously trying to reconstruct Silcarez's voyage? I'm telling you, Reshwim's accounts aren't reliable!"

Jhobon's indistinct, rambling reply was lost beneath Ylaen's louder drawl ("What else is there to do? Besides, we like looking at the pictures.") and Elaram's high-pitched giggling.

Nheras would have lain in the dark, listening to every word they uttered.

Nheras was still awake.

Eventually, Rahelu said: "The box we stole…"

Was there a slowing in the pattern of inhalation and exhalation?

"…it held an obsidian crown."

Nheras didn't reply.

Fine.

It wasn't like Rahelu had asked a question. No question, no reply—all fine, very acceptable, even if some sort of acknowledgment would have been nice.

But next time, she would save her breath. If Nheras chose to exclude herself from their company, then Rahelu had no obligation to keep her apprised of significant developments that occurred when she wasn't around.

The air down here was dead; so was the ambient resonance, thanks to their dreamwards. Toss about as she might, Rahelu couldn't get comfortable. She shut her eyes and turned her focus inward until the unison throbbing of her leg wound and resonance-backlash-induced headache and her heart grew so loud it drowned out the House-born chatter.

She nearly missed the whisper:

"A chain."

"What?"

"It's a chain," Nheras said.

"No, it's not. It's shaped like a—"

"All crowns are chains."

A chain. A black chain. Black chain and black knives and bloodied crystal and a glittering black gem that matched the—

—gold-flecked black crown inside a wooden, velvet-lined case—

In a flash, she knew: Onneja's Augury.

She braced herself for pain and seized the realization, pushing for the full memory to unfurl itself. There was some connection here, between the fragments of the future she had glimpsed and not understood, and the artifact they sought.

Evocation resisted her—her own mind resisted her, hiding behind a swirling black haze. She pushed harder, visualizing a strong puff of cleansing wind that would part the smoke and reveal the memories behind. The harder she pushed, the more substance the smoke gained until it felt like she was pushing a large boulder uphill.

She was so very tired.

And it was so very heavy.

Rahelu let go and sank into shadowed sleep.

18

SORRY

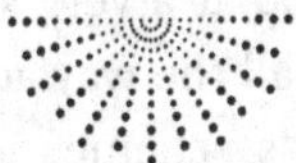

THE 3RD DAY OF EARLY HARVEST, 530 A.E./A.F.

ELARAM HEAVED A GREAT SIGH AS SHE DANGLED from the mast.

She should have been exceedingly bored by the endless blue expanse that stretched east and west and north and south and up and down and every other direction in between.

She should have been incredibly annoyed by the nagging, repetitious, uninspired noises of the sea: the slapping of waves upon the hull, the flapping of ropes, and the snapping of canvas as the wind blew and the sails billowed.

She should have found life aboard the *Sooty Gull* agonizingly dull for its routines were far more strictly regimented than the ones at home, and Mother had, once, during fourth year, scheduled every waking quarter-span of her summer break when it had become apparent that her marks in Seeking meant she would be graduating alongside her brother with an acceptable Guild rating after all, and therefore worthy of being dragged to meeting after meeting after meeting to be paraded before potential sponsors who were *drab* and *humorless* and—most unforgivable of offenses—so godsdamned fucking *respectable*.

The sea, however, was not boring or annoying or dull.

It was ever-changing, mysterious, and beautiful.

And it was awful, just simply awful, that she had missed out for so long. She'd grown up in Ennuost Yrg! Right on the doorstep of the Aleituan Sea! The Kuath Bay was visible from her bedroom window! Albeit as a very small shimmer of Isca blue and only if she stood at a very specific spot, on tiptoes, craning her neck to look all the way across the city.

But between Mother's schemes and her brother's plans and her own lack of any ambitions in particular, other than to have the best fun possible as much as possible, Elaram had never given the sea a second thought. Ships had always seemed to be a great inconvenience rather than a great method of conveyance. The ones Mother deemed safe took so very many people to get moving; the ones that looked like they were full of fun and stories made port at the Lowdocks and Mother always got so upset whenever she heard that Elaram had so much set a toe anywhere outside Westgate, Sunset, or Northpoint without an escort. Mother had had such a fit when their unconscious bodies had been brought home in the family palanquin that Lhorne (kind-hearted, well-meaning, but willfully oblivious to how the world actually functioned) had summoned, then had pretended to nearly faint herself when she had learned the two of them had been there, in Market Square, right at the center of *'that awful, messy, religious affair that good obedient children had no business being involved with in the first place'* just so she would have an excuse to clear her *entire schedule* and see to it that neither of them would get to leave her sight to see or do anything interesting or worthwhile with their days—or lives, for that matter. Father had had to step in and remind Mother that there was no need to accompany them to Cseryl and Lhorne's party on the pretext of *'paying a congratulatory visit'* to *'a dear old friend'* on the *'happy occasion of her daughter and nephew successfully Petitioning'* (when everyone knew that Mere Ideth would rather permit her son and heir to make his inadvisable choice of consort than to allow Suurynn Issolm into her presence) since she was owed several favors, whereupon Mother had put away her richest robes and let them go alone—after they had sworn private oaths in blood and upon crystal that they would not associate with anyone other than the other Supplicants-to-be and that they would absolutely not set a foot outside their palanquin to go anywhere other than the Ideth estates.

Gods be thanked for Ana.

Still, Elaram hadn't been overjoyed about getting on a boat. You couldn't easily stop a boat and get out to look at something that had caught your eye the way you could in a palanquin. One time during the summer break in their third year, Rualk of Isonn had invited her to go river boating on the Suusradi and she had lasted two whole days before she'd been bored sick. The Isonn barge had no sails so it had to be pulled upstream by teams of plodding oxen so slow that she could have covered twice the distance on her own feet in the same time without breaking a sweat, and there'd been no entertainment aboard to speak of, other than those third-rate hired musicians who would only play the yawn-inducing traditional ballads Rualk preferred, and Rualk himself had spent the whole time lazing in the sun, answering all of Elaram's questions with monosyllabic words, and Rualk's uncle had kept telling her no, they could not stop every kual to watch the river traders negotiating with the eel trappers or the rice farmers or go look for baby deer in the scrubby forests. That night, she'd secretly swallowed a few drops of lymwort syrup which had caused her to vomit her dinner all over Rualk in a most *spectacular* manner and Rualk's uncle had charged his daughter Enith with seeing Elaram safely back to Ennuost Yrg the very next day, seeing as how she and Rualk were no longer on speaking terms after the incident.

In revenge, Enith had taken their raft down a section of the Suusradi her father had explicitly ordered them to avoid for fear of upsetting Elaram's delicate stomach further and you couldn't even be mad at her for it: the ride through the churning white rapids (and the subsequent ride that followed) had been *thrillingly delightful*.

And thus, Elaram had felt perfectly justified in concluding that boats and sailing were for dull people with dull lives. Even the *Winged Arrow* hadn't changed her opinion much. While Isonn's fastest ship was undeniably very pretty—

(Jhobon had kept marveling at the ship's 'fine lines' and 'sharp hull' and had spent considerable time sketching the complicated system of blocks and tackles and ropes and pulleys for its forest of sails which apparently required a full complement of thirty hands to manage—an exercise that he had had to give up on account of Captain Csorath tearing out a third of his notebook and confiscating the pages when he noticed they contained laboriously attempted recreations of the great cabin's schematics, inclusive of its impressive Obfuscation barriers.)

—it was still rather like living at home, for all that it was a building that floated on the sea, except Elaram was stuck under the watchful eyes of two senior mages upon whose whims turned the success or failure of her budding career instead of her absent-minded parents, only five other people who were deemed to be socially acceptable company, without the option of being able to go somewhere else and just two nights free to do any socializing whatsoever.

That had been before she had stepped aboard the *Sooty Gull*, and—oh!

Climbing up, up, up to perch at the very top of the swaying mast, feeling the lift of the wind at her back, seeing the scintillating sparkle of sunlight upon the sapphire sea, hearing the rush of the white-frothed waves pushing the hull, meeting the curious pods of dolphins and whales that swam alongside as she flew with the *Gull* and the happy flocks of visiting seabirds as they all chased the horizon…

Elaram spread her arms and legs, arching backwards, letting the ship swing her by her rope in a gentle arc above the deck. If she hadn't already known from the moment Ana had confirmed they were on the most fucking epic mission ever, this would've made up her mind.

She was in love.

Ship life was the best life and the *Sooty Gull* was the best ship—not that you'd know it from the others.

Dedicate Csorath hardly spoke except to give orders. Possibly because captains weren't allowed to insult vessels under their command or, more probably, because he was too tired and grieved and busy to do anything but.

Neither the Elder nor the Guardian seemed to fully exist in the present. They had claimed—or Csorath had relinquished his claim on—the entire tiny aftercabin. So far as Elaram could tell from eavesdropping on their muffled conversations through the aft bulkhead (which made for a very limited, imprecise dataset, seeing as she couldn't very well physically peek into the aftercabin or get past the Obfuscation barriers Maketh had installed), the Issolm Elder and the Imos Dedicate spent most of their time hunkered over the small selection of books Ana had brought from her personal library and the wooden box stolen from Ruarem's shop and the black crown inside.

There was a haunted aspect to Maketh's haggard face whenever they periodically surfaced to sit cross-legged at the prow, hands cupped around pulsating focus stones as they recharged their mage pendants.

Ana, on the other hand, drifted through the waking spans

as though she walked through a dream. (Perhaps she did. Between all her Auguries and her never-ending contemplation of the crown, perhaps it had become difficult for Ana to tell the difference.)

Jhobon, when he wasn't tending the sails or obsessively staring at the sky, hid himself in the hold and his nose in his notebook. Ylaen called the *Gull* 'an ungainly excuse for a single-masted cutter' and spent a lot of time hurling knives into its wood. Rahelu complained about its rigging being 'unnecessarily complicated' for its size and lamented its lack of decent nets. Whenever Nheras handed off the captain's battered bronze spyglass to Elaram, she did it grim-faced and white-knuckled, and whenever Elaram passed the precious instrument into her brother's care, he always gave it the stink eye.

Silly sourpusses, all of them.

Not one had cheered with her when *finally*, after days and days and days of begging the captain—and a lot of gentle urging over mealtimes from Anathwan—her efforts paid off: having left the trade routes behind, Csorath begrudgingly allowed some of the Supplicants to take turns at the *Gull's* tiller, starting with Rahelu, Jhobon, and then Ylaen, all while hovering over their shoulders, preemptively correcting their steering the whole time.

When Jhobon had asked, "Captain, perhaps if you would just let us see the charts..." Csorath had fixed him with such a severe stare that Jhobon had begun mumbling apologies before the captain finally cut him off with, "There are no charts." Jhobon was so shocked he kept repeating "How can there be no charts?" over and over to Ylaen—who bore it with affectionate tolerance—and to Rahelu—who was briefly surprised, then annoyed, until she eventually snapped (as she was wont to do) and yelled some nonsense about how charts were a privilege and a crutch used by lazy House-born and rich merchants who were too soft to use their brains. Personally, Elaram thought Jhobon had been rather rude. Obviously, there had to be charts; they just happened to live inside Csorath's head; of course he wasn't going to let anybody from House Imrell in on Isonn trade secrets.

Still, the next time all three senior mages were on deck for the midday meal, Elaram offered to brew up a fresh pot of heartleaf tea, and a wan and pale Ana had gratefully accepted.

The aftercabin was filled with clutter.

Tea, yes, and plenty of it.

Books; boring ones—esoteric textbooks on obscure resonance theorems and House Issolm histories detailing the line of succession and the circumstances of each Atriarch's rise to power since its founding, with all of the gossip and drama redacted—masquerading as the interesting adventure stories and romantic ballads that they weren't behind light Seemings anchored to resonance crystal seals hidden underneath the thick endpapers glued to the covers.

Sketches of the cultists' ritual knives and the stargem Rahelu had found littered the desk. Fragments of erotic-sounding poems mixed with bits of creepy scripture and temple prayers scribbled in the margins. The wooden box they had stolen sat on top, its lid open, the black crown inside looking even duller and more unimpressive than when Ana had revealed it last night under the moon and starlight.

Exactly nothing had happened when Elaram had tried it on.

There were, indeed, no physical charts.

Unfortunately, no amount of cozying up to Csorath moved him to let her have a turn at the tiller; a decision that would have been completely unfair if he hadn't agreed to teach her how to fly instead.

Which was why she was currently hanging from the top of the mast, swaying in the wind at the end of the short rope looped around her ribs and underneath her armpits, trying—and failing—to get the attention of *any* of the ten or so seabirds currently within her Seeking range.

"Give it up, Ela," Ghardon said from aft of her. He had threaded both arms and legs through gaps in the rigging—which didn't look the slightest bit comfortable—so he could cling on like overgrown moss; his face was practically the same color. "You're making me nauseous, swinging about like that."

"You're feeling nauseous because you keep looking down," she said. "Chew on the ginger I gave you"—she used the toe of her left foot to spin around and push off the mast so she swung right past her brother—"and look out over the water."

Too fast.

As she passed the mast again, she gripped it briefly with her feet to take off some momentum.

"You are supposed to be"—she snaked her left hand through the square hole of ropes framing his green-tinged face—"on Seeking duty!" and gave his nose a good, firm tweak.

"Ow!" He tried to swat her back but had kept his elbows hooked onto the shrouds so he couldn't have possibly reached her and anyway, she'd swung well clear by then. "You miserable little monkey, I—" and then he forgot all about reprimanding her for reprimanding him because the heavy bronze spyglass slipped from his clammy grasp.

Elaram caught it. Midswing. With her bare feet, like a proper acrobat.

And now she could try to flip it up into her hands, spinning end over end like some of the baton tricks she'd seen street performers do, but Csorath had taken his hawk-sharp eyes off Rahelu's steering to watch them and she remembered she was supposed to be trying to fly the other way.

Also, she should probably practice with something less breakable from a height that was less likely to cause severe damage to the deck (and possibly the hull) and impair their ability to successfully navigate the crossing if she were to drop the spyglass.

Maybe Nheras would let her borrow her baton.

And maybe pigs might fly.

"Sorry." Elaram contritely offered the spyglass without even wiggling it in her brother's face as the situation begged her to do. "Why don't you ask to switch duties with Rahelu? You won't even have to worry about steering—the captain will take care of that—just the ropes."

Also, Rahelu was better at Seeking than he was. As a matter of fact, so far Rahelu was doing better at everything on this assignment than Ghardon was, which had to be why he walked around with a perpetual air of injury. His ego must be on its deathbed. Ordinarily, Elaram wouldn't have worried, but Rahelu was in her element and Nheras was determined to take his place. The fawning, obsequious way Ilyn had attached herself to the Elder whenever she had the opportunity was utterly transparent, but Ana was not her usual self. If Ghardon wasn't careful, if he didn't figure out how to cope soon, he was going to drop straight from the top down to the bottom of Ana's rankings, level with her, and Nheras would be the one ordering them around unless Rahelu suddenly grew wise to the play for position.

And maybe fish might fly.

But she was trying to cheer her brother up, not make him feel even worse, so Elaram stopped swinging around and held still.

He wiped his shaking hands on his shirt—twice—before he took back the spyglass. Ghardon didn't comment on her suggestion (which meant he knew she was right) but he also said, "They don't like what you're trying to do."

'*They*' meaning the seabirds.

That meant he was mostly fine since he was back to giving her big-brotherly advice on things he knew nothing about.

"I almost had it before." She pouted at the birds in question: a cluster of five or seven gulls just aft and to port, coasting along on the thermals inside their collective resonance aura of sky-blue contentment. "Then you came and interrupted me."

She chewed on her lip as she contemplated the gulls. The little flock had flown with the ship ever since they'd left Peshwan Yrg, thanks to Rahelu's bet with Ylaen. Elaram was very proud of Rahelu for coming up with the idea—

(They were going to have so much fun once they got back from the end of the world with the artifact they were chasing and Elaram could present her sister properly at the next Issolm dinner party. With a fashionable wardrobe and a better hairstyle and the reputational clout that would accrue with pulling off this mission, the former fisher girl was going to puncture *so many egos* once you aimed her in the right direction, and Elaram was very good at aiming weapons of blunt destruction at puffed-up targets from a distance. Cseryl of Ideth would be their first casualty.)

—for she could think of no fate Ylaen was more deserving of than to be bombarded with bird shit.

She was disappointed (but not surprised) that Rahelu hadn't thought to consult anyone first. Fortunate that Csorath had interrupted them before they could get started, and doubly fortunate that she and Ghardon were there because '*every gull in the harbor*' was the worst possible parameter Rahelu could have set for herself, and '*mob*' and '*take you flying*' weren't much better. Thanks to her timely intervention (and, she supposed, Jhobon's; he had spotted six out of the seven ambiguities she'd tried to introduce in Issolm favor) the terms of the contest were now governed by a two-page document and the betting pool was currently at twenty-six silver kez with four-to-one odds in Rahelu's favor. Ylaen's skill with Projection was obviously superior but he had the harder task of convincing at least fifty- or sixty-odd birds to do the extremely unnatural thing of picking Rahelu up by her hair and clothing simultaneously and flying her once around the ship. Also, Rahelu had some Isonn-like affinity with the gulls: two or three of the braver birds had taken to regularly perching on the toprail within arm's reach of the tiller when-ever Rahelu was on watch, their snowy heads cocked in attentive poses as she spoke softly to them in Chanazian, and at least a dozen or so were starting to void their bowels in Ylaen's general direction whenever he ventured up on deck. The first time it had happened, Elaram had wondered whether Csorath would punish Rahelu for it, or punish them all for encouraging the contest, but the captain simply ordered the decks scrubbed more frequently. Which nobody, other than Ghardon and Nheras, minded because it was something to pass the time.

Unfortunately, the side effect of the contest also meant none of the gulls were inclined to listen to Elaram at all.

Not even the one Rahelu had said was the youngest and most impressionable of the flock. Its ruffled coat of scraggly gray, the light brown speckling on its slightly fuzzy-looking white head and neck, and its lack of black flight feathers made it easily distinguishable from the rest of the sleek, well-groomed, monochrome birds. Rahelu had named the bird 'Nelavonezra' (which she said was Chanazian for *little nuisance*') for its noisy, persistent begging, but Nheras had named it 'Little Fishguts' (supposedly for its favorite food) and Little Fishguts was the name that stuck.

If Elaram wasn't so sure that Nheras was up to no good, she would have been rather proud of her other sister's sly, underhanded brilliance. It was fittingly Issolm, except the joke had been at Issolm expense, which made it not very Issolm at all and was therefore proof that Nheras really was up to no good and thus not truly her sister at all.

"I did not interrupt you, and you were not remotely close to getting it," her brother said. "Csorath told you to 'reach as you would with Seeking', not Projection, and—"

"'Make contact as you would to form a Concordance'," Elaram said. "Yes, I know; I was there." (She didn't say, *'and you weren't,'* because she could be subtle if she wanted to be.)

Right now, Little Fishguts—as distinct from Big Fishguts down on the tiller, holding an impenetrable conversation with Csorath in fluent Chanazian of all things, though it did make sense that the captain of the Dominion's diplomatic flagship would be fluent in many languages—was playing drop-catch in the thermals with a toy fish Rahelu had woven out of dried eel-grass two days earlier.

Ghardon sighed. "If you haven't got it by now, you're not going to get it today. Try again tomorrow." He lowered his voice to a whisper. "Ela, I know you're unhappy."

"Don't be silly."

She was not. Not in the slightest. If she were, she would be doing something appropriately sulky, such as moping about when it wasn't her watch and brooding as she stared off into the distance with a tragic air, like Ylaen was.

Which was very unfair of him, considering that she'd decided to forgive his inadequate performance (it had been their first time together after all, so how was he to know what she preferred when they didn't trust each other enough to be using Seeking?) since he'd helped her carry her brother all the way back up to the citadel. She'd even suggested that perhaps they could go down to the festival fires in the fields and find solace together, but he had looked at her with such, such—she had no word for the dreadful expression on his face (which, in itself, was incredible, considering that she'd spent the last five years learning how to categorize every single human expression)—and then left her standing awkwardly in the hallway outside Ana's apartments without saying a word.

"What did Mother say to you before we left?" he asked.

"Nothing."

Mother hadn't said one gods-cursed thing to Elaram. She'd been far too busy fussing and fretting over her golden boy. As usual.

"Was it Father then?"

"Of course not."

Father hadn't been home. As usual.

"I see," he said and did not see at all.

But he was trying, which was more than Mother and Father ever did, so she gave him her best smile.

"Stop worrying, big brother, I'm enjoying myself." Elaram set herself swinging again. "You should too. Life's too short to be miserable."

She concentrated on the joy of flying through the air, the wonder she felt at the glorious, spectacular view of the world curving below her, and sent her resonance senses soaring out, skimming over the brilliant blue-green waves then up, up, up to meet Little Fishguts halfway through its dive:

—fish-sea-fall—

Her wings cut the air.

—wind-fly-fall-fish-spin—

Her target tumbling towards the water.

—beak-open-chase—

Little yellow-and-white starbursts in her aura accompany the flutter-thrill swell in her stomach. She smiles wide wide wider as she hurtles down down down—

—sea-pull-strong-wind-feathers—

Three heartbeats to impact.

SNAP!

A burst of golden triumph as they catch the fish, like sunlight breaking through clouds.

—flap-beat-flap-beat-flap-beat—

Tremendous force straining her wings.

—tired-sky-pull-flap-beat-fly-soar—

SO MUCH FUN!

—tired-wind-push-fly—

AGAIN!

—tired-climb-fly-climb-sky-rest—

Wind caressing her feathers.

—tired-sky-rest-keow!

LET'S GO AGAIN!

—tired-rest-keow!

COME ON—

A small flash of bone-white terror.

Somewhere distant: a hot, prickly sensation. Orange-red clouds boiling back over the sun.

"Ela." Noises. "Ela, stop it." Human noises. "You're scaring them."

Unimportant.

COMEONCOMEONCOMEON—

She wanted to fly and fall and fly into the sky the waves the sky—

AGAIN!

Keow! Keow!

KEOWKEOWKEOW—

Rage lanced through her mind, breaking her connection to Little Fishguts.

A heartbeat later, a large gull swooped at her head.

"Hey!" she cried out and ducked, trusting her rope to swing her out of harm's way. "There's no need for that."

"Ela, I think you'd better apologize," Ghardon said. Chalk-white pallor chased the green tinge out of his face as the flock of ten became twenty, then thirty, then a thunderhead-like mass of churning gray-and-white. "And quickly."

KEOW! The gull wheeled around for another pass. *KEOWKEOW!*

"For what?" Elaram ducked again. "We were just having some fun."

Thwarted, the gull flew off to rejoin the flock. A dull, red glow flickered around them.

"See?" Elaram said. Little Fishguts wasn't visible in the

knot of birds gathering astern but a quick Seeking confirmed it was hovering somewhere in the middle. "We're fine."

Two more gulls came shrieking towards the ship, white feathers turned pinkish-gold by the faint haze of reddish-orange in their little resonance auras.

"Captain? Rahelu?" Ghardon called as he conjured an Obfuscation barrier around them. Not his usual one of shining gold but the watery bubble of gray-blue calm Rahelu preferred except he'd made it much, much bigger: a sphere of influence three strides deep in every direction that stopped just short of the greater Obfuscation barriers Maketh had put around the whole ship.

The two gulls crossed the edges of Maketh's barriers, then Ghardon's barrier...and kept flying.

"How do we get them to stop?" His voice climbed higher and higher with every word. One gull landed on a ratline right in front of his nose to stare at him with beady yellow eyes. "And leave us alone?"

"Wait," Rahelu called back. "Usually they stop once you leave their territory and show that you're no threat. Or you can try to scare them off." She paused, then added: "Maybe you guys should get down from the rigging."

"Alright," Ghardon said, eyeing the gull eyeing him. He eased himself down to the next rung. "Ela, let's go."

"I don't want to."

She liked it up here. Being down on deck was boring: you couldn't see as far and Csorath was sure to make up some mind-numbingly dull task for her, like checking every crate of vegetables in the hold for signs of rot.

Besides, she wasn't going to let some birds drive her off.

The second gull sat on the crosstree above her, next to the other end of her rope. It was rather cute when it wasn't squawking at the top of its lungs. Maybe it would let her pet it.

She added, "Let's just wait," but she did get back on the ladder before she cautiously reached out a finger.

Bubble of calm or no, the gull pecked her.

"Ow! You horrid little skyrat."

"Ela, don't," Ghardon said, already halfway down. "We're trying to—"

She grabbed a tiny measure of the pain from her bleeding finger...

"—defuse the situation here, not escalate things."

...and swatted the gull back.

Not hard, and not with her hand—she wasn't cruel—just the smallest of formed Projections, like a little puff of air.

Ghardon groaned as the gull tumbled off its perch and gave an undignified little *aaark!* before spreading its wings and flapping away.

Good. That ought to teach it not to bite people.

"Why, Ela, why?" He'd stopped climbing down to rest his forehead on the back of his white-knuckled grip on the ratlines. "Why do you keep doing things like this?"

Five more gulls darted forward, their wings whipping up an orange-red haze in the ambient resonance.

"If you haven't noticed, brother, your barrier isn't doing any good." Elaram pulled on the gulls' budding anger-alarm; pieces of resonance came to her in wispy trails like skeins of dragon's beard candy. "What are we going to do if the whole flock descends on the ship? Just sit here, completely surrounded? You can't keep broadcasting forever and the moment you stop is the moment they'll mob us. It's better to scare them off now before they work themselves up into a real frenzy."

She lobbed the resonance back at the gulls as two marble-sized warning Projections—she didn't really want to hurt the silly things after all—but she was a bit out of practice so instead of skimming past harmlessly, her Projections struck one gull in its head and another in its breast.

Their tiny hearts seized. The two birds jerked in midair, then plummeted towards the waves.

Oh. Oh no.

The next set of gull cries was deafening.

"No, no!" she blurted out. "I'm sorry; I didn't mean to!"

Words couldn't come fast enough. She switched to Projection; a burst of sharp, black-blue grief. *I didn't mean to! I didn't mean to!* Human noises; human concepts. She tried to bridge the gap with Seeking, reaching out to encompass all those little minds in the flock, sending them the golden joy and beautiful sky-blue wonder she'd felt before. *I just wanted—sea-fall-wind-fly-sky-fall-beat-flap-soar—*

KEOWKEOWKEOW!

The flock's crude Concordance shrilled out an alarm over the open sea. The distress beacon rippled through the ambient resonance for at least one, perhaps two, kual.

Distantly, a handful of echoes: *keowkeowkeow!*

Nonononono.

I'm sorry! Elaram sent. *I'm sorry, I'm sorry, I'm—*

Air roared and thundered in her ears.

The flock struck.

A furious storm of small feathered bodies swarmed the topmast. She shrieked as they dove at her face, lifting her arms to protect her eyes, squeezing them shut. Sharp beaks tore at her hair, shredded her sleeves, scored her unprotected skin. Heavy wingbeats assailed her; a rain of fierce blows that pushed her off the ladder.

Fear surged.

"Help!" Elaram screamed. *HELP!*

The flock wheeled around and shrieked back. They flew in for their next onslaught; bodies armored with the hard, ugly yellow gleam of vindication.

A second swell of calm flooded the air with deep, slow-moving currents. For a moment, Elaram recalled lying on a bamboo raft that drifted down a lazy river, breath riven from her lungs by fierce white rapids. Rahelu's work; it seemed to lull the oncoming gulls into a hover.

Oh thank gods.

Then: "All of you will stop," Csorath ordered.

"But Elaram—"

The Seeker-captain overrode Rahelu's protests. "She hurt one of their young and killed two of their number. The flock will not stop now unless you slay more of them, and that would be an unconscionable use of your resonance skills. Not to mention that there are worse things out there, hoping to find us."

The river wavered, then vanished. And while Elaram understood why Rahelu didn't want to kill the gulls she loved, the betrayal hurt more than she thought it would.

It cut deeper than the second round of cuts the gulls laid in her scalp.

Her brother fought on but he was losing the battle: his Obfuscation barrier shrank and shrank as wave after wave of gulls attacked. There must be hundreds of birds now, with more and more converging from every direction. Every time one flew at them, its aura blazing red with anger, its flight path left a molten wake in his bubble of calm.

It didn't take long before that calm crumbled.

The only resonance left to draw upon was the terror pouring out of her aura into the ambient resonance. Any moment now, he would condense that swirling bone-white mist into a ring of protective spikes around her and make those awful birds go away, like he'd always made anything and anybody that hurt her go away.

But he didn't.

He didn't.

The birds kept on coming, striking her over and over with their wings and their beaks until her sobs were as loud as their shrieks, and Ghardon just...he just clung to the ropes and let the gulls vomit and shit on them both until the last one finished hurling the contents of its stomach and bowels at her and flew off.

Ghardon came back and caught her mid-swing.

"Come on, little monkey, climb on me," he said. "Let's go get cleaned up."

He carried her down the mast and onto the solid deck and tried to set her on her feet.

She kept her arms and legs wrapped around his neck and shoulders and waist and clung on.

Rahelu started forward to meet them, but one stern look from Csorath sent her scurrying back to her post.

"Go back aloft, boy," Csorath said. "Your watch is far from ended."

"Captain." Very carefully, so as not to bump her, Ghardon bent down and set the spyglass on the deck. "Permission to be excused. My sister is in need of urgent care."

Silence reigned.

Elaram buried her face in her brother's shoulder and tried very hard not to think about anything at all.

"Um, Captain?" Rahelu asked. "The wind is holding steady for the present and Ghardon seems unwell himself. Permission to go aloft in his stead?"

"Very well," Csorath said. "But I'll have no more of this immature conduct. This business"—he waved his arm; an expansive gesture that encompassed the three of them, the dispersing flock, and the horizon—"ends now."

"Aye, Captain." Rahelu lashed the tiller in place and scrambled up the rigging with the spyglass.

"Aye, Captain," Ghardon echoed.

Elaram felt Csorath's eyes and Seeking upon her as her brother turned towards the cargo hatch.

"Aye, Captain," she whispered.

Csorath dismissed them.

Ghardon carried her down into the hold, where the other three Supplicants lay asleep in their hammocks.

She said nothing as her brother helped her remove her soiled shirt, rinsed out her hair and washed off all the blood and half-digested food and dung with the rest of his water ration, applied a liberal coat of stinging antiseptic balm over her cuts, and then swaddled her up like a baby with a bolt of blue silk from the stash they were supposedly smuggling.

"Ela," he said.

She hugged her shins with both arms and rested her chin on her knees, sniffling. He'd drawn out and gently lilted the syllables of her call name the way she did when she was calling the ship's cat which meant he was about to use his '*I-know-you-don't-want-to-but-we-need-to-talk-because-it's-important*' voice on her.

"Someday you're going to have to learn how to stay out of trouble. I won't always be around to keep you safe."

What Elaram heard was: '*You shouldn't be here; you shouldn't have come.*'

"Go away then," she said, staring at her feet. She wiggled her toes; the nails were getting long again. "Leave me."

He sighed. A great, world-weary sigh. He was doing a lot of that lately.

"Kyrosh said yes."

"What?"

"Kyrosh said yes," Ghardon repeated patiently.

"He said yes?" She felt very stupid parroting his words but she couldn't help it. "When did he say yes?"

"The night before we left."

At Ideth's party? "How did I not hear about this?"

"You were busy."

Oh. *Oh.*

"But he won't join us." Her thoughts moved sluggishly, crawling over each other like snails. "Myreil won't let him."

"No," Ghardon said. "So you'll get your wish, little sister. I will be leaving you."

"When?"

"When we get back."

"I meant"—he was so stupid; how could he be so stupid?—"when did you tell Mother and Father?"

There was no way they had agreed to this. They would have stopped it.

"I haven't."

She stared at him. "You haven't."

The floor seemed to drop out from under her, or maybe the ceiling had fallen on her, or maybe some giant hand had picked up the whole ship and thrown it because everything was spinning and nothing made sense.

"No," he said. "You're the first to know. Please don't tell, little sister; I need some time to work out how." He stood up. "I'd better finish my watch. I'll wake Jhobon and ask him to keep you company."

"He won't want to."

Ever since solstice, ever since that night aboard the *Winged Arrow*, Jhobon had avoided her like she was poison.

"He will. As long as you don't bite."

19

WORDS

*****

J HOBON LOVED PROBLEMS.

The only thing better than having a problem dropped in his lap was being the first to discover it. That meant he could hoard all of the wonderful intellectual challenges it represented, taking his time to dissect them, mulling over possibility after possibility from angle after angle. The mental *click* as pieces fell into position. The sudden flash of insight. The glimpse of elegant reason behind chaotic unreason. Then: illumination. *This* because of *that*; *that* because of *this*; the *if/then/else* architecture building *inputs* into glorious *result*.

And then there was nothing to fear. Once you understood how the result was derived, you didn't have to live with it if you didn't like it. You could change the parameters or change the equation; and if your first few attempts didn't work, well, it just meant you needed to try something else.

A solution—multiple solutions—always existed.

It was just a matter of how long it took him to find it.

And since he kept a record of every problem he'd ever solved and how long it had taken him, his estimates were accurate to a confidence level of eighty-five percent.

Not bad. Not bad at all.

Simple problems—like how the *Sooty Gull* managed to achieve an average speed of two to three kual per span though Captain Csorath had them sailing ten degrees south of the main sea routes where the trade winds were scarce—took him around four to eight spans.

(Solution: the *Sooty Gull's* shipwright and sailmaker were mathematical geniuses whose sail plan and design for the *Gull* translated to a total sail area one-and-a-half times greater than another sloop of comparable size with only an additional ten percent increase in mast height and girth; not to mention the cunningly constructed running bowsprit.)

Complicated problems—like figuring out where, exactly, Csorath had taken the *Gull* and how far off from Tsorek-fa they were when he had no charts, no compass, and no visible landmarks to reference—took him about a week.

(Solution: the *Sooty Gull's* little namesakes had an average range of a hundred kual and their annual migratory route crossed both the Aleituan and Abmerduan Seas. None were interested in aiding Ylaen to win his bet with Rahelu—'why-no-wings-want-fly?' the flock had responded; then, after the matter had been explained to them, offered the unsolicited advice of, 'must-sing-dance-hunt-fish-win-mate-pair-bond'—but they had permitted Ylaen to join their crude Concordance from time to time so, eventually, Jhobon had been able to cross reference the flock's scent-map of the course they had taken from Peshwan Yrg against his star readings and hastily reconstructed working copy of the *Winged Arrow's* charts to pinpoint their approximate location.)

He'd told Ylaen the very moment he'd worked it out. Rushed up on deck a full span before he was due for his watch, short snatches of staccato whispers in Free Speech that Nheras wouldn't understand pouring out like dawn light over dark water. Good news: we're about three hundred kual or so off the coast of Tsorek-fa. Csorath's giving the city of sails a wide berth—you'd have to steer a north-north-westerly course for at least three to five days before we're in range of any clan's scout ships—and he's taking us well clear of the Dragon's Teeth. We won't have to sleep with our eyes open, you won't have to run a Seeming non-stop, we might just be able to fly by, swift as a questryl, slip through the present without ever touching the past or the future, we can go to the Desolate Isles and come back and be away again, Zovresh and Xya will never even know that we were here—

His tsol-na, leaning back against the steering post, eyes shut against the sunrise, steering by feel alone, had let him go on expounding his theories for another span, until full light brought a yawning Nheras down from aloft, a bright-eyed Elaram bounding up from below, and a serene Rahelu who went straight to the bowsprit to meditate. Ylaen had watched her go through cracked eyelids.

Memory flashed through their tsol-bond:

—he leaves the temple at the solstice's zenith with half his soul deadened to go down to the sea and finds solace in hurling the tsol-blade into the black depths—

"They know, tsol-ek," Ylaen murmured.

The sea had refused Ylaen's sacrifice and given the tsol-blade back. It now lay wrapped in a packet of embroidered white silk, its presence muffled under five layers of Obfuscation barriers Jhobon had anchored to the resonance crystal beadwork on the unwanted shirt.

"Achwa-te-gish-no, Jhobon; I cannot avoid it. The sages named us true."

Jhobon had laid his hand on Ylaen's white-knuckled one. "The ocean is wide. Do not give up on hope. Not now. Not when you've seen that no Augury is certain."

More and more, his tsol-na seemed to need the reminder. The sages had their own secretive methods, but those could not be so different to how Anathwan worked, which meant if the Elder could be wrong, then the sages could be wrong.

His thoughts drew forth a tired smile—and a lie. "Perhaps you are right," Ylaen had said, before relinquishing the tiller to him and following Nheras below.

Jhobon had spent the rest of earthwatch thinking.

He needed better words.

They needed a better solution.

But complex problems—like the one Ghardon had, quite literally, just dropped in his lap—were difficult to solve.

He'd been jolted awake by a rough hand. While he'd blinked bleary eyes, still groggy with sleep, Ghardon had dumped him out of his hammock and said: "Get up."

Jhobon had panicked as the deck rushed toward his face.

First, he had put his hands to his pockets for chalk and crystal but he had none on him: he'd slept in his loincloth because his clothes had still been damp at the end of his watch so he'd left them sunning on the deck. Next, he'd tried activating Dethiram's Shield—he had thought long and hard about what kind of barrier would work best against the Issolm Supplicant—but he'd drained most of the power in his focus stone by trying Evocations on Reshwim's illustrations and had yet to recharge it. Then finally—finally!—the reflexes Ylaen had relentlessly drilled into him kicked in. His body had tucked and rolled him to his feet, brought his fists up...

...and Ghardon had put a sniffling, silk-wrapped, soggy Elaram into his arms.

He'd staggered from her sudden weight. "I—"

"Yes, you. I need you to look after Ela," Ghardon had said, and stalked away, before Jhobon could ask a number of vitally important questions, such as *'what happened to her?'*, *'where are you going?'*, *'why me and not one of your other sisters?'*, and—

"What's wrong? How do I fix it?"

"There's nothing to fix. She's a person, not a construct."

Jhobon knew that. It was why she terrified him.

Elaram, for her part, had said nothing at all.

"I—"

He'd stayed frozen to the spot, thoughts whirring, as she buried her face in his neck. Water trickled from the loose ends of her damp hair; strands of it stuck to their skin, smushed between the soft curve of her cheek and her ear and his shoulder. The astringent scent of numbweed balm; beneath that, the faint copper tang of blood.

"Tell her a story."

"The Skymother's mirror? But I don't know that story!"

"Then tell her a different one. Or make some shit up." Ghardon's voice had faded as he disappeared up the companionway. "Romantic stuff. Grand adventures. Tragic heroes. That kind of thing."

Romance, adventure, and tragedy? That was Ylaen's area of expertise. But he'd not even taken one step towards the hammocks before she'd whispered, "Don't! Oh, don't," so they'd ended up on the deck: he leaned against the portside bulkhead with his knees up, and she curled like an oversized cat, wedged into the valley between his torso and thighs.

Time crept by, heartbeat by heartbeat, while he tried to think of something comforting to say, but he had never been much good with words. Words were an imprecise medium for expression—their effectiveness depended on a foundation of shared cultural understanding between speaker and listener, and Aleznuaweithish vocabulary was so limited.

Projection was better. It didn't confer the complete understanding of the tsol-bond, but you didn't have to worry about shaping your intent to fit into words and phrases; you could simply throw the whole, complicated knot of emotions lodged in your chest at someone and they would get the gist.

Except Elaram didn't seem inclined to do that. She had scrunched her aura down as tight as it would go and must be wearing some variant of Rahelu's resonance ward too, because he couldn't feel a thing except the quiet rise and fall of her breathing and the loud thrumming of his pulse. (If that bothered her, she didn't show it.)

Which left him with Seeking. Seeking would tell him what she wanted to hear, as well as what she needed to hear, but Seeking was also the last thing he would want someone to try on him if he were her because sometimes sharing the shadows in your heart meant darkening the rest of their days.

That sent his thoughts skittering to the first problem he had ever encountered. A wicked problem. He hadn't been able to solve it then—just shuffled the pieces around for half a decade or so—and he was no closer to solving it now.

(Often, Ylaen said: "We should run." Sometimes, Jhobon answered with: "We already have." Other times, he asked: "To where?" His tsol-na had no answers for that; save to fall back on saying that they hadn't run far enough; that they ought to have kept going after Ennuost Yrg—north, south, west; it was all the same to him so long as it wasn't back *east*. The stars could ordain whatever they pleased and the sages could proclaim whatever they liked but nobody could force him to his fate if they couldn't lay a hand on him in the first place, and hadn't Jhobon been the one to propose that theory? To which he had pointed out there was nowhere on the Ngutoccai continent they could run from the Houses, which was why they had stayed in Ennuost Yrg. They'd gone through the motions of that old, old argument right up until their Atriarchs had yanked on their leashes. They'd whined like two whipped dogs but were, in the end, obedient to their collars and got on the *Winged Arrow* as ordered, and then Elder Anathwan had given them the secret of Seeming, and, for a day or two, Ylaen had been as giddy as he—the clans knew nothing of Seeming—and then, the solstice, and after that, another devastating cycle of raised hopes and crushed dreams when Jhobon's theory of Revocation had not borne out. And now? His tsol-na was back to alternating between bouts of melancholic brooding and maniacal practice sessions with knives interspersed with periods of obsessively pursuing distractions in a fatalistic attempt at acceptance.)

But just because he didn't have a solution didn't mean there wasn't one; he simply wasn't looking at the problem from the right angle, which pointed to a flaw in his approach.

So: what was he doing wrong?

The Starfather worked in patterns. Complex patterns, but patterns nonetheless. And human behavior was the most complex pattern of all: rooted in logic, yet without the consistency of logic. Every time Jhobon had failed to solve a problem, it had been one that dealt with human behavior.

Like the game of tiles.

The last problem he'd tackled but failed to solve.

Nheras had said his failure was because he was reading the tiles, not the room. He hadn't understood what she was saying at the time, but Elaram had tried explaining it to him: "People don't think before they act; they act first, then think up reasons for it afterwards."

But he hadn't been listening to her pleading with him to open the door of the ship's study. That would've been the logical thing to do—listen to her apology, verify she meant what she said, accept the overture, problem solved, honor satisfied all round, return to the cabin, resume the game and cordial relations, and so on. Instead, he'd stuffed his ears with wax and fetched his ink stick and inkstone and brush pen and opened up the notebook Elder Anathwan had given back to him because it hurt to hear Elaram's voice with all that laughter still ringing in his ears so he'd left her out in the passageway to talk at him through the door because he knew it upset her and he'd been glad it upset her because then she felt a little of what he felt without him having to use Projection outside of a sanctioned duel which would have made him no better than a child throwing a tantrum and that had made him feel all the more ashamed; ashamed and angry at himself, for being a thoughtless hypocrite, and at her, because it wasn't his fault—she'd pushed him to it—and, even worse, just a little bit attracted too, because she'd begun to look at him differently and that had been strange and novel and terrifying and a variable he'd very much prefer not to factor into the wicked equation he was trying to solve.

So he'd doubled down on his original solution for the problem of Elaram—avoid her at all costs—only that hadn't worked. The more he tried, the more circumstances conspired to throw them together, until they'd ended up as watch partners. There was only so much space on deck; there was only so much he could pretend to be preoccupied with at the tiller; there were only so many ships she could sight from aloft and sense with her Seeking, especially now that they were so far from land. When all was said and done, there were still three-and-a-half spans of silence left to fill in a four-span watch and Elaram had filled in all of those yawning gaps with rapid-fire questions, always darting off to consider and voice the next question before he had finished contemplating the implications and the limits of the one she had just raised.

Perhaps...

Perhaps that was the angle.

Jhobon looked for his notebook; it lay out of reach underneath his hammock where it had fallen.

No matter. He didn't need it. Gods knew he had spent long enough poring over Reshwim's accounts that he could recite most of the notable passages forwards, backwards, or in strict chronological order without Evocation.

He tried to look down. Couldn't; not without digging his chin into the back of her head. Her breathing was light and regular now. Like someone asleep. He knew better, though, for he was well acquainted with—they all were, by now—what she sounded like when she was truly asleep.

His turn to fill the silence, then.

"I've been wondering about Revocation," he said.

She went on as she was—even breath; suppressed aura; body tucked tight against his chest—but there'd been an encouraging fractional lengthening of the pause between those breaths and so he went on:

"Revocation is to Evocation as Fortunement is to Augury, isn't it? Similar, opposing concepts mirrored about the axial present. Like Projection and Obfuscation."

An even longer pause.

"Have you ever wondered why the Guild only teaches five core resonance disciplines? First Seeking. Then Evocation and Augury; Projection and Obfuscation. Don't you think it's odd?"

Elaram stirred but didn't speak.

"Seeking doesn't fit the pattern. It's odd."

That got a reaction. "It isn't," she said, into his neck. "Seeking is the foundational discipline; it lies at the heart of the other disciplines which are derived from its principles."

"Only because the Guild teaches it that way. Every discipline has its opposite and Seeking is no exception. Don't you see?" he asked. "Seeking's opposite is Seeming—one reveals truth; the other conceals it. On the surface, they seem like opposites because one is antecedent and is concerned with existence while the other is descendant and is concerned with possibility. But conceiving of them as opposites isn't the right frame of reference because there's no true symmetry; they're more alike than unalike. Think about it, Elaram. If

Seeming is to Seeking as Fortunement is to Augury, that means Revocation—"

She reared her head so suddenly that she knocked it against his jaw and snapped his teeth shut.

"—ow!"

He ran his tongue gingerly over the throbbing indentation in his lower lip and tasted copper; touched his fingers to his mouth to double check and his fingers came away with blood. Looked from the blood to Elaram, torn between making an obvious statement of fact and asking an obvious question, then noticed her even more obvious misery.

"I'm sor—" she began, and that brought up—

Her Seeking flashing orange; raucous laughter chasing him and his bruised aura out of his own cabin—

"It's fine," he said. He clamped down on the stirrings of his involuntary Evocation and closed off his resonance aura with two Obfuscation barriers to make sure it wouldn't happen again. "I'm fine," he said, "no harm done."

Wide eyes stared accusingly at him and his brain filled in the words she didn't say: *I'm a Seeker, stupid; why are you lying to me?*

"S-sorry," he said, and was about to elaborate, but the last time he'd tried elaborating, he hadn't been able to say it quite right. Therefore: keep to simple clarification. He said, "No lasting harm done," and mentally resigned himself to a week of careful chewing and avoiding as much salt in his food and drink as possible. Repeated: "I'll be fine," and put her down so he could get up and look for a handkerchief.

She burst into tears.

Shit.

What was he supposed to do? How did he fix this? If he were Ylaen, he would use Projection, but also: if he were

Ylaen, he wouldn't have made the mistakes he had; and anyway, Elaram had been quite vocal in her opinions about people solving problems with Projection—

"R-really," he insisted. Courtesy dictated that he should give her the handkerchief he'd found but her arms were encased in that cocoon of damp blue silk. "It-it's alright." Drop it in her lap? That seemed awkward. "It was an accident." Perhaps try dabbing her eyes with the bit of cotton? That stirred up another set of memories from solstice he'd been trying to get out of his mind and feelings that he'd rather not feel so he laid a third barrier on top of the two he'd already conjured. "Y-you didn't m-mean to—"

She cried harder.

He was making things worse.

He wasn't supposed to make things worse; he was supposed to make them better but he didn't know how; he never did, not when people were involved; that was why he couldn't solve something as simple as the tile game, let alone something as complex as Elaram, and that meant Ylaen was right; Ylaen was right and he ought to give up searching, they ought to do as they were bid and stop running, and he ought to enjoy what little life he had left instead of spending it on puzzles that stumped scholars who had devoted decades to studying them instead of mere years.

He was the problem. And since he was the problem—

He dropped the handkerchief and backed away.

"Sorry," he mumbled. "I'll—I'll go get your brother."

"No!"

No? He tried to remember a time when Elaram had needed help and Ghardon hadn't come roaring to his sister's rescue at once. Failed. Sages only knew what had happened.

"Your sister, then?" Neither Nheras nor Rahelu seemed the comforting type; both were more likely to put an end to

Elaram's misery by biting her head off rather than consoling her but it wasn't like he'd had much success either, and—

"No!"

"I—" Who else was there? Who would know what to do? Then he knew: "E-Elder Anathwan, then."

His body knew what to do too: it set one foot on the first rung of the companionway, then the other on the second, and he was running, running—

NO!

And bound up in Elaram's desperate Projection was an outpouring of resonance. The pale purple-white bolt slammed into his triple-layered barriers and tore straight through. Neither Evocation nor Seeking nor Seeming but some in-between admixture that blurred past wounds and present loss and future fears:

—running away from her, like he did before, like he will again—

He hadn't thought to shield against regret; he'd been so full of it himself. She'd pierced his defenses and now...now the whole dammed-up mess pushed against the breach. He willed his barriers to reseal themselves, but her bolt had lodged deep in his aura, providing a channel for his own regret and an opportunity for the involuntary Evocation he'd been suppressing to unspool:

He flees as she cries 'Jhobon...Jhobon, wait!', stumbling over his clumsy feet as laughter chases him through the Winged Arrow's passageways. He can feel the very ship itself laughing too—deck thrumming through his bare soles, the bulkheads vibrating against his fingers and palms—as he shuts himself up in its study.

She is a whirlwind: suddenly here—

Hammering her fists and palms against the door: it rattles, shakes, trembles before her; he rattles, shakes, trembles before her and her chanted refrain. ('Jhobon, please come back; we were having fun, weren't we? Just a bit of fun, just a joke or two or several. Please come out, please let me in, please talk to me, please...')

He sits in the dark with his eyes shut and ears stuffed with wax, wondering through 'what-ifs': what if she is sorry what if that sharp yellow-orange mirth comes in with her what if he just stays here until they forget about him (surely they'll forget about him surely they'll find something else to laugh at) and she really does sound very sorry.

Perhaps it mightn't be such a bad thing to let her in...

He opens the door a crack...

—and suddenly gone.

He remembered looking out into the empty corridor, vacillating between slinking back to his cabin (full of loud, drunk Supplicants sniping at each other with their loud, drunken jibes) or following her to hers (the rest of Issolm were still with Ylaen so Ghardon hadn't raised his barrier yet, though even if he had, Jhobon had been seventy percent confident he could have dismantled it) and trying to explain, at length, the way she had, that he was sorry too—

—yet the gap between where he stands and where she goes and who she is and what she must want and who he must be is too great a distance to bridge so he closes the door and spends the rest of the night redrawing Reshwim's diagrams from memory, because it wasn't what she said, it was a death ritual or a summoning ritual or something else they didn't recognize—

—and now she looked at him and his bleeding resonance aura, through the ghostly form of that other him crouched over an insubstantial notebook that overlapped with his real notebook, her wide, wide eyes and Seeker-sharp senses drinking in his regrets. A delicate ringing, barely audible, at the edges of his resonance senses. Silver-purple resonance surged—

His feet descended the ladder…

…stepped through the study door and found their way to hers…

—shifted—

His knuckles rapped against a phantom door…

…it opens, and he blurts out, 'I'm sorry too…'

—coalesced into memory:

He wakes in a tangle of silk sheets underneath the cover of an Issolm white-and-black quilt in a bunk decidedly too small for one, let alone two, to the sight of Elaram: chin propped up in her hands, her elbows digging into his ribs, wispy ends of her loose chestnut hair tickling his collarbone, her warm weight straddling his flanks.

She beams her dazzling smile. Says, "Hello." Asks him, "Want to do it again?"

He jerked to a stop. "Th-that, that—"
"Didn't happen, no," she said softly.
"Wh-what, what—"
He took a deep breath.
Saw her sitting where he had left her, her half-dried hair still a dark brown but its ends starting to lighten and curl around her pale shoulders, patches of damp blue silk stuck flat to her skin. Flushed and would have turned away, but that wouldn't have helped with the new memory-that-wasn't-memory which was sending all sorts of signals he didn't want interfering with his thought process right now.
So he sat down where he was, facing her, cross-legged.

Realized immediately how that must look; flailed for a moment when his hands and arms tried to do one thing while his legs insisted on another; then gave up—what was he trying to hide for when she'd just seen and felt much, much more?—and dove into mage trance.

The, the—hallucination—yes, that was the correct term for it—sat strangely in his mind. Even though the beginning and end of the vision slotted perfectly into the timeline, there was an unstable feel to the superimposed image. He prodded at it with his resonance senses. It felt…different. Like looking at a manuscript where the author's original text had been overwritten by some other scribe.

He hadn't thought of running an Augury while he'd been staring out into the dark from the ship's study (though now he wished he had; that was important data!) but if he had, this scenario felt like a possibility he might have glimpsed.

It didn't break causality. It was plausible; perhaps even likely, had he but the courage to follow her at the time.

A Seeming?

No. Seemings started to fall apart the moment you became aware that they might not be what they, well, seemed, and this hallucination wasn't falling apart. If anything, it was becoming more substantial.

He *wanted* to remember that night differently.

"It's hooked into the real memory somehow," he said. "Like a parasite. It's feeding on the original to make itself stronger." He blinked as he surfaced from mage trance and scrambled for his notebook. "We've got to get rid of it before it overrides the original."

And before it could mess up their minds any further.

Elaram whispered: "Would it really be so awful if that happened?"

"Yes!" She reeled back, resonance aura bruised black and blue, like he'd struck her. "No, no!" he cried and dropped the notebook. "I didn't mean that you are—that I don't—that it wasn't—"

Words, stupid words; he knew so many of them and none of them were ever the right ones.

Words could go to the eighth hell.

He kissed her.

All thoughts stopped.

For a breathless moment there was only blessed silence and Elaram, beautiful, warm Elaram, in his arms, melting against him in a tangle of silk and—

Reality caught up in a burst of copper that tainted the sweetness; so did his sense of time and space and propriety and Ylaen and Nheras close by, asleep but tossing in their hammocks, and Ghardon and Rahelu exchanging barbs about ropes and knots and hairstyles and bathing preferences on the deck above, and the indistinct murmurs of Captain Csorath and Elder Anathwan and Dedicate Maketh right on the other side of the stern bulkhead, and—

Back away from the bulkhead and Elaram and the blue silk puddled around her hips; back to his notebook and his terrible, inadequate words.

"I'm sorry," he said.

"You're not," she said. That beaming smile again. "I'm not either."

"You're not?"

"No."

So: they sat there.

Breathing.

Looking.

Thinking.

Eventually, he said, again, "It didn't happen."

She said, "It could have—"

"But it didn't."

Her, with the courage he lacked: "But I wish it had." A pause. "Don't you?"

"...Yes." And that one little admission made it easier to go on with the next. "I don't want to get rid of it."

"So don't," she said, as if it were that simple. "Keep it."

"But it's not real! It didn't happen!"

"You wished it and I wished it and if I say it did and you do too, then who's to say it happened otherwise?"

"Reality!"

He called up an Evocation, on purpose this time, to prove the point...

...and saw himself waking up to Elaram all over again.

Gods. *Gods*. Was the original memory gone? No, it was still there, obscured by the hallucination. He poured more resonance into the Evocation; the vivid recollection of Elaram and her cabin disappeared, replaced by dark shapes that suggested a slight, wiry figure hunched over a notebook in the *Winged Arrow's* study. The details—the truth!—resisted his summons, as if he'd tried Evoking a memory ten years removed instead of ten days.

"I..." He let the Evocation go. "Reality is more malleable than I thought. Like...like knife-cut noodle dough."

Elaram giggled at his poor joke. He smiled and joined in despite himself, then trailed off as the implications sank in.

Revocation was no myth.

It was real.

Somehow, they had serendipitously stumbled onto the right combination of factors and undid the past. Well, not literally— they had changed their recall of a specific sequence of events that had unfolded in a defined space between two defined moments in time, which meant the physicality of the alternate events (yes, there was the page where he had copied Reshwim's diagrams, and he could not help the thrill that ran through him even as he verified the thought) had not occurred; had not actually superseded the physicality of the original—but, as Elaram had pointed out, wasn't the altered memory just as good?

No, because if the physicality of the event mattered, then Revocation was useless. As he had surmised, Revocation was to Evocation as Fortunement was to Augury and Seeming was to Seeking, but since it was on the wrong side of the temporal divide, it couldn't directly affect the physical world the way Fortunement could influence someone towards a particular probability.

Or could it?

If you altered someone's memory, would that not alter how they would act?

He looked back at Elaram looking at him looking at her; felt the familiar rise of heat creeping into his face and wanted to flee.

But this time, he also remembered the feel of blue silk in his arms, chestnut locks tickling his ribs, and her warm weight beneath a white-and-black quilt, and besides, that other version of her had given him the right words.

He flipped past his recreations of Reshwim's sketches to a fresh page and asked, "Want to do it again?"

She crawled over on all fours, mischief dancing in her eyes. "Do what?" She batted her eyelashes as she reached him. "Change more of the past?" Slid her palms up the inside of his knees to rest on his upper thighs. "Reenact our new past just to check how well the Revocation compares to the actual, physical experience?" Lowered her head down to his lap and took a corner of his notebook between her lips; flipped back to the previous page to reveal his copy of the drawing that had fascinated her so ten days ago. "Try to invent some more mathematically optimal positions?"

"...Yes." The word came out as a low half-groan.

"Mmmn," she said as she kneaded his thighs some more, "but yes to what?"

"All of it." He grabbed her hands and put them somewhere more productive.

She blinked as she suddenly found her hands full with his notebook. "Jhobon!" She pouted. "Might I suggest that given our current state, the most efficient thing to try first would be to—"

"Document everything we can remember about the moment of initial discovery?"

Her pout became more severe.

"I know it's not as exciting as...as o-other options, but it will save us so much time later. Experiments with significant, world-altering potential first."

"Investigating the difference between Revocation and reality seems pretty significant to me."

"Later," he promised. "We need to capture everything that just happened while it's fresh so we can identify all of the possible variables and figure out what we did and whether it's reproducible and what the limitations might be and—"

"Jhobon, answer me honestly: do you or do you not realize that I am currently without my clothes?"

"Oh. Yes. Your brother left them in a pile...there." He frowned. "Mine are still drying. Where is my brush pen?"

"I," she said as she pulled on her loincloth and trousers, "am seriously considering Revoking that Revocation." She gave him another overexaggerated pout as she shrugged her arms through the sleeves of her shirt.

He put his brush pen down on top of his notebook and stopped searching for his inkstone long enough to pull her close by her hips.

"Elaram," he said and did what he had seen the apprentice do to her on the summer solstice, except he went about it in reverse. In between kisses, he said, "I promise I will make the wait worth your while."

"Only if you also promise me that this discovery can be our secret."

"I promise." He finished buttoning her shirt.

Then realized that he'd lost track of which knot was meant to be paired with which loop and how many of the pairs he'd done up.

Now she was giggling as his fingers seemed to forget how to undo them again; now his ears burned at the sound of her laughter; now she was pulling him back, back to her, her cool hands soothing the hot flush in his cheeks, his neck, his chest; her sweet tongue silencing his stutter and his hands suddenly finding their way to—

"Elaram," he groaned, not quite sure how they'd ended up horizontal when they'd been sitting upright just heartbeats before. "This is not helping."

She grinned at him, unrepentant. "Don't you think we'd concentrate better if we got a few distractions out of the way first?" She trailed her fingers down his flank and walked them over the knot on his loincloth. "We could be quick about it."

"Elaram, please," he begged. "We don't have much time." I don't have much time. "And I want to take my time with you."

"Oh," she said, with a shimmer in her bright, bright eyes. "Well, alright then." Mollified, she picked up his brush pen and notebook. "Let's start from the beginning."

20

LISTEN

"SKYMOTHER'S TEARS!"

Ghardon glared at his most stubborn adversary yet, which was really saying something, considering how much he had suffered over the last few weeks: evil cultists, Maketh's mind block, Ruarem's door, those blasted gulls, and of course, his infuriating sisters.

He ignored the *creak-thud* behind him as the cargo hatch swung open and shut, and the *slosh-thumps* announcing Rahelu's half-slide, half-hopping entry because he had a mind to dole out some thumping of his own.

"Listen, you unfashionable excuse for a chamber pot: if you do not start cooperating, I will break you into ten thousand pieces and feed you to the sharks."

The clay cooking pot blurped sullenly at him and the smoky fire beneath it belched out a handful of sparks.

"Give me that." Rahelu snatched the wooden ladle from him before he could bang it against the side of the pot again and set down her bucket. She poked around at the dubious-looking gloop bubbling away inside and scraped up an awful-smelling, brown-black mouthful of something with the same consistency as the gull shit and half-digested fish he'd spent the rest of their watch rinsing out of his clothes and hair.

To his horror, she put the steaming hot gloop in her mouth. Made a face, and then—instead of spitting it out like a normal person—*still swallowed it.*

"How in the eight hells did you fuck up congee, Ghardon? It's a very simple dish: one measure of rice to seven of water; bring the pot up to the boil, then set it aside to simmer."

He turned his glare on her. "You did not tell me that."

"Yes, I did."

"You did not. You told me to get the fire going"—he pointed to the roaring flames merrily consuming the six logs he'd laid on top of the coals—"put the rice in the pot"—she hadn't specified how much so he'd done the logical thing and measured out one serving for every person on board with a small wooden bowl—"and fill it up with water." There hadn't been much room left for water, seeing how nine bowls of uncooked rice had filled up more than half the pot, but he liked his congee thick and velvety so it seemed right.

She slammed the ladle down across the rim of the cooking pot and stalked off towards the hammocks. Bits of burnt, half-cooked rice flew everywhere; he yelped and jumped back in disgust.

"Might I remind you that congee was your idea? I said we should make soup—hey!" he protested as she came back armed with his only decent shirt: the fine linen one he'd smuggled aboard so he'd have something comfortable to sleep in. "What are you doing with that? No," he said as she shook it out, rolled it lengthwise, and wound it around her hands. "Do not—"

She shouldered him aside to take the pot off the hearth and he wanted to weep. His poor shirt; there were going to be singe marks where it had touched the hot clay.

"If you're going to mourn something, mourn our dinner."

Rahelu tossed his shirt aside with the same regard she gave the cleaning rags used to scrub the decks. It landed on top of the still-twitching fish in the bucket by her bare feet.

"That's it." He rescued his shirt before it could suffer further injury. "Nheras is now officially my favorite sister."

Until Ilyn showed her true colors.

"I'll be sure to pass on my congratulations, except I don't think either of us will survive your cooking. Are you trying to poison us?"

"No." Not only were there smudges of ash on the collar, the sleeve, and a large swathe of the shirt front, there was also a small tear in the back. Sure enough, he spotted a loose thread caught on the dorsal fin of the most vigorous fish thrashing around in the bucket. "But I am beginning to give the thought serious consideration."

Rahelu beat one of her fists softly against her forehead. "Ghardon," she said. "Why don't you go check on Elaram?"

He raised his eyebrows at the suggestion, tilted his head in the direction of the hammocks, and waited.

A fit of choked snort-gasps, then a loud, tortured *aaaaah.*

"Ela's fine," he said.

He had come straight down after sunwatch prepared to wear his voice out with fireside stories that included plenty of fantastical monsters and no birds whatsoever, only to find Ela fast asleep—*holding hands*, of all things, with Imrell (also asleep, in an adjacent hammock), of all people, godsdamnit.

Jhobon should've been far too shy to let Ela do anything.

Putting his questionable House aside, Jhobon Imrell was a far inferior match, politically and magically speaking, compared to her last choice, but seeing as Ylaen Imos was about a hundred times more of an asshole and Ela had had a...rather unhappy experience, Ghardon hadn't had the heart to separate the two slumbering sweethearts.

"Since you haven't fallen down dead yet," he continued

before Rahelu could give him any more grief about the congee—he was already full of grief, thank you very much, for his shirt, "I assume the congee is also fine." He picked up the bucket and unsheathed his belt knife. "Now what do I do with these fish?"

"You give those goldtrout to me," she said. "I don't trust you to not ruin them too and that'd be a waste; they're hard to catch."

He handed over the bucket with its churning contents but kept the fish that had destroyed his shirt for himself. Vengeance was due.

It stabbed him.

"Ow!"

Those fins were *vicious*. He checked for injuries immediately: no slices, thank the Starfather, but he had pricked his thumb on one of the many ridges along the fish's spine and now it was bleeding.

Rahelu glanced up sharply with what almost looked like concern, then rolled her eyes when she saw him sucking on his thumb while his fish flopped around in front of him.

He stabbed back at the fish's eye; it dodged. "How do you gut these things if they keep moving?"

"You hold it." Her fish lay perfectly still, trapped between her palm and the bench. "Then slice here, here, and here."

Her knife flashed. Her right hand darted in and out. Suddenly, there was a dead fish with an empty belly on the bench and a pile of fish guts bobbing in the bucket.

"Got it?"

Absolutely not; she'd moved too fast.

But since the Earthgiver had blessed him with an exceptional capacity for learning in addition to good looks, an impeccable sense of fashion, and more resonance talent for Evocation than anybody ought to be born with...

"Got it," he said.

Her turn to raise her eyebrows. "Show me."

The arrogant little scaled monster in front of him flipped its tail and flailed its fins, taunting him. *'Do your worst, human,'* it seemed to say, bristling the points of the larger bones that gave its slimy, translucent flippers structure.

He would. He would do his very worst. Except his head still ached from the resonance backlash those gulls had inflicted on him and they were due back on starwatch in another three spans, so vengeance would have to wait. He didn't want to fall from the rigging in a dead faint because he'd pushed himself too far to gut a fish flawlessly.

"You should go to sleep," he said instead.

"I'm fine." She rinsed her knife and grabbed the next fish.

"You've been up every day before dawn, even when we're not on dawnwatch," he pointed out. "The bags under your eyes are getting big enough to be mistaken for bruises. And if your eyes become any more bloodshot, I guarantee Nheras will start calling you 'Fishdemon' instead of 'Fishguts'."

"This may be news to you, Ghardon, but 'before dawn' is when normal people wake up and go to work." Rahelu whacked her fish square in the head with the hilt of her knife. "We don't have the luxury"—a savage slice—"of lying about"—a swift yank—"in silks and feathered quilts until high sun and summoning servants to bring us our breakfasts on a lacquered tray."

Splish. The next handful of fish guts went into the bucket.

Still stuck in her old narrative.

"Hmmn. Someone bringing you breakfast on a lacquered tray? That sounds oddly familiar. Why would that be?"

She didn't meet his eyes; she bent down to snatch up her third fish, resonance aura sullen red with shame.

"Oh, that's right!" he continued. "That was me, coddling you, after you nearly brought dishonor upon us all by disrespecting a Dedicate. Was that normal behavior?"

"I—"

And since they were on the subject: "Was accepting an heirloom mage pendant without providing an equal exchange normal behavior?"

Rahelu eviscerated her fish. "It was a gift."

Still stubbornly ignoring the obvious.

The other Houses liked to sneer at House Issolm for being mercenary—which was the word idealists preferred to *'pragmatic'*—but with House Issolm, you always knew exactly what you were getting into with all of the terms and conditions clearly spelled out in ink.

Manipulating a starry-eyed fisher girl with some hoity toity *'I'm such a pure-hearted, genuine soul'* bullshit? That took Ideth pretentiousness to pull off.

"It was the prelude to a trade. You said you sold fish to pay your way through Guild training; you should recognize when someone is manipulating you with a charming little story because they want you to buy what they're selling."

She stood there, chest heaving, bloody knife in a white-knuckled grip.

"Come on, Rahelu. A friendship gift? Just how naive are you?" Normally, Ghardon would leave it at that, the implications being self-evident, but his common-born sister was so resistant to good sense it was better to spell things out: "His words, not mine."

She glared at him, resonance aura crackling, but refused to admit he was right.

"Why did he follow you to the Lowdocks? How does a match between the two of you make any fucking sense from a political perspective? What—"

Rahelu moved, her arm blurring in a swift arc. He brought his knife up to deflect her attack—

THUNK!

—and had to pull his counterattack.

She'd rammed her blade straight through the eye of his fish, pinning it to the bench. Black hair fell forward to hide her face as she slumped and asked the floor, "Is it so absurd to believe that Lhorne might simply just like me for myself?"

Ghardon sighed. "I think you know the answer to that."

Her shoulders quivered.

"Listen, little sister." He put his knife down, wiped his slimy hands on the shirt she had ruined, and parted her curtain of long black hair with his fingers. "He likes you. He always has; nobody disputes that."

Their Guild intake had always wagered on the *how* and *when* with respect to Lhorne of Ideth and Rahelu—nobody had ever put coin against the entire notion. Ideth had been infatuated with her from the first, though anybody with the slightest wit for politics could see it was a bad match. Atriarch Ideth was probably *extremely pissed* he'd gone ahead with the whole *'friendship gift'* thing, what with her heir refusing to put his Isca lover aside to make a proper match with Isonn, but Mere Ideth hadn't become Atriarch without knowing how to turn unexpected twists of fate in her favor.

Also, wasn't it interesting that of all the captains at House Isonn's disposal, Csorath—the only one who was Ideth-born —was the one who had been chosen for this expedition?

And Csorath had had a lot to say to Rahelu in Chanazian.

"You can keep on pretending that's all there is to it. Everybody has their own delusions so I won't begrudge you yours."

Still looking at the floor. He crouched down and put his face in front of hers; held her red-veined eyes with his.

"But you're not in the Lowdocks anymore, Rahelu. We don't do gifts. So don't let your personal delusions interfere with your professional decision-making—or your sleep." He tapped her nose. "I distinctly remember someone wise telling me to get a full night's rest the last time I accepted an unusual assignment."

She blinked.

"Sensible person, whoever it was," he added. "Smart and ambitious, too. That person lived for something and did whatever it took to achieve their goals." His fish was quite dead and still now, thanks to her, so he jabbed the tip of his knife into its belly. "Would have been nice to have that person here instead of a grumpy fish demon that goes wherever the current flows."

Ghardon sawed away at the fish as he waited for her retort. It'd probably be something about how no amount of flattery would get her to give him part of her water ration to *'waste on stupid, frivolous House-born shit like lemon-scented baths'*.

Perhaps it was stupid; perhaps it was frivolous; but being able to rid himself of the grime and stink of dried salt and sweat and bile that inevitably accrued on his skin, his hair, and his clothes no matter how hard he tried to steer clear of unnecessary physical labor was the one brief, bright spot of joy in his otherwise cheerless days so there was no way he was giving up *his* personal delusion of being somewhat clean and well-groomed and *not* somewhere between fifty and one hundred and twenty-five kual away from home in…wherever the fuck they were.

While he waited, he prepared the usual remarks about how a rinse did not qualify as a bath because a bath implied immersion; how her personal hygiene and grooming left a lot to be desired; how true waste would be actually drinking most of his water ration since there was plenty of wine and most meals involved some kind of soup or soup-like food (primary exhibit: the pot of steaming congee congealing off to the side) so his intake of liquids was more than adequate.

But a whole twenty heartbeats went by without Rahelu

saying any of that—or taking issue with how he'd mangled her precious goldtrout.

He nudged her with his elbow, then grabbed the next fish.

"Tell me exactly how to cook the fish and sleep, Rahelu. Even if I ruin them all, you've already saved the congee."

Now, a touch of Evocation as he used her knife:

Thunk!

His archery instructor would've deducted marks for not nailing the slippery creature through the center of its pupil but it ought to be enough to reassure Rahelu he knew what he was doing.

He took up his knife again. "Or I can just slice them up raw, like we get for our dinner parties."

"I can't sleep."

He waited some more. When she didn't elaborate, he laid down his knife and said, "Ela's got some—"

"I know."

"It didn't work?"

"No. It's—" She paused. "Have you been dreaming?"

'*Why, yes,*' he wanted to say, '*this whole mission has been one, long nightmare and I keep wondering when I'll wake up,*' but that wasn't what she needed to hear.

"Have you?" he asked.

She nodded.

"Your dreamward?"

She pulled her collar open and dragged Ideth's pendant out of the way. The dreamward was there, combined with the complicated suppression ward she always wore, all of the strong, confident lines smooth and intact. He trusted that she knew what she was doing; besides, Anathwan would not have let her leave Peshwan Yrg if her skill with wards wasn't up to Maketh's standards.

Still, it was better to be thorough and check, just in case. "Have you told the Guardian?"

She pulled her shirt closed and shook her head.

"Do you want to tell me?"

"Not much to tell."

At the rate this conversation was going, he ought to put out the fire, stick his little finger in the ash and redraw his eyebrows right next to his hairline to save himself the trouble of raising them, then putting them down over and over.

"Tell me anyway," he said.

"The usual horrors."

Very specific. He prompted her with another look.

She shrugged. "Blades. Blood. Chains."

Their murder investigations had given him his own dreams. "Dharyas?"

Another nod. "Hzin," she said.

The fishmonger.

"And Xyuth," she added.

The scrivener who had helped her and then died for the stargem she'd been carrying around. He darted a glance at her trouser pockets; if she still had it, he couldn't tell.

"You didn't go see a healer?" He had gone as soon as he'd completed his reports for that assignment and he had made sure Ela had too.

Violet-black slipped into her resonance aura. "I didn't want to forget."

Indulging in unproductive self-flagellation. He resisted the urge to beat his forehead with his fists like she had, because that wouldn't help either.

"Is it getting worse?"

She went silent, which was confirmation enough. He was about to drag her off to see Ana, but then she turned towards the front of the ship and cocked her head.

"Listen," she said.

He heard: Ylaen's lazy "Seeking?" directly above their

heads and Nheras's laconic "Clear!" from aloft. From the swaying hammocks: Ela's loud snoring and Jhobon's quieter half-mumbles. Behind him: nothing from the senior mages in the aftercabin—another Projected conference then; that or they had gone up to meditate and recharge their pendants while Csorath took his turn to sleep.

"Do you hear it?" she asked.

He strained his ears.

Cables snapping against canvas as the wind shifted. The *Sooty Gull's* incessant creaking as it lurched through the waves. And some sort of rumbling in its timbers.

He frowned. "The *Winged Arrow* didn't make that noise."

"It's not a noise," she said. "It's a note."

A note? "Show me."

She took his hand and a shaky Concordance bloomed.

He'd been right—she was just as drained as he; perhaps slightly more so. Half-healed leg injury aside, he had no idea how she was staying on her feet, let alone function enough to catch and gut fish.

Rahelu didn't send their focus up and spiraling outwards in a standard Seeking pattern; she pulled them inwards so they sank into the watery blue-gray depths of her mind. And there, right on the edges of his perception, he sensed it: a low, ringing tone, but muffled, like a gargantuan temple gong sounded underwater. A massive vibration moving so slowly through the ambient resonance that it seemed not to move at all while rattling the marrow in his bones at the same time.

"Skymother's veil!"

If that had been knocking around inside his head, he wouldn't be able to sleep either, and he already had enough trouble sleeping as it was.

He broke their Concordance to check whether he could still perceive it clearly without her.

He couldn't.

His senses only registered the faint rumbling that he hadn't otherwise questioned.

"How long have you been hearing that?"

"Hard to say." She rubbed her face and left a smattering of loose fish scales around her eyes. "It got clearer once we sailed into the Aleituan proper. Five weeks? Give or take?"

That was it.

"Hammock," he said and pointed. "Now. You've been very good at pretending so far, so close your eyes and pretend some more."

Once he got her to go lie down, he was going to go look for the ship's medical kit (Skymother only knew where Nheras had stashed it because it wasn't where he had left it at the end of his last inventory) and dose her bowl of congee with heartroot so she would sleep straight through the night. It wasn't like there was all that much to do during starwatch—they hadn't sighted any other ships for two days; just kual upon kual of empty ocean— so he'd be fine on his own and she could return the favor by letting him sleep through earthwatch later. Besides, if anything was the slightest bit amiss, Captain Csorath would be up on deck without anyone needing to alert him.

"It's not going to work."

"Maybe it won't, but maybe it will. Either way, I'm not giving you the choice. You can go of your own accord, or I can haul you like a sack of turnips, or I can ask Nheras to compel you with Command." He picked up his ruined shirt. "Which one will it be?"

Her gaze stumbled from the three neatly skinned and gutted fish in front of her (heads, tails, and fins still intact and attached to their gleaming golden scales) to the uneven chunks of translucent, reddish-gray flesh and the dying fish feebly smacking its tail against the bench in front of him to the clay pot to her hammock and eventually swung back round to meet his eyes.

"I—"

Rahelu blinked but didn't resist as he wiped her face and hands with the last clean bit of linen, then turned her around and gave her a light shove.

"What are you going to do to my fish?" she mumbled as she toppled into her hammock.

"I," he said, "am going to surprise you."

———

GHARDON SPENT the remaining span until dinnertime slicing up the goldtrout into perfectly uniform cubes and arranging them in a pleasing spiral stack on the lid of an empty barrel, the closest thing he could find to a suitable serving platter.

He ate three cubes (randomly selected) to confirm they were, in fact, palatable; lost five more to the ship's cat, who had pounced the moment he had turned his back to set a cast iron pan full of oil on the coals to heat and search for the crate of limes; lost another handful to Ylaen of Imos, who sauntered down well before the change of the watch to fill two flagons from the wine cask ahead of dinner—and then had the audacity to throw the spice tins into disarray while volunteering criticisms on his selections.

"Powdered garlic, chilli flakes, sesame, ground kelp." The Imos Supplicant grabbed a tin and flicked its lid open. A fifth of the contents—star anise—tumbled into the wine with tiny *splishes*. "And citrus peel. Not this—"

Ylaen put the tin down and wet his index finger.

Caught up as Ghardon was between defending the platter against the ship's cat and obsessively checking that none of the fish skin frying in the pan had burned, he did not succeed in snatching the mortar away before Ylaen managed to stick a finger into the spice mix he'd spent a quarter-span grinding to a fine even powder.

"You're disgusting," Ghardon said. "We all have to eat from that."

His stomach rumbled. He really did not want to eat anything Ylaen of Imos had touched. But he also didn't really want to throw it away and start over; blisters were developing on his fingers in places where he didn't have his archer's callouses.

Ylaen licked his finger and blanched. "Ugh. What is that?"

"Poison." If only. "Obviously, it's five-spice."

"Five-spice does not taste like that."

"As if your savage palate is refined enough to appreciate anything other than the taste of overcooked, charred meat."

"Is that so?" Ylaen drawled. "I thought your sister tasted—"

Ghardon very calmly put down the pestle somewhere that was not Ylaen's face and said, "Utter one more word about my sister—either of my sisters—and you and I can settle our differences in the circle."

"You'll be waiting a long time, then." Ylaen smirked. "Or doesn't your precious handbook forbid dueling over personal grievances during missions?"

...fuck.

"And you'll have to excuse my savage upbringing. Correct me if I'm wrong, for counting, you understand, is difficult for us savages. I was, however, under the impression that you are fortunate enough to be here with three sisters."

"You're welcome to Nheras, seeing as she is the only one who doesn't expressly disdain your company. Only the Skymother can fathom how and why."

Ghardon reclaimed his space by leaning forward until his

nose was right up against Ylaen's face, his hands on the verge of shoving the two heavy flagons of wine over and off his counter. He chose very blunt words and enunciated them very clearly, for Ylaen was evidently incapable of interpreting the glaring 'FUCK OFF' signals written in resonance.

"But leave Ela and Rahelu alone. Or I'll put enough arrows into those arms you're so proud of that you'll be mistaken for a large, exceedingly misshapen, winged monstrosity."

"Ghardon, Ghardon." Ylaen pressed his face forward and smiled. "You don't have to go to such lengths to get me to listen. If you want my company, just say so."

According to the Issolm *Supplicant's Handbook*, unprovoked attacks fell under various categories of misconduct, depending on the severity of any resultant injuries. But the *Handbook* also made allowances for accidental injury in hazardous environments and circumstances and, in Ghardon's opinion, the galley of a barely seaworthy ship ranked fairly high as far as hazardous environments went.

He wondered whether breaking a tooth would constitute a minor or a trivial injury and whether he ought to run the risk of incurring Maketh's wrath after he had already been disciplined earlier by Captain Csorath.

But Ana was not exactly enamored of Ylaen Imos and she was the one who would be evaluating their performance, anyway.

"You're really not his type."

Ela's cheery voice rang out from the hammocks before he could see whether Ylaen's smirk would be quite so supercilious if he were missing several teeth. His sister wandered over, dressed in her spare clothes, hair all a-tangle and sticking up at odd angles from having gone to sleep with it damp and unbrushed. She blithely broke their stand-off by pushing her wide-eyed face in between theirs and rapping her knuckles unceremoniously against Ylaen's forehead.

"Wooooooooow," Ela said, her widened eyes full of feigned innocence. "It echoes like an empty cavern."

A cursory once-over revealed nothing untoward in her resonance aura. Oh, it still held a trace of her earlier distress —if that had been absent Ghardon would have dug deeper with Seeking—but it was largely superseded by a bubbling orange-gold anticipatory glee that was four shades darker than usual, thanks to an undertone of smugness.

Ela patted Ylaen on his cheek. "Try again when you've got a thing or two of value in there," she said, "my brother likes them smart," then continued on without a breath as she looked at the platter of cubed fish and frying fish skin. "Have you recreated that dish from that fish stall? Gods, that was delightful, and I'm positively *starving*."

The cat yowled plaintively as Ela lifted the platter high and went to rouse the others with that mannerless little fiend stalking in her wake.

"Darling kitty, I know the fish smells divine, but this isn't for you, though if you're good and hop quietly onto my shoulder, I'll let you have a few bites of mine. No? Very well. Jhobon! Jhobon, will you come and get the wine? Rahelu, fetch the plates and bowls and pass them up to Nheras, won't you, and then perhaps you can find the spoons and eating sticks and bring those. Brother, dear, that fish skin looks ready now—goodness, I can taste the crunch and spices already—no, don't try to carry anything else; I'm sure Ylaen will have no trouble managing the pot with those muscles."

Cajoling and teasing by turns, Ela got them all out of the hold just as the senior mages were concluding their silent conference.

Elder Anathwan beckoned for the off-duty Supplicants to

lay out the evening meal. Ghardon was about to sit down in his customary place when Nheras called out from aloft:

"Sails! Sails to the south and east!"

Everyone froze.

Csorath gestured sharply at Ylaen—move!—and cast an impatient eye at Nheras's ginger descent—hurry!—as he strode to the tiller and held out his hand for the spyglass.

Several hundred heartbeats passed as Csorath scoured the horizon, the spyglass glued to his eye.

Eventually, the captain said, "A Belruonian vessel, I think. Perhaps thirty-five or forty kual distant. I sense no barriers, but the rate of accumulating resonance suggests some fifty or sixty souls aboard."

"How certain are you?" Anathwan asked.

"At this range, there is no certainty. But I mislike the sight of strange sails from that direction. We are too far from the main sea routes to encounter Federation or Dominion patrol ships. It is possible that they are honest traders blown off course by some ill luck wishing to exchange tidings. Or they may turn out to be another factionless Free Territory ship, ready to give chase without signaling."

Csorath shook his head and put away the spyglass.

"All things considered and given the choice, I would rather not pit the Gull against the unknown when our imperative is stealth and speed."

The captain's crisp orders came via a series of precisely controlled, tight-beamed Projections that traveled directly to each individual he targeted, and no further, and the Supplicants scrambled to carry them out.

In less than a third of a quarter-span—

Decks: cleared.

Sails: furled.

Ship's barriers: readied.

Ship's wards: intact.

—the *Sooty Gull* sat still in the waves, bobbing gently, as the Skymother lowered her lamp into the sea.

Csorath's plan, as far as Ghardon could gather, was to hide in plain sight.

Good thing those birds had scattered and flown off; he couldn't imagine a more obvious sign of their presence than a knot of twenty or thirty shrieking gulls clustered about the ship, *keowing* as they fought over the food scraps that Rahelu habitually discarded over the side after every meal.

He doubted that they had gone far, though. Those greedy, vicious little skyrats never left them alone for long.

Maketh glanced up at the sails with a frown. "Ought we not press on ourselves? Light, sound, and resonance all travel far too easily over open waters. If they discover our presence…"

Csorath shook his head again, looking to his left, out over the water to the ship's…right? (Bow? Stern? Port? Whatever.) "The *Gull* is a far smaller vessel and well shielded. Unless they have talented Seekers and lookouts, they should not be able to spot us in turn." The Seeker-captain glanced at Anathwan. "I advise against conducting Augury. If it is a Belruonian ship, Augury would draw attention from their mage-priests faster than a wide broadcast."

The Elder nodded. "Very well." She glanced at the dishes Ghardon had prepared, lying on the deck, forgotten. "What of the evening meal?"

Csorath mulled over the question. "They are also hove to for the night." A pause as he considered the platter of fish. "I think it safe to have our usual meal, particularly when so much effort has gone into its preparation," he allowed. "Full stealth protocols may wait until starwatch."

Ghardon exchanged uneasy looks with Rahelu.

Full stealth protocols meant the captain would send everyone below and stand watch alone until dawn, both to minimize the amount of stray resonance that might escape the ship and betray their location, and maximize the number of rested mages he had available in the event of combat.

Csorath had not enacted full stealth protocols since the last time the *Gull* had been pursued—and narrowly escaped—the Free Territories raider.

"Skymother hide us with the veil of night," Rahelu muttered as the Elder motioned for everyone to seat themselves.

"And may the Starfather blind them to our presence," Ghardon added, then frowned.

Nheras Ilyn had taken his usual spot in the cross-legged circle—on Ana's left—and had also taken the honor of serving up the food *he* had prepared to the Elder. Why, he ought to—

To what? What was the point of tussling over a position he was going to vacate soon, anyway?

Ilyn could have it.

To Ghardon's culinary triumph, everything he'd prepared was devoured in short order. (Save for the burnt congee—only Rahelu was stubborn enough to make a point of eating that while wearing her *'I'm-so-senselessly-frugal'* look of superiority, though he did appreciate her show of Issolm solidarity in keeping her true opinion of how disgustingly inedible it was to herself.)

To his annoyance, however, the small bowl of seasoning he'd prepared for the crispy fish skin had been tampered with. Somebody—Ghardon glared across the circle at Ylaen Imos, who almost but did not quite dare to make his response as lewd as he certainly would've if the three senior mages weren't present—had added at least seven other ingredients, including one that made his eyes water, numbed his tongue, then set the insides of his mouth afire with a heat that was exacerbated with every swallow of spiced wine.

He stewed as he choked his indignation down; defeat had never tasted so delicious.

Two spots to his right: Ela—vivacious, expressive, the centerpoint of their hushed conversation. If she had made a point of sitting between Ana and Jhobon instead of him and Rahelu; if her questions, interjections, and retorts were a little tamer and less ribald; if her giggles were a little less frequent and more muted; no one remarked on it.

When his sister was next entranced (by Csorath's account of all the sea creatures he'd seen before), Ghardon caught Jhobon's eyes and nodded in Ela's direction.

Thank you, he sent.

The Imrell Supplicant's cheeks, ears, and resonance aura lit up with a ferocious blush as dark as the spiced wine but he nodded back. *I am glad I could help*, Jhobon sent, then gulped the rest of his wine.

To Ghardon's left: Rahelu, looking considerably more rested but on the verge of falling asleep, cradled her near-empty bowl of congee.

He nudged her with his shoulder. "Is that all you've eaten?"

She blinked very slowly. "I had one cube of goldtrout. And one bite of the fish skin."

"You don't like it?"

"It was fine."

"Tastes better with the spices."

"Then I'd have to drink the wine; I hate that wine."

"There's tea."

(Csorath had declined the wine too; had gone down into the hold himself and come back up with a tray that held a freshly steeped pot of heartleaf tea and eight clay cups for them, and a flask for himself. "That's enough," the captain had said when Ylaen made to pass the second flagon of wine around. "I'll suffer no drunkenness aboard; you'll drink tea, every one of you, or drink no more.")

"I hate that tea."

He mock-scowled at her. "Do you hate my surprise too?"

That got a short, drowsy laugh out of her. "No. It was a fine surprise. I just..." Blinked again. "That night when we... you know."

Ghardon didn't remember much of the night they'd stopped the cultists, seeing as how he and Ela were both near-unconscious towards the end. His final report had focused on writing up the results of his inquiries with the merchants at Market Square and hers had documented what their Concordance had found in their last Seeking.

Ela hadn't felt the need to review anybody else's work because their assignment had been indisputably completed to all requirements. He hadn't felt the need to check over what Lhorne and Rahelu had submitted either, not truly, but with Kyrosh and everybody else still busy with Petitioning, he'd read over their final reports anyway.

When he had finished, he'd gone straight to his bath, then the healer, and then booked himself in for a four-day retreat at the Golden Grove in Sunset.

"Hzin," Rahelu continued in a slurred voice. "I never liked him. He was a sick, greedy man. Made my mother's life miserable on a daily basis. He sold Bzel for that new fish stall, you know? Sold his own fucking son to a..." Another long blink. "Tseiran was waiting for him at the door. She must have seen my mother pass. She saw me, my spear, my bloody hands, the stupid goldtrout I was holding—started screaming at me: 'Your fault! Your fault!' and wouldn't stop. I—"

"You didn't kill him."

"I let him die."

"It's not the same thing."

Rahelu closed her eyes. "I thought he deserved to die." A pause before she went on in a voice so low he had to lean in close to listen to what she said. "People like that; they're—"

She lapsed into Chanazian; a long, liquid phrase of mostly vowels and hardly any consonants that his ear had trouble separating into individual words.

It was a while before his struggle registered with her, and she switched back to Aleznuaweithish.

"With the Skymother's gifts, we can know each other's hearts; with the Starfather's, we can glimpse the fortunes that lie ahead; and with the Earthgiver's blessing, we can choose whether we get and bear a child when we couple. Tseiran chose; *Hzin* chose; but Bzel never got to choose. What Hzin did, it's—it's—"

She couldn't seem to find the words she wanted.

"Why does your language flatten and disconnect everything?" she cried, then stopped trying to translate for him. "Anmabanelavelanaz. Children are supposed to be gotten in love, borne in love, and raised with love, for love's sake. They are the future made flesh."

Rahelu looked at—through him, with unseeing eyes that shimmered with the seeds of involuntary partial Evocations.

"My parents starved themselves so that I could eat; and if that hadn't been enough, they would have gladly cut up their flesh and boiled their bones and fed that meat and broth to me because they *chose*." She set her jaw and firmed her voice. "Hzin did not live up to his choice."

Ghardon didn't know what to say to any of that.

He didn't know the first thing about her family's history with this Hzin or Bzel or her life in the Lowdocks—that had been abundantly clear when he'd made a flippant remark about getting some murdered soul's blood on one's clothes and it turned out that that had *actually happened* to her.

If it were Ela, with her face and aura all wretched with

self-loathing like that, he would have hugged her close without a thought. But Rahelu preferred to keep everyone at arm's length (Lhorne included); whether that was due to her Lowdocks-ingrained wariness against pickpockets, thugs, and the other disreputable dregs of society or some Chanazian taboo, he wasn't entirely sure.

Rahelu slumped over until her head rested on his left shoulder.

He went very still.

Tentatively, he leaned his cheek on top of her head.

She didn't move; she had fallen asleep.

Once all the fish had been eaten and the tea drunk and the rest of the congee disposed of over the side (with no gulls nearby to make war over it), Anathwan directed Maketh and Csorath to secure the ship and bid them good night.

Above: Maketh's triple-layered Obfuscation barrier dimmed the starry sky into gray gloom.

On deck: Csorath ordered absolute silence, lights out, and everyone below as he returned to the tiller.

One by one, the other Supplicants stood. They unbuttoned their shirts and presented bared throats and chests so Guardian Maketh could verify their personal wards were adequately chosen, properly drawn, and fully operational.

Rahelu did not stir at Maketh's approach; not even when Ghardon shook her gently by her shoulders. (Hopefully, that was simply due to her exhaustion and not because he'd dosed her with too much heartroot.)

Ghardon looked at the Imos Dedicate making his way down the line and started rehearsing some appropriately politic words while unbuttoning his collar.

"Guardian," he said as Maketh stopped in front of them and eyed the sleeping Rahelu, "my sister showed me her wards earlier. Full dreamward, fifth variation; combined with an advanced suppression ward. I can vouch that they are properly drawn and fully—"

"Yes, very good." Maketh barely glanced at his Evocation of Rahelu's wards. "You, on the other hand, could do with further practice. Stop sketching your lines and draw them with surety."

He grimaced. "But the proportions—"

"Are done by feel, not formula."

Ghardon wanted to debate the point, but a yawn threatened to overwhelm him. He managed to stifle it by clenching his jaw tight, then forced a quiet, "Yes, Guardian," through his teeth—only for a second yawn to pry his jaws back apart wide enough to swallow the moon.

Oh gods, had he just *yawned* at a senior mage?

He needed to bow; couldn't, with Rahelu's head still weighing his shoulder down. "Forgiveness, Guardian! I meant no disrespect. I—"

Maketh held up one hand. "It is late. You are tired. I will make allowances for the circumstances." He paused, then asked: "Have either of you had trouble sleeping?"

Ghardon looked down at Rahelu, drooling on his shoulder.

Remembered experiencing her sheer terror at finding herself locked inside an interrogation chamber somewhere deep inside a restricted area of the Guild he hadn't even known existed, slicing her wrists open on the resonance crystal cuffs that shackled her to a table while Maketh Imos accused her of being a Conclave spy in front of two Elders and an Atriarch.

He kept a firm grip on his emotions as he met Maketh's eyes. "No more than usual," he said.

Maketh regarded them both steadily.

Ghardon waited.

He didn't have to wait long for the third yawn.

"Go," the Imos Guardian said. "Get some rest."

Somehow, he managed to carry her below without falling off the ladder. The yawns came one after another now, so thick and fast that his eyes were closed more often than not, though it hardly mattered; the hold was so dark.

Ghardon automatically reached out with his resonance senses. Not the same as physical sight, but it was better than nothing—at the very least, it would help him figure out which of the hammocks were theirs.

He couldn't feel a thing.

That made no sense.

The other Supplicants were down here. True, they were also warded and probably asleep, and his skill in Seeking wasn't as refined as Ela's, but Captain Csorath wanted them off the main deck for good reason: sustained resonance would eventually get through the wards so he ought to be getting something. There ought to be—he ought to be...

They fell over.

And lay there. For what seemed like a very long (or was it very short?) time. It was peaceful. Almost like drifting off in the hot spring caves at Meruaz Yne.

Something brushed against the edge of his mind. An insistent, high-pitched note of urgency. Faint; almost too soft to hear, as if coming from very far away.

Ghardon tried very hard to listen.

Listened.

But all he heard was silence.

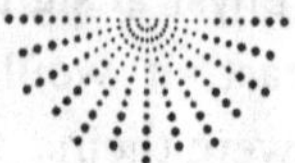

21

SHADOW

Starlight above. Dark sea below. Crimson rivulets running down the channels carved in the ebon altar-throne. She kneels over the butchered body, a blade in her blood-soaked hands.

She should look at the face.

She does not want to look at the face.

To look upon that face is to remember love and she does not want to remember love like this. Love would not want her to remember like this. Love would want her to remember the why; the stars would remember the rest.

She cannot look at the face.

She keeps her hands and knife steady, working by touch alone to excise her mortal eyes; eyes that had seen so much and yet not enough, never enough, for they could not see beyond the smallness of mortal concerns.

Even in this moment, her mind holds death's after-echoes as close as love had held her in life. Perhaps she should excise her heart as well. Cut it out, all the better to examine every flaw, so she can remake it in the image of her ideals.

She bows in prayer, a supplicant before the Starfather's celestial gaze, and begs for the blessing of wisdom, born of infinite sight.

Help...

...me.

WHITE-HOT PAIN PIERCED RAHELU'S STOMACH.

She needed to breathe; couldn't—ribs and diaphragm resisting her lungs as they struggled to inflate against the weight of the limp, heavy body crushing her against the deck.

Dark; it was so dark.

A second stabbing sensation tore through her gut and she screamed: a near-soundless whistle that went nowhere.

Gods, it hurt; it *hurt*.

Pain gave her strength to push the body off her, curl her knees to her nose, and press both hands against the wound, the knife, that had to be there, had to be sticking out of her body, she hurt so much—

...lp me.

Nothing.

No knife, no wound; only her own abdominal muscles, tight with tension, as her insides roiled and rumbled.

Out. She had to get out. Which way was out? Never mind getting on her feet when the world tilted side to side; she wanted—she needed the bracing four-point stability of hands and knees so when the next waves hit—

(and...*there!* A triple strike of pain and nausea and unsteadiness)

—she shook and trembled beneath their fury but did not fall.

She did not fall.

...help me.

She got up.

Staggered over to the companionway, one hand over her mouth, cheeks bulging, body doubled over from the nausea and pain—*ah, the pain!*—lancing through her gut.

Her stomach rebelled before she made it to the hatch. Bitter bile and bits of burnt congee that she had swallowed whole rather than chew and taste spurted from her mouth.

The sick smell set her heaving again.

She clung to the ladder, dizzy, and clenched her stomach out of habit. Food was food; too precious to go to waste simply because it didn't agree with her digestion.

Help me.

She screwed her eyes shut. No; she would not give in, would not relinquish her right to rule her body, would not sit here, retching over and over until there was nothing left for—

Rahelu came to, lying in the middle of the deck, shivering.

Her tongue felt thick and unbearably dry; her throat scraped raw. She needed water, sweet water, to rinse her mouth and replenish the liquid she had lost and was about to lose when the twitching pangs in her bowels eventually swelled into a single explosive point.

Bouts of severe cramping hampered her blind crawl sternward at a snail's pace. She located the water cask by smell and the feel of its wide base. Whimpered when the spigot refused to turn. Waited until her shudders subsided enough for her to pull herself up and cursed when she found the ladle missing.

Which fucking idiot had misplaced it? She didn't care if it was the captain himself; she would bludgeon the culprit with it until their skull caved in and made for a new ladle holder.

It took four tries to pry the lid off. Precious water spilled through the gaps between her cupped, stiffened fingers before she could drink.

Fuck it.

Rahelu plunged her head into the cask and didn't surface until she had guzzled enough to settle the roiling in her stomach and reduce the water level by two finger-widths.

She wiped her eyes and mouth on her sleeve. Stripped off her vomit-drenched shirt and blew her dripping nose into it for good measure. Draped herself over the open cask and closed her eyes again, forcing her twitching muscles to relax.

Breathed.

Cool, fresh air soothed her. Deepnight's quiet—now that she no longer disturbed it—was a welcome respite. The rhythmic lullaby of waves slapping against wooden hull did wonders to calm her, even if the same song sounded different upon the Aleituan Sea than it did upon the Elumaje.

Stormbringer. She hadn't reacted so badly to a meal since she was fourteen when a Free Territories ship had brought a plague of rats into the Lowdocks. The rats had gone everywhere, spreading disease and dysentery across the city, until every common-born citizen spent half the day squatting in the streets, squeezing out bloodied stools. Twelve hundred and eighty-six people—a full third of them from the Lowdocks—had died before the Houses had allowed the Healers' Hall to shut down trade, institute quarantine measures, and put together a task force to purge the city.

Gods.

Rahelu shuddered—at memory, this time—and scrubbed her eyes. Finally, she looked up.

Thick gray fog smothered everything.

She couldn't see more than a few strides in any direction; even the shape of the *Gull's* mast and furled sails were obscured. There was no hope of seeing the sky, of drawing peace and comfort from the Starfather's benevolent gaze—not when the Stormbringer had dropped a dense woolen blanket over the world. The salt-laden fog deadened and distorted her senses of sight, sound, and resonance. All her Seeking found was a bleak stretch of endless emptiness, utterly devoid of...

Rahelu shot to her feet, heart pounding in her throat.

She was the only one on deck.

All quiet; all wrong.

Where was the captain? Csorath had nightwatch; he ought to have met her with the spyglass in hand when she came up to interrupt his ceaseless prowling of the ship's perimeter. And, full stealth protocols aside, the night should be noisome—filled with Elaram's erratic gasp-choked snores, the softer sounds of Nheras's nasally whistling; Jhobon's nonsensical murmuring; Ylaen's occasional coughing; the rattle and squeak of iron loops on iron hooks as Ghardon tossed and turned in his hammock—for she had left the cargo hatch open in her panicked flight.

She trawled through her memory of dinner. Everyone had eaten from the same pot of congee, the same platter of fish; drunk from the same pot of tea—

Bitter, Rahelu thought. Everything she'd eaten had been bitter—the bowl of burnt congee; the sip of heartleaf tea—except for the fiery bite of spice-dusted fish skin, and the sour-sweet cube of goldtrout. All other details were indistinct; the chronology between eating and waking a blacked-out blur that segued in and out of nightmare.

Shouldn't there be someone else staggering after her, groaning in pain, squirming around, clutching their belly?

Listen.

She strained her ears and resonance senses.

Heard the eerie creak and moan of timber and taut cabling as the *Sooty Gull* ran into the next swell at the wrong angle. Felt the ever-present alien song's teeth-itching, bone-aching frisson running through her mind. Looked for the soft, stately hum of Maketh's triple barriers, its bland harmony smoothing out the sporadic bursts of accumulated resonance leaking through their dreamwards, containing it from spilling out beyond the *Gull's* deck. Found—

Nothing.

Maketh's barriers were down.

Rahelu rushed to the starboard toprail, hands grasping along the rim. Row after row of dulled resonance crystals passed under her fingers. Drained. She reached the prow; sank to her knees; found the cluster of stones—the formation's lynchpin—embedded in the *Gull's* planks.

Cracked.

Shit. Shit!

Panic rippled through her, its frothy edge bubbling past her ward, into her aura, spilling out into the ambient resonance as a molten orange glow. It lit up the night, bright as a bonfire, visible to any Seeker within ten kual.

She extinguished that ill-timed beacon with an Obfuscation barrier of blue-gray calm. Held it for a count of a hundred and a hundred again, resonance senses and ears tensed for the telltale tingle of a Seeking or the sound of waves parting beneath the hull of an approaching ship.

For a thousand counts: nothing.

Rahelu sagged as her panic ebbed and faded with her barrier, replaced by sweet relief. Once she stopped trembling, she forced herself back on her feet. Find Csorath first, she decided. The barriers' failure was significant enough to qualify as an emergency demanding the captain's attention. Perhaps he knew already; perhaps he had already gone below, to wake Guardian Maketh to take care of the repairs.

Be ready.

A muffled *BANG!* from below. The aft hatch flew open and a coughing shadow scrambled out.

"Captain!" Rahelu gasped as she hurried over. "The barriers—"

Resonance surged from the aftercabin.

ATTACK!

She flung up a hand instinctively (idiot! What good is a hand against Command?) and drew deep on Lhorne's pendant. Smooth blue-gray calm surrounded her—too little, too late. The Command pierced her Obfuscation barrier, sure as a spear cast, and slammed into her skull.

Rahelu reeled back two strides, then tottered forward and stumbled to one knee.

Push. *Push!* Push back against the unwelcome intrusion before you lose all awareness of it because this was not happening, *this was not happening*, not again, never again—

MOVE.

Rahelu moved.

The deck was slick with condensation; her bare feet slipped and slid on the wooden planks as the Command sent her after the fleeing shadow, hurtling sternward on unsteady legs. Panic flared anew—she couldn't see anything; she was going too fast; she was going to trip and fall and break something. She tried to dig her heels in but her body refused to listen and the next misstep sent her straight into the mast.

Pain and shock joined panic; Command overrode them all. Move, she had to stop lying there, get up, move, move—

MOVE!

The Command yanked her to her feet and onward; made her seize the tumultuous flows of burning red, brilliant yellow, and molten orange pouring out of her aura. She wasn't sure why, but she was sure that it was important—

vitally important—that she got hold of and kept hold of every last bit. She had to...she needed to...to...

Prepare.

...to prepare.
For what?
Certainty surged within her.

Danger.

Yes, that was it.
Danger.
Where was it?
She couldn't see; couldn't *see* through all this fucking fog. Seeking! That was what she needed—Seeking and all the range she could get. Stop jumping at shadows and playing with the coalescing resonance. Turn the fuck around and go back towards the mast and up—*up*, damnit, *up UP UP!*—the rigging to...
What was she thinking?
Danger had been stalking them. Danger was a strange ship on the horizon, on a heading set to intersect with theirs in the night. Danger had snuck a stowaway and a tracking beacon on board and caused Kerg to slit his own throat. Distractions, done in hopes of...of...

Betrayal.

Betrayal?
Bitter food. Barriers down. Not a soul on watch.
Yes. Betrayal.
Anger simmered. Csorath had been right—there *was* a traitor in their midst.

A lily-livered, false-faced, lying, sneaking traitor who relied on drugs and poisons to enact their treachery instead of honest combat.

How dare they? How dare they!

Resonance condensed in her open palm.

Who was it?

Nheras?

No, not Nheras. Nheras wouldn't stoop to poison; Nheras would stab her in the back, then spin her around and stab her in the front, just to make sure she knew who was responsible.

Tangled red pain-ribbons straightened, thickened into a shaft radiating soul-searing heat.

Ghardon?

He'd been so insistent she sleep; so insistent on preparing dinner himself; so delighted at the sight of everybody eating and drinking.

Could some skilled interloper have fooled them all with a Seeming?

No!

Rahelu recoiled as viscous orange panic clumped at one end of the Projection-shaft like a gather of hot glass; sharpened into a wicked, wedged blade.

Not Ghardon. Not him; not Elaram; she refused to consider the possibility. They called her *'sister'*; they'd cared for her like she was one of them—she would *know* if they were not who they were.

Ylaen. It had to be Ylaen.

Or Jhobon.

But they, too, had eaten the fish and drunk the wine and swallowed the tea.

No. It didn't matter who the traitor was—that could be dealt with later.

Yellow shock raced from her aura to her hands up the haft

to spark off the gleaming, razor-edged spearpoint.

Right now, she had only one job.

ATTACK.

She swung the Projection-spear.

Hit nothing.

Fuck this Stormbringer-sent fog.

She couldn't see; couldn't hear; couldn't Seek worth a damn with all those salt-laden droplets distorting the ambient resonance.

Where the fuck had that cowardly shadow crept to?

There! A tall shape beside the tiller.

She swung again—missed *again*.

Nothing? Fuck!

Rahelu snarled as she whipped the Projection-spear up and down from stern to bow; spinning, slicing, stabbing at shadow-opponents who stretched tendrils through the dense gray fog to snatch at her goose-pimpled skin. They left their marks in trails of sweat down her shoulder blades and flanks; in shivers that robbed her arms of sure strength; in the bone-white ghosts that rose out of their demise.

The *flap* of the mainsail unfurling.

She sprinted aft.

Slipped; righted herself again. Cast her resonance senses ahead in a Seeking, feet and ears and eyes racing to catch up. No way for the traitor to escape her now: she had them cornered; she had their position; she had the dark shape hunched and clinging to the mast above in her sights—

Rahelu yelled; hurled her Projection. The tri-colored spear soared skyward, shedding yellow sparks in its wake. Red-orange-white brilliance set the fog aglow, illuminating mast, stays, haul lines, mast, clews, sail, mast—

A swirl of fog and shadow from behind.

Shit.

Rahelu thrust her left hand up as the traitor whipped a

doubled length of fishing line over her head. The makeshift garotte bit into her fingers; jerked her off her feet.

Lowdocks instincts screamed and her body reacted. Rahelu threw her weight back with the attacker's momentum to ease the pressure on her throat, went to turn so she could take the throttling on the side and back of her neck where the fishing line would bruise and cut instead of strangle—

Some deeper, familiar, inner voice arrested her shoulders and torso mid-twist; compelled her to reach for resonance instead.

The chokehold tightened.

Dread settled into the hollow pit of her stomach in place of her earlier nausea as her half-formed Projection bled away. The only thing keeping her conscious was her trapped left hand but it wouldn't last long. Once her attacker compensated and wrapped the garotte around her neck...

Turn. Turn!

Her rapidly weakening muscles refused to obey.

Turn, gods all be damned, she needed to—

ATTACK.

Realization dawned with horror.

LET GO OF ME! she raged as dread flowered into full-fledged terror.

Anathwan had no right to do this to her. There were laws against the abuse of resonance skills; that was the whole point of the Guild and the Houses and the Dominion itself. Bone-white mist broke past her sweat-eroded ward, past the flickering Obfuscation barrier anchored to her pendant, and flooded into the ambient resonance as she thrashed, helpless as a deer caught in a nheshwyr's coils.

LET GO LET GO LET GO LET—

Rahelu, Anathwan sent. *Trust me.*

How could she?

Twice, no—three times; this was the third time—the *third*

fucking time—the Elder had reached inside her mind with Command and puppeted her around like a game piece on a board. Even Mere Ideth had asked—not demanded—her free consent, and that had only been for a direct Seeking. So much for all that high-minded talk of bringing forth the future, of making the right choices and not forcing things, of true success founded in shared vision instead of coercion.

More urgently, insistent as ever, but fainter, with a desperation Rahelu had never sensed from the Elder before: *Trust me.*

Her mother would tell her to submit.

Rahelu owed Anathwan obedience as a senior mage of her sworn House and the hand of the Exalted Dominance himself.

Anathwan was her Elder in every sense of the word; possessed of wisdom and experience and knowledge that Rahelu lacked.

What practical difference was there between Anathwan giving her orders and her following them, and Anathwan Commanding them of her, except that she got to say 'yes'?

She got to say 'yes'.

Was she willing to die over something so small?

She didn't know.

But if the Elder had used Command, then she needed Rahelu alive. You couldn't Command the dead, so Anathwan wouldn't let her die. Not like this.

And that meant Rahelu held the upper hand.

Trust me first, she sent.

Blackness crept into the edge of her vision as the last of her breath wheezed from her lungs. The pressure in her mind grew stronger, tighter than the line wrapped about her throat; the overwhelming urge to give in, release thought, relinquish reason so great she could think of nothing else.

Fuck. Fuckfuckfuckfuckfuck!

She was going to die. Anathwan was going to let her die.

She didn't want to die.

Rahelu emptied her mind.

And let Anathwan Command.

Bone-white mist erupts in the ambient resonance and swallows them both.

Control the emotions.

She feels the pure, distilled terror in the clamminess of her palms and the bottoms of her feet; the wetness of the cold sweat and fog beading on her skin; the sudden heat of piss running down her legs; the way her heart is vibrating so fast that it feels as if it will burst; how her lungs have seized so she cannot act, cannot scream, cannot think, cannot perceive anything other than the very worst fears in the darkest recesses of her mind made tangible.

But terror cannot rule her when someone else rules instead.

Control the resonance.

She seizes every tendril of terror close.

She cannot see or sense the traitor's resonance signature behind their wards, but she knows—by their height, their weight, the set of their stance, the lack of ridged, raised scars on their arms—it is not Ylaen or Jhobon. Taller than her and Elaram; slighter and lighter than Ghardon; slimmer than Nheras, but no less ruthless.

She does not need her pendant or her hands or air for this; only her will and a simple visualization.

One moment, her resonance aura is as smooth as the Elumaje in winter—pale clouds swirling over blue-gray calm; the next, ten thousand jagged spikes of fear-ice sprout from the misty waters at her back to pierce the traitor.

Their death grip falters.

Precious air rushes into her lungs.

She twists; throws her weight forward until her feet touch the deck once more. Slips free and tears the fishing line from the enemy's hands. Free! She was free! She—

CONTROL THE WORLD.

—calls forth the power stored in the pendant around her neck until it glows and burns like a star even as she stretches out her right hand to reclaim the terror still lingering in the ambient resonance. Someone else's skill, gained through decades of practice, guides her. Heat crackles through her focus stone. Resonance rushes to her; more power than she can safely handle alone, faster than thought. A bone-white spear manifests instantly in her palm: as tall as she is and half her height again, capped with a large-bladed point three hands long and boasting twin, wicked barbs.

There is nothing left in the ambient resonance for the traitor to draw upon, for she controls the world.

They will have to draw upon themselves.

Behind her, the traitor summons an Obfuscation barrier: cold as the Unomelaje glacier, vast as the skies, dark as the deepest depths of the Earthgiver's heart.

RAHELU'S PROJECTION WAVERED.

No Supplicant—not Ghardon; not Jhobon; not even Lhorne wielding the pendant she now wore—could create anything approaching that...that impenetrable defense.

Dedicate Maketh Imos was the fucking traitor.

(But his shadow...surely his shadow would loom larger?)

It *had* to be Maketh. Who else had the skill? Who else would dare move against Csorath? Who else was in a position to betray Anathwan?

Wisps of terror smoked off the Projection-spear's blade and haft as her control frayed. What could she do against Maketh? He had greater skill, greater experience, greater stamina and power built up over decades—

Steady. Did Anathwan seem weaker? I am with you.

She had tried to defy him before, twice, and twice, he had shown her just how pathetic her defense was.

Run—*run!*—she had to run (but there was nowhere to run) or hide (where could she hide from him?) or—

We are Issolm, *Rahelu; we do what needs to be done.*

The shining bone-white spear in her hand steadies. Sight; sound; sense—all are distractions.

Rahelu shut her eyes.

She is a weapon—and she is well-aimed by her wielder.

RAHELU SPUN and hurled her spear.

Bone-white terror slammed into blackened dread. The high-pitched static whine of interference—shrill and sharp, like the *screech-scrape* of metal against glass—sheared through the ambient resonance and rent her senses.

She lost the sense of Anathwan's presence.

The shining greatspear plunged through the barrier, which rippled and swelled as it tried to devour the Projection. Bit by bit, the dread overwhelmed the terror until all that was left of her Projection-spear was the last two handspans of the shaft. Soon, even that would be swallowed up and she would have to face Maketh alone again.

Anathwan had Commanded her to fight like a mage.

Fuck that. Rahelu would fight to live.

She dug her feet into the deck, and charged.

A futile move against Ylaen; against Maketh, it was suicidal. The Imos Dedicate might be older, but he was still a man in his physical prime: taller, broader about the shoulders and chest, and heavier compared to the Imos Supplicant. But since Maketh harbored exactly zero tender feelings for her, the alternative to suicide was certain death. If Rahelu was going to die, she'd rather dictate the terms of her end.

Her only chance was to strike first: hard, fast, and low.

And snatch the dagger in his belt.

Focused as he was on holding against the fearsome Projection Anathwan had helped her unleash, he didn't see her coming until it was too late.

Rahelu's shoulder rammed straight into his gut.

At best, she hoped to wind him; at worst, she would be grappled, or bounce off, dazed by the impact. But he was not ready, he was not braced, and the two of them sailed five strides through the air.

They crashed into the portside bulwark—hard; as though Maketh weighed no more than petite, slim Elaram—and Rahelu heard the satisfying *smack* of skull against solid wood, followed by a distinctly feminine cry of pain.

Impossible.

Her eyes flew open. And finally, through the fog, the dark dread of his crumbling Obfuscation barrier, and the last brilliance of her fading Projection, she got a clear look at the traitor's flickering face.

Rahelu gaped. "Captain?"

The shock in her resonance aura radiated through the ambient resonance in a raucous clangor and her mind fell into the familiar as soon as she named him: *'Yes, that's him; that's Csorath, gods all be thanked, you've found him at last'*.

His features began to stabilize.

No, she forcefully reminded herself, and lashed out with Csorath's true resonance signature. *This is impossible.*

Seeking contended with Seeming for control over reality.

Focus, Rahelu, on the feel of the body beneath you; the shoulders nearly as narrow as your own, the compact frame beneath the muscles, the yielding softness of the chest.

Remember who Csorath Isonn *is*. He does not have the brusque manner, harsh temper, or large build of Maketh Imos, but he is no slack-handed sap who commands his ship from a silk cushion; Csorath has the robust, well-muscled frame of a practiced sailor who has worked his way up from unranked deckhand to captain of the *Winged Arrow*.

"Who are you?" Rahelu asked. "Who sent you?"

Plausibility collapsed.

The traitor's Seeming unraveled, exposing a young woman with cropped black hair and a sharp blade of a nose paired with a large, thin-lipped mouth. Her front was dusted with a light powdery substance that had left chalky streaks across her palms.

Rahelu's thoughts skidded to a halt.

The woman wielded no focus stone in the form of a mage-staff, pendant, or ring—not even the smallest earring—yet she had conjured a terrifyingly capable Obfuscation barrier equal to Maketh's best efforts and a Seeming as thorough and enduring as any of Anathwan's.

"Conclave." The Chanazian word slipped out of its own accord; Maketh had been right all along. "You're Conclave."

Wandering eyes as dark as her own, set wide below a full forehead, snapped back into focus.

Steel flashed in the woman's hand.

Instinctively, Rahelu went for her own belt knife; cursed when she realized she didn't have it. She threw herself clear in a savage roll across the deck; rolled; rolled again to avoid the slashes aimed at her sides, to put distance between the two of them. She swayed as she scrambled to her feet. Poured what power was left in her pendant into her fading Obfuscation barrier until the space between her eyes throbbed in time with the fresh stirrings of nausea and the resonance crystal grew dangerously hot once more.

It would do her very little good. Her odds against a

Conclave-trained mage were…well, *'severe disadvantage'* was a mild way of putting it. She'd have a better chance of out-dueling Maketh.

Rahelu ignored her mounting resonance backlash and roiling gut to fall into a defensive combat stance and back away towards the mast.

The ambient resonance was still thick with glittering yellow-white shock—there was hardly enough wind to stir the mainsail—yet the Conclave mage made no attempt to control it. She merely followed, poised on the balls of her feet, raised dagger parting the resonance-filled fog before her, a shark announcing its presence in the water with its fin.

"I will make this easy for you"—Rahelu had thought Csorath's liquid Anazvelan accent that rounded off most of the hard consonants when he spoke Chanazian was the product of expensive language tutors; not because the speaker hailed from Anazvela itself—"for I understand you are merely upholding your oaths."

And that dagger—*that* was strange. Whoever heard of a Conclave-trained mage fighting with physical weapons? Such a common, crude thing was beneath them.

Evidently, the dagger was part of the disguise—Csorath was Isonn-sworn and when he wasn't masquerading as a smuggler, he practically qualified as a walking armory. The woman's form was good; Rahelu had narrowly missed being stabbed twice. Even now, the Conclave mage held her stance, though her limbs and the point of her dagger were unsteady and she was not watching Rahelu.

"Go and lie in the hold with the others," the woman said. "Wait until dawn comes. Then rise with the sun and follow it home. I have what I came for, and I wish you no harm."

Something was off.

The woman's eyes kept sliding from the dim glow of the pendant around Rahelu's neck to the mast, and then to the lost horizon beyond. Her free hand hovered protectively over a dark, glassy hoop hanging from her belt. A piece of the night that drank up the faint light refracting through the fog.

The crown. The key.

She was stealing the crown, but not the ship—she didn't need the *Gull* because there was another ship out there, a Chanazian ship, waiting to retrieve her.

But why not call that ship with Projection? Why leave Rahelu's Obfuscation barrier intact? Why allow Rahelu to gather resonance uncontested? Why was Rahelu still standing when she had done for everyone else?

Why delay the inevitable with talk?

Either it was intended to be a statement of supreme confidence...or her enemy had exhausted all other options—in which case, the situation was entirely different.

It didn't matter how skilled the other mage was in close combat; it didn't even matter that she was armed and Rahelu was not. No physical attack—no matter how skillfully wielded—could hope to prevail against resonance skills. For perception begets emotion and emotion becomes thought; thought translates to intent, which, in turn, becomes action.

And thus: wars are won first in the mind and then upon the battlefield.

"I don't think so." Rahelu leveled the beginnings of a new, crackling yellow-white beam coalescing in her hand at the woman, doing her best to keep it steady and level despite her racing pulse. "How about you drop your weapon and what you've stolen instead? Allow yourself to be bound and submit to a direct Seeking and then we can see about convincing my Elder to permit you to be ransomed."

The Conclave mage eyed her Projection warily. "The weapon you can have." She released the dagger and it clattered to the deck. "But I cannot agree to the rest."

Fine. Time for a display.

"I don't think you have a choice." Rahelu spun her half-formed Projection in a basic spear drill. Each pass left a hollow trail behind as her Projection soaked up free resonance, gaining in substance and length as she pushed the woman back. "Would you not prefer to retain your dignity?"

"Go home to your anma and aban, nelan," the Conclave mage repeated. She gave no further ground, for she was right up against the starboard toprail now, and the tremors in her hands and knees were obvious. "Seek not the Endless Gate."

"There is one person in this world who has the right to call me that," Rahelu said. "And you are not her."

"Do I not?" The woman gave her a long look. "Do you deny Onneja's teachings?"

Rahelu froze.

The shock-spear she clutched in her right hand fuzzed and crackled, but shock was an unruly source of resonance to begin with; sparking and spluttering was in its nature.

The ripples in her Obfuscation barrier were more difficult to conceal. She thought of Nheras and covered her lapse with borrowed disdain. "Those lessons have not saved you."

"But they might save you. You are in great need of them."

"I am in no need of saving."

Her words rang hollow. She knew the value of Conclave training: every lesson Onneja had taught her had saved her life in one way or another. The meditations that kept her centered when anger threatened to overwhelm good sense; the early demonstrations of Seeking that kept her family from falling prey to unscrupulous Lowdocks scams and extortion rackets; the resonance wards that made her as valuable a team member as any of the House-born Supplicants.

"Were that the case, you would not rely on that crutch."

She resisted the urge to cover up Lhorne's pendant with her free hand. "It is not a crutch."

"If you were a true apprentice of Onneja's, she would

separate you from that pendant at once, so it cannot limit your potential."

What?

"But focus stones are the pathway to greater power!"

"If you will not go home, then go to Anazvela and learn the truth for yourself. For the Houses do not delight in sharing knowledge; their power comes from hoarding it."

She couldn't. Could she?

Tsenjhe had once seen the sum of her life, had she but apprenticed to the Conclave. She had changed the world.

"Come with me," the woman said as she extended the hand that had previously held a dagger; it shook with barely suppressed tremors from the onset of severe resonance backlash. "Onneja would be pleased to see you again."

Rahelu wanted to see Onneja again, too.

She wanted to sit at Onneja's feet the way she had sat at Anathwan's, somewhere lonely and high above the surging sea, spill out all the secrets and darkness and questions she had been keeping inside, and listen to the steady wisdom that had never steered her wrong.

"Leave the Houses to their petty squabbling, Rahelu. What have they done for the good of the world?"

Nothing. The Houses professed to uphold the Dominion's ideals—equality, fairness, prosperity—but it was a lie. Petitioning had proved that. And Lhorne had confirmed that the system had been deliberately designed that way.

Her family had given up everything, had traded their peaceful life by the Elumaje for five years of eking out a miserable existence in the slums of a city that branded them as foreigners just so they could kowtow and fight for the crumbs and leavings brushed off from House-born tables and tossed out into back alleys.

And she was one of the Starfather-blessed ones. She and

Tsenjhe had made it—two out of how many common-born hopefuls who had flocked to the Dominion?

"What do you care for them?"

Dharyas had asked her a similar question, once: '*Why do you want to join one of the Houses so much?*'

Rahelu hadn't been able to give a good answer.

She didn't give a shit about which House was Exalted or their stupid dinner parties or which silk-draped, glitter-painted fool ranked above another in their convoluted pecking order. To her, the Houses had never been more than a means to that promised end of a better life. Unlike Lhorne, she neither knew nor cared about what each House purportedly stood for, and her choice hadn't been based on any principled belief or nuanced analysis.

There had been one paramount consideration in her mind when she weighed Anathwan Issolm's offer against Mere Ideth's offer: Anathwan was paying her ten times as much.

"What do they care for you?"

Nothing! Her thoughts fell into the litany of injustices she had witnessed against common-born: the House Isca landlord seizing the majority of Xyuth's few assets and leaving nothing for his consort and daughter; the extortionist fees charged by the Guild—fees that were trivial for wealthy House-born but amounted to an entire week's income after expenses for her family.

Not one clerk or bailiff had ever shown compassion when her family had come up short on their payments because there were too many boats in the harbor and not enough fish.

House-born didn't care about anyone beyond themselves.

Except...

Except that wasn't true.

Dharyas had cared.

Lhorne cared. He had cared from the very beginning; had interceded on behalf of a sorry, common-born nobody. She would never have been accepted into the Guild for training if it had not been for his kindness.

Ghardon cared. He was miserably seasick, homesick, and magesick, and still looked out for her as much as he looked out for Elaram; he'd tried to *cook* something nice to cheer her up even though he was not remotely adequate to the task.

Elaram cared. Elaram had invited her to dinner with her family before she'd been accepted by the Houses; Elaram had convinced Ghardon they ought to team up with her; Elaram had cared about stopping the cultists before they killed more people; had understood it was not a game.

As for Ylaen, Jhobon, and Nheras: they weren't friends and given the option, she'd avoid their company to do just about anything else, but they were a team and she wouldn't leave them behind. She figured they felt more or less the same about her, and that was fair.

Beyond that, Tsenjhe cared. Keshwar cared. Anathwan cared. Perhaps even Maketh cared.

Who was this woman, who had lied about who she was and betrayed their trust, who couched her attempts at manipulation in the language of her heart, who dared claim the bonds of venelanaz, who thought it would be easy to tempt Rahelu into betraying her oaths with a simple appeal to a yearning for a shared ancestral homeland?

Stormwinds. This was going to hurt.

The glow of her pendant winked out. With it went her Obfuscation barrier. Rahelu dropped her combat stance and Projection, letting fizzling yellow-white sparks rain on deck and eddy around their feet with the fog.

She took the Conclave mage's shaking hand, bare palm to bare palm, and readied Seeking. "You know my name, venaz. Will you gift me with the knowledge of yours?"

The woman returned her searching look. "Venoru."

Venoru. Its truth rang loud and clear to her Seeking; it was woven through the woman's aura, suppressed though it was behind wards that must be as complicated as her own.

"Venoru," Rahelu repeated. "I assume you know what the Houses plan. Will you share what the Conclave intends?"

She kept the visible part of her resonance aura as calm and placid as the Elumaje on a windless day. This was her only chance; she dared not slip up.

"Gladly," Venoru said. "Once we are safely away." She pulled her hand free and stepped sideways so she could circle back to the mast. "Go, nelan, and pack your things while I light the signal lantern."

Venoru bent down to retrieve her dropped dagger; Rahelu stepped on the hilt first.

"That seems inefficient, venaz," Rahelu said. "This fog has reduced visibility to less than a kual; they might search all night and still not find us. Why don't you tell me their rough position and the codes to broadcast? If they're within ten kual, I'll—"

A muffled *thud* from amidships.

Venoru whirled to face the new threat, one hand on the crown at her belt.

Ylaen Imos stumbled out of the fog with his knife drawn and left hand raised. His eyes swept over Rahelu, blinked in confusion at seeing her out of stance, then landed on Venoru.

He snapped off a gesture; looked surprised when nothing happened.

In the space between that heartbeat and the next, Rahelu saw the shift in Venoru's resolve and Ylaen's intent, and froze with indecision.

Lightning-quick, Ylaen whipped his knife straight through Venoru's throat.

But not before Venoru ripped the crown from her belt and tossed it into the Abmerduan Sea.

22
GONE

RAHELU LUNGED THROUGH THE FOG. GRUNTED AS
the toprail smacked into her midsection. Eyes, ears, arms,
resonance senses straining, hands snatching at empty air as
she scanned the dark.

Gone.

It was gone, the crown was fucking gone; whatever sound
it had made as it hit the waves drowned out by the gurgling
and groaning coming from the two laid out on deck behind
her so there was nothing to mark where it had sunk.

All because of that *idiot*.

She trembled with barely contained rage as she stalked
past the dying Conclave mage. Held the fire in her smoldering aura close, wrapping it around herself like a second
skin, lest she let off yet another beacon for the nearby
Conclave ship. She seized the dropped dagger and swore at
the quivering, moaning, belly-clutching pile of uselessness
vomiting on the deck in front of her.

"What the fuck is *wrong* with you? I had the situation
under control until you charged in and started throwing
steel! If it weren't for your act of terminal stupidity, I—"

"Under control?" Ylaen gasped between fits of heaving. "Is that what you call it?"

"If you disagree with my characterization, let's hear your reasons for killing our navigator and the spy in our midst instead of capturing her for questioning."

He made a choked sound; she couldn't tell if it was supposed to be a laugh or a cry of pain, so she ignored it and turned her attention inward, trying to stem the rising tide of panic inside.

The crown was gone.

Both hatches were open.

Anyone who was onboard and awake would have been conscious of the disturbance in the ambient resonance and any mage in full or even partial command of their faculties would have been woken up by the repercussions of her mage fight against Venoru—as Ylaen had.

Yet no one else had joined them on deck.

Maketh had not materialized at the prow to fix the barriers. And Anathwan had fought Venoru through Rahelu instead of fighting the Conclave mage herself—and then faded from Rahelu's mind.

Gods in the four heavens and eight hells.

If the Elder was dead...

What the fuck were they supposed to do?

What the fuck was *she* supposed to do?

Rahelu closed her eyes and clenched her fists, jaws clamped shut so the scream rising inside her would find no voice, torn between wanting to kick the living shit out of this supposed Harbinger who had used his knife when he ought to have used his brains and now—

Now Ylaen had his knife back in his hand as he swayed on his knees. He was saying something, words that interrupted her thoughts and sent them skittering away, like rats fleeing before a hungry cat.

"If you fault my decision-making, then I find equal fault with yours. I saw you. I heard the two of you—"

Shit. How long had he been lurking in the fog, listening to her exchange with Venoru? How much had he understood?

"—greeting each other, with your hands clasped like comrades. Venaz, you called her. Elder sister of my heart."

Her rage melted away (it would not help now) as she fumbled around for something else. Calm was beyond her, so shock, perhaps—she'd gathered so much of it before, little yellow-white stars falling from her hand like shining coins to dance around her feet like fireflies—or exhaustion. No, no; nausea; nausea and gut-wrenching pain; see how he's struggling to stay upright, see the erraticity of his resonance aura and the pathetic Obfuscation barrier that sputters out as soon as he summons it, now make it worse, make it much worse, make it so he wishes he'd never been born, and—

Geometric patterns blazed in the night.

Ylaen's scars, glowing with molten light.

Ah, *ah!*

Rahelu doubled over, half-formed Projection collapsing, its green-brown sludge-like resonance washing back over her, slipping out of her grasp with the dagger as she retched.

Gone, all gone; gone like the crown, lost in the fog and the night like it had never been. She was left with only pain. Resonance backlash lancing through her eyes and severe cramps wracking her abdomen, as though Ylaen had hurled his knife into her gut instead of Venoru's throat. She blinked away tears and found him looming over her, with that same blood-drenched blade in his unsteady hand, poised to strike.

"So, love." Tingling as his clumsy drug-addled attempt at Seeking bumped up against the edges of her aura. "How did you know not to eat or drink anything last night? Open your heart to me. Why have you conspired with the enemy, Rahelu of Issolm. Or, should I say, Rahelu of Chanaz?"

"I didn't!"

She put what she had left into Projecting sincerity, but if she had little control left of her resonance abilities, he had none at all. His Seeking fell apart and his scars went dark. The whites of his eyes rolled, agitated, as her whisper of a Projection sank into his aura, uncontested.

His knife wavered closer.

She hurriedly cut off the Projection, before he could construe it as a hostile attempt to influence him.

"Listen to me." Talk fast—faster. Simple sentences. Simpler words. Plain Aleznuaweithish, as her mother spoke it. Complex concepts reduced to simple ideas anyone would understand. "I was fighting her. She nearly killed me. She had the crown. That ship Nheras saw was hers. She was about to raise a signal. I delayed her. I was trying to lull her into a false sense of security so she would let down her guard."

Ylaen Imos stared at her, weighing every word, frowning at the way she rounded off and softened her consonants, the only trace of her tendency towards Chanazian pronunciations in her otherwise near-accentless Aleznuaweithish.

Oh, Skymother.

He was trying to decide whether he could believe her without Seeking, and suspicion—no doubt well-ingrained in him by Maketh, and heightened by what he'd witnessed due to his ill-timed arrival—was winning.

"Please," she begged. If she could not reach him through empathy, then she would try appealing to self-preservation. "We need to rouse the others. We need to repair the barriers she destroyed. We need to get the *Gull* away from that Conclave ship before it finds us. Find out if"—she swallowed—"if Anathwan and Maketh are still alive."

They must be alive. *I have what I came for, and I wish you no harm.* Whatever Venoru had slipped into the wine or the spices or the tea last night had merely been debilitating, not deadly—Ylaen was proof of that. It had to be resonance back-lash; it *had* to. They just needed a few more spans to regain their strength. That was all.

A great shivering in the ambient resonance.

Some chilling and powerful presence swept across the ocean to pass over their defenseless little sloop…then swung back to settle upon them, like a blanket of snow.

The Conclave Seeker—or Seekers—had found them.

Ylaen cursed.

"It wasn't me!" she cried.

He reversed his grip on his knife and brought its hilt down. Rahelu rolled. Took the blow meant for her head on her forearm, then grabbed at his wrists.

Listen to me! she sent and laid his right hand over the streaky charcoal lines of her faded resonance ward. Her heart thrummed in sync with his; she could feel its pulsing beneath her fingers, and she prayed that he could feel hers, beneath the crushing pressure of his palm. *I am not your enemy.*

Please, Skymother, please let him sense the ring of truth.

"Swear you aren't lying to me," he said.

"I swear it."

He made no move to relent.

"I swear it!" She looked deep into his wild eyes and did not flinch when he increased the pressure on her ribs. "Stormbringer strike me down if I lie."

"Then you'll mark it in flesh and seal it with blood, in the sight of the sky, the stars, and the sea?"

"Mark me as you like."

Ylaen took her at her word.

A slash of his knife; a shallow score across her upper chest, crossing two of her ribs, his blade so sharp and a cut so light she very nearly didn't feel it through the rest of her pain. Then he let her up and said:

"Alright, love; let's fly."

ONCE THEY HAD the *Gull* sailing on a broad reach, they collapsed beside the steering post, nursing fierce resonance-backlash-induced headaches. In between gybes, they took turns to retch into the bucket they had specifically designated for that purpose, and to run and squat above the hole in the beakhead with their heads draped over their knees, arms clutching shaking legs, trousers around their ankles.

Span by span, Rahelu's strength returned and her resonance backlash subsided. The cramps remained. She whimpered as the first summer rays slid over the portside bow to warm the deck, her legs, her belly, before anxiety subsumed her once more.

It was dawn. No one else had risen with the sun.

She wiped off blood and loose, watery stools and pulled up her trousers for the tenth time, then staggered aft to put the *Gull* through another gybe.

The feeling of being watched eased as the *Sooty Gull's* stern swung through the wind. But as soon as the sloop completed the maneuver, that watched feeling returned.

She did not bother raising an Obfuscation barrier. What little reserves she had recovered would not stop a Conclave-trained Seeker's probe, and Anathwan had made her drain Lhorne's pendant of power in fighting Venoru.

Besides, the enemy Seeker was only watching. Why waste the effort on probing when they were sure to catch the *Sooty Gull* in a matter of spans? They hadn't been able to sight their pursuit through the fog, but they could feel the Conclave vessel inexorably gaining—a half kual for every quarter-span. No matter how much Rahelu adjusted the tension in the backstays or how cleverly Ylaen steered, they could not seem to pull away. Even if they could, there was still that blasted Seeker, tracking their flight across the Abmerduan.

"Hey, Imos," she said. "This isn't working."

They had to stop treading water.

They had to risk losing a kual or two—or more—of their narrow lead in the next span, if they wanted to have any chance at escaping.

"Did you hear me?" she asked, louder.

"I heard you."

Ylaen lay like a corpse himself two strides from Venoru's fallen body, his bloodied knife still clenched in his fist.

"And?"

"And what?"

"You're not even going to try and think of some other solution?"

A slight twitch of his shoulders.

"What the fuck was that?" Rahelu stared, incredulous. "You can't even muster up the will to *shrug* properly? Are you so weak and easily defeated that you're giving up without a fight?"

"Why fight the inevitable?"

Were all House-born this soft?

Finally, she said, "I would not be here, a dozen dozen times over, if I had given up every time someone told me my failure was inevitable."

He muttered something. What, she did not know and did not care, because she deliberately stomped all over his words —loudly, with vicious satisfaction each time her heel smacked against the deck—as she headed for the cargo hatch and sat on the very top rung of the companionway.

"Ghardon?" she called, listening, just listening, as she descended ass-wise into the deathly quiet dark of the ship's hold. "Elaram?"

No answer.

"...Nheras?"

She braced herself for backlash and tried again—*Ghardon?*

Elaram?—throwing names out as general Projections into the vicinity of the cargo hold.

Nothing.

Gods.

She was going to have to check each body for signs of life, and if they were all dead, she would have to—

Her mind shied away from the thought.

What...?

The groggy mental voice she heard wasn't one she would have preferred, but at least she and Ylaen were not alone.

Rahelu crawled to the closest berth, where a shaking Nheras hung out of her hammock. Her skin was clammy; patches of chilled sweat rubbing off on Rahelu as she half-carried, half-dragged Nheras onto the deck.

"Sort yourself out, then get the healer's kit ready." She left Nheras to find her own way to the bucket or the head.

If Nheras had survived...

Rahelu shook the others one by one.

"Gods, my head." Ghardon groaned as he sat up woozily. "What time is it?" He gagged at the stink of vomit that hung around her, then stuffed his forearm into his mouth.

No such restraint from Elaram.

"First span," Rahelu said, as Ghardon suppressed a second bout of retching. "Get Elaram up to the deck, now."

"What happened?" Ghardon asked. "I remember that I..." Short, sharp headshakes, like he was trying to clear his ears of trapped water. "I thought I heard something. Like a call for help but I couldn't sense—" His resonance aura roiled with panic. "Why can't I sense anything?!"

"It should pass." Assuming she was right about what Venoru had done. "Start running Evocations as soon as you can."

Jhobon seemed to be doing an inward search of some sort. Not Seeking. Whatever it was, it made his resonance aura light up with a similar orange glow and he lunged out of his hammock only to fall flat on his face. "Why is Ylaen—"

"Forget him," Rahelu snapped as she pulled on a clean shirt. "He's not a priority. Go see to the barriers."

And since she was down here...

Rahelu steeled her courage and went to check the water casks.

The first one she opened was empty. So was the second. A chill chased over her when the whole row proved the same—she had to break open the seal on eight more casks before she found one that was only half empty. She took a sip and spat it out immediately. Faint bitterness lingered on her tongue. Casks nine through twelve were also bitter but casks thirteen and fourteen, which Nheras had made the mistake of stowing right up against the forward bulkhead behind a mixed assortment of crates, were merely stale.

She went back to the first cask and shifted it clear of the others. There, turning it slowly in the shaft of sunlight coming through the open hatch, she inspected every finger-width until she found what she was looking for: a series of small cuts—no bigger than the length of two finger joints—in the sealing caulk at the very base of the cask on the side that had been hidden against the second row.

She stuck her head inside one of the tainted casks and inhaled. Underneath the tang of vinegar and the stale smell of standing water, there was the bitter scent of what she suspected was heartbane.

In small quantities, it was used as a sedative by healers for complicated mental treatments to prevent a patient from inadvertently lashing out with resonance mid-procedure.

In larger amounts, it was used as a poison.

A dozen new thoughts crowded out her other concerns: When had Venoru tampered with the water stores? How long had they all been drinking the heartbane-tainted water? Was two-and-a-half casks the only good water they had? What of their food? Much of what remained was dried; most of the fresh supplies had been consumed and the pickled and fermented stuff might be contaminated, too.

Rahelu scrambled out of the hold, fearing the worst. Sure enough, Ghardon and Nheras both hung over the open top of the water cask, guzzling its contents by handfuls, letting stray trickles splash down on Elaram, who was drinking from the half-turned spigot.

"Stop!" She rushed over to pull Nheras and Ghardon away, slammed the lid closed, and shut off the spigot. "We need to save that water."

Ghardon sank down beside Elaram. Nheras ignored her and went back to trying to pry the lid open again with shaking fingers.

Rahelu would deal with that later; it wasn't like Nheras was getting anywhere.

Jhobon, the only one sensible enough to take a single scoop of water and sip at it, slowly, had put the ladle to Ylaen's lips and was urging him to do the same.

"Jhobon," she said, interrupting his examination of Ylaen's eyes.

He started, spilling the ladle.

"The barriers," she prompted him. "Remember?"

Jhobon blinked. "What barriers?"

"Exactly." When he still didn't get it, even after she swept both arms wide and gestured skyward, she elaborated: "They're broken; Ylaen's not. Stop hovering by him like he'll expire any heartbeat and go fix our fucking defenses so we can get the fuck away from the Conclave ship hounding our wake instead of presenting our asses to them—and whoever else might be in range—with our trousers down."

That had the desired effect; Jhobon dropped everything so

fast that Ylaen's head knocked against wood twice: once against the base of the water cask and once against the deck.

Good.

Next Rahelu said, "Ghardon."

He didn't respond.

"Ghardon."

He was too busy holding Elaram's hand and hair back as she disgorged all the water she had guzzled, so Rahelu prodded him none too gently with her foot.

"Ghardon!"

"What?" he snapped and finally deigned to meet her eyes.

She glared back and pointed to Venoru's corpse. "We have a dead Conclave spy on our hands."

He paled. "Right," he said weakly. "I'll just—" He dropped Elaram's limp hand to cover his mouth as he cast about for the bucket.

Rahelu didn't wait to see if he found it in time; she turned to the only other Supplicant who seemed to have regained a modicum of resonance ability along with consciousness.

"Follow me," she said.

Nheras did not follow her to the aftercabin.

Rahelu growled, her limited stores of patience gone. She stalked back to grab Nheras by her hair; hauled on it like she was pulling in a full catch.

Under normal circumstances, she never would've been able to drag the other girl bodily to the aft hatch. Fortunately, whatever combination of drugs Venoru had dosed them with had sapped Nheras's strength so her efforts to break free were about as effective as a fish's flailing attempt to escape once it had been reeled in. But it did make things harder and that was the last thing Rahelu needed.

She took a quick detour to port, shoved Nheras against the bulwark and forced her upper half over the toprail and down into the spray.

"Would it kill you to listen to me just once in this life-time? I'm not doing this because I hate you; I'm doing this because if I don't, we're all going straight to the Storm-bringer's realm. So stop treating me like I'm some piece of shit clinging to your high-heeled sandals and pay attention. Or I'll drop you over the side and see if you can, in fact, outsmart a fish in not sinking to the bottom."

Nheras didn't say anything in reply, but she did stop struggling, so Rahelu released her and stepped back.

She gave Nheras thirty heartbeats to pull herself together and grab the healer's kit, then said: "Let's go."

THE AFTERCABIN WAS A SHATTERED MESS.

Elder Anathwan had collapsed against the stern bulkhead by the small chest tucked under her sleeping berth. The chest was open. Its contents—books and loose pages of notes— were scattered across the cabin sole like leaves. The wooden box from the Bronze Turtle yawned, clam-like in her lap, its empty velvet-lined interior exposed. Next to Anathwan's limp hand was a cracked glass bowl containing three small wooden spheres, each spotted with blood. A fourth sphere lay in her curled palm and bore her bloody fingerprints.

A physical struggle, in addition to the magical one Rahelu had expected. Dark liquid stained the planks; two particularly long arcs of splatters originating from a splotchy half-circle and terminating at a pair of lacquered wood tea cups that had rolled away to settle against the prone form of Dedicate Maketh, in the very middle. His breath was labored, coming and going in fitful wheezes, and his resonance aura—a flick-ering, shapeless blue-white corona riddled with black cracks —barely extended beyond his skin.

Anathwan's aura was nonexistent. Her upright body

seemed as devoid of resonance as Venoru's corpse as if it had all leaked away or crystalized in her heart. But her chest and the gleaming pendant that rested on her breast still rose and fell, and the vein in her neck pulsed like the stumbling footsteps of a drunkard who had lost control of their body as thoroughly as the way home.

Neither of the senior mages had visible wounds.

Rahelu swore. "Stormwinds!"

They were alive. Anathwan and Maketh were both alive— and no good to anybody.

Relief and fear flooded her in equal measures, pale gold and ivory twined and knotted together like rope. The strands immediately melted. Anger heated the pale gold into a fierce coal-red and fear darkened into cobalt hurt. The scream she'd swallowed earlier, along with her nausea, uncoiled from her belly; a large, hard lump rising up up up in her throat as she stared down at Anathwan's composed blank face.

Nheras was saying something, but Rahelu couldn't hear the other Supplicant over the singular thought repeating itself in her mind:

I trusted you. I trusted you. I trusted you.

The overwhelming urge to shake the comatose Elder seized her—didn't you spend every waking span wandering the myriad futures so something like this wouldn't happen; did you know Csorath wasn't Csorath; you must have, you must have seen it in an Augury; didn't you say to me, velaz; did you actually have a plan or have you been making shit up as you go; were you going to warn us or were you always going to keep us in the dark; why, why wouldn't you tell us anything, how can you ask me to trust you when you won't trust me; how dare you ask me to trust you and then abandon us like this; we're fucked, we are so *fucked,* do you hear me; there's a Conclave ship chasing us through these Free Territories raider-infested waters, and we don't know where we are or where we're going or what we're supposed to do when we get there, and *we have no water*, so you'd better wake the fuck up, *Ana*, because I won't take this silence for an answer; I'm going to shake you and shake you and—

Somebody jerked her back.

"Don't touch me!" Rahelu snarled, as she wrenched her arm free and reached for Anathwan.

Nheras smacked her hand. "Don't touch her!"

Rahelu whirled around, fist raised. "I said, don't touch me!"

Pure white resonance bloomed as Nheras grabbed her by the arm. Again. The icy Projection rippled out from that point of contact, soaking through her sleeve, thickening as it ran up underneath her collar and dripped down her sides to collect in her waistband and run down her legs until every part of her skin was coated with it. Cold logic tightened around her, constricting her coruscating aura.

Rahelu threw her punch.

Nheras ducked, so she threw another.

Her fist slammed into the unyielding cover of the Issolm *Supplicant's Handbook* that Nheras was brandishing as a shield, then it was her turn to dodge as Nheras hurled the handbook at her midsection and countered. The open palm strike caught Rahelu on the side of her head as the hefty black tome struck her squarely in her half-healed thigh, then landed on her toe, and before she could howl in pain, Nheras snatched up the bloodied wooden sphere from Anathwan's hand:

Stop.

Her muscles froze at the Command. Only for a moment, but a moment was long enough for Nheras's Projection to take hold and douse the madness that had seized her.

Rahelu sat down, ears ringing.

"Sorry," she muttered as she clutched her throbbing leg and bruised foot to her chest. "I won't do that again."

Nheras sat on Anathwan's other side and dropped the wooden sphere into the cracked glass bowl with its fellows. "'Sorry' isn't going to get us out of this disaster, fish guts. Can we just do what we came to do?"

Somehow, the other Supplicant appeared perfectly calm (except for her aura, which was laced with identical bands of anger-pain and fear), while she—now that Nheras's Projection had worn off—struggled to sit still, having to grind the heels of her palms against her forehead to keep herself from smashing the nearest breakable object.

That would be the plain, serviceable clay pot of tea the senior mages had been sharing. It sat undisturbed on the tray balanced across Anathwan's open chest.

Rahelu pulled off the lid and sniffed; wrinkled her nose at the bitter scent of Anathwan's medicinal tea. She dipped the first joint of her little finger into the tea, brought the suspended droplet to her mouth, and sucked it.

It tasted exactly like heartleaf tea was supposed to taste: awful.

But now that she knew what she was looking for, and what to expect, she felt it, eventually. There was something dragging on her senses, a slight dulling in her perception of the ambient resonance that could've been easily attributable to ordinary fatigue, and a...loosening—she didn't know how else to describe it—of her mental focus.

She refilled one of the fallen teacups and offered it to Nheras. "What do you think?"

Nheras gave the tea a hesitant sniff of her own before gingerly taking the barest sip. "Heartbane," she concluded. "Two-thirds of the standard concentration. Maybe even half."

They exchanged grimaces.

The independent validation of her theory didn't make her feel any better. "How many cups did you drink last night?"

"Three."

"I had one sip. What about the others?"

"Two cups for Ylaen; he only started drinking tea after he ran out of wine. Jhobon had four. Ghardon and Elaram had at least six each." Nheras shut her eyes briefly, then reopened them. "I remember pouring for the Elder and the Guardian, but I don't remember seeing them drink during dinner. I didn't have to refill their cups once."

"I don't think they had any." Rahelu nodded at the spill then showed Nheras the pot: it was still almost full. "At least, Anathwan didn't," she said, then gave Nheras a summary of the fight against Venoru. "She couldn't have done that if she'd been heartbane afflicted. Could she?"

Nheras frowned, then shrugged as she set the cup back on the tray. "Only one way to find out," she said, and actually refrained from adding any backhanded commentary like, *'But I can't help you with that, because I just had to drain myself stopping you from doing something incredibly fish-brained stupid.'*

Nheras simply got on with picking through the wreckage for mundane clues, so Rahelu allowed herself one final glare at Anathwan to placate her misplaced resentment, then sank into the three-count meditation pattern for Evocation.

Her efforts yielded a smear of fleeting impressions:

—he speaks; pleads; listen to me, Anathwan, listen; listen—

—lips in a thin line, eyes fixed upon the glittering black crown in her hands—

—expressive; impassioned, even, as he never is before the Supplicants—

—she reaches for her belt knife—

—he reaches for his pendant—

—we must stop—you must stop—this greed and hubris will doom us all—

—the hatch creaks open—

—they turn—

—a rain of stars scything through the darkest night—

—a blinding bolt—

—a wall of light—

—three shadowy bodies struggling as torn pages fly through the air—

—BANG!—

—choking, choking—

—can't see, can't see, where is the—

—staggering, falling to the—

—arm flails, graceless, hand rooting around for—

The next scrap Rahelu managed to squeeze from the past erupted in a soundless white flash that left her blinded.

"Fuck!" she yelled.

What a stupid fucking waste of time.

Maketh had put too many extra barriers and wards on the aftercabin, all of which interfered with the ordinary accumulation of resonance in the ship's timbers so she couldn't use them as her focus, and the mage fight that had taken place between Anathwan and Maketh and Venoru meant there was simultaneously too much and too little lingering resonance.

Oh, yes, she could put those fragmentary glimpses into a neat little timeline, but too many critical moments were missing and she couldn't form what she had into a coherent scene for analysis. Who had attacked whom? Maybe Anathwan had attacked Maketh; maybe he had attacked her; maybe the reason neither of them had drunk Venoru's poisoned tea was because they'd been too busy eyeing each other with suspicion, so even though the Conclave mage's plan hadn't worked as intended, she'd been able to steal the crown from under their noses anyway, while the Elder and the Dedicate had been working at cross purposes.

That left the senior mages themselves as the only possible options for a focus, but raising a direct Evocation without consent was tantamount to an attack. She'd been Starfather-blessedly lucky to survive her confrontation with Venoru, and she was in no condition to revisit a contest of wills with Maketh, even in his current state.

Especially in his current state.

As for Anathwan...

Rahelu seethed as she groped around for something to throw.

The Elder was *gone*, just like the crown. Her body lived and breathed, but it was bereft of thought and feeling and intent and therefore of no use as a focus for Evocation. What Rahelu needed was Anathwan's mind, but what she had was an empty, soulless husk. Every Seeking found no trace of Anathwan's resonance signature, not even when she tried channeling her efforts through the little wooden sphere that bore the Elder's blood, once she had finally recognized the object as hers. That token had been Rahelu's invitation from House Issolm to a private audience with Anathwan during her Petitioning; an item of personal significance that had allowed the Elder—and then Nheras—to focus and concentrate their Commands on her.

Unfortunately, the connection didn't go both ways.

Rahelu's fingers landed on the refilled tea cup and she flung it at...she didn't even know, because she couldn't fucking see, and resonance backlash made it impossible to sense anything.

"Very helpful, fish guts," Nheras said as the cup clunked off something harmlessly and cold tea splatted everywhere. "They're so useful, these tantrums of yours. Let me know when you're done sulking so we can get on with our jobs. Next week, perhaps? Or are you going to come help me lift the Elder sometime today?"

"I thought you said not to touch her."

"She fell. They both did. She could be bleeding to death inside for all we know, and you were going to shake her. You might have killed her!"

'And she might have killed us!' Rahelu wanted to retort, but Nheras wasn't wrong, so she bit back the words.

Nheras went on: "There's no way to get them up the ladder and out of here safely so the best we can do is make them as comfortable as we can in here, and then see if there's any method of rousing them." She paused, choosing her next words carefully. "The first standard cure for an overdose of heartbane is to flush it out of the body with fresh water."

A course of action so obviously not viable it didn't merit a response. She obediently moved as Nheras directed until they had wrestled Anathwan's limp body back into her berth.

They paused, breathing heavily.

Rahelu brushed the sweat from her brow. Her hands ached. She looked down. Frowned as she ran her thumbs over the pads of her fingers. They were coated with a residue. Dust? She tried to wash it off by rubbing her sweat between her palms, but that only made them feel grimier.

When Rahelu looked up, she saw Nheras absently wiping her own hands on her shirt as she eyed Maketh's bulk, the distance to his berth, on the forward side, and the height of the berth from the cabin sole.

"We'll have to leave him on the floor," Nheras said at last. "We'll roll him onto his back and drag him here, where we can wedge him so he'll stay put even if the ship rolls, then turn him on his side so he won't suffocate or choke."

Rahelu grunted in assent.

Tugging and heaving and pushing by turns, they got the Dedicate to roll over. His face and the front of his robes were caked with a gritty white substance. He'd been lying next to a pile of—what was that? High-grade warding salt? Chalk?

Neither, she realized as momentum flopped Maketh onto the pile and a cloud of fine white particles filled the air.

Belatedly, Rahelu covered her nose and mouth but her muscles and resonance aura had already begun seizing up.

"Get out," she cried, over his hacking cough. She scrabbled back as the deadly powder unraveled his overtaxed control and his aura shredded itself. "Get out now!"

She didn't wait for Nheras; she hurled herself up the ladder as fast as her failing limbs would take her. Away from Maketh, and the swelling miasma of swirling dust and roiling resonance gathering force around him like storm-whipped waters in a gyre. Kept going past Ylaen (still lazing on his side by the water cask), past Elaram (tied up aloft, in a Seeking trance), until she reached the portside toprail, where Jhobon was replacing shattered crystals and Ghardon was gripping on for dear life, his aura and face tinged green.

Ghardon's eyes widened as she collapsed at his feet.

Nheras wasn't far behind. As soon as she had made it out of the aftercabin and onto the deck—with a book, of all things, clutched under her arm—she went for the hatch.

"Don't!" Rahelu rasped. "We need to let it dissipate or—"

"No." Nheras heaved the hatch shut and sank onto the deck beside Ylaen, limbs twitching. "We need to keep it contained and make sure we don't share their fate."

"What?" Ghardon's aura flared a bright orange in alarm.

Ylaen bolted upright. "What fate?"

"Heartbane," Nheras said as she stared up past the sails. White clouds, their hazy bottom edges gilded gold by the sun, drifted lazily across the sky. "In powdered form, mixed with resonance crystal dust. They're as good as dead."

"Which is not the same thing as actually dead," Ghardon said. "If you find it hard to tell the difference, I suggest you take a closer look at this," and he jerked his chin over his shoulder at Venoru's corpse.

Ylaen scowled at the reminder but did finally bestir himself to shamble over to the body. While his attention was diverted, Rahelu caught Ghardon's eyes and raised her eyebrows. *Did you and Elaram…?*

Ghardon shook his head. *We caught the gist of your fight, but there's no trace of whatever happened before. That Conclave mage erased everything between sunset and you waking. Couldn't glean a thing from her corpse either; it's got none of the usual resonances that ought to linger after death. What of our Elder?*

Indisposed, Rahelu sent, along with an image of Anathwan and Maketh's comatose forms obscured by swirls of heartbane powder in the air, her sense of their erratic heartbeats, and the missing crown.

Fuck. Out loud, he said, "We can't leave the Guardian and the Elder down there."

"There's no safe way to move them, and they've breathed in too much of the stuff. Nheras is right." She sat, leaning against the bulwark. "There's nothing we can do for them."

He joined her.

They watched Jhobon finish patching the last break in Maketh's barriers in silence.

The Imrell Supplicant sagged in relief—they all did—when one barrier after another flickered to life. He straightened his shoulders, began to crane his head over the toprail to cast an eye down the resonance wards painted along the *Gull's* topsides, then shut his eyes and shook his head like he didn't want to know.

Rahelu agreed. They had bigger problems.

Like the Conclave ship and its Seeker, a cold presence only twelve or thirteen kual distant now. She had put on as much sail as the *Sooty Gull* could carry but they'd covered less than a kual in the last span.

And Ylaen. Dispirited no longer, he looked two heartbeats away from giving himself a nosebleed as he stared down at the dead mage, a dark scowl on his face and his resonance aura unreadable: the colors too muddled and indistinct to call and the patterns lacking both defined form and texture.

"Let it go," Rahelu said, halting him on the verge of another fruitless Evocation. "Stop trying to raise her shade just so you can kill her twice and make yourself useful like the rest of us. Best as I can work out, we're twenty kual south and east of our position yesterday."

"East?" Ylaen's wild eyes snapped to her at once. "You took us south and *east*?"

Jhobon jumped up and hurried to his side. "It's alright," he said. "It's—"

Rahelu didn't relish another fight, but she wasn't about to let the supreme idiot responsible for their current situation try to make her look bad in front of everybody else. "The current is flowing south and east."

"*You* took us south and east. How fish-brained stupid do you have to be to—"

Her temper flared. "Go look in a mirror and finish the rest of that sentence. I've been working to get us out of immediate danger since dawn, while you've spent most of your time lying about, whimpering for your mother."

He seethed but said nothing and let Jhobon drag him off towards the tiller, where the two of them would presumably apply themselves to working out where, exactly, they were and how far they might be from the nearest safe port.

Ghardon said, "I need a drink."

When she didn't respond to that remark or his subsequent elbowing, he swore.

"How bad?"

"Bad."

When the *Sooty Gull* had sailed from Peshwan Yrg, she had counted a hundred and ten casks of fresh water, enough to supply a season's worth of cooking and drinking water for ten people. Enough excess that Rahelu had not thought it odd for Csorath—Venoru—to turn a blind eye to Ghardon, Elaram, and Nheras sneaking an extra flask or two of the stuff every few days to wash.

"'Ghardon-you'll-need-to-restrict-yourself-to-one-bath-a-week' bad, or 'we're-going-to-die-of-thirst' bad?"

"I haven't checked everything but that cask"—she nodded at the one they'd nearly drained before she had stopped them—"and two more might be the only good water we have left."

Shock radiated through his aura. When Ghardon spoke again, his voice was controlled. "That's plenty, isn't it? We don't go through more than two flasks a day each."

From further aft, Nheras snorted.

"There was only supposed to be another week or ten days of sailing left to the Desolate Isles," he insisted.

"Look."

At the tiller, Jhobon and Ylaen were holding an agitated conference that involved a lot of guttural phrases that bordered on outright growling and repeated gestures at different quadrants of the sky and the sea.

Rahelu tilted her head back and squinted to gauge the angle of the rising sun herself.

"I'm looking."

"In which direction lies the Desolate Isles?"

Ghardon pointed. "There?"

"No." She took his arm and moved it in a fifty-degree arc until his finger pointed slightly off true north, in the same direction as the Conclave ship. "There."

A pause. "Oh." Then, "Shit." Even more quietly, "Shit!"

Rahelu said nothing because there was nothing else to say. She straightened her right leg, letting out a muffled whimper as the pressure on her thigh wound eased, and slid further down the bulwark until she could easily reach into her pocket and draw out the only thing she carried that was still useful to their survival.

Ghardon wasn't done though. "What about food?"

It started with a snort. A quick, involuntary inhalation through her nose, followed by tiny tremors that originated in the back of her throat, bubbling up her windpipe to make their escape as a snigger. Soon, the tremors spread until her shoulders shook and she had to press her forearm to her mouth to keep her giggles contained. That stopped the sound, but not the amusement that burst through her resonance aura, a sunny yellow so utterly incongruous that it caused Ylaen and Jhobon to break off from their disagreement to stare at her.

"Even if we don't have much water, we've still got plenty of food. Right?"

Poor Ghardon. He clung to his line of questioning as if gathering enough facts and applying sufficient logic could get them out of their current predicament. He looked so thoughtful, so determined, so bewildered by her behavior that she couldn't keep the wild mirth back any longer.

He never should have left the city.

None of them should have left the city.

Still choking on her hysterical laughter, Rahelu scooped up Venoru's steel dagger. She turned over the Conclave mage's hand so it lay palm up.

"Rahelu?"

Cruel lines marred the flesh where the fishing line had bit into Venoru's fingers—thin, triple bands of dark bruises that matched the ones on Rahelu's.

"What are you doing?"

Rahelu held the hand down by the wrist and scraped the sharp point of the steel dagger down the edge, from the base of the palm, up the fleshy part, along the outer side of the smallest finger until she found the gap between the first and second joints.

A gentle slice—just the slightest placement of pressure on a keenly honed edge poised over a weak point in the bone structure—and the fingertip was separated cleanly from the hand.

"You asked about food," Rahelu said.

She tied the severed fingertip to the end of the fishing line that had nearly strangled her and held it out to Ghardon.

"Here's your answer."

2 3

COURSE

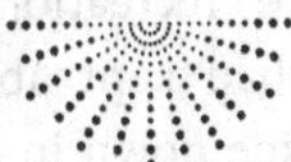

THE 4TH DAY OF EARLY HARVEST,
530 A.E./A.F.

SIX SPANS LATER, THE ENEMY SEEKER'S COLD regard swung away from the *Sooty Gull*.

GHARDON FORCED himself to swallow each unpalatable mouthful of their belated breakfast (grilled fish and rice boiled in diluted seawater) as he listened to his sisters' circular debate and watched Ylaen Imos and Jhobon Imrell hold an impenetrable discussion in their savage speech while the sun went down and the stars came out.

He craned his neck to get a better view of the Imrell Supplicant's ever-present notebook. What he saw bore no resemblance to a map. Just numbers. Lots of numbers and a host of dots—solid and hollow—joined into odd groupings by short, thick lines. These were scattered across some two dozen, unevenly spaced columns, delineated by thinner lines that spanned the pages from top to bottom.

It took some squinting at one of the shapes (three dots connected by a straight line, bisecting an arc connecting two others) and observing Ylaen (who alternated between glowering at the page and glowering at the heavens, as if by doing so he could change one or the other) to figure out what he was looking at.

Presently, Ylaen flipped the pages back to the beginning.

There, finally, was something Ghardon knew how to read: a very rough, mundane recreation of the Imbued map Csorath—or 'Csorath'—had kept aboard the *Winged Arrow* with the word '*Two*' upside down in a corner. Further down, in the margins, were several lines of scribbled notes. One was simply the phrase '*sacred Belruonian relics*'. Written underneath the heading of '*Mistranslation???*' was a larger section that included an equation balancing '*Eternal Gaze*' with '*Endless Gate*' and a sketch of two sets of similar-looking runes. The differences were highlighted with faint circles in charcoal.

Ylaen's next barked question needed no translation: '*So where are we?*'

Jhobon answered with a vague waggle of his finger.

'*Here*' turned out to be some hundred square kual of empty sea, smack bang in the middle of the Abmerduan Sea. A blank, uncharted expanse lay to the north. Beyond that would be the Desolate Isles. To the south and east was the Divine Kingdom, though Jhobon had only sketched a small portion of the massive Belruonian continent's sprawling coastline. The island archipelago of the so-called 'Free Territories' of Abmerdu lay directly west, closer by an order of several magnitudes. However, Ghardon gathered, from the very light, indirect Seeking he paired with his close observation of Jhobon's sweeping gestures at the sky and sea, the archipelago was actually much farther away than it appeared, owing to the winds and the ocean's currents.

Closest of all was a scattered grouping of smaller islands —he'd almost overlooked the tiny, seemingly haphazard dots until his mind registered that their configuration didn't match the pattern of a stray ink splatter.

Ylaen Imos quietly swore.

With that, the two scarred Supplicants abandoned further discussion and devoted themselves to steadfastly chewing down mouthfuls of rice and fish while piling the bones into the world's tiniest spire. Neither objected as Ghardon put his empty bowl aside and grabbed the map. He eyeballed the scale, measuring out distances with his knuckles while trying to convert the barrels and casks and sacks he'd counted and the eight fish he'd caught (and the possibility of catching another eight every day) into per-person rations and comparing the result to the estimates Jhobon had notated along the dotted lines of their possible routes.

Home, Ghardon realized with a pang, was impossibly distant.

"...telling you, they're gone," Ela said, her half-eaten bowl lying forgotten in a pool of fish juices on the deck in front of her.

"Can't be." Rahelu stabbed the points of her eating sticks into her fish, down the lateral line and just below the edge of the dorsal fin. The entire top half of the fish's left side flaked away from its bones in one neat piece of flesh. "Ships don't just disappear," she insisted around the rim of her bowl, as she shoveled half her fish and a third of her rice down her throat in one go.

"They've chased us unmasked for more than a day and a night. It makes no sense for them to shield now, all of a sudden, and that is the last time I'm repeating myself." Ela leaned against the mast, closing her eyes and the subject. "If you're not done doing the same, I hereby give you permission to use a direct Evocation and examine the evidence from my perspective. My assessment, however, is not going to change."

Bluff called, Rahelu pivoted to interrogate Nheras. "You're sure you can't see them?"

"They're gone," came the tart reply as Nheras climbed down from the rigging. "There's nothing out there except for more of these blasted birds of yours, and they haven't seen anything either."

The sharp, beady little eyes of the returned gulls shone in the dusk as they gathered on the toprail, squawking and shuffling along in a feathered gray-and-white chain.

"Maybe you're not asking nicely."

His common-born sister was so fixated on arguing that she didn't notice a clump of half-masticated food fall out of her mouth.

Two of the braver birds hopped down to venture closer.

"I did."

Nheras's retort came laden with a series of quicksilver impressions:

—rapid wingbeats; the barren, briny scent of empty sea; a familiar, crawling sensation that ruffles all his feathers as it judders him from beak point to tail tip—

The none-too-gentle Projection roused a round of sympathetic flinches from Rahelu but not any actual sympathy, for her speech grew clipped and terse. "Ask again."

Keow! Little Fishguts spread its wings and gaped its beak in an obsequious, begging gesture.

"I have."

Greedy little devil. He scraped up the fallen morsel with the flat of his belt knife and flicked it overboard before he could be swarmed again.

The gulls, thankfully, followed.

"Properly."

"If you—"

"Enough," Ghardon said, cutting Nheras off before she and Rahelu could get into an even more unproductive argument about gull etiquette. "It makes no difference whether the Conclave ship is truly gone or not."

He had kept quiet during the sea chase and let Rahelu make the decisions when immediate peril had threatened the *Sooty Gull*, but now it was time for someone capable of thinking beyond their mere survival to take charge.

He was not the Elder, but he was the eldest.

Ghardon stood.

"If it's a ruse, it's a damned good one. We've already proven that we're not equal to piercing whatever Obfuscation barrier or Seeming they've put in place, so further attempts are both futile and wasteful."

Rahelu glared but could make no reasonable arguments, for what he'd stated was the unvarnished truth.

"If they catch us, they catch us. Unlike the ship clans, the Conclave will be civilized about it: they won't traffick us for Suborned slaves and they'll abide by the Houses' ransom protocols if we invoke them."

He omitted any mention of Maketh's mind block; the leadened weight on his consciousness was reminder enough.

"If it's not a ruse, then we're fucked. There are only two viable theories as to why the Conclave might abandon the chase when they were so close. Would any of you care to venture a guess?"

Ela didn't open her eyes. Rahelu's glare remained unchanged. Imrell wasn't even looking at him; he had taken possession of his notebook again. Nheras was, but she was also wearing that doll-faced mask of hers, and that strutting Imos ishtrel actually dared smirk back as he folded heavily scarred arms.

Ghardon swallowed the urge to lecture them all—why waste his breath if they weren't going to listen?—and cut to the conclusion. "Either they've realized we don't matter, or we're about to run into something worse. We need to come up with a plan."

Red light glinted off bared steel as Ylaen Imos also stood. "I have a plan."

Gods damn the bastard for skipping past verbal sparring and escalating straight to veiled threats. But Ghardon kept his voice measured and even. He was not going to be pushed into dueling. "Then let's hear it."

"We head west and make for the city of sails."

"I fail to see how sailing to a lawless haven for free-booters and smugglers will help our cause. Our original destination was the Desolate Isles, in the north. The Elder may not have fully briefed us but any idiot can deduce our mission objectives by now: the Exalted Dominance commanded us to sail east, find the strange artifacts of power used by that splinter cult to disrupt Augury, and secure the possession of these supposed legacies of the heavens for the Dominion."

"The crown is lost, Issolm. The mission is over."

"Per the Elder herself, the crown was but an advantage, not the goal. It may be lost, but the last artifact is still out there and there must be other ways of locating it—I'd stake ten thousand gold kez on *that* being the true reason the Conclave have abandoned chase."

Ylaen paid him no attention, too busy making a show of pressing the edge of his knife against the inside of his left forearm. A thin line of blood welled up and dripped onto his makeshift altar of fishbones. "Our captain and navigator turned out to be a Conclave spy and is dead—"

"No thanks to you."

"—and our senior mages have been rendered incapacitated and poisoned with heartbane powder. We only have food and water left for four days. Twelve, if we move to quarter-rations. That's enough to get us to Tsorek-fa, based on Jhobon's calculations."

Imrell jumped in, on cue, blathering on and on, in impenetrable nautical language, about star readings and sun positioning and bearings. The more the Imrell Supplicant said, the less Ghardon liked what he heard.

Someone was trying very, very hard to make one particular course of action sound more appealing than the others.

His theory was confirmed moments later, when Jhobon—after forestalling Rahelu's initial pushback on his estimates with an overly detailed breakdown of their remaining food and water supplies—concluded, "Ylaen is right. The best course is to head west. The island of Tsorek-fa has several permanent navigational beacons we'll be able to orient to once we're in range, and we'll be able to plot a safe course for the city of sails. From there, we can lean on our original disguises as smugglers, offload most of our diversionary cargo, and resupply."

What Ghardon saw, he liked even less.

Ela's worried follow-up—"How long will it take?"—was quickly soothed with: "It's only one, maybe two weeks sailing," which conveniently neglected any mention of the underlying assumptions that the Stormbringer would send them good winds and favorable currents.

Next would be a textbook pretense at candidness to foster trust. And sure enough...

Nheras asked, "Realistically, what are our chances of avoiding capture if we sail there?"

The two scarred Supplicants exchanged looks.

Ylaen shrugged and Jhobon said, "Three in ten."

Ela blinked. "That's...not encouraging."

Ylaen shrugged again. "Fleets are hungry things and seaworthy ships are always in demand. Even this little toy boat would be worth a clan's time to seize—it's all packed full of crystal and silk and spices and steel weapons and Suborned slaves in the making."

By maneuvering the conversation away from the strategic into the tactical considerations, and getting them all to think through the practical steps involved in sailing to Tsorek-fa, Imos and Imrell were slowly but surely solidifying their preferred course of action as the only reasonable course of action in everybody's minds, when that was not the case at all.

Worse, his sisters were falling for it.

Ela had taken over Jhobon's brush pen and notebook and was nonchalantly doodling a series of large serpentine squiggles following a line of small, deformed triangles pointed west—a very bad rendition of a dragon chasing the *Sooty Gull* across the Abmerduan Sea to the city of sails.

Nheras had followed Jhobon. As he went about undoing and redoing Rahelu's work with the sails and the tiller to bring the *Sooty Gull* around, she interrogated him about fleet alliances and the feasibility of passing themselves off as ship clan instead of Dominion smugglers and the availability of rare ingredients missing from the ship's healing kit: powdered tortoiseshell and jade and a long list of herbs.

Rahelu had been diverted, but not in the direction he had hoped. Not only had she added her fishbones to the miniature altar Ylaen and Jhobon had improvised out of theirs, when Ylaen held out his blade, she used it to contribute her own offering.

"I'll—" Rahelu yawned. She rubbed her partially recharged pendant as she looked blearily at the headings Jhobon had marked in very faint lines of charcoal, then at Ylaen. "I'll stand nightwatch and dawnwatch if you take earthwatch and sunwatch," she said, as though the matter of where they were going was settled.

Ylaen eyed her critically as she stood, then yawned again.

"I'd better take nightwatch," he said. "Elaram can stand dawnwatch with me and you can have earthwatch with this lackwit. You managed to teach him how to fish; maybe you can teach him to face reality too."

That was it.

"I don't think I'm the one in need of the lesson," Ghardon said, "since I am, apparently, the only one committed to pointing out the stark realities of our situation."

He snatched the notebook from Ela, flipped over to the first page he'd seen, the one with all the dots and the numbers, and thrust those pages with Jhobon's damning calculations in Ylaen's face.

"You've no idea how far south the current's taken us. Nor have you been able to accurately account for how far east or west we may have drifted in that fog. So, unless I'm mistaken in my reading of these calculations, it will likely take us much longer than your prediction of twelve days to reach Tsorek-fa."

Rahelu frowned.

Ghardon dropped the notebook into her hands. He looked askance at the tiny fish bone altar, then back at Ylaen. "Praying to the Stormbringer for rainwater and fair winds to speed us to the shore's embrace is not a plan."

"It is universally the only plan possible when you're lost at sea." Imos mockingly proffered his knife, hilt first. "You should join us."

"In superstitious idiocy? Why don't I just slit my own throat and save myself the agony of dying from thirst?"

"Please do. Lifeblood goes quite a long way to earning favor from the gods and there would be one less burd—"

Ghardon pushed the knife away. "If we turn back now, we'll have ceded control of the artifact we've been Seeking to the Conclave." A pause for effect, then extra crisp diction to underscore the reminder. "That's treason, Imos."

"It's also suicide. Do you know why they're called the Desolate Isles? Here's a hint: they're desolate. No fish swim in those seas. No birds fly there to roost. And the ships that return bear no one living." Ylaen wiped his blade clean and sheathed it, but left his arm to bleed. "It's the city of sails or nothing; we don't have a choice."

"Oh, I think we do." Ghardon tapped the scattered grouping of smaller islands northeast of their estimated position with the toe of his boot. They formed a dotted, meandering line that pointed north, towards the Desolate Isles. "These are closer, by at least forty or a hundred kual, and they're in the same direction as the current."

Both Imos and Imrell had the temerity to immediately shake their heads at him.

"We've been there once," Ylaen said. "The Dragon's Teeth are atolls. Shallow waters with unpredictable currents and sharp coral everywhere. One wrong steer and we'll gouge a hole in the hull faster than you can blink."

"Most of them are uninhabited," Jhobon called from his position back at the tiller. "If we stumble upon one that is, it might be a ship clan hideout. Either way, we won't find any help there."

Rahelu looked up from the notebook and said, "But some of these larger ones might have springs."

Skymother be thanked! One of his sisters had finally seen sense. At Rahelu's whistle, a gull flew over to perch on her shoulder. It cocked its head, *keowed*, then pecked at one of the splotches.

"That one has water," Ghardon said. He didn't bother hiding the golden gleam of satisfaction in his aura as the gull shared some more impressions. "And, look. Judging by our little friend's account, it's only three days' sailing to the east, as the flock flies, instead of Starfather only knows how many to the west."

Ghardon allowed himself a triumphant smirk as Ylaen clenched his jaw in the first visible sign of anger he had shown since they had all woken up from their drugged sleep.

"We're not going east."

"Why's that, Imos?"

"Land truces don't apply in the Dragon's waters. The moment we're spotted, we'll be boarded and captured."

"They'd have to find us first," Ghardon pointed out, and that prompted Ela to ask, "Just how good are their Seekers?"

Ylaen looked them up and down. "How eager are you to find out?" When Ela wavered, he drawled, "I thought not."

"Surely it would be impossible for any ship clan to find us," Ghardon said, "considering that their Seekers lack formal mage training and given what a very thorough job your uncle has done with our barriers and wards." That got another reaction out of Ylaen—a sharp flare of his nostrils—so Ghardon went on: "For a man who's Imos-blooded, Maketh does have the unusual distinction of being reputed for his ability to reliably perform. Unless there's something you'd like to confess?"

Ylaen laid his hand on the hilt of his knife. "Here's a dose of reality for you, Issolm. Only three people here know how to sail. You're not one of them. And of the three, only Jhobon and I know these waters." His voice dropped to a low growl. "We're not going east. If you'd like to contest that, you can challenge me for the captaincy of this vessel."

Ghardon hated pulling rank—it was a move that revealed weakness of position even as it asserted primacy—but if Imos and Imrell weren't going to back down, then he had to do whatever was necessary to ensure they stayed the course, and the House oaths they'd all sworn meant that Issolm had the majority to enforce his rightful claim to authority.

"This vessel," he stressed, "is a Dominion ship, temporarily given over to House Issolm command under the terms that govern joint missions which have been ratified by all eight Houses. House Issolm leads this mission, by the Exalted Dominance's decree, and therefore, this vessel operates according to House Issolm policies and procedures. Our chain of command is based on merit, determined by reference to the applicable emergency protocols, not some barbaric contest of physical prowess that has nothing to do with leadership ability or sound decision making."

Briefly, he wished he had his copy of the Issolm *Supplicant's Handbook* so he could literally throw the entire volume in Ylaen's face, chapter and verse. He detested the kind of crude and blatant theatrical display Imos loved—it was all sensational spectacle, no substance; just a cheap appeal to the base thrill of shock.

Alas, personal preferences had no part to play when what mattered was effectiveness and winning. He had to win this argument, decisively so, and an orator's grave delivery of said chapter and verse would impress no one here.

But spectacle—*with* substance—would.

"As the next highest ranking member of House Issolm present, *I* am in command of this mission, and as Supplicants, we are bound by our oaths: duty to the Dominion; honor to the Houses—I trust you can recall the rest. When we are charged with a mission, we do not abandon it at the first sign of difficulty. *We do what needs to be done.* So take heed and listen."

They were all staring at him. Good.

Now: how had Ana done this?

"We are looking for the Endless Gate."

Let the pronouncement hang in the air, buoyed by the silence that sheer incredulity provoked.

Let the weight of his words sink in until...

Nheras snorted. "The Endless Gate is just temple-speak

for the temporal horizon; it's not a real place. Please stop confusing your fireside stories for facts."

Let Ilyn look around expectantly for agreement—and find none.

At the very mention of the Endless Gate, Ylaen Imos had dropped his knife and destroyed his fishbone altar; Jhobon Imrell had abandoned the tiller in favor of snatching his notebook back from Rahelu, who was busy exchanging guilt-ridden glances with Ela.

"You can't be serious," Nheras said.

Ghardon waited.

"It's real," Rahelu said.

Ela added: "Or at least there is a real place known by that name."

All that was left to do was show them.

Ghardon reached for Rahelu's hand. She took it, her clasp clammy with cold sweat.

Black serpentine knives descend in relentless arcs. Blank, dead faces; five in all. Some are familiar—like Welm and Hzin and the woman who had died in place of Xyuth's consort—their features wrought with vivid clarity; the rest are occluded. All the butchered corpses are meticulously arranged in an identical manner: a constellation of five-pointed stars.

Black-robed cultists argue over a missing stargem and heathen adepts and their ritual to open the Endless Gate in the wreckage of a scrivener's shop.

The Seeming of Csorath dissolves into Venoru, her trembling hands on the obsidian crown. Her words echo through the fog: 'Seek not the Endless Gate.'

Time to drive the point home while the vivid echoes of their Evocation still lingered in the ambient resonance.

"That Conclave ship is gone, bound for the Endless Gate. If we sail west, they win. They will gain uncontested control of an inconceivably powerful artifact, capable of granting any desire."

With Ela and Rahelu firmly behind him, Jhobon distracted, and Ylaen's challenge to his authority defanged, Ghardon bent his gaze on Nheras.

"We cannot allow that to happen, no matter the cost."

Choose, Nheras. Can I count you as my sister? Or will you reveal your true colors?

Nheras did not disappoint. "You've lost your mind."

Ela sighed. "If there is one thing my brother is good at, it's being correct; it is—by far—the most annoying of his many annoying habits."

"There's no sound basis for his conclusion. He's shown us a disparate collection of memories, that's all."

"And if you had been paying more attention to what Elder Anathwan was engaged in while you were doing your best sycophantic impression of a cushion, you would have noticed she spent all her time running experiments on that crown we stole, arguing theories about sympathetic resonance with Guardian Maketh, and analyzing at least six different versions of Enjela's Ballad, the first volume of Silcarez's memoirs, and every major translation of Belruonian scripture ever published, in addition to attempting her own translation. Every version of the legend agrees: when Enjela set out in search of the Starfather's wisdom, she had to pass through the Endless Gate to enter Fortune's realm." Ela snapped her fingers as she recalled the next part: "And when she returned with the stars, bearing the sign of divine favor upon her brow, she was no longer able to look upon the world with mortal eyes." A mishmash of paraphrases instead of an exact quote, but it conveyed his point, so Ghardon let her state-ment stand, uncorrected. "The artifact we're looking for has to be inside. Why else would Anathwan be cross-referencing every mention of the Endless Gate she found against the descriptions of each island Silcarez mapped in the Desolate Isles?"

"By all means, you two can invest in his crackpot theory. But I am no little girl with an overactive, drama-starved imagination who's so desperate to escape her dismal life that I'll be swayed by nothing more than suppositions and half-guesses. Nor do I have fish shit for brains."

"I am not—" Ela began as Rahelu bristled, but Nheras was about to cross the line that divided *personal attacks* from *insubordination* so he was duty-bound to give her due warning.

"Think carefully on what comes out of your mouth next, *sister*."

Nheras quieted.

Ghardon drew himself up to his full height to address Imos and Imrell. "Turn this ship around."

Ana's lessons and Ana's manner—absolute belief in holding absolute authority—gave him a scaffold to cling to and an example to emulate.

"We're sailing east."

The two scarred Supplicants stared at him for a full five heartbeats before they broke out laughing.

Fuck.

"Gods!" Ylaen exclaimed, slapping his knee. "The Elder's pet parrot thinks his bluster has bite! Cute speech, Issolm. How many times have you practiced reciting that before a mirror? No, don't answer; enumerating your pedantry would take you far too long, and I've no interest in being bored by your bureaucratic babble."

It hadn't worked. Why hadn't it worked?

Ghardon's thoughts raced frantically as he desperately sought some way to recover, some way of forcing the pair to obey him. His mind could only come up with memorized excerpts—he was right, no matter how you cared to interpret the laws of the Dominion and the policies of the Houses—but those provided him with no leverage over ship clan scum who laughed at the strict discipline of the Houses.

"I'm not unreasonable, however." Ylaen tore off a strip of his shirt to bind the cut on his forearm and added, "If you can find a solution to the problem of how we can locate a mythical destination that no one knows how to get to, we can go and Seek this Endless Gate. But until you present me with one, I'll not consign my uncle to death nor risk scuppering my ship on a pleasureless cruise through two or three thousand kual of treacherous reefs chasing a delusion unless Anathwan herself wakes up to Command it of me."

The Imos Supplicant strode off to join Imrell at the tiller, still snickering.

Since his strategy had failed, Ghardon struck out with Ela's favorite weapon: the truth.

"You won't go east because you're afraid."

Ylaen froze mid-step.

"The sky is vast and the ocean is wide." Ghardon gestured to the horizon and the barriers and wards Jhobon and Rahelu had recently restored. "If—somehow—in all that wide, wide ocean, with all these protections, we should have the misfortune to be glimpsed by a ship clan vessel, surely a Harbinger capable of making Rahelu pass for one of theirs up close would have no problem doing the same for the rest of us, given that no one else has quite so many inadequacies they need to cover up with *decoration* for flaunting as y—"

Thunk!

Ylaen's knife sprouted from the deck between his feet.

Ghardon yelped as sudden shock and the ship's motion conspired to land him flat on his back.

Fuck. He hadn't even seen Ylaen move.

Who did that? Who went around answering perfectly valid remarks by throwing knives?

He dragged a breath into his lungs; forced his ribs to expand so his heart had room to hammer away inside. When he looked up, his chest and aura seized again with unadulterated panic at the sight of Ylaen looming over him with *another* fucking knife.

The Imos Supplicant's dark eyes shone with a crazed glimmer; his pupils grown so large in the fading twilight that the irises seemed to have disappeared altogether.

"Was that a challenge that I heard, Issolm?"

Ghardon swallowed. "No," he croaked through dry lips, eyes tracking the silver gleam of naked steel as Ylaen idly spun his knife.

There was no reasoning with insanity.

"Ah. Just the cry of a passing seabird, then." Ylaen plucked the first knife out of the wood. "My mistake."

Ghardon didn't dare move. Not while the point of a bared blade rested against his groin.

"Now," Ylaen said conversationally, "just so I don't make another: which way do you suppose we should go?"

"West," he whispered.

"What was that?" A delicate jab pricked his skin. "You'll have to speak up for the others to hear you."

"West!"

"Very good, Issolm. We're going west and if you want some scars to blend in, just say the word: I've plenty of knives."

POOR GHARDON.

While the others were busy playing Ylaen's game by giving the Imos Supplicant the exact kind of attention he sought, Elaram gave her attention over to puzzling a way out of their current bind. With Rahelu's help, she got her dazed brother to sit up.

Getting him to calm down, however, was a different story.

"Did you see it?" he kept asking them, over and over. "Did you see that mad look in his eyes? He's going to get us all killed if he doesn't kill us all first. He's got to be stopped."

He might not like it, but Elaram decided to keep her arms wrapped around his shaking shoulders. If Ghardon had fallen back on the passive *'he's got to be stopped'* instead of the active *'we've got to stop him'*, then that meant he was really upset.

After she'd had that thought, he leaned against her—actually leaned against her, so she had to shift and brace to accommodate his weight—when he was usually so careful to avoid putting pressure on her right collarbone ever since Rahelu had broken it all those weeks ago even though the fracture had mostly healed by now.

Ghardon was really, *really* upset.

And instead of doing anything helpful, Rahelu only said, "Stormbringer save us," which was more of a curse than a prayer, and exacerbated his frenetic distress over nearly being gutted like one of her fish by adding more spilled blood of her own.

Elaram pressed his head to her shoulder so he wouldn't be able to look at it. "Don't be so glum, brother dear." She patted him on the back, stroked and smoothed his mussed hair, and said all the kinds of trite things his bruised and fearful ego needed to hear, such as, "I thought you made some excellent points."

Gradually, his tremble reduced to the occasional shudder

and his thunderstruck, bleached-bone aura ceased ringing against hers like a gong.

Then Nheras had to go and open her poisonous mouth.

"Yes, well done," said the Ilyn Supplicant. "Of all the possible ways to handle Ylaen Imos, you found the shittiest one and somehow concluded that was the approach you ought to try."

Elaram shot Nheras a dirty look. She agreed with the sentiment of course, since it was the truth, but done was done and there was no point to cutting Ghardon down further for utilizing a tactic that—on another day, under ordinary circumstances, with a different audience—would normally have been effective.

"Don't you be a bitter bitch either. Ghardon found a way out; that's what matters."

You could say many things about Ylaen Imos—she would know; she did so, frequently, and she had a whole list of his attributes, both attractive and unattractive (of late, the latter far outweighed the former)—but fourth in the column itemizing the attractive things was *'keeps his word'*, which made everything quite simple.

Waking Anathwan was impossible.

Consulting her, however...

Elaram looked past Nheras and Rahelu and their tiresome tussling to consider the aftercabin.

("Stop indulging his delusions," Nheras was saying, "unless you want to end up like him," and Rahelu shot back with, "Better than ending up like you. He's right, and we all know it, and yet you deliberately chose to undermine him.")

When Nheras and Rahelu had gone to investigate what had transpired between the senior mages, they'd been able to walk around the aftercabin unharmed, cataloging the scene, running Evocations, shifting Anathwan into her bunk. It hadn't become dangerous until they had tried moving

Maketh and thereby disturbed all that heartbane powder, which had set them both tearing out of the cabin with…

Something nudged Elaram's attention back to the argument in front of her.

"Am I the only one with a conscience?" Nheras thumped Jhobon's notebook. "If we sail east, we doom Anathwan and Maketh! A strategic retreat is in order; heartbane is an awful way to die."

Rahelu's savage retort was immediate. "You're talking about betting six lives and the mission's success—and thus the security of the Dominion entire—on the slim possibility of saving two. That's the worst trade I've ever heard of."

Curious, Elaram forced her eyes back to the aft hatch. She squinted at an innocuous-looking oblong patch of shadow—and found her gaze pushed towards Nheras again.

Who drawled, "Well," as she tugged at the silver chain around her neck until it popped free of her collar for moonlight to glint off the focus stone and the resonance crystal ring on the taut chain looped around her finger. "You would know, wouldn't you?"

"I don't know what you mean," Rahelu said, every muscle in her face gone rigid. "I have no regrets."

"I have regrets," Ghardon said, straightening. "I regret that—"

Huh.

Elaram stopped listening and started Seeking.

The little patch of shadow morphed into a thin, shabby volume. Small and cheaply bound, the faded title script on the cover declared it to be a collection of ghost stories and other fanciful tales of old Aleznua, from before the Dominion's Founding—but that, too, was a lie.

Well, well, well.

Ana had been sneaky.

Nobody paid Elaram any attention as she got to her feet.

Ylaen and Jhobon were too busy doing something to one of the sails, and Rahelu was too busy egging Ghardon on as he blistered Nheras with his condemnation of her conduct, each complaint fully cited according to chapter and verse.

"Shut up," Elaram told them on her return, "and behold!"

She presented the book with her left hand so her right was free to give a street performer's exaggerated gesture, and the looks on their faces as the Imbued Seeming gave way beneath her Seeking and the battered cover melted to well-oiled leather beneath her hand was worth more than gold.

"Guess who found Ana's maaaaaaaaage journal!"

That was worth another good flourish, so Elaram brandished its true form in their faces, like a banner, before riffling through the pages.

She skipped over sketches of the cultists' ritual knives, the stargem, the crown, and pages of cramped writing until she found the odd one out: thirty brushstrokes combining in elegant sweeps and swirls in shimmering black resonance ink that called to her. They formed a single Chanazian character that exuded a gentle green-tinged-gold warmth and a coded resonance signature. A tiny candleglow of spelled trust lighting the ambient resonance, pushing back the dark.

"Well?" Elaram asked. "What does it say?"

Rahelu scowled.

"No, sister dear, don't get into one of your moods. None of us can read Chanazian characters, so you're our only hope."

"It's 'velaz'," Rahelu said shortly.

"Which means…?"

"Lots of things. It changes, depending on the context in which it's used."

"Like…?"

"Like—"

Rahelu rattled off several sentences, all of which included

'velaz' and none of which anybody else understood, though, thankfully, she was cognizant of that, and gave literal translations in Aleznuaweithish without further prompting. Those, however, also made no sense, so Elaram was obliged to pester her for figurative translations, too: *'the sight mastery requires'* (which seemed a self-evident tautology) or *'the sight that masters'* (an even stranger construction that had to be an artifact of translation) or—

"That one!" Elaram said. "Ana means 'the master's sight'. Come on, let's go."

"We already tried Evocation," Rahelu called after her. "We didn't find any answers."

"Well of course you didn't. You weren't asking the right way."

Ghardon's head snapped up at her words. "Ela, no."

"Why not? It's a valid strategy."

"It's a first-level violation of personal rights!"

"Mission protocols make allowances for extenuating circumstances."

"It's an indefinite suspension of your mage license with a ten-year exile!"

"If you haven't noticed, brother,"—she spread her arms out wide and did a very wobbly pirouette—"we're currently lost in the middle of the Abmerduan Sea. I don't think any reasonable Adjudicator would allow the argument in the Hall of Justice. It's out of jurisdiction."

"The Hall of Justice is one thing; the council of Elders is another. You're proposing a resonance assault on our superiors—"

Elaram pouted. "I'm not a fool and you're not a genius," she said. "No, I don't propose we test ourselves against Guardian Maketh's formidable defenses—he'd likely obliterate our minds without even being aware of it while he's fighting the heartbane—or give House Imos any excuse to haul us before an inter-House disciplinary panel. Besides"—she waggled Ana's journal in front of his nose—"Ana already consented to a direct Seeking."

"You presuppose that's what she meant," Ghardon said slowly. "What if you're wrong?"

"You presuppose that she would object." Elaram grinned at him. "How much are you willing to stake on that supposition? Six lives? Eight?"

Indecision churned in his resonance aura. Finally, he nodded and said, "Two."

Yes! The giddying sense of *rightness* moving through her—as her brother grasped her hand and she pulled him up and the two of them turned to confront danger together again, hand in hand, an inseparable team—was so powerful that Elaram could float all the way over to the aftercabin on its lightness if she wanted to.

"Wait," Rahelu said. "Make that three."

Even better! You could run 'Break and Enter' with two, but three was ideal because then you'd have one to guard and one to anchor while the third unearthed the answers and she couldn't *wait* to get a glimpse of all the secrets Ana had kept hidden from them.

Elaram beamed. "Three should do it."

Nheras stood to go with them.

"No," Ghardon said. "Your time would be better spent elsewhere." He glanced from the sail to the tiller to the fishing line Rahelu had abandoned to the Conclave mage's corpse, which they had shoved unceremoniously to one side of the vomit-covered deck, to the vomit-filled bucket and the dirty cookpot and scattered fishbones from the remains of their meal. "Since you can neither sail nor fish, perhaps you'd best start making yourself useful by cleaning up this mess."

Nheras flattened her lips into a thin line. "I did you the kindness of not exposing the flaw in your claim to authority earlier, but don't presume to give me orders on that illegitimate basis. House Issolm mission protocols dictate decisions by majority vote in the absence of a direct instruction from a superior, not seniority. You have no true authority over me."

"I suppose not." Ghardon held Nheras's eyes. "But I do recall a bet where the stakes were servant's duties, with the loser doing the winner's bidding for a day and a night."

Nheras reddened. "That bet was never—"

"Then let's call a vote. Who will second my suggestion?"

All this squabbling was taking far too much time. The longer they took to get answers, the further west they would sail, and while Elaram very much wanted to see the city of sails, she wasn't completely irresponsible: clearly, they had to take care of whatever Ana had set out to do at the Endless Gate first.

Elaram snuck a glance at the tiller—Jhobon and Ylaen still had their heads together—then said: "Seconded."

Three was plenty; they didn't really need Nheras.

And, honestly, Nheras deserved to be excluded. House Issolm looked after its own. Teasing your siblings when they made asses of themselves was just fun and games; so was playing on different teams, provided you were working to advance Issolm interests and gave each other fair warning. Standing aside when they were in active conflict with other Houses? That was something else altogether.

Betrayal deserved punishment. Obviously.

So when Ghardon asked: "All in favor?" Elaram put her hand up in one synchronized motion with his, and when Rahelu didn't, Elaram reminded her with a pointed look.

Rahelu quickly amended her error.

"Carried," Ghardon announced.

He used one foot to hook the pile of soggy, torn linen that had previously been Rahelu's shirt and flung it into Nheras's face. Nheras jerked away and caught the stinking bundle, but the sodden, vomit-covered sleeves still slapped her full across the cheek.

Elaram winced inwardly. He really shouldn't have done that, but her brother had his *'I-warned-you-but-you-didn't-listen-so-I'm-going-to-bludgeon-you-with-your-mistake-until-you-recognize-how-wrong-you-were'* face on and she wasn't about to get in between Ghardon and the target of his vengeful scolding.

"Get scrubbing, sister dear," he said and smirked at Nheras's distasteful look, "unless you want to go back on your oaths. Do you require a refresher on the penalties for insubordination as well?"

The ambient resonance shivered as dull embers sparked off Nheras's resonance aura. "No need," she said, biting off each word as she got down on all fours. "You've made my options perfectly clear."

"Great, fantastic," Elaram said. "Can we go already?"

Ghardon didn't move until Nheras was carrying out her assigned task to his satisfaction: head bent close over the deck, hands scrubbing the wooden planks of the weather deck along the grain, the anger in her resonance aura faded away and replaced by steely gray focus.

"That," Rahelu said to Ghardon as the three of them tied strips of sea-dampened linen across their faces, "was not a good idea."

"This entire mission has been a series of fucking terrible ideas," he said, voice muffled through his makeshift mask. "What's one more?"

Fun, though. Elaram smiled as she tugged the rough cloth higher over the bridge of her nose and lower so it covered her chin in addition to her mouth, then lifted the hatch.

"Alright," Ghardon said as he shifted his resonance aura into a shining barricade of golden pride and they descended into the aftercabin. "Let's try not to die."

2 4

DIVE

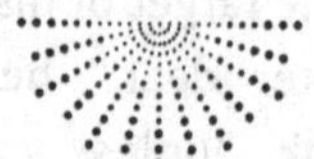

RAHELU CROUCHED BEHIND GHARDON AND ELARAM and did her very best not to breathe.

Though they had sealed off the aftercabin for the better part of two arcs, heartbane-infused resonance crystal dust still swirled around inside. Every movement stirred up new glittering plumes; every breath caused a fresh layer to settle onto the damp linen tied over their faces. The powdery grit clung to their hair, their clothes, and every inch of exposed skin, collecting on the slopes of their foreheads and in the slight hollows where the base of their eye sockets met the tops of their cheeks. You could not help but want to brush off the constant, feathery sensation, which only shifted the stubborn substance around and intensified the irritation.

Each particle contained only a trace amount of malicious resonance—individually so insignificant that she would have had to really concentrate to pick out the disturbance from the general fluctuations in the ambient resonance. If the spill had happened up above, on the open deck, the wind and the sun would have made short work of the vapors and the dust. Down here, poisoned powder caked their makeshift masks within twenty heartbeats. Soon—in a span, perhaps less—the fabric would be coated so thickly they would be trying to breathe through mud.

Yet the dust was not the true danger.

Worse than the lightheaded feeling of steady suffocation, worse than the pin-sharp itching that urged her to beat her hands against her skin, worse than the insidious fraying of her command of her muscles and her aura, was the resonance storm born of the Guardian's deterioration.

Maketh was right where Rahelu and Nheras had left him —lying on his back, in the middle of the aftercabin—but now his mage pendant glowed a sickly pus-like yellow beneath the ghostly steel-gray Obfuscation barrier surrounding him, weeping thin trails of noxious green that matched the twin trails of blood dripping from his nose. Every few heartbeats, his resonance aura erupted with unconscious Projections that lashed out in all directions, sending bone-white terror and red agony arcing through the ambient resonance like lightning. The Projections shattered on the heartbane-powdered bulkheads, breaking apart to recombine in a restless, surging current that threatened to topple them over as it battered away at Ghardon's barrier and their concentration.

Her copious tears should have kept her eyes clear, but heartbane dust had clogged her eyelashes and every blink felt like she was dragging a curtain of glass shards over her eyeballs and shoving them into the corners where they dissolved into her skin. The damage was subtle—practically indistinguishable from her fatigue. Did she stumble over the shards of the broken teapot because she had gone for twenty-four spans without sleep? Or was it the heartbane at work, a barely audible murmur of dissonance inside her veins?

Belatedly, Rahelu realized they should have blindfolded themselves, too.

"Eyes closed," she yelled and promptly shut her own eyelids to rely on resonance senses alone.

They crept across the aftercabin with Ghardon taking point behind a partial Obfuscation barrier of shining gold that shielded them from the worst of Maketh's Projections. The ring on his right hand blazed with power as he seized Anathwan's pendant with his left. He yanked; the delicate silver chain snapped and there was a sensation of something wrenching apart in the ambient resonance as the soft blue glow of Anathwan's pendant died. Just as quickly, the pendant lit up again, this time with a brilliant gold.

Ghardon's shield expanded into a thick wall that encircled the four of them, an island of temporary peace.

Rahelu risked a peek. Heartbane dust rose in deadly little puffs as Elaram hastily undid Anathwan's shirt.

"What is this ward?" Elaram's hand hovered uncertainly above the elaborate lines inked over the Elder's heart. "Should I break it?"

Eight concentric layers of suppression wards nested within eight more layers of diffusion wards. The intricate formations done in black resonance ink were mirrored on the inside of Anathwan's shirt in copper thread that shimmered in Rahelu's resonance sight.

She leaned in and brought her hand to hover next to Elaram's. This close to Anathwan's heart with the stitched ward out of alignment, she could finally detect a faint flickering outline around the Elder's comatose form and the churning resonance beneath her skin. Stray wisps of resonance—black-blue sorrow, lilac regret, and silver-gray resolve—were beginning to escape the bounds of Anathwan's ward.

"No," Rahelu said. "Break it and we'll have worse to deal with than Maketh's Projections." She laid Elaram's palm across the bared skin of the Elder's left breast, in the exact spot where the heart of the mirrored ward on Anathwan's shirt would have been. "This should give us enough of an opening. Can you sense it?"

"Yes," Elaram said. Her fingers trembled. "Ready when you are."

Left hand clutching the pendant around her own neck, Rahelu drew on its power as she entered the Concordance. Her perception expanded immediately: resonance signals amplified from whispers to clearly audible rhythms; the muddied, washed-out colors of the current running up against Ghardon's Obfuscation barrier sharpening into alternating bands of red, orange, and blue. Through the heightened awareness of Concordance, coupled with her hand on Elaram's hand on Anathwan's heart, she sensed the Elder's suppressed resonance signature as a faint rippling.

Beneath it all, the oscillating tone of the alien song.

Rahelu visualized the bulk of her mind as an anchor: solid, heavy, and unyielding as black iron sunk into bedrock. The rest of it—the part that was melded in shared purpose— she envisioned as a coil of braided fishing line that knotted itself securely around the honed, compacted shape of Elaram's mind.

"Go!" she said, and Elaram slammed their combined focus through the gap in the resonance ward.

They tore through the outer layers of Anathwan's consciousness like a crossbow bolt through paper screens, ripping through the few fragmentary thoughts that still lingered despite the corrosive effect of the heartbane: meditations from Unevazobaru's manual, snatches of verse from Enjela's ballad and Belruonian hymns, the haunting melody Maketh had hummed.

Elder Anathwan? Elaram quested out.

The coded resonance signature from the Elder's mage journal rippled away, signal deadened by silence.

That didn't stop their headlong dive into the depths of

Anathwan's mind, Seeking the Elder's resonance signature through the abstract thoughts and complex emotions littering the middle layers: orange-yellow impatience, so well bridled beneath Anathwan's composed exterior that Rahelu would have bet gold on its absence; simmering frustration that burned low but steady, its bubbling restrained by a wide, smooth border of acquiescence that covered all else. They sank into that deceptively soft environment—a sea of heavy fog tainted with the bitter scent of heartbane that yielded as easily and swallowed them.

Inside the smothering pale gray void, they lost all sense of time and space. The boundaries of her mind expanded forcibly until the outer membranes of her concept of self were stretched thin, exposing the contradictory emotions that whirled around the inner constructs of her identity.

Somewhere, beyond this insubstantial mental realm, were their bodies, chained by their physicality to the passage of time, their frail flesh the only bond that connected past and present and future. Somewhen, she—

—lifts a dark crown with elegant, ring-clad fingers that are not her own—

—grips a black serpentine dagger with scarred hands—

—drives it towards her heart—

The edges of their joined consciousness were dissolving away in the searing fog of...memories? Desires? Fears? It was impossible to distinguish between them, for this deep below the conscious mind, memory and emotion were one and the same—how one related to the other and the strictures of reality made no difference to how the soul perceived them.

Anathwan? Elaram sent. Again, but in the high, lilting tones of a very young child: *Ana, where are you?*

The fog shivered.

Sixteen tall, fluted pillars and large, block-like steps took gradual form and hollowed out the void's mist-filled center into a grand hall. The massive columns stood in doubled rows and stretched impossibly high: they seemed to curve together into arches whose tops merged with the clouded ceiling, yet when Rahelu drew close to one and spiraled up round and round its height, she found no deviation in its form. Indeed, looking down from above, it seemed to her that it was the base of the pillars that were curved as if they shared a single root.

Ana!

Their Projection rippled through the hall of mist—*Ana-ana-na*—a partial manifestation patterned after Anathwan's resonance signature. Instead of compressing their focus, Elaram diffused it, stretching their Seeking after the leading edges of their Projection as it swept through the substance-less pillars and steps. The strain of the Seeking pulled their minds as taut as the skin of a drum, sensitive to the least vibration.

They waited.

For one heartbeat or ten thousand, they waited in trembling Concordance until an answering echo came from the farthest corner.

Anathwanathwanathwan...

Elaram released her tensioned hold over the empty, unresponsive regions of their Seeking and their Concordance zipped across the expanse of the clouded hall, drawn to the echo like iron to a lodestone.

Upon a pale marble dais sat a polished chest that gleamed with its own pallid yellow light. Its blank sides and top were wrought from a single piece of ivory, finely carved in the likeness of white oak. There were no seams, no hinges, no visible gaps where they might be able to enter; even the ever-present corrosive heartbane had not etched its surface in the slightest.

Anathwan had withdrawn herself inside her mind block.

It did not open to their Evocations.

Whenever they manifested the character, velaz, and placed it on the empty space where a lock should be, the dark glittering brushstrokes wriggled and fell apart to slither away into the shadows.

Eight hells, Elaram sent. *That wasn't the key. We need our brother for this.*

We can't, Rahelu sent. *If I pull Ghardon into the Concordance, we won't last long enough to come back.*

If you don't pull him in, we won't get any answers.

You're assuming he can get in. Guild medals and trophies aside, Ghardon is not on Maketh's level—you said so yourself. Think, Elaram. Anathwan got herself in; she must be capable of getting herself out. We just have to give her a reason to do so.

Out of nowhere, a massive Projection struck. The tenuous mist-form of the hall—Anathwan's mind—shook and trembled, then its clouded ceiling melted. Foreign resonance poured through in a tremendous crimson flood that swept the pillars and the steps and every other visible edifice away.

All save the mind block, which shone like a beacon through the agony-waves—the only point of stability left in the crumbling thought realm.

Ana! Elaram cried in her child's voice as she clung tight to the chest and left Rahelu to hold their Concordance together.

The chest sat there, as motionless as ever.

Outside, from a long way away, Rahelu felt another tremor coming; and a distant alarm not her own.

Elaram, she sent urgently. *Elaram, we need to go.*

She steeled her will, renewing her grasp on Elaram's mind

as she prepared to haul them both back up to consciousness along the thin connection anchoring their Concordance to Lhorne's pendant.

Ana, I'm scared. Please...

The chest flickered. Had she imagined it?

A roar.

The sound of rising thunder.

Bone-white lightning crackled through the void, seared the remnants of the gray fog into nothingness, and shattered the dais. A hundred smoking fragments whirled around in a maelstrom, terror arcing from one sizzling fragment to the next, and became a net, a cage, a prison constricting around them.

We're going. Rahelu flexed her mind, envisioned a dozen hooks that sank into Elaram's presence and yanked on their anchor to reel them away from the still, silent chest and towards the rapidly shrinking gap in the terrible lightning.

But Elaram would not let go.

Ana! she screamed as the lightning closed around them, and then they were both screaming as it flayed their minds, releasing buried terrors that choked them with burning shadows. Existence shattered and reformed wrongly: five emaciated figures with bloated faces lying in the hold of a tattered, half-drowned ship careening wildly on a black sea. The rotted visage wearing Elaram's face wept blackened blood from its empty eye sockets as it shook the corpse with clumps of long, golden curls slumped over the ivory chest and screamed again.

ANATHWANATHWANATHWANA—

The ivory chest blazed—

Hush, Ela. Fear not, for I am with you.

—and the corpse that was Anathwan opened its glowing eyes. Cool white light streamed from the Elder in a sweeping radiance. The world steadied: the ship's bucking lower deck transmuted itself back into polished ivory, bloodstained wood becoming decorative whorls in the natural patterning of the dais holding the locked chest; the cramped hold expanded into a vast hall with sixteen fluted pillars and grand steps; Anathwan, Elaram, and Rahelu herself, all wearing their Issolm garb and armbands and kneeling, hand in hand in hand, around the locked chest.

But their faces were still the faces of the dead and Elaram still wept blood. *Ana.* Her mental voice trembled and Rahelu added her own to bolster it. *Anathwan*, they sent in their doubled voices.

Memories poured out of them in a rush of jumbled images because words took far too long.

Anathwan breathed in what she could, and what she could not, she allowed to sink in through her waxen skin. Then:

My brave, courageous daughters, the Elder sent. *You have done so very well. Stay the course. You must not turn back. Do not allow yourselves to be swayed by young Imos. Go through the Dragon's Teeth and follow the Dragon's Spine to the Desolate Isles. The Endless Gate has been opened. We cannot lose the artifact to the Conclave.*

Even if doing so means death for you and for the Guardian? Rahelu asked.

Even so—but it shall not come to that. Heartbane poisons the mind and the soul; it poses little immediate danger to the body. I can endure a while longer. As for the Guardian...

Anathwan paused. *House Imos holds high ambitions.*

With that one phrase, Rahelu was forcibly reminded of the conversation she had had with Mere Ideth in that deserted warehouse, when she—a common-born applicant— had dared accuse the Atriarch of House Imos of plotting treason, and the Atriarch of House Ideth had merely nodded and asked, '*Do you understand why?*' then told her that her answers were, '*True, but wrong.*'

At the time, she'd simply thought it a test, to plumb the depths of her knowledge of the Houses and the extent of her ability to parse the motives behind their political maneuvering.

She ought to have realized: the greatest living Augur in the Dominion would not ask an academic question.

For the sake of our mission, Anathwan continued, *it may be best if Dedicate Maketh does not recover. Your study of his notes must suffice.*

That implicit, longed-for recognition of her skills was a partial fulfillment of the promise Anathwan had made in the *Winged Arrow's* great cabin—and with it came the sudden, crushing weight of the Elder's expectations.

How could she, with her self-taught approach to resonance wards, hope to perform at the level of Maketh's abilities?

The notion was absurd.

Just the very thought of it unsealed her panic, and the first of the countless obstacles that stood in their way tumbled out of her mouth along with her rotted, blackened tongue. *But we've no charts!*

We have Reshwim's accounts. When Silcarez's fleet sailed in search of answers to Enjela's fate, they made a great many maps. Though the seas have changed, the stars have not, and Jhobon Imrell has proved himself quite adept at reconciling the two. All he wants is the key.

But that's just it, Elaram sent, miserable. *We've lost the crown. That Conclave spy threw it into the sea.*

A trinket, Anathwan sent. *Listen.*

The low, sonorous tone that haunted Rahelu swelled.

That is the starsong. It led Silcarez to an island in the North Ocean. A dark cone on the horizon, its base wreathed in white frothing waves. *A broken mountain lies at its heart.* Black sand on glassy black rock. *Inside the mountain*—a circular abyss with four gargantuan ebon obelisks carved with deep scars—*the Endless Gate*.

Shock burst from her in a shower of brilliant yellow sparks. Their anchoring connection trembled; their Concordance fuzzed—she felt the distant hammering of her heart, heat pouring off Lhorne's pendant as she tightened the grip of her left fist, a sudden awareness of being submerged chest-high in the volatile resonance spurting through the cracks in Ghardon's thinning Obfuscation barrier.

"Hurry," he was saying, fending off another strike from the unconscious Guardian. "Gods, please, hurry..."

She shut out his words, his fear, her thundering heartbeat, the uncomfortable sensation of wearing a hot coal around her throat, and wrenched that piece of her mind back to the depths of Anathwan's subconscious mind.

...do when we get there? Elaram asked. *How do we reverse the ritual those cultists began when we don't even know what the ritual is or what it does?*

Velaz, my daughters. Anathwan smiled. Flame spurted from her skull's rictus grin, charring bloated flesh to bone. *You found my journal; our House has already supplied you with the key. Bind my mage pendant to my body and place it upon the altar-throne at the heart of the Endless Gate. I will do the rest.* The Elder pulled them to their feet with bony hands and pushed them away from her as the hall shook from another blow. *The future of our House and the Dominion depends on it.*

Go, she Commanded them, and the force of her will sent their Concordance spinning upwards.

Rahelu seized the thread of their anchor and called to Lhorne's pendant madly. Imagined the comforting blaze of its resonance signal as a beaconfire upon a rocky shore and they a drowning swimmer on the end of a very long line glimpsing the promise of air and warmth through murky waters.

Protect us, she thought.

Power surged down the connection, turning a gossamer thread into a sturdy rope.

Below, Anathwan jerked her corpse arms high. The sleeves of her pristine white robes fluttered in the wind whistling through the columns. Pale blue calm gathered in the cage formed by her stiffened fingers and swelled, enveloping the dais in a glassy bubble. Her gaze never left them, even as a gigantic pulse of terror obliterated half the hall, snapping pillars and scattering them like matchsticks.

Go! The Elder flung them through the jagged hole in the cloud-covered ceiling. *And remember: beware Im—*

Maketh's uncontrolled Projection met Anathwan's hasty Obfuscation in a deafening *boom*. Black cracks ran up along the last of the fluted columns in an awful silence as the clash of resonance shredded the misty hall.

One moment it was there and the next it was not.

Someone was screaming, Rahelu knew; whether it was Elaram or herself, she could not tell because she could not hear anything, could not sense anything as they flew through the chaos reigning in the layers of Anathwan's consciousness until their Concordance pulled free of the vortex.

Rahelu's working disintegrated under the strain at last— their minds snapped back into their bodies with such force she reeled backwards.

The high-pitched *clink-smash* of shattering clay and *fizzle* of vapor unleashed from dissolving powder. Shards of broken pottery sliced through her shoulder; the cuts burned—not like fire, but like acid as the corrosive taint of heartbane-corrupted resonance dust leached into her blood.

She needed to get up; they had to get out; she forced herself to roll over by shoving her elbow against the blood-splattered, poison-soaked floor. With her last shred of control, she tapped into her pendant and flared what power she had left to its limits. Her ghostly, blue-gray Obfuscation barrier lit up the aftercabin:

—there was Ghardon, kneeling between them and Maketh's wildly coruscating resonance aura, the golden shards of his splintered Obfuscation barrier falling from his scorched, ringless right hand as his left hand grasped Anathwan's smoking pendant with blistered fingers—

—there was Elaram, bleeding from her eyes and ears and both nostrils, pulling him to his feet, fingers dug deep into the soft, fleshy part of Rahelu's upper arm, the three of them staggering to the rickety ladder—

—there was the square hole above, gateway to the endless stars, each glittering pinprick of light in the Skymother's cloak an unborn possibility—

Rahelu threw herself up, up, up towards that dark starlit sea because diving was easier than climbing and she could smell the open water and the clean salt air. There were shadows; slithering, sneaking, scarred shadows surging towards her, with smoky limbs and a low voice that gushed like the floodwaters: rounded sounds truncated by harsh, guttural stops as jarring as the sharp rocks that stuck out of the Suusradi. *Safety*, it promised her with its glowing green eyes, *safety, peace, warmth, love*—it reached for her with long, misshapen arms as it crooned its siren song—*safety, peace, warmth, love, you will be safe*—the song rushed over her aura, set it humming in sympathetic resonance—*you are safe you are safe*—the shadow slid forward, smoky wisps skimming across her skin—*with me my love come my love to me*—and the pull of its warmth was irresistible.

She had been here before.

—look at the stars look at my face look at me, love, and remember our night by the sighing sea—

She knew this moment—had lived it over and over in her

mind a hundred times, each time searching the past for a different path.

This lie was not the truth.

She aimed a punch at the shadow's head but her fist would not close and her arm sailed forward in a feeble circle that fell short by a good stride or three. Panic flared up unevenly across her resonance aura. She dragged it together in dribbling clumps, lacking the control to even shape her Projection into the semblance of pebbles, let alone the spear she preferred.

Tiny gobs of orange arced through the air like droplets of molten lead; sputtered. Died before they ever reached the shadow.

It flowed towards her; an eager dance partner that followed her stumbling retreat. She could not outrun it upon the *Gull*; she could not outmaneuver it with her graceless limbs; she could not outfight it—for how do you fight a thing without substance?—so she did the only thing she could.

Rahelu turned, vaulted over the rail, and threw herself into the ocean's embrace.

25
LIES

SHE STRUCK THE SURFACE BELLY-FIRST, unresponsive limbs trailing like fins.

The impact drove the air from her lungs. Cold water closed over her head as she sank, leaving a trail of diminishing bubbles in her wake. Instincts that should have kept her nostrils closed and her mouth shut failed her; she gasped like some landbound idiot who had never seen the underside of the water before.

The pain of her sudden plunge shocked her senses awake.

Seawater rushed in, stinging her throat and nose and shoulder with a hundred thousand tiny needles; she tried to spit it out as she frantically flailed upwards (was that up? She could not tell the difference between the seabed and the sky), waiting for the initial burning sensation to subside. The agony only got worse: the surrounding water sizzled and hissed as clouds of bubbles burst from her skin, her eyes— her eyes!—as if it were boiling, boiling her alive.

Rahelu wanted to scream—

Don't scream, idiot—

(His...? No, not his voice.)

—you'll drown.

—so she did.

She opened her mouth and drank her fill of the sea so it could burn her clean from the inside out while she screamed and thrashed against the leviathan that had seized her—

Don't fight me.

—about the waist with its sinuous, ridged, tentacled limbs—gods, she would rather be torn to pieces by a bharost than be swallowed whole and devoured in its maw—she beat her fists against its body—once, twice, thrice—to no avail; clawing at it with her fingernails did no good either—

Don't fight me!

—if she had drawn blood, she could not tell, for there was blood in the water already; blood weeping from her shoulder and rinsed off her arms and corrupted resonance leaking from the corners of her mouth and eyes and nose and the pores of her skin, though when she sank her teeth into its muscled flesh she tasted copper, copper and a firm, utterly un-squidlike texture. It dragged her down, relentless, powering through the depths with short, sharp strokes of its other limbs until they broke through the sea into air.

Air!

Air, sweet air. The limb that had her gave her stomach a fearsome squeeze. Bitter seawater spewed from her mouth and nose in a furious gush. She spluttered. The desperate need to breathe warred with the visceral urge to purge the corrosive poison remaining in her body by vomiting. A sudden drop left her stomach somewhere above her ears and her head spinning. A violent upward heave. She tasted copper again as the force of her chin snapping against her collarbone caused her to bite through her lip.

Freed from the drag of the water at last, she kicked blindly for all she was worth, shoving and pulling at the limb locked around her waist as tight as the iron bands of a Tide-locks shackle until her captor flung her away.

She dredged as much air as she could into her lungs, ignoring the way her ribs protested at the sudden, forced expansion. No time to orient herself properly for a dive; she simply kept her eyes squeezed shut, curled up, tucked her head to her knees to her chest, and braced for—

THUD!

She slammed into the wooden deck; rolled once, twice, then came to a shuddering stop against the mast. Something else landed on the deck with two more wet *thuds*. She tried forcing her stinging eyes open—her vision swam, the moonlit outlines of the ship's rails left glowing reddish-blue afterimages as the *Sooty Gull* rolled—as the thing squelched its way towards her with a horrid *drip-dripdrip-dripsplat*.

She scrambled away, crablike, on her ass, hands scrabbling behind her for a line, a bucket, a knife (hadn't she left her knife here?), her vomit-soaked shirt—anything.

"Stay back!" Her hoarse cry came out garbled. "I'll kill you!" Her right hand closed upon a fistful of needle-thin spikes—the makeshift seaspire of fishbones. She hurled them at the dark blob towering over her, at the pale glimpses of rolling white where the thing's eyes should be.

It deflected the fishbones easily with a casual swipe of one limb and said, "Thank you, Ylaen, for helping me get my brother and sister out of the resonance hell we willingly walked into, to prove a point that didn't need proving."

She blinked.

"Thank you, Ylaen, for hauling my resonance-mazed ass out of the Abmerduan Sea instead of leaving me to drown." His blurry figure stretched out on the deck beside her, clutching his arm. "Sorry about biting you."

Eight hells.

Rahelu gave up trying to make her eyes work and concentrated on not coughing her lungs out instead.

Breath in. Breath out.

Focusing on the simple two-count meditation brought back a semblance of control. After a hundred heartbeats or so, her limbs stopped trembling. After five hundred, her lungs stopped seizing. She needed five hundred more before her resonance backlash faded enough for coherent speech.

"Thank you," she rasped.

"And...?"

The deck felt rough against her cheek. "And sorry."

"And...?"

"And what?"

What else was she supposed to say? She tried peeling her eyelids open again, an endeavor they objected to—they were swollen with irritation, heavy with exhaustion, and the full moon was far too bright—but eventually she managed.

"You know, when Symezosh saved Enjela's life, she was a whole lot more grateful." Said while wringing out his shirt. "Heapings of praise for his bravery and good looks." A very pointed pause. "Offers of generous gifts in reward. Pledges of undying devotion from her allies."

Hollow footsteps approaching from amidships marked Nheras's arrival. "Symezosh tamed a dragon so he could fight the Stormbringer in the heart of his own realm and returned with the technique of Command. You went for a pleasant swim and came back with some fish guts."

"By all means, let's try it again," Ylaen drawled. "Will you play the dragon? Or shall I?"

Rahelu's thoughts wheeled away from their sniping banter, up towards the heavens. The sign of the bell hung directly over the bowsprit; the *Gull* was sailing close-hauled into the light wind. A quarter- or half-span had passed at most, but it might as well have been a night and a day.

Another glance around located Ghardon and Elaram. Both were out cold next to the aft hatch. Her heart lurched at the sight of their pale resonance auras guttering like candles in a stiff breeze, just as Maketh's had been.

Fuck.

They'd gotten the answers they needed, but the heartbane had gotten Ghardon and Elaram too. Someone—Nheras, most likely; Jhobon was busy dismantling the temporary hoist used to haul her and Ylaen back on board—had washed their faces and stripped them of their powder-caked masks and clothing, and covered them up with blankets.

Neither of the Issolm siblings looked like they would be waking up any time soon, which left Rahelu as the only one who knew what Anathwan's orders were:

Go through the Dragon's Teeth. Follow the starsong to the Desolate Isles and secure the Endless Gate. Take the Elder's body inside its heart.

And beware Imos.

Had Anathwan been referring to Maketh alone? Or did her warning extend to his Supplicant?

But Anathwan had not trusted her Supplicants with the particulars of their mission until she had been forced—and only because they'd risked a direct Seeking. If Maketh was Atriarch Hnan Imos's hidden instrument, wasn't it only logical that he would keep that intention buried too?

And yet...if there had been one traitor, why not two? If you were going to commit treason, why not use a team?

When it came to a straight fight, Ylaen was the most formidable of the Supplicants; his command of Projection combined with his combat skills made him a dangerous opponent. Thus far, they had only sparred under controlled conditions—never with resonance and combat skills combined—and he had never revealed the full extent of his capabilities in any of those bouts. His overall Guild ranking was somewhere at the bottom of the top quartile—respectable enough that Petitioning would not have been a problem for him, but not high enough to make him particularly remarkable. Not that she had ever paid any attention to him—his flirtatious manner, his flamboyant disregard for propriety, and his obscene wealth were all things that made her dismiss him as a spoiled and callow House-born with the depth of a puddle.

And what of Jhobon? It was easy to overlook his presence when he spoke little and revealed even less; easy to forget that he was every bit as capable as Ghardon—perhaps more so, for where Ghardon took every opportunity to flaunt his potential, Jhobon underplayed his abilities, content to hide in Ylaen's shadow. But House Imrell had sworn vassalage to House Imos and where Ylaen led, his shadow followed.

Rahelu had never been so conscious of the body beside her before.

A knife—not hers; Ylaen's; the same one he'd nearly gutted Ghardon with not a span ago—lay two strides away, next to the slashed line used to haul them out of the ocean.

Her limbs twitched; his immediately tensed.

Fuck! She had to bury her visceral recall of him kneeling on top of her—and her overwhelming urge to lunge for the knife—with an exaggerated shiver.

Confronting Ylaen might be suicidal. Even if Elaram was right, that—if presented with incontrovertible proof that there was a reliable way to find the Endless Gate—he would keep his word and sail east, the Imos Supplicant hadn't been wrong in his assessment. They could follow the gulls to the

Dragon's Teeth, but that would only extend the inevitable. Yes, in theory, the starsong would lead them to the Endless Gate—if Jhobon could solve the puzzles Silcarez had left in Reshwim's accounts, if they could find enough water and fresh catch to sustain them, if Ghardon was right about their ability to slip past any ship clan raiders with Maketh's barriers and wards, if the Stormbringer sent them good winds, if they covered some fifteen to twenty kual a day, if they didn't have to spend spans and spans navigating around the deadly reefs Ylaen had spoken of...

If, if, if. Then what?

Presume the Houses are right: that the artifact they chase exists and has the power to reshape the fabric of the world.

Presume Elder Anathwan is right: that she can endure until they reach the Endless Gate and the artifact, which will provide the power and means necessary for her restoration and completion of their mission.

Presume that Ghardon is right: that the Conclave are already on their way there, to seize the artifact's power for themselves, and that they—mere Supplicants—are the Dominion's sole hope of preventing that disastrous outcome.

Cast in those terms, Rahelu had no choice: she had to carry out Anathwan's orders. And why was she prevaricating, anyway? Hadn't she already decided when she had rejected Venoru and her temptations?

But, whispered the insidious part of her that refused to stop questioning her duty: what if the Conclave arrive first? How will you fight your way past a ship full of mages like Venoru, with the Elder's unconscious body in tow? What if you're too late and the artifact is gone and Ylaen is right and the Desolate Isles are well named and you have no food or water to return...

Lhorne's furious words echoed through her mind once

more: '*...send you to die on a suicide mission at the other end of the world!*'

Better to go west, that voice insisted. If she held her tongue, who else would know? Nheras had not been with them, and Ghardon and Elaram were not awake to gainsay her.

Heading to Tsorek-fa, though, was a different kind of suicidal. Three in ten chances of avoiding capture? Rahelu didn't like those odds. It was one thing to masquerade as renegade Guild mages looking for hire on a smuggler's boat when they were fighting fit and capable of dissuading raiders from acting on opportunistic inclinations; it was quite another to limp into a foreign harbor where the Dominion held no sway, half-dead from thirst with a hold full of valuable cargo they couldn't defend and advertising they had two —four—mages in desperate need of a healer.

They might as well paint the words 'FREE FOR THE TAKING: ONE SHIP, ITS GOODS, AND EIGHT SLAVES' on the *Gull's* topsides and sails and hope whichever clan seized them first would outfit them with comfortable collars.

And if Ghardon and Elaram should wake up to discover that she had, after all, betrayed House and Dominion...

Clap!

Rahelu blinked, eyes refocusing.

"Well?" Nheras asked.

She looked so *strange*. Weeks without access to her combs and hair oils had stripped the shine and bounce from her tight brown curls. A halt in her daily application of perfumed creams gave her salt-flaked, peeling skin like a molting plum tree when patches of pale red wood showed through the brown bark. Dark splatters marred the front of her shirt. Her sleeves were rolled up to her elbows; her hands red and raw from scrubbing, which recalled to mind Ghardon's distrust:

Nheras Ilyn is a painted doll who has never had a thought in her head that wasn't placed there by Lynath Ilyn. If she's sworn to House Issolm, it's because she was ordered to.

Where did House Ilyn fit in all of this?

"Were you able to rouse the Elder or the Guardian?"

Rahelu needed time. To think; to plan; and—gods help her—figure out whether she could trust Nheras.

"No," she said.

Which, strictly speaking, was true.

Talk to Nheras first, she decided. That meant getting the two scarred Supplicants out of the way for as long as possible.

Rahelu looked at Ylaen. "Tell me you have a plan for getting us in and out of the city of sails that doesn't involve us blithely sailing in during broad daylight and presenting our necks to the first raider that runs across our ship for Suborned collars."

With a perfectly straight face, he said: "I have a plan for getting us in and out of the city of sails that doesn't involve us blithely sailing in during broad daylight and presenting our necks to the first raider that runs across our ship for Suborned collars."

He was a fucking terrible liar and she told him so.

"You wound me," Ylaen said with a hand to his heart. "I had no intent to deceive, merely an intent to please."

They were not going to go there.

"Either way, you failed."

Rahelu dragged herself semi-vertical and crawled over the freshly scrubbed deck to paw through the things Nheras had brought up from the hold.

"Jhobon." Rahelu waved a water flask at him. "You and Symezosh here need to go deal with the Guardian."

"For what purpose?" Presumptive as always, Ylaen spoke

as if she had addressed him. "That resonance storm chewed up the three of you and now you want us to put ourselves at risk? How do you think you'll fare trying to sail this sloop single-handed? No." He shook his head. "We'll wait until my uncle tires. And he will tire, eventually."

She seized upon that familial relationship; concern for Maketh's well-being had, purportedly, been one of his reasons for sailing west. "The longer his body goes without being purged of heartbane, the worse he'll get. Leave your uncle to suffer and he might do himself permanent damage. But get enough clean water down his throat, and it might sufficiently dilute and mitigate the heartbane's more damaging effects and give him a chance to regain control."

Ylaen flinched but it was Jhobon who said, "I still don't think that's a good idea."

Fine.

She tried a different tactic; the one Elaram had proposed. "Anathwan couldn't be roused, but we did glean the answer you wanted. There is a way to reach the Endless Gate without the crown. Listen."

Rahelu closed her eyes. Opened her senses to the music that haunted her dreams and let it suffuse her resonance aura the way it rumbled through the ship's planks until every mote of her being thrummed with it. Frisson lanced through the ambient resonance at the starsong's glacial warble as it modulated from one low frequency to another. Eight tones, repeating in an endless cycle, never in the exact same sequence and never shifting in the way she anticipated.

When she opened her eyes again, the Imrell Supplicant's jaw had struck the deck.

"'As the stars sing and the heavens toll'," Jhobon breathed. "The melody that led Silcarez to Enjela's shrine. You hear it!" He abandoned the mainsail to rush over. "How long have—why can you—no, no; that's not important. Where, Rahelu? Which way does the starsong say to go?"

She looked past Jhobon's frantic, pleading face to meet Ylaen's flat stare. "East."

A flicker in the dark depths of his eyes—oh, he *was* afraid.

"East, then north," she said, shifting her focus back to Jhobon. "To the Desolate Isles. With the starsong guiding us, we'll be able to reconcile Silcarez's descriptions to your star maps and find the Endless Gate. Or so the Elder believed."

Jhobon turned. "Ylaen," he said, "this could change everything. All is not lost. If we—"

"No!" Ylaen's sharp gesture nearly knocked Jhobon over, and he quickly grabbed him before he fell.

Their next exchange was in rushed Free Territories speech, too low and too urgent for Rahelu to parse much of the meaning, other than Ylaen's general, vociferous sentiment: *'No, no; I won't risk you.'*

But Jhobon had taken the bait; Jhobon evidently believed in the starsong and now he was seriously considering the case for going east, and that gave her the leeway and a margin of safety to attempt Ghardon's failed tactic again, for clearly the only thing that seemed guaranteed to provoke Ylaen Imos into doing anything was outright ridicule.

"Coward," she said.

Ylaen stiffened. "I am not a coward."

"Your lies aren't getting better with repetition."

"It is not a lie."

"Prove it."

"I just saved your life."

"It doesn't count."

His turn to stare. "How does it not count? You would have drowned in these razorfang-infested waters."

"I'd rather drown than deliver myself into slavery. Which is what sailing west amounts to, since you have no fucking plan on how to avoid being captured and no intention of trying to come up with one."

Three long heartbeats passed before Ylaen spoke again. "You have no idea what a fool you are."

"Maybe not," Rahelu said. "But I'd rather be an honest fool than a lying coward. At least a fool tries to accomplish something with their life. We got you your solution, yet here you are, refusing to keep your word out of fear. I wonder how the crowds will greet you upon your return."

She racked her brains to recall the specific verse he had referenced, then twisted all of the lines where Enjela had praised Symezosh's courage into a vicious condemnation. The words she supplied didn't quite fit the rhythm or the tune of the ballad he so loved, and heartbane and seawater and bile had burned her throat so her pitch was far off from true, but what she mockingly sang was recognizable enough that his expression darkened with every line that passed her lips. And when she reached the final crescendo—the famous couplet that meant one thing when performed in the Sunset district's songhouses (and quite another in the lustier entertainments found in rowdier establishments)—Ylaen finally shoved himself upright.

Rahelu taunted him with the water flask as he advanced upon her, his resonance aura aglow with the coal-red heat of his anger. "Was Maketh right? Do you not have any true skills beyond a few showy tricks for the dueling circle? Perhaps you're as inadequate a mage as you are at pleasing your lovers?"

He glowered and she laughed, even as his resonance aura scorched her sea-chilled limbs.

"No," Rahelu said. "I don't think I'll sully myself or my reputation by associating with a treasonous, oath-breaking, lying, incapable coward. You want to be rewarded with my gratitude? Go down there, get your Guardian under control, and earn it."

Ylaen plucked the flask out of her hand with a growl. Searing lines of crimson light raced across his arms and torso as the innate defenses carved into his flesh flared to life.

"We're still not going east," he hissed, before stalking off towards the aftercabin.

Jhobon shot her an exasperated look and followed, with Ylaen's sodden shirt in hand and his own scars afire.

Whatever.

They were gone so Rahelu could finally turn her attention to Nheras, who leaned with her back against the starboard bulwark, elbows on the toprail as she regarded Rahelu with equal intensity. Sensibly dressed, without her face painted like a mask, Nheras actually seemed…approachable.

Right up until she opened her mouth.

"You three fools were thrashing around, sending corrupted resonance up through the hatch, screaming loud enough to summon a shade." Dark green-brown scorn shone clear in her aura. "Ylaen was all for barring the hatch before you could call down a fleet of raiders upon us."

Rahelu chose her next words carefully. "I'm glad you were here to prevent him from doing that." That was true.

"Who says he tried? And if he did try, who says it was me who stopped him? I think he should have left you in the sea, where you belong."

"I thought we agreed to begin anew, in sisterly affection."

"I was not the one who reneged on our agreement." A pause. "You voted against me."

"*That's* what's got your scales in a ruffle?" Rahelu tried reaching for Seeking to plumb Nheras's intentions, but doing so brought on twinges of pain and tears to her eyes. "If I had voted otherwise, I would've prolonged the deadlock, and what good would that have done? Besides, what use would you have been down there?"

"If you have to ask that question, then you really do have fish shit for brains."

Perhaps she did. Certainly, Ghardon would never approve of what she was about to do. But with Seeking ruled out, there was no better option than to take inspiration from the Elder's example.

"Shut up, get down from your lacquered folly, and come here." She held her palm out. "Not everything is about you."

Nheras made her wait so long she had to brace her arm with her other hand that, in turn, was propped up by her knees.

Resonance flared from the open hatch—Ylaen's Projections and Jhobon's barriers clashing with Maketh's subconscious onslaughts.

"Nheras," she said as her arm was about to fall off. "*Please.*"

The moment Nheras extended her swollen fingertips, Rahelu seized them.

"Wh—"

Rahelu visualized a narrow inlet to a blue-gray lake; a trickling brook bordered with carefully placed river stones, ankle-deep and wide enough to dip two scooped hands in.

Don't waste time, she sent. *Seek!*

Rahelu pressed Nheras's blood-streaked fingers to her damp forehead, letting her sift through the memories floating on the surface of her mind:

Anathwan's final Command and exhortation, redolent with warning.

A song that tolls unending in her sleep. A cone-shaped island; a broken mountain; the ebon gate. Her dreams of blades and blood and—

Sharp fingernails dug into her temples.

"Enough!" she yelped and ripped Nheras's hand off her face. "I trust you understand our orders."

Now, the test:

Provoking Ylaen into dealing with Maketh was one thing; convincing him to sail to the Desolate Isles instead of Tsorek-fa was another. Since her best attempt at goading him hadn't motivated him to change course, Rahelu was at a loss for further ideas to try. But Nheras would know; Nheras had spent three weeks hunting smugglers with Ylaen and Jhobon during Petitioning.

Let Nheras figure it out. She had, after all, wanted to help.

Rahelu wanted—needed—to sleep.

But first, she needed to mend her ward. She got as far as undoing the third button on her shirt and half her right shoulder out before the sting of sea-soaked cotton peeling away from open wounds brought fresh tears to her eyes.

"Help me get this off and my shoulder rinsed," Rahelu said, "and I won't ask why you look like you've decided to apprentice to a butcher."

Nheras obliged. "This is going to need a healer," she said. "Clean, shallow cuts, but—"

"Seawater," Rahelu gritted out as Nheras prodded away at her shoulder. Poke, poke, poke—each one drawing another hissed breath through her clenched teeth.

"—you won't want to risk binding it up when there's still traces of heartbane in the wound and—"

"Seawater," she repeated, louder. "And would you mind your—"

The poking stopped. Rahelu breathed a sigh of relief as she heard the unmistakable *clompclompclomp-scrape-splash-clack-clomp* of Nheras hauling up a fresh bucket.

"Wash it out with—"

She coughed and choked anew as Nheras dumped the

bucket's contents none too carefully on her shoulder. There was an audible *hiss* as her wounds sizzled.

"Skymother's tears, that hurts!"

It took six rinses before the cuts no longer felt like they were on fire, and eight more for the stinging to subside entirely. (At least, she didn't feel the stinging any longer.)

"You've the Starfather's own luck," Nheras said. "How did you know to use seawater to purge the body?"

Rahelu shrugged. "Salt and running water both interfere with resonance." True. "Jumping into the sea was logical." And had nothing to do with her heartbane-induced hallucinations of tentacled leviathans with gaping maws.

In a rare moment of empathy that Rahelu had not believed Nheras was capable of, the other girl tossed her Venoru's clothes, followed by a spare stick of charcoal from Maketh's crate, then went to crouch beside Elaram and Ghardon. (Both the shirt and the trousers were two sizes too large, but at least they were still relatively clean and dry. Venoru's body was nowhere in sight.) Nheras frowned and began poking at their faces and lifting their eyelids.

Rahelu absentmindedly redrew her ward as she watched Nheras douse the other two. Their bodies spluttered on instinct as the caked heartbane residue in their hair rinsed off in frothing rivulets, but neither showed any signs of rousing.

Eventually, Nheras rocked back on her heels and said, "It must be too deep in their blood now." She hesitated, then went on to add, "If they do not wake in the next six spans, it may be worth trying direct infusions."

"With what?" Rahelu asked. "There's no powdered tortoiseshell or jade in the medical kit—you said so yourself —and even if there were, that's advanced Healing. We'd likely do more harm than good."

Silently, Nheras reached into her trouser pocket. She

pulled out a lumpy crystal the size of her fist and set it on the deck.

Rahelu's gorge rose. Memories flooded her—*a serpentine blade sawing through glistening ribs; a gloved hand gripping a still-beating heart*—and tainted her resonance aura a sickly yellow-green-brown. She couldn't tear her gaze away from the obscene sight of the newly harvested crystal; her jaw flapped open in the wind while the *Gull's* creaking lines kept time for a good count of thirty-five.

This was definitely not what Ghardon had had in mind when he'd set Nheras to cleaning. Violating the bodies of the dead like this ran against every Aleznuaweithish custom.

Nheras stared back, defiant. *Go on and judge me*, her gaze seemed to say. *If you dare.*

She didn't; she couldn't; she never would. More than once, when her family had fallen short of their repayments, Rahelu had given serious thought to watching the back alleys of the Lowdocks. The Yellow Fangs and the Blackbones paid a finder's fee to anyone who reported deaths to them first, instead of the city guard—and generously covered the expense of the deceased's funeral rites. (They took their cut, of course, in the form of whatever resonance crystal the deceased had left behind. A gamble—but all life was a gamble.)

Once Rahelu had recovered from her temporary bout of squeamishness, she gave Nheras a tight nod of approval.

The new resonance crystal was an opaque blue-gray with naturally angular, smooth facets and no flaws. (As one would expect of a legacy from such a powerful mage.) It would make a first-class focus stone fit for a senior Dedicate, perhaps even an Elder, after further cutting, polishing, and grinding by an experienced artificer. Even in its raw state, it would serve Ghardon well enough as a replacement for his ring, which had exploded from resonance overload during their excursion below.

Or if they could somehow distill the heartbane from the dregs of Anathwan's poisoned tea or tainted water casks…

A skilled Harbinger might be able to pick apart the specific resonance frequencies it distorted—and then compose the correct counter-frequencies to neutralize its effect. Not as good as having a healer, but as far as field treatment went, not a bad option either.

"What do you—" she began, but was interrupted by the growing murmur of Ylaen and Jhobon's voices from the hatch. They were speaking in the Free Territories tongue again, disagreeing again. Rahelu caught the words *'sages'*, *'fate'*, and *'father'*, but their context was utterly lost on her.

Still, she mouthed what she had understood at Nheras and cocked her head in query.

The other Supplicant shook hers in answer.

A short, guttural negation cut through the air and they both flinched at its sudden loudness. Yellow bolts sparked through their resonance auras a heartbeat later as they registered the protest was in *Ylaen's* voice—not Jhobon's—and the hasty reply that followed was drowned out by the sound of clay smashing.

Eight hells.

If nothing and no one—not even Jhobon—could convince Ylaen to sail east with words, then they were out of options.

So be it.

Rahelu picked up his knife and reached for the crystal. She would go and challenge him and they could dance one last time in the circle.

No. Nheras's hand snaked out and arrested her by the wrist. *We're not going to squander more time and effort on ineffective tactics. We're going to get this ship pointed in the right direction, then figure out what House Imos has been planning, and come up with a way to defeat those ambitions.*

Go yank on some strings then, Rahelu sent back. *My part is done.*

Hardly, Nheras sent. *You promised Ylaen a reward; he'll want to collect.*

I promised no such thing.

Nheras arched one eyebrow. *He thinks you did.*

I don't care what he thinks. He can go—

You should, Nheras sent. *Discovering what he thinks is necessary to our task. Wars are won first in the mind and then upon the battlefield.*

Don't patronize me with principles from first-year subjects. I—

Win the mind, win the battle, Nheras continued, her authoritative lecturing every bit as insufferable as Ghardon's when he was in full spate. *To win the mind, you must know the mind; to know the mind, you must learn its reason, for reason is what the mind uses to make sense of madness.*

You saw what happened when Ghardon tried, she sent. *There's no reasoning with madness. The only thing Imos will be moved by is force.*

And how well has a combative approach served thus far?

Rahelu fell silent.

We must cross thousands of kual to reach the Endless Gate. You and I cannot sail this boat by ourselves and they cannot find it without us.

'Us' being Rahelu, since Nheras's reaction to the starsong's revelation had been one of surprise, but in typical Nheras fashion, she was going to take credit for it anyway.

We can't trust them. That was the ugly truth. *This water situation? That Conclave spy may have been the one to contaminate our supplies, but she couldn't have been responsible for the leaks in the casks.*

Who said anything about trusting them? What we need is a

temporary alliance, founded on common purpose. I will persuade Jhobon to change course; he will listen to me and, between the two of us, we will be able to persuade Ylaen—but only if he is amenable to being persuaded, understand? Since you're the one who riled up his blood by insulting Imos honor, you must be the one to placate him. Then you will spend the foreseeable future ingratiating yourself with him so they will not discover our knowledge of their intended treachery and we may avoid being blindsided by their scheming. As you've neither the skill for scintillating conversation nor the requisite pedigree for valuable political connections, I suggest you start by offering him recompense in the form of a suitable place to sheathe his other kni—

No. Rahelu had heard enough. *You want Elaram for that.*

Of course I do; Elaram is the far better Seeker, Nheras sent. *He, however, doesn't want Elaram. Nor is she available. Also, Elaram has the subtlety of a thrown brick.*

Subtle? Amusement flared, along with the remembered sight of Nheras, ever circling, kept at bay by Cseryl's firm back; the glittering, unnoticed splendor of cloth-of-gold over cream and pale blue silk robes. *Very well; you do it then, since you've had so much practice. After all, your strategies have always worked so flawlessly for you before.* Out of pure habit, before she could keep the cruel thoughts back: *If you're worried he won't have you either, don't be. Imos will happily bed you with or without your jewels and silks and perfumes, as long as you offer him a warm, wet, and willing welcome.*

None of Nheras's bitterness showed in her resonance aura, though Rahelu felt the sting of it through the hand on her bare wrist. *All the more reason you should do it.* She scooped up the crystal and pocketed it without releasing her grip. *And don't you worry; the next time you look into Ideth's puppy dog eyes, you can still swear to him under Seeking that this was neither your idea nor did you have any choice. Besides—*her lips curved in a sneer—*you're warm enough for a fish, you're already wet, and you've been willing ever since—*

Rahelu didn't need to hear the rest. "Fuck you," she said and yanked her arm free with a vicious twist.

"It's pronounced 'thank you', sister dear," Nheras said, "though I expect Ylaen won't care how you say it as long as you do. Be sure to take all the time you need and best make sure you're very, very thorough."

With that, Nheras began to get up, but Rahelu wasn't done with the conversation. She grabbed the silver chain that had slid out from Nheras's shirt and said: "I want my ring back."

"How unfortunate for you—I don't want that horrid rotten driftwood bucket of yours back."

Rahelu did not let go. "Ghardon needs a focus stone."

Nheras mulled over the words, then smiled. "You once offered me a favor, with no conditions."

Suspicion, so recently extinguished, ignited once more. "I thought you needed no favors from me."

"A favor from a fish is worth very little on land. At sea?" Nheras shrugged. "That is a different matter. Do we have a deal?"

Rahelu hesitated. "I will not be compelled by this to act against my oaths."

"Why, I wouldn't dream of demanding such a thing," Nheras said. "We are, after all, both loyal and obedient daughters."

Muted footsteps sounded behind Rahelu—Ylaen's light, surefooted tread upon the companionway.

"Agreed," she said, and jammed the ring onto her finger the moment Nheras detached it from her necklace.

Ylaen sauntered into view with his arms spread wide, face and hair completely swathed in copper-embroidered linen, now caked white by fizzling powder. "Here I am, returned in triumph over the storm." He unwrapped his head and dropped his shirt into Nheras's bucket, where it bubbled and frothed. "The fearsome Guardian of the depths slumbers peacefully, at last. But Jhobon could use some help with locating Reshwim's accounts. We'll need those, regardless of our destination." An order, worded as a suggestion, and addressed to Nheras alone. "Most of the books in there are disguised by Seemings and at least half are rigged with traps."

"Congratulations, Stormbane, on your victory." Nheras drew a new bucket of seawater and placed it before him. "I suppose I should do my part."

"Indeed." Ylaen dipped his hands into the fresh bucket and splashed the cupped handful of seawater over his face. He gave Rahelu a sidelong glance as Nheras disappeared into the hold. "Let us all do our part."

He sat down next to her, close enough for their auras to touch.

Rahelu scowled and twisted her ring around and around her finger with her thumb, while Nheras returned with Anathwan's journal tucked under her arm and her head swathed—in silk, no less; quality linen wasn't good enough for Nheras; oh no, she had to have fucking *silk*—and swept up her discarded rags and bucket and went to join Jhobon in the aftercabin, without giving either of them a passing glance.

Ylaen didn't say a thing. Just sat there, radiating smug satisfaction and body heat, waiting for Rahelu to eat her earlier words.

Fine.

"I'm sorry for calling you a coward."

"And...?"

"Thank you for saving my life."

"And...?"

"I'm very grateful you did."

She was also a fucking terrible liar and they both knew it.

A slow smile played on his lips. Right on cue, Ylaen recited: "'For you, I have slain the storm; for you, I have conquered the sea.'"

Gods. He was enjoying this far too much. Maybe if she threw herself back into the ocean, her face would stop feeling like it was on fire. If Tlareth could see her squirming now, she'd be screaming with laughter.

In case you've forgotten, Nheras sent, *Enjela's lines are: 'With you, I shall defy the heavens; with you, I am—'*

Rahelu gritted her teeth. *I know what the fucking lines are.*

She just couldn't bring herself to actually say them.

Not to him.

She closed her eyes.

Recalled the floral perfume of the Ideth gardens. The length of his body, pressing hers to the deck. The warmth of his muscled thigh against hers, their bare skin wet with solstice rain.

Breathed deep.

No trace of cedar and sandalwood answered this time; his scent was the clean scent of brine and ocean air. The smell of a similar moment in another time, another place.

She reached for him without looking; without looking, she rushed through her utterance of Enjela's stupid lines— imagined she spoke them to someone else—then said no more, for her lips were on his.

Salt; with a hint of bitterness from a faint dusting of heartbane that had escaped his quick rinsing. The taste burned her tongue and scorched her throat as she swallowed, her mouth somehow both dry and wet at the same time.

He drew her close, callused fingers and ridged scars chasing their way down her bared back to cup her buttocks and lift her up and over until she sat astride his hips. Wisps of rose-red mist gathered and blossomed in the ambient reso- nance. She welcomed the heat of it and its gift of loosened inhibitions; found herself drawing on the power in her reclaimed ring to stoke its strength and keep it from drifting away. (Elaram would turn her nose up and call it lazy; Elaram and her romantic notions could go and rot in the sixth hell.)

They had no audience this time, so he did not bother with any preliminaries. He didn't even reach for Projection to aid her efforts. Whether that was because he had spent his strength on subduing Maketh or because he felt no need to exert himself was a mystery.

Either way, she didn't care. She was done with caring.

Unprompted, his hands found the flimsy tie that held up her borrowed trousers—its simple knot was no bar to his practiced fingers—and their removal gave her an excuse to mount him in reverse. The position limited his range of movement, it suited her mood and best of all, she could open her eyes and stare up at the sky and still pretend anything she liked without the illusion being broken by such incongruent sights as intricate scars that did not belong on his body or the absence of red hair and green eyes.

It was terribly selfish—and terribly gratifying.

No danger of temptation here; he knew well what her thoughts were—had *invited* them for his own benefit. It was a purely transactional exchange of mutual convenience that harmed no one; and if they each had ulterior motives, well, she could think of far worse sins to commit.

This was a means to an end; an end she found several times over.

After all, Nheras had demanded she be thorough.

26

HOLLOW

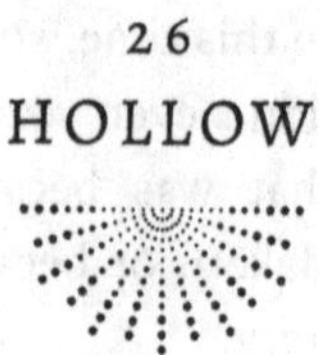

YLAEN HAD BEEN SO SURE IT WOULD BE DIFFERENT
this time.

There *was* an allure, a special something, an intense intoxication to playing predator instead of prey; his father and his uncle had been right about that. Certainly, the heady, seesaw tension of the chase almost rivaled the thrill he felt whenever he stepped into the circle to face a new opponent—toes curled and knives drawn before either of them made the first strike—when a world of possibilities existed for the duel.

About everything else?

Either they were wrong, or there was something wrong with him because he felt nothing of what he'd seen flashing in their eyes and auras when he'd witnessed their moments of victory.

There was supposed to be a fierce joy, a powerful rush, a sweetness more addictive than dreamleaf when the chase turns to capture.

Well.

In Ylaen's opinion, victory tasted no different to defeat: bitter as the traces of heartbane that still clung to him.

So much for that experiment.

The empty realization almost made him give up.

He would have given up, if not for the damage that might do to the shaky Imos reputation. Never mind the blame for those jokes could be laid entirely upon his uncle's failures (though Hnan Imos, of course, would never admit it). And if his...enthusiasm for his reward hadn't already flagged the moment Rahelu had closed her eyes, it definitely had now.

It hadn't taken much for the jokes and snide asides to spread.

One night—he had had one bad night. One lapse in judgment at Ideth's party had led to humoring Ghardon's flighty little sister after weeks of her stalking. One mistake had undone years of work, for she had promptly turned around her opinion of his reputation and began running her mouth on the subject of her dissatisfaction like a Chronicler announcing the ascension of a new Atriarch.

Sages, he had been stupid.

"Half a span!" Elaram had whined to anybody slow enough to be snared by her as she downed cup after cup of wine and made good on her parting threat to him. "Do you know, I was down there, on my knees, for half a fucking span before it seemed like he might be able to give my own fingers some competition?"

He would have Commanded her to silence if he'd thought it would do any good—but he knew it wouldn't; uncle Hnan had tried a very similar thing not long ago and found whispers were cursed inconvenient things to be rid of...though his current consort seemed to have learned the lesson. (Number four? Or number five? Ylaen had stopped keeping track of the women's names and bloodlines; his uncle changed them so frequently. Still, there was never any shortage of candidates willing to yoke themselves to Atriarch Hnan Imos for the sake of power and position.) So far, she had kept a circumspect tongue despite her barrenness and all of House Imos clamoring for Hnan Imos to produce a suitable heir and if he had sired any of Atriarch Imrell's three children—

Well. Chenya Imrell was ship clan to the bone, so she kept clan traditions. She took no consort, acknowledged none of her children as her direct issue (despite the fact she *had* birthed each of them being a matter of public record for none of the three had yet earned all of their scars), and did not entertain questions regarding their parentage.

Which left poor uncle Hnan with the practical but unpalatable solutions his Elders favored: either admit his impotence and general incompetence and relinquish the leadership of House Imos to his elder sister (who ought to have been Atriarch in the first place) or confirm Ylaen (her bastard savage-blooded son) as heir.

Some had even agitated quite vigorously for Maketh, the youngest brother, to be named the direct successor to the Imos throne.

As was often the case with Hnan Imos whenever he was presented with a sensible proposal, he punished those who benefited, no matter how loyal, then proceeded to butcher the implementation by only taking the parts he liked and adding new twists that undermined what little good remained.

So: here Maketh was, dead to the world for all intents and purposes, and here, too, was Ylaen.

He tried to put his resentful thoughts out of his mind and concentrate purely on the physical sensations alone. That wasn't supposed to be hard; he was supposed to be; he was supposed to want this—

Good thing that Rahelu could not see his grimace; good thing she was so lost in the pretense he'd encouraged that she wasn't paying the slightest attention to him; good thing that all he had to do was lie there and pretend he didn't mind her painting over the ship's deck with an Evocation of a pallet in a tiny inn room where a kettle steamed over a merry fire, and facing away so she wouldn't have to confront the jarring dissonance of his scars.

How long would he have to last before his current performance would be enough to dispel any credibility to Elaram's slander?

He supposed if he were the heir his father and uncle wanted, he should do something. Take control of the situation, put Rahelu in a position where she had to acknowledge present reality, revel in the sight of his victory and her loss sinking in, drive the point home and...and delight in her cowed submission.

He didn't want that.

What was wrong with him?

That cursed question had haunted him his whole life so his mind did what it had always done best—shrank from the question and left the hollow shell of his body behind to cope on base instincts.

At least this time, Jhobon was close enough that he could flee through their tsol-bond, instead of losing himself in the stars.

Ylaen exchanged his consciousness of one set of physical sensations—the chill of the sea-soaked deck; the heat of Rahelu's empty embrace; her near-wordless cries (which sounded, to his ear, like they were one consonant off from a name that was not his)—for another:

The stuffiness of the cramped aftercabin, made stuffier by the damp shirt wrapped around his head. (Nheras, for some reason, had pulled the hatch closed after she'd gone below.)

The gritty sensation of powdery heartbane residue rubbing off on his shaky fingers as he wiped a damp rag over the faded and cracked black leather cover and tarnished silver clasps of...Solmoram's mage journal, apparently. (Jhobon, for some reason, was exceedingly unnerved though most of the heartbane powder had now resettled.)

And Nheras's measured, nasally tones.

"...been considering our little water shortage problem," she was saying as she gestured to the bucket of seawater she had brought with her. "And it occurred to me that perhaps the problem is not as dire as we believe."

She knows, Jhobon was thinking. *I didn't clean up the traces quickly enough.* His relief as he felt Ylaen settle into his familiar, logically ordered thought patterns was palpable enough to draw Nheras's attention.

She did not remark on the ripple of pale gold resonance in Jhobon's aura. Relief was, after all, a natural enough reaction to being told that there might be a feasible alternative to 'sailing on without a plan'.

Stall, Ylaen suggested. *She might be bluffing.* Ilyn was very good at pretending to be what she wasn't; she was possibly better at it than he was.

"It isn't?" Jhobon asked.

Never one to use words when blunt action sufficed, Nheras picked up a fallen cup and tilted its mouth so they could see a spoonful or so of cold tea still remained, thanks to its bulb-like shape. Faint, barely visible traces of discordance—heartbane vapors—smoked off the surface. She placed the cup back on the tea tray, scooped up an equivalent amount of seawater, and let it trickle into the cup from her palm.

The tea sizzled and foamed as the heartbane reacted to the salt in the seawater...and the resultant compound calcified into a white chalky deposit.

She took a sip, then offered the cup to Jhobon.

The clear blue liquid tasted both salty and bitter—like someone had tried to sweeten heartleaf tea with sugar but had picked up the wrong jar—but he didn't lose control of his limbs or his resonance senses.

Jhobon said, "That doesn't solve the problem; it merely delays the inevitable."

Nheras shrugged. "I never said I found a solution. I'm merely pointing out that we do, in fact, have a supply of sufficiently potable water that would last far, far longer than twelve days, even on full rations."

...*Damn*, Jhobon thought, and Ylaen was inclined to agree.

His uncle's plan had relied on House Imos's most loyal Dedicate usurping control of the mission from House Issolm, backed by the authority of Alozei Imrell's ship clan allies, waiting in the Dragon's seas. Then the Conclave had intervened and Maketh had had to improvise and now they were stuck with Alozei's very recognizable, commandeered sloop.

His father's plan had relied on a desperate need for water to drive them towards the city of sails, where the clan's superior numbers could take the weakened mages as hostages and use them to find the artifact. And Xya had gone to great lengths to issue him with reminders of his father's expectations, through Kerg's example.

Neither Atriarch Hnan Imos nor Zovresh of the Crimson Storm cared much that Ylaen (*or Jhobon*, his mind was quick to add, but if the two men cared little for Ylaen, they cared even less for Jhobon though Ylaen would have died long ago if not for him) didn't want anything to do with their plans.

What about our plan? Jhobon thought.

Ylaen didn't like their plan either; it involved a whole lot of guesswork about the true nature of the Endless Gate based on Silcarez's ramblings hinging on Reshwim making a critical error in translation, and there was a high risk of them both ending up in the exact situation they'd fled all those years ago. Aleznuaweites might believe that no Augury was certain, but the sages—

The sages had never been wrong.

You said you didn't have a solution.

I didn't then; I might now.

Jhobon's thoughts shifted back a day.

It took Ylaen five heartbeats to identify the unfamiliar emotion that prickled him as he witnessed Jhobon's entire recollection of events from Ghardon's charge to Elaram's acquiescence.

Jealousy.

None of his lovers had ever looked at him the way Elaram had looked at Jhobon in that single moment of startling discovery—one soul recognizing its own vulnerability in another—let alone go on to try forging that temporary connection into a new bridge.

(*There was solstice,* a part of him insisted, *when Rahelu looked at you through the dark and the rain—*

Fool! scoffed another part of him. *That was moonlight in her eyes; she can't bear to look at you. Not then, not when you saved her life, not moments ago, not now; and if you doubt it, you could crawl back inside your own body and see the truth for yourself.*

Which he very much did not want to do.)

It was small-minded and petty of him to begrudge Jhobon this one thing when he got to have everything else—especially when his tsol-ek never held anything back, never once looked at him with resentment—but he couldn't help the immediate, visceral surge of envy that screamed '*why him and not me?*' and the shame that followed after.

(Shame that was met with Jhobon's empathy—for who else knew, intimately, what it was like to live in someone's shadow?—and burned all the more fiercely for it.)

Useless milk-blooded spawn. All these years and the echo of his father's disappointment still cut sharper than his knives. *To think I roused the fleet and searched every ship on the seas for* this.

Stop sniveling and seize your fate like a man before I decide the sages were mistaken in their reading of the omens.

He breathed—they breathed—and focused on the issue before them.

They said, "Tsorek-fa is a surer destination."

"But in the wrong direction." Nheras waved a hand dismissively. "I find myself persuaded by my brother and sisters: since there is a confirmed source of freshwater on those smaller, nearer islands, we ought to sail for those."

"There's no guarantee we'll find a sufficient supply on that island."

"Considering our circumstances, any supply is better than no supply. That island is but one island, among many. We are as likely to succeed in finding more as we are likely to fail, and our chances are considerably improved if we bring those pesky skyrats along. And while the rest of us take stock, you can apply yourself to studying the starsong and puzzling out a viable course to the Desolate Isles."

"But the reefs—"

"Aren't actually a problem either, are they?" Her calculating gaze didn't waver. "Ylaen said you've both been to those atolls before. You know a safe path through the Dragon's Teeth."

Left unsaid: *'You know which islands have water.'*

They did, and their silence was as good as confirmation for her.

"So." Nheras picked up and wiped off the last dust-streaked volume that lay on top of Anathwan's bedsheets with her rag. Another thick, black leather-bound tome with silver clasps—twin to the one in Jhobon's hands—that, apart from the semi-dried white streaks on its cover and spine left behind by the heartbane residue, was in otherwise pristine condition. She idly flicked through the pages of the Issolm *Supplicant's Handbook.*

"Any particular, compelling reason why we should disobey explicit orders from the Exalted Dominance and our Atriarchs, given to us via our mission directive, to make a detour to the city of sails, when we have the means to continue at hand?"

They could overpower Issolm right now, but if they wanted things to stay that way, they'd have to kill at least two of them and they weren't prepared to go that far; Ylaen had already killed someone he shouldn't have.

Damned if they did; damned if they didn't.

Not if your uncle doesn't find out until after we succeed, Jhobon thought. *It's a long, long way to reach from Ennuost Yrg and he has to rely on my Atriarch's arm to do it. The ocean is wide.*

The ocean was wide…but so was Zovresh's shadow.

If they didn't sail the *Sooty Gull* straight to Tsorek-fa…

Mother, Ylaen thought.

Too late to despair over that; Hnan Imos had sent Rysere Imos away. Far, far from Ennuost Yrg; as deep inland as one could go into the heart of the Ngutoccai continent without actually venturing into one of House Isilc's mines. He didn't know which was more ludicrous: the thought that Hnan Imos might bury his enmity with Relk Isilc long enough to strike a deal (the possibility *had* crossed Ylaen's mind…and been ruled out by the uncle who didn't hate him or his mother) or the idea that a few hundred kual of land might stop Zovresh from taking what he wanted just because his deep-hulled warships couldn't sail up the Suusradi or the Tsojo rivers.

No. All that Hnan Imos had accomplished by banishing Rysere Imos was to deepen Ylaen's long-standing resentment into hatred.

Three weeks ago, after Petitioning had concluded but before the Houses had made their final decisions, Ylaen had gone straight from handing over the ringleader of the smugglers whose illicit business had been undercutting House

Imos's margins in the dreamleaf trade into the custody of the sub-commander of the city guard's southern district to being summoned to his mother's receiving chamber.

Rysere Imos had greeted him with a choked cry of, "My darling son," and squeezed the breath out of him in a vise-like embrace before saying, "There's such wonderful news!" (The joy in her voice had not matched her red-rimmed eyes or her closed-off aura or the sight of her half-packed trunk.) He hadn't had the chance to respond; a young Guild trainee had arrived on his heels, puffing from her run, to drag him from the upper levels of the Imos estate down to the work-rooms below ground where Rysere's youngest brother had been waiting.

"No theatrics, Ylaen," Maketh Imos had said, stern and serious as sharpened steel. "Not a hint of disrespect, under-stand? Not a word, not a look, not a flicker in your aura. He's after any excuse to get rid of you; don't gift him one," and before uncle Maketh had finished saying all he had to say, both of them had been summoned by his other uncle's most decorated lackey to an audience in the Imos throne room.

Atriarch Hnan Imos had made a point of receiving his nephew according to ancient Aleznuan tradition dating back to before Exile: Ylaen had had to leave his knives, strip naked, and walk the full three hundred strides from the doors to kneel before his uncle's towering golden throne with all the Elders of House Imos standing around as witness to his Supplicant's oaths and the one-sided conversation that followed.

"Stop flinching, boy," Hnan Imos had said, while four priests—one from each of the temples—chanted benedictions and waved censers stinking of frankincense and poured blessed waters over Ylaen's bowed head and bled his arm. "It's a shallow cut, not a mortal wound."

One of the attendant Elders had pointed to his unscarred back and whispered into his uncle's ear.

Hnan Imos frowned. "That would have been pertinent to know before we began this mummery. Alas. Pray, then, for my son."

'I am not your son!' Ylaen had wanted to shout.

But uncle Maketh's warning was fresh in his ears and anyway, the man who ought to have claimed Ylaen as his son had not wanted him. So he had sat on his heels and let the priests carve their ugly line through the older scars on his right arm, growing increasingly light-headed as he watched his blood drain into a stone bowl while uncle Hnan nattered on and on about his expectations.

"And there will be no more of your wandering around in torn shirts like a homeless beggar," Hnan Imos had proclaimed. "You will dress as befits the heir of a great House."

Meaning: *'Hide those barbaric scars.'*

Ylaen had looked up at the old man—a gaudy, gem-encrusted gold monstrosity sat upon a larger, gaudier, even more gem-encrusted golden monstrosity—and said, very evenly, "As my Atriarch wills it."

Another slight frown from Hnan Imos had been all it took before the first Elder piped up.

"Supplicant Ylaen," Elder Nhorwen had said, "Show some filial piety."

He'd almost snarled back, *'I will, when my mother sits upon that throne,'* but by that time Rysere Imos and her personal effects had been hustled out of the Westgate by a small entourage of guards bribed to be loyal to Hnan Imos on the fastest horses House Imos could borrow, so all his defiance would have earned him was a night in the cells with only his satisfaction to keep him warm.

And possibly a bunch of hired knives aimed at his mother.

"I beg my father's forgiveness," Ylaen had said, eyes on the floor.

That had not been a lie.

Nor was it a fantasy; Zovresh *would* forgive and recognize him—if he lived up to his name.

Ylaen missed the Free Territories and the city of sails, but if he returned without redemption—without earning his scars—he would return to a life just as hollow as the one he had now. The thought of that clanless, empty existence turned his stomach worse than any punishment Hnan Imos might order; worse than what he would have suffered if Jhobon hadn't saved him from the sages.

You're sure you have a solution? Ylaen asked.

He waited as Jhobon's thoughts stepped him through the likely scenarios; fretted nearly as much as his tsol-ek was fretting beneath Nheras's increasingly suspicious stare as they delayed in their reply.

Twenty-five percent sure, Jhobon concluded.

Not as good as the odds of success on either Hnan Imos's or Zovresh's plans, but those were the best odds on their plan yet.

Alright, Ylaen decided. *Our plan.*

Stormbringer willing, may the audacity of it make his true father proud.

There was no need to bend the future if they could rewrite the past.

Our plan, Jhobon acknowledged as Ylaen withdrew through their bond and left him to distract Nheras with details on how, exactly, they were going to negotiate the *Gull's* safe passage through the Dragon's Teeth.

Ylaen regained his sense of his own body just in time to register Rahelu collapsing on top of him in the shuddering aftermath of her release.

Well, good.

He didn't care if she was pretending or who she pretended he was anymore, because now it was his fucking turn.

She made no complaints as he rolled them over with a grunt—because she was asleep.

He wilted instantly.

She couldn't even do him the courtesy of waiting until he was done too?

Fuck her.

'*You tr-iiiiiiii-ied,*' Elaram's singsong voice sneered at him in his head, '*and you faaaaaiiiiiled.*'

Fuck Elaram too.

Before his mind could conjure another cutting retort on Elaram's behalf, Ylaen picked up Rahelu and the trousers she had discarded and stowed them both in the closest hammock below before he found the spyglass and settled himself aloft for the three-and-a-half spans that remained until dawnwatch because he wasn't the inconsiderate jerk Elaram made him out to be.

So when Nheras eventually came out of the aftercabin clutching one of those Issolm handbooks to her chest like it was a lifeline and pleaded with him most eloquently to reconsider and revise his earlier decision, it was easy to respond with a light, carefree shrug and say, "Very well, love, you've convinced me: we sail east, through the Dragon's Teeth and the Desolate Isles to the Endless Gate, as the Dominion demands."

NHERAS WATCHED Ylaen slide off his perch and stroll aft from the corner of her eye.

Once he was busy making whatever adjustments were needed to bring the *Sooty Gull* around and point its bow towards their new heading, she made her own shaky way below. There, in the absolute dark she detested, safe under the precautionary wards and barriers Maketh had laid down in the cargo hold, she opened Anathwan's copy of the Issolm *Supplicant's Handbook*. Counted until she found the section she wanted—'EMERGENCY PROTOCOLS' under 'MISSION PROCEDURES' beginning on page two hundred and seventy-seven—five pages from where she had left off perusing the volume in front of Jhobon at the first tingle against her fingers.

Nheras held her breath as she ran her hand down the center of the page.

Nothing. Just an ordinary page.

She turned it over and tried again with page two hundred and seventy-nine, her pulse fluttering as fast as a butterfly's wings.

This time, her fingertips encountered several things.

One: rough, ragged edges. Like someone had hastily gouged a circular, finger-deep hollow in the heart of the book.

Two: a thin arced band of glassy stone. Cold—warm?—to the touch, its surface dusted with tiny raised bumps.

Three: a glittering black resonance seal in the center. Intact, even if the brushstrokes of the character 'velaz' were smudged, like the ink hadn't been given enough time to dry.

She touched the seal and fed it the correct coded signature from its twin in the Elder's mage journal and triggered a warm Projection:

Rahelu, the message said in Anathwan's voice. *Keep the key safely hidden until the appointed time. Do not use it before you reach the heart of the Endless Gate. Remember my promise.*

INTERLUDE II: DEVOTION

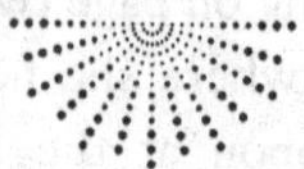

ONCE, UVESHT-MO HAD WALKED THE PATHS TO eternity at will.

He had been a younger man then; his faith strong, his body unbroken. As a greater adept of Enjela, the earth, the sea, the void—all existence—had been bound to him, blood and soul, and entry to the Starfather's realm was guaranteed through devotion alone.

No longer.

The vessel that staggered up the twisting slope of the tall sea cliff overlooking the west was a wretched creature. Folds of wrinkled skin, scratched and bleeding from spans spent worming through the thick, old-growth trees on this remote isle, hung loose upon his bony, stooped frame. His unsteady feet tripped on roots and slipped on dirt. With every step, the mountain threatened to throw him off its slopes.

Devotion might have propelled him to the summit, but it was a humble walking stick that kept his body from being dashed to pieces upon the sharp rocks in the churning surf below.

High above, beyond the edges of mortal hearing, the

heavens still sang. Reclaiming the symbols of his servitude had enhanced his ability to join with the holy hymn that filled him with power. It suffused his mind and spirit with a vitality his body no longer possessed, reduced sensations like pain and fear and hunger to distant concerns, and brought back the blessings he had forsaken:

Knowledge. Connection. Sight—

Where is my heir ascendant?

—amongst other things.

Stars gleamed in his mind as they rose, each scintillating point an anchor for the myriad threads of fate that linked soul to soul to soul to soul. However diminished he was, however forsaken his faith, his unending delight in the divine beauty of the Starfather's intent remained: pure, unadulterated, brilliant as the constellations of Fortune, twisted though they had become.

Where are my faithful?

No, devotion alone could not carry him to the Endless Gate to see Enjela damned and her works destroyed.

For that, he needed a ship.

Uvesht-mo wrenched his mind from the concerns of heaven. He wept as he perverted and bent the future further from true. He rearranged events; found the results unsatisfactory and so rearranged them again, splicing probability after probability in differing combinations until every divergence he could track had circled back to a grand convergence.

Soon, very soon, he would see the aborted xuuqoshtalogte rite fulfilled.

You have strayed far, beloved.

He would make the last sacrifice.

Repent, and be saved.

And, Starfather willing, that would end Enjela's cycle of sin.

So wracked was his body by the aftermath of his Fortunement and the deep knells still reverberating through the fabric of existence that it took a day and a night to descend the mountain.

When he returned to the shore, he found a ship at anchor. Crimson-sailed; captained by a woman: tall, heavily scarred, and soul-bound; come as supplicant and armed with many offerings.

He accepted them and he accepted her, along with the burden of her faith.

No, devotion alone was not enough.

But it could be exploited.

PART III
THE ENDLESS GATE

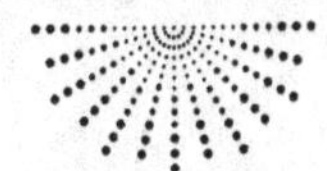

27

FAULT

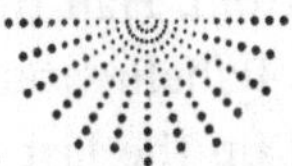

THE 5TH DAY OF EARLY HARVEST, 530 A.E./A.F.

WHEN THE SUN ROSE THE DAY AFTER THEIR emergency consultation with Anathwan, Ghardon and Elaram did not rise with it.

So Rahelu (shouldering the bulk of Ghardon's weight, as Ylaen sulked and refused to do more than help take his legs) and Jhobon (clutching Elaram to his chest like a precious bauble) moved them into the aftercabin, which Nheras had turned into a makeshift sickroom. The whole place and all its contents—indisposed senior mages included—had been scrubbed to spotless, heartbane-residue-free perfection with seawater and soap.

Very, very thorough of her.

Rahelu left Nheras to tend the comatose mages while she tended the ship with Ylaen and Jhobon.

They agreed on an inverted watch rhythm—eight spans on, four spans off—dictated by the severely reduced number of capable hands, the continued necessity of maintaining an active Seeking at all times, and the new demands of the sickroom's vigils.

They drank brackish water, obtained through a tedious

guesswork-filled process that involved scrubbing out an emptied cask with ash, filling it with heartbane-tainted water, adding boiled seawater, stirring until the sizzling, foaming mixture turned pale and occluded as rice water, then leaving it to settle overnight, before pouring off the clear sapphire-blue liquid for drinking and cooking, and scraping the chalky white residue off the bottom. Half the dregs went to Nheras for her attempted cures; Rahelu would have tossed the rest, but Jhobon, having used up the last of Maketh's supplies to repair the *Gull's* damaged wards, insisted on keeping it for experimentation. (The product turned out to be a reasonably functional substitute for both chalk and charcoal—though not for resonance crystal dust.)

They tiptoed in and out of the aftercabin at the changeover of their watches, bringing Nheras whatever she ordered. Clean cloths. Rations. Dishes of resonance crystal dust and powdered heartroot and other medicinal ingredients (none of which Rahelu could name). Their veins. The infusions Nheras mixed from their blood samples had to be forced into the invalids with as much fresh water as could be spared (which was nowhere near as much as their bodies required) through a combination of physical force and Command to ensure they swallowed, rather than choked on, every precious drop.

None of it worked.

On the fourth such day, Rahelu glimpsed green-tinted clouds and lighter patches of water through the eyes of a gull. The flock soared ahead. Ylaen and Jhobon dropped everything to reduce sail and slowed their sloop to a crawl. They hove to three ship-lengths shy of the reef's edge—and the burned-out husk of a submerged wreck.

The sunken ship had been a fearsome vessel, judging by the enormity of its broken hull. The canted deck, shredded canvas, and snapped branches of red coral embedded in the smashed planks told a clear tale of its untimely end: crippled, then pulverized, by broadsides from stem to stern, the damage exacerbated when the ship had run aground at speed and dashed itself to pieces upon the coral. There, it must have been boarded, crew taken captive, decks plundered of worthy salvage, banners and signal flags and hulk fired to leave nothing by which it could be identified, and left to succumb to the inexorable grip of the Stormbringer's fist.

Half a fathom straight down through the crystal clear waters, the remains of the drowned rested on the sandy seabed. Naked bones gleamed white beside the silver flash of weapons—picked clean by the razor-toothed, venom-spined, myriad-finned sea creatures teeming in the shallows.

When the waves washed a splintered spar against the *Sooty Gull's* hull, Ylaen appropriated one of her nets to fish it out.

"How long ago?" he asked.

Rahelu turned the spar over in her hands. Saltwater had leached away any trace of resonance. "A week or ten days, give or take." Stole an uneasy glance at the empty horizon, then shrugged. "Maybe as recently as two. Hard to tell."

He exchanged grim looks with Jhobon, then flung the spar over the side.

There they floated, above the watery grave, memorizing the twists and swirls of the currents as they watched the broken spar drift away, waiting an eternity for clouds to clear, tide to turn, and the Skymother to move her lamp so it would cast no deceptive shadow on the water's surface. Heartbeats stretched into spans as they negotiated the treacherous coral-fanged pass, leaving her nerves scraped raw. When they found safe anchorage at last, Rahelu would have cried, had her salt-wicked body any moisture to spare for tears.

Salvation was a scrubby, crescent-shaped cay.

No bigger than two or three kual long from end to end.

Five hundred strides across at its widest point and gorgeously trimmed with generous borders of sparkling white beaches dotted with the drowsing, unruffled forms of their feathered guides. Alert breeding pairs of glossy white questryls met them—four clumsy, shambling invaders—with flurried wingbeats and clacking bills while herding their goggle-eyed, fluff-balled, speckled-feathered offspring away from the water's edge.

They slaked their thirst on the tiny spring bubbling up through the sand, then stripped the islet and its shallows of everything it had to offer. Scrub and salvaged driftwood for fuel. Eggs purloined from sea turtle nests, along with several sun-basking juveniles. All the sweet water they could bottle with flagons and flasks and a couple of casks before the incoming tide drowned the spring.

Not enough; not nearly enough, but nobody dared linger.

Early skyarc found them hurriedly weighing anchor to catch the very end of the slack tide that permitted safe egress to the open sea:

Rahelu—sun-blinded and dazzled by reflections—mistook a coral head for a cloud shadow.

Jhobon—eyes similarly strained and further fatigued from spans spent reconciling ancient star maps to current readings by faint moonlight—called out the correction from the bow a heartbeat too late.

Though Ylaen threw his weight against the tiller at once, he was not quick enough.

Below, Nheras shouted in alarm.

The *Sooty Gull* shuddered as its hull was raked from prow to amidships. Somehow, by the Stormbringer's mercy, they suffered no leaks. Later inspection, however, revealed the Dragon's Teeth had left an indelible mark: a swathe of finger-deep gouges along three strakes on the starboard side, which had been scraped clean of barnacles and algae and kelp.

The very next day, while Jhobon was cross-examining Rahelu's interpretation of the directional vector and intensity of the starsong incessantly shivering her bones:

"Give me your pendant, fish guts," Nheras demanded, wiggling one set of expectant fingers.

All Rahelu heard was the echo of *'Give me your Petition'* reverberating across time and the empty ocean with the starsong's tolling.

If Ylaen had not been lounging close by at the tiller—

But he was, wearing nothing on his upper half in the sweltering heat save for his scars and his sly, self-satisfied smile, his dark eyes drinking in the rising tension in her aura.

So Rahelu had to rein in the instincts clamoring for her to slap the smirk off Nheras's face (*'See! See!'* that expression had gloated. *'Let him come to you; here's how I shall take him away again.'*) and reiterate to herself:

We are sisters, sisters; I said we should let go; we agreed not to quarrel in public and so shame our House—especially not in front of Imos fucking No-sleeves—and I owe debts; debts of duty and obedience to Anathwan for the duration of this mission; debts of gratitude and affection to Ghardon and Elaram for...for...

(*Three days*, memory reminded her, *they took turns tending you in the aftermath of Maketh's wrath for three fucking days!*)

...at least a month, quite possibly a year, or perhaps even longer, after we return home.

(*If*, logic interjected yet again, with another unhelpful inventory of their dwindling supplies. *If you return home.*)

Rahelu surrendered the mist-filled focus stone to Nheras, though it near flayed her insides to do so, then unleashed her ire on Jhobon.

"Challenge me on the direction of the starsong's origins one more time, and I will cut off the four fingers on your brush hand, fashion them into a compass, and sew them onto your face so you can remember which way we're supposed to go—north, as the gull flies—and don't you dare veer from it again."

"That's not how compasses w—"

"Keep arguing and I'll cut off your thumb, too. Then Elaram will be *very* upset by the loss when she wakes."

When she wakes, when they wake, Rahelu repeated to herself over and over again as she watched Nheras disappear into the aftercabin with her pendant. *They are going to wake, they will they will they will—*

She abandoned a cross-eyed, tongue-tied Jhobon to his contemplation of *that* particular puzzle in favor of filling a flagon with some wine.

Ylaen followed.

To her flagon, he added the last of the honey and dream-leaf and gods only knew what kind of spices.

The wine tasted cloyingly sweet as they poured it down each other's throats.

Everything dulled. Her disquiet thoughts. The intensifying starsong. The inner voice that branded her a traitor for passing around the pendant Lhorne had entrusted to her like the heirloom resonance crystal was some common tool. Everything, except the pleasant hum in her veins that sent her floating through a carefree void.

She swallowed and swallowed and swallowed.

Then all too suddenly, the flagon was empty. They were reduced to licking the splashes and trickles of wine they had spilled on each other and dribbled out of their mouths.

By the time an utterly drained Nheras came down to the hold to return an equally drained pendant with a shaky Ghardon on her heels, she was too drunk to care that Nheras had accomplished her goal, and she had not.

(*Hah!* sneered a part of her that was all ugly spite and

jagged jealousy. *Didn't manage to heal the senior mages too now, did she?*)

She was also far too busy doing what Nheras had pushed her into doing.

Very, very thoroughly.

"Oh," Rahelu said when her eyes managed to focus on Ghardon's disapproving ones at last. "You're awake!" Then, "Oh. Oh!"

She soon forgot about saying anything else; Ylaen had redoubled his efforts when he realized they had an audience.

From somewhere vaguely overhead: the soft *thump* and faint *clatter* of Jhobon's notebook and brush pen falling to the deck; the softer *thud* of him sitting down; and his very soft, low groan of "Ohhhhh..." that answered Elaram's high-pitched, playful giggling and rather enthusiastic slurping.

Ghardon said, "Congratulations, Ilyn. You are now officially my favorite sister."

To that mortal insult, Nheras replied, "Don't you dare try and kiss me too," while poking through the remaining slices of preserved fruits Ylaen had cut up but neglected to put into their flagon of wine.

"I'm grateful, but not that grateful; you'll have to content yourself with Ela's thanks and if you feel stinted, I'm sure she'd be happy to express some more of it."

"If she tries it again, I will put her straight back into that heartbane coma."

"Fuck!" Rahelu said and kept saying it, louder and louder, until Ghardon and Nheras finally got the message and took their citrus wedges, soaps, hair combs, and dripping disgust with them.

Plenty of disgust remained behind; some of it was even hers.

Fucking uppity House-born.

"Harder," she snapped at Ylaen.

He slammed her shoulders against the bulkhead for it.

"Is that all you've got?"

That taunt earned her a pinning by the throat with his forearm.

"Harder!" she rasped.

Slam.

"Is that"—*slam*—"hard"—*slam!*—"enough"—*SLAM!*—"for you?"

A metallic tang in her mouth; the world spinning.

She'd bitten through her lip.

Ylaen's next breaths came in great, gasping gulps that were harsh on her ear and cheek.

"Try harder," she panted.

Ylaen tried harder.

When they were done, his hipbones had well and truly blacked and blued her thighs; her spine and sides sported far worse.

She had rewarded him with ten claw marks down the lovely, smooth, no-longer-unblemished expanse of his back, some lovely new half-moon scars on his neck and shoulders, and lovely mottled bruises of his own.

Ghardon rewarded them both with his unwanted judgment and pointed glances at the Ideth pendant she'd immediately looped around her neck once more.

Not fair.

Especially when he turned such a blind eye to Elaram's carrying on with Jhobon. Especially since Rahelu hadn't been the one to come up with this stupid scheme in the first place.

Nheras's idea; therefore: Nheras's fault.

Not hers. Not hers.

That said, the arrangement was not without its perks.

Ylaen's claim to possessing "excellent hands" had been no idle boast, and it was not difficult to prevail upon him to use them for her benefit.

There was physical solace to be found during the times their off-watches overlapped in the brief but restful naps that followed after she took her pleasure from him. (He, she assumed, took his at some subsequent point while she drifted into slumber, for searing passion now preceded the blades and blood and chains in her half-remembered dreams.)

Sharing a hammock, too, was convenient. As harvest waned, so did her ability to shut out the starsong's susurrations. Soon, whenever sleep—that most precious commodity after water—flitted away, it would invariably leave her in restless thrall to the alien reverberations thrumming through her veins. That ceaseless, insistent melody-that-was-no-melody tormented her; made her body flush and her resonance aura tense with the agony of suspended resolution; wracked her entire being with a desperate, aching need that drove her to reach for him in search of ease.

And if what she got from their frantic, wordless coupling was emptiness instead of wholeness—

So what? Pain could drown regret as effectively as any pleasure.

After a while, she forgot the difference.

KUAL BY KUAL, the *Sooty Gull* chewed up the sea.

The sea chewed at them.

They could not swallow the sea, so they chewed on each other instead.

"SAGES' sake, Rahelu!" Jhobon shouted at her from his seat by the steering post, red-faced with sunburn and resonance aura bloodied with frustration. "We can't sail through the Dragon's Spine that way, do you hear me?"

"Starsong says that way."

"The currents are too swift; the waters are too shallow; the wind is blowing the wrong direct—"

Rahelu shouted back: "I don't give a shit!" Crossed his squinty skyward glare with a flinty one aimed downward from where she roosted and roasted in the rigging. "That"—she jabbed at the horizon—"is where we need to go, so figure it out, genius. Silcarez did."

Loose pages fluttered out as he shook his notebook at her. "Silcarez had three astronomers, five scout ships, two years' worth of provisions, and teams of Seekers quartering the seas, partnered with seabirds trained from the egg! He wasn't reliant on a flock of wild gulls as he blindly followed some mystical starsong nobody else could hear—"

"Elder Anathwan heard it," Ghardon said. The only time he had spoken up to participate in any conversation she had initiated these last two weeks. "So did I." Obligatory show of Issolm solidarity complete, he went back to retching over the port toprail.

"—which, by the way, is impossible unless we're talking about encrypted transmissions through a long-range Obfuscated network. That technology only became stable enough for cross-continental relays in the last eight—"

"Five," Nheras corrected absently. She turned a page in Anathwan's mage journal.

"—five years and even then, there are no transmission nodes located in the middle of the Desolate Isles that would bridge that kind of distance! You'd need—"

"I hear it as well," Elaram said softly from within the circle of Jhobon's arm, which shut him up until she added, "Sometimes. Usually loudest at deepnight, as starrise waxes," and set him off again.

"That doesn't make any sense! Why can you hear it and we three"—a wild gesticulation of his hands at Ylaen, himself, and Nheras—"can't?"

Another *crinkle* as Nheras turned the next page.

"Perhaps," Ghardon said, "we're more"—he retched again—"perceptive."

Nheras snorted.

Jhobon said, "*You're* not; you're just sensitive. And neither of those attributes have anything to do with—"

"You want to hear it again?" Rahelu asked. "Listen, then!"

She reached for Projection.

May he, too, have the joy of being assaulted by the hair-raising, bone-itching, incessant alien emanations that haunted her, night and day.

The ambient resonance warped. Twenty gray ribbons, dark as thunderclouds, streaked forth from Ylaen's hand like the Stormbringer's own lightning.

"Behave." Ylaen stepped forward as exhaustion struck her. "Or I'll make you behave."

Rahelu fell out of the crosstrees and into his waiting arms, unable to reply as he carried her below deck.

Nobody else seemed inclined to reply on her behalf either. Nheras turned another page, Ghardon continued to commune with the waves, and Jhobon went back to scribbling notations on his charts and explaining them to an eager Elaram.

WHILE SHE WAITED for Ylaen to release her, Rahelu considered whether she ought to reply.

Decided no.

Her head, her heart, and her lower belly ached too much. She could not muster the thought and willpower and energy needed for a reply; she'd used it all up, bit by bit, over the last twelve days.

Two fucking weeks of expressing very, very thorough *thank-yous* had gotten her no closer to discovering the exact nature of the treason House Imos plotted. Ylaen was as close-mouthed as a clam about everything: his past, his future, his House.

Even now, as he laid her down in their hammock, he had nothing useful to say.

"Are you done lashing out at people who don't deserve it for things that aren't their fault?"

Rahelu made a low noise in her throat.

"What was that?"

"I said, go away."

Ylaen did not go away.

Ylaen climbed in with her, all hard muscle and simmering amusement, his resonance aura clear of the anxiety that was ever-present in the rest of theirs.

Ylaen had not finished taking liberties either: one excellent hand kneaded her lower back as the nimble fingers of his other excellent hand brushed her hair off the nape of her neck, then crept underneath her shirt.

"I know an infallible cure"—murmured in her ear, followed by a nibble at her earlobe, then a whole trail of kisses that ventured down the side of her neck—"one that's guaranteed to chase the pain away."

"Stormbringer strike you down, you absolute ass. I could have died."

"Rahelu, love, if I were trying to kill you, you would know." He tugged gently at her shoulder.

"Not in the mood, Imos."

"That's easily addressed." Rose-red mist stirred in the ambient resonance as he pressed himself against her back. "I don't mind a little blood."

She reached down between their bodies. "What about when it's yours?" Yanked—more firmly than he preferred—and dug her nails in.

He yelped, hands freezing where they were.

"I could give you another scar here"—she squeezed, twisting her grip as she did—"to match the one you've been cutting into your arm."

He'd made a start on the new scar the day after they'd resolved to sail for the Desolate Isles as Anathwan had directed: a thin, sinuous, dashed line that originated at the base of his throat and wove its way past three other patterns to curl around his left wrist. Unusual in its broken design, when every other scar he bore was contiguous.

"No need." His voice came out strained, a good half-octave higher than normal. "One talog-te at a time."

That was more information than he'd ever volunteered before. She relaxed her grip fractionally; he let his breath out in a *whoosh* of air.

"What's talog-te?"

His turn to pull away, but she had him so he didn't go far, especially when she rolled over to face him after all.

"What are these"—she ran the fingers of her other hand along the bumps and ridges of the largest scar: a closed spiral centered over his heart, with forked lines that branched off in every direction—"if they are not just mere decoration?"

"A clan secret," he said. "One we don't speak of to the uninitiated."

"Is that so?" There was a sense of symmetry and balance to the placement of his scars and how each section interacted with its neighbors that spoke of some overall purpose.

"Mmmhmm." His slow smile returned, and so did his wandering hands. "Shall we play trickster's truth?"

"A Harbinger matching wits with a Seeker?" She laughed. "You will pay more forfeits in answers than I will in kez."

"Kez? What use is kez while we drift through the Storm-bringer's domain? No," he said. "I will have your forfeits in kisses." He lowered his head to demonstrate exactly where he'd like them on her body. "Kisses and one night without you hiding behind that pendant or numbing your mind with wine or losing yourself in your false Evocations."

Give him free rein to her secrets?

"I don't think so." A little honey to soothe the sting. "Kisses and a wager on the result."

"What will you wager? A favor?"

"One whole and complete truth for another."

"...that's a rather disappointing prize."

"Do you have no interest in learning of our mission's true purpose?"

Not a lie; merely a question. A question they had all asked, more than once. A question they still had no answer for, despite the spans upon spans they'd spent poring through the senior mages' notes.

Besides her sketches, Anathwan had left shorthand summaries of Silcarez's memoirs and extensively annotated passages of Belruonian scripture that nobody (save Jhobon) had the patience to parse and cross-reference to Reshwim's accounts. The Elder had also left what appeared to be a series of visualizations intended as the foundation for a complex Seeming of Ennuost Yrg. Detailed visualizations. Exhaustively so. The chain of plausibilities extended some five, ten, fifty years into the future.

Dedicate Maketh had left eight pages, glued together by their edges into a larger, rolled-up sheet: a design for a sprawling resonance ward of unknown purpose and massive scale.

Ylaen stilled. "You said you couldn't rouse either of them."

"We couldn't."

A pause. "Very well." He leaned back. "Ask away."

She picked one of his scars at random.

"This one"—she traced the grid-like design of nine lines in a cross-hatch—"resembles a repulsion ward." A simplified version; a proper repulsion ward would have used twice the lines, all of them shaped to counter incoming resonance from a specific trajectory. "You have one at each shoulder, joined into a greater form that looks like a distorted sigil of Protection."

"Power, actually, but you're close enough that I'll pay it. Go on."

"This one"—an intricate, geometric pattern of angled lines that covered his left arm from shoulder to elbow like armor: they resembled concentric nested arrowheads but, upon close examination, you could see each triangular 'scale' was connected to the next; all part of a single line—"works like an amplification ward. This part concentrates resonance and that part passively harnesses them. That's why the Projections you channel through your left hand manifest with greater strength."

"Top marks."

Ylaen pointed. One rose-red ribbon flew towards her from the index finger on his left hand. The slender Projection—so concentrated it gleamed like silk—twined itself around her right wrist: a very impractical bracelet.

Heat spread through her lower belly; swept the pain away and rushed straight to her loins.

A slight crook of his finger and her hand went willingly to his belt buckle.

"Curious that the same design isn't there on your right."

He tilted his head but didn't answer.

Fine. That wasn't the secret she was after.

"But this one"—the fingers of her left hand drifted over to the partially healed cuts he'd spent each night repeatedly carving into his flesh—"does not fit with any resonance ward that I know. Yet it must have some purpose."

"Wrong." He loosened the knot on his loincloth. "I'll have the first of your forfeits now."

Strictly speaking, her statement didn't qualify as a guess, but indulging his interpretation made him more amenable to the tentative beginnings of her Seeking, so she didn't bother to argue the rules of trickster's truth.

There, beneath his surface emotions of desire and frustration, was a hint of fear. Fear and grief and yearning all tangled together in a knot of ivory, black-blue, and silver-violet wire.

Forfeit paid, she said: "I know little of the Free Speech and even less of your customs, but I have heard of achwa talog-te."

His muscles grew taut beneath her fingers.

"It cannot be tsol-ek-na, for Jhobon's scars are unchanged. And it is not tsol-mal-ek."

"Why not?" He traced the line of her collarbone and the plane beneath it, where his blade had scored her. "I've marked you." The arch of her back. The curve of her breasts, her waist, her buttocks. "Many, many times."

She looked. "Seems faded to me. Fitting for a temporary diversion that neither you nor I will care to remember or mourn when it ends."

"Cruel of you. Would you not miss our sparring?"

"Your skill with your spear is sadly lacking." The burst of indignation in his resonance aura had her laughing again. "I can't have been the first to tell you so; surely Elaram made her disappointment clear. If you want somebody to stroke your...ego, you can go back up on deck and cry to Jhobon, though I suspect he'll be unavailable."

"That's not what—" Ylaen began and then cut off whatever he was about to say. "Whoever taught you of our customs, they explained tsol-ek-na poorly."

She sat up. "Educate me then."

He sat up too, eyes narrowed. "Is that the secret you wish to know?"

"No." She readied her Seeking, focused it squarely on him, alert for the slightest fluctuations in his resonance aura, and stated: "You have begun achwa-te-gish-no."

There it was: a brief flicker of surprise that tinted his resonance aura yellow, matched by an involuntary flutter of his eyelids.

"And you have begun it without your ritual knife"—he'd done it with the point of his dagger; not the ornate, gold-hilted steel weapon he had carried aboard the *Winged Arrow* with its distinctive, waved blade—"without witness"—on the nights when he had starwatch, he had stolen away from her side only once her limbs had grown heavy and languid—"or song."

Ylaen regarded her steadily with a level of intensity that he never displayed, not even in the sparring circle.

Rahelu's heart beat faster.

He got up and stalked towards the companionway.

She harried him the whole way up onto the main deck.

"What is the great task you have sworn to complete, marked in flesh and sealed with blood, in the sight of the sky, the stars, and the sea?"

He continued aft without another word, startling Jhobon and Elaram apart from their cuddling beneath the mainsail with his loud, long strides.

Ylaen had no intention of keeping his end of the bargain.

"Coward!" she yelled after him. "Impotent sot!" She picked up a bucket and hurled it at his head—he ducked and she narrowly missed striking Ghardon as he emerged from the aftercabin. "Honorless, limp-dicked spawn of a wharf rat!"

Unfair of her, but she'd just invested two fucking weeks of her life into Nheras's stupid plan—one that would have worked far better if their roles had been reversed—and now that Ylaen had finally let something slip, she was loath to let him go.

"Answer me, Imos!"

They passed by the drink barrel. She scooped a double handful of precious water to rinse the taste of him out of her mouth, but the brackish liquid only deepened the salty tang on her tongue, which made her all the more angry.

When they were clear of the boom, she launched herself at his back.

He whirled around so fast that she flew straight into his grasp, but he hadn't had time to set his stance properly so they tumbled to the deck. She'd never won a single bout against him in the sparring circle whether they had knives or not—he had the advantage in weight, in reach, and strength—but there was no circle now, just the urge to break his skull into pieces and tear the truth out of him.

Again, he slammed her shoulders against the wood. Again, he pinned her by the throat with his forearm.

This time, she had no compunction about crossing the line from indirect to direct Seeking. She shaped her focus into a needle-thin point to drill past his resonance ward and the spiral etched over his heart through a tiny gap, imperceptible to the naked eye, that she'd only discovered after days and nights of tracing its lines in the dark.

His fault; it was his fault: he had reneged first. This was revenge; this was self-defense.

Why did you really kill that Conclave mage? Anger gave her Projection sharp edges, even as her vision darkened. *What do you know of Maketh's plans? How deep does your House's treachery go?*

She burrowed through the outer layers of his mind, Seeking the buried fear/grief/yearning she'd sensed earlier. Found it. Now! Evocation to bare his secrets to the world:

Horror lurks inside the Winged Arrow's hold.

Kerg holds his rejected tsol-blade; the steel is blooded on both edges. A long scarlet slash runs from wrist to elbow on Kerg's left arm—the first mark of tsol-ek-na. The snatches of intricate polyrhythms superimposed upon the staid beats of Kerg's resonance signature that speak of a home and a claim in a language he has tried to cleave from his heart.

Recognition sparks in the wild eyes of Csorath's third mate.

'Hello, little cub.'

He despairs.

Xya has found him at last.

'My, my. How you have grown.' Kerg uncoils from his rigid stance with a lethal grace that belongs to another. 'Come closer, love, and let an old woman get a good look at you.'

To move is to accept Xya's challenge; to accept Xya's challenge is to accept the name the sages gave him. But no power under heaven, however mighty, is worth losing his soul.

He does not move. 'Release him and begone, Xya.'

'Oh, ho-ho!' A mock shudder. 'What a fierce growl you've learned.'

The tsol-blade advances. He retreats. They circle.

'Come, little cub! Show me your fangs and claws; I would see whether you've inherited the mettle to match your sire's spitting image.'

Blood drips steadily from the mate's bleeding arm and scribes a broken line in their tracks.

'Begone, Xya,' he says again. 'This man has sworn other ties; he is no part of the clan.'

'Tsol-ek-na,' is her unequivocal answer. 'His soul is bound.'

'Through no consent of his!'

'That does not matter—as you well know.' Quick little thrusts of the tsol-blade between each word; feints to test his guard. 'But I am not here to debate the forms.'

'Why are you here?'

The circle is complete. He backs away, and away again, careful not to cross the line. There can be no return if he does.

'To bring my son warning.'

Envy stabs him to his core, and yet—

'I will tell him,' he says, for there are no secrets between tsol-na and tsol-ek.

'A new sage who wields ancient powers has come.'

How Jhobon will rejoice when he hears that his theory has been proven correct.

'Zovresh has changed his mind.'

Meaning: Zovresh has tired of waiting.

'Your milk-blooded kin will find no allies waiting in the Dragon's Teeth, for the Stormbringer's judgment strikes swiftly and without mercy.'

Xya's next thrust is aimed at his throat and carries the full power of the first mate's matured strength and heavier weight behind it. He deflects the blow—just. Is forced by the recoil to twist the wrong way.

Now he has nowhere to run.

'A failed achwa talog-te is not the end. You may still redeem yourself. Bring this ship and its bounty to Tsorek-fa. Offer them as tribute to Zovresh, and demand achwa-te-gish-no. Prove yourself worthy of your scars with dance and song, by blade and blood, before witnesses, and he will claim you as—'

GET OUT GET OUT GET OUT—

Her mind slammed back into her own body. Shadows swam before her eyes; her breath wheezed in her bruised throat. The fierce, staccato clangs of a knife fight cut through the roaring in her ears, followed by a gasp of pain and subsequent clatter of someone being disarmed as the roaring slowly resolved into overlapping shouts:

"—fucking traitor, Imos! You knew that—"

"—was a misunderstanding, no harm—"

"—stand aside, Jhobon, he's a—"

"—'s death was not my fault! I didn't betr—"

Her limbs trembled as she rolled over. She crawled forward anyway, towards the mast, where Jhobon fended off a spitting Elaram and her Seeking while Ghardon and Ylaen were locked arm-to-arm, grappling over the fallen knife.

"Stop!"

Her squeak carried no further than her own ears.

Stop! she sent.

That, too, went unheeded.

STOP.

A sudden blast of confusion swept across the deck with the force of a late harvest gale. The four Supplicants fighting forward of the mast staggered, then fell to their knees; Rahelu, already down on all fours, simply froze in place.

Where were they?

What was she doing?

Why were they fighting?

She puzzled over those questions until the gray fog clouding her mind dissipated and she saw Nheras, standing over Ylaen with her hand pressed to the back of his neck and one sandaled foot pinning his knife to the deck.

Jhobon lunged for Nheras but was hauled up short by Elaram and Ghardon.

"My sister asked you a question, Imos." Nheras crouched. Orange-white resonance shaped like wire sprouted from her fingers, the bright lines thickening and weaving until they formed into links of a glowing chain that slowly tightened around his neck. "I suggest you answer her."

He glared at them through his fall of black hair. "My name, Issolm," he snarled, "is *Ylaen.*"

His resonance aura shivered, shrank in on itself, then exploded with anger. Not the smoldering rage Rahelu knew, but a cold one, its bite sharp as the icewinds that blew from the Unomelaje in truewinter. Implacable as the storm.

One moment, Nheras commanded the deck; the next, Ylaen's Projection shattered hers.

Still on his knees, he brought his left fist up; twisted and struck Nheras square in the ribs.

She crumpled to the deck without a sound.

Bad. Very, very bad.

But still, Rahelu could not let it be.

"Imos," she said, enunciating for all she was worth. "We had a wager and you lost. I'll have your forfeit, or I'll have blood."

Foolish bravado. He was at least twenty strides away and armed again, having just flattened their best offense, and she had no spear.

"I have already paid my forfeit twice over," he said, scars glowing with an ominous dark light. "Once in blood and once as promised." Impossibly, every word rang true. "Your understanding was not part of our bargain."

Ylaen raised his knife. Resonance coursed along his arm and surged up the blade, blackening the steel.

"Let go of Jhobon." His voice was a low, flat monotone. "Now."

Once Jhobon reached his side, Ylaen sheathed his knife. As the two scarred Supplicants passed Rahelu on their way to the hold, he sent her a final warning:

Don't try another Seeking on me, ever again.

28
NAMES

WHILE ELARAM DARTED FORWARD TO SNATCH UP Jhobon's notebook, Ghardon immediately rushed to Nheras's side. He gently lifted her crumpled form in his arms, then followed Elaram to the aftercabin.

Claiming it as Issolm territory, Rahelu supposed, before Ylaen and Jhobon remembered that Maketh was inside.

No one returned for her.

Rahelu looked up through the spare sails and sacrificial bolt of blue silk stretched to catch the slightest drizzle and soak up the sea's breath at night.

Crosstrees.

Masthead.

Brooding sky.

Not a bird in sight.

Too far to climb.

She could crawl though, so crawl she did. Slithered over the planks on her belly until she could tumble over the prow and lie in the netting underneath the bowsprit.

The flock of gulls carved into the ship's stem made for poor company. Their feathers were hard and cold, their open beaks silent; and they were only here with her because they could not fly away, like their flesh-and-blood counterparts.

The empty fathoms below were worse.

Dharyas's face stared back from the depths. The Isca girl's right side was serious and whole with a born Augur's far-sighted look in her eye; her left side was a blinded, caved-in ruin by the crossbow bolt still lodged in her skull.

Again and again, Dharyas asked: *What do you strive for?*

Kez, she tried to say.

That was the honest answer. Callow and callous; cold as coin.

She could not get the whisper past her bruised throat.

Anyway, that answer would not please her dead friend. Rahelu tried again with, "My family," but the eloquent rebuttals she'd used to defeat Lhorne's arguments so soundly in the Sable Gull's inn room faltered before the condemnation of Dharyas's shade and the memory of Tseiran's screams.

Gods. Had Lhorne been right?

How were her choices any better than Hzin's?

What had she sold herself for?

For as long as she could remember, her entire existence had been pointed towards a single goal. Her parents had dreamt of a better life and she had been the means; she had sworn a child's solemn oath to bring their dreams to fruition. All that she had learned, she had learned to do in pursuit of that dream.

Now that was done and over the moment she had sworn a Supplicant's oath to House Issolm. Years of Guild training had shaped her into a mage the Houses wanted; a tool that suited Anathwan's needs.

She had not learned how to choose.

Weapons go where their wielders will; they do not determine their direction. Much like how they had to rely on dead reckoning and the starsong to set the *Sooty Gull's* course when clouds blanketed the signposts of sun, moon, and stars in the sky, Rahelu had to rely on Anathwan's vision.

She borrowed House Issolm words and told Dharyas: "I did what needed to be done." Repeated Anathwan's assertion: "I made the right choice," and ended it with: "Velaz."

Dharyas—who did not speak Chanazian; who had not understood and would never understand the fundamental subordinate nature of the lesser 'I' descendant from the greater 'they'—held Rahelu's eyes with her sorrowful one until she could bear it no longer.

Rahelu shut her eyes.

Dharyas asked: *What is that chain you wear?*

A gift, a gift; it is a gift!

But Dharyas would recognize Lhorne's pendant; Dharyas had been there when he first gave it to her; Dharyas would believe him, believe her, believe it was a friendship gift.

Did Dharyas mean the bruises Ylaen had left on her neck?

Dharyas asked: *Who are you?*

"Rahelu of Issolm."

Dharyas asked: *Who is Rahelu of Issolm?*

She had seen herself reflected so clearly in Nheras's hand mirror—combed hair, immaculate uniform, head held high —but she couldn't visualize that image now. Easier to imagine the peace she would find by slipping over the side to float away upon the currents like the fish Nheras named her.

Her own words came back in Dharyas's voice to mock her: *You don't know?*

"I know what needs to be done."

I do what needs to be done; the Elder will do the rest.

One task at a time to survive.

Follow the starsong. Find the Endless Gate. Take the Elder's body inside.

Don't think of what comes after until you know there will

be an after. Keep your eyes on what's in front of you or you won't live to see another day.

No matter what Ghardon said, she didn't believe the Houses could be so different from the Lowdocks. Besides, the open sea was of neither: it belonged to the Stormbringer and the Stormbringer's judgment was swift and merciless.

"I swore an oath," she told Dharyas. "And I will not break it."

With that, Rahelu flung herself into the widest search pattern she knew for Seeking, right to the very limits of her ten-kual range, so she would not have to stay here, feeling and naming every single ruinous emotion on board.

EXHAUSTION WAS A GOOD BALM.

If she was too tired to think, she would be too tired to feel, and that was good because there was no more wine.

RAHELU RETURNED to herself at the end of skywatch and found open hostilities were in effect.

Battlelines had been drawn over the aft hatch: House Issolm had a fortified position and a hostage and they would cede no quarter to the Imos-Imrell alliance demanding the return of their Dedicate. Elaram, being Elaram, had chosen to go nose-to-nose with Ylaen, and he had his knife out again. Their height difference would've made the scene comical if they hadn't both looked murderous.

"For the last time," Ylaen was saying, "you will—"

Elaram glared. "You do *not* get to—"

MOVE!

Elaram moved.

She tore her shirt open to the waist and thrust her chest forward; took one step, then another until his bared steel kissed the side of her trembling throat.

Ylaen goggled, as stymied as Ruarem's apprentice had been on summer solstice's eve.

"Your move." Said to Ylaen with a sunny smile in that provocative tone of hers—like they were all still drinking wine and playing stupid games back in his cabin on the *Winged Arrow*—but the bright shimmer of her eyes was for Jhobon.

Ylaen did not move.

"What are you waiting for? You've threatened my brother repeatedly and struck down my sisters. Why stop there? Go on; go for your favorite move—the Chroniclers and the gossipmongers will eat up *that* story: 'Savage-blooded bastard of House Imos loses his fucking mind! Commits unprovoked slaughter!'"

"Unprovoked? Unprovoked?!"

The blade shook in Ylaen's grasp and Elaram gave a fearful little gasp, but her eyes and resonance aura glittered with the pale gold of triumph as Jhobon put a restraining hand on Ylaen's shoulder—and Ylaen allowed himself to be disarmed.

The reprieve was short-lived.

"*She* assaulted *me*." Ylaen shrugged Jhobon off—the closest thing to rough treatment Rahelu had ever seen from tsol-na to tsol-ek. "*She* committed a first-level violation of *my* personal rights!"

Ghardon fired right back. "Turns out *she* had *cause*." Tension crackled in the ambient resonance; the Issolm ring she had given him flared with golden light. "You treasonous piece of shit."

How had things come to this? How had the tenuous alliance that had seen them through the travails of the Dragon's Teeth and the Dragon's Spine dissolved so thoroughly in a matter of spans? How was Rahelu the one standing by, aghast at the prospect of further violence, instead of being the first to the fore?

They *couldn't* fight.

Not now, when resonance backlash would soon set in.

And not without Nheras.

Rahelu thrust herself in amongst the House-born. Put her back to her sister and her brother, her face in front of Ylaen's, and said:

"Your watch."

She shoved the spyglass into his chest. Which was bleeding. He'd been carving more lines of his achwa talog-te.

What a way to demonstrate one's commitment to treason!

Ylaen didn't take the spyglass. Forced her to another choice: contest his will by holding it there (her arm; it hurt—she hurt), concede his win and take it back (no, no—she had won, he had refused to concede, so she ought to win again and he ought to concede—properly!—this time), or call his bluff.

Rahelu let go.

The spyglass shattered against the deck.

No. Oh no.

"I want my uncle," Ylaen said, giving no sign he knew the spyglass existed.

Barely checked power smoldered around Ghardon. "It's your watch."

"I won't repeat myself again."

"Jhobon may come in," Elaram said with another sweet smile that jarred. "If he also disarms and submits to a Seeking."

Ghardon nodded. "Strip, Imrell. Then you can nurse his traitor Guardian."

Ylaen twitched. Resonance gathered around his left fist.

Then Jhobon shouldered past Ylaen and Rahelu both to stand before Elaram and Ghardon, shedding crystals and knives, clothes and wards and barriers, as demanded.

Ylaen walked off without another word.

Seeking complete, Elaram yielded way to Jhobon and ushered him below.

"Rahelu."

She did not realize that she was still standing there, head tilted and ears straining after the soft tread of Ylaen's receding feet over the rising starsong and muffled *clinks* nearby, until Ghardon spoke again.

"Rahelu."

She blinked.

Ghardon had cleaned up her mess. With his shirt. The fine linen one she had ruined by using it to protect her hands from the scalding hot pot of congee he'd fucked up so badly. Now it was bundled up around the remains of the spyglass she broke, and she could no longer see the small tear in the back and the ash and fish juice stains down the front.

"You need to sleep."

She did.

But she didn't want to sleep down in the aftercabin. It would be overcrowded with seven people crammed inside, the air stale and full of distrust.

She couldn't sleep in the hold either; that was Imos-Imrell territory now.

Eight hells.

Maybe she ought to go take one of the hammocks and hang it on deck; Ylaen and Jhobon didn't need all six of them. But Ylaen was on watch, vengeful as a nheshwyr-bitten bharost, resonance aura roused like the hackles on a snarling jhalyx and those sharp knives of his still unsheathed.

Rahelu said, "One of us should watch him."

Ghardon sighed.

But he didn't object.

RAHELU CALLED herself half a dozen different names as she headed forward.

Clumsy.

Idiot girl.

Stupid.

Fish guts.

Fool.

Fish-shit-for-brains.

Her scan found: an unsightly bulge in the mainsail, disordered ropes, a scattering of brushes abandoned partway through scrubbing the deck (you could see uneven patches of clean oiled wood alternating with grimy planks), fur from the ship's cat that had clumped or matted together, water casks shoved here and there along the bulwarks because while everybody was happy to go to the effort of bringing up full ones, nobody could be bothered hauling empties below, especially as they could always do with more room in the hold...

Csorath—the real Csorath—would never have permitted the *Sooty Gull* to fall into this disgraceful state of degeneracy, no matter how much he despised the Imrell-owned ship. It had been, after all, a vessel under his command.

Doubts assailed her immediately.

How would she know what Dedicate Csorath, Seeker of House Isonn, would or would not do?

Had the captain ever been Csorath?

Or had he always been Venoru?

Was the real Csorath still alive?

"There you are, my love."

Syzemosh's line. The next, wordless snatch of Enjela's Ballad drifted out of the sag in the foot of the mainsail: Ylaen had improvised a hammock for himself by putting in quite a bit of slack so he could lie on his back along the boom and stare up at the heavens. One unsheathed knife rested on top of a red-spotted rag inside an untidy coil of rope below his dangling feet.

"Come for vengeance?" he asked.

Rahelu held both hands up as she sat by the port rail, where she and Ghardon had left the fishing equipment beside several buckets: one for bait, one for catch, and one for rinsing. The first two were currently empty; the last was half-filled with dirty seawater.

"No," she answered. She took up the heap that was supposed to be a fishing net, her practiced fingers slowly straightening out the sorry tangle. "Just air." *And understanding*, but what she said was, "And to apologize. I should not have done as I did."

She should have waited until he was deep asleep and disguised her Seeking amongst his dreams.

"What other truths will you twist to your ends this time?"

"What have I ever told you that was untrue?"

"Name one thing you have said to me that was true."

"Everything I said to you, I meant."

She had meant it; every word, every syllable, for even the untrained could sense an outright lie, and though he was no Seeker, he was still a graduated mage.

"Ah, so you are as cruel as any House-born," he said. "How quick you've been to mold yourself to their example." A pause, then he added: "Their ways don't suit you. I liked you better when you were trying to gut me."

That set her resonance aura humming again. "You are House-born."

"I was born on a ship—a sloop rather like this one, in fact —and the man who sired me claims no House."

"What does that matter when your mother's wealth and connections and lineage paid for your Guild fees, secured you your private tutors, and guaranteed you a sponsor for your Petition?"

"Should my mother love me less than yours?"

"Such love makes the world unequal."

"Is that why you are so miserly with yours?"

The accusation stung. "I know this may be news to you when you can conjure love as and when you like, but believe it or not, the world does not owe you love."

"The world, perhaps not, but you do. At the very least, you owe me some semblance of it."

"Why?" she asked. "We exchanged no gifts; we swore no oaths; we shared no blood."

"I saved your life."

"For which I have expressed my gratitude. Repeatedly."

"And every time you said the words or lay with me, it was not me you were thinking of."

Oh, piqued was he?

"You did not care before," she said. "Unless it was you who lied."

The sound of waves beating against the hull. Then, very softly: "I did not lie."

"Is it a life debt you mean to collect or a consort you hope to woo? Because if it's the former, I'm fairly certain I've caught more than enough fish for you to repay it, and if it's the latter, then you can forget about it, Imos. I'm not interested."

"Is it my House that you hate, or me?"

"Did I say I hated either? I said I'm not interested."

"Why?" he demanded.

She looked at him, incredulous. "Does there have to be a reason?"

"Yes."

Fine. "You and your uncle are plotting against the Dominion!"

"Are we? What proof do you have of our supposed plotting?"

"I—you—"

All she had was a nod from Mere Ideth and Anathwan's word; all his stolen memory had shown was him doing his best to resist the temptations offered by someone who shared the part of his heritage the Houses despised, spoken in the language of his heart. Her fingers flew towards the faded mark he'd given her; as soon as she realized what she was doing, she turned the instinctive reaction into a purposeful motion—a casual tucking of stray hair behind her ears.

She fooled no one.

"So you have no proof. What, then, can your objection be? Atriarch Imos is also my uncle on my mother's side—he has no heirs of his own and if any of Atriarch Imrell's three children were sired by him, well, she won't acknowledge it." Ylaen reared up on one elbow. "He named me heir to House Imos when I swore my oaths of Supplication, you know."

"Congratulations on your impeccable pedigree and undeserved rise in station," Rahelu said. "What a pity that I don't care."

"For someone who doesn't care, you spend an awful lot of time holding my birth against me."

"Your father and your mother fucked, and then you were born. So what? You didn't earn a thing."

"I graduated as the top-ranked Harbinger in our intake."

"Ghardon's been the top-ranked Evoker since first year; he graduated with five Guild medals. By that logic, I ought to consort with him."

Ylaen snickered. "He wouldn't have you."

The sentiment was mutual; they would drive each other mad. So, more to the point: "Lhorne bested Jhobon to graduate as the top-ranked Guardian in our year."

She didn't need to say anything else. At the mere mention of Lhorne's name, Ylaen scowled, eyes fixed on the pendant glittering around her neck, and obligingly filled in the silence himself: *Lhorne would have me, Lhorne has had me, Lhorne would happily have me again; perhaps you've had me, but only as him, never as—*

"He's not even the Ideth heir!"

She shrugged. "So?"

"So? So?!" Ylaen sat up, looking taken aback. "One day, I will be Atriarch."

"And if we die out here, you'll go no further than Supplicant."

"We will not die out here," he said, with conviction. "At least, I will not."

"No Augury is certain."

"No Augur perhaps, but the sages are never wrong."

There! He'd given her an opening.

"What—"

"No," he said. "Not unless you give me something in return."

"Are you not bored of this game?" she asked. "Because I am."

"I don't understand how; I'm far better looking than he is." He was utterly sincere too. "But if it's lies that you prefer..." His features wavered in the fading light.

Not this again.

Rahelu sighed gustily, dropped the net in favor of the rinse bucket and tossed its contents at him. His Seeming puffed away as dirtied seawater drenched him from head to waist: fish scales glittered in his hair; fish guts dripped down his face; and thinned fish blood stained his linen trousers a pale pink.

"You were supposed to try and gut me!" he spluttered.

"Too much effort for the same result. You may assume that I duly attacked, and you were, of course, fully prepared when I did, and that after a suitably long struggle over your knife during which you disarmed me and both of us accumulated further unneeded injuries, the fight ended when I upended the bucket over your head."

"Why should the fight end then?"

"If you find simple theory insufficiently illuminating, I can supplement it with a practical demonstration if that's what it takes to get through your thick skull." Rahelu hefted the empty bucket in her hands and held it ready, arms trembling from the effort. "But I'm tired, so can we please skip past all that? I came to talk."

He paused in the middle of wiping gobbets of congealed fish blood off his cheek. "Talk?" he asked, as if the concept was completely foreign to him.

"Talk. Make conversation." Never in ten thousand years did she think she would come to this, but here she was, borrowing Elaram's words. "Become acquainted with each other."

"I have spent months becoming well acquainted with you."

"With my body, not me." She hurled the bucket at him, putting her full weight into the follow-through. "There's a difference, Imos."

"*Ylaen.*" He caught it a handspan away from his groin in an awkward two-handed fumble and glared at her. "Why is it so godsdamned hard for you to call me by my name?"

She glared back. "Because I don't know who you are!"

Heartbeats passed in silence, one after another, until he

looked away. "I heard that in Chanaz names are earned, not given."

"Only some."

"Was yours?"

She shook her head. "Birth names are prayers."

"Omens?"

"Prayers." She picked up the net again. "From your parents, if you have them."

Anma and aban must have moved out of the Lowdocks by now. It was strange to think that when—if—she returned to Ennuost Yrg she would not immediately know where to find her parents. They had the sloop, of course, but she'd also left enough coin that they could hire one of Isonn's drydocks for a season and spend the winter months snug and warm for a change.

"And if you do not?"

"You make your own." The last tangled part came undone. She added, "Rahelu means 'to leap the sky'."

"A good prayer." He watched her fold up the net. "Your parents have high hopes."

She thought of her mother, pressing a cream-and-gold envelope into her hands, and the Ideth pendant around her neck.

"Higher than you know," she said, adjusting the silver chain.

Or perhaps not; a corner of his mouth had turned up in a knowing smile.

Memory flashed through her mind—*gold torc, gold bracelets*.

"Ylaen." She drew out the syllables as she sounded them carefully. "That is not an Aleznuaweithish name."

"No."

If she understood the Free Speech better, she could try deriving its meaning, but it was a mongrel of a language with a mishmash vocabulary of words rooted in Aleznuaweithish,

Chanazian, and Belruonian that followed some other syntax for tenses and grammar. The closest guess she could come up with was 'wandering get of an octopus'.

Privately, she thought her guess an apt moniker, but she doubted he would share the sentiment—not the supposed heir to House Imos. How much of that was truth and how much of it was his arrogance? Atriarch Imos had made no official proclamations to that effect, though that did not necessarily mean anything. Succession plans for some Houses, like House Issolm, were highly confidential, known only to the House's council of Elders.

Temptation beckoned; a light Seeking trance would give her a better sense of the muted colors in his resonance aura. She didn't, however, want to risk the fragile rapport of the moment.

So Rahelu stayed where she was and tipped her head back to watch the Skymother change her cloak while he went to change his trousers, doing her best not to drift off.

She waited.

Waited.

And waited, until the sign of the bell, hanging low in its arc across the heavens, blurred in her eyes.

He returned after the sea breeze had used up its very last stores of the day's warmth. But his footsteps passed her by and when she dragged open bleary eyes, she saw him staring off into the east, scarred arms draped across the rail, a dark shadow against a darker horizon.

She picked up his knife and bloodied rag and limped over. Past the drooped mainsail and the flapping stay-sail—she glanced up out of habit and noted that one of its seams was starting to unravel in the middle. She ought to fix that now, but she was tired, so tired.

"Keep your secrets then." She held out his rag-wrapped knife. "I won't ask again."

He took it without looking at her.

She was halfway to the aft hatch when he spoke.

"The storm comes."

"We have time," she called back. "Wake me in two spans and I'll help you switch to storm sails."

A distant rumble of thunder.

"No, love," he said. "My name."

That drew her up short. "That's what your parents prayed for?"

Who would pray for a storm, of all things? Whisper too loud and the Stormbringer might hear you.

Ylaen made a short, bitter noise—a sound like a whipped dog. It took her several heartbeats to realize it was supposed to be a laugh. "My father, perhaps, but no. In the Free Territories, names are omens, chosen by the sages."

She hissed through her teeth. "What did you do to earn such a curse?" And curse it was to anyone dependent on the sea; they all lived and died by the Stormbringer's mercy.

"I?"

The breeze stirred up his unbound hair in long writhing locks; became a wind that snatched each word as he voiced it, carrying his answer to her ears despite how softly he spoke.

"I was born."

There was a raw edge to that admission, an echo of the buried grief she had been Seeking earlier that manifested as a ghostly halo around his shadowed form.

She turned back, intent on coaxing more out of him, but the pale light of his resonance aura winked out. A gust rose as if he had summoned it, pushing her back.

"Go sleep, Rahelu," Ylaen said. "The storm will be here soon enough."

SCREAM

'WHERE ARE YOU, MY LOVE?'

> Here; I am here.
> Here I wait, beneath the stars.

'There you are, my love.'

> Where else would I be?

'Here, beloved, silk to dry your tears.'

> You have taken my city.
> You have taken my people.

'The battle is done and dawn is near.'

> But your war is not yet won.
> For you have not taken me.

'Here, beloved: wine. Will you not drink with me?'

Yes, I will drink.
I will drink my fill of you and be joyful.

'What is it, love? What do you see?'

Her blade in his heart.

See, Starfather, see—

His blood on her hands.

—the proof of my devotion!

See how the world trembles—

—breaks.

I will put it back together.

She puts the stones of her shattered city back together and finds…

…rubble.

She puts her people inside her walls of rubble and discovers…

…suffering.

She pours herself into her people and creates…

…harmony.

Listen.

Listen.

Listen to the song of the stars.
Listen to their cries.
Listen as they die.

Something is very, very...

...wrong.

WIND KEENED. Lines and pulleys rattled; clacked to the irregular *flap* of luffing sails. The sea's caresses turned to slaps. Her heart thumped with every shudder of the stressed hull; her aura stretched taut and rigid as the tensioned rigging. Instincts honed over a lifetime spent on water responded before conscious thought and propelled her out of the stuffy aftercabin.

The ship pitched and she stumbled.

Shit. Too much canvas; they needed the storm sails.

Rahelu squinted against the spray. Where was Ylaen? She'd told him to wake her.

FLASH.

Lightning forked through the dark clouds massed in the east. She blinked rapidly, trying to clear its brilliance from her vision. Her ears caught the dull roar from the wind-whipped sea just as the next wave surged over the toprail.

SMACK!

The icy shock of the Stormbringer's fist jolted her out of her sleep-addled state. Saltwater burned her lungs her nose her throat as she spluttered and forced stinging eyes open.

Frenzied swells.

Mainsail, staysail, and jib still fully hoisted.

Ylaen, asleep at the tiller.

Fuck.

"Up!" she roared. *WAKE UP WAKE UP WAKE UP!*

Five resonance auras flared in panic. Ylaen started awake so fast he nearly jumped out of his own skin. He blinked at the sky, then ran for the bow, cursing the whole time.

Good.

She sprinted to the hold, snapping out orders as she yanked open the hatch.

Jhobon, help Ylaen take the headsails down now. *Nheras, we need to tie down every loose thing in the hold. Ghardon, Elaram—do the same in the aftercabin, senior mages included. Truss them up like chickens, roll them in hammocks if you have to, but for the love of the four heavens, make sure they're secure or we'll lose them to the storm before we lose them to the heartbane.*

Where were the *Gull's* storm sails and sea anchor?

Low cursing behind her announced Nheras's arrival.

There was no time to find and light the storm lantern so they both fumbled around in the dark. How had they let the ship's stores become such a disaster? They should have broken down all those empty crates and barrels, stacked and lashed them at the back of the hold for later reuse, not left them scattered about. Now she was paying a handsome price in stubbed toes and bruises as she caught her hands and shins on every sharp edge and corner.

The ship rolled to starboard and an open crate slid across the tops of its empty fellows with an ominous *scraaaaape*— she went to throw her weight against it but tripped over the sack with the last of their dwindling rice.

She fell.

Was immediately pummeled about the head and shoulders by a shower of rotting turnips; would have been knocked unconscious if Nheras had not seized the crate before it could crush her.

It took another four bruising encounters to locate the correct, rolled-up lengths of waxed canvas and an eternity to struggle out of the hold. Dark clouds raced towards the *Gull*, dragging a heavy wall of rain, blotting out the waning moon and half the stars in the sky.

Jagged lightning illuminated the deck with a searing white flash.

Count the heartbeats.

Jhobon, wrestling with the tiller, trying to get the *Gull* to come around to port and point its bow into the waves.

Ylaen, slashing at the staysail's lines.

One.

Knees soft to take the rolling motions of the ship's deck.

Head down against the rising gusts.

Eyes half-closed so she wouldn't be blinded by the sharp ends of her hair whipping into her face.

Two.

She was running, Ylaen was running, then they both grabbed at the jib's lines as another wave rose to starboard.

"Idiot!" she yelled. "We need to switch to the storm trysail—"

Thunder overhead, so loud it felt as if the world itself had cracked.

Three.

"Too late for that!" he yelled back. "We trim the—"

Water flooded the *Gull's* deck as it careened heavily to port, forcing them to clutch at the forestays.

Their curses lit up the air along with the next flash of lightning. She left him to back the jib; snatched up the fallen staysail he had hacked down, set it off the bow as an improvised sea anchor, and ran for the mainsail.

"No!" Ylaen shouted again. "Reef it!"

"Are you insane? We'll be tossed around like dice until the mast rips off."

"We don't have time!"

She filled her lungs to the brim as the sky rumbled and the ship groaned. "SO—"

Thunder shook the world again.

"—HELP ME!"

Her scream and uncontrolled release of bone-white-and-red resonance cut through the hush of the two-heartbeat distance between the glow of the Stormbringer's spear and booming laughter.

He winced, but his hands never stopped moving on the halyards, easing off the peak to lower the gaff, then easing both further still.

"Son of a goat!" She grabbed the nearest line as the ship slewed up the curve of the next wave. Which fucking line was this? "Do as I say, or I'll toss you off the stern as a second sea anchor."

The *Gull* tumbled off the wave's crest into the trough.

"Ylaen!" Jhobon cried. "I—"

Rahelu screamed again as she slammed against the mast and desperately flailed for another handhold.

CRASH!

The whole vessel shuddered.

The world ablaze.

When she could look again, eyelids dripping and vision warped by the afterglow of the lightning, she found Ylaen had abandoned her and flown to Jhobon's aid because he was right—*he was right*—so she quit arguing and set to reefing the mainsail as he'd ordered.

The waxed canvas was slick with rain and stiff from cold; her hands and arms the same. The slippery reef ties fought her like live eels. She couldn't see how the others fared through the driving rain, though she could feel Jhobon and Ylaen battling with the tiller through the ship's tortured turn into the wind. Surely Ghardon and Elaram and Nheras would've secured everyone and everything by now. If not, they'd have no food, no water, and lots of cracked or broken ribs.

Gods, oh gods, please keep us safe, Rahelu prayed.

The three below had better be praying too—to the Stormbringer for mercy, to the Earthgiver for strength, to the Starfather for luck, and to the Skymother for sun. No Obfuscation barrier could keep out the wind; no Projection could propel them out of the storm. Even the most powerful Fortunement had no effect on the natural world.

Knot by knot, she took the mainsail down to the first reef, then the second. When she tried for the third, the peak halyard stuck. She tugged; it refused to budge. The line had chafed against the sheave and parted, jamming the block.

Damn Ylaen for leaving her to reef the mainsail alone. Had they but worked together, the job would already be done and she wouldn't be here, teetering atop the crosstree on her toes, struggling to loose the frayed halyard with her fingertips because the Earthgiver had not seen fit to bless her with a little more height. And—

The world tilted again as the ship heeled to port.

—she slipped.

Terror surged as her hands heedlessly grasped for a line—any line!—and mercifully found one. Cold sea spray struck her face and she choked. Coughing brought her out of her paralysis. Her heart thudded against her ribcage in an uneven rhythm as if it had forgotten how to beat.

One thick line stood out from the writhing tangle of the rigging by its frayed middle, swinging towards her as the ship struck the next wave. She cried in sheer relief, bitter tears mingling with sweet rain and salt as the peak halyard came to her hand at last but its twisted strands of hemp were still stuck fast. Rahelu could only pray some more as she sliced through the jammed halyard and returned to the deck in a reckless slide down the shrouds.

She was no longer alone.

Nheras, dainty Nheras, who didn't know her halyards from her sheets, had joined her. Pissing rain had plastered her brown curls to her skull and soaked her through to the skin, sticking the threadbare cotton of her once-fine shirt to her willowy curves.

Thank gods! was Rahelu's first thought; then, *hurry, idiot, so both of you can go below*, but cold practicality won out.

"What the fuck do you think you're doing? You shouldn't be here!"

Not that Nheras could hear her over the *boom-crash* of the thunder and the waves, but she was right and it felt good to be right and to yell at someone as she yanked frantically on the throat halyard until the whole mainsail came down.

"Go below before you get yourself killed!"

Nheras shouted something, but the wind stole each word away as soon as she uttered it, so Rahelu gestured wildly at the storm trysail as she secured the boom, hoping her pantomime made sense. It was cut short; they both had to grab onto the boom as the ship leapt from the crest of another wave—airborne for two long heartbeats—before crashing down into the swell of the next.

The moment the *Gull* leveled off, Nheras seized the fallen storm trysail by its clew.

"No, no!" Rahelu screamed—all she seemed to be doing was screaming and screaming. "Not like that!" Why hadn't they drilled Nheras and Ghardon and Elaram on the ropes and sails? "You need the head. Here, give me that. Take this" —she thrust the cut halyard at Nheras, then shoved her towards the boom—"and lash the mainsail as tight as you can."

Slow; they were too fucking slow. Rahelu's chilled fingers refused to flex the way she needed them to in order to get the trysail hoisted and Nheras hadn't known how to flake the main along the boom so now the bunched-up canvas resisted her attempts to tie it down. Their shared frustration and terror rose faster than the stormwinds; gushing torrents of blood-red and bone-white resonance so thick they seemed to be drowning in a second sea.

Rahelu screamed wordlessly into the gale.

Who was the blind idiot that had failed to spot the first signs of the fraying halyard? Ylaen, it had to have been Ylaen. *He* had seized captaincy; therefore, he was responsible for the ship—and that would've been true even if he hadn't decided to throw his knives around. Nheras spent her days in the aftercabin, her efforts divided between sporadic attempts at healing the senior mages and studying Anathwan's mage journal; Jhobon hadn't so much as touched the sails, wholly consumed by the difficulty of navigation; the burden of shoring up Maketh's Obfuscation barriers and wards had fallen entirely to Ghardon, for Rahelu and Elaram had to keep their attention ever on the horizon—and Ylaen still kept second-guessing their reports about the ships and sails they sighted. Who did that? *Who did that?!* If he had minded his own fucking responsibilities—

Ylaen ought to be here, undoing his mess, instead of Nheras; Nheras, who couldn't tie a proper fucking knot because she didn't know a half-hitch from a reef. All Rahelu could do was cling to the mast as she wrestled the trysail, snatching worried glimpses of Nheras struggling with the fucked-up mess she'd made while the loose halyard tail and dangling edges of the mainsail flogged about.

Rahelu shouldn't've trusted Ylaen to look after the ship; she should've insisted on storm drills; she should've listened to Lhorne and not accepted this gods-cursed suicide mission—

A tidal wave of pale blue calm swept across the deck from tiller to prow. Its undercurrent was the ice-white clarity of reason and the steel-gray shine of determination. The massive blast of concentrated resonance was so potent that although the wind still shrieked and tore at the sails, the storm seemed powerless in comparison.

Rahelu cut off her scream.

What had she been so upset about?

So she was wet and cold; what of it? It wasn't like she'd actually fallen into the ocean. Even if she had, she was a perfectly good swimmer.

Beside her, Nheras had one arm wrapped around the boom with the massed mainsail: eyebrows furrowed and white teeth worrying at her full lower lip, brown eyes narrowed in disbelief that something as common as mere canvas and rope dared defy her will, nostrils beginning to flare in disgust. Such was the control Nheras had over her emotions that the Projection flowed over her resonance aura but did not change its composition, the same way a flooding river ran over a boulder lodged in its course and changed no more besides wetting its surface.

Then the ship rocked over another wave and they fell. Loose canvas burst free and sheeted over their heads. Nheras squealed as the waterlogged mainsail smothered them, neat as an Isonn squarekeeper bagging up rabid strays.

The ridiculous image of Nheras being plucked up by the scruff of her neck and shoved into a sack like a spitting, yowling cat stuck as the two of them lay prone beneath the unbunched folds of the mainsail with their cheeks resting against wet planks, ears ringing in the impromptu quiet.

Rahelu couldn't help herself: she laughed.

"Eight hells." Her chortling turned edged and wild as the effects of the Projection faded; however strong Ylaen and Jhobon had made it, the resonance couldn't pass through so much heavy canvas and rain. "Look at us. Look at us!"

Her laughter died as suddenly as it had begun.

"We're pathetic. Why the fuck are we even here? We have no fucking idea what we're doing."

"Not we," Nheras said quietly. That trace of envy in her resonance aura again, but touched with a curious kind of wonder. Resignation set in and hardened her voice to the harsh tone Rahelu knew so well, though she had never known Nheras to aim it at herself. "Just me."

The unflinching admission struck Rahelu like a blow. It was a sentiment she had felt so keenly and so often that it might as well be carved upon her bones and her mind filled in the next set of words unprompted:

I don't belong here.

Something in her ached with sympathy.

Nheras, lost and alone in the great hall crowded with Petitioners—

Nheras, weeping in a pavilion, unable to go home—

Nheras: aboard a ship; in an unfamiliar city. Ever excluded from the camaraderie between the other three Issolm Supplicants and the tsolbond that binds Ylaen and Jhobon in ways beyond House ties.

How many such tiny moments had Nheras suffered? Thousands, surely; both subtle slights and outright insults borne with such unbreakable composure—except for that once—that Rahelu had always assumed they never touched Nheras at all.

If she had not clung to her personal dislike; if she had not given in to her stupid, petty reasons; if she had been willing to set aside their childhood grudge in truth—

Too late to wonder how events might have unfolded differently, but not too late to learn from her earlier mistakes.

"We can fix that."

Her palms prickled as they breached the boundary of

Nheras's resonance aura. Rahelu pushed past the frisson of the instinctive defenses they both raised to grab Nheras by her wrists. The tingling spread to her wrists and forearms; skittered through their intersected auras and shivered their bodies. A stinging sensation that was both painful and sweet, the way blood burned and wakened a numbed limb when its circulation was restored.

Rahelu breathed.

Calm, she told herself as she formed her visualization: a simple raft tied up to the sturdy dock of a placid lake.

Nheras's hesitant Seeking hovered at the edge of her opened pathway. Uncertainty bloomed. Sympathetic resonance thrummed through their half-mingled minds, a restless wind that ruffled the smooth lakewaters—and the intimacy of shared memory answered:

Colorful paper lanterns line the fine gravel pathway that winds its way between the rustling trees. Half hidden in their living curtains of silver-green leaves is the newcomer: freshly washed, clad in plain but quality attire, and faintly perfumed with rosewater.

She looks down upon the glittering company gathered in the garden but does not join them—for she belongs and yet does not belong.

Another arrives, robed in jeweled splendor.

They make an exchange—words, coin, and crystal—and take their leave, each satisfied with what they have wrung from the other.

Both diminished, though they had not known it then.

Rahelu said, "Come here," and reached. Not with Seeking, but the beginnings of a Concordance: offering up knowledge and skill that she had and Nheras didn't.

Nheras recoiled. "I can't!" she kept saying—scared, Rahelu decided, but there was no time for Nheras to be scared, and no reason for it either. "I can't—"

"You can." She cupped her hands around Nheras's face, bypassing their resonance wards through direct skin contact. "Because I can."

Rahelu pulled Nheras close; distilled a lifetime of knot-tying and storm sailing into one swift Evocation, and gifted the spirit essence to Nheras.

Nheras hissed as she absorbed the weight of those memories, then cried out. In pain? Surprise? Something else? All of the above? Rahelu didn't know; maybe Nheras didn't either, and they didn't have time to worry about it now.

"Come on," she urged. "Quick! Before it fades."

They crawled out into the raging wind, which threatened to knock them over with its fury.

But the artificial hush of Ylaen and Jhobon's combined Projection lent them the necessary presence of mind. Moreover, Rahelu was no longer alone and Nheras was no longer a liability on deck. Years spent dissecting each other's movements as they clashed in sparring circles, fought in the training yard, and brawled in the streets endowed them with a keen sense of how the other thought that granted an unspoken synchronicity.

No need to argue about what needed to be done first or how they should accomplish it when they were prompted by identical instincts. Nheras could view the situation through the lens of Rahelu's experience and Rahelu could read Nheras's assessment simply by the set of her shoulders, in the line of her stance, and her decisive trajectory—and intuitively understand why.

It was not the same conclusion Rahelu had reached but Nheras's reasoning was impeccable.

Rahelu veered from the dropped trysail and grabbed the clew of the flapping main as Nheras found the tack. In less than thirty heartbeats, they had the mainsail flaked along the boom; in another ten, it was lashed flat with neat half-hitches at even, half-stride intervals. Lightning flashed as they raced for the trysail; thunder cracked as they reached it. Up Rahelu went to shackle the head to the spare halyard; lines flew as Nheras rigged the trysail's sheets. Down Rahelu came in a reckless slide-drop, then both of them were hauling for all they were worth, hands flying, muscles straining in unison.

Wind filled the newly hoisted trysail with a loud *snap*.

Nheras turned to Rahelu with a grin so wide that it had to hurt, her resonance aura bursting with pride. Not the unapproachable gleam Rahelu normally associated with all Houseborn; just a soft glow like sunrise.

Rahelu hugged Nheras tight as their auras melded harmoniously in a golden song of satisfaction. "You did it!"

"We did it," Nheras said. "Skymother, that was amazing!"

A last surge of serenity passed over them—from Ylaen and Jhobon's incredible sustained Projection—then vanished.

The light of their shared victory persisted; faint as a wavering candle flame in the echo of stillness left behind.

Then the world tilted astern as the ship ran up the swell of the next wave. The swell they climbed turned into a mountain, the mountain into a sheer cliff, then that clifftop began to curl and bubble, spitting froth and foam that splattered onto them like the saliva of a slavering leviathan.

The sudden shift sent them slipping sliding flying aft to where Ylaen and Jhobon still strained against the tiller—and the glow of their confidence snuffed out, plunging them back into the fury of the storm.

The tremendous roar of rushing water clashed with the sound of their screams. A coil of loose rope unraveled as it fell past. Rahelu seized it tight—*Starfather, please let this be attached to something*—and wrapped it once, twice, thrice around her left forearm, then hurled what remained of its length up at Nheras.

The wave broke.

Nheras's desperate eyes met hers as the rope whistled through the air towards her outstretched fingers—

Darkness.

Hold on! Rahelu sent, then repeated her useless Projection: *just hold on—*

Terror.

—for no good reason because Nheras couldn't hear her everyone knew resonance couldn't travel through seawater —*holdon-holdon—*

Pain.

—just like everyone knew better than to pray to the Stormbringer for mercy when—*holdon-holdon-holdon-holdon—*

Words and thoughts crumbled beneath the Stormbringer's judgment as the immense weight of the ocean crushed her against the deck. Rahelu clung tight to the rope wrapped about her left arm, twisted until her right was just as thoroughly trapped, cherishing the searing pain of rope burn because it meant that *she was still holding on,* hoarding precious air in her lungs until the third toss of the waves heaved the ship level again.

She gasped, blind; shook the seawater out of her eyes. Her blunted resonance senses detected frantic movement; one, two, three panic-filled auras besides hers on deck. Her ears cleared half a heartbeat later; registered—

Jhobon, screaming something incomprehensible at Ylaen as the *Gull* pitched about uncontrollably in the bottom of the trough between two enormous waves.

Nheras, rigid beside her, resonance aura blazing white-hot as the lightning that forked all around them, breath coming in quickening gasps.

—the ocean's roar.

The next deluge smote them like a broadside. Water devoured the deck as the sea encircled the *Sooty Gull* in a deadly embrace. The deck began to tilt they were slipping as it was tilting and then they were all sliding as the *Gull* tilted further and further as it threatened to dip its rails in and flatten its mast to lie starboard side down on top of the waves.

Ylaen relinquished the tiller and drew his knives. Drove the steel blades into the soaked planks to arrest his seaward slide, then clawed his way gracelessly up the near-vertical deck, grabbed the toprail, and threw his weight over the side.

Wind howled. Water raged. For one dizzying moment, Rahelu and Nheras dangled and spun in midair, bare toes kicking at the spray instead of the deck, suspended above the churning depths from a single length of rope while Jhobon hung from the tiller by his elbows and Ylaen clung to the portside rail.

With a groan, the *Sooty Gull* slowly righted itself.

Gods. *Gods.*

Rahelu struggled to free herself from the line that had both saved and snarled her. Someone needed to go to help Jhobon. They weren't safe, they wouldn't be safe, not until they could straighten out the tiller and get the prow pointed square towards the swell. Better if it were Nheras instead of her, for Nheras was taller and stronger, but Nheras was back to being useless and paralyzed now that the short-lived effects of Rahelu's Evocation had faded from her mind.

The storm shook the *Gull* in its teeth like some mad beast savaging its prey. The maintenance debt accrued from weeks of short-handed sailing when they had neglected everything other than the most pressing duties came due. Burdened beyond tolerance, the rigging snapped. Rapid *cracks* underscored the next *crash* of thunder as lines and canvas ripped themselves free and loose shackles clacked against each other and the swaying mast.

But that was alright, it would be alright, sailing bare-masted could work, would work, had to work—

FLASH.

One—

BOOM.

A deafening hush.

CRACK.

Bone-white terror blazed as the mast snapped.

FLASH.

Lightning seared the image of Jhobon onto her eyelids. Fear and awe were written across his upturned face; recognition too, as if he had expected this moment. All three emotions wavered as he let go of the tiller, then resolved into acceptance. He gathered up his wiry body like a coiled spring, feet and shoulders turned towards starboard, fingers closed around the hilt of one of the knives Ylaen had planted in the deck. The thin, raised scars on the back of his hands and arms glittered in the cold, blue-white glow.

With the inevitability of the headsman's ax, the mast fell. It smashed through the toprail as it toppled into the water, trailing torn sails and tangled rigging. By some thankless miracle of the Starfather, some of the lines held, and the weight and drag of the broken mass jerked the *Gull* to a stop.

Jhobon ran forward as the ship balanced on the edge of the Stormbringer's mercy.

No!

Ylaen's Command was absolute in its denial, a negation so profound that the world seemed to still in the wake of its reverberations. The storm tamed—for a heartbeat, for an eternity—as Symezosh was said to have done.

The ship canted sideways as the next wave rose.

Denial and despair drenched the deck with it, a maelstrom of resonance blacker than the storm-riven night that turned Rahelu's limbs to lead and her will to wax.

She stopped fighting.

They were going to die. They were all going to die. The

storm would sink the *Sooty Gull* and they would pass through the depths into the Stormbringer's realm.

Against that darkness, jagged bolts branched and spanned the heavens to form a cage of lightning. Blue-white brilliance raced along Jhobon's scars until he burned with it.

He alone could move.

Steel glinted in a bright arc. Tensioned rope twanged as the lines that tied them to their doom were cut, one by one.

The *Gull's* keel slammed back into the water.

The sudden motion tossed Rahelu and Nheras to and fro until they smacked into what was left of the mast in a dazed, crumpled heap. Through blurred eyes, Rahelu watched Ylaen leap over the portside rail and streak across the deck, hands reaching for Jhobon, sawing away at the very last strands of the line towing the submerged mast top and sails alongside.

Another wave swallowed the ship.

With a sickeningly swift lurch, the *Sooty Gull* shot free.

When they surfaced, all Rahelu could see was Ylaen, grasping for something beyond the rail, heedless of the swinging tiller, resonance senses stretched out in Seeking, head up, swiveling, scanning, searching the churning surface of the sea. He wrenched every meager drop of power left from his focus stone until the crystal dimmed and his aura blazed, brighter than the lightning, a beacon sweeping around and around and around in the staccato burst that was Jhobon's resonance signature.

Only the thunder answered his grief.

Jhobon was gone.

30

WOUND

A CHILL SO BITTER IT NUMBS HIS BONES.

A CRUSHING ache inside his chest that grows heavier and heavier yet will not explode into pain.

A VORTEX that spawns a disorientation and nausea beyond physical discomfort for it comes from the great, gaping wound in his soul.

31

ALONE

When reason returned, Ylaen found himself lying in the hold. Trussed inside his hammock, in fact, with lengths of thin rope. How he had gotten there, he had no idea, but he knew whose hands had tied those knots.

Let me go.

His weak Command bounced off Rahelu's Obfuscation barrier.

"No," she said. "Not if you're going to try and follow him into the Stormbringer's realm again."

Had he done that? And if he had, how dare she stop him?

"Then leave me be."

She was silent for a very long time. When she spoke again, her voice was rough. "I know it hurts. But you should not be alone right now. Trust me in this, if nothing else."

Faint anger stirred. How could she possibly know? The draw from the void above. A pull from the void below. And nothing to anchor him except the yawning void inside, for half his soul was gone.

"Then come here, love," he drawled, "and make me feel something else."

Surely that would drive her away.

"That I can do." She climbed in, shifting until she had curled her body around his.

Fucking Issolm. Every one of them contrary as cats. This one was even purring.

No, not purring. Humming. The melancholy refrain from what she had called Enjela's Lament with the additional lines uncle Maketh had added from the nameless lay he loved. Slowed down so that the tune was matched with a stately pulse of what must be the starsong—

(How was he hearing it now? Was she Projecting? No; it was because she had wrapped him in her arms and her resonance aura was suffused with it.)

—and the two blended in an achingly beautiful harmony.

He did not realize he'd been crying until she brushed the tears from his face.

Sages.

Still the sentimental weakling Zovresh despised.

Ylaen closed his eyes and jerked his head from her hand; tried to wriggle away from the familiar contours of her body and her sphere of influence.

He could not afford to be comforted like this; to be petted and coddled and swaddled up in the soft yielding blue-gray calm of her resonance aura as if he were some lost little babe. But the sobs kept coming no matter how tightly he clenched his jaw and so did the hot, shame-filled, guilt-ridden tears and through it all she kept humming that haunting, plaintive melody that sang of love and loss and sacrifice as her fingers stroked his hair and before he knew it, he had buried his face in the soft curve that lay betod ween her neck and her shoulder as he relived the moment Jhobon had been ripped from him over and over again.

The moment...the moment that...that...

No. Don't think it. To think it is to name it.

Better to blame himself; he had been warned.

His mind tore apart *what happened* and tried to reconstruct the alternative *what might have been*: if he had not fallen asleep on watch, if he had rigged up the storm sails weeks ago, if he had maintained his refusal to sail anywhere but to Tsorek-fa—

"Stop."

—if he had pawned the gold torc and bracelets his mother had passed to him and they'd fled to the Cloudspire Peaks; if Jhobon hadn't saved him; if he had never been bor—

He felt the next three syllables form before they fell from Rahelu's lips—a direct transmission that passed from the lowest register of her vocal cords through her flesh and bones and the ear he had pressed against her throat.

"Ylaen."

She spoke his name as his tsol-ek would have spoken it—the soft '*y*' that also began '*you*' with the emphasis on a long second syllable that sighed into the third instead of accenting the first and turning it into the hard, short '*Ih*' prefixed to every House the way Aleznuaweites did. Whether it was an invocation or a summons, he couldn't tell, but its reverberations struck the very core of him.

She had never called him by his name before.

He opened his eyes to see the fractured past. Partial Evocations swirled around the aftercabin like mist, events jumbled and chronology distorted from his attempts to unwind the chain of causality.

Rahelu pulled away from him despite her promise, putting distance between their bodies as she did every night, and again said: "Stop."

She seized the pieces of his butchered Evocation and swept them away, all but the one that showed the back of a wiry figure dwarfed by the ship's broken mast against a thunderous sky. The vision was occluded by rain and thick with dark clouds and despair.

That moment she held in her left hand. Magnified; every heartbeat slowed until they could track the birth and crackle of lightning across the heavens the same way you could watch a heavy raindrop run down a glassed window.

"This is not how you should remember him."

"That is how he—" His voice cracked twice before he could steady it. "That is what happened."

"No. It's not."

Again with the *'no'*. He was sick of hearing *'no'* from her all the godsdamned time.

"Do you want to know?" she asked.

His turn to say it: "No."

He already knew—that was both the gift and the curse of their tsol-bond—but she wouldn't know that.

"I think you should know."

The remnant of his Evocation rippled, the angle of the scene shifting to her perspective. She untied the knots restraining his left wrist. Took his hand in hers, then turned the memory she held over into his cupped palm like it was a precious thing so he could see Jhobon through her eyes:

Recognition. Fear. Awe. And, at the last, acceptance, before the black
sea rises up and—

He crushed the Evocation in his fist; felt a brief flare of satisfaction at her jaw drop as he spurned her misguided comfort.

"I said no." Let her choke on refusal for once. "It's a word you should understand, considering how often you say it."

"No, I—"

He raised an eyebrow as she proved his point. She flushed but went on to finish her sentence anyway.

"—don't."

"Really? Get out."

She scowled. "No."

Time for a smirk. "Shut up."

"You shut up."

He snorted. "Still counts as a 'no'."

"No, it doesn't."

"It does and so does that. Unless..." And now a deliberate leer; a long, luxurious one that traced a certain pathway—from earlobe to jawline to parted lips then down and beyond—that he knew she liked very much when he explored it with his tongue instead of his eyes. "Do you mean it as an invitation?"

She stiffened.

Success at last.

Then he remembered the last time they had done that, he had looked up to watch her and she had not been watching him; she had had her eyes closed and the hand he hadn't claimed had been gripping Ideth's shitty little pendant.

Suddenly he couldn't stand being trapped underneath her.

"Get off me before I throw you off."

She didn't move.

"Get. Off. Me." He flexed his free hand in warning.

She still didn't move.

Well. He had warned her. Twice. So his conscience was clear as his hand shot out to give her a great big shove in the chest that would send her tumbling out of the hammock.

She deflected his strike with her forearm, then pinned his wrist with her knee. "Are you quite done?"

He met her irritated gaze with a bland, carefully neutral expression. "Are you?"

Go on, he thought. *Tell me 'no' again.* He was tired, so tired, of games within games within games. He had never wanted any part of them, but no matter how hard he tried, his fate kept dragging him back in. His control slipped and all of his pent-up resentment flooded his resonance aura.

She climbed off him as abruptly as she had climbed on.

"What are you doing?"

In answer, she put her hands and feet on the ladder and began to climb some more. It was what he had said he wanted but his heart shook at the thought of being left alone.

Reflexively, he reached through the dark to find the soul that anchored his. Found absence where there ought to be connection. Prodded and pushed at the wounded place in his mind where the tsol-bond should be but was not.

That sense of wrongness spread until he felt himself trembling.

He didn't know how to be alone. He had never been alone. Not for as long as he could remember.

DON'T GO.

This time, it halted her—then she aligned her will with that cursed pendant around her neck. The Ideth focus stone flared in response and shattered his Command as if it had been no stronger than spun sugar.

"Please." To the eight hells with what Hnan Imos or Zovresh or anyone might think of him begging. "Please," he repeated in a hoarse whisper then shut his eyes and prayed. *Please.*

Nothing.

Nothing for a very long time.

But nothing, in this case, meant that she was still halfway up the ladder which was not quite *'here'* with him but not quite *'there'* either. And that was good enough for she had not left him to be utterly alone.

He relaxed. Lay with his eyes closed and listened to the starsong and allowed its slow cycling to lull him to sleep. And if at some point in his hazy half-dreaming the solitary starsong became a duet with a hummed melody…

Well. That was more than good enough.

WHEN YLAEN NEXT WOKE, Rahelu was gone.

He debated rising.

He could if he cared to; she had left his hand free.

He did not care to.

HE WAS STILL LYING in the hammock when Nheras came to intrude on his brooding.

"Have some food," she said, shoving a warm bowl at him. "Ghardon didn't burn the congee this time, and he remembered to flavor it too."

The 'congee' was so thin that it amounted to a spoonful of disintegrating soggy grains suspended in 'broth' the color of rice water, and the 'flavoring' was two charred pieces of preserved pork sausage and a single dried mushroom that the sea had apparently reconstituted for them.

"I'm not hungry."

"Eat," she said and put the bowl to his lips with a touch of Command behind her insistence.

He ate, then resumed his staring at the deck overhead.

"It's been five days, Ylaen."

Five lifetimes, for him.

"We've been very, very lucky. Starfather-blessed and Stormbringer-favored lucky."

"Don't bring the gods into this."

"How else could we have survived? We've just two minor injuries among the lot of us—three cracked ribs for me, and a mild concussion for Fishguts."

Nothing about uncle Maketh or Elder Anathwan's condition, but he did not press her on the omission.

In a pathetic, transparent attempt at levity, Nheras added: "Hard to tell with her though."

Ylaen did not smile; he knew their survival had not been due to luck.

It was his curse.

"And," she continued, undeterred by his lack of reaction, "we've only the one casualty."

Deliberately blunt and callous to rile him. A small part of him considered taking umbrage; another part admired her unflinching courage to put it so plainly.

In the end, he let her remark pass.

She nattered on some more about other insignificant things, like the fact that their problems were now reversed: plenty of rainwater, but no food.

"The gulls haven't returned," she said, as if the comings and goings of some stupid birds should concern him. "The fishing lines and nets are coming up empty. No sign of true land either."

Nheras paused to look at him expectantly.

He gave her nothing, so she spelled it out for him.

"We think that storm must have swept us beyond the Dragon's Tail and the edge of the North Ocean, to somewhere near the Desolate Isles. The others say the starsong is very loud now. Even I can hear it sometimes."

Well, good for them and good for her.

"Closest thing's a sandbar Elaram spotted, about three kual northwest of our position. Looks barren but we're heading there anyway, as soon as we can catch a breeze. We've got a hole in our hull. Rahelu's patch is holding but the *Gull's* still taking on water."

Resentment stirred—so they had imprisoned him here for nothing!—then faded just as quickly. A lifetime here was but an instant in the Stormbringer's realm, which lay beyond the temporal horizon. By the sounds of it, they would all join Jhobon there soon.

Abruptly, her tone turned apologetic. "We can't really give him the full rites. There's no true earth there, just black sand—"

More to the point, they had no body. That was alright though; ship clan traditions dictated a sea burial anyway.

"—but we've fuel enough to build a small fire." Very delicately: "His notebook. May we…?"

He didn't flinch; only wondered why she had spent so long tiptoeing around the subject.

"Yes."

What use were their audacious plans now? There was only one event he cared to Revoke, and the few experiments Jhobon had quietly conducted with Elaram had all resulted in the same finding when it came to changing the past:

Physical reality could not be undone.

You could only rewrite someone's memory of the event.

He could not simply go back to the night of his Supplicant's oaths and exchange his decision to get into the lesser grand palanquin and attend Ideth's party for what he should have done instead:

Command his uncle's ever-present spies to stop lurking around every corner with their eager eyes and ears and Seeker's senses ready to report the smallest transgressions in his behavior and go jump off the Eastcliffs.

Summon Jhobon through their tsol-bond to meet him at the Highdocks.

Run. Straight to the nearest jeweler to pawn the gold torc and bracelets his mother had foisted on him for kez. Throw the lot at the captain of the fastest ship in port and sail. Upriver. Away from the city, the sea, and the Dominion.

Even memory could not be reshaped so easily. No matter how he tried or what his mangled soul wished, he couldn't construct any alternative realities that could seamlessly fit with the observable facts. He couldn't even conjure any Seemings of Jhobon—they all melted away, shredded apart by causality.

His tsol-ek was dead.

He knew this incontrovertible fact in his soul.

"Will you come?" she finally asked.

Go and watch them burn Jhobon's incomplete life's work as if that would honor his spirit?

"No."

He'd rather cut his own heart out.

Nheras left without another word.

———

SPANS LATER, Rahelu returned from starwatch with a smashed basket and Anathwan's bitter herbal tea. After his third refusal of the offered cup, she shrugged and drank it herself—dregs and all—while she picked apart the basket and wove the pieces anew into two reed lanterns.

Rahelu did not ask if he would come with her; she simply hung one of the lanterns on the hook above his head and padded out of the hold with the other.

She did not come back.

———

HE STARED at the lantern and tried to think of nothing for a time.

Was still awake, long after weariness had silenced the Issolm Supplicants' murmuring voices.

Eventually, he got up to do what he ought to have done

the moment he woke: found the greater resonance crystal Nheras had harvested from the Conclave imposter; retrieved the silk-wrapped tsol-blade, oil, whetstone, and polishing cloths packed at the bottom of his seabag; and went to sit cross-legged beneath the sky.

YLAEN STEELED what remained of his soul against the flensing to come as he prepared to peel away the tsol-blade's cover.

Five Obfuscation barriers instantly dissolved at his touch. Each layer was precisely designed to channel the resonances released into the delicate crystal beadwork that had been its anchor. Sigil after sigil warmed, glowed, then flashed beyond existence as the flow of resonance overloaded the tiny stones, leaving their afterimages seared into his vision.

Courage. Strength. Power.

Embroidered white silk smoked. Caught fire. Crumbled to ash that was whisked away by the wind to reveal the blood-quenched blade within.

He wept again.

Jhobon had thought of everything.

The sinuous steel shone mirror-smooth in the moonlight, its perfection marred only by faint flecks of rust that had accumulated over months of neglect and a tiny nick on the edge of the third undulation from its base.

He scoured away the rust with smooth, patient strokes. Touched the nick gently with the heart-finger of his left hand, then filed that imperfection away too until the only way you could tell it had ever been there was to look closely at how one side of the wave had been slightly flattened so it was no longer symmetrical with its opposing twin.

When the moon rose in the second quadrant, Ylaen was as ready as he would ever be.

He set the point of the tsol-blade over his heart.

This was right.

This was how it should end.

The only sure way to avoid one's fate was to seize it by the throat and cut it free from the Starfather's design.

Besides, ritual demanded it.

Jhobon was gone. How could he go on alone?

He did not realize he had been listening for a rebuttal that would never come until the wind changed and the sail snapped in protest. And the words he wished to hear—

Well. Jhobon had offered him no parting words for they needed none; his tsol-ek had spoken them all long ago.

The only things that had come through their tsol-bond at the very last were his patient love, his quiet strength, and his unwavering belief that fate could be undone. The pain of their separation, the sorrow of their failure, the dread of what was yet to come—all those things and more Jhobon kept to himself and took with him to the Stormbringer's realm.

Ylaen's hand shook.

Wrong, it was all wrong.

They had tried so hard to run from fate, yet fate had ensnared them anyway. In the end, Jhobon had fulfilled the promise of his name.

Perhaps it was time Ylaen fulfilled his.

The first cut was the hardest. The next seemed no easier. Yet no pain he could inflict on himself could compare with that of their broken tsol-bond or the thought of abandoning their solution—though of course he could not carry out what they had planned now that he was alone —and he came to relish the sharp clarity of focus it brought him.

The stars slipped by overhead as they bore witness.

By the time he set down his knife, the deck was stained with his blood.

"I will not fail," he vowed aloud.

The heavens made no answer.

Ylaen cupped the imposter sage's resonance crystal with sticky hands. Breathed in the slow seven-count for Seeking as he drew on its power and sank into mage trance so deep it felt almost like the tsol-bond. (Almost.)

A ruddy glow bloomed between his fingers. It soon became a white brilliance that shone with the fierce heat of a newborn star. He closed his eyes against the piercing light and welcomed its burn.

This was it. There would be no turning back.

Ylaen dredged up every scrap of power within his grasp—the raw emotions he bled, the refined resonance accumulated in crystal—and sent it arcing across the vastness of the ocean in a tightly focused beam that was both beacon and Command until the crystal shattered in his grip.

The horizon answered.

With daylight and crimson sails.

———

No amount of prayer had prepared Ylaen for the wellspring of emotion that choked him at the sight of his father's ship.

The *Stormbringer's Judgment* was just as he remembered: a five-masted behemoth that didn't so much as cut through the sea as the sea seemed to part before the snarling bronze snout of the dragon head mounted on its bow.

He felt lightheaded despite the blood-strengthening tea he had drank. Only his white-knuckled grip on the railing saved him from the ignominy of fainting. Even at this distance, the ship's aura gave off an almost physical pressure that—combined with the memory of his shameful departure from its decks—ought to have brought him to his knees, gibbering in fear.

But, fool that he was, all Ylaen could think was: *Home*.

Home, whispered the wind as it filled the great finned sails cut from silk as crimson as blood.

Home, his spirit sang as his eyes drank in the unmistakable lines of the warship's graceful prow and tall stern.

Home-home-home, hammered his soaring heart at the sight of the brilliant paintwork that rendered legend and clan history into dazzling murals on the sleek strakes. His new-made cuts seemed to throb in time with his racing pulse.

"Home," he said, trying out the sweetness of the word.

It sat awkwardly on his thickened tongue. Of course it did; the word was Aleznuaweithish and his mother's language had no place in the seas and islands Zovresh claimed.

"Home," Ylaen said again in the Free Speech. "Home." Discomfort remained.

No matter. With time, with repetition, and with incontrovertible proof of his right to bear the scars that marked him, discomfort would surely fade.

"Home," he affirmed, then went to gird himself for battle.

———

RAHELU STRODE up on deck at the first span after dawn, towing a pack of scowling, half-asleep Issolm Supplicants in her wake, shouting expletives and demanding to know how in the eight hells a Free Territories warship had known where to find them in the middle of the Desolate Isles.

By then, Ylaen had discarded everything about him that marked him as Guild or House or Dominion.

The looks of stupefaction on their faces as they checked

themselves two strides short of him—just outside of an easy lunge—made him want to toss them all overboard. Unfortunately, that would undermine his already weak bargaining position and he needed every scrap of status he could get if he wanted Zovresh to accord him a modicum of respect.

So he spread his arms and obliged their staring with a slow spin.

Let Rahelu mark the change in the shape of the talog-te that wound its way through the gaps of his old scars and measure the blood he had spilled.

Let Nheras absorb the significance of his decision to don the gold torc and bracelets his mother had foisted on him.

Let the world recognize he was done with quiet defiance. Hnan Imos was not here to cow him with threats against his mother; uncle Maketh was unaware and unable to counsel prudence; and Jhobon—

Well. This was their plan. The best Ylaen could make of it, alone.

"Don't just stand there ogling me," he said when none of them had picked their jaws up off the deck after a whole ten-count. "In a quarter-span or so, the *Stormbringer's Judgment* will be close enough to board us." He raked them over with his eyes; shook his head and *tsked.* "You'd best be quick about making yourselves presentable."

Of course, Rahelu and Ghardon and Nheras chose to ignore his advice to go gawk at the warship on the horizon. Elaram, however, did not look; she stared into the depths with reddened eyes.

Sages. This would be so much easier if he had Supplicants from more biddable Houses to work with. Well. At least Issolm would usually orient themselves in the direction of self-interest, assuming they could figure out the calculus.

To their credit, it didn't take very long.

Rahelu instantly recoiled as she took in the *Judgment's*

eight gleaming cannons, the immensity of its hull (over a hundred strides long and near thirty in beam), and the crew swarming its decks with practiced precision, their collective resonance aura crackling with the bold orange of battle-readiness. Nothing got past her resonance ward, but her hunched shoulders, flaring nostrils, and fidgety fingers (tracing lines of warding along the toprail) suggested a small prey animal one heartbeat away from flight.

Not that there was anywhere for her or the *Gull* to flee to.

Nheras, on the other hand, gathered up the edges of her resonance aura close like the trembling white-cored blue flows of awe and terror were simply folds of a particularly voluminous set of formal robes she had chosen to wear. She repeated Rahelu's question in the same tone of idle curiosity she typically trotted out for dinner parties: "How did the Crimson Storm find us?"

He shrugged. "Does it matter?"

"The ocean is wide." Nheras's voice remained calm, almost unnaturally so. White-blue resonance shaped like wire sprouted from her fingers, the bright lines thickening and weaving until they formed into links of a glowing chain-noose. "As you have often told me."

"The ocean is wide," he agreed. *But so is my father's shadow.*

"Yet here they are." Nheras had not attacked him but neither did she release her Projection. "What curious twist of Fortune brings a Free Territory warship to chart a profitless course so far away from the fat, cargo-laden vessels traveling the established sea routes?"

"The storm comes, and the Stormbringer's judgment strikes swiftly and without mercy." Rahelu had her eyes on the tsol-blade he carried once more. "You knew this would happen. You knew they were there."

The guise of calm Nheras wore so well did not fit Rahelu. He preferred her riled with irritation and spitting spirited curses, her cheeks rosy with color and her baleful black-eyed glare sparking anger.

"You knew they were looking," Ghardon said. "And you…"

Watching the two Evokers-in-training piece it together filled him with delight and dread. He could almost see the thoughts turning over in their minds: the locations of the disparate ship sightings, the vectors of vessels they'd hidden from, comparing the patchwork of those resonance signatures to the ones currently bearing down upon them…

"You called them." The flatness of Elaram's accusation—and the none-too-gentle Seeking accompanying it—stung.

He could deny it but what would be the point?

Four against one.

He waited for the logical presence that balanced his emotional weakness to speak up with cool observations like: *'Elaram poses no threat without her crossbow'* and *'Nheras can be convinced'* or *'Ghardon will demand a ritual duel'*.

Silence from the void.

Only Rahelu was intemperate enough to wager all on a sudden attack—and he had her measure. He could kill her.

He did not want to kill her.

He did not want to kill any of them.

Perhaps he should let them kill him.

So: "I called them."

His simple admission split their alliance.

Nheras set aside her burgeoning anger and let her Projection dissipate. She kept back a touch to reinforce the veneer of composure that owed more to the paralyzing qualities of fear and awe than to true calm. No trace of betrayal bruised her aura as she contemplated her options.

Elaram relapsed into staring blankly at the water with listless eyes and a deadened aura.

How dare she? How dare she pretend to a grief greater than his?

Ghardon said: "Treason done in service of your House, I could understand—"

So very Issolm of him.

"—but this? This goes beyond treason. The Stormbringer should have taken you instead."

Gods. Gods! Ylaen could not agree more. So he said nothing and did nothing as Ghardon denounced him with what sounded like every epithet ever set down in Chronicler records of Aleznuaweithish history before he pulled an unresisting Elaram away by her elbow.

Rahelu, though.

"Which god cursed you with such stupidity?"

There was that beautiful temper.

"We were supposed to be a team." Said like she actually meant it. "We had a plan." Each word bitten off so sharply you could hear them crunching against her teeth. "You had no right to act without consulting us first." As if any of them would have listened or understood.

Ylaen laughed; there was no other response he could make. "What was there to discuss? Look around."

A jury-rigged mast that creaked in the moderate breeze.

A lone sail—severely cut down from a larger spare and hastily stitched—in place of the former five. It fluttered weakly in a rather convincing impression of a wounded wing.

The miasma of sickness wafting out of the aftercabin.

"Forgive me for assuming that you would prefer living over dying slowly from thirst or starvation or drowning when the Stormbringer finally sinks this miserable wreck."

"Nevertheless," Nheras said. "I don't care for your presumption."

"And I," Rahelu spat, "already told you I would rather drown."

"As you will." He gestured over the rail. "I won't trouble myself to save you this time. If you're lucky, the razorfangs might tear you to pieces before the *Stormbringer's Judgment* crushes you with its hull."

That silenced her but it wasn't enough. Not when she had mocked him so thoroughly before.

"Why the hesitation, Rahelu? Will you not stand by your word? Or are you afraid to die?"

Her sharp intake of breath made her answer plain.

"Oh, don't look so wounded, love; I won't brand you a coward for it."

Rahelu glared at him, unable to deny the truth but unwilling to concede defeat.

Nheras had no such qualms.

"Done is done." Nheras let that overture hang in the air as she ran her hands through her hair and over her wind-chapped, sun-burned skin in the first self-conscious action he'd seen from her in months. "We should wash and dress so we may present ourselves as valuable 'guests'." She frowned. "Will they honor the ransom protocols under Stormbane's Treaty or shall we prepare ourselves for imprisonment or enslavement?"

"I recommend hoping for the former, though it does not rule out the latter." Ylaen checked over his knives, then selected one. "Depends on the knife toss." He sent it spinning towards his target.

Struck the dead center of the bloodied rag pinned to what was left of the original mast—with the blade's hilt.

He'd misjudged the distance.

Three heartbeats of disbelief reigned, then Rahelu said, "That's not funny, Imos." When he made no indication that it was a jest, she said, to Nheras, "You do not ever—ever!—get to tell me that I am the one with fish shit for brains, ever again."

He picked a second knife; tested its balance. "As I recall, 'drunken knife toss' was your solution to a very similar problem. At least mine is rooted in tradition."

Threw again.

Thud.

Dead center, again.

...clatter.

Not enough force.

"That's your great plan?" Rahelu demanded. "To bet our lives, our freedom, and our whole mission on a single knife fight against the captain?"

"Oh no, love. Not the captain. I haven't earned that right. What's more, I wouldn't last more than two steps in that dance. No; the first mate will challenge me for the right to take my ship and my crew. If I win, then I may bargain for your lives and your freedom, captain to captain."

"And if you lose?"

"Then I will join Jhobon in the Stormbringer's realm, and you will do as you must."

Nheras lifted her chin by another fraction and said, "I hope you know what you're doing," then strode off towards the cargo hatch.

Rahelu did not follow. Just stood there, clenching and unclenching her fists, eyes darting between him and the water and the massive, sleek bulk of the *Stormbringer's Judgment* as its advance ate up the sky.

She looked as though she wanted to try and throttle him.

He raised his eyebrows at her as he began limbering up with stretches. "Care to dance? It may be our last."

"Not with you," she said, and left him to meet his fate alone.

3 2

JUDGMENT

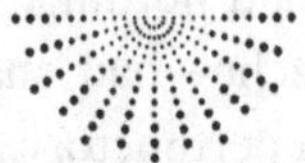

THE 16TH DAY OF LATE HARVEST, 530 A.E./A.F.

RAHELU STORMED INTO THE HOLD IN SEARCH OF the cache of weapons they were supposed to be smuggling, fully expecting to join the others in gearing up for combat.

Perhaps not Elaram.

Elaram was not well.

But Nheras would have already located the crate, and picked out the best of the deadliest options to supplement her lead-cored baton, while Ghardon would have his bow strung and gloves on, in the midst of treating his arrows with heartbane as he readied his quiver.

Instead, she got an eyeful of them all standing stark naked around one of the rainwater barrels taking turns with the soap and frantically sluicing rice water out of the cooking pot and over their heads. Every seabag had been ransacked for clean clothes. Those deemed acceptable were laid out on the benchtop in neat piles along with Ghardon's ivory combs and cut wedges of preserved citrus.

Incredibly, one of those piles seemed to be intended for her.

"What in the eight hells are you doing?"

"Hurry up and get out of those stinking clothes," Nheras said. Her nose creased in concentration as she worked a comb through long wet strands of tight brown curls until they shone like silk.

"And wash your hair," Ghardon added, "or else you won't be able to braid it properly."

Even Elaram—who said nothing, her resonance aura one dull, tight, suffocating ache—had shaken herself out of her stupor long enough for a perfunctory scrubbing.

They were actually taking Ylaen's facetious suggestion seriously.

Unbelievable.

She ought to scour the lot of them with the stiff-bristled brush used to scrub the decks like she was scaling a fish to see if that House-born silliness might flake off to reveal some competent Guild-trained mages underneath while screaming, *'We're about to be boarded by a lawless crew of cutthroats who won't give a flying fuck! They'll just as soon as shave our hair off before they throw us into their slave pens!'*

But:

Elaram was not stupid.

Ghardon was no coward.

And when Nheras Ilyn—no, Nheras *Issolm*—set her mind on a purpose, she pursued it with methodical ruthlessness.

Fine.

"Explain, using simple words for the benefit of my simple fish-brain, why we should swim right into this trap without a fight."

Nheras's nostrils flared with a disdainful little *hmmph!* that generally meant, *'No, because it's perfectly self-evident so I won't be wasting my breath.'*

Rahelu smothered the sharp cobalt pang of disappointment that prickled at her resonance aura and started looking for a spear.

Why had she bothered? One extraordinary instance of Concordance-aided rapport did not undo five years of hostility.

Nheras said, "We can't fight our way out of this one."

"There's four of us and one of him. Best I can work out, Ylaen Projected that beacon as far as twenty kual for half the night; he's got to be close to drained. I went over that warship from prow to stern: it might have sixty—"

"Seventy-two," Elaram said.

"—crew but none are mage-trained. At least, no one cared to defend against my Seeking and no one is controlling the resonance gathering on deck. If you're half the Harbinger you claim to be, you could—"

"I could what?" Water sloshed behind her. "Go out there and Command them to lay down their arms and sail away?"

"Yes!" It was, after all, the bleeding obvious solution. "You've got a reliable ten kual working range; just hold it for half a span. By the time it wears off and they turn around to come after us again, Ghardon and I will have the wards and Obfuscation barriers back up."

"And Ylaen?"

"I said I would gut him and so I will."

The outright snort Rahelu half-expected didn't come. "Swear to the Skymother that you've got better than a two in five chance of taking him down and we'll do it your way."

Just as Rahelu opened her mouth to say, *'Of course I bloody can,'* Nheras paused in the midst of drying her hair to fix her with a stare and a raised eyebrow.

The brash boast died in her throat and she was forced to replace it with a fairer assessment. "One in ten."

Maybe. They'd sparred quite often now, with fists, feet, and knives, but every bout so far had ended with him on top and the last time they'd exchanged blows had...not proceeded to plan.

"If you distract him."

"While she's simultaneously holding seventy-two people in thrall?" Ghardon asked.

"She linked twenty crystals into an Intermediate Obfuscation barrier formation and held it while defending against a coordinated assault from four Guild-trained mages—Ylaen included—without the aid of a greater focus stone. Why would seventy-two untrained be a problem?"

Nheras's eyebrow climbed higher. She pursed her lips. Put down the comb. Finally said, "I didn't know you held my skill in such high regard."

"I don't like you. All the face paint and jewelry in the world can't make up for your personality; I'd rather bed down in a nest of nheshwyr than spend time with you." An exaggeration—five years of matching insult for insult was a hard habit to break—so Rahelu quickly softened it with, "That doesn't mean I'm stupid enough to confuse dislike for incompetence."

Nheras's eyes glittered. Dear gods in the four heavens, was she about to cry?

"Alright, fine." Rahelu held up a hand. "I accept that you can't do it; don't bore me with the technicalities as to why. But Elaram is very good with a crossbow and a Concordance would—"

"We *could* fight."

Resonance shivered at Nheras's words:

Their ghost-selves find arms and charge out of the hold to fling themselves at Ylaen. Fourteen times they betray themselves—the pattern of their footfalls recognizable as footwork that preludes combat; their shadows announcing hostility with silhouetted weapons raised in attack—while another three attempts are doomed to failure by the vagaries of ill-timed wind and waves.

Her *'one-in-ten'* estimate had absurdly overstated their prospects.

Still, a chance was a chance; she had faced less likely odds and triumphed over the dictates of Fortune before. Rahelu reached out to the futures Nheras had conjured with her resonance senses, the way Anathwan had shown them, hunting for the singular strand of possibility that hummed with the syncopated beat of anticipatory elation as skill and stars aligned.

It could work; it should work.

It *would* work.

Ylaen's reflexive Augury negates their advantage of surprise. A Command targeted at Elaram sets her crossbow sights on Ghardon, forcing him to flee. Ylaen ducks a staff blow from the butt of Rahelu's improvised spear as he draws his knives. He deflects the lead-cored baton Nheras aims at his skull with the flat of his dagger and drives her back with the longer, serpentine blade.

Outcomes trembled beneath her examination: Rahelu-shadows winked in and out of existence as she altered her intent, setting off a cascade of corresponding Nheras-shadows even as Nheras wielded her own intent against the changes. The resonance of a future where the *Sooty Gull* slipped away from the warship went from a murmuring whisper to a head-splitting clangor in two heartbeats. An instant later, four-fifths of the paths leading to that possibility died:

A hundred phantom Rahelus faint from resonance backlash; a hundred more stumble to a standstill as her Obfuscation barriers collapse under Ylaen's Projections. Ten straighten at his touch; the familiarity of their recent, physical intimacy lends him an easy path past her defenses. Her newborn regard for Nheras is no match for the old rage she has nursed for over half a decade.

His Commands take hold.

Ten Rahelus fall in beside the Ylaens and array themselves against Nheras as the few Elarams who do not fall to thrown knives fall to Command and fill the Ghardons full of crossbow bolts.

Nheras remains. Nheras loses. Over and over and over and over—

Twenty variants of their coordinated assault played out in succession.

All ended in defeat.

"Fuck." Rahelu's temples throbbed. "Fuck!"

The lack of any other possibilities in their joint Augury proved Nheras right.

Nheras sighed and said to Ghardon, "How do you stand it? She's so dull that she can't conceive of any possibilities that don't begin with punching people in the face."

Instinct and habit aligned to rail against her resolve to demand she do exactly that.

The twitch of her fingers did not escape Ghardon's notice.

He frowned.

Rahelu almost laced her hands behind her back to stop them from clenching into fists. But that was too close to the way a child would offer proof of good behavior by sitting on their hands after a sharp rebuke, and folded arms—the adult equivalent—would be no better for salvaging her dignity.

She poked at the comb intended for her instead. "So we don't fight. That's no reason for me to—"

"You're wasting time, Rahelu. Shut up and do as Nheras says." Ghardon was already dressed. Water dripped onto his collar from his slicked-back, already-fastened hair as he swiftly braided and coiled one side of Elaram's hair while Elaram did the other. "Ela, let's go. We've got to destroy

Elder Anathwan's notes and Guardian Maketh's schematic before they get here."

Away they went.

Rahelu grimly reached out to the last, eerily familiar vision of a Suborned version of herself throttling a gasping, purpled-faced Nheras floating midair between them and crushed that instead.

Nheras, in the tones of the extremely put-upon explaining the self-evident truth to the slow-witted: "We need a new ship. And an able crew fit to sail it."

Her headache multiplied tenfold; Nheras was making no fucking sense. "You just proved that it can't be done."

"A ship goes where its captain commands." Fingers danced as they twisted water-straightened brown locks into strands that shared a closer resemblance to elaborate knotwork than simple braids. "This one is no different. Whoever Commands the captain—"

Rahelu was pretty sure that the Free Territory ship clans did not hold with the same obedience to duty and respect for authority that the Houses held sacred.

"Ship clan captains are elected to lead by unanimous consent, Nheras; crew are not Suborned to them."

"Crew are made of men and women. They can be convinced."

Nheras propped the hand mirror up against the hearth chimney, craning her head this and that way. Wrinkled her nose at her own powderless face and unpainted lips with the distaste she usually reserved for Rahelu.

"The game," Nheras said, "has three choices."

This time, when Nheras turned her head, Rahelu saw the dark gleam of onyx and the bright glint of silver swishing from her earlobes—a matching pair of little caged songbirds holding crystal in their beaks. A soft bloom of rose pink bloomed in smooth cheeks that should be roughened by salt breezes and harsh sun as vivid vermillion blushed her lips.

The veneer of Seeming was so slight, the image of House-born poise and sophisticated beauty so naturally suited to Nheras that, had Rahelu not known otherwise, she would have assumed Nheras was vain enough to have brought her jewelry and cosmetics along, despite orders to the contrary.

Guttural shouts above.

An answering ululation from Ylaen.

They were out of time.

Rahelu stopped trying to puzzle out what Nheras had in mind and started looking for a place to hide. A dozen options, each worse than the last, jostled for her attention. She dismissed the empty barrels (too obvious) and the hidden compartment just below the forepeak (ideal, except Ylaen knew of it) and—

No. She was a good swimmer. Ylaen was probably exaggerating about the razorfangs. The *Stormbringer's Judgment* was approaching from the *Gull's* leeward side. They had lost much of their ballast in the storm so the sloop was riding higher than it had been. There was room enough in the hidden compartment to swing the hatchet they used to split firewood; from there, a small hole cut into the starboard side of the hull ought to come out just above the waterline. The raiders wouldn't notice one small figure clinging to the side or bobbing at the end of a fishing line. They would be too busy securing the wallowing sloop with towlines and stripping its hold of consumables, valuables, and ransomables— an endeavor which wouldn't take long seeing as Ylaen had invited them and the others were preparing to welcome their unwanted guests with open arms.

All she had to do was remain concealed until the raiders returned to drink and dice on their warship, sneak on board, discover where they were keeping their Stormbringer-sent gift of two defenseless senior mages (most likely in the ship's apothecary, under a healer's care), three new captives (most likely in the slave pens, in the hold), find some way to steal one of their boats and, and, and—

Stupid, stupid, stupid!

No Augury was certain, but there were no viable alternatives here either. She couldn't win a fight. She had nowhere to run and no place to hide.

But she would not be like the others, grooming herself for captivity like some biddable prize sheep.

Rahelu went for the crate of weapons and found a length of bamboo and a dagger suitable for her requirements. Using spare fishing line to lash the long, flattish hilt tight to the makeshift haft was not ideal, but the dagger's barbed quillons and wicked, serrated blade would do well enough. She backed up to the middle of the hold where she would have room to test her improvised spear and adjusted her grip.

Already, she could tell it was poorly balanced.

The sheep in front of her curled blood-red lips back to bare white teeth in an almost feral smile at the mirror. Repeated: "The game has three choices."

Hah.

"We can't fuck our way out of this one. Not even Elaram would think so."

"Who said anything about fucking?"

Rahelu halted mid-thrust. "You can't be serious."

How could Nheras even contemplate an alliance, right on the heels of Ylaen's betrayal?

The two elegant eyebrows arched at her said otherwise. "They're mercenaries. It's a valid option."

"It is not." Disbelief welled up in her resonance aura, garish yellow bands that constricted her lungs and robbed her tongue of eloquence, reducing her protests to statements of the obvious. "We swore *oaths*."

Her vows to House and Dominion—writ in resonance, sealed with blood, and heavens-witnessed—resounded in her head even as her ears cataloged the signs of boarding: *thunk-thunk-thunkthunkthunks* of metal biting into wood; the *creeeeeaaak* of the *Gull's* timbers at its sudden lurch leeward.

"So we did."

Nheras breezed past, garbed in illusory Issolm whites and blacks, smelling subtly of soap and citrus. Her scent—real and sweet and reminiscent of the floral fragrances she typically preferred—made Rahelu recall another day aboard another ship when Nheras had sat in front of that very same mirror wearing a similar mask.

"Did you forget what those oaths were?"

"Have you forgotten which House we swore those oaths to?"

That was an insult no self-respecting Evoker would tolerate. Her makeshift spearpoint snapped up. "I forget nothing."

Nheras's eyes flickered down. Disappointment twisted her features.

Something in Rahelu twisted too.

"Out of my way, fish guts," Nheras said and stepped forward.

Into the square of sunlight—shining down into the hold to crown her braided hair with gold—and Rahelu's spear blade.

One little jab and she could end this. Cut Nheras a second, more silent mouth incapable of spouting anything other than blood. Her blade was right there, a finger-width from the jugular; one serration had already bitten through skin. A single ruby droplet glided down the slant of Nheras's throat to glimmer in the hollow between her collarbones.

No.

Don't look there.

It reminded her too much of the weight resting against her heart.

Rahelu looked up. Saw—

Eyes: wide; unblinking. Face: perfectly composed. Resonance aura: riddled with chalk-white fear, bound and bridled into a flawless Seeming.

—past the mask.

Who was she trying to convince with her posturing anyway?

Lhorne wasn't here.

She hadn't sworn to Ideth; she had sworn to Issolm, and Issolm honor was as flexible as it needed to be.

Rahelu dropped her spear and took up a comb.

"How the fuck do you braid hair?"

IT FELT wrong to just stand there, weaponless, with her resonance aura bound as tightly as the braids pulling at her scalp, while eight heavily scarred, heavily muscled raiders bristling with knives, sabers, and axes swarmed up the boarding ladder and onto the *Gull's* deck.

But when Rahelu had gone to tuck the dagger in her belt, Nheras had smacked her wrist and said, "We are daughters of Issolm; Anathwan's favored Supplicants." Next, a spritz of lime juice had stung her eyes. "We can strike them down with our minds if we choose."

Glossing over the Augury of the certain failure awaiting them if they chose was an all-new level of personal delusion that surely didn't fall under the category of those Ghardon considered excusable.

"Today," Nheras had continued very emphatically with an even more emphatic prodding of long nails down Rahelu's spine to force it into a line that felt overarched though she had seen in the mirror it was merely straight, "we do not choose, because they are more useful to us this way."

Calm, Rahelu reminded herself, and visualized a mirror-smooth expanse of blue-gray water. Not enough to call an Obfuscation barrier into existence—Nheras had insisted doing so would undermine their appearances as surely as bearing arms—just a veneer like Nheras's Seeming; one that muffled but did not negate her churning emotions.

("Why would we need to carry weapons?" Nheras had scoffed when Rahelu had wished for her spear. "We are weapons." Never mind that their resonance crystals consti-tuted weaponry, though she supposed Nheras would contend they weren't technically armed with any, since they had all either swallowed their focus stones or secreted them away as a precautionary measure against being searched.)

Wars are won first in the mind and then upon the battlefield.

The leader of the boarding party, a weathered man missing his left ear, barked at the other seven raiders. They paid no attention to the five Supplicants clustered before the mast, swarming around them as if they weren't there.

Ylaen paid them no attention in return as he strutted forth to meet One-Ear.

Naked to the waist with gold glinting at his throat and wrists, the Imos Supplicant flexed his muscles and flaunted his scars in such a cocksure display of overcompensating that he ought to have fully committed and swaggered out with his dick swinging too. The long melodic phrases he exchanged with One-Ear had the cadence of poetry despite the rough, guttural sounds of the Free Speech; the theatrical manner in which Ylaen thumped his right fist upon his left breast and One-Ear's mirrored gesture at the end of the exchange suggested the conclusion of some formal ceremony.

Rahelu did not like the look of One Ear's appraising eyes as he considered the four Issolm Supplicants.

"Tsol-ek-na?" One-Ear asked.

Ylaen smirked. "Tsol-an-mak."

She did not like the expansive sweep of Ylaen's arm as he gestured behind him any better. But she suffered One-Ear to draw close—so close she could smell his sour breath—and traded him stare for stare instead of spitting in his face.

Because Ghardon held his ground even as his throat bobbed nervously in a dry swallow.

Because Elaram plastered a wide, sunny smile on her face: a brittle thing that didn't square with her reddened eyes.

Because Nheras met One-Ear's inspection of her with cool eyes and a slight inclination of her head, as if the two of them had just been introduced at a dinner party.

Nheras strode the deck of the storm-beaten sloop, descended into the bobbing boat, and climbed out of it wearing unassailable confidence the way she wore cloth-of-gold and silk. So straight and tall was her posture that you hardly noticed the crossbow digging into her back (left of the spine, below the shoulder blade, directly over the heart); so relaxed and graceful her strides that it was more accurate to say that she glided rather than walked. At no point did Nheras spare a glance over her shoulder or to her side—not for her raider escort, not for her House siblings, and not for the two comatose senior mages being ferried over in bundled hammocks like corpses.

So Rahelu swallowed her spit, clenched her quivering stomach muscles like she was preparing for a body blow, and didn't acknowledge the sharp point of the crossbow digging into her back either as it urged her past cannon after cannon, scarred warrior after scarred warrior.

THE DECKS of the *Stormbringer's Judgment* were not stained red by the blood of a thousand fallen foes. Only one segment was: the large sparring circle burned into the planks between main and mizzenmast.

Everything else, however, appeared to be true.

Sun and salt and time ought to have leached color away, fading the bloodstains to the browns of rusted iron, patched with grays and blacks, yet the wood inside the circle remained as bright a crimson as the ship's sails. Flickering after-echoes of the past dances that had painted the deck still dwelled in the ambient resonance within. Here, there, and there; Rahelu could trace the marks of the shadowy combatants' death throes to the merciless matches preceding their gory end. Individually faint, the impressions were no clearer than the suggestive outlines left behind when inkless brush-strokes dried on heavy paper. But sympathetic resonance turned the collective weight of those final moments into a vivid tapestry of violence whose stomach-churning emanations could be felt from ten strides away—where she knelt in a neat row along the starboard side with her brother and sisters.

All around them, the ambient resonance hummed with the anticipatory thrill of the gathered audience as One-Ear and Ylaen approached the circle with matched strides.

They exchanged words.

Too low for her ear to catch over the speculative buzz of seventy-one voices jabbering in short, guttural phrases of the Free Speech. Ceremonial posturing as ship clan members called wagers and placed odds, Rahelu decided, and—her stomach did another flip—those odds were not in Ylaen's favor. Many of the assessing looks aimed at him were dismissive, and she could not disagree.

One-Ear stood half a head taller, was as stout as an ox, and muscled like one. His scars covered his arms, his torso, most of his back, and his legs. He joked with those standing near him as he stretched and did not look at his opponent.

Weeks of low rations had reduced Ylaen's naturally lean frame to whipcord thinness. The gold torc and bracelets on his arms were looser than they were designed to be and jangled noisily as he limbered up. His tan had fled after days of grief-stricken stupor spent lying in the hold, leaving his skin with a sickly pallor. Sleeplessness had given him sunken, bloodshot eyes, and fatigue, combined with too much wake-leaf tea, endowed his hands with faint tremors. Proximity to the sparring circle and its shades made him jittery with nerves, and the lack of any ritual scarring on his back emphasized his youth and vulnerability.

That lack also seemed to be the focus of the derisive whispers rippling through the crowd.

Against the older man, Ylaen looked and sounded like an unblooded boy. Quick and plenty talented, as evidenced by the way he handled his knives, but untested by experience. He cast a glance up towards the quarterdeck at the captain's chair, a massive throne of carved rosewood grand enough for any Atriarch. Registered that the chair was unoccupied—and nearly fumbled one of his weapons.

Guffaws through the crowd.

Rahelu nearly groaned aloud; Ghardon actually did.

Nheras did not look concerned, but that was the entire point of her mask. Without Seeking, there was no way for Rahelu to know whether Nheras felt the same rising tide of panic that threatened to overwhelm her resonance ward.

(Seeking was another thing Nheras had forbidden, as its use would mark them as insecure. Augury, too; not that she had ever had much skill with that. The litany of *'don'ts'* had gone on and on until Rahelu had cut Nheras off with an exasperated, "May I breathe? Or is that too much to ask?" The answer had been: "In the basic four-count only." Sorry she'd asked, Rahelu had endured the rest of the list without remarking on the increasingly urgent demands of her bladder because Nheras would probably have said, "Piss? Not unless you can draw a suppression ward with it at the same time.")

Rahelu couldn't even hold to the false hope that, somehow, this would play out as part of some pre-arranged, devious strategy in a hidden game of House politics she had missed, or the betrayal Elder Anathwan had warned her to expect. The Crimson Storm, as far as they knew, was not one of the ship clans under contract to Houses Imos and Imrell.

"There is no plan," Nheras had said. "Only purpose. To go in with a plan is to blind ourselves to opportunities."

The Earthgiver must have blessed her with nerves of steel and a heart of stone. How else could Nheras keep her head so high? There were seventy-one pairs of eyes calculating her worth, weighing the value of a House-born Supplicant's ransom against the value of a Guild-trained Harbinger sold to a Suborned den—or kept chained for their own use.

Next to Nheras, Rahelu felt untried and unworthy of Anathwan's promise.

Across the circle, One-Ear raised his knife in salute, signifying his readiness. A hush swept across the warship. The crowd stilled and Elaram momentarily perked up as Ylaen raised his knife in answer.

One-Ear grinned, showing two crooked rows of stained teeth. Spat his wad of chewed herbs to one side and strode into the center. His acquisitive eyes roved over the chests, crates, and piled bolts of cloth from the *Sooty Gull* and down the line of kneeling Issolm Supplicants. Something shivered in the ambient resonance as his gaze swung over to Rahelu: a charged tension that raised the hair on her arms and made her skin prickle.

A blue-gray corona flickered very briefly into existence around her as she reflexively flooded her resonance aura with a calm she did not feel. Almost immediately, she forced it back, but the damage was done.

One-Ear snorted; said something that contorted Ylaen's controlled expression into anger and incited the crowd's malicious laughter. Heckles and jeers were followed by obscene gestures and leers that transcended language. Her fragile composure cracked. Molten shame hissed through the fissures in her resonance aura and earned her more ribald laughter.

Bone-chilling fear struck the crowd with the force of a truewinter blizzard.

Laughter died.

"Mal-ek," Ylaen said quietly. *Mine.*

One-Ear's reply was nonchalant. "Achwa talog-te, ki-na e Zovresh?"

The Imos Supplicant stepped across the circle's warding line. His saunter was gone—he moved too lightly on the balls of his bare feet. Gingerly, as if he walked on burning coals.

"Ze, Vaaqin," Ylaen said. Resonance shimmered. Crimson fire ignited along the intricate geometric patterns of scars that covered his torso like armor. With rage, came defiance: "Achwa-te-gish-no, e *Ylaen.*"

Across the circle, One-Ear's scars shone with their own fiery light.

Their knives met in a ferocious *clang.*

YLAEN AND ONE-EAR did not dance.

Nor was their fight a duel.

It was brutal, savage judgment in the space of two hundred heartbeats.

YLAEN STAGGERED TO HIS FEET, weaponless, as the glow of his scars winked out, leaving rivulets of blood to run down his dangling left arm and drip from limp fingers.

He should finish Vaaqin. Zovresh expected him to—Vaaqin expected him to! Achwa-te-gish-no was, after all, a death-dance.

But:

Vaaqin was well loved.

Vaaqin had taught him to see beauty in the dance itself when Zovresh had only trained him to focus on its goal.

Vaaqin looked at him with Jhobon's accepting eyes.

No. *No.* The sages might never be wrong, but they could be more than what the omens ordained. Wasn't Chenya Imrell proof of that? She had changed her fate, somehow, and Jhobon had thought he'd found her secret.

Anyway, Ylaen had used up all his knives.

He swayed.

No, no! He couldn't fall. Couldn't show a hint of weakness now.

Straighten up. Stand tall. Spin around—slowly!—and meet every eye. See what I have made of Vaaqin; listen to his pitiful cries. He is mine, his life is mine, his fate is mine to decide.

"Mal-ek!" he shouted to the heavens. *Skies and stars be my witness.*

Like grass bending before the wind, the assembled crowd bowed their heads.

"Na-lek!" Feet stomped and fists thumped in a thunderous chorus. "Ylaen! Na-lek!"

He basked in the clan's roared affirmation.

This victory...

This victory was sweet and bright.

Ylaen savored the tang of copper and salt and stinging

pain as he staggered out of the circle. He left Vaaqin pinned to the deck with both of his knives through his shoulders.

A mercy.

The only mercy Ylaen could afford to give. For now. Later, once Zovresh had rendered judgment, he could come back and release Vaaqin.

He stopped five strides from the quarterdeck companionway that led up to the captain's chair. It was occupied by a tall, heavily scarred woman whose long, corded limbs sprawled languidly across its carved arms.

Ylaen's mouth went dry at the sight of Xya in his father's seat.

"Hello, little cub."

Aleznuaweithish, for the benefit of the captive Issolm Supplicants lined up against the starboard bulwark on their knees, and that damned diminutive instead of his name.

His heart sank, heavy with foreboding.

This victory was not enough.

White-lipped, white-faced, Ylaen abandoned the speech he had rehearsed to lower his eyes and bow, fist over heart.

"Xya," he replied in the same language. His right hand wouldn't close properly. "Xya, I—"

Xya uncoiled. Each deliberate tread of her boots as she descended the companionway seemed ominous as thunder; the hiss of her serpentine knife clearing its sheath loud as a scream.

"Where is the crown?"

"Lost," he confessed. "It lies at the bottom of the Abmerduan Sea."

"And your tsol-ek?" Steel pierced the skin at the base of his throat; opened the lines of his achwa talog-te to bleed afresh. "Does my son also lie at the bottom of the Abmerduan Sea?"

"Yes," he whispered. "Jhobon fulfilled the promise of his name."

The point of Xya's blade skimmed up the length of his windpipe to rest under his chin, forcing him to meet her eyes. He looked for some sign of emotion in that ice-pale gaze. Anger he could use; grief he could share; pride—

Foolish to hope for that.

Abruptly, she said: "A good dance," and took her ritual knife away. "You may keep your ship and pretty playmates."

He almost sagged in relief right then and there—but he needed more than that to make this gambit worthwhile.

"I have further terms."

"Name them."

"My ship repaired and fully reprovisioned, in exchange for all its trade goods," he said immediately.

The *Sooty Gull's* hold had been emptied and he would wager every remaining kez in the House Imos coffers that the prizes would soon be divvied up according to the outcomes of four or five dozen dances due to take place in the lesser circles below. Best get what he could.

"Granted."

"Guest-rights for my crew."

Xya *tsked*. "I judged them yours already; do not insult me and mine by implying otherwise. None will touch them, save at your command or by their consent."

He didn't dare look to confirm that: break eye contact with Xya now and she could construe that as a further insult. But a brief, narrowly focused Seeking showed him the Issolm Supplicants were on their feet once more, shaking out cramps and massaging stiff muscles, the four crew who had escorted them disappeared about their ordinary duties.

Well done, Nheras sent.

Very well done, Elaram added.

Ghardon, of course, gave off only dissatisfaction (which

Ylaen attributed to his slow, dawning realization that he never had, and would never have, a chance at victory against him in the circle).

Rahelu also said nothing. He did, however, sense a grudging admiration from her silence and a hint of concern. Not in her resonance aura, which was warded (when was it not?) but in the tilt of her chin and the covert glances she used to tally his injuries.

"Your healers to tend and restore my heartbane-afflicted to good health."

Xya mulled over that stipulation for a long time. "Granted. For a price."

Her next words were in the Free Speech: "Your heart."

Gods, no. Not this.

"Is it weak and divided still?"

Don't look at the others.

"My heart is strong and whole." It was his soul that was broken.

"I believe you—"

She didn't, she didn't; that was patently false. What Xya did have was a glimmer of hope: a delicate, pale gold thread worked through her resonance aura like the filigreed hilt of the heavy cutlass at her hip.

"—but Zovresh requires more concrete proof."

"What proof does he desire?"

"His exact words were: 'Tell that useless, milk-blooded boy to earn his scars.'"

Xya offered him her knife.

Ylaen took it, numb.

He went to Vaaqin first. Ylaen owed Vaaqin much, but he owed Maketh more.

Would Zovresh care how Ylaen killed so long as he did?

Blood pooled beneath the old man. Vaaqin no longer

struggled to free himself—he no longer had the strength—but he had plenty of opinions left to offer.

"Weakling," the old man gasped. "Coward. Sentimental, soft-hearted fool. Spawn of a—"

Vaaqin died with a sneer on his lips and Xya's knife in his gut.

See, father? I can be strong. Stronger than you.

One nod of approval from Xya was all it took for uncle Maketh to be carried below to the healers' apothecary.

Good. *Good.* He had never liked Vaaqin anyway.

As for Anathwan...

Did he need her?

Yes. Yes, he needed her; none of them had managed to fully decipher her notes, which were destroyed now. It would be foolish to reach the Endless Gate and be thwarted by a lack of knowledge.

He considered her Supplicants as he retraced his steps out of the blood-soaked circle.

What would uncle Maketh advise? Whose life could Ylaen spend, to prove his loyalty lay with his clan and his father, instead of his House and his mother?

Whose life would Anathwan spend?

Elaram was the obvious choice. Maketh had named her a liability to their mission and she was: she had nothing to offer in terms of offensive or defensive capabilities; her skill in Obfuscation was so non-existent that she couldn't even defend herself reliably; she was childish and silly and thoughtless and rude to the point of occasional cruelty, and she wasn't even supposed to be here anyway! She had begged and begged until Anathwan had relented; had wished to see the *Stormbringer's Judgment* for herself—

Well. It would be a fitting fate. Ghardon would hate him for it but Ghardon hated him already. Nheras would understand; or if she did not, he could make her understand. Rahelu…

Rahelu had made it very clear that he was nothing to her. So her opinions ought to be nothing to him.

"Come here, Elaram," he said.

Ylaen extended his free hand—or tried to. His useless left arm didn't respond, and neither did Elaram.

Couldn't blame her, really. He did not look his best right now.

"I'm not going to hurt you." *I'm going to kill you.* The thought, the decision didn't seem real, so he repeated it: *I'm going to kill you.* "I promise."

Not a lie; he knew exactly where to cut her to make death quick and painless. Throw in a strong, sustained Projection and all she would feel was the ecstasy she had insisted he was incapable of arousing.

"Jhobon wanted me to tell you something."

Curiosity. Yearning. Both stronger than caution.

Elaram came to him.

Warily.

But she came.

"What is it?" she asked. Caught his despairing glance down at his left hand and took the useless appendage with her slender fingers. "What did he say?"

"He said…he said…"

She's here, you have her, you have Xya's knife; just tell her what Jhobon needed you to tell her, then do what you're supposed to do, what you have to do. And then—then—

The heavy foreboding lodged in his heart expanded. Pushed the air out of his lungs so he could not speak. Grew so immensely strong that it took up all the space inside his aching ribs, leaving no room for his heart to beat as the world spun about the axis of the moment upon him and his Guild-trained resonance senses screamed—

Augury invaded his mind:

He has no words for her, for his tsol-ek left none. What he has is a feeling, stolen from a shadow-painted memory experienced through their tsol-bond—

Blessed silence.

Warmth and blue silk.

Sweetness.

—a beautiful, bright talisman his tsol-ek clings to as the Stormbringer's fist crushes him in its watery grasp: comfort for his pain, light to dispel his terror, and love to defeat his despair.

Words have gone to the eighth hell.

He kisses her; as he had never kissed her; as his tsol-ek had kissed her (but would never again) and through that kiss, he tells her what his tsol-ek would have told her, had he but found the words:

Sorry, he said sorry; sorry I ran from you; sorry I broke my word; sorry I will leave you I am leaving that I left that I am gone and I will never, ever come back.

'Oh,' she says and folds her arms around him.

Just like that, he crumples and drops Xya's knife. Makes the same fucking mistake all over again, undoing his victory. This time, there is no hiding his weakness for the whole clan is here to witness his shame, and that—that is an even worse betrayal of his tsol-ek's memory than running her through.

He can still redeem himself.

She is distracted now, howling out the grief she has bottled up right along with him. Their legs give out underneath them so she and he sit on the deck and wail like two bawling babes, insensible to everyone and everything.

The hilt of Xya's knife digs into his right calf.

But oh, oh—

His tsol-ek had held her, just like this.

He remembers her looking at him, just like this.

—and he can't; he can't; he can't he—

He did the next best thing:

Scraped up every bit of the bleak despair weighing him down. Forged it into four Projections that resembled thick lengths of chain. Slapped the makeshift Suborned collars around the unwary Issolm Supplicants' necks, then tightened his control over them until they fell on their knees and bowed their heads once more.

Ylaen wiped Vaaqin's blood off Xya's knife on a lock of Elaram's hair, then faced the presence seated in his father's rosewood chair.

"That woman is a Harbinger and an Elder of the Houses, and the one in charge of the Dominion's mission," he announced. "Her focus stone belongs to me now, and she is to be placed in the mage cells for questioning. As for these four, they're worth more alive. Put them in the slave pens." Ylaen looked deep into Xya's eyes and addressed the presence lurking behind her stare. "My gift to you, Zovresh."

Thunderous silence as the clan awaited judgment.

"Ylaen," Zovresh-as-Xya said, then crushed him close in a father's forgiving embrace. "Welcome home, my son."

33
SEARCH

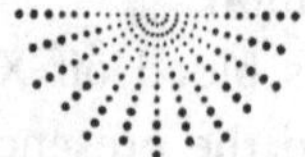

EARLY WINTER, 530 A.E./A.F.

GHARDON WAS QUITE CERTAIN THAT THE accommodations he shared with his sisters were undesirable by any reasonable standard.

The slave pens were cramped, dark as pitch, fetid with the stench of unwashed bodies and human filth, and far danker than how he had imagined the part of the sewer network that ran beneath the Lowdocks. (Upon hearing him express that sentiment, Rahelu had, inexplicably, laughed until she cried and then cried until she began to laugh again for a whole span.) There were no windows (they were well below the waterline) or light wells (with three decks overhead) and very little fresh air (the sole entry point was a small hatch located at the center of the long narrow corridor).

The slave pens were also filled with Ana's screams.

The Elder had been chained up at the opposite end of the hold. There, in a separate saltwater mage cell, the ship's healers had attempted their many cures. After some weeks of mending her body, they discovered heartbane poisoning was not the sole reason for the Elder's uncooperative state.

The captain was not pleased.

She dismissed her healers and threw her eyes and arms ceiling-ward. What followed, Ghardon assumed, was an extended and colorful bout of railing at the Starfather's capriciousness punctuated with the expletive "uvesht-mo!" until Rahelu told him Captain Xya had cried out to the heavens for wisdom, and that one of the curse words was a name and the other actually meant 'sage'.

The captain's appeal had summoned an entity straight out of the eighth hell. More apparition than human, the black-robed sage resembled a bundle of shadows given twisted form. It *flowed*, rather than walked, the spidersilk-delicate silver sigils stitched on its robes rippling in an unseen wind. The accumulated resonance in the much-to-be-desired ambience had parted before the creature's measured approach as though repelled by its presence. The scraps that failed to flee in time had been quickly absorbed...by the black serpentine knife that hung at its waist.

Oh gods, Ghardon had thought. Gold flecks, suspended in the knife's glossy ebon surface, caught the lamplight and trailed sparks across his vision. *That sage is one of* them.

Beside him, Rahelu had emitted a most un-Rahelu-like whimper as the hunched figure turned its cowled head in the direction of their cell.

At such a distance (fifty strides, well within comfortable bow range, if only he had his bow) and in such a gloom, the cultist's face ought to have been obscured beneath its hood, but Ghardon would swear to anyone who cared to question him under Seeking that what he saw was two glittering black gems set in weeping eye sockets staring back.

"Blades. Blood." Rahelu had shuddered as the cultist drew its ravenous weapon and her aura had shuddered with her, its fear-spiked edges piercing his aura as the four of them huddled together. Sympathetic resonance had brought his own nightmares back with a vengeance. "Chains."

Ana had cried out as the cultist approached. Her body had arced and spasmed and thrashed while the serpentine knife rended her resonance aura to ribbons and her Supplicants cowered in the farthest corner of their cage.

The captain was zealous in her search for answers:

"Where is the Endless Gate?"

"What does the artifact look like?"

"What powers does it grant?"

"Who can wield it?"

"How does one wield it?"

"Can it be controlled without the crown?"

Sometimes the interrogation lasted only a quarter-span; sometimes it seemed to span an eternity. Always, it elicited terrible screams from Ana, screams that lingered long after the captain and her bloodied ritual knife departed.

But Ana did not break.

The rest of them, however...

Ela had sunk straight back into despondence.

Nheras alternated between bouts of flinching at every *chitter* and *scritch* of the creatures scrabbling in the shadows and periods of unnatural calm that involved muttering to herself under her breath: "This isn't happening. This isn't real. It's not happening. It can't happen to *me*."

Ghardon had never wanted to shake the both of them more while yelling: *'Wake the fuck up! It's real, this shitty nightmare is real; stop pretending that it isn't and we're not absolutely, totally fucked!'*

But Rahelu had already done enough yelling for all of them. She had begun captivity by embracing her element: explosive, senseless rage. The moment Ylaen Imos had released his Projection, she had launched a flurry of pointless attacks: kicking and biting and snarling curses in three different languages and flinging pathetically weak Projections that amounted to little more than annoyances for her guards.

They, in turn, had clubbed her to the point of near unconsciousness, then shackled her hand and foot before physically dragging her below deck.

(The rest of them had had the privilege of being shackled right before they were tossed inside their cell.)

And now Rahelu was beginning to make him question what, exactly, qualified as 'reasonable standards'. In a final bid to cling on to the very last shreds of his sanity, he had embraced the debate with gusto, only for her to crush his opening arguments by pointing out the hammocks in the *Sooty Gull's* cargo hold were not an appropriate benchmark, them being his sole point of reference for low-status shipboard accommodations notwithstanding, since the sleeping quarters of a free crew were not remotely comparable to a storage area for unwilling and dangerous live cargo that had to be drugged into docility.

"The Tidelocks," she said in a far-off, dreamleaf-induced lilt. "They should be our reference point and they're far worse than these cells." Then she went on to wax lyrical about the fact that the raiders had given them *straw—*

("Our bedding, obviously," he had concluded as the cell door *clanged* shut behind them, though how four people were going to fit on what amounted to an armful of straw was concerning. They'd have to take turns.

Rahelu had stirred. "No, idiot, it's for toileting," she'd replied and struggled upright. "There's no piss bucket."

"What else are we to sleep on?" he had asked. "Certainly not on that floor"—he'd lifted one foot to inspect the bottom of his boot and had instantly regretted it—"in that scum."

"It's called a deck," Rahelu had retorted. "You should know that by now." Then she had preemptively ended their discussion by dropping her trousers and loincloth to squat and soak *their accommodations* with what seemed to be an entire canteen's worth of urine and wipe her ass with a handful of *their bedding*.)

—because the Tidelocks didn't have straw. The Tidelocks flooded twice a day. The Tidelocks had slimy sea moss and hungry little crabs with hard spiky shells and sharp pincers that scuttled in when the tide washed out so the prisoners could never sleep for fear of death by drowning or death by being feasted upon by a thousand tiny crustaceans—

"You're right, you're right!" he said hastily. "This is far better than the Tidelocks."

They did *not* need to augment the waking spans in their hellhole with further horrors; his resurgent memories from Petitioning, added to the fresh agony of Ana's suffering—and the foreknowledge of all she would still suffer and was yet to suffer—had already poisoned his dreams.

(Those always began innocuously enough: dozing beneath a lovely warm quilt. Then: irritation caused by the shafts of second-rate duck down feathers poking through the silk covers to prickle and itch his skin. Finally: terror, as he woke to discover the quilt had morphed into an army of rats crawling all over him as he slept.)

Later, after they'd repelled the most recent rat invasion with fists and feet and what faint Projections their low heartbane dosages allowed them to produce:

Rahelu announced, "I've changed my mind." She tossed a dead rat into a corner filled with the corpses of its fallen comrades and their shit and used straw. "You're right; this is far worse. The prisoners in the Tidelocks have access to an endless supply of clean seawater and fresh crabmeat. It tastes better than raw rat meat."

Ghardon did not ask how she knew what raw rat meat tasted like; he feared hunger might drive him to discover it for himself. The idle thought had crossed his mind the last time the healer's timid apprentice had come by on one of her occasional rounds to wash and clean Ana's body and cell, and to supply the Supplicants with sea sponges soaked in an astringent liquid so they could scrub themselves.

Towards the end of their stint aboard the *Sooty Gull*, after they had eaten all that the storm had left them and starved for a time, he had, eventually, overrode Rahelu's objections and shot down several gulls, after they had extracted what navigational information they could. (No other seabirds—questryls, especially—had been willing to venture near.) When lines baited with gull parts caught no fish, they had eaten the stringy remains themselves.

Raw rat meat could not possibly taste worse than sun-roasted gull. Surely if he gave the rat a good scrubbing, it would be clean enough to eat. In fact, if he subscribed to Rahelu's 'add-enough-salt-and-it'll-taste-great' theory (ignoring the fact that said theory had been thoroughly disproved by his last culinary experiment), it would taste better than the slop they were given.

When Ghardon next woke to Ana's screaming, covered in rats and screaming himself, then found himself salivating as he seized the wriggly little creature trying to burrow inside his trousers, he knew things had gone too far.

His mind was not what it was, after eighteen days of privations measured by slops and screams.

(Or thereabouts. 'Eighteen days' was a best estimate with a margin for error measured in days; a margin so wide he didn't know why they bothered to reckon the passage of time, save for the fact that Rahelu would not let the issue go.)

That was when the next idle thought occurred: perhaps he ought to confess that he could hear the starsong too.

He couldn't hear it *now*, obviously; hadn't heard it since their second meal in these cells, after Rahelu's failed attempt at taking down one of their guards with Projection had gotten heartbane added to their food in addition to the dreamleaf. But if they stopped drugging him…

He would hear the starsong again.

He could tell them where to go.

Better yet, he could provide them with the Elder's notes.

Take him out of this hell; give him a hot bath, a comb, and clean clothes; allow him a few days of recovery in a nice hammock (he did not dare hope for a soft bed); lay out inkstone and parchment and put a brush pen in his hand, and he could reconstruct every page of the documents he and Ela had burned with one hundred percent accuracy. After that…

He could look for an opportunity to free the others.

He could save them.

Undoubtedly, Ylaen Imos—

(No, not Imos. That bastard didn't deserve a House name, even if it was a traitorous one. While coups were always bloody affairs—and any coup of Atriarch Hnan Imos's would be doubly so—it was still far more restrained and targeted as a move than, say, manipulation of trade to engineer the wholesale economic ruin and thus toppling of a House entire. And, in all truthfulness, Ghardon wasn't opposed to somebody else replacing Atriarch Relk Isilc as the Exalted Dominance. Theoretically, that would change, with his oaths, but he wasn't sworn to House Isilc *yet*.)

Undoubtedly, *No-sleeves* had thought the same. (He hadn't been wrong; they were all here, still very much alive, and thus 'saved'.)

No-sleeves, however, couldn't hear the starsong, and thus couldn't lead the Crimson Storm to the Endless Gate. The captain's increasingly urgent daily visitations and line of questioning were proof of that. Fleets were hungry things, and the Desolate Isles must be desolate indeed. Ghardon's mind might be muddled on how long they'd spent in captivity, but his stomach had no trouble tracking the size of their meals. The portions, which had never been generous, had grown noticeably scanty as of late.

Nor did No-sleeves have any idea of how to exploit the artifact, supposing he ever found it.

Whatever theories Jhobon Imrell had left behind in his as-yet-unburned notebook were, unsurprisingly, not substantial enough—though that may not have been Jhobon's fault. Ghardon could not say for certain. The only pages he'd committed to memory and crystal had been the maps. Everything else he'd left unexamined, out of respect. (Everything else had been written in code.) He'd wager fifty gold kez that No-sleeves was having no success with deciphering Jhobon's notes, since there was nothing between that strutting ishtrel's ears except for two lists—one itemizing his knives and the other detailing his conquests.

Which meant Ghardon could, actually, save them.

All it would cost was his loyalty to Ana and to House Issolm...which was worth—what, exactly?

How much was an oath worth, when you knew you would soon be swearing a different one?

That, right there, was when Ghardon decided he could no longer trust his own thoughts.

He withdrew inward, contemplating the mind block Maketh had laid on top of the very foundations of his consciousness. Wondered if he ought to try retreating inside, as Ela and Rahelu had told him Ana had done, then eliminated that as a viable option too, seeing as how he had neither the ability to slip past the seamless walls Maketh had constructed nor had Ana's mind block prevented the cultist from doing...whatever it was that had been done to her.

Ana yet resisted.

Her example ought to inspire him. But all he could think of was how they had failed, and he had failed, and how she—

She had failed too, and most critically. If her way was the

right way, then her methods would have worked. Ylaen Imos would have listened to him and Jhobon Imrell wouldn't be dead and he and his sisters wouldn't be here; they would've made it to the Endless Gate with the Elder's body and she would've done whatever stupid fucking working the Houses needed her to do, to reverse whatever horrible ritual the cultists had fucked up, and in fucking up, fucked up Augury for the whole world, and she and they and he would be halfway back across the ocean by now, on the way home to—

No, no; it was time to let go of that delusion; it was interfering with his decision-making, suggesting courses of actions that would compromise his personal integrity and making them look more and more attractive by the span.

Ghardon gave up and joined Ela in her despondence. He ceded the corner they'd designated for sleeping to his sisters and bedded down in the middle of the piss-soaked floor.

Because why the fuck not? No rescue was coming.

Like it or not, this miserable cage would define the borders of his existence for the foreseeable future, so the benefit of regaining his personal space was entirely worth it.

WHILE ELARAM and Ghardon spent every waking moment in a daze, Rahelu and Nheras watched and waited.

Their only visitor was the newly promoted first mate who appeared at unpredictable spans to deliver their meals. A nonchalant man at least two decades younger compared to his predecessor, One-Ear, he had a burly torso that was only one-quarter scarred but his face...

His face was a different story. Strong and unflappable despite his apparent youth, and well-versed in every trick, threats slid off Scarface like a blunted spearpoint on a polished steel shield. While he was happy to banter in heavily accented Aleznuaweithish, he never prolonged his visits no matter how prettily Nheras entreated him to stay. Their feeble attempts to overpower him physically were about as successful as trying to stay dry while swimming, and he was far too canny to provide anything that might be turned into a tool or a weapon—he ladled burnt clods of congealed congee scraped from the bottom of the cookpot straight into their cupped hands with their water ration.

The powdered heartbane and dreamleaf that laced their meals numbed their aches and stinging cuts, set their minds wandering, and dulled their resonance senses so much that the only auras Rahelu could perceive in blurry detail were those of the others, and the starsong was silenced altogether.

She tried very, very hard to dismiss the inner voice that insisted on blaming Nheras. (*All that trouble to clean yourselves up and for what? You ended up in the slave pens anyway.*')

Ylaen being a treasonous unnomobunezra was not Nheras's fault. Nheras was fucking terrified and yet she was still *trying*. She made appeal after appeal to Scarface—

(Surely the great Zovresh already had plenty of Suborned mages. Surely the crew deserved some recompense for giving up an entire season's worth of profitable raiding on the Aleituan Sea to chase some silly legends about an artifact that they wouldn't get to use and benefit from personally. Surely they'd prefer to have some gold—nice, tangible, spendable gold—in their pockets instead.)

—until he agreed to suggest to the captain that she might consider making an inquiry with the Houses regarding their possible ransom through the standard relay channels.

Word came back swiftly...and came at a cost.

Scarface lingered during his next visit to watch them lap up their next meals with their tongues like dogs. It did not take genius to figure out what he wanted. With Elaram and Ghardon still catatonic, and Nheras having proven herself incapable of seeing such endeavors through to their end, Rahelu resigned herself to the unpleasant task and got on her knees, unasked, as he approached.

"Not you," Scarface told her. "He's boasted of having you and I don't want his leavings, 'specially as he says you bite." He beckoned to Nheras. "You. Let's see if your mouth is as sweet as your voice."

Nheras did not sound very sweet as she gagged and choked.

Nor did Scarface look like he was enjoying himself, but he did keep his word. When he withdrew, he handed Nheras a scrap of parchment containing the Houses' response in someone's untidy scrawl:

> *Salutations and greetings to Captain Xya of the Crimson Storm. The whereabouts of Elder Anathwan Issolm and Supplicants Elaram Issolm, Ghardon Issolm, Nheras Issolm, and Rahelu Issolm are known. We regret to inform you that the individuals claiming to be the individuals so named in your inquiry are imposters; renegade mages skilled in the art of resonance forgery. Our policy prevents us from engaging with such criminals further.*

The Houses' refusal to recognize them in favor of pointlessly maintaining that stupid fiction about conducting a regional audit in Peshwan Yrg to preserve the no-longer-required secrecy of their mission was not Nheras's fault.

So they continued to watch and wait and meditate and stretch their limbs as best as they could in the limited space they had while debating their next move in endless circles.

"It's now or never," Rahelu insisted.

Nheras kept telling her, "Not yet. The circumstances aren't right. Even if we succeed, we won't get far, and that will land us back here—minus the element of surprise—which is a net loss, fish guts."

"If not now, then when?" she demanded. "There's a limit to what the mind and the body can withstand."

Right on cue, the captain arrived with her knives.

The healers subsequently informed Xya that they would be able to revive the Elder's heart but once more, for the apothecary was depleted of all but the most basic of healing herbs and bandages, and the prisoner would most assuredly die if she lost blood faster than her body could replenish it.

Next time, the captain brought a hammer.

"I am reliably advised by my healers that scholars of medicine reckon there to be some two hundred bones in the adult human body," Xya said. "Shall we count yours?"

Anathwan's screaming began anew.

Rahelu won the argument.

For a week, she and Nheras did no more than lap at their rations—just enough to moisten dry tongues and parched throats, leaving the rats to hide the evidence and Elaram and Ghardon to keep watch, drug-addled out of their minds. Within a half-span, they would regain their command of resonance to sink deep into mage trances, channeling whatever scraps of power they could gather into the focus stones they had kept hidden away.

When Scarface next appeared, they were ready: Rahelu kneeling by the bars, hands cupped in her lap and head bowed, as the others feigned sleep: Nheras curled on top of what remained of the straw, Elaram and Ghardon propped upright against her legs, their hands entwined behind their backs where they could not be seen from the cell's door.

Scarface lifted his long-handled wooden ladle and threaded its brimming bowl through the narrow bars. As he began to tip congee into Rahelu's hands, the Nheras-led Concordance flickered into existence.

A whip-thin Projection lashed out at his head.

Rahelu surged forward and thrust her arms through the bars.

An Obfuscation barrier of steel-gray flared to life around Scarface as her hands closed on empty air. A heartbeat later, Nheras's Command bounced off the barrier and the dripping wooden ladle slammed into the side of Rahelu's head.

They could have borne his anger; they could have borne derision. Even pity would have given them something to work with. But Scarface simply clucked like an anxious bird discovering its chicks had fallen out of its nest. He barked, summoning three younger crew, and unlocked the cell. His helpers crowded in and seized them. One by one, they were inspected: two sets of hands restraining them while the third stood ready with a bared cutlass as Scarface sliced through tattered clothing to strip and search them at knifepoint. His fingers were cold, rough with calluses and ragged nails that scraped her insides as he probed the depths of every orifice with the same alert detachment that the horse traders at Market Square used to inspect a potential purchase.

Satisfied they had no more surprises stored away, Scarface forced congee down their throats until they choked, then left.

He took all the focus stones with him: the Issolm ring she had loaned to Ghardon, the ring she had reclaimed from Nheras for herself, Nheras and Elaram's necklaces, and her gifted Ideth pendant.

Nheras did not say, *'I told you this was a stupid fucking plan, fish-shit-for-brains.'*

She did not need to.

Perhaps Augury might have forewarned them of the points of divergence to avoid; perhaps it could have helped them find other paths that led to escape. Augury, however, had become impossible: none of them could muster the necessary mental state to move beyond the present, let alone explore the more remote probabilities.

Even if they could, they no longer had the means or the opportunity. Three crew accompanied Scarface each time he came to dole out their drugged rations now, their presence serving as both unspoken reminder and threat, and they did not leave until every mouthful had been swallowed.

During their fourth, awful, supervised meal:

Anathwan screamed as Xya crushed another bone.

Elaram and Ghardon mechanically went through the routine motions of eating while Rahelu weighed whether the satisfaction she would gain from flinging her congee through the iron bars would be worth the humiliation of Scarface forcing her to lick it off every surface it had splattered across —him and his helpers included.

Nheras walked right up to their cage door and rattled it.

"Enough. Enough!" she shouted at the tall figure backlit by the circle of lamplight by Anathwan's mage cell. "Captain Xya, if you wish to find the Endless Gate, you will release me at once. In return, I will deliver that crown into your hands."

What?

The screams cut off.

"What game do you play now?" Rahelu hissed. "The crown is fucking *gone*."

Nheras had to be lying. Of course she was lying; of course a soft House-born like her would spin a lie about the crown in a desperate, transparent attempt to win free of their miserable cage. Rahelu would too, had she the wits to think of it, but she'd seen Venoru throw the crown overboard with her own eyes so the possibility had never crossed her mind.

('*Because you're a dull, unimaginative, terrible excuse for a mage,*' sneered the part of her that spoke with Nheras's voice, and she could not dismiss it for the statement was true. If it weren't she would have freed them by now.)

Then: "Nheras…"

Anathwan, speaking for the first time in months, in a

horribly weak, papery rasp that somehow carried across the length of the hold.

Footsteps echoed.

"The crown?" A growing circle of light burned away the shadows, then blossomed in their faces and blinded them. "The crown that Ylaen swore lies at the bottom of the Abmerduan Sea?"

Over Anathwan's faint protestations of "Velaz, velaz," Nheras said, "The true crown was never lost; merely hidden."

Fury that Rahelu had believed beyond her roared in her ears, swelled in her veins, and bled into the ambient resonance. She forgot the congee and Scarface and the captain and hurled herself in the direction of Nheras's voice.

"You fucking—"

The cage door creaked open. Someone slugged her from the side. She landed, rolled, and ended face down in shit, with Scarface's boot planted in her shoulder blades and the tip of his cutlass pressed against the base of her spine.

"My crew found nothing in their search."

"Perhaps they weren't looking in the right places."

"My crew are quite thorough."

"Then perhaps they lack the eyes to see."

"Bring that mage's chest. And summon the sage."

One of the crew ran off to obey. The other two joined Scarface inside the cell to keep the loyal Issolm Supplicants mute and subdued, and that traitorous bitch joined the captain outside to talk terms.

First: guest-rights for her as Nheras of Ilyn—not as a member of Ylaen's crew.

In addition: uncontested possession of the focus stones Scarface had confiscated. New clothing. Her own furnished cabin on the uppermost deck, with a window and private wash facilities. Three meals a day at the captain's table instead of the mess. Freedom of the decks. All to be fully paid in kind by services rendered while onboard as a Guild-trained Harbinger answerable only to the captain. Her first duties would consist of assisting the captain and Ylaen with their study of the crown and answering any questions they had regarding Elder Anathwan's original plans, which she had, of course, analyzed extensively when she had had the opportunity to do so prior to their destruction and she was, therefore, uniquely suited to contributing valuable insights on how those plans might be adjusted to benefit the Crimson Storm as well as the Dominion.

Finally: safe passage to Tsorek-fa and a transfer token that would grant passage home from Tsorek-fa to Ennuost Yrg, in exchange for bearing an encrypted message from Zovresh of the Crimson Storm keyed for Atriarch Lynath Ilyn alone.

"I think life aboard the *Stormbringer's Judgment* will suit you," Captain Xya said as she and Nheras sealed their bargain in Free Territories fashion: fresh cuts along the inside of their forearms, clasped together for a ten count so their blood could mingle. "You negotiate well."

"You are very kind to say so, Captain."

When Anathwan's white oak chest arrived—

When Nheras revealed she, alone, had been deemed worthy to bear Anathwan's trust—

When the cowled, hunched, black-robed cultist confirmed the true crown had been hidden all along inside Anathwan's copy of the Issolm *Supplicant's Handbook* behind a clever, anchored Seeming of Nheras's making—

Still Rahelu lay there, her mouth full of Nheras's shit, outrage and hurt and her resonance senses reeling from the vicious smugness of Ghardon's vindication (*'I knew it! I knew it! Why else would the granddaughter of Lynath Ilyn swear to Issolm?'*) warring with the denial and hope (*'An act; it must be an act.'*) as her eyes searched that perfect mask for some sign: a flicker of the eye; a twitch of the nose; some other, fleeting expression; some hint, knowable only to those who had spent months living together in close quarters, that—

"This crown is priceless. Yet you do not negotiate anything for your House-sworn siblings and your Elder."

"The crown may be priceless but generosity and goodwill are not limitless. You are no fool, I know Ylaen to be unforgiving, and—if he resembles his sire in temperament as much as he does in his looks—I do not dare ask anything that might be displeasing to the great Zovresh."

"Wise of you."

"Not my wisdom but my grandmother's; she taught me to bargain with the future in mind."

"Wiser still, then, to heed her teachings."

"Call it payment in kind. My companions have never treated me as their true kin; I am but doing likewise."

Every word rang true.

Every. Single. One.

Nheras Ilyn was not—and had never considered herself— their sister.

Rahelu was a fool to have ever believed otherwise.

All the fight went out of her.

She ceased to mark the passage of days and settled into numbed nothingness. Not the peace of true meditation—that escape, too, was denied her. Just a dull state of suspension where she felt neither alive nor dead; a sensation of being untethered to the world, mind floating in an emptiness that should have been thick with ambient resonance, yet shackled to her body by a heaviness that lay on her skin where her aura should be.

***

TIME PASSED in a long monotonous blur.

One day, the *Stormbringer's Judgment* stopped moving.

Elaram was first to stir. "What is happening?" she rasped.

It took a moment for Rahelu to register the question. The Aleznuaweithish words were so sweet on her ear that she wanted to weep. For the first time in...in...

Long enough, was the only specifics her mind could supply.

Rahelu untangled herself from their huddle and crawled to the far side of their cage. There, she cupped both hands around her ear, pressed it against the hull, and listened:

Cannon wheels rumbling as they trundled over the gun decks. Rapid *thudthudthud-thudding* of bare feet dashing to obey orders. Voices, many, many voices, raised in the call and response of work songs. Inadvertently, she found herself mouthing the words along to one: the rousing oar chant Jhobon had taught them so long ago, during those beautiful, sunlit, fish-filled days on the *Sooty Gull*, when they'd sat round the fire hearth in an unbroken circle—

Music she had forgotten; the sounds of life and freedom.

She wanted to see it all, breathe it in, immerse herself— lose herself—in the world outside the awful dark. Was that a whiff of fresh air wafting through some invisible crack in the hull? Did she imagine the sizzle of fat dripping on hot coals that set her mouth to watering? For a moment she tasted salt and smelled roasting meat; cried, thinking of the platter of skewers she had devoured in Peshwan Yrg; then realized the salt she tasted was from the tears running down her face.

She reached out with Seeking, not truly expecting to sense anything other than the dead, blank nothingness that kept her cut-off from resonance. Forcing her way through was like swimming in mud: resistance met her in every direc-tion, and the more she struggled, the greater its opposition. But unlike all the other times, this time she felt a glimmer of something through dulled resonance senses.

Rahelu pushed. Felt the blankness yield before her prod-ding like the stretching of a thick membrane. Whimpered as she flailed against it, dashing her mind into the drug-induced barrier over and over again helplessly.

A small hand threaded its slim fingers through hers.

Elaram, she thought, and got a faint pulse in return.

When she pushed at that membrane again, it thinned noticeably to a sheer veil, through which blurred shadows and distorted emotions could be glimpsed.

Another hand, the clasp of its callused palms and fingers rough against their skin.

Ghardon, she thought.

His answering pulse was clear and distinctive.

Their Concordance emerged slowly, like hauling a handcart that was stuck fast out of its rut. Unstable. It needed to be anchored; needed a steady flow of power to sustain it but Scarface had taken their focus stones.

Only one way to get it.

Rahelu turned her arm over, exposing the blue tracery of veins coursing beneath the skin. Pressed her wrist against her mouth; gagged at the taste of soured sweat and urine.

Bit down before she could change her mind.

Coppery blood flooded her tongue, a crude but direct conduit to the power in her veins, and she cast her mind back six years ago:

We stand upon the deck.

(She had first beheld the grand harbor of Ennuost Yrg from the bow of a riverboat, on a day when the Skymother had hung her blazing white-gold lamp high.)

Sun warms our eager faces.

(Blue skies, beautifully clear, stretched to infinity in a gradual curve.)

The beckoning shore.

(Bird calls, sea breeze, wave song, and market cries blended in a welcoming chorus.)

At last, at last! We are here.

Rahelu honed in on the emotions defining that memory: hope, burning fierce and bright; the steadfastness of clasped hand in hand in hand, rooted in the ties of family.

Past and present blurred; did not quite merge—but the sympathetic resonance was enough.

Their Concordance snapped into place.

Rahelu's Evocation flared; crumbled; its power used up.

And Elaram sent their combined focus soaring out, out, over the sea:

A breach in the shining horizon.

Unrelievedly black.

Unnatural in its geometric perfection: a symmetrical triangle with equal sides; a perfect cone whose peak is evenly broken, as if some divine hand had decapitated a mountain in one clean swing.

No seabirds soar above the slopes. No gentle harbor softens the fury of the waves breaking upon the jagged basalt reefs lurking beneath the surrounding shallows. No rustling grass relieves the severity of the bare, rocky sides which slant in such regular angles from the sharp rim to the foam-wracked surf that you couldn't have drawn a straighter line with a ruler.

The dead islet is an inverse hole, punched through the empty stretch of ocean on Jhobon's maps to wound the eartharc sky.

"Oh! It's just as Silcarez described," Elaram breathed. "The Endless Gate."

34

SOLUTION

WINTER SOLSTICE EVE,
THE 14TH DAY OF TRUEWINTER,
530 A.E./A.F.

YLAEN WATCHED, MESMERIZED, AS THE SEA frothed and churned and threw up sulfurous spray that stung his eyes and skin, his idle hands fidgeting with the glittering black crown in his lap. Up close, the Endless Gate still looked as impossibly inaccessible as it had from the aftercastle of the *Stormbringer's Judgment*. No marks of weathering or erosion marred the unnatural geometrical perfection of its massive basalt columns, despite the ferocity with which the turbulent waves tossed themselves at those sheer cliffs.

Ostensibly, he sat in the lookout's seat at the prow instead of taking the stoker's position at the first oar because he was leading the landing party.

In reality, he had been relegated there, by his injury.

Minor nerve damage, the healers had told him. If he'd been a fraction slower to dodge Vaaqin's knife, he would have lost the use of the arm entirely. One half-hearted move in the circle, to disarm instead of stab, and now? All his fine control —gone. Oh, the arm still moved, the fingers still closed, he could still grasp a knife by the hilt in a convincing hold. But his grip was weak, his range of motion severely curtailed. The next time he had to step into a circle…

Best not think of that.

Ylaen braced for pain and gritted his teeth. He forced himself to pass the time by doing the exercises the healers had given him. First: the hand. Then: the arm. Finally: the shoulder. Winced as muscles, tendons, and ligaments protested at the strain required for the slow, steady movements.

They spent four precious spans cautiously circumnavigating the islet at a prudent half-kual distance before he spotted the signs described in Silcarez's memoirs: a gap in the surging swells, where the ebb and flow hinted at a narrow channel cut through the submerged reefs ringing the treacherous shoals.

"There!" That useless left arm shook as he fought to keep it pointed in the right direction. "Steady on the oars as you take us in."

A sharp chorus of "ayes!" answered.

Voices rose in a new chant as Ruan urged them to pick up the rhythm of their strokes. The boats steadily gained momentum until they seemed to fly, skipping over the choppy waters like a cast stone. Soon, the *splash-splash-splash* of wooden blades heaving against the current and the *beat-beat-beat* of the waves upon the hull merged with the other, insistent tone that had haunted Ylaen ever since he had taken up the crown.

'*Humming*' was not the right word to express what he heard but neither was '*singing*'. '*Itching*' perhaps. A constant niggling at the very edge of his resonance senses that made him want to jam his fingers inside his ears. The signal seemed to come from everywhere and nowhere all at once: a contradiction of long slow pulses, so low in frequency they seemed to emanate from the entire islet, and a thin sustained whine so high-pitched it raised the hair on the back of his arms and juddered his bones. Sometimes, he thought he could detect a speech-like pattern to those irregular fluctuations. Like a call. Or a summons. When he had mentioned it, offhand, to Nheras, she had looked at him as though he had lost his mind, so he had shrugged and did not mention it again. But at night, safe in the privacy of Vaaqin's—his—cabin, he kept darker thoughts at bay by allowing his imagination to pair the restless rise and fall of the starsong with words as he brushed his finger over the sweeps and curves of the crown's edges, counting the tiny raised bumps the way he used to count the stars when he had trouble falling asleep.

In the end, Ylaen decided he was right.

The starsong was a call. One full of unbearable, unknowable, desperate loneliness that he now recognized as the mirror of his own grief-stricken, wounded, soul-torn cry to the void.

Come back.

He shut his eyes and did not open them again until he heard the *crunch* of wooden hull against pebbled shore.

The moment he set foot on the islet, the entire world trembled.

Fearful whispers rippled through the crew.

The pressure in the ambient resonance flashed from a subtle stir to a choking squeeze; the next instant, the gentle vibrations beneath their feet became a groaning quake. Cries of surprise and pain and alarm rang out as they toppled over, then turned to coughs and curses as they saw the fine black sands had scattered into symmetrical patterns, like some great celestial hand had stretched out a thousand thousand finger-knives to mark the virgin beach with naming scars. The few who had gotten to their feet were knocked down again as the constant background hum of thwarted longing swelled into the foreground and drowned out all sound.

For a long, long while, the starsong was the only thing anyone could hear until a harsh croak rasped against that beautiful, terrible melody.

"Divine One."

Uvesht-mo had knelt, facing the sheer slope of the mountain that lay at the islet's heart, and prostrated himself upon the humming sands.

Ylaen hurriedly adopted the same pose and signed for the rest of his landing party to follow.

"Your faithful have returned and your heir has come."

Uvesht-mo's ritual words seemed to be the answer to a question asked long ago. The starsong shivered, then stilled, and that hush was louder and all the more oppressive for the absence.

From somewhere beyond the long-silent void in his mind: a wordless echo stirred.

Ambient resonance burst into starsong anew.

The discordant melody rose and rose and kept on rising, modulating through eight tonal centers until the unrequited tensions flowered at last into harmonious resolution: a single grand exultation that reverberated through their collective resonance auras for a fraction of a breath—

Come.

How much time passed before he could speak again, Ylaen did not know. What he did know was just how thoroughly he and Jhobon had miscalculated.

The legacy of the heavens was not inside the Endless Gate.

It *was* the Endless Gate.

The gods must be laughing.

"All hands to your appointed tasks!" he snapped. "Get these boats unloaded and follow the sage; you can keep staring at the mountain while you take these crates and barrels up to the shrine. Mind you don't spill any offerings on the way unless it's your blood. Ruan, see that the sage has everything he requires and the special goods are distributed as the captain directed. You can have everyone except for these four." Ylaen pointed. "You two, take the shoreline. You two, take the first boat. I want a complete and accurate survey of this place and the surrounding shallows done within the next two spans so we can take it to the captain, bring the ships in, and have them docked by high sun."

They went at it with alacrity.

Ylaen paced back and forth along the gleaming dock of ebon stone extending out into the sheltered cove, counting each stride from shore to sea:

Three hundred and eighty-eight.

Twelve short of the round figure of four hundred that had been written down in Reshwim's accounts.

He drew his tsol-blade, unnerved.

What else had they gotten wrong?

Too late to wonder. He was committed; they all were. The only thing Ylaen could do was pray. He grasped his ritual knife by its blade. Borrowed the form and the words from the sages' version—the true version—of Enjela's ballad to beg the Starfather's favor:

By my blood on this blade, I petition you for safe passage through the door to Fortune's realm. I, Ylaen Imos, son of Rysere Imos and Zovresh, am come as supplicant, in search of the divine wisdom found in your Eternal Gaze. I dedicate my life to the fulfillment of the vow I once made before my elders, and now make again before the gods, in sight of the sky, the stars, and the sea. Let this sacrifice be a sign of my devotion and faith to that exalted purpose.

Ylaen held still, held his breath, held his bleeding hand

out over the end of the dock until the bright shining steel in his grip dulled to red. Then he gathered every scrap of fear, envy, indecision—all the impurities that had plagued him from birth—and channeled them together with his desperate need.

Exhaled.

Power flowed out from his veins. Light and searing heat flashed through his fingers; his next intake of breath carried the scent of smoke and charred flesh. Resonance flowed over the surface of the blood-coated blade and ignited, radiating a brilliance that left him blinded.

Ylaen hurled the tsol-blade into the sea.

It sank beneath the waves.

He fell to his knees and bowed four times, overwhelmed with relief. Sacrifice accepted. He could have laughed; could have wept; limited himself instead to a hitched breath somewhere between a sigh and a gasp. Dried blood flaked off as he flexed his throbbing left hand and plunged it into the waters.

Warm as a heated bath.

He got up.

Faced the deserted shore. Strode forward with shortened strides. Stopped on the count of four hundred and looked down to see the toes of his boots touching the sand. Looked to the sky and at the black mountain ahead.

Even the sunlight did not seem to truly touch this place.

The bright eartharc rays shimmered briefly upon the dark stone but illuminated no details other than the razor-thin, jagged rim against the gold-and-rose-tinted clouds, and the small, heavily ladened procession led by Uvesht-mo wending its way up the steep slope.

In the back of his mind, the starsong murmured—

Come to me.

Ylaen shivered.

Checked that the crown still hung on his belt, then dragged his attention back to the task at hand: frantically trying to think of some solution to salvage his plan.

He couldn't spirit away an entire fucking islet.

Securing and holding the Endless Gate was equally untenable. The islet was too barren to support life, too remote to feasibly run supply lines to, and too big to defend with only one warship, even if it was the *Stormbringer's Judgment*. Oh, he had no doubts regarding the result if all they had to worry about was a mundane ship-to-ship battle. Xya was a skilled, wily commander, and her crew were disciplined, raid-seasoned veterans whose belief in her leadership was absolute. Any ordinary ship that dared pit itself against the *Stormbringer's Judgment* would soon be a smoking wreck. (As those poor souls aboard that Imrell ship had discovered, in the Dragon's Teeth.) But those advantages meant nothing against enemy ships bearing Conclave journeymages, like that operative who had impersonated Csorath, and Belruonian magepriests who wielded the same uncanny powers as Uvesht-mo.

Wars are won first in the mind and then upon the battlefield.

Fuck!

If he wanted to reshape his future, he had to do so here—now—or not at all, and *he was not ready*.

It had taken weeks of study and experimentation before he recognized one of the threads in Anathwan's notes—the immense vision of Ennuost Yrg the Issolm Elder had summoned aboard the *Winged Arrow*. From there, he and Nheras had been able to extrapolate the rest: a future where the borders of the Dominion began and ended with the oceans that surrounded the Ngutoccai continent; where the eighty-eight federated states of Chanaz had been subsumed by the Houses; where the Conclave's Tower in Anazvela had been torn down and its shining stones repurposed for new Guild halls; where the scattered isles of the Free Territories became trading outposts along the maritime routes that joined the Aleituan to the Abmerduan Sea; a giant hand of wood and canvas stretching out to enfold the Divine Kingdom on the other side of the world within its grasp.

Not Fortunement as the Guild had taught them—the slow, careful analysis of existing possibilities through Augury and the painstaking manipulation of their probabilities—but the deliberate construction of a reality that did not already exist as a possibility.

The Houses' collective will made manifest.

A Seeming.

It hadn't made any sense.

He had glared down at his notes, torn between wanting to shred them for tinder and wanting to reshuffle them to check his conclusions from a different angle, as Jhobon would have done. Seemings were built on phantasmal *what-ifs*. They existed in the liminal space of what *was not* but what one *wanted to be*. Seemings were, in a word, invitations. They offered the heart a convincing escape from what the eyes and senses perceived, but they weren't real.

The loud *rap* of someone's knuckles against the cabin door had interrupted his thoughts.

"Did you hear me?"

That muffled voice was female. Loud and sharp with annoyance that teetered right on the verge of flaring into anger, so he had kicked aside the untidy heap of books and loose papers that threatened to bury him beneath the weight of his failures and got up. His heart had skipped a beat at the shape of her silhouette out in the corridor before his wits pointed out the incongruences in height and bearing and posture and his eyes readjusted to the dimmer light.

"The captain's asking for a report on our progress."

Nheras eyed the mess on the cabin sole behind him. "I'm not going to be the one delivering the bad news again."

He had scowled. Said, "Tell Xya if she wants to see progress, she needs to stop interrupting. She'll get her report when there's something to report."

Then he had slammed the door in her face and leaned against it, listening in vain for the sound of fists beating the wood, because it was not her, it couldn't be her, since she was down in the slave pens where he had consigned her.

Insight had struck with the force of a spear thrust to the gut:

So long as the lie was more desirable than the truth and there was no reason to question it, the heart would believe. If the heart believed, the mind would act and the body would follow.

The lie becomes the truth. (As Rahelu had proved to him, night after night.)

Now: apply the principle at scale…

Ylaen had laughed then; a full-bellied laugh—one that had gone on and on, for whenever he stopped to catch his breath, the sheer ridiculousness had struck him afresh so he began laughing all over again.

The Houses had, quite literally, sent them to go stand in a magic circle and make a wish.

He had thought he'd found the solution then. To be is to *want*. If it was simply a matter of *will* and *desire*…

Stop trying to be Jhobon, with his patience and love of cryptic puzzles. Stop trying to decipher the pages upon pages of esoteric references in Anathwan's notes. Stop trying to decompose the Elder's chain of plausible events into their causal components. Take Anathwan's visualizations. Overwrite her intent by shoving all those existing, competing *wants* pulling you apart into her elegant construction of the future and make it your own. Alter key details to paint a different version of tomorrow, one that will serve Zovresh's goals and fulfill the sages' omens while preserving your mother's life and obeying the letter of your Atriarch's orders; orders that you—that Maketh—are bound by, through oath and duty and blood and crystal:

Fill the Kuath Bay with crimson-sailed ships.

Substitute the purple and black banners of House Isilc lining the marble halls of the palace in Ennuost Yrg with the gold and ivory of House Imos.

Replace the corpulent man upon the throne.

But—like most things Ylaen wanted—it was not to be, and he was a fool for thinking otherwise. The only futures he brought forth that didn't immediately fall apart were ones that stained his hands with blood.

Even when he stood upon the shores of the Endless Gate.

High above, the tiny, ant-like figures scaling the mountain disappeared over its rim. Beneath him, the black sands shifted as the islet thrummed. Old lines were erased with a flicker; new ones emerged. All around, the worst of the worst possibilities he had manifested swirled in the ambient resonance; half-formed, mutated echoes that were neither proper Evocation nor true Augury:

Kerg: dead, from a slashed throat. Csorath: dead, from a thrown knife. Rahelu: dead, windpipe crushed beneath his forearm. Jhobon: dead, taken by the storm. Vaaqin: dead, from a gut wound. Elaram: dead, still smiling, still embracing him even with his blade through her heart. Ghardon: dead, unrecognizable, his face half-eaten by rats. Anathwan: dead, every bone in her body broken. Nheras: dead, severed head rolling to his feet. Xya: dead, a white-and-black fletched arrow lodged in her eye. Father: dead, from a gift of poisoned wine. Mother: dead, ambushed by assassins masquerading as bandits in the Westwoods. Maketh: loyal to the end and dead, lying at the foot of a towering golden throne, and Hnan—

Hnan is still alive, Hnan laughs as Ennuost Yrg burns—

No, no, no, no, no!

The world didn't need him to spill more blood. What it needed was someone who knew how to solve problems, and all he had ever done was create them. The world needed—he needed Jhobon, and Jhobon was *gone*, Jhobon was *dead*, and no power in existence could summon him back from the Stormbringer's realm.

Despair consumed him, an uncontrollable dark tide that dredged up memories of every futile attempt to escape the fate that had been written in the stars. Shadowed resonance flooded out of him; an inescapable maelstrom that trapped him in its vortex.

He forced his breathing into a simple two-count; wrenched his tattered focus into a blunt Seeking so he could hack apart the nightmare he had conjured. But the visualization of his tsol-blade and its keen edge would not hold—the knife was gone, drowned beneath the wind-whipped sea— and the starsong's scream howled through his mind the way he had howled into the wind when the storm had torn his tsol-ek from him and when he threw himself at the mountainous waves, the corpses surrounding him rose from their unrest upon the shore to seize him with their cold hands and accusing eyes. Clothes rotted. Eyes devoured. Faces bloated but bodies recognizable from their death wounds: Kerg, with his slit throat; Vaaqin, with his spilled-out guts; Elaram, with her red-painted side; Rahelu, with her bruised neck; Maketh, with a black, serpentine knife protruding from his chest; Jhobon—

Jhobon opened his mouth and the ocean poured out.

Back in the terrifying black depths of the storm. Thunder-deafened. Lightning-blinded. Choking on seawater and fear. In his head, a scream that was not a scream: *Save me!*

A dozen ice-cold hands dragged him down, down, down, to the Stormbringer's realm.

You didn't save me—*I tried!*—his jaws wouldn't work—*Why didn't you save me*—his throat had been slit—*I tried, I tried to follow you*—*You chose to save yourself*—*I didn't!*—he thrashed, limbs restrained by knotted rope—*You could have saved me!*—guilt as heavy as the weight of the water pressing him into the seabed—*You should have saved me*—he should have; he should have—*I died so you would live*—*no, no; you should be the one who lives*—*I had to die so you could live*—he had; they had always known that—*Why do you get to live? Why you and not me?*—*I never wanted that*, he thought, and as he thought it, realized how inadequate and selfish a defense it was—*You could have changed that*—that cool, inescapable logic cutting through his tangled emotions—*If you had loved me as I loved you, you would have chosen your death instead of mine*—*I did; I do love y* —but he couldn't finish the thought; couldn't deny the truth: he'd been too cowardly to make the choice, so he had simply run away, hoping the choice would be made for him, and—oh it had; it had—*And for what, Ylaen?*—for…for…—*What did I die for?*—a vow…he had made a vow, hadn't he? Marked in flesh and sealed with blood, in the sight of the sky, the stars, and the sea—*What good will you do to make my death worthwhile?*—but what, what exactly had he sworn to accomplish? He had had an answer for that but it eluded him, like air—

I tried!

Useless, so useless.

I'm sorry, he thought, but *'I'm sorry!'* was worse than

useless. You could be sorry that the Stormbringer had been ill-tempered that day; you could be sorry that the Earthgiver had withheld the season's blessing; you could be sorry that the Starfather had not seen fit to grant your heart's desire. 'Sorry' was a thing you said when you could not comprehend the actions of gods—it could not right wrongs, Revoke the past, or return what was lost; it was simply one mortal acknowledging the heavens-inflicted pain borne by another. 'Sorry' was another fresh wound in an old one that would never heal; a selfish plea for forgiveness.

Ylaen let the corpse-hands tow him along with the ocean currents towards the shadowed mouth of the ivory mountain looming large in the distance.

Maketh's mind block.

What would happen if he triggered it? Would it leave him as a shadow of himself, identity intact but unable to function, as Ghardon had theorized and feared? Or would he find oblivion, which was another word for 'peace'?

Would anything change if he did?

If Zovresh had no omen-marked son with a claim to a Dominion throne for the ship clans to rally around; if Hnan Imos had no puppet heir of Rysere's blood to quell the factions agitating for his abdication; if all Ylaen had ever been was an empty vessel for the ambitions of others, a symbol whose choices mattered less than the fact of his existence...

The simple clarity of that conclusion stilled the turmoil in his mind.

Jhobon had been right; there was always more than one solution.

THE FIRST BETRAYAL came easier than he thought.

The *Sooty Gull* had docked, but the *Stormbringer's Judgment* had not. When Ylaen returned to the warship's aftercastle to report unqualified success, he discovered Xya had ordered a change of plans.

"We're leaving," she informed him as he fell into step beside her—without preamble and without hearing his report. "The Conclave'll be here within the next twelve spans with the mage-priests on their wake and I won't have us trapped inside this rat hole of a harbor."

Both Seeking and a brief Augury confirmed what Xya said.

Ylaen objected nonetheless because she expected it of him. "We can't leave yet."

"We can, and so we will, my lad."

"But Uvesht-mo is still at the shrine, preparing for—"

"Then he will remain. I sought out the sage in hopes of saving my son and that bargain is done. Sage he might be, but Uvesht-mo has not bled for the clan and so the clan will not bleed for him."

"They are but two ships. What are their two ships against ours, and the power of a god? Put Nheras on the *Gull* with every available raw talent and let the rest join my uncle in raising the *Judgment's* defenses while I wield the Starfather's blessing with the sage's guidance. We can—we *will* defeat them. I will make sure of it."

"I do not presume to lecture you on magery, so do not blather at me regarding naval tactics. Were I captain of that Conclave ship, I'd wait until half the crew and all the mages are encamped upon that desolate rock. I would let those eager fools do the hard work of retrieving this legacy of the heavens. I'd sail up during the dark of the moon and have my mages Command every hand not sworn to my Tower to leap overboard so the waves may dash them to pieces on these jagged reefs while my boats take the warship. I shall wait at leisure for the pretty plump pigeons to return, every one ripe for plucking. And then: sail away uncontested, artifact in hand, with some three dozen fresh prisoners to work my oars, and a brand new warship for my fleet.

"No, my fierce little cub"—she put a finger on his lips to forestall further protest—"remaining here is folly and Zovresh does not abide fools. We will sail home with the prizes we've already won, rather than lose all for the sake of greed."

Scowl at the dismissal. Clench that useless fist, as though you're tempted to do something bold and rash. Then: breathe out all that tension in a great rush of air until your shoulders droop in defeat.

And when she takes her finger away, make no mention of the glaring error—the same one you made—that mars her otherwise impeccable logic.

"Give me the night, Xya. I won't have it said that I had a sure victory within my grasp but chose to return home without seizing it because I fled from the shadows of foes who had not yet appeared on the field of battle."

"Ylaen." Xya smiled at him, almost fond. "None here doubt you any longer. If it is condemnation you fear, then fear not. We were witness to your courage and we will provide testimony of it to any who still doubt your right to bear your scars."

She handed him a palm-sized resonance crystal.

"Choose two you trust to accompany you on the *Gull*— you can have anyone save your uncle, your pretty friend, or Ruan, for I will need them with me."

Ylaen examined the crystal in his hand. It was a control node. One Maketh had constructed out of his own mage pendant during the protracted weeks of his recovery, against the healers' orders. Maketh had steadfastly refused to lay eyes on or speak to his nephew, preferring to painstakingly chip away at the outer edges of his focus stone until it had been reduced to less than half of its former size. Those hundreds of linked resonance crystal fragments had been given to the ship's alchemists to be blended with the eight kegs of black powder he had wheedled out of Xya.

The eight kegs he had directed Ruan to precisely distribute all over the Endless Gate, in the form of carefully planted explosives.

"As soon as we are clear of these cliffs, overload the network. Detonate the nodes on the south side last. Then rejoin me and take charge of our magical offensives. Perhaps we can sink a ship or two whilst the Tower and these so-called Chosen fight over crumbling stone and ashes."

The second betrayal was harder.

Ylaen offered the control node back. "Send Nheras. Her work with linked crystals is better than mine, and I am more familiar with the resonance wards my uncle uses."

That was true.

Xya frowned. "I would prefer to keep the Ilyn girl close."

Suspicious then. Good.

"Then strip her of focus stones. Say that I will require all of them for the upcoming battle. Send her with Ruan to act as your eyes and ears—and hands too, if need be," Ylaen suggested. "He's already proven himself capable of subduing her when she's recalcitrant."

(Words, just words; so long as he didn't think about Ruan boasting of *'her sweet mouth'*.)

Step forward with Xya as she rests her hands on the toprail to consider the problems: the islet which must be destroyed before they can depart, the ominous presence and steady trajectories of the enemy ships closing in from beyond the horizon, and only three fully trained mages who are not of her crew.

Nheras, who has given her absolute obedience thus far— but whose loyalty has proven variable, when subjected to sufficient pressure. Whose strength as a Harbinger might pose a considerable problem if her loyalties were to shift again while Ylaen was not there to act as a deterrent.

Maketh, who has given her good counsel, but whom she cannot risk—because he is Ylaen's guest; because he is leverage—and, ultimately, cannot trust because his loyalty is unshakeable.

And Ylaen, who has given her grief, who is the very image of her tsol-na, whom she cannot look at without being reminded of her dead son.

Now: gently, very gently, tease out those threads of doubt and suspicion in Xya's resonance aura; twine it with some of your own grief and your own longing for your own mother as you bring your hands up to the toprail. Let the useless one hesitate, hovering above hers for a fractional moment, before you put it down, less than a finger-width away.

A distance so small it ought to be trivial, made inviolable by Jhobon's absence.

Ylaen said, "I will gladly entrust my ship to Ruan if it will allow me to stay and learn from you."

Her forehead creased as she furrowed her brows in an expression that was achingly reminiscent of Jhobon's.

Say 'yes', Xya. The subliminal visualizations he needed to sway her came effortlessly, for she had already imagined them and they were rooted in memory. *Don't hold me at bay any longer, just because I'm not him. The two of us have been—were— inseparable since birth; you raised me, as much as you raised him.*

"Very well." Xya clasped his left hand. "Inform Nheras of her role. See that she remembers the fulfillment of our bargain is contingent upon her continued satisfactory performance. Instruct Ruan that he is to return without her should there be...complications."

He gripped Xya's hand as tightly as he could, then let go, not trusting himself to say anything else as he departed in search of Nheras.

AFTER HE DELIVERED her new orders, the control node, and a rough map of the islet, Nheras grew very still.

"Why is the captain assigning this task to me, and not you?"

"Didn't ask. Now, your focus stones, if you don't mind? I'll need time to acclimatize to them."

She ignored him. "Xya had the decks cleared for action whilst you were away, and when you came back, you came back with your landing party one short. Soon as you dismissed them, they all rushed to bleed themselves at the ship's shrine. The whole crew's whispering that the islet is no holy place but a cursed one, haunted by hungry shades eager to snatch any living body they can, and that's why Uvesht-mo hasn't returned to cast the omens for the battle."

Ylaen would have called them *grumblings*, not *whispers*.

"Those who were part of the landing party swear they saw it with their own eyes: that they had Uvesht-mo in their sights the whole time they were climbing the mountain. 'We heard him loud and clear', they say, 'conversing with shades in the old tongue', but insist they saw no sign of the old cultist when they reached the top. 'Disappeared,' they say, 'as if swallowed by the void'."

Ylaen had nothing to add to that account.

Nheras held up the map he'd given her, the one Maketh had carefully annotated with the locations of where the explosives were meant to be placed. "They're sharing muddled, untrained Evocations of the strange visions they had—the dead come to life again—and saying that they had to drop everything to flee, for fear that they would be next."

Yes, that had happened too.

"And when they returned to the beach, Ruan told you they would sail any sea for Zovresh, fight any battle with Xya, follow any order you might give, save for the one to go back and finish the task they abandoned, because 'this is a dead place for dead things, and we are living souls.'"

"They're untrained." Ylaen shrugged. "They're easily spooked. You'll have my uncle's ward to protect you, and Seeking to disperse any rogue visions."

The parchment trembled faintly.

Fear, he noted, from the slight paling of her fingers and resonance aura, but there was a touch of anger, too, in the faint blush staining her cheeks and lips and neck.

She said, very flatly: "Xya still doesn't trust me."

There was the hint of bitterness he was looking for.

"Why, Nheras, love, whatever makes you think that? Xya is trusting the most important part of the plan to you. It would do neither the Dominion nor the Free Territories any good if we were to sail off while the Endless Gate remains intact for the Conclave to exploit."

That earned him a snort.

"If what the crew says is true, I'm being sent to finish the work of fourteen incompetents. Alone. Ruan has orders not to leave the *Gull* to assist me, does he not? And to sail without me, if I can't get it done in time." Nheras cast him a contemptuous glance over the top of the parchment before she crumpled it in her fist. "Xya is removing what she believes to be an unpredictable element from the board."

"We're facing two enemy ships, love. We can't afford to leave the *Gull* out of combat." Ylaen left a brief pause, just long enough to imply whose idea the next part had been. "You'll have a boat if you need it."

"Oh, a boat! A boat that I'll have to row myself through a treacherous passage while fending off Conclave Projections and Belruonian Auguries and ducking cannon fire!" She sneered as he held his hands up in a placating gesture. "How generous!"

Ylaen took a deep breath as he braced himself to commit the third and final betrayal.

"Trade me."

"What?"

"Trade places with me."

She narrowed her eyes. "Why?"

"Why?" He put his hand over his heart. "Because it upsets me to see you in such distress."

"Don't feed me any of your songhouse lines, Ylaen. Why do you want to trade?"

Now: show her the wound.

"Because I can't live without him."

Silence from Nheras as he looked away. Out through the window of her cabin, across the desolate beach at the mountain, a black void that drank up the very last dregs of skyarc light as the Skymother lowered her lamp into the sea and the starsong keened.

Come back to me.

"I can't leave this place without trying to—"

He broke off the sentence. Left her to fill in what he had not said.

Did she understand?

He didn't dare look—that would give the game away—but he did venture a covert indirect Seeking.

"Will you let me go?"

"Will you come back?"

"What do you think?"

"Ylaen."

"Oh, Nheras, there's a whole night to pass before our enemies are due to descend upon us and, according to Xya, they wouldn't do anything so foolish as to sail into 'this rat hole of a harbor'. I've practically an eternity to accomplish everything."

"*Ylaen.*"

This time, her voice held an edge he could not afford to test, so he dropped his flippancy and told her the truth.

"I will, if the gods will it so."

He doubted they would.

Nheras tilted her head. "What do I get for letting you go?"

"My complete trust and your guaranteed escape aren't enough?"

"I can fool Xya with my Seeming, but I won't fool Maketh for long. He may not notice in the chaos of battle, provided I keep well away from him, but the moment it's over, he'll know. Then I'll find myself stranded on a different—but no less desolate—rock."

"You won't," he said, with total conviction.

"How do you know?"

"Because you'll be able to give him the truth."

And, he thought to himself as she mulled over his proposition, *because you won't be able to resist the opportunity I've just handed to you.*

Sure enough, Nheras smiled, and when Ylaen smiled back, he was smiling at himself.

"Well, love," she drawled at him in his own voice, with his own mannerisms. "How could I possibly refuse your delightful offer when you've thought of a solution for everything?"

35

CHAINS

SCARFACE DID NOT RETURN.

But the rats and Rahelu's sense of the starsong did.

"GODS DAMN them all to the sixth hell!"

Rahelu slammed her fists against the unyielding, unhelpfully rust-free iron bars for the *'seven-eight-why-the-fuck-was-she-even-counting-ninetieth'* time.

The cell—the entire hold!—was rich and saturated with weeks of soul-shaking terror; debilitating despair; knife-sharp agony; glorious, righteous rage—and none of that resonance was any use because fucking *nobody* was coming down to check on them and that meant they had nobody to manipulate into getting them out of this stupid fucking cage.

If they had Nheras, it would be different.

But they did not have Nheras because Nheras was too fucking accustomed to being on the winning side that she couldn't abide being on the losing one—not even to keep her oaths—so Rahelu and the others remained well and truly trapped since none of them could shape a passable Command.

What good was having her resonance senses back?

Seeking and Obfuscation couldn't get them *out*; Seeming was useless until they *did* get out, and Augury and Evocation were both fucking impossible. Visions came and went in snatches with the ebb and swell of the starsong. Best they could tell, whatever was inside the Endless Gate warped time and resonance and causality until you could not distinguish between the concrete past and unrealized futures.

Manual searching revealed no secret weaknesses in the cell's construction to exploit. The planks beneath the rotting, piss-soaked straw were structurally sound. The door's hinges were stoutly made and firmly attached to the frame, nail heads hammered in until they were flush so no fingernail could be edged underneath. The keyhole of the lock was too tiny for even the tip of Elaram's smallest finger and—absurd songhouse fiction or not—Rahelu found herself belatedly wishing that she had not been so quick to decline Nheras's offer of hairpins when they'd hastily braided her hair.

All they had to show for two spans of Projecting calm and curiosity at every rat they could entice within arm's reach was a palmful of resonance crystals so laughably low-grade and flawed that they wouldn't survive a single working.

Right now, Rahelu would trade every scrap of resonance ability for a nice hefty hammer.

Or a rock.

Or anything slightly more resistant to injury than her own squishy fists.

SLAM!

"Stop that!" Elaram snapped.

Rahelu ignored her—the way Elaram had ignored the entire world when she'd let herself go to pieces—and slammed the bars again.

Nothing.

"We are *trying* to *not* draw the *wrong* kind of *attention*—"

SLAM! The bars were set into wood, not drilled and mortared into stone. *SLAM!* The iron might not bend or break but if she did this hard enough for long enough, even the solid cedar frame would have to splinter.

SLAM!

"*—and* you're *scaring* Snuffles!"

Not one gods-cursed hairline crack. She needed more of her body weight behind each blow. If only her stupid shackles would stop jerking her up short every time she tried.

"You've *named* it?" Ghardon shuddered as he gingerly poked through the useless pile of bloodied crystals. "Why, Ela? It's a dirty, disease-carrying, disgusting little pest."

"Shhh!" Elaram hissed. "You'll hurt her feelings." She flipped her voice a whole octave up into a syrupy coo aimed at the black ball of fur trembling in her cupped hands: "Don't listen to him, little one. You are brave and beautiful and—"

SLAMSLAMSLAM!

"Fuck!"

That *hurt*.

"Ra-heeeeeee-luuuuuuuuu..." Elaram's annoyance grew, and spiky orange bubbles joined the dark red haze in the ambient resonance. "I'm waaaarning yooooouuuuuu..."

She needed something—anything!—harder than her fists. "Ghardon, give me your boot."

"No, I need it." Plainly a lie for he wasn't wearing it; he'd taken it off, set it down by his knee, and then laced it back up again with a tidy bow. "Use your own."

Fine.

"Do *not* use your boot or *anything else*, Rahelu. We need someone to scout; someone who is free and willing and able to go anywhere and look at anything on this ship, and all that noise is making it hard for Snuffles to concentrate. Don't you look at me like I'm being silly and stupid; I am being totally, utterly serious. You need to—"

CLANG!

Equally fucking ineffective, but it didn't hurt as much. So she took the other one off too and put both boots on her hands like a pair of very ill-fitted gloves.

CLANGCLANGCLANGCLANG—

Crack!

The unexpected force of Elaram's slap jerked her head right. She gasped, tears welling up in her eyes at the sting in her left cheek. "Elaram, what—"

CRACK!

She reeled. Elaram had put her entire shoulder into that. "You. Need. To. Stop."

A very emphatic *squeak!* punctuated that pointed rebuke.

Nestled securely on Elaram's palm against Elaram's chest with Elaram's left arm raised above it—readied for a third slap—the rat glared at her with its beady little eyes and actually dared to bare its teeth.

Rahelu glared back.

"Now apologize to Snuffles or I'll let her bite you."

No fucking way.

"Bite me and I'll swallow you whole," she told the rat.

But she did plonk her ass down in the corner where she slouched, massaging her aching fists. Rat bites were no joke.

"You don't want to do that, sister dear," Elaram said. "Snuffles might decide to chew her way out of your stomach."

Rahelu snorted.

Eyed the mound of rat carcasses in the opposite corner, then sat up very, very straight.

"How many friends does Snuffles have left?"

SNUFFLES HAD A *LOT* OF FRIENDS.

But the *Stormbringer's Judgment* was built of very thick wood.

In the end, three spans of Projection-fueled work (that left Rahelu wrung out with exhaustion) done in rotating shifts by a colony some two hundred rats strong yielded a small hole.

Snuffles wriggled through.

Guided by Elaram, the rat made it two decks up to the passageway with the officers' cabins, before it froze outside Scarface's door.

———

"EXPLAIN YOURSELF, RUAN."

Nheras ducked through the beaded curtain of raw bone, teeth, and uncut resonance crystal guarding the entrance to the stateroom, glad she wasn't the one inside, quailing beneath Xya's stare.

"She-she said she knew what our orders were," the first mate stammered, "and that she'd seen the kind of power a Conclave journeymage could wield. Told us a single blade wielded by a sure hand might be what makes the difference between defeat and victory, and that being the case, there was no point in us standing round idle and that we ought to go back straightaway, for you'd need us. So we did."

"But you came back in the boat."

"Aye, captain."

"And left the *Gull.*"

"Aye, captain," the first mate repeated, his resonance aura gone gray with bewilderment. Tiny sparks of yellow-green anxiety whirred around him, like fireflies, as he darted a sidelong glance at Nheras.

She batted her eyes back at him, all perplexed innocence

as she sank languidly into the cushions of Ylaen's customary seat at the map table and draped her legs over its carved arm.

Her entrance, thank gods, drew no attention from the fourth person in attendance: Dedicate Maketh Imos, who kept his eyes fixed upon the map table, even though he ought to be thoroughly dosed with soporifics and left to rest in bed.

Ylaen might have wrung guest-rights out of Xya for his uncle, but only after the healers had reassured the captain that any exercise of resonance ability on Maketh's part would be at his risk, for each time he did, he flirted with the possibility of doing himself permanent damage. The Guardian's presence was expected—Xya's direct orders, so she could "consult his considerable knowledge". The captain liked to keep him close, but she also liked to relegate him to a stool in the corner.

Nheras feigned her own study of the map table as she considered Maketh through her eyelashes.

Right now, he did not look like the threat Anathwan had warned her Supplicants to beware of in secret. He did not even look much like a mage, let alone the battle-tested Guardian he was reputed to be. He looked like someone who had hollowed himself out to the point of death, only to be told that he was not allowed to die yet. (Rather like a pet hound. One that had been wounded so it could no longer hunt, but remained too valuable to be put down, so its owner kept it leashed, collared, and muzzled in order to continue making use of its experienced instincts and keen nose.) His pallid brow, so characteristic of the Imos bloodline, was dotted with beads of sweat. Traceries of blue veins stood out starkly beneath his skin, like patterns on fine porcelain.

Watching Maketh try to breathe in shallow gasps and listening to the way air wheezed through his damaged lungs made her own chest feel tight. Whenever he wiped the blood-flecked spittle from his lips, she grew conscious of her own papery tongue, and when she tried to remedy the dryness by swallowing, she thought she tasted iron.

Trapped, Nheras decided, by his protracted illness, his affections for his nephew, and the oaths he had sworn.

There was nothing Maketh could do to speed his recovery, for no known resonance art can force the body and mind to heal faster. And, despite their estrangement, he would not support any course of action that might jeopardize Ylaen's well-being. Nor would he object to working with the Crimson Storm so long as Xya was committed to destroying the Endless Gate. That, after all, was an acceptable outcome for the Houses' joint mission; the one he had advocated for most strongly, against Anathwan's preferences.

Which meant if Nheras chose to act on her current opportunity (and she wasn't sure she should; the circumstances weren't right—yet), Maketh was still going to be a problem. *'Trapped'* didn't mean *'tamed'* or *'toothless'*.

Best she remained wary.

Threat assessment completed, Nheras gave her full attention over to the map table, where the colored shells and their placements relative to the lines carved into the damp sand represented the last known positions of the four ships in the vicinity of the Endless Gate.

Either the Conclave had slowed or the Belruonian mage-priests had closed the gap in the spans since.

Promising. If every hand aboard the *Stormbringer's Judgment* was preoccupied with the enemy ships...

"She asked if we wouldn't mind switching," Ruan continued, "for she can't row well but had been trained to sail the sloop. I thought there were no harm, the *Gull* not being a fighting ship, and seeing as we can always use the extra boat for another boarding party."

Gods damn you, Ylaen, Nheras thought. Their guises were

flimsy enough without drawing additional scrutiny. She hurriedly intervened before Xya interrogated Ruan further.

"The fault is mine. Ruan is usually so capable that I assumed—well. Nheras has a persuasive tongue." A pause to seed a little doubt. Later, she could see about cultivating it further. "It would not be the first time she managed to sway him with her pretty arguments." She let her eyes drift over the correspondence on Xya's desk, stacked beside the long-distance communication relay node, before meeting the captain's gaze. "I see now that I should have been more specific." Stood. "I will retrieve—"

"No." Xya waved Nheras back into Ylaen's seat. "We shall use this." To Maketh: "You say these wards and barriers, once activated, can mask our presence from their Seekers completely? And that the resonance flux from the Endless Gate prevents the effective use of Seeking within the cove?"

"Yes," he rasped.

"Good." The captain hunkered down over the map and rearranged the painted shells. "We shall use the *Gull* as bait. They know we are here; a vessel docked in plain sight will allay their suspicions, even if they cannot accurately gauge how many are aboard. Our enemies must approach cautiously, for they will expect opposition, but they cannot be too cautious, for the islet has only a single approach and they cannot afford to cede the advantage to each other.

"Once the detonations begin, they must abandon caution if they are to seize any piece of the prize. So we"—Xya moved the red shell representing the *Stormbringer's Judgment* until it sat to one side of the narrow inlet, tucked away behind the curving cliffs—"will lie in wait, like the nheshwyr, to see who triumphs first. Then we shall strike at their backs.

"Now, I will hear your objections."

THE CONFERENCE CONCLUDED ONE-AND-A-HALF-SPANS LATER, after six rounds of tactical revisions.

Xya gave Maketh permission to adjust the wards, sent Ruan to oversee the very important but tedious duty of blacking every sail and reflective surface so no gleam of moonlight nor starlight would betray their presence, and approved Nheras's request for wakeleaf and other mental stimulants.

Saunter, don't scuttle, Nheras ordered herself as she exited the apothecary.

Remember who you are: Ylaen, son of Zovresh, who has earned his scars and clan-rights and thus can go anywhere aboard the *Stormbringer's Judgment* to do anything he pleases.

Her shoulders straightened. Her strides lengthened; then slowed as she headed forward to Ylaen's assigned station on the deserted foredeck. A quick Seeking confirmed Ruan was still amidships, seeing to the mainsail. Xya and her second and third mates were at the helm, with the Seekers, and down in the galley with the rowers, maneuvering the warship into its new position. The fourth mate was with the alchemists and the gunner teams, readying the cannons. The healers, having rushed her out with her fulfilled requests, were preparing the apothecary and its adjacent rooms as infirmaries, and—

Mrow!

She stumbled and nearly tripped over one of the ship's cats. The black-and-gray striped female that had kept her company on her first night after being freed; the one whose belly was heavy with unborn kits.

"Go away," Nheras hissed.

Another *mmmrow!* Louder, more insistent, and accompanied by a gnawing sensation in her stomach. Nheras had to push back with a gentle nudge of fear before the cat would keep her distance. Nevertheless, the stubborn feline followed, leaving a trail of sullen, reproachful hunger to mark their passage.

She ought to get rid of the furry nuisance with a proper Projection. But it was comforting to have another soul padding along on her heels and besides, she hardly noticed the cost of stretching the boundaries of her Seeming a little further and wrapping up the cat in a small Obfuscation barrier. No one would wonder why Ylaen, who disliked cats (and was disliked by them in return), had one twining about his ankles, so long as the cat kept quiet about her hunger.

Her hunger.

Their arrival at the Endless Gate had disrupted all routine. The cooks had prepared but one scanty meal—they'd been reduced to half-rations for the last week—and every crewmember, from the captain and her officers to the lowliest deckhand, had eaten lunch as they worked.

No one had remembered to feed the prisoners in the slave pens.

That—that changed things.

Nheras pivoted mid-step. Her lantern—the first thing she had requisitioned from the quartermaster—bobbed and swayed as she turned into the passageway leading to the officers' cabins.

A scrabbling noise ahead.

What in the eight hells?

She swung her lantern forward.

The dim pool of golden light illuminated a large black rat, caught in the middle of the very un-ratlike behavior of trying to squeeze itself through the too-narrow gap underneath Ruan's door, and—instead of scampering off into the shadows—the rat froze.

Nheras stepped forward for a closer look at the bits of resonance sparking off the ends of its fluffed-up fur. Mixed in with the miniature frantic *pops* of orange alarm fizzling against the wood were larger spots of steel-gray determination and a too-familiar shade of red anger that overrode the rat's natural instincts to flee.

The new development set her pulse racing.

The game has three choices; two of which look much alike during the course of play. She had begun the game with no plan; only purpose and an alertness for opportunity.

Now the circumstances were right.

No one, save Xya, had the authority to question Ylaen, and with Ylaen himself gone ashore and Maketh under healer's restrictions, there was nobody with a sufficient level of resonance skills left to oppose Nheras. Even supposing she had underestimated the ships' Seekers, she had not one but six focus stones, including two mage pendants, to draw upon for any Projections she chose to unleash.

She could still win.

Her thoughts flashed ahead to possible futures she had previously dismissed as unviable. And while she was preoccupied with mapping out the quickest, surest path to realizing the most favorable outcome, the Seeker on duty raised the long-anticipated alarm—

Enemy ship on the horizon!

—and the cat pounced.

<hr>

FUCK. *Fuck!*

Rahelu had, perhaps insensibly so, actually thought the plan might be ridiculous enough to work.

When Elaram burst into tears, Rahelu joined her.

Ghardon did not.

He'd been focused on smashing the tiny, useless crystals they had harvested from the other dead rats with the heel of his boot into tinier, even more useless fragments, and engaging in an activity that was not only useless but actually counterproductive in the event they could get their hands on Scarface or the keys: jamming them inside the lock to his shackles.

"That's not going to work," Rahelu said once she could stop her sniveling. "Even if you can get the right shape, you won't be able to get enough leverage. The matrices of these stones are too flawed to withstand the compressive forces generated by the ward springs and—"

He smirked.

A smirk!

A real patronizing one, of a caliber he hadn't directed towards her in months—not since before graduation. One he had generally reserved for whichever unfortunate happened to finish the term with the lowest grades.

Resignation fled before her irritation. "You are a fucking—"

Ghardon filched a pinch of the crackling orange resonance from her aura, squeezed it into a glowing, vaguely key-shaped Projection, and shoved it inside the lock.

And every single crystal fragment simultaneously went *boom!* as he overloaded them.

His shackles fell open.

So did Rahelu's mouth.

"*Genius*, brother!" Elaram squealed. "Do mine next!"

GHARDON'S TRICK did not work on their cell door.

Low-grade crystals harvested from rats simply didn't contain enough power to generate sufficient explosive force, no matter how many they packed inside the heavier lock.

Rahelu wrapped her loose chains around her knees; hugged her knees to her chest; tucked her chin into the coiled links as she shammed sleep and sank into the familiar *in-out-in-out* rhythm of the foundational four-count meditation. The discipline of it soothed her nerves, renewed her frayed patience, and steadied her focus. Inside that imposed state of detachment, she let her mind float on the surface currents of the ambient resonance, observing the random patterns formed by the percolating emotions around them, gathering the beautiful strands of simmering coal-red anger to coil them around her weakened limbs like bandages until she felt flushed and strong and invincible from the heat sinking into her very core.

Soon—*soon!*—Scarface would come.

And now...

Now they had weapons. Now those currents had reversed direction. Now resonance flowed towards the other end of the slave pens.

Then: a Command so strong that Rahelu nearly got up and tried to walk through the cage's iron bars even though it was not meant for her.

Come.

NHERAS RATTLED down companionway after companionway to the lower decks, moving as fast as she dared.

She ignored the long, flat dagger tucked into her waistband underneath her shirt and how its barbed quillons and serrated blade pricked her with every step. Ignored, too, the ungainly crossbow at her belt and how its bulk would interfere with her ability to quickly grasp her baton if she needed it in a hurry; the way its heavier weight kept dragging her off balance when she had to duck and twist her body to avoid bumping and scraping the shortbow and quiver on her back against the bulkheads of the narrow passageways.

She could not, however, ignore her lungs.

The further she descended, the more the bulkheads seemed to close in. Fine carpentry had shaped the *Stormbringer's Judgment*; every gap perfectly caulked with powdered shells and tung oil so that no air, much less water, could get through, which meant she needed to take deeper and deeper breaths the further and further she went just to keep the dizziness at bay.

Gods help her if she had to fight.

But she would not have to fight.

You won't get away with this, whispered a corner of her mind. *Everyone's on high alert. If you turn around, right now, and go to Xya instead—*

No.

That might have been the best option before, but it was definitely not the best option now. If she hurried, she could still frame her actions in the right light...

Here I am, a true daughter of Issolm, so devoted to doing what needed to be done that I was—am—willing to be branded a traitor, for the sake of House and Dominion.

Any fool can swear fealty; anyone can claim stubbornness as a virtue. But true loyalty lies not in an impressive display of unbending martyrdom, but in actions that produce results.

That was what Lynath Ilyn taught and Anathwan Issolm struck Nheras as someone who valued those capable of producing results.

Like completing their original mission.

Still, Nheras prayed to the Skymother that she had not wagered wrong; and if she *had*, that the Elder would at least permit her the chance to speak the arguments she had prepared in her own defense:

I had to do it. Because she hadn't been able to bear it any longer. *I had no other way of earning Xya's trust.* Which she had still failed to do regardless. *I had to play the part of pet Harbinger and Dominion turncoat perfectly, to get myself into a position where I would be free to act when the opportunity came.* She just hadn't expected it would take so long for one to manifest. *I, alone, was equal to the task.* Elaram had been useless from the start, Ghardon had broken rather than bend, and Rahelu had neither the brains nor the stomach nor the cold-hearted calculation required—to smile sweetly when she would rather snarl; to yield complete obedience when she would rather hurl defiance; to inhabit the lie so it was a lie no longer, but merely an aspect of truth. *I may appear to have broken faith with House and Dominion but I never forgot my purpose. See? Here are the keys, and here are your weapons; this is what they have planned, and this is how we shall slip away.*

The inconvenient voice in her head refused to quiet, so she drowned it out with the minutiae of practical concerns.

Keys and weapons would do no good if the others could not move under their own power. Stimulants she already had in plenty, but she would need to raid the apothecary for clean water, clean rags, clean bandages, clean *clothes*, poultices for infected wounds, and elixirs to relieve pain.

So: stride into the apothecary, order their immediate release and treatment, upon your authority as the mage in charge and Zovresh's son. Would the healers obey her? Or would they find it suspicious? Did it matter if they did? If the others had their resonance abilities back...

Yet all the bandages and elixirs in the world could not instantly heal broken bones or restore withered limbs. The main difficulties in Anathwan's backup plan had always been logistical ones; transporting the Elder's comatose body to the heart of the Endless Gate, past entrenched enemies, would have been challenging even when all the Issolm Supplicants had been physically fit. How were they supposed to go about it now, if everyone (except for Nheras) might be limping around on crutches?

Better to bring extra muscle instead of crutches; crutches could only be turned to so many uses.

Nheras found Ruan standing on the foredeck, one hand gripping the rail, the other resting on the hilt of his cutlass, his head cocked and eyes staring out to sea. She tapped him on the shoulder and gestured, hoping that she had gotten the hand sign for '*slaves*' right.

The first mate's facial scars flickered briefly, outlining his worried features in dim orange. His hands were a blur as he signed a query back.

Too complicated for her to follow, let alone reply. She couldn't mouth the words at him either; despite her best efforts, she had not been able to learn enough of the Free Speech to talk in anything other than broken sentences.

Projection it was.

She sent Ruan a string of stripped down memories: one-sided snippets of Projected conversations she had had with Ylaen, all sliced up and rearranged so that his words and imagery formed the meaning she wanted in his mental voice with his resonance signature underlying the message: *Did you neglect to feed the slaves? Because I sense them stirring.*

No more needed to be said.

On their way down, they crossed paths with Maketh, who shuffled along the warship's perimeter, double checking the lines and circuits of the anchor crystals to his wards and barriers.

Nheras instantly averted her eyes.

She and Ylaen had both been present when Maketh had first returned to himself—she because she had an academic curiosity to satisfy in regards to how a patient in a severe heart-bane coma ought to be revived, and Ylaen because he had gone from his duel straight to his uncle's bedside and had not moved from it since. Maketh had stared at Ylaen and the glittering black crown on his lap and the angry, half-healed scars carved into his chest with a mute, horrified fascination. No amount of pleading or Projection from Ylaen had moved him to speak. The Imos Dedicate had simply looked at—then through—his nephew, as his horror subsided into a keen disappointment.

Nheras had caught a glimpse of Ylaen's expression as he rushed off: he'd looked as though he wished he had been the one to die in the dueling circle.

Uncle and nephew had kept their distance from each other ever since. But, for some inexplicable reason, Maketh chose to breach that distance now.

The rapid *bada-bada-bada-bada* of her heart accelerated as his firm footsteps broke their rhythm to come after them.

Her Seeming shivered as they disappeared down the companionway.

Ruan did not notice—far too fixated on rectifying his oversight—but Maketh's tread could be heard on the stair behind them so Nheras threw up a basic Obfuscation barrier of slate-gray indifference: the clearest *'I don't want to talk to you'* signal she could send whilst still respecting Xya's orders for absolute silence.

A moment later, she felt the polite tap of his determined mind against her barrier.

Shit.

Maketh had something to say to Ylaen, and it was apparently of such vital importance that he was prepared to violate the healers' orders and shove the unwanted message into her skull when battle was nearly upon them.

The game was up.

Ylaen.

Nheras gasped in pain, as indifference buckled beneath

the force of the Imos Dedicate's targeted Projection and her Seeming crumbled.

Ylaen, I—

Maketh's mental presence reared back in surprise as she preempted him by dumping all of the answers he would've probed her for straight into his consciousness as a disordered deluge. While he was still frantically sifting through the information for the *wheres* and *whys* behind Ylaen's disappearance, she seized Ruan.

Help me.

An enormous shadow lunged past her. A series of scuffles and grunts followed, before she heard a *thump!* that restored the tense quiet.

Nheras trembled, but forced herself to keep moving.

They found the door to the apothecary ajar, the healer unconscious, and his little apprentice and keys missing.

Oh no.

She abandoned the caution that characterized good sense and rushed headlong into the dark. The *clank* and *clatter* of her weaponry and boots rang through the passageways, loud as the ship's bells, but louder still were Ruan's lumbering steps as her Command dragged him along.

Loudest of all: the erratic thumping of her heart.

First impressions mattered. If she did not get there before the apprentice; if hers was not the first face Anathwan saw...

Ahead: the hatch to the slave pens, still closed.

Thank gods!

Nheras breathed.

Breathe.

In just a moment she would open the hatch. Expose a square of deeper black on black that led down into an unlit void as formless and full of despair as the depths of the third hell and every bit as noisome with Elaram's snoring, Rahelu's restless tossing and turning, Ghardon's muffled moans,

Anathwan's labored breathing—a little *tsssssst* with every inhalation, then a low-pitched *uuuuunghhhhh* tearing through the Elder's hoarse throat and the ceaseless *rattle-rattle-clank* of chain on chain, regular as the lapping waves and, less often, the *clink-thunk-splash* as she thrashed in her saltwater mage cell—

Breathe.

Creeeeeeeaaaaak.

Eerie silence.

Send Ruan on ahead so the horrors below may fall on him first. Then you can beat them away with your baton and Projections until there's only you; you and a pile of broken bones that can't hurt you.

When nothing befell Ruan, she eased herself down the ladder.

Nheras breathed.

In.

Out.

In.

Out.

The Guild's basic four-count meditation calmed her racing pulse and gave her eyes the time they needed to adjust.

She nearly screamed once they did.

"Look at me, Nheras," rasped the broken horror that had stolen Anathwan's voice.

There were new lines in the Elder's face—lines that dragged down the corners of her mouth and nose so she looked twice as old as she did in Nheras's memory. Up close, you could see her hair was matted with dried blood—so much of it that you would never have guessed it ought to be the color of ripened wheat. Half of those golden curls had been hacked off when someone (probably the captain) had made all those slices in her scalp. Very little remained of her clothes other than irregular, narrow strips of blood-soaked cotton that had never quite dried out; those stuck to the long open cuts that ran from collarbone to navel and lower. Underneath her scanty attire, the Issolm Elder was skeletal from deprivation. Her skin was covered with weeping sores from weeks of being submerged in stale seawater; her arms hung limp by her sides; her shoulders were sunken and misshapen, dislocated from days of thrashing around while being suspended by her wrists. Her once-elegant hands now terminated in stubby, swollen fingers that were streaked with blood and bare of rings—and fingernails.

Captain Xya had done her work well.

But Anathwan's eyes were as intent as ever and she still smiled at Nheras.

Her Supplicants did not.

"Now, tell me: what purpose lay behind your…initiative?"

Easy to feel confident in her arguments when she had merely been rehearsing them in her head. But now she had to speak them aloud:

To Ghardon, who was savvy to the conversational techniques that had been drilled into her, for he had been trained by the very same tutors.

To Elaram, whose focused Seeking illuminated the statements she used to shade her motives as the partial truths they were.

To Rahelu, who had already made up her mind the moment Nheras had handed over the crown.

To Anathwan, who had explicitly told her: "Velaz." Whom she had disobeyed.

She sounded unconvincing even to her own ears.

"I—Forgiveness, Elder." She sank to all fours, offering up their focus stones without another word.

One did not cross a Dedicate's will and expect to walk away unscathed, much less an Elder vested with the authority of the Exalted Dominance.

"You claim you had no choice but treason." Anathwan paused. "Your brother and sisters faced the same difficulties, yet they chose differently. So, my Supplicants, I would hear your thoughts: how do you judge her?"

"Guilty," Elaram said immediately, snatching up her ring. "When Nheras betrayed us, she had no greater plan of deception in mind, only the thought of saving herself." Abruptly, she dropped her accusatory tone to add, "But she fought harder and for far longer than I did, and she came back. That's what matters. So..." A long inhale and exhale. "I forgive you, sister."

"I don't know," Ghardon said. "Treason requires intent and that is not the same as weakness. I don't think Nheras is guilty—but I won't call someone I can't trust 'sister'."

She hadn't expected he would.

But just as it had warmed her more than she thought to hear him say things like, *'you are now officially my favorite sister'*—even when he had meant it as an insult to Elaram and Rahelu rather than as a compliment to her—it hurt her more than she thought to hear him disavow her.

Anathwan nodded, her expression still serene, as though they had all the time in the world for this little mock trial when they ought to be arming up and getting out. "Rahelu?"

Rahelu remained silent as she looped the Ideth pendant around her neck and did up the silver clasp.

I came back for you, Nheras thought, praying that Elaram's opinion would hold more sway than Ghardon's did. *Like you came back for me. Remember? Remember how we agreed to begin anew; remember what we can accomplish together; remember that—*

Nheras looked up as Rahelu plucked the ring Lhorne Ideth had bought from her fingers. *Remember that you owe me a favor, with no conditions.*

A jolt of frisson as their auras intersected.

Rahelu. Nheras held still as the other girl searched her

eyes; saw her own quaking reflection—all brittle hope and terrified eyes—before Rahelu pulled back. *Please.*

Rahelu said: "I don't have the wisdom to decide. I defer to your judgment, Elder."

Her last hope crumbled. But, favor or no favor, she could not blame Rahelu for abstaining. Anathwan would judge Nheras as she pleased, regardless of what her Supplicants thought, and they would all stand by her verdict.

"Then," Anathwan said, "I will serve justice for House Issolm and for the Dominion."

Oh. Oh no.

SUBMIT.

Her Command of the first mate unraveled with her resonance aura. Ruan seized his cutlass—

No! Nonononono. Nheras grasped at the shards of her chalk-white fear quivering in the ambient resonance. Just one —*one*—of those shards would be enough to stop him and allow her to resume Command.

Resonance eluded her.

Control eluded her.

Independent thought eluded her. Slipped through her fingers like moonlight her body turned to water her soul to ice because Anathwan willed it and reality itself obeyed.

Her terror grew unchecked; suffused the ambient resonance; illuminated even the farthest, darkest corners of the slave pens with its bleached bone brilliance. And this was as it should be. After the fire dies, the light of terror is the only way to keep the shadows at bay.

See the ghosts all around you.

Scream, Nheras.

Scream as loud as you like; no one will save you.

A thousand overlapping echoes screamed with Nheras as Ruan swung his cutlass at her neck.

RAHELU COULD NOT BREATHE.

If she breathed, she would choke.

Was this justice?

She should look at the face; she owed Nheras that much.

Rahelu didn't want to look at the face.

If she looked at the face, she would see what it is and remember what it was and know the two were not and would never be the same again.

But Elder Anathwan did not permit them the choice.

So they looked and did not flinch from the head as it rolled away from Scarface in his executioner's stance, while blood ran down his cutlass and his statue-blank eyes stared, while the equally unseeing, unthinking healer's apprentice worked.

A thousand thoughts fought each other in Rahelu's mind.

Had she ever imagined Nheras's death? Of course she had; you could not survive five years of merciless bullying without such fantasies. A freakish training accident; a casualty of House politicking; a routine assignment gone wrong. But not an end like this, this, this...

Murder, one whisper insisted. This was murder, plain and simple. Nheras was a daughter of Issolm and Anathwan had Commanded another to strike her down. Anathwan had dealt death to a Supplicant of her own House; a penalty that far exceeded the punishment warranted by disobedience.

But:

It wasn't simply disobedience, another protested. *Nheras betrayed our mission!* Nheras had sworn a Supplicant's oaths: obedience to her Elders; loyalty to her Atriarch; to bring honor to her House; to do her duty to the Dominion. In trading away the crown, the thing Anathwan had protected above all else, not only had Nheras broken those oaths by putting herself above the interests of House and Dominion, she had delivered the key to power that could control the world into the hands of the Dominion's enemies.

She had given away the Dominion itself.

The laws say:

Traitors deserve to die.

Therefore:

Nheras's death is just.

No, no, her mind whispered again. *A clean death, dealt in a single stroke? That is not justice; that is* kindness.

Anathwan ought to have shackled Nheras and brought her to be tried before the Hall of Judgment for grand treason. Had the evidence of Nheras's betrayal been put to the Adjudicators, she would have suffered the full extent of the penalty for treason: one hundred days of one hundred lashes, each blow struck by a different citizen, for treason was a crime that did equal harm to everyone in the Dominion.

Who would prefer that awful fate over being mourned as a Supplicant fallen to an enemy's blade while on assignment?

This reduced punishment, then, this shallow truth is Anathwan's grace.

Who would care to ask further questions?

Yet:

Nheras came back!

If she were truly a traitor, invested only in her own skin, she would not have braved the dark she so desperately feared to return to the slave pens with their stolen focus stones, dragging the first mate and his keys and a crossbow for Elaram and a shortbow for Ghardon and the dagger Rahelu had once fashioned into the blade of an improvised spear that she had set down and never wielded on Nheras's advice.

Advice Rahelu had not agreed with.

Advice that had landed them *here.*

(No, fish-shit-for-brains; that was Ylaen's doing.)

Stormbringer. No matter how she examined the evidence and weighed the factors, Rahelu could not decide what was right.

Velaz. *Velaz.*

No Elder of the Houses would act without cause or reason.

Rahelu had to believe that.

"There," Anathwan said, and crouched down by the headless corpse, heedless of the blood. Stretched out a newly bandaged hand (every finger shortened by a knuckle) to stroke the dead body in a macabre gesture of comfort. "The lesson is done. I trust that I will not have to teach it again."

The corpse began to tremble.

Its back spasmed, as if possessed with life, or perhaps Nheras's lingering shade, for Rahelu recognized the way those shoulders curled inward over those knees, how the long-nailed fingers on those flattened palms dug into the deck, and suddenly, suddenly she could see, *she could see—*

"Nheras made a choice," Anathwan continued. "A poor, if understandable, choice that was dictated by fear rather than informed by faith. Fear, however, cannot rule without diminishing so to submit to fear is to submit to weakness. If you are afraid, then be afraid! But let faith, not fear, guide your actions."

Relief bloomed in the ambient resonance: a pale gold halo wrapped around a sobbing girl. Head still very much attached; no longer pressed to the deck in the lowest form of obeisance but buried in Anathwan's lap.

"Rise, my dear."

The Nheras that got to her feet looked so shaken she'd probably fall over if someone breathed on her. But get up she did, with assistance from Anathwan and her bandaged hands.

"Now," the Elder said, her voice so full of compassion and

understanding that it warmed the heart like a hearth. "Let us also be done with fear."

Why, then, did Rahelu feel so cold?

"Know that the heavens themselves smile upon the Houses and look upon our mission with favor, for tonight is the eve of the winter solstice, the most auspicious and sacred of nights to the Starfather."

Power rushed out from Anathwan, sweeping through the ambient resonance like a gale.

"Tonight we shall pass through the Endless Gate and into the heart of Fortune's realm."

For one dizzying heartbeat or a hundred or none at all—Rahelu couldn't tell—she lost her sense of self.

It didn't matter.

The Elder needed her help.

"Tonight, my Supplicants, we go to bring forth the future."

36

DRAW

MAKETH WAS NOT AROUND TO CALL THE ALARM, SO Nheras led them across the deck of the *Stormbringer's Judgment*—in full sight of Xya's crew, secure under the protection of her Seeming of air and nothingness—and straight to one of the small boats: the one Ruan had unwittingly returned in and was now obliged, by the Elder's Command, to row back to the islet.

No one spoke to Nheras.

But Elaram—who had instigated and gloated over her public humiliation in front of everybody on the *Winged Arrow* —had hugged her fiercely as she distributed weapons.

And Rahelu—who had not been willing to risk her estimation in the Elder's eyes to speak up on her behalf—had gripped her hand in silent apology.

Even Ghardon—who steadfastly clung to his distrust of her—still caught her as she stumbled in the shallows of the islet's black sand cove.

Best of all, Anathwan had not truly punished her.

Oh, the Elder's lesson had been harsh, yes—outright disobedience such as hers could not be allowed to go unrebuked, lest the example encourage further disobedience—but it had been no harsher than the ones she had learned from her grandmother, and Lynath Ilyn had not tempered her lessons with any affection. So Nheras smiled as they staggered ashore, though her muscles burned from the unfamiliar effort of rowing and her vision blurred due to the strain of holding the Seeming, for Anathwan had embraced her anyway, then told her privately: *Show me your faith, Nheras, and give me another fine display of strength; and I will show you how promising your future can be as a daughter of House Issolm.*

She no longer cared that she had been cast out from House Ilyn; that she would not be able to buy her way back into her grandmother's good graces with the promise of a new alliance; that she hadn't, in the end, managed to prove herself better than Rahelu or the others.

Anathwan accepted her.

Which meant so long as Anathwan succeeded, Nheras won.

WHEN ANATHWAN SIGNALED A REST, Rahelu gladly collapsed onto the coarse black sand with her eyes squeezed shut, the knuckles of her thumbs dug into the dull ache building behind her forehead, and—

—resonance thrumming through her bones.

She should get up.

She *needed* to get up; needed to do her part in dragging the boat further up the beach, away from the high tide mark. Already, the waves ate away at the shoreline beneath her legs; already, the wet sand had leached the pleasant warmth from her body. Soon her boots and trousers would be as waterlogged as her shirt; soon the trembling of physical exhaustion would turn to chills. But getting up meant moving her arms (both sore and heavy, limp as noodles) and pushing herself up with her hands (*those* were blistered and cramped from pulling the oars) so *fuck* moving.

It was so good to simply lie here, listening to the *rush-crash-gurgle-hiss* of the incoming tide running over rocks, feeling the *dum-dadum-dadum* of her heart beating in time with the mesmerizing starsong—

—echoing the rhythm of the waves.

Up, urged an inner voice.

No. She deserved to take a fucking break for ten fucking heartbeats. Ten spans—no, ten *days,* at the very least. Perhaps even a whole season.

Urgency washed over her with the next wave.

Rahelu got up.

"Renew our wards, Rahelu," Anathwan said, as Scarface— his will now entirely supplanted by hers—slung the Elder over his shoulder. "Elaram, ready Seeking. Ghardon, let Nheras raise the barriers; I require you to hold your strength in reserve. From this point on, believe neither your eyes nor your senses, but only in me. Do not be tempted by the Endless Gate.

"Now, come. We must reach the summit, undetected, before sunset, and make a fortified camp by nightfall, where we may bide in safety and ready our strength, for we shall have but one opportunity to attempt this working, and it must be attempted at the very zenith of starrise."

Anathwan set a brutal pace.

The Supplicants followed.

Ash stirred and pebbles crunched underfoot as they jogged across the beach in a ragged line, cutting across a set of footprints that meandered, doubled back, and crisscrossed themselves on their roundabout trek inland.

Ahead, the mountain loomed; a dark, forbidding mass against the dusky clouds. The only way up was the massive stair cut into the glassy black stone that formed the mountain's bones: wide enough to accommodate two palanquins, each tread two strides deep, each step rising as high as Rahelu's navel. It ran straight as a ruler from the foot of the mountain to the rim of its broken peak. Every tenth step bracketed by prayer gates carved from the same black stone; every tenth gate twice as large as the rest. Their ascent was a graceless scramble up the smooth, slippery ledges on their elbows and knees, like children who had not yet learned how to walk. Rahelu hugged each step so she could not see how slowly the beach below receded or contemplate how very far they had left to climb.

Don't think.

Focus only on what's in front of you.

Tally the cycles and patterns of rote movement through gates, the sound of laborious panting, and—

—bare rock humming beneath her fingers.

Inhale. Up. Pain.

Ringing in her ears.

Exhale. Forward.

Rushing waters below.

—a surge, a melody, song without beginning or end—

Earth and sky—

Inhale. Up. Pain.

—alight with spinning starfire.

Seven hundred fucking steps—

Exhale. Forward.

—her hands, outstretched, meeting—

—empty air.

Thank gods!

They dragged themselves up to the razor-thin, jagged, black rim of the crater and flopped onto their bellies, gasping for air like dying fish as they crawled forward.

Then: Nheras's sharp intake of breath, followed by Ghardon's, "Skymother take my eyes!" while Elaram's mouth hung open. The only thing that escaped was a glittering stream of brilliant blue sparks drifting up on the wind from her aura, headed towards the twinkling stars.

"It's real," Ghardon murmured as he craned his neck forward in a lean so slight that you could only call it leaning because his nose was technically further out relative to the position of his toes. "It's actually real."

Head swimming, Rahelu forced herself to stand with the others.

Looked down into the mountain's heart.

The inner slopes of the crater walls fell away into a dark lake that could have swallowed the city of Ennuost Yrg whole. Rising from its depths were four gargantuan obelisks that spanned heaven and earth.

Visceral recognition slammed into her with the next swell of the starsong.

She knew this place.

Its image had been seared into her mind, along with the other fragments of the possible futures Onneja had conjured in the sky above Stormbane's Rest. At the time, she'd been too overwhelmed to register more than general details—a sky full of strange stars; a circular abyss; four dull pillars, black as night.

Now?

Rahelu trembled anew, breathless. White mist spilled from her resonance aura to pool at her feet. You could not stand here on the very threshold of the Endless Gate, behold the immense size and the impossible grandeur of its obelisks, and feel anything other than dread and awe. Their pointed tops soared into the infinite sky; their bases stretched down into the black waters. Evenly spaced around the perfectly circular shore, positioned precisely at the major cardinal points; anchors in a rudimentary Obfuscation formation. The red rays of the setting sun glinted off the carved ebon surfaces. Patterns that were neither modern sigils, resonance wards, nor Free Territory ritual scars, yet were akin to them —an ancient predecessor.

Alive with eldritch light and music.

Those curling pale mists coalescing upon the water...

The lake called to her.

Come, it sang.

Come to me.

The Elumaje looked just like this on clear harvest evenings. Rahelu remembered it well:

She races Anenje along the sands with armfuls of lakegrass.

She dives with her mother into the blue-gray waters to dig up shrimp and clams from the silty lakebed.

She paddles her raft after her father's as they look for trout where the warmer shallows mix with the cooler depths. He sings to her as he casts his net, his rich baritone carrying out over the sunlit waters, and she sings back to him in her childish treble as she casts hers. Line after line, their voices chase each other across the lake—verse, refrain; verse, refrain—again and again until her voice grows strong and sure in the words and melody and she can sing the whole ballad on her own, beginning to end and back to the beginning so he can teach her the harmonies. When the sky dims, and her voice and arms tire, and their baskets bulge full, her father lashes their rafts together and speeds them to shore as he sings on, alone, until a whole joyful chorus answers—come to me, come home to me, come home, my love, to me—*her mother's and every voice in their little village soaring through the air to greet them.*

A pinprick of orange light glimmering in the distance. Faint strains of laughter and music on the air.

Come to me.

Those figures standing on the other shore...
"Aban?" she whispered. "Anma?"
How they must miss her!
She had never been away from home so long.

Come home to me.

When had the night grown so bright?
Her eyes hurt.
She squinted; tried to see past the brilliance of the swirling resonance rising from the lake in silver-edged lavender mists.
A cookfire!
That was the warm glow of a cookfire in the distance; that

was the mouthwatering scent of the fat trout they had caught being grilled over hot coals.

Come home.

She moved towards it.

"Rahelu, no!" Someone yanked her back. "Stop!"

A youth in ill-fitting, mismatched clothes streaked with ash and dirt. He had dirty chestnut hair that hung limp over his eyes and ragged nails and his skin was covered with rat bites and scratches. His face looked vaguely familiar, gaunt and hollow though it was, and he gripped her around her ribs so hard she thought she might faint.

Annoyance flared; sparked into anger in an eyeblink.

How dare he touch her? How dare he try to stop her? She let her anger surge out past her resonance ward to drown him, but he had raised a barrier of his own: a thick, jagged wall of icy fear to counter her Projection.

Damn him.

Hot as her anger was, his barrier would take time to burn through and she didn't have time; aban and anma were waiting for her to come home.

Rahelu threw her weight forward and elbowed him in his groin.

He grunted, then cried out as his boots teetered on the ebon rock, but he did not let go as they fell down, down, down the ash-covered slope in a cascade of chalk-white terror and coal-red anger and bits of sharp gravel—

A woman's commanding tones from behind: "Follow."

—slipping sliding tumbling in a tangle of locked limbs. Her toes kissed the edge of the abyssal lake as they finally rolled to a stop beneath the shadow of the closest obelisk; sent ripples across that mirror-smooth plane towards the squat oblong shape at its heart.

The woman's voice again: "Wards!"

Mist-filled ambient resonance shivered.

Two whisper-thin darts of blue-gray resonance struck her and the boy directly in the temples. Cool clarity froze, then shattered the sentimental yearning that had fogged her mind.

She stopped grappling with Ghardon at once.

"Sorry, I'm sorry!" Rahelu panted as they helped each other up. "Thank—"

A shadow stirred at the heart of the Endless Gate.

"Eight hells!" Ghardon swore as they scrabbled away from the whatever-the-fuck apparition that was lurking by the altar at the center of the stone platform in the middle of the lake. Back from the water's edge; back to the relative safety of the crater wall and the others, the others who were running, running to meet them.

Behind them, more shadows surged.

"Wards!" Anathwan shouted as the two of them skidded to a stop to avoid bowling everyone else over. "Wards now!"

"Which ward?" Ghardon asked as Scarface dropped the Elder in a heap next to him, but Rahelu was already moving.

How she wished she had her spear! A spear would have helped her draw this circle swiftly and neatly. She would've been able to plant the iron-shod butt into this cursed gravel until she found solid stone, then sweep it around to mark out a clean even line, instead of limping around dragging the heel of her boot in this wobbly squiggle that was supposed to pass for a foundation line.

"Dreamward!" Rahelu barked even as Anathwan said: "Maketh's grand ward." At Rahelu's incredulous look—how were they supposed to reproduce that eight-page monstros-ity?—the Elder added, "This is not subject to discussion."

Rahelu's jaw snapped shut. She did not want to be the object of Anathwan's next lesson.

"Ghardon, recall the design. The rest of you: clear the site of detritus. Quickly! Before the Endless Gate's temptations gain further strength."

Anathwan closed her eyes as she set Scarface to work, then lifted bandaged hands to summon an Obfuscation barrier of pale gray calm. It was weak, almost pathetically so —its feeble light rendered near invisible by the stronger glow from the obelisks—and the effort required to hold it visibly cost her.

Blood began to drip from Anathwan's nostrils.

Rahelu joined Elaram and Nheras in kicking at the gravel. They scraped the edges of their boots across the ground until they could see their distorted reflections in the glassy black stone beneath; heaped the gravel and rock dust into a laughably frail, ankle-high bulwark against the wakening darkness while Ghardon stretched his hands out in front of him, palms down, and called on Evocation:

Ash stirs. Flames leap. Torn scraps of paper fly into the air. Twist. Reassemble themselves into eight pages with their edges glued together.

All around them, the desolate landscape *rippled—*

Ghardon knelt and touched his hands to the earth. Black stone shimmered; bleached to pale ivory until they seemed to stand upon a giant unfurled parchment. Intricate lines— vivid, glossy red—bloomed outward beneath his fingers.

—as the shadows quickened.

A gleeful Dharyas rushes out from the workshop. Years older. Dressed like a Supplicant in gray and copper—a combination of colors that belong to no House. Her eyes shine with excitement. 'It worked, it worked, it worked! I told you I could make it work!' She reaches over and shuts the account books spread out over the shop counter. 'Leave those sums to Xyuth,' Dharyas says when Rahelu protests and hustles

her—ink-stained fingers still holding an abacus and brush pen—to the
workshop door. 'I need you to help me test it! Come—'

Her heart leapt at the sight of Dharyas.

Dharyas! Alive! Whole and hale and unscarred, except for the long, spiraling ritualistic lines decorating her arms.

Rahelu stilled, the piled gravel before her forgotten. She ached to step into that lost future, where Xyuth and the Tattered Quill had not been torn apart by the murderous cultists because she had never taken the stargem they had sought; where she and Dharyas had spurned what the Houses had offered to make their own fortunes; where—

'—meet my parents,' Elaram says, her pale yellow silk robes fluttering as she tugs a nervous Jhobon, sweating in his formal Imrell robes, past the open gates of the Issolm estate. Ghardon and Rahelu stroll through on their heels in matching robes of white-and-black. Rahelu says, 'Twenty silver kez on Jhobon dying of embarrassment before the sixth course,' and a laughing Ghardon accepts as—

"Jhobon?" Elaram's voice quivered. "Jhobon. Jhobon—" Ghardon looked up at the sound of her breaking voice.

—he follows two Supplicants, one a girl arrayed in the lilac-and-black splendor of House Isilc and the other a youth dressed in Issolm white-and-black with a coiled whip on his belt, through the dim hallways of a Sunset songhouse to where a dozen more Supplicants, dressed in the colors of all eight Houses, await them inside—

He faltered.

Illusory parchment dulled, blackening in patches as the half-completed lines of Maketh's grand ward which he had so flawlessly reproduced began to fade.

Some part of Rahelu knew she ought to act, ought to help

him keep the precious Evocation from slipping away by shoring it up with a Concordance. But her feet wouldn't move; she couldn't tear her eyes away from the sight of Dharyas, Dharyas smiling, Dharyas beckoning her to come closer—

—closer, Rahelu, come to me—

Nheras's baton cracked against her shins. She fell, one stride short of stepping through Anathwan's thinning barrier, next to Elaram, also on her knees, crying as she lashed out at the visions surrounding them with Seeking.

"You're not real, you're not real, you're not real—"

Vision after vision shattered.

The fragments warped. Split. Reformed into countless variants. Broken glimpses of infinite futures through occluded eyes, like reflections in the hanging shards of a mirror shrine.

"Stay in the circle, fish guts!"

Nheras knelt beside Ghardon and laid her hands on his, eyes closed against the vision of:

—a private tearoom where a much younger Nheras, dressed in the plain clothes of a common-born, plucks at a zither. Her small, nimble fingers dance over the strings; they conjure a burst of melody—

Crimson lines steadied as Nheras barked, "Start drawing!" over a bright swell of music that was sweeter than birdsong, each sparkling note as beautiful and brilliant as the droplets of a sunlit waterfall.

—the screen doors behind her open, revealing—

"With what?!" Rahelu asked while Ghardon said, "Hurry the fuck up! We can't hold this forever."

—sixteen soaring pillars in a grand hall. Anathwan, splendid in white-and-black robes of heavy silk brocade with a matching ebon circlet crowning her golden hair, glides past the stately fluted columns to approach the white marble dais with its empty—

No resonance crystal. No salt. No wood.

—towering golden throne whose silk cushions are—

The only stone, other than those eerie obelisks, was the unyielding ground beneath or the loose gravel scattered on its surface.

—soaked with blood that drips—

The entire landscape within their circle and beyond the edges of Ghardon's Evocation was a desolate waste.

—from a black, serpentine knife—

There was only ash, ash everywhere, and Rahelu had no water or oil to cast it with to make the finished ward last through the night.

"I've nothing I can use!"

—in Ylaen's hand—

Another pulse of resonance from Elaram splintered the vision.

"Use blood," Anathwan said as her barrier winked out.

Blood?

Rahelu stared at the daunting network of ward lines that surrounded them. She would need buckets of it. Her throat tightened. Did Anathwan mean for her to bleed herself dry?

She glanced down at the Elder.

Broken body supine on the ground. Two dark lines running over her lips and chin. Splatters all over her shirt front. Anathwan looked like a dying woman, but her eyes were calm and cool and trained on a spot above Rahelu's right shoulder.

The scrape of someone's boot on bare stone from behind.

Rahelu turned, fumbling at her waist for the dagger Nheras had given her.

Scarface came towards them, bared cutlass in hand. His eyes were no longer blank; they blazed with barely contained rage. He was the very image of the Earthgiver roused to fury: craggy face fractured by scars that glowed the molten red of erupting lava, a hulking titan bent on destruction.

Oh, fuck.

He swung while Rahelu was still trying to draw her weapon. It wouldn't come out—the dagger's barbed quillons had caught in a fold of her shirt. She went to dodge, then realized if she did, that would leave the Elder unprotected.

Rahelu might owe an Elder her obedience; she might owe her sworn House her loyalty; but Anathwan herself?

Rahelu owed Anathwan her freedom, thrice over.

And freedom was worth everything.

Starfather, grant me luck, she prayed. She ducked under Scarface's swing to grasp his forearm. Dug her heels in. Heaved; pulled with all the might she could muster and her body weight.

His steel blade struck rock, a handspan shy of Anathwan's throat.

Cracks spidered across the ground and ripped through the fraying Evocation Ghardon and Nheras struggled to hold in place with their Concordance. Chips of ebon stone flew. One cut a gash in Elaram's forehead as she tore apart another of the Endless Gate's visions; another, palm-sized piece sliced Rahelu's fingers as she snatched it up and drove the razor-sharp triangular fragment into the side of Scarface's neck.

The fragment stuck.

He didn't seem to feel it.

Fuck. Fuck!

Scarface seized Rahelu by her throat. Her eyes bulged and her vision dimmed as she felt herself lifted bodily off her feet. She kicked; connected with air. Raised her hands and made claws of her fingers to rake his face, searching for the soft, vulnerable eyes where she might dig in her nails and force him to release her. But she was weak; weak and thin from weeks of imprisonment and he enraged beyond rational thought. He held her at arm's length, viselike grip cutting off her breath, letting her choke herself with her furious struggling to the point of near unconsciousness before flinging her away to lift his cutlass once more.

The Elder sighed.

A needle of doubt, thin as spider silk, pierced Scarface's eye.

His fingers spasmed.

The first mate dropped the cutlass with a metallic *clang*. He shuddered and moaned as his hand, against his own volition, reached for the fragment of stone embedded in his throat and yanked it out.

Blood gushed from the wound as Scarface toppled over.

"Now, Rahelu," Anathwan whispered. "Draw."

RAHELU DREW.

Long after Elaram collapsed.

Long after Ghardon succumbed to resonance backlash.

Long after Elder Anathwan shuttered her eyes and Nheras's strength gave out and the Evocation guiding her died with the guttering daylight.

Rahelu kept drawing.

Relied on ordinary, unaided recall to tell her shaky hands where to smear line after sticky line across the bare rock glistening in the flickering light of obelisks and the ghostly possibilities swarming at the edge of her vision.

At last, she closed the final loop.

Had it worked?

She sat back on her heels; dazed. Blinked bleary eyes, trying to look and yet not look at the shifting resonance outside the grand ward of blood and gravel. At one point, there had been thousands upon thousands of realities, so vivid and strong they had blotted out the present. Now—with twenty warding lines between them and the shadows and every soul (save for Rahelu) sleeping the dreamless sleep of the utterly exhausted—those possible realities had thinned to mere dozens.

All faded but lingering, still, under the fitful light of the obelisks and the new moon.

Dharyas smiled. Waved at her through an open workroom door. A gray shadow limned with copper light from the small forge behind her.

"You're dead," Rahelu said.

Her words became a crossbow bolt and killed Dharyas all over again.

The revenant rose and looked at her with a reproachful eye.

"I'm sorry—"

Your fault, Dharyas mouthed at her. *This is your fault.*

"—I'm sorry!"

You're not sorry.

"I am!"

Tell that to Xyuth. He had a consort and a daughter, did you know? A little girl who—

"They were going to die. He wanted to save them. He helped me so I could save them."

Did you?

Gods.

She didn't know.

She didn't know.

How could she not fucking know?

Because she'd been so caught up in her own giddy relief and self-loathing that she had not stopped to care about anyone else. No; worse. After bearing the brunt of Tseiran's grief and hatred for Hzin's death, she had decided to take her family and sail as far away as they could get from any reminders of the part she had played in the misery of others.

Where was that little girl now? Would she thank Rahelu for interfering? Or would she, like Tseiran, blame her for meddling?

You killed him.

She had, hadn't she?

In one breath, she had warned the scrivener of the folly of trying to avert Augury and the arrogance of assuming that well-intentioned action always aligned with intended consequence. In the next, she had disregarded those warnings.

You killed him.

"I *helped* him—"

For a few sheets of parchment and some ink—

"—so he would help my family."

—and you're not sorry.

She was and she wasn't.

She was sorry that he had died and sorry his consort was left to raise their daughter alone, but she was not sorry that she had used every method at her disposal to save her family.

She had warned Xyuth of the risks but she had given him the choice.

And he had accepted.

Ylaen had had the right of it after all. Why should she love her family less?

"No. No, I'm not sorry." In Chanazian, she added: "Their blood in my veins; their breath in my lungs," though Dharyas had not understood before and would not understand now. "Before I owe the world anything, I owe my parents."

Guilt stared at her with Dharyas's face. Her Dharyas, with the caved-in skull and mangled ribs—not the Endless Gate's lie—asked: *What is the world but the greatest family of all?*

"I hate pointless riddles," Rahelu said, dredging up a scrap of resonance from her wrung-out aura. "And you're dead; the dead should stay dead."

The shade of Dharyas puffed away at her brief pulse of Seeking.

She shivered, cold now that the wild fear and frenzied physical exertion that had sustained her had passed. What heat the ground had soaked up during the day had dissipated with the last of the daylight. Though the breeze remained gentle, it seemed to have a new bite as it blew over the arbitrary stretch of bare, windswept rock where they had been forced to make camp on the uncertain lakeshore bordering the Endless Gate and the mountain's crater walls.

In the center of the grand ward, Elaram and Ghardon snuggled up against Anathwan for warmth like two jhalyx kits curled up against their mother's flanks. Even Nheras—unconsciously formal with her hands at her sides despite her exhaustion, the strong planes of her face thrown into sharp relief by the cold, steady light of the yellow-blue crescent above—had been drawn into that pile of humanity for Ghardon had not let go of her hand.

At the ward's very edge: Rahelu, covered with Scarface's blood, his drained, stiffening corpse at her feet.

She grimaced. Threw her dagger to the ground with a *clatter*. Rolled the corpse over and over with her boot, past the outermost line, clear of their warded camp so she wouldn't have to look at it, and went to sit on the opposite side where she could keep watch over the Endless Gate and its specters until the winter solstice was nigh and it was time to wake the others.

THE SKYMOTHER SPREAD her jeweled sable cloak across the heavens.

Beneath it, the obelisks glowed.

There was a mesmerizing beauty to the play of resonance across those ancient runes. A pattern. A signal. Now and then Rahelu could recognize small sequences: fractal compositions of varied color, texture, duration, and length, repeated over and over in combinations. Sometimes they matched the thrumming of the starsong; sometimes they skipped between the great beats of the ever-present drone in counter-rhythm.

The spans of stormwatch slowly slipped by.

Rahelu passed them by guessing at the changes in the runelight.

It was like trying to hum the next lines of a song she didn't know written in a language she was hearing for the very first time: she grasped enough of the rise and fall and shape of the melody to intuit when a shift was imminent but the complexities of the harmonic structure eluded her. Surely, she would think to herself, those flame-like ripples of passion must be followed by the soft bloom of joy, only to see them chased off by deep purple bands of bitter regret or eaten away from the edges by dribbles of black despair.

Not once did she correctly predict a change for the whole of the pattern was beyond her ability to grasp. But the puzzle diverted her mind from the gnawing of her empty stomach and the exhaustion that kept dragging her eyelids down; helped her ears stay alert in the flat, eerie quiet.

Clouds rolled in from the west as stormarc became stararc; a second veil that dimmed the moon and the Starfather's infinite eyes, leaving only the faint glimmer of runes.

The night should not be this quiet.

She listened but could not hear the wind (there were no scrubby trees or tall grasses, not even the smallest patch of vegetation); could not pick out the background whine of insects buzzing and chirping (only the constant niggle of the starsong that seemed to come from everywhere and nowhere all at once); could not sense a single seabird nesting in the crevices of the rain-carved gullies in the ebon rock that formed the bones of this islet or on the black sand beach far below, so far below that even the ceaseless rush and crash of waves upon its rocky shore was muted by distance.

The night was so cold.

She rubbed her hands and feet and arms and legs. Got up. Took her boots off. Jumped up and down and jogged in place. Felt an absolute fool. Put her boots back on again. Paced the perimeter of the grand ward—to stay awake, to move, to get warm, to do something that felt purposeful instead of futile —and flinched at the loudness of her heels striking rock.

Idiot, idiot!

A sharp sound like that would travel far in this silence.

So she took her boots off again and completed her circuit on bare feet, squinting as she inspected the ward lines, whereupon she sat down and hugged her knees to her chest, drenched again—this time with sweat—and no warmer than before.

The night was too dark.

Rahelu could barely make out the obelisks now—their looming presence had faded into the still black waters and the empty black sky. She felt as if she sat suspended at the heart of a void in existence. She closed her eyes—

Darkness.

She opened them—

Darkness still.

Closed.

Opened.

Closed and opened: no discernible difference.

Had to lift her hands. (Where were they? She couldn't see them; had to trust that they existed and they were moving by the slight sensation of the earth pulling on them.) Put them over her eyes to feel the flutter of her eyelashes against her fingers to confirm that yes, she still had a body and it was responding to her commands, but even though the exercise was a success, she wasn't entirely convinced by the results so she reached out with Seeking, sending her mind spiraling up and out in a pattern reminiscent of a questryl's flight.

The only resonance signature she sensed on the islet was hers; hers and the four others in the warded circle with her. (As it should be.)

Yet something—something that was not the starsong— flickered at the very edge of her resonance senses. A long slow pulsing that she felt in the marrow of her bones? Or a thin, sustained shiver so high-pitched that drilled through her ears and itched at her teeth? Rahelu could not tell which it was; whenever she tried to hone in on the signal, it oscillated from one extreme to the other, and she ended up chasing it across the spectrum like one of the Yellow Fang's hapless marks lunging for their purloined coin purse in a Lowdocks back alley.

Whatever it was, it carried a living warmth that was a welcome respite.

Pleasant heat seeped into her chilled limbs.

Slowly, slowly, the coiled tension in her muscles thawed.

When had she last felt so relaxed? In those first song-filled days after Peshwan Yrg, upon the Aleituan Sea? Before she had sworn her Supplicant's oaths, when she had convinced her parents to steal a week away from their debts and obligations to sail far, far beyond their usual fishing waters on their little sloop? During those happy spans laughing and catching up on lost years with Tsenjhe in her workshop? Or had it been even longer? Perhaps before they had arrived in Ennuost Yrg, or before they had crossed the border from Chanaz, chasing a dream.

Well, that dream was reality now.

All those years of work and sacrifice had made it so, and relaxing for a moment or two could not take away from the achievements that had secured and guaranteed her family's future.

And, if Rahelu thought back to that very first moment when Elder Anathwan had outlined her expectations in the *Winged Arrow's* great cabin, hadn't she accomplished so much more since?

She had: appropriated the box from Ruarem's safe without the act being traceable to the Houses; resisted a Conclave agent's attempts to sway her loyalty; survived the Stormbringer's wrath in crossing the Abmerduan Sea; withstood and escaped the subsequent ordeal of captivity; assisted—more than assisted—in the construction of a grand ward that ought to have been undertaken by a senior mage; had done so under the pressure of an incredible, relentless resonance assault. Their presence here, the fact that the others could rest and regain their strength peacefully while camped upon the very threshold of the Endless Gate, was due in no small part to Rahelu's efforts.

And soon—in a few spans at most—they would seize the

crown back from Ylaen, Anathwan would call upon the power of the Endless Gate, and then they could all return home, with their mission a resounding success, to the Dominion.

Perhaps it was time for a new dream.

Rahelu let her eyes drift to the west.

Imagined sailing into the future, standing upon the bow with her brother and sisters by her side, watching the wide harbor and the familiar walls of Ennuost Yrg come into view.

She would not need to search the Isonn fleet for her family's sloop. Her parents would not have sailed out into the Kuath Bay. They would have had all the coin they needed to take a season's rest from fishing. The news would have spread through the relay networks like wildfire as soon as they made port at Peshwan Yrg so her parents would be there, part of the crowd lined up along the pier waving as the *Sooty Gull* came in and tied up at the Highdocks. And Rahelu, dressed in her Issolm whites and blacks with her hair braided neatly and her Supplicant's armband prominent on her left forearm, would stride down the gangplank as part of Elder Anathwan's retinue, looking for a globe of golden resonance that outshone the high sun, for at the very heart of that glow would be anma and aban, standing tall and straight with pride, their eyes glistening with unshed tears of joy.

She would not be able to go to her family immediately.

There would be palanquins and a retinue of guards to escort and usher them into the presence of the Exalted Dominance and the other Atriarchs gathered in the throne room of the palace. There would be a very grand ceremony that she would have to suffer through—though it would, in truth, involve very little suffering for Nheras would have coached her through how to stand and what to do while the Houses bestowed them with honors and accolades and Elder Anathwan kept her promise to elevate them as Dedicates, and the boring political speeches would be rendered comprehensible by Ghardon's explanations and made bearable by Elaram's cheeky irreverence.

And she would not go to her family alone.

Somewhere in that crowd of faces would be another friend. Perhaps, with time, when that friendship was rooted in more level soil, it could blossom into a more equal partnership.

No, Rahelu thought. *Not merely a dream.*

A possibility, a close one, founded on so much truth that she could not tell if the vision before her was a Seeming she had unconsciously willed into existence or an impromptu Augury of her most likely future.

Whichever it was, it was more real than anything else in the void. The darkness that had seemed so all-encompassing before was a mere screen; the filmy silk of the Issolm palanquin's gauzy black curtains. Beyond it, she could hear handcarts clattering over cobblestones; the sharp *whiiiist-crack!* of corded leather striking pack animals. Voices, many, many voices, raised in shouts—not just the guttural tongue of the Free Territories, but the long, multisyllabic phrases of Aleznuaweithish mixed with the rounded, river-smooth, song-like speech of her homeland—a harmonious clamor of greetings and farewells; exchanging news of the weather, the tides, their triumphant return from their quest to the other side of the world; dockside vendors hawking their wares to couples promenading along the wide, elegant boardwalk: seafood, new-mended clothing, trinkets—

A voice, drifting out from behind the curtain:

Rahelu.

She shot to her feet.

Opened her eyes. (Were they open? Yes, yes, they were open.) Spun around, holding to her Seeking, lifted her hand, pulled away that curtain, searched the lush green hill of the parkland overlooking the Highdocks until she could make out a tall, broad-shouldered, robed figure through the trees in the distance, waiting for her at the heart of a bower with four pillars that held up the Skymother's star-studded cloak.

Come to me.

Her heart soared.
Please.
Not a command.
A prayer.
One she could grant.
Help me.
Rahelu stepped into the dark moonlit waters.

37

KNIFE

But not silent; never silent. Always, there is: the steady beat of her heart; the rush of her blood in her ears; the slow, musical burble of air as she slips through the cool embrace of the black waters.

Familiar.

Effortless.

Home.

Ahead and behind, only shadows; all around, banks of frilled weeds that greet her with waves and caresses. Stay; stay. The tendrils tangle her wrists and ankles. Her skin tingles at their touch.

Do not go; do not leave.

But she must, she must—

Help me.

—for he is calling her, he needs her, and he cannot swim.

She tugs against the weeds that have snared her, but they hold her fast, tight as iron shackles, and draw her down.

Down, towards the silty bed.

Down, away from the rippling sky.

Down, to rest among the bones.

She thrashes. Twists. The waters around her roil.

Where is her knife? She never dives without her knife; she swore to never go without a weapon again. Get the knife get the knife and cut yourself free. Distance softens the telltale signs of her struggle; distance and the dizziness that comes with the breathlessness of your last gasp. It is dark, so dark, and despair will drown her before the waters do, for she has failed and he will go on, thinking that she did not answer because she does not love him in return.

She is wrong.

His love keeps no ledger.

He finds her now, as he had found her before. His defiant scream scythes through the silent sea; his knife slashes through the seagrasses that dared try to keep her.

Free!

She is free; he is free; they are free!

Silt stirs and swirls as they hurl themselves skyward, swift and sure as a spear throw, shattering the still, glassy surface of the lake and the still, moonlit night with noisy gasps.

The heart of the Endless Gate holds a circular platform. They stagger out of the depths onto solid ebon stone, made soft by pale, fine-grained sand. It takes twenty-five strides to reach the very center and flop against the squat, oblong rock.

The rock is warm.

The rock is also humming.

She looks up.

Even in the Lowdocks, the stars are bright and beautiful.

Here, safe and secluded, in this perfect circle of gleaming black stone cradled by silvered waters high above the murmuring sea, she can relax.

And simply be.

The thought is as delicious as the warmth seeping into her limbs.

Water beads; drips from their skin and sodden clothes. Little splatters in the sand, like the Skymother's first tears. Bone-white grains *darken; clump into tiny rounded discs. In the dim, flickering light emanating from the four pillars holding up the star-stitched lacework stretched across the heavens, the splashes look like the clotted blood that still clings to her shirt.*

Her skin and her hands, though, have been washed clean.

Gone, too, is her resonance ward.

Good.

She has no need of wards. Not with him.

'Rahelu.' *His voice is rough and tight; so are the fingers gripping hers. His skin is hot—feverish—but his body is shiver-wracked with chills.* 'Rahelu. You came for me.'

His left arm looks odd hanging like that by his side.

'Are you hurt?' *she asks.*

She urges him to sit on the warm rock.

'Yes.' *He buries his face in her shoulder.* 'Yes. It's been months and it still hurts. Why? Why do I still hurt?'

*His grief is a cold, dark tide—*Rahelu oh Rahelu please please all I can feel is this suffocating crushing sucking ache in my chest*—dragging at their lungs, stopping up their throats, burying them with the weight of the ocean—*please stay please help me make this emptiness go away please I don't want to be alone—

Why had she left him to shoulder that grief alone?

'I—'

She should have stayed by his side to bear witness as Dharyas burned.

'I'm sorry,' *she says. Words; inadequate ones, no matter how much she means them.* 'I would Revoke it if I could.'

'It can't be done. I've tried. The heavens forbid it. The dead,' *he says, with a soul-racking sob,* 'are meant to stay dead.'

Oh, avela.

'For you,' *she says,* 'I would defy the heavens.'

His right hand grips her left so hard it hurts.

'You would?' *he asks.*

'Yes.'

Yes.

A thousand times, yes.

He sits up, pulls back. Looks at her with hope sparkling through his blackened aura, brighter than the stars.

'Will you stay with me?'

'Yes.'

Yes.

And I will not leave you again.

'And help me bring him back?'

Help me.

'Ye—'

Wait. *Him?*

STUPID—SHE was so fucking stupid!—to have fallen for his tricks.

No more.

Rahelu launched herself at Ylaen.

Her knife.

Where was her knife, the one Nheras had given to her?

Shit.

She'd dropped it—dropped her bloody weapon like a bloody fool because she hadn't liked the way the grip had stuck fast to her fingers after...after what Anathwan had asked her to do, after what had to be done—so she had best grab hold of his knife before he did and hope he had lost the others in the lake.

Her hand snaked down towards his belt.

Found a handle. Yanked.

The soft *hiss* of a sharp blade sliding out of a leather sheath.

Discovered the knife he carried was one of *those* horrid black knives—and drove the serpentine blade into his injured left shoulder anyway, before he could use the grip he still had on her hand to twist them around and pin her to the ground.

He didn't cry out.

Didn't fight back as she straddled his chest.

Didn't even flinch as she pulled the knife free and held it to his throat.

"I told you not to lie."

She had warned him. Often. Loudly and repeatedly. This time, she really would gut him from hip to hip, then cut him open from navel to collarbone and leave his entrails and organs for the seabirds to feast upon.

Ylaen said, "We all lie."

"Shut up."

What the fuck was she waiting for? When had she ever hesitated to do what was necessary? She had killed before, for many reasons. Ignorance. Arrogance. Inaction. Protection. What difference would adding another name and another reason to the list make, other than requiring her to begin using two hands to tally the total instead of one?

Damn him to the seventh hell for forcing this choice on her.

How can she cut his throat if he simply lies there, unresisting, looking at her like that?

"To ourselves, if to no one—"

"Shut up!"

He did not, of course, shut up. "That was not my lie. The

Endless Gate feeds on desire; you saw what you wanted to see." A corner of his mouth quirked up into a self-deprecating half-smile. "So do I."

The sweet ache of longing filled the ambient resonance with silver-purple mists. The void around them shifted—

His hand on the tiller of a familiar sloop as it surges through the waves like a frisky, overeager pup. He wears a threadbare shirt over linen trousers cuffed short at the knee and an open smile. From the mast, Jhobon's steady hands sheet in the luffing sail. From the bow, Elaram squeals in delight as the next wave slaps the hull and soaks her with sun-drenched spray. Beside him, humming a song matched to the sea and reeling in a net full of jeweled-toned fish: her.

—and some part of her—the part that had, not so long ago, yearned to leave her family's debts and obligations behind to sail a sloop across the sea, all the way to the other side of the world—answered:

Seabirds wheeling overhead by green-tinted clouds. Sunny day after sunny day following the shoals of fish and steady currents to scrubby cays trimmed with blinding white sands, and starlit, song-filled nights being rocked to sleep by the sea or the wind, wrapped in the warmth of someone's arms.

Detail after detail embroidered and broadened the idyllic vision, underpinned their imaginings with Evoked realism until the original possibility she had been chasing seemed... limiting, instead of logical.

Did she really want to go back to a life governed by rigid rules she did not know, dictated by people she did not like, to enmesh herself in a net of House machinations for political ends she did not understand?

For here, before her eyes, was another life she could lead.

No debt; only the Earthgiver's good abundance of fruit trees that give shade and sustenance. No coin; only pretty discs of metal that chime pleasantly against the seashells strung above their hammocks.

Existence reduced to its barest essentials.

It couldn't possibly be that simple.

If the world was so simple, they would not be here in the first place.

Rahelu wrenched her emotions back under control. Without her Evocations to fuel his longings with substance, the vivid possibility faded into a gossamer imprint on the void.

"A pretty lie."

"It could be the truth—if you allow it to be." He coughed; the movement pulled at his bleeding shoulder and scored a thin line across his windpipe. "Well. I suppose it doesn't matter."

He wasn't looking at her any longer; he was looking past her, to a point somewhere behind her. "Go on, Rahelu." A tremor shook his body; a shrug? No. A silent sob. "Do what you will."

Heartbeat after heartbeat passed beneath the black, serpentine blade's quivering edge, and still she could not force it down to where it needed to be.

His death was entirely justified on some level, she knew. If she stopped to think about it, she could likely come up with a list of offenses as long as the road from Ennuost Yrg to Peshwan Yrg. The first three alone—betrayal of their mission, conspiracy against the Dominion, grand treason; the very same charges Nheras ought to have faced—gave her every right to condemn him.

But:

Without a trial, there could be no execution.

Without a fight, there could be no self-defense.

That left murder.

"Give me the crown," Rahelu found herself saying. She took the ritual knife away from his throat and sheathed the horrid thing—she was *not* going to ask where in the eight hells he had gotten his hands on a weapon like that; she neither needed nor wanted to know—and let him up before she could second guess her decision. "And the *Gull*. Then take your uncle and your ship clan and your father's warship and go home."

"Home," Ylaen slurred.

The Aleznuaweithish word came out with its consonants rounded off and unbalanced by his heavier emphasis on the vowel, so it sounded one syllable removed from the Chanazian equivalent.

"Home," he repeated, then brayed in laughter. "Home!"

He smelled like the sea but his breath stank of cloves and cardamom and star anise; just how wine-addled were his wits?

Softly, Rahelu, softly.

Try—for once—to resolve this without punching anyone in the face.

Tell him whatever he wants to hear; give him whatever he asks. Then you can take the crown to Anathwan so she can unlock the Endless Gate and do what she came to do—good job, well done, mission fulfilled—and you can all get the fuck off this dead black islet with its time-warping, mind-bending siren visions and you, too, can go home.

"Yes," she said. "Home."

The ambient resonance stirred. And for a moment, just a moment, she—

—kneels at Onneja's feet atop a tall spire surrounded by ice and wind and cloud—

—strolls through a silk-garbed crowd, robed in pale green and sky-blue brocade with jade and sapphires in her braided hair, arm in arm with Lhorne—

—stands at Anathwan's right shoulder behind a white marble throne—

—dances with Ylaen in a chalk circle, her bared arms marked with twisting scars that mirror his—

Ylaen's wild laugh cut off as suddenly as it had begun. "I can't go home. If I do..." He shuddered and tore his eyes away from whatever vision was playing out behind her. "I can never go home. It's in my name, Rahelu; do you understand?"

Not one bit; this conversation was shifting faster than gang vendettas in the Lowdocks.

Cautiously, she said: "You said your sages cursed you."

"Jhobon never believed it—he always said that a blessing and a curse were two sides of the same coin—and he thought we could change the omens; that it was like the seven-piece puzzle: just a matter of finding another way to put the same shapes together to make a different picture.

"I tried, you know—I tried! For weeks I studied the notes that he'd made and copied the visualizations in Anathwan's journal and changed them to what I wanted. First chance I had, I took that crown and I came here and made my offerings and knelt before Enjela's bloody throne and prayed and begged the Starfather to show me a future that doesn't end with more of my family dead at my hands and a line of chained corpses strewn in my wake and a grief-stricken city burning to the ground."

He arched his brows and stretched his lips into a grimace

—a toothy mockery of his usual flirtatious smile—and asked: "Would you like to see?"

No. She had had enough of dreams filled with blood and blades and chains; she didn't care to add fire to them. "If you want to show me."

The sloop-dream returned:

Kual upon kual of an empty blue void surrounds him. Gone is the easy hand on the tiller, the carefree smile, the harmonious ebb and flow of sailing from shore to shore, following the shoals in their migratory cycle season after season. The sloop drifts, pushed from one horizon to the next by fickle wind and capricious currents in an aimless gyre until a fierce spring squall ends the tedium by tipping the tiny vessel hullside up and smashing it to driftwood.

It, too, had the feel of true Augury.

"Storms in the middle of the sea," he said, tipping his head back to stare at the stars as black bands of self-loathing rippled through his resonance aura, "pose no danger to anyone except those foolish enough to seek them."

Another line from another ballad (not one she knew). Its inherent pathos made her want to immediately ridicule him. Which would...do what? Rouse him to action? And what action did she want from him, exactly?

She'd spent so long using mockery as a goad that she had forgotten her mother's lessons in negotiation.

What did he want to hear?

"Keep the *Gull*. May you both fly swiftly." Gods. That empty platitude made her sound so cold and impersonal. "It's hard to be alone."

What else could she say to assuage that awful sense of loneliness in his last future?

"Ylaen." She laid a tentative hand on the shoulder she had stabbed, trying to soften her voice with as much grief and understanding as she could summon without turning to Projection. "Ylaen, I'm so sorry."

There.

"Oh, don't pity me, love," he said. His eyes were shuttered; his voice barely above a whisper. "I don't need your pity; I need your help. Then you can fuck off with what you want and I won't be alone."

Rahelu flinched.

She was not ashamed of her motives but hearing him cut through her attempt at empathy to state them so baldly was…uncomfortable. He made her sound as manipulative as Nheras.

"Fine." They could both pretend this was just an ordinary business transaction. "I'll help. What are we doing?"

"We're going to summon Jhobon's shade."

They were going to do *what?*

Twenty objections crowded into her head, aggravating the resonance backlash she had almost forgotten.

"You've lost your fucking mind."

"Wrong. My mind's still here, and it's perfectly fine. What I've lost is half my soul. But I'm no Evoker; I can't bring him back on my own."

She couldn't either. Shade summoning was no party trick to be undertaken lightly and they were short of everything required. But there was no way to break that news to him gently, so she didn't even try.

"No. Pick something else."

"Stop telling me 'no'. You promised to help."

"I want to help you. I do. It's just…"

Where to even begin?

Problem number one: "I hardly knew Jhobon and we don't have a focus."

That notebook of his would have been ideal but Ylaen had come empty-handed, except for that knife.

"Even if we did have an object of significance to use as a first-hand reference, it would be a passive focus. If you want me to summon something that's more than an ordinary Evocation, I need an active, willing focus in possession of the necessary mental faculties to guide me through the summoning—"

Which brought her to problem number two.

"—and Jhobon is *dead*."

"*I know*."

Cruel and tactless of her to say it—stupid, too, for if Jhobon were still alive, there would be no reason to try this in the first place—but they were running out of time, so she winced, then moved on.

"If we can somehow obtain a single unbroken chain of causality then maybe—maybe!—we could get it to work."

If they had enough power.

"We have me."

She scowled. "We need an intact past. His past; not yours. A complete chronology of every event of significance in Jhobon's life—as *he* experienced them. Do you understand?"

"We were tsol-bonded, Jhobon and I," he reminded her. "My soul remembers his."

A valid point.

"Fine. Let's assume you can contribute the lifetime of memories we need as a starting point. But cobbling them together in an imitation of a living mind with its own purpose and desires..." Rahelu grimaced. "We need a larger Concordance. Ghardon—"

"No."

"Why?"

"I don't trust him."

She refused to be deterred by his very unreasonable refusal. "Maketh then. Tell your stab-happy clan captain you need him here."

"Xya wouldn't allow it." Another bark of laughter. "Besides, my uncle hasn't said a word to me since his recovery. I do believe I've finally disappointed him beyond all hope of redemption."

"Elder Anath—"

Ylaen sat up and glared at her. "Quit dickering with me over crumbs when I've offered you an entire meal. Either help me or kill me, and if you won't do either of those things, then give me back the knife so I can end this!"

"For fuck's sake, Imos!"

Her voice shook; she made an effort to steady it instead of giving in to the urge to yell Beginner principles that he ought to have remembered from second-year Evocation studies at him until they got through his thick skull.

"I am trying to help you. But I'm not Enjela or any of your songhouse legends. Even if I were fully rested and had the use of an archmage's staff, I don't have the power or the skill or the stamina to recall the entirety of a person's life, tragically short though Jhobon's may have been. And even supposing I could, you don't have a suitable target stone for me to bind the Evocation to!"

She jabbed a finger at the focus stone on the worn leather thong around his neck. It might be a top-quality stone (first class, rose-pink, attuned to Projection) but it was a lesser focus stone nonetheless.

"That matrix has the capacity for—what? Five or six years out of eighteen or nineteen? Choose then: would you have Jhobon as the child he was, or do you want him as a puddle-deep facsimile of the person you remember?"

He went to open his mouth again so Rahelu raised her voice.

"And the working will still fade over time! You might have three seasons—four at most—if you're lucky."

"Then I'll count myself lucky."

Before she could list off eight more complicating factors and the shortcuts she would have to take to get around them, he seized her wrists and yanked her forward. Her hands landed right on top of the great, half-healed gashes over his heart. The wound throbbed, the flesh hot and swollen beneath her fingers.

"Enough delaying," he hissed.

She tried to pull away; only succeeded in wrenching one hand free. Her left, caught in Ylaen's right fist, remained imprisoned, as surely as if he'd shackled it with iron.

"You need a focus? Use me. You need something to anchor it to? A power source that won't easily run out? *Use me.*"

Anchoring a shade to his own mind? That meant insanity. You'd risk corrupting your memories; start thinking you were somebody else.

"Absolutely not. There's too many fucking—"

"Yes, I'm well aware of the risks, and no, I don't fucking care. I want you to Evoke every heartbeat of every span of every day he ever lived and then sew the whole damned lot to my soul until it's whole again."

He wasn't going to listen.

Rahelu made one last-ditch effort to dissuade him. Why she bothered, she wasn't sure, other than that she didn't want to be held accountable for the damage done when it all inevitably went wrong—she carried enough on her conscience to burden her for the rest of her life.

Let the Skymother witness that this was his choice.

"You realize it won't really be him."

A shade was just an intelligent simulacrum that could interface with and interpret a record of Jhobon's memories. You could interact with it like you would interact with the original person, but it wasn't a person at all. Merely an imprint of their soul.

Ylaen shrugged off her warning. "We sit at the heart of the Endless Gate, Rahelu, and I have the key to its power." He patted the altar-like stone. Right underneath him was the crown. Slotted, apparently, into the grooves of the ancient sigil carved into the stone's surface. "Anything is possible in a temporal nexus like this."

Panic fluttered as she felt him reach out with his resonance senses; she dropped verbal speech and fell straight into direct Projection.

No, no! Wait! she sent. *You're—I—we're not ready!*

His aura shook. *I've waited long enough.*

Shit.

Rahelu scrambled for calm, for apathy, for fear, even—anything she might be able to shove into his skull to make him pause for half a heartbeat because, dear gods in the four heavens, this was a fucking terrible idea.

She came up short because she had drained her entire fucking pendant during their escape from the *Stormbringer's Judgment* and he was taking everything from her and from him and pouring it into the crown.

Shit!

Nothing left to do but leverage the connection of their physical skin contact and past intimacy into a Concordance so she could exercise some semblance of control over the Evocation.

He hissed as she dove through the breach in his scars; flexed his mind against her mental intrusion and nearly threw her out again, so she smacked the idiot right across his pretty face.

"Let me in, you selfish coward, unless you want this to go awry."

"Fuck you," he said, but let her in so they could begin at the beginning:

Two babes swaddled together in a single cradle: the wailing one already sage-marked; the other already his silent shadow. They grow into children sharing a snug berth on a ship with crimson sails: boys who play at being men and mages while drawing wooden blades and chalk circles with driftwood sticks and charcoal, minds and bodies acting as one with a thousand small rituals forged through constant companionship.

Seasons pass.

They exchange wooden blades for steel, and writing sticks and sand trays for brush pen and paper.

At the height of their tenth truewinter as the moon wanes: the ship sails.

The clan gathers into a vast fleet—a city unto itself, floating at the center of the world—a circle of silk and incense and steel to bear witness in the sight of the sky, the stars, and the sea.

They go before the sages to receive their omens.

They enter as children—nameless; powerless; naked flesh anointed with lines of vermillion ink—in hopes of leaving as clan.

The Evocation wobbled as Ylaen trembled. Unsteady now as the child he was in the past.

Stand still beneath the ritual blade whose edges are waved like the sea.

Stand still as it carves the marks of lineage and power into their skin.

Stand still for a thousand cuts.

Stand.

Remain, as those who entered with him leave the center with their names and the bloodied blades that have marked them to join the circle, for the sages and omens and his sire are not done with him. They tell him:

Hold.

Hold for a thousand and a thousand and a thousand cuts more.

Hold to your strength to your courage as the tracery of thin, red lines on your skin turn to open seams in the fabric of your soul.

Hold tight to your pain your fear your desire to please your need to be worthy of the name of the blood of the pain the fear the blood the blood welling up to overwhelm the intricate patterns of spiraling lines and twisting angles that disappear as droplets bead together to clothe him in a crimson shirt of pain pain oh gods the pain it hurts he hurts they hurt flee flee flee the pain and hide hide hide away find a place it cannot follow—listen to the stars—it cannot follow him to the— listen to the—void the place between the—stars and the moon— bright points of one reality and its myriad variations—and the song the song the song—where he burns they burn the world burns oh gods the sky is burning the ships are burning he is burning for there is fire in his veins in his lungs in his hands and all that he touches turns to smoke and ash and screams.

The tie that tethers his soul to his body snaps and he loses himself in the stars.

Shock from the souls bearing witness as the empty vessel crumples to the deck.

Silence from the sages who cursed him.

A sigh from the man who sired him—the blade in his hand still dripping blood still moving still falling—and a shout from the wiry boy who has been his shadow.

*Still staggering from paying the price for his own naming scars, the boy takes the blow meant as a killing stroke on his arm; mirrors that wound on the matching arm of other body with his knife as he reaches out to the void and calls—*Ylaen, Ylaen, you are Ylaen— *over and over until the lost wandering spirit answers—*here I am, here, I am here—*and the body shudders, jerks upright, and says—*

"Jhobon."

The grief Ylaen had held wadded up inside exploded. Tore a deep, ugly, throbbing wound in his resonance aura as it burst and saturated the ambient resonance like a sudden downpour, a flood, a black tide that knocked the air from her lungs and the strength from her legs as her stomach heaved itself into her throat. Rahelu choked as she tried to double over and retch and stand and suck in new breath at the same time while her knees threatened to buckle from the pressure that grew heavier and heavier and her head swam from the dizzying, lurching sensation of careening through freefall, of being unmoored from a world that somehow still existed though a central part of it was gone.

The cohesive narrative they had spun out of Ylaen's memories frayed and bubbled as precious defining moments—

(*two terrified boys stumbling through a maze of underground tunnels*)

—surfaced themselves—

(*the sloop-dream, again, but different: the Ylaen at the tiller is older and steers with his right hand; his shoulders and chest and forehead are broader, his back also scarred, his features sharper, his mane of wavy black hair longer and silver-streaked in the sun, and his left arm encircles a milk-skinned woman cradling a sleeping babe*)

—in disorderly pops—

(*the oars of a sailboat splashing in a river*)

—dribbles—

(*of wine, heavily spiced to mask the bitter taste of numbweed*)

—and spurts—

(of blood, more blood, always blood, blood to bind heart and mind until they are tsol-ek-na; one soul in two bodies)

—as Ylaen gave into his emotions and the sheer strength of them wrenched control of their Concordance away from her.

The stars, the moon, the Endless Gate: all darkened.

What the fuck are you doing?! Rahelu shrieked. *If you taint this Evocation with your emotions; if there are memories missing or joined together in the wrong order, I can't guarantee that—*

The Evocation dimmed to a shadow of a shadow on the verge of dissolution until only loss remained. Bitter, aching, overwhelming loss: a pain that numbed and burned at the same time; a regret so raw, a hurt so deep it seemed impossible to heal.

Jhobon!

He was weeping, Rahelu knew, even if she could not see him or hear the sobs that must rack him from inside out because she could feel hot tears splashing down on the back of her palms and her wrist to roll down her arm and drip from her elbow to water the sand and the erratic racing of his heart beneath her fingers as he flung everything he had into the utter blackness of that void.

Come back!

For a count of ten:

Nothing.

Then:

Silver-purple resonance stirred; roiled and branched into—

Jags of lightning in the raging sea. Fallen mast and snapped lines and torn canvas fly out of the water fall into the sky mend and stitch themselves into working wings...

Ylaen's lingering grief morphed—

...the waters rise, lift up, and spit out a smoky form...

—contracted—

...etched with bright blue-white lines that crackle and burn.

—manifested as—

Shadows.

"Ylaen?"

Jhobon's loving intonation, overlaid with Jhobon's hallmark hesitation; a whispered invocation of hope that broke their Concordance and froze Ylaen just by the sound of the voice—

(Yes, voice! That was the sound of human speech. The—*'thing'*, whispered her dread, and she had to forcibly correct it to—*'living memory'* they had summoned was speaking.)

—that was not Jhobon's voice, for that tentative name had come out of Ylaen's throat. It birthed echoes of *'Ylaen-laen-aen'* that ran across the darkened expanse of the Endless Gate's bare stone platform, the syllables separating and refracting into a wordless murmur. Frequencies doubled and distorted until the very lowest rumbles quickened the quiescent starsong; the familiar melody an insistent call that demands response as it rises (rose and will rise again) with the points of light that wink into existence. Scintillating constellations above, mirrored in the silver-flecked, glassy, ebon rock beneath until they seemed to stand upon a second sky.

Heaven and earth reflected; sea and sky reversed.

Stars reemergent, tolling once more in perfect time with their heartbeats.

A third pulse thrumming in the ambient resonance.

"Jhobon," Ylaen whispered, and let her go.

Rahelu's breath caught in her throat as she backed up a

step to examine the shadow that had separated itself from the others to drift towards him.

The shade's resonance signal was unmistakably right—it had the staccato pattern that she remembered as Jhobon's resonance signature—but its shape lacked definition and its features lacked fidelity.

Just as she had feared.

"Don't—" she began, but Ylaen had already embraced it.

The shadow sank into his flesh.

Ylaen sighed.

The throbbing red-black pain in his resonance aura vanished—consumed by the corona of purple-edged gold flames writhing around his body as he slumped over on the stone, spasming in a joy so intense it bordered on ecstasy.

"Rahelu." *Rahelu.*

Jhobon, speaking with Ylaen's voice, yet that caress of a Projection was all Ylaen, and the soul that looked at her out of Ylaen's eyes...

It was him but it was not him.

He bared his mind.

"Finish it." *Finish it.*

She tried.

Grabbed at the bits of shifting shade crawling around under his skin. Took tendrils of Jhobon's fragmented memories and wove them into stable shapes.

A simple doll.

A braided rope.

A shitty overhand knot.

Something compact and self-contained she could squeeze into that ragged corner of his mind and nail it down by strategically stitching together a handful of common moments the way you would disguise two offcuts as whole cloth by carefully matching the grain of the edges.

She might as well have tried to weave smoke.

Her shapes held for a breath; a breath later, they collapsed back into mist. And each time one dissipated, the shade lost a little more substance.

"Like this." *Like this.*

Jumbled images—strikingly, confusingly familiar… instructions?—spilled into her mind: ink and charcoal depicting two naked figures with writhing limbs and overlapping bodies and resonance auras so fused and intertwined they appeared as one being joined in many anatomically impossible places.

Something shifted in her mind.

Intuition blossomed. Fundamental assumptions—built atop one another like a stack of perfectly balanced stones: so simple, so stable, so sensible that she had not been able to conceive of them as anything other than obvious truths—crumbled and their remains rearranged themselves into new configurations.

Tsol-ek-na.

Soul-bound.

She'd been trying to squeeze two souls into one body when they had been one soul that had existed in two bodies.

Jhobon's shade didn't need her to anchor it to existence—Ylaen by himself was anchor enough. The shadow coiled over and around his limbs like some sort of bizarre pet, trails of afterecho-like mist snaking in through his watering eyes and coughing mouth and running nostrils. Though it choked him to do so, he clung tight to the shade, made a cage of his resonance aura to bind its wispy form, took in more of those great, gasping gulps, the same way a dreamleaf addict huffed on his last pipe. But his body kept rejecting the shade; sweated the foreign resonance out of his pores and spewed it back up as bile—because Ylaen and Jhobon's tsol-bond had been established based on a pattern, and that pattern, now that she understood its origins, was a unidirectional one.

They had the wrong body.

The only way to swim against the tide was to cut through it.

She heaved his dead weight up with a grunt. Struggled to get him laying still and centered on top of that squat, oblong dais, then climbed on top of him to keep him there.

"Shhh," she said as she drew the knife.

Whether it was due to the familiarity of her voice or their position or something else, he did, at last, suppress the worst of his shudders. It was far too dark for her eyes to pick out the intricacies of his scar so she resorted to using her hands, running them over the many whorls and ridges until she found the first one, the one Jhobon had given him, the one that burned like hot coals and slashed through it.

Blood met stone. The polished ebon slab began to glow. All around them, the starsong rose and rose, the individual notes piling up into a cluster of unearthly intervals accompanied by an inward rush of air and resonance.

Shade and body stilled as the unresolved chord droned on.

"Ylaen?" She shook him. Then, hesitantly: "Jhobon?"

No answer.

She put her cheek against his nose and her fingers in the hollow of his throat; felt a ghost of warmth and a very faint heartbeat.

Oh, thank gods! She hadn't killed him.

Giddy relief made her kiss him (he tasted like copper and bitter salt); guilt shrieked at her (what the fuck are you doing, he's fucking unconscious!) until she recalled her senses and turned her mind to what came next.

Bind his arm and shoulder first. No sense in wasting all that effort by letting him bleed out. She would have to shift him over a bit to get to the crown, but she wouldn't bother with moving him somewhere else—her part of their bargain was concluded. She had summoned the damned shade he wanted, and stabilized the chaotic frequencies into a manageable equilibrium; what came after that was his business, not hers, and if he was still here, when she returned with the others to finish the job, well, that was his concern. Her concern was getting the stupid fucking crown out from the stone—the band fit so snugly into the channel that she couldn't get her fingernails into the gap to lever it out.

She tried the knife.

Its bloody point stuck in the crack.

Putting sideways pressure on the hilt resulted in ominous crackling accompanied by hairline fissures that spread through both blade and crown to an alarming extent.

Great. Just great.

She balled her hands into fists; beat those fists against the stone in a futile attempt to jolt the crown free; only succeeded in dislodging the knife which fell onto the pale sand that had accumulated around the base of the glowing altar-stone. Looked up at the heavens. Cried—why, gods in the four heavens, why; why did every fucking thing always have to come at such a high fucking cost—and cried as the starsong cried with her as she prayed—

HELP ME!

Help me!

Help me...

—though to *whom* she did not know and did not care, so long as someone heard her prayer.

Sympathetic resonance answered.

—she kneels over the butchered body—

—holds death's after-echoes as close as love—

—bows in prayer, a supplicant before the Starfather's celestial gaze—

Sparked a conflagration of light and heat and resonance and song that rippled outwards from the heart of the Endless Gate.

Her resonance aura iced over as another shadow moved.

"Very good, little meddler," rasped a thin, weak voice in heavily accented Aleznuaweithish.

The flow of resonance *parted* around the shadow, revealing a hunched, hooded figure in rippling black robes.

Uvesht-mo said: "Your offering is accepted."

Deep alarm rang in her bones.

What had she—they—just done?

Like a wave gathering shape and strength and momentum as it crosses from the depths into the shallows, the starsong's background hum grew into a crescendo as it rolled out over the still black lake, rushing up along the curved bowl of the crater's walls to rebound and converge in a thundering chorus ready to crush the three of them—she and he and his superimposed shadow—with the weight and fury of the resonance storm tearing apart the divisions the Skymother and Starfather had decreed since creation.

Time stopped as silence smote them.

All of existence imploded in united cacophony.

Locked past; branching present; multitudinous futures—eternity itself—compressed into a singularity.

Uvesht-mo said: "The hidden Gate has been opened. It is time to pay the price."

Quick, quick! Scramble off the glowing stone slab and leave him—can't leave him like that he's bleeding through those bandages—leave him!—and pick up that knife from the sands. Oh fuck, it isn't there; oh, *fuck*, the cultist has it!

Don't look; run! The heart of the Endless Gate has no walls or steps; it is a smooth, circular stone platform fifty strides wide, suspended in the center of a crater lake no deeper than the—don't look!—shallows of the Kuath Bay so close your eyes, shut your ears, squeeze your aura tight and run, damnit, run! It's twenty, eighteen, twelve, six strides to the water's edge and a quick swim back to the safety of the grand—don't look!—ward and the Elder and your brother and sisters if you would put your head down and dig your heels in and hurry the fuck up before your mind breaks trying to make sense of the strobing noise and the gyrating mosaic of history, tradition layering event upon event for century upon century with brushstrokes of cowled, black-robed—not real; not real not real not real this isn't real—figures chanting swaying repeating in motifs of descendant blades and ascendant shades that are blood-veiled, chain-crowned, star-blind, fate-bound, divinity enfleshed—

A wizened hand seized her by the roots of her hair. Dragged her eyes up, up until she stared into the shadowed depths of that hooded face.

Two glittering black gems stared back out of weeping eye sockets. Rahelu saw herself reflected in the cultist's false eyes—a thousand refractions across a thousand tiny facets—and screamed.

Uvesht-mo said: "I will help you make the last sacrifice."

Fuck. Fuck!

Rahelu twisted; threw her fists up and her weight forward.

Black robes skimmed her knuckles; swished over the sole of her foot; swept across her face as Uvesht-mo sidestepped and spun with her in perfect synchronicity. Every blow dodged. Every move anticipated. There was a surety to the cultist's motions, an almost-inhuman swiftness to their reactions that you could be forgiven for thinking this desperate, flailing exchange was some choreographed dance rehearsed well past the point of mundane muscle memory.

The Projection she hurled in the direction of the impromptu Issolm camp rebounded off the grand ward she had drawn.

*Fuckfuckfuckfuck*FUCK!

Orange-edged panic rose in her resonance aura as she was dragged, elegantly but inexorably, back towards the center—a living echo of a dozen translucent silver-robed initiates gliding over seamless stone to prostrate themselves in supplication before the brilliant, hazy figure hovering above the runelit altar.

A woman.

A woman who wore an obsidian crown, her face veiled by blood.

Swirls of sparking shards became a brittle bone-white shroud over a noxious, churning, black-brown bog. Rahelu made only the briefest attempt at visualization before she concentrated every drop of horror within a half-stride radius and flung it at the cultist.

Her sloppy, barely formed wave of resonance rushed forward—then reversed direction. The deluge of her concentrated fear added further strength to the unrelenting hand that forced her to her knees and put her eyes level with the blood pooling underneath Ylaen's arm to fill the carved channels, freeing the crown from the stone.

Move!

She couldn't move—*she couldn't move.*

Terror kept her pinioned in place as the cultist jammed the blood-drenched crown onto her head.

Come.

A searing, stabbing sensation, like a hot iron poker in her

skull. Cold gripped her insides, a chill so fierce it melted her fear. A sudden, visceral pull. Hooks in her heart, strong as the draw of the earth.

Impossible to resist.

"Ascend the throne," urged the cultist. "Divinity awaits."

And pressed the handle of the black serpentine knife into her hand.

HELP ME.

Rahelu mounted the altar.

Sank into the hovering figure.

Speech poured from her lips: words she did not know in a sequence that made no sense with a tongue she did not speak—one that sounded strange and familiar all at once; a gurgle of sonorous, flowing vowels and sharp consonants that bubbled up from her throat like the language of the drowning; ancient as the obelisks. Their meaning shook the temporal horizon and broke the stillness of the singularity.

History released a hundred thousand reverberations of the same ritual, air and ambient resonance thrumming with the power of a thousand voices raised with Uvesht-mo's in song, a sympathetic resonance whose urgency drove her chanting to a feverish pitch as stars blazed where she had seen no stars earlier in the night. Their fiery tails scored the heavens as they fell.

The four obelisks lit up in response to the celestial rain, their gargantuan tops catching with silver flame that bleeds through the scarred channels.

Cannon fire and shouts in the distance.

Starfall thickens, spearing the earth with so many shafts that they blur into a sheet of light.

THE BLADE.

Her hands move of their own accord.

One smooths the black silk of his red hair to cup his upturned, flickering face. Look away, look away; do not look at the face. *His eyes are closed as if in peaceful slumber*—he dreams, he dreamed, he is dreaming—*his hands crossed over his breast in a funeral repose*—he is but a dream, her dream—Rahelu, Rahelu, open your eyes, open your eyes and wake—

Her thoughts dart around and around in a useless circle, berating her with her mother's voice. *Idiot girl. Always so easily distracted. All that expensive Guild schooling and still stupid as a slug.*

Stop, Rahelu, stop. You're going to kill him—

The other holds a knife—the knife; the black, serpentine knife—*and thrusts it into the sky. The dark blade drinks in the summoned power, glutting its thirst on the celestial light until it blazes brighter than high sun.*

—and he will die.

Not quickly, as Xyuth and Hzin had. Not on his feet, fighting, as Dharyas had. Not in service of his House, as Jhobon had, or in defense of his clan, as Scarface had.

No; he will die like Welm, like all the others who had been slaughtered for this ritual, his body broken, bled, and gutted like a helpless fish—and she will be the one responsible.

Nonononono.

This is not the end she sought.

THE HEART.

No! she rages against the implacable will forcing her arm to murder. *I won't do this. I won't! I'll kill myself first.*

Drop the elbow. Rotate the wrist. One easy slash across her throat.

Her body pays her no mind.

First, her outstretched arm refuses her order to bend, then her fingers refuse to release their grip on the hilt. Her thighs and calves remain locked in a straddle over his hips.

The blade descends in a sun-bright arc.

Gods. *Gods.*

She shuts her eyes—that much she is allowed.

The relentless trajectory sears through her eyelids anyway: unhurried, deliberate, carefully calculated to terminate in his heart.

What else can she do?

Can she open her mouth?

Yes, yes she can, so she does and fills her lungs. All she needs is one more good, wordless scream and the others will come and Anathwan will put an end to this disaster.

Instead, her voice cries out: "Xuuqoshtalog-te!"

And her arm plunges the knife towards his chest.

38

FAITH

SOMETHING HURTLED THROUGH THE LIGHT AND clipped her shoulder. She lurched. Felt the sharp shock of knifepoint meeting bone travel up her wrist anyway.

Blood.
Blood on her hands again.
Blood everywhere.

Distant voices screaming in the night.

(Not hers, for all that she wanted to, and not his, for all that he ought to be.)

HELP! Rahelu sent. *PLEASE, HELP!*

Hold him; hold him still.

Help must be coming. Whatever ritual they—she—that cultist—had completed, it had warped the local ambient reso-nance so thoroughly that even the untrained in the harbor would sense it. The leading edge of its emanations formed an omnidirectional beacon detectable from hundreds upon hundreds of kual away—most assuredly so in Ṭsorek-fa; quite probably in Peshwan Yrg or Ennuost Yrg; possibly even as far as Anazvela—because it had set the heavens themselves on fire.

Gods oh gods dear gods.

How could there be so much blood?

The knife had penetrated but in a different spot and at an off angle. Instead of slipping between his ribs to pierce his heart, it had scored a shallow slice parallel to his sternum through three of his scars until its point found a narrow gap and lodged fast in spongy marrow then went no further, for the blade's twisted orientation and widening of its sinuous length had prevented that. Now, it jutted out of his chest and there was no end to the stuff welling up from the wound. She could feel the blade quivering in her steady hand (let go let go let go why could she not let go) with each rise and fall of his breath (a good sign; if he's breathing, he's still alive) in a way that didn't look or feel right (a giggle—a giggle!— escaped her at the silly thought; how could a knife sticking out of his ribs possibly look right?) because there was too much of everything: blood and light and built-up pressure as the knife drew the coruscating resonance to her in a wild rush.

Alien starsong thrumming in her veins.

Melody as its own counterpoint, overlapping upon itself to form a swelling harmony more beautiful than the sunlit waters of the Elumaje.

Glorious.

Heat flashed between her hands and through the blade to cauterize flesh. Skin sizzled; fused; sloughed off in sheets. A delectable scent like frying pork set her mouth watering while her nose twitched at an acrid, metallic stench as her gorge rose and she jerked—

The knife!

—back reflexively.

The knife was burning her hands were burned she burns

with overwhelming need as starfire enfolds her limbs eclipses her aura burrows beneath her skin to consume her from the inside out and it was her turn; her turn to spasm and sigh as a golden flare of incandescent ecstasy sealed the long-delayed union of flesh and spirit.

Ah!

To be in possession of a body again!

Her heart thumped erratically in time with the wild pulsing of the resonance crystal resting at the base of her neck: *da-dum ba-da-dum da-ba-da-dum* and each breath, each heartbeat, brought a fresh onslaught of sound and sight and sensation:

Voices in the shadows.

We're coming, Rahelu.

The pounding of many feet upon bare rock.

Don't do anything else fish-brained stupid.

"Enjela."

She won't! There isn't anything else stupid enough left for her to do.

The Stormbringer's kiss.

"Rahelu? Rahelu!"

The iron tang of blood.

Such hate in that hiss.

The skull-splitting resonance backlash that spun the world and drowned out purposeful thought and a heart-shattering guilt sharp as—

The knife!

—the knife whistling past her ear.
A girlish shriek: "Get away from her!"

The singing steel rain of crossbow bolts and arrows.

"Stand down, Supplicants!" Stern words, robbed of strength by the wheezy baritone. "We have larger concerns at hand."
Whiiiiist—

—whiiist—

—clatter-clack!

A woman's ringing voice: "Velaz! Do not allow yourselves to be swayed. Above all, remember our purpose."
"Xya, n—"
The silver-gold slash of a swinging cutlass.
Cries of protest, cut off by—

Clang!

Pain radiating across her blistered palm.

—another distant *BOOM!* of cannon fire.

Skin and sacred blade ripping free—

The knife!

—from her resonance-scorched fingers.

She savored each and every sensation for sensation meant she was alive—alive!—laughing and crying as vertigo toppled her newly acquired vessel from her throne, into the black-robed arms of her waiting Chosen. They tumbled down together in a dizzying rush of sky and sea and sand and stone.

How good! How good to be alive!

But even as she relished the intoxicating, dizzying rush, she was displeased. Only one of her Chosen had come to stand guard over the earth, the sky, and the sea. What of her other faithful? Where were her silks? The rest of her sacred instruments? Her incense and perfumed oils to sweeten the air and the cleansing water? The tender cuts of meat, well-seasoned with rare spices and salts, to break her fast, and the wine to quench her thirst?

In addition, the vessel given to her had not been properly trained or consecrated; it had not been prepared with the customary anchors to receive her divine self; and its small, savage spirit railed against her presence instead of meekly submitting to her will.

LET GO OF ME!

She shunted it aside.

True, the forms did not matter. The xuuqoshtalog-te ritual she and her soul-bound had devised did not rely on such inconsequential trappings to function; her first ascension had taken place with no ceremony at all. But ceremony, as she had discovered over the course of centuries, was the foundation of faith and divinity could not exist without such devotion.

How long had she drifted in the eternity beyond the stars as a disembodied dream, leaving her realm unguided, for her faithful to stray so far?

A lifetime? Several? An eon?

GET OUT!

Her displeasure grew.

Be silent.

The little spirit shrunk at her Command, so she permitted its retreat to the lower levels of the mind, where it could look after the baser needs of the body.

Later, she could attend to the matter of subsuming its substance; first, she had to discover the fatal flaw that had led to the previous botched attempt at the ascension rite.

The full power of her throne and the Endless Gate's matrix was denied to her—she could not open the door to Fortune's realm through such a weak, untrained vessel—and so she had to grope feebly after the strands of fate, like a mortal, sifting through the memories of this poor substitute for glimpses of the answer.

Her heir ascendant: lost. Her soul-bound: missing. Her faithful: scattered. All this by the hand of one Uvesht-mo in mere seasons.

Seasons!

Wroth though she was to discover the impermanence of her works, she would not punish the mortals. Such transgressions were in their nature, for they lacked what she possessed: the Starfather's blessing of infinite sight.

(That was the nature of mortality.)

Thus, she must be as she ever had been and ever will be. Strong enough to bear the weight of their sins. Wise enough to mend their broken ways. With grace enough to love them despite their foolishness.

(That was the nature of divinity.)

GET OUT GET OUT GET—!

No.

Great was the work that had been undone; greater still was the work that must be done. For too long, she had been content tending to her faithful, leaving those outside her Divine Kingdom to govern themselves and allowing disharmonious beliefs to proliferate.

No more.

She and this Uvesht-mo landed in a sensuous tangle on a bed of bone-white sand. Her new vessel was young, strong, sensitive to touch. She luxuriated in the feel of the fine soft grains rubbing against her bare calves and toes; the silken caress of his silver-stitched robes; the heat of his fevered breath on her cheek, the crush of his body on hers, and the wild drumming of their synchronized heartbeats through their ribs.

Ah, youth! There were so many pleasures she had forgotten.

She reached inside his hood and arrested his attempt to rise by gripping his wrinkled throat. "Uvesht-mo, he who was once Chosen: do you confess your sins?"

If he was penitent, she would grant him mercy.

His rasping voice was thick with true remorse. "My sins are as innumerable as the stars and my torment eternal."

"Let go your mortal fears." In her absence, his understanding of doctrine had become so twisted that he no longer believed in the fundamental tenets of her faith, which kept the world in peace and prosperity. "Turn your eyes and heart back to me and embrace your devotion once again. Then may you rejoice, for I shall make all things right."

She silenced his whimpers by putting her mouth on his.

How his hands tremble as he cradles her close!

How sweet the salt of his tears!

How—

A sickening *crack* as he smashed her skull against the

ground and splintered her crown. Fresh pain exploded behind her eyes, multiplied the severe strain of resonance backlash, and robbed her of vision.

He dared? He dared to strike *her*?

So surprised was she at the sacrilege that she temporarily lost her hold on the wilful little spirit. It surged out of the dim recesses of instinctual memory she had relegated it to, shrieking—

GET THE FUCK—

—as it contested her control and placed her continued existence in great peril, for Uvesht-mo had recovered the dropped soul-blade from the sands.

He came at her stunned vessel with his resonance aura warped and the ritual blade aimed at its heart. Both blazed with the same cold light of the obelisks, as did the two stargems that served as his eyes.

In his misguided zealotry, his gaze sought forgiveness— not from her, but from the heavens. "I beg you, Starfather, to accept this last sacrifice."

Though it angered her, she had to admire his daring.

How clever, Uvesht-mo!

To strip her of her supplicants, her sacred instruments, her soul-bound; to force her into this inferior, limited form; to stay his treacherous hand until she had come into full possession of the vessel but before she had gathered the rest of her being; to disrupt her means of effecting an efficient transfer of her greater consciousness by breaking the key; so he might sever the bonds she had forged to existence with one of her own sacred blades.

— OUT OF MY BODY YOU—

How clever and how blind!

Of course, she could not permit such a thing to come to pass. The continuation of her divine reign had been delayed long enough; she would consummate the ascension now.

But oh, how it would destroy her to destroy one of her children.

—DERANGED PIECE OF SHIT!

Wars might be won in the mind but battles are fought with bodies—and his was no match for hers.

Instincts bred and beaten into the vessel throughout its short life (and thus so deeply embedded it would require months, if not seasons, for her to subjugate them) caught his killing stroke; reversed it into his gut.

OH GODS.

A hot wet stink assailed her as his entrails spilled out onto the sand and Uvesht-mo crumpled at her feet. Her heart sorrowed at the waste as she took back her blessings. Knowledge. Connection. Sight. All these things and more she wrested from him—

OH GODS WHAT—

—as she wrested the stargems from his eye sockets.

Ah, Starfather!

—ARE YOU GOING TO—

What a soul-bound he would have made, had he but kept his faith! His foul utterances reminded her that he still had a voice and a tongue capable of swaying the heathens with blasphemous speech—

—DO TO—

—so she took that too.

—GODS. GODS! YOU'RE A—

"Poor, wayward child," she told him. "It is not the Starfather to whom you should pray, but to me. Before you return to the stars, you shall witness and believe again."

GHARDON! ELARAM!

His moaning softened into choked gurgles that died away.

LOOSE! LOOSE NOW, YOU NEED TO KILL—

This vessel's recalcitrant spirit, however, was not worth the bother.

Perceptions *stretched.*

A brief *wrench* of the world as something was *ripped* free and discarded to float and bob upon the ebbing resonance like fish guts on the water.

Physical awareness flaked away.

The temporary thrill of battle fatigue, the bone-weary exhaustion manifest in the deep, incessant trembling of atrophied muscles pushed beyond reasonable endurance—both vanished. As did the agony in her head and hands, the heat in her bones, and the thudding ache of resonance backlash.

All replaced by the loose, giddy, aimless sensation of fading.

Oh. Oh *no.*

She held tight to the stubborn refusal that had carried her through the impossible before, knotted that determined denial into a shining net cast out around the disparate parts that had peeled away from the core of her being, tugged them back into a unity:

Rahelu.

I am Rahelu.

She tried to remember how that intrusive presence had slipped past her guard to take root in her dreams, her mind. Envisioned her rebellious body as an empty shell and she a crabling accidentally jolted out of it by an unexpected wave. Poked and prodded at the boundary between where her body ended and her aura ought to begin in search of some break, some breach she could squeeze back through—*let me in—let me in!—LET ME IN!*—beat and battered at the vicious shade that had usurped her, visualizing her spirit as the Storm-bringer's closing fist, a dark curling wave that engulfed and swallowed her body whole.

All to no avail. Her body continued to laugh and cry without her as reinforcements and enemies alike finally arrived.

Fuck!

She hurled herself at her body again—bounced straight off again. Fucking stupid, to do the same thing and hope for a different result, but she didn't know what else to do.

Why couldn't she get back in?

Was it because that *thing* was in there?

Was it actually a shade or some freak unintended conse-quence of this temporal nexus, a crazed amalgamation of echoes that had accumulated over the centuries from ritual after ritual that had somehow coalesced into a semblance of a shade without guidance?

Rahelu wanted to cry and couldn't because some shitty temporal echo had tossed her out of *her own fucking body* and she didn't even understand how it had happened, only that it had and that cultist was responsible and they wouldn't even be able to question him now because *that fucking thing* had used *her body* to tear out his tongue and gut him exactly like an oversized fish and she—

She could only hover by, helpless to do anything other than count up the auras:

The captain's. (Tight with thwarted vengeance.)

Guardian Maketh's. (Ruddy with rising anger.)

Elder Anathwan's. (Gray and cool, like ash.)

Her three House-sworn siblings'. (A riot of fear and confusion.)

The cultist's. (Blackened, fading fast.)

Ylaen's. (A shifting, twinned gold-blue—so did that make eight or nine?)

Finally, *hers*. The smoking, writhing, foreign resonance twisting around her body—her giggly, insensible body that was scooping up crimson-swirled, bone-white sand and letting the dusty grains pour through her fingers, then staring in fascination while rubbing the remaining sticky, wet clumps and the dry residue that crusted and clung together between her palms—made ten.

Rahelu herself was everywhere and nowhere: disembodied, adrift on the sea of distrust and discord that surged back and forth between the divided ranks.

House set against House.

Dominion against the Free Territories.

Subordinates against their commanding superiors, who had eyes only for the lingering after-echoes that chronicled the two disastrous rituals.

Any moment now, the sudden hush and uncertainty imposed by the shocking scene must snap. Hostilities would resume. Too much blood had been shed for too many betrayals which had been heaped on top of oaths made and bargains struck like corpses on a mass pyre until they were strained to the limits of their interpretation. She could sense the break coming in:

The tight pull of Elder Anathwan's flattening lips.

The frenetic flicker of Nheras's eyes.

The white-knuckled grip of Captain Xya's hand on the filigreed hilt of her slowly rising, still-bared cutlass.

The rigid tension in Ghardon's arms as he kept his nocked arrow trained on her throat and held his bow at full draw.

The cold, crackling white-tinged bolts building in Guardian Maketh's resonance aura as his eyes raked over the three scattered bodies.

Ylaen's: laid out cold upon the altar-throne; bits of dried pus and black blood caked on his bare chest.

Rahelu's: staring vacuously at the moon, now well past its zenith and beginning to set.

Uvesht-mo's: innards strewn everywhere.

The longer Maketh stared, the heavier his scowl grew until it weighed down the corners of his lips into a full-blown snarl.

Then Elaram—irreverent, irrepressible, irresponsible Elaram—threw convention and caution to the wayside with her crossbow to break ranks. She charged across the sands, mussed braids and tears streaming in her wake, embraced the grinning, blank-faced doll that was no longer Rahelu, and cried:

"What in the *holy fuck* just happened?"

That single, unanimously held sentiment ushered in a strange, bewildered kind of truce that saw Xya sheathe her cutlass and Ghardon lower his bow as they rushed forward too.

"Get rid of those," Ghardon said to his sister, holding Rahelu's lolling head and heaving shoulders down, even as Elaram picked out fragments of the broken black circlet out of her scalp and asked, "Can you feel that…that *wrongness* in her resonance signature?"

It's not mine! Rahelu sent. *It's, it's*—she didn't know whose it was—*please, just get rid of it.*

Nheras remained where she was, tethered to Anathwan's side as her sole means of support, while the Elder of House Issolm and the Dedicate of House Imos stood still, busy exchanging silent, Projected thoughts and identical looks of, of—

Whatever it was, Rahelu couldn't put a name to it. Something between resignation and vindication that was thoroughly mixed up with what resembled grudging respect and disappointment.

"It appears," Maketh rasped in a slow, measured speech that was all the more unsettling for how utterly at odds it was with his ferocious displeasure, "that these two"—left unspoken: *'empty-headed, brash, incompetent, unschooled, idiotic excuses for Guild-trained mages'*—"decided to raise the dead."

Captain Xya's fingers stilled in the crook of the throat of the blood-splattered youth lying on top of the altar-throne. "Did they succeed?"

"No," Maketh answered, even as Anathwan contradicted him with, "Yes."

While Xya demanded they elaborate, her sister and brother said, "Rahelu, Rahelu," over and over again as they shook her body. "Can you hear us?"

Yes! she sent, desperate. Rahelu circled round and round the two of them like a restless gull. *I'm here; I hear you; can you hear me?*

Her plea went unheard and unanswered.

She wasn't getting through to them; why wasn't she getting through? Were her Projections too weak? Too unfocused? Was she a shade now, was that why she couldn't touch anything or anyone? Was she doomed to a discorporate exist—

She cut off her spiraling thoughts, grasping the edges of her consciousness and pulling them in before more of her could expand and diffuse into the ambient resonance.

Just in time to catch the non-technical half of Maketh's explanation.

"We cannot say for certain but we can surmise some things based on the after-echoes. When Rahelu and Ylaen attempted to summon Jhobon's shade, they unwittingly mirrored a different rite, the—"

Maketh floundered as he stumbled over the next word.

"The xuuqoshtalog-te?" Ghardon ventured.

Maketh nodded. "Similarities between the workings triggered sympathetic resonance and brought back another leftover fragment of consciousness."

"Whose?" Nheras asked.

When Maketh hesitated, Anathwan cut in. "Enjela's. We think."

Slack-jawed stares from every Supplicant, Rahelu included, at her deceptively still body, which had apparently succumbed to sheer physical exhaustion.

"*Enjela*," Elaram squeaked, "is in *there*?"

"A version of her," Maketh said, gesturing to the obelisks. "One that has been distorted and destabilized from the extended duration it has spent trapped in the array."

He had no idea how much he was understating the facts. Rahelu's very brief stint in occupying the same mental space as the shade had been utterly terrifying: Enjela was certifiably *insane*.

"Where is Jhobon's shade then?" Elaram asked. "Did—"

"Ylaen lives," Xya interrupted. "Does that mean my son is—"

"Alive?" The Imos Dedicate grimaced as he paced out a

measured circuit of the Endless Gate. His thick eyebrows were pushed low together, like gathered thunderclouds, and his deep-set eyes had narrowed to black pits as his gaze and shockingly clumsy Seeking swung from obelisk to obelisk. "It depends on your definition of 'alive'. As well as on your definitions of 'Ylaen' and 'Jhobon'."

Was Maketh Imos, somehow, searching for her?

Here! Rahelu screeched. She trailed him, feeling uneasy as her substance stretched thinner and thinner the further he went from her body. *Guardian, I'm here; I'm here!*

He didn't so much as blink.

Shit.

She couldn't get through to Maketh either.

Perhaps it was their lack of personal connection—she had made a pet project of staying away from the Imos Dedicate when she could and avoiding his attention when she couldn't.

There was only one person here whose life had been so thoroughly tangled with hers that surely, surely, they would know each other anywhere.

Rahelu flew back towards the heart of the Endless Gate.

Past the gutted cultist.

Past the hand-linked duo of Elaram and Ghardon, trying something with a Concordance.

Past the wan, slumping figure of Anathwan propped up against the side of the altar-throne with her legs curled up underneath her and her eyes far off in mage trance, toying with the shards of the glittering black crown and the glassy serpentine blade in her lap as she stared west, into the future.

Interposed herself right in the middle of the charged stare between Captain Xya and Nheras—a finger-width from Nheras's nose—and shrieked: *Nheras!*

No wrinkle of that nose.

NHERAS!

No pursing of those lips.

Eight hells.

Fine. Fuck courtesy, fuck the mutual respect they had so recently built, fuck everything. Rahelu dredged up every drop of hostility she had ever felt for the granddaughter of Atriarch Lynath Ilyn and flung it in Nheras's face.

Look at me, you spoiled, lily-footed, gold-gilded, hollow-hearted, overperfumed, overpainted, overpriced Ilyn bitch!

A slight crease formed between those elegant eyebrows but that was all. And that could've been entirely due to Captain Xya's pointed remarks concerning bargains and blood debts.

That left Elder Anathwan.

Anathwan had told Rahelu, "You are a daughter of Issolm now and may speak freely with me."

Running through that conversation:

'Excuse me, Elder Anathwan. It's me. Rahelu.' (The Supplicant you've had to rescue from her own incompetence three times.) *'Sorry to interrupt your vitally important Augury of how we're going to get out of this fuck up.'* (My fuck up. That I am incapable of unfucking. Please save me a fourth time.) *'You trusted me to ward us against hostile influences so that nobody would go insane in this gods-cursed place.'* (After I lost control and thus forced us to camp in the worst possible spot. Shit. That's four, not three, times you've already saved me.) *'But I was feeling lonely and sorry for myself so I got wrapped up in counting our profits before we had realized them and allowed myself to be seduced by the Endless Gate* (twice, even after you warned us of its temptations) *and let Ylaen Imos trick me into helping him with his ill-thought-out plan.'* (Because I have fish shit for brains.)

Rahelu quailed. There was no reason why Anathwan would consider her to be anything other than a waste of two hundred and fifty gold kez plus expenses, but she didn't want to be stuck like this forever, so she gathered up the fraying tendrils of her being and sped closer to the altar-throne.

The youth lying there beneath the captain's fierce regard stirred. His mouth made a little gasp of pain as Xya's other hand dug into his shoulder, but his face twisted into an expression of wonder—an expression that Rahelu had only ever seen Jhobon wear, never Ylaen.

"Mother?"

Ylaen's voice, inflected with Jhobon's hesitation. Whatever else he might have said was lost in the crush of Xya's embrace and—

Boom-boom-BOOM!

The sudden rounds of cannon fire drew all heads sharply to the dim orange glow radiating from the harbor.

Captain Xya stood.

Dying cultist, escaped slaves, turncoat Harbinger, stone-faced Guardian—she disregarded them all in favor of the youth in her arms. Swift as a shearwater a-wing, she cut through the ominous hush with her sure strides seaward, dodging an outstretched arm and a low, "Xya, please, wait!" from a visibly pale Maketh on his way to rejoin the circle of mages on the sand.

"Captain," the Elder called. However diminished Anathwan's physical stature might be, the strength of her voice was unaffected. "Hear my proposal."

The captain did not slow; in fact, Xya sped up as she sloshed through the lake with her precious burden. "Speak, then. And best hurry, if you wish to be heard."

"Extend the bargain you struck with Supplicant Nheras to myself and the rest of my Supplicants. I offer our resonance skills to defend you and your ship against Conclave and Belruonian offensives until the *Stormbringer's Judgment* reaches the safety of your home harbor at Tsorek-fa, and one permanent working of your choice from a given selection to be negotiated at a later time."

If Rahelu still had control of her eyes, she would have widened them until they fell out of her skull. Forget the Supplicants; the services of an Elder alone were worth— Rahelu didn't know how much, exactly, but the correct answer was *'a lot more'* than four weeks of free board and passage, and the permanent working itself was unheard of. However, considering that they were all a sneeze away from keeling over from severe resonance backlash and Xya controlled two ships and their crews and would have to fight her way out of the harbor, the unprecedented offer was probably warranted and—

Fuck. She'd gotten distracted and as her thoughts had started to drift off, so had she. With an effort of will, Rahelu pulled herself together again.

Xya's immediate reply rang out over the black waters. "Do you—kin and House and Dominion—renounce all claims, whether they be ties of blood or name or memory, to the one you call Ylaen of Imos?"

"I do so renounce him for the Dominion," Anathwan said, just as swift.

Maketh looked as if the Elder's words had sliced through him. For three long heartbeats, the only sounds that disturbed the night were more explosions and the *slop* of water on gravel as Xya emerged from the lake onto the far shore.

"Dedicate?" Anathwan murmured.

In a voice robbed of inflection, Maketh said: "I do so renounce him for House Imos. As brother to Rysere Imos, I do so renounce her blood claim to her offspring."

Captain Xya's white teeth flashed in the moonlight. "Accepted. We leave now."

"Not yet."

"Defying me already? Well." The captain shrugged. "I suppose our bargain is not yet sealed. Come or stay as you please; it is no concern of mine."

Then Xya waited no more and they were gone.

Rahelu gathered herself in the lull that followed for a firm but subservient Projection; an image of her body prostrate before the Elder in proper supplication: forehead and nose in the sand, fingertips together, palms flat, arms squared to the shoulders—none of which her body was currently doing.

(It was preoccupied with humming contentedly to itself as it rubbed its palms and cheeks and chest along the top of the altar-throne in a cringe-inducing imitation of a kitten not old enough to be in full control of its limbs rolling around in catnip, causing Elaram and Ghardon and even Nheras to dart many concerned looks at it whilst they conferred amongst themselves.)

Forgive me, Elder, I beg your—

"Anathwan."

Had anyone ever heard Maketh speak the Elder's name stripped of her honorifics? She didn't think so. And the way he said it...

Rahelu was glad she could not shiver.

"We must get our charges and ourselves safely aboard the *Stormbringer's Judgment* before the turn of the tide. Xya will not tarry and her ship—"

"Will wait upon the needs of the Dominion." Anathwan's voice remained cool, composed, and pitched to carry; the voice of an orator. "In accordance with the agreement we struck."

"The Conclave—"

"Are already here, pitting their journeymages against the might of the Divine Kingdom's Chosen in the harbor while the Free Territories scavengers peck away at both. Let us not squander the opportunity the Starfather has given into our hands."

Maketh's jaw worked furiously. "There is no time. The resources we were given, the strategy we were required to adopt—they left us with no margin for error and we have erred, repeatedly!"

If he wasn't careful, he would break a tooth. And if he didn't hurry up and stop monopolizing Anathwan's attention, Rahelu might lose herself entirely.

"Had the Houses been but willing to set aside lesser concerns and send more Dedicates—"

"Peace, Maketh. It is what it is. This is not the time to rehash those arguments." If Anathwan was displeased with the Dedicate, she gave no sign of it; her attention was wholly on the pieces of the broken crown she held, the serpentine knife in her lap, and the altar-throne. "As you said, there are larger considerations at play."

"You cannot use the Endless Gate as planned; we no longer have all of the necessary mages, the access key is broken, and its power has been drained!"

"Will you have us return empty-handed when we stand upon the very threshold, uncontested, without making a single attempt?"

"I would have us return. All those who are able."

"As would I."

"Then cease this obsession of yours." His voice softened. "Ana. Whatever prize you may salvage is not worth the cost. Look at us—look at them—"

Yes; yes! Please!

Attention had never been something Rahelu enjoyed, but she found herself desperately wanting, needing, craving the vicious weighted regard of public judgment that came with making a spectacle of herself because then it would mean that someone had heard her, seen her, knew that she was *out here* instead of *in there*.

Look at me! Rahelu begged. *LOOK AT ME!*

"—look at *her*"—a jab of his meaty finger at Rahelu's body now (oh gods) licking the stone—"and tell me that this is not a failure."

"This is not a failure," Anathwan told him calmly. "We have not attempted all possible measures."

Maketh cast one glance at the Elder, mapped the trajectory of her gaze, and lost the little that was left of his composure.

"No."

"It is not your decision."

"She is—"

"A daughter of Issolm."

"—a *child*, Anathwan!" A whole host of scathing insults packed into that one word.

"And lost to us."

The two senior mages were nose to nose now. Neither willing to back down, and neither willing nor able to sense Rahelu's increasingly frantic protests that she was not, in fact, lost, but *right fucking here*.

Out of ideas and full of frustration, she hurled herself at them. She promptly rebounded off Anathwan, the Elder's innate defenses rejecting her intrusion much as Enjela (if it really was Enjela who had usurped her body) had rejected her attempts, but Maketh—

"Not lost," he insisted. "Not irretrievably so."

He had held onto that clumsy Seeking of his the whole time. Clumsy, because it was not a perfect match for her true resonance signature; somewhere along the way, he had confused the pattern of who she was. But he must have been monitoring the Issolm Supplicants' latest effort to restore her: they had huddled in a ring around the altar-throne, Ghardon and Nheras forcibly holding her struggling body still while Elaram had pressed their foreheads together and cupped Rahelu's face in her hands.

Little by little, Maketh's Seeking had shifted closer and closer to the true signature Elaram was using.

And since Rahelu was *out here* and not *in there*...

The same inexorable will that had captured and dragged her effortlessly into the Guild's interrogation chambers caught her as her fraying presence made contact with his aura.

Maketh *pulled* as he announced, "I have her."

Most of her.

There were pieces missing, she knew; pieces that had strayed into the void. Those she grabbed not long after their escape seemed mostly unaltered; those she found later were a little strange, embedded with other bits that she didn't think had ever been her to begin with.

Something flickered in Anathwan's expression—a mild flash that passed far too quickly for Rahelu to pinpoint—then the Elder said, "Make haste."

The Guardian barked, "Supplicants! Listen carefully."

Spans and spans of studying and working under his close supervision made them all jump and hop to the directions he rattled off.

They dug through the matrix of the pendant Lhorne had given to her—the pendant he had used twice to call her wandering spirit back when she had lost herself before—and found a deeply buried Projection that he had left and she had never noticed, one that was more prayer than message:

Be safe, Rahelu. Come back home.

They amplified it and the Endless Gate responded. Sympathetic resonance recalled her dream of watching the terraced city of Ennuost Yrg rise out of the west and striding onto the cedar boardwalk of the Highdocks and blended it with the timbre of Lhorne's voice and her resonance signature.

All the lost pieces of her came back, drawn to the pendant like iron filings to a lodestone.

Suddenly, Rahelu had form in addition to substance again, a translucent copy of her body as she had imagined herself in her dream: dressed in immaculate Issolm whites and blacks, her Supplicant's armband on prominent display; her face and skin made smooth and clean and fragrant from washing with scented soaps; her hair combed and oiled to a glossy shine, coiled and pinned up in simple braids with silver ornaments.

Thank you! she sent, and this time, they heard her. The tears that she wept were illusory, but the rush of gratitude that accompanied her drop into the lowest form of obeisance was not. *Thank you, thank you, thank—*

Another round of cannon fire reminded everyone that Captain Xya must be well down the mountain by now, if not already on the beach and preparing to row out into the ongoing naval battle in the harbor, and if they had any intention of finding a way off this islet, they needed to join her as soon as possible—which meant she needed to get her fucking body back so they could get the fuck out of here.

Rahelu dove at her heart.

She slammed into a resistance so firm that her dream-image ended up smeared across her body like a particularly poorly constructed Seeming.

Fuck!

How do I get back in? she asked.

Maketh shook his head. "You can't. Not now."

What?!

But it's my *body!*

"And it's suffering from a biological form of resonance overload. Your body has absorbed too much foreign reso-nance to allow you back in, and because the foreign resonance occupying your body is a shade; it is, for all intents and purposes, capable of responding in a manner that approximates sentience—which includes the desire to maintain its independent state of existence. It must be purged before you can return."

The obvious question—*how long might that take?*—went unasked between the next blasts of cannon fire because they all knew the answer: too fucking long.

Nheras glanced at her translucent form. "And if it can't?"

Elder Anathwan added, "Rahelu may be able to sustain a sort of existence in limbo, as Enjela has done. A lapse in her will may result in her dissolution. Or it may not, if she is anchored strongly enough. Regardless, all precautions must be taken; an unstable mage—particularly one with access to an archmage's abilities—is a threat that must be managed. If it cannot be managed, it must be eliminated."

Rahelu couldn't breathe because she had no body and therefore no lungs but felt like she was drowning all the same because she couldn't hold back the tide of her rising fear and panic any longer.

Precautions. Managed. Eliminated.

Fuckfuckfuck—

"Supplicant Rahelu." The circle of Issolm Supplicants and Maketh shuffled around the altar-throne to make room for the Elder, who knelt so their eyes would be at the same level and took her hand. "Be at ease."

Anathwan's warm voice with its honeyed tones cut through the frantic maelstrom of her overwhelming terror.

Though she couldn't really feel the fumble of that imperfect clasp (the Elder's mangled, once-elegant fingers could not quite thread themselves through Rahelu's twitching ones properly), she could imagine it, and that small gesture gave her comfort and courage.

"I am with you."

The complex swell of tangled emotions that came with Anathwan's unexpected gift of absolution near unraveled her again.

Forgiven. She was forgiven.

If she could be forgiven, then—

Can you fix me? Rahelu asked.

The senior mages exchanged glances.

"The interaction between the body and the spirit is a delicate and complex thing," Guardian Maketh hedged. "A senior healer, given the opportunity to properly assess your condition, would be best placed to advise on possible remedies and a potential timeline for recovery."

Translation: no fucking idea.

In the interim, they would drug her body back into oblivion, return her to those slave pens or perhaps that saltwater mage cell, and keep her under heavy guard. Her jailers would have orders to shoot her full of crossbow bolts the moment her body or its resonance aura twitched in a way they didn't like, then when they got to Tsorek-fa, they would slap a Suborned collar around her neck at the first opportunity.

Elaram leapt to her feet. "Then what are we waiting for? There are healers aboard the *Stormbringer's Judgment*."

"We cannot leave yet," Elder Anathwan said.

"Why not?" Elaram cried, looking like she was on the verge of stomping her foot. "We've failed, haven't we? There's nothing left here except for rocks and ghosts—and we'll be bringing two of those with us!"

But Ghardon said, "Ela, the mission directive was 'secure or destroy'. Since we don't have the numbers to secure the Gate…"

"We have to destroy it," Nheras concluded. "Otherwise we'll be leaving its secrets for the Conclave to exploit."

Some part of Rahelu was aghast at the thought.

There was an unearthly beauty to the Endless Gate and

the ancients who had built it possessed a mastery of the resonance disciplines beyond present-day understanding. Its capabilities bordered on the miraculous: the runes alone would merit decades of study; the construction of the obelisks several lifetimes.

And they were supposed to tear it all down?

No one else seemed appalled in the slightest—which made her realize she'd been an oblivious idiot.

From the very beginning, Anathwan had said: '*You should not be here.*'

The Dominion had never intended to secure the Endless Gate.

At least, not publicly.

If seizing the artifact had been the priority, the Exalted Dominance and the Royal Council would have ordered half the Isonn war fleet to sail with every Dedicate who could be spared from essential duties organized into specialist teams, a sizeable leadership council of Elders drawn from every House to oversee and coordinate the efforts, and an Atriarch —most likely Atriarch Isonn—in command of the expedition.

But the Houses had sent a lone Elder, with only two Dedicates and six new Supplicants to support her, on a leaky Imrell smuggling sloop, which meant Anathwan's true orders were to prioritize the artifact's destruction at all costs.

That way, neither the Conclave nor any other faction would be able to wield its power and the Dominion was no worse off, save for the loss of a handful of senior mages (who would be inconvenient but not impossible to replace) and a third of the city's latest Supplicant intake (well within the usual turnover for first-year Supplicants).

More importantly, the relative balance of power within the Dominion remained unchanged.

Except...that meant none of the Houses stood to benefit either, and a House that risks nothing is a House that will soon be surpassed. But a House that succeeds in pulling off a long-odds gambit, such as a single, high-risk, supposedly impossible working to bend the future in favor of the Exalted Dominance's current expansion plans...

Anathwan had two sets of orders.

That was why she and Maketh had argued the night Venoru struck.

"But we can destroy it on our way out," Elaram protested. "Didn't you say Ylaen's landing party had hauled up several kegs of black powder and you were supposed to use some sort of control node to detonate them remotely?"

"They never finished the job of placing all the charges," Nheras said quietly. "And Xya took the control node with her when she left."

Elaram's gaze unfocused as she shifted her perceptions outward. "I'm no Augur, but I don't have to be to know that if we don't rejoin the captain soon, she might not have any ships left."

The Seeking Elaram Projected into their midst showed the *Stormbringer's Judgment* trapped in a losing battle it should have easily escaped.

Boxed in by the islet's treacherous basalt reefs and two enemies—one a mid-sized merchant vessel draped with vertically hung banners sporting Chanazian characters; the other an immense, narrow longship with a broad sweep of oars—the Free Territories warship had no sea room to maneuver.

Bereft of their captain (Xya was still half a kual away, rowing against the tide) and her first mate (Xya had, somehow, managed to drag both Scarface's corpse and Ylaen's comatose body down those stairs, across the beach, and into the boat with her), the crew's uncoordinated response was exacerbated by their lack of active resonance defenses. Half were stunned or otherwise disabled from the backwash of dissonant frequencies resulting from the clash of the massive

Projections hurled in the mage battle between the Conclave journeymages and the cowled mage-priests; the other half were split between trying to steer, aim, and fire broadsides and trying to keep their resonance-mazed fellows from sabotaging their efforts.

Elaram wasn't wrong. Without a contingent of trained mages to shield the crew, the *Stormbringer's Judgment* didn't stand a chance.

The *Sooty Gull* had already been blown apart.

"Even so." Maketh stood. "As you have quite correctly observed, Supplicant Elaram, we have failed to achieve our primary mission objective. Let us not exacerbate that failure by also failing in our duty. Come, Supplicants. The charges must be evenly distributed about the obelisks and this central focal point to ensure that..."

The Guardian gestured as he spoke, assigning quadrants to Elaram, Ghardon, and Nheras. He left the altar-throne in the center to Elder Anathwan and the final quadrant for himself.

He did not assign anything to Rahelu (for obvious reasons) and the omission stung.

"Commit the details of every square stride you have been assigned to crystal. Be thorough—the Atriarchs will want to review the Evocations personally—but be quick; I will start destroying the anchors as each section is completed. Reassemble here to assist Elder Anathwan and Supplicant Rahelu in departure as soon as you are able." Maketh's brows furrowed further. "Supplicant Rahelu's body will have to be placed under heavy sedation before we can safely transport her."

Already, he was treating her like...like a piece of inconvenient baggage. Deadweight that had to be carted around, instead of a functional member of the team.

No, not deadweight; a liability.

One that would be hushed up owing to *'the sensitive nature of the matter'* and glossed over in official reports—assuming there were any (and Rahelu wasn't certain there would be, considering the nature of their mission, the original requirements for absolute secrecy, and the fact the Houses had already denied them once)—which would be necessarily brief.

Would any of her achievements even merit a mention?

No, she decided. The Atriarchs and the other Elders would be concerned with the result (astounding failure) and assessing the potential fallout (unknown); they would leave the assessment and ranking of the Supplicants to the Elder and Dedicates leading the mission. Her name would likely be relegated to the appendices with Jhobon's and, probably, Ylaen's, in the brief section relating to injuries and casualties that all teams were required to file as a matter of standard procedure, and that nobody ever read.

How ashamed her parents would be to see her shuffled down the gangplank, a disgraced prisoner in chains!

She'd rather that they put her body in a crate like it was some sort of rabid animal and pretend she was another piece of cargo. But cargo implied worth and liabilities had none, except...

Except she *was* worth something.

They had, after all, set out to locate and secure a priceless, powerful magical artifact and those didn't come in much more priceless and powerful varieties than an intact shade of a long-dead, legendary archmage that had obligingly packaged itself into a container that the Houses already controlled, ripe for research and experimentation to 'ascertain its true capabilities'.

Well, fuck.

The Houses were never going to let her go, were they? Even if they could separate Enjela from her body, even if a healer could put Rahelu back in, they would never let the sole surviving specimens of the Endless Gate's effects walk free.

How would they explain her disappearance?

Would they redact House and Guild records to show that there never had been a common-born Guild-trained mage graduate named Rahelu who had sworn a Supplicant's vows to House Issolm and sailed to Peshwan Yrg on the *Winged Arrow*?

Hah. She was getting ahead of herself.

They didn't need to alter records; they could simply tell anma and aban: *'We regret to inform you your daughter…'*, include details of *'a fierce harvest squall'* and *'Supplicant lost overboard'*, end with, *'she fulfilled her duty to the Dominion and brought honor to her House'*. A simple Seeming crafted without resonance, made of mere ink and deceptive phrases her parents couldn't read, and whoever they paid to read it to them wouldn't have the resonance skill or context to discern the truth it hid.

Wait, Rahelu sent, as the rest of the Supplicants moved off to do Maketh's bidding. *Elder Anathwan…didn't you say we might still be able to salvage success from this mission? That there are measures that we haven't tried?*

All eyes swung to the Elder.

"You have read my mage journal."

She had.

"You know the shape of my working."

She did.

"Do you understand its purpose?"

I—Yes, Rahelu sent. *Harbingers bring forth the future.*

"Indeed." Anathwan chose her next words with care: "But I cannot do so alone. You know how much power such a working demands."

Incredible power.

Power on the scale of archmages. Power such as the real Enjela had wielded, if her legend were true. Power that Anathwan could have called upon through the Endless Gate...except she and Ylaen and that cultist had squandered most of it.

Rahelu glanced from one senior mage to the other.

Anathwan met her scrutiny, expression resigned yet resolute while Maketh steadfastly avoided it. His face—usually so impassive—was a study in conflict; his gaze skipped around from obelisk to altar-throne to obelisk as if he could, by the sheer force of his glares, intimidate them into collapse.

Oh gods.

All of Maketh's muttered imprecations clicked into place. And it made sense; it made too much sense for there was one, very obvious, very viable source of power, quite literally in their midst:

Power that came from sacrifice.

The tension grew so heavy that it made the air seem a tangible thing, even in her disembodied state.

Rahelu waited for the inevitable order but it did not come.

Anathwan was letting her choose.

39

SISTER

Maketh Imos was first to break the silence.

"I cannot condone this."

The Dedicate's cold, crackling anger was back. Each word he spoke was so precisely enunciated and carried such righteous, ringing conviction that Rahelu was certain that Captain Xya, out on a rowboat headed towards the middle of three ships waging a pitched sea battle, would surely hear it through all the cannon fire.

"Supplicant Rahelu is..." Maketh's jaw jutted forward as he searched for an adequate label. Too honest to say *'alive'*; too unwilling to give her false hope with *'not dead'*. Eventually, he settled for: "...not beyond saving," which wasn't much better, since he made no reference to the odds and difficulties involved, but Rahelu had no trouble supplying wild suppositions to plug that glaring omission herself. "We have a duty of care to our charges—"

"Supplicant Rahelu is my charge." Anathwan's voice was calm, asserting House Issolm's claim on her as the incontrovertible fact it was. "And all of us owe a greater duty to the Houses and the Dominion."

Rahelu knew debt. And she knew duty.

It didn't make the choice any easier.

The Guardian locked gazes with the Elder. Something flitted between them: a tight beam Projection she only detected because his stone-carved features cracked into an expression of guilt for a fraction of a heartbeat.

And just like that, the moment of confrontation passed.

Maketh's shoulders slumped. "Then this is a matter for House Issolm." He bowed his head briefly—to Rahelu, not Anathwan—then said: "I will ready the black powder."

His ponderous footsteps were heavy as he retreated into the distance.

Ghardon jumped in next.

"Is there no other way?" Her brother's voice was ragged. "Is there nothing else we can try?"

Anathwan's answering smile was sad. "We can refrain from attempting this working, destroy the Endless Gate, and depart as Guardian Maketh has advocated, but it will mean the end of House Issolm. Failure—particularly failure on this scale—does not reflect well on His Exalted Dominance. Atriarch Relk Isilc will want to make an example."

Stormbringer. That explained why Rahelu had been offered a short-term contract. She hadn't thought it possible for the stakes to be so high.

Neither had Ghardon, it seemed. Anathwan's frank admission quelled him, but not Elaram.

"Please, Ana. *Please*." Her sister's eyes and cheeks were wet. "I—we have lost Jhobon already. Ylaen too. Can we not try to save Rahelu?"

"My dear Ela, if you truly count Rahelu as your sister, as a worthy daughter of Issolm, you must honor her choice."

Anathwan spoke as if Rahelu had already agreed, as though there was but one path before her.

Indignation stirred—and then faded just as quickly.

She had been willing to accept the risk of death in exchange for coin; she had been willing enough to die before to avoid being forced to murder.

Was she really going to balk at being asked to die for a cause?

Didn't she believe in Anathwan's vision? Didn't she wish to see the city that had been such a beacon of her family's hopes and dreams prosper? Was she no better than the House-born society she despised? Willing enough to revere and recite the Aleznuaweithish ideals the Dominion was founded upon but unwilling to commit to the necessary actions to make those ideals a reality simply because they disadvantaged her personally—even when the alternative was to linger on as a shade, an experimental subject, reliant upon the Houses' continued goodwill to keep her body drugged and collared like a Suborned slave so there would be no risk of Enjela running amuck, slowly losing her sanity and becoming a twisted version of herself.

"*What* choice?" Elaram shrilled. "You're talking about killing her or keeping her drugged and shackled like she's some sort of monster!"

"Ela." Ghardon laid his hand on their sister's shoulder. "It is what it is. Don't—"

Elaram shook him off. "No, don't *you* 'don't' me! This? This is *gullshit*, is what it is. Rahelu shouldn't have to—"

"Be *kind*, Ela," Ghardon said, without grabbing her again. "Don't make this harder for her than it already is."

"There's no fucking kindness in any of this!"

"Supplicant Elaram," Anathwan's voice was chill. "You are overwrought. I am prepared to make some allowance for the unfortunate circumstances, but I expect you to recover decorum, or I will be forced to revise my earlier assessment of the value of your presence." With that ominous rebuke, the Elder turned to the last member of their circle. "Supplicant Nheras. What reservations do you hold in your heart?"

Nheras's expression was inscrutable. "I would like to know how Supplicant Rahelu would like to be honored. Or what she would consider a kindness."

If only Rahelu knew herself!

What reasons did she have for clinging onto an uncertain existence, other than selfish ones?

She was getting so agitated that she was losing hold on her form again, her thoughts whirring around in frenetic circles as she gusted one way and then the other in a mockery of someone pacing.

The worried faces gathered around her blurred as the sky slipped away and the horizon slid into its place. In the late spans of stararc, when the stars had begun to dim but the sun was yet to rise, everything seemed surreal.

To the east, the vastness of the empty ocean.

To the west, flickering firelight from burning ships. A reminder that the tide would not wait.

The tide would not wait.

Rahelu looked down at her still, still body, lying on the blood-stained, gold-flecked ebon altar-throne as though it were a bier, her scorched hands clasped around the pulsing pendant. Its soft murmuring refrain of *'be safe, Rahelu; come back home'*—Lhorne's voice, interwoven with her resonance signature—was the only thing that kept her from dissolving into the void.

The uncanny sight made her remember something else he had said:

> *I refuse to believe that the point of the past two weeks was for you to sell yourself for pocket change so Issolm can send you to die on a suicide mission at the other end of the world!*

A tremor ran through her. The tremor turned into a shudder and the shudder turned into short sharp shakes that would've been gasps of laughter if she still had her body but she didn't she didn't and she might never again the shakes were rattling the core of her being the way hailstones in a spring gale ripped shutters loose to be buffeted by the wind that blew the wind that tickled the wind that danced with the world as it spun her wildly about and made her shattered pieces shake all the harder still.

None of this seemed real.

This must be a dream.

And in a dream, she could dive into the depths of the sky.

When she woke, surely she would find herself in her parents' little ramshackle hut in the Lowdocks with the parchment of her Petition stuck to her cheek, her drool having made a mess of the answers she'd written in diluted squid ink in her cramped, messy hand...but no—that was all done: Keshwar himself had sponsored it; she had sat inside the Ideth heir's fancy palanquin with him and Tsenjhe cramming her full of advice that she couldn't remember and that night she had dreamed of blades and blood and then she had seen her mother die, her mother's blood on a blade like the one she had held, the one now in Anathwan's hand; she, too, had died by a blade like this before when it had carved apart her ribs; Dharyas had died by these blades and there had been blood, so much blood that it had covered the floor of the Tattered Quill like the ocean that had snatched Jhobon away, his face all—

Rahelu.

Obelisks.

Infinite stars above and below.

An endless void filled with endless possibilities:

Rahelu, neat in sky blue and pale green,
elbow-deep in sheaves of parchment and crystal nodes.

Rahelu, submerged
in the shallows of the Elumaje,
blowing bubbles at
a babbling babe
who grasps her index fingers
with chubby hands.

Rahelu, soaked to the skin in the summer solstice rain,
kissing a Supplicant in forest-green.

Rahelu, counting out silver coins
behind an ink-stained counter.

Rahelu, kneeling before
a golden throne.

Rahelu, lighting a vine-and-
iceflower wreathed bier.

Rahelu, thrusting her spear
into a tall, pallid man's gut.

Rahelu, a bruised child in ragged clothing,
wearing a gleaming crystal ring.

Rahelu, pressing her lips
against the forehead
of a blank-eyed Bzel.

Another *pull.*
"Rahelu."

She started at the sound of Anathwan's voice.

"Have you made your choice?"

First and most importantly:

What of my contract? Will House Issolm consider my oath of Supplication fulfilled if our mission is complete but I fail to return?

"The terms did not contemplate this situation—and I can make no guarantee that what we attempt will be successful. But, as the mission would otherwise be a total loss..." Anathwan considered, then nodded. "I do not think the council of Elders will object to me ruling your oath fulfilled."

That was good.

Not only would her family receive the other half of the five hundred gold kez Anathwan had promised her for this mission, but they would not be beholden to House Issolm for anything else.

Aban and anma could start over. Leave Ennuost Yrg. Exchange the sloop for a one-way fare to Anazvela. Her mother was still young enough to bear another child, if she chose to. Rahelu's death would buy them the comfortable life they had always dreamed of, and the Conclave apprenticeship they'd wanted for her but had not been able to afford.

Yes, her parents would grieve.

But they were as hardy and resilient as the reeds that grew along the banks of the Elumaje, surviving no matter how fiercely the storms raged or how many times they were uprooted.

However...

The Ideth legacy I bear.

Lhorne had given it to her as a gift—not as barter for some other, traditional exchange that she had yet to make good on in return—and the gifting had been verified by Anathwan and subsequently confirmed by Mere Ideth herself, which meant House Issolm could mount a rather persuasive claim to it.

Will you return it to Supplicant Lhorne of Ideth?

"No." Anathwan did not qualify or explain her response.

Rahelu had not expected a different answer.

Despite being able to trace its history back to the Year of Founding, House Issolm had accumulated few enduring legacies of its own. Solmoram's legacy, which had been passed down in an unbroken line from founder to heir to be borne by every Atriarch of House Issolm since, was the one of the very few Rahelu could think of that was of a matched caliber to the one currently around her neck.

Anathwan would be a fool to let such a treasure go—but it seemed so wrong, however justified the reasons.

The pendant belonged to Lhorne.

What of mine?

Any legacy of hers ought to be returned to her parents.

The Elder's pause was not reassuring. "If this succeeds, I do not know if there will be sufficient accumulated resonance remaining for a legacy to take form."

The world fuzzed for a moment as Rahelu tried to process the idea that she would leave nothing behind to be remembered by. The sum total of her life—gone. Used up in an experiment that Anathwan wasn't even confident would work.

"But you will not be forgotten," the Elder added. "I will go to your parents and tell them of what you have done for the sake of us all, so that they may bestow upon you a fitting name. And I will see that name and your deeds enshrined in the songs people will sing of the legend we make today."

Now that—that was a poor trade.

What was it that Mere Ideth had told her? That she would do no good if she wasn't willing to speak up and act. And Lhorne and her mother both had warned her not to value herself so cheaply.

I want more than a name and a song, Rahelu sent.

If the Houses were going to use her blood to fuel the changes they wanted to make to the future, she ought to get a say in it. Somebody had to make sure at least one of those changes would directly benefit those not fortunate enough to be born to a House.

I want that working modified. I want the Guild to reserve at least one place in every trainee intake at every single one of their locations throughout the Dominion for a common-born applicant. In perpetuity. And I want those places to be fully funded by the Houses, with no portion of the related Guild debts accruing to those trainees.

A small thing to ask in exchange. A change that would make no noticeable difference to the operating budget of the Guild or the Houses, but one that would make all the difference to families like hers.

"I will see it done," Anathwan promised.

Rahelu drifted back. *I am decided then.*

"Very good."

There was compassion there in Anathwan's ice-blue eyes as she gently smoothed the strands of sweat-matted, sand-gritted black locks that had stuck themselves to Rahelu's forehead.

Compassion, yes, but also implacable resolve.

"No!" Elaram cried as she threw herself over Rahelu's body. Instead of gripping her hand, she seized the pendant in her fist and sent a fierce Projection along the tether that still bound Rahelu. *She can ask but—*

Elaram, Rahelu sent back. *Sister.*

—you don't have to do this.

I know.

You don't have to do this!

I want to.

Better to decide her own fate and seize it than to leave things to chance.

Don't you dare leave me too!

We are Issolm, Elaram—

Exactly! Elaram glared. *We don't do martyrdom! Martyrdom is for losers, duty-blind dullards, and stupid people who don't know how to have fun, and we're none of those things. So you're going to tell Ana 'no fucking way' and we're going to get out of here so the healers can fix you and—*

Rahelu tore her gaze from her sobbing sister to look for her brother. *Ghardon…*

He was already there, urging Elaram to let go.

"I don't want to! *I don't want to!*" Elaram shrieked and slapped him as he dragged her away. "You can't make me!"

"Oh, grow up, Ela," Ghardon snapped. "Stop making a scene; this isn't about you."

Elaram twisted out of his grip and shoved. He staggered. His boots caught on his bow, which lay forgotten on the ground, and he tripped. Arrows spilled out of his quiver.

"Of course it isn't—it's never about me—and that's just fine!" Elaram snatched up her dropped crossbow, going out of her way to stomp on and snap as many of his arrows as she could. "But what do you care? It's all good; it's all fine; doesn't matter what happens and who suffers so long as you end up with some shiny medals. But I won't stand here and watch while she—"

"Rahelu is my sister too," Ghardon said, his voice tight.

"That's a lie." Elaram leveled her crossbow at him. "You can go and fuck right off, Ghardon of *Isilc*; you're no brother of ours."

Isilc? What? Elaram wasn't making any sense, but Ghardon's face had drained of color.

He got up, bow in hand but held loose at his side. He left his scattered arrows where they were; said nothing as he dusted himself off. He looked at the broken Issolm circle around the squat obsidian stone, eyes roving from Elaram (who still had her loaded crossbow pointed at him) to

Rahelu, hovering over her body. He swallowed as his gaze slid past Elder Anathwan and Nheras to the empty space that he should have occupied, then swung back to Rahelu.

She cast about for something to say but struggled to think of something that wasn't overly sentimental because that would just embarrass them both.

Farewell.

That was easier than *'goodbye'.*

Thank you for—'for putting up with me,' she wanted to say, but that seemed inappropriately flippant so she went with another truth instead—*for pushing me to do better.*

His mouth twitched. "Little sister, I'm proud of your choices."

He looked as though he had more to say, but Guardian Maketh had returned, bearing a heavy keg on his shoulder, so Ghardon limited himself to an abrupt nod. Then he turned his back and headed to his assigned quadrant.

"Fine!" Elaram yelled after him while furiously scrubbing at her eyes with the back of a wrist. "Be like that!"

"Enough theatrics, Supplicant Elaram," Anathwan said. "As you cannot apply yourself and be useful here, you will go and keep watch by the boat."

Elaram's shoulders and chest heaved as she sucked in a deep breath and opened her mouth.

The Elder did not say another word. Did not fall back on Projection or Command. Did not raise her hand or lift an eyebrow. Anathwan simply held Elaram's defiant eyes until she lowered them, swallowed whatever retort she had been about to blurt out, and whirled around to run for the stairs, crossbow clutched close.

Anathwan raised the black, serpentine knife. It looked awkward. Her bandage-swathed fingers couldn't close all the way, couldn't grasp the handle tight so she had to clamp it between her mutilated hands.

"Are you ready?"

No.

Yes, Rahelu sent. Despite her resolve, fear stirred in the ambient resonance. Little white frost-like flakes precipitated from her edges and drifted down to bury her face. *What do I need to do?*

"There is nothing more for you to do." A soft gold river of resonance flowed out from Anathwan to surround her. The warm blend of pride and gratitude soothed away the prickles of cold fear and quivering dread. "What you have already done is enough."

Rahelu basked in those wonderful words and that warmth and let herself melt into them. She was done—Anathwan had declared it thus—so she could drift away on those currents and let them buoy her soul skyward if she wanted to.

The stars were calling.

She didn't have to watch Maketh and Ghardon scurry about from quadrant to quadrant, their eyes averted from the center as they measured out black powder and packed it around the base of each obelisk.

She didn't have to witness Nheras bind her limbs to the altar with strips of cloth torn from the hem of the cultist's robes and tied into shitty knots, or linger to observe when Anathwan's repeated struggles to get the knife properly positioned against her ribs woke the shade and her body began thrashing against its bonds.

No, Rahelu had done her part. There was no reason for her to stay.

The knife slipped.

Blood ran from her side.

The shade in her body screamed.

A *clatter* followed by Anathwan's hiss of pain and frantic words: "Supplicant Nheras! Take the knife; I cannot wield it properly so you must."

The shade's rage poured forth in an explosive incandescent surge that ignited the ambient resonance and coated everything with crimson light until the heavens above, the world beneath, and the obelisks of the Endless Gate that spanned the space between all bled with flame.

Rahelu looked down.

Chaotic resonance crackled and roiled in the vast emptiness above the altar-throne. In the midst of those red-and-black clouds and jagged, white-hot spears of lightning:

A familiar city takes shape. Buildings sprout; expand beyond the walls. New walls ring them even as more dwellings and market stalls and private shops and larger places such as temples and guild schools and trading halls and smaller gated estates and public parks and new docks spill out across the land; a tide of timber construction and quarried marble and paved stone that flows from the sea in the east to overrun the rivers north and south and the woods in the west until it crawls up the foothills of the mountains and punches through them.

Below the vast, sprawling city:

Anathwan. Doubled over on her knees, dark liquid running from her eyes and nose, bandaged hands grasping at the glowing, smoking shards of the shattered crown, gasping, "Hurry!"

Nheras. Straddled across her body's bucking hips, left forearm braced across her body's straining shoulders while the right fist clenched the hilt of the black blade, eyes wide and wild with panic. "I–I..."

The shade. Arching and twisting every which way in an effort to free her body, cursing in that strange tongue, hammering the Elder and Nheras with Projections and Commands that bore the force of an avalanche.

Somehow, they both resisted.

The focal point of Anathwan's working shifted. Expanded

from a city to a continent until it encompassed the world: a network of glowing lines that connected the myriad bright, shining lights floating in a flickering sea, an earthly mirror of the constellations above. Expanded again, into a twisting geometry that was impossible for naked eye, unaided mind, and raw resonance senses to follow exactly how the Elder simultaneously pruned away the rogue probabilities branching off from the three-dimensional not-too-distant reality she had constructed while bending the certainties that reality was causally dependent on into shapes that reinforced the overall shape of the design.

Power dwindled rapidly.

Anathwan's working was draining resonance from the Endless Gate at an incredible rate; far faster than the flow of blood—and therefore power—coming from Rahelu's body. Hampered by her mangled hands, Anathwan had not managed to stick the knife in between the ribs thanks to the struggling shade so the sharp point had only opened up a shallow slice down her flank.

And Nheras was just sitting there, frozen—the same way she had frozen in the Ideth pavilion, in the Bronze Turtle's vault, in the dark of the storm—as working and Elder both wavered, right on the brink of collapse.

Oh no. Nonononono.

Desire became thought; instantaneously transmuted to action.

Rahelu reached out to the pendant, touched her mind to the tether that joined her to the resonance crystal, and willed herself back towards her body.

Nheras, she sent urgently. *Nheras Issolm! Finish the job!*

"I can't—"

You have to—

"—I can't!"

—because I can't.

Nheras trembled—her dark pupils so enlarged that her golden irises had shrunk to a thin border—and the reality Anathwan had conjured trembled with her. Cracks appeared at the edges of the vision as the glow of the obelisks guttered out like snuffed candles and the Elder crumpled.

One by one, the lights in the working's shifting constellation withered as Anathwan abandoned large chunks of the design, leaving gaping holes in the brilliant pattern.

Laughter pierced the air.

It came from Rahelu's throat, an eerie, erratic, unhinged sound that oscillated rapidly through the gamut of squeaky high-pitched giggles, throaty growls, and full-bellied roars, and sent her body into paroxysms of coughing and cackling.

"Ah!" Enjela gasped. "You poor, blind, foolish children. How you stumble in the dark!"

Come on, Nheras!

With no other option remaining, Rahelu flung herself at Nheras, hoping that the shock of having a shade either pass through or bounce off her would spur her into action.

We need to act now!

Several things happened at once:

Distant sparks flared at the base of the obelisks as Maketh and Ghardon lit the black powder.

The barrage of Projections and Commands aimed at Nheras ceased as Enjela brought the full force of her will against Anathwan to contest the Elder's control of her working.

Nheras looked at Rahelu.

Saw her. Knew her. Welcomed her.

And Rahelu slipped inside Nheras's body without the least resistance.

A CELL. *A storm. A locked door.*

Test after test pits one against the other, each devised to divide them and divide them again, until the immeasurable complexity of the whole is reduced to the manageability of singular dimensions.

This one is talented. That one is tenacious. This one is insecure. That one is ignorant. This one is led by fear. That one is driven by anger.

Tally their strengths. Magnify their flaws. Toss them into a furnace for forging; see which one shatters and which one tempers.

Score them. Rank them.

Encourage them to cut each other down and quench themselves in blood—dull weapons serve no one well—so they will learn to measure their worth by wins and losses and the game, the contest, the outcome becomes everything.

This—

—or that.

Us—

—or them.

Me—

—or you.

Why?

Why what?

Why is it always one or the other?
Why is there no concept of 'we'?

But we are.

Here; now; we are.

I would that we WERE *sooner.*

Two girls meet in a crowded street.
One caged in a palanquin; a doll dressed in silks.
The other wears plain cotton; a foreigner on foot.

Does it matter?

…it matters.

They meet again on the Guild's sandstone steps.
Their worlds speak different tongues.
They possess nothing in common.

I think I would have liked a friend.

Friendship begins with giving.
Giving requires no words;
only action.

I know I would have.

I'm sorry; I should have done things differently—

They make an exchange.
Gifts instead of insults.
Ten pieces of dried fish for a jeweled bangle that sparkles like
the sea.

I'm not sorry.

No?

No.

Oh.

We chose what we chose;
we are who we are.

So what are we?

Whatever we choose to be…sister.

THEY WEPT as they rammed the knife home.

RUSHING IN THE AMBIENT RESONANCE.
The world ablaze with light and music.

A scream of rage.

Something *yanked*; flayed soul from soul, *pulled* her from flesh to focus stone and kept pulling until her anchor gave way and she *snapped* back into her own body.

Pain assaulted Rahelu—

Searing, rending pain in her hands, her side, her head, her eyes, her limbs from the burns, the gash, the resonance backlash that felt like her brain had been riven in pieces by a thousand rusted nails, the makeshift bonds that kept her tied down to the stone beneath the weight of the willowy girl crushing her abdomen, the knife—*that fucking knife!*—the knife in her chest whose blinding brilliance pierced more sharply than its blade.

—and its sudden intensity stole the breath in her lungs.

The Endless Gate stole the rest.

Fear.

Anger.

Pain.

Despair.

Every last manifestation of independent emotion flowed out of Rahelu with her blood—all except one.

Regret lingered.

Its silver-violet wisps clung to the resonance crystal pulsing against her heart in a pattern that was achingly familiar. The pendant's glow flared fitfully; trying to surround her with an Obfuscation barrier even though the focus stone that powered it was empty; trying to protect her to the very end.

He had found her when she was lost.

Easier than she thought to hear his voice over the star-song surging in her veins and the shade's dissonant snarls as it breached the outer reaches of the pendant's matrix and burrowed into the focus stone's heart.

She had found him when he had fallen into the pitch-black sea.

She held onto that sense of him as her mind plummeted into the jumbled cacophony of chittering noise, colliding frequencies, and clashing possibilities swirling in the vortex of timelines that Anathwan had summoned and was now weaving together.

They could find each other again.

Her veins had run out of blood and now she was bleeding power: raw resonance manifesting as rivers of light that flowed through the channels carved into the glowing altar-throne and obelisks to Elder Anathwan and into the grand working.

Rahelu poured what remained of herself into one final Seeking:

A cheap inn room. He sits in a nest of tangled sheets with his eyes squeezed shut and one hand clutching the lesser pendant around his neck. Behind him, two figures huddle in a corner: a man wearing a chain of black iron around his neck, arms wrapped protectively around a gibbering woman thrashing about in mage trance, her hands clasped around a glittering black gem.

A jolt of recognition.

Rahelu. *Relief smooths out the lines of tension in his shoulders and forehead as he senses her presence. Beneath the wash of cool gold in his aura, there are twisting coils of worry. Where are you? Are you—I dreamed that you—*

Yes. Inadequate, so inadequate, but there was no time to gather her thoughts and find the right words. *Goodbye, Lhorne. Tell my parents I—*

The shade's greater power flung her aside...

...and fled through the temporary bond she and he had forged.

Oh, shit. Oh, *shit!*

His pendant pulses. Erupts with a blinding light that coalesces into the shredded outline of a silver-robed woman superimposed on his beautiful aura.

Her heart lurched; her stomach plunged; her horror announced its birth with a burst of bone-white mist in the already volatile ambient resonance.

Stupid, sentimental, fish-brained fool!

It would have been better not to say goodbye.

Rahelu immediately dredged up every bit of that newborn strength and channeled it. Visualized a hundred grasping hands reaching into her pendant and through his, to seize that shade and rend its collected substance into motes of memory that would have no power over anybody—or, at the very least, haul it back into her failing body so it would die with her.

Near and far; above and below:

Crack—!

—*crack-crack-CRACK*—

CRACK!

The starsong howled, the glory of its haunting melody distorted beyond music into shrieks.

The obelisks shattered.

Distantly:

A tide of triumph.

Their connection snapped.

Heat exploded in her chest. The scent of smoking flesh.

Water sizzled as slabs of splintered stone smashed through the tranquil surface of the lake and sent plumes of steam shooting into the air. Shadows encroached; shouted; scrambled about. Scooped her up—a limp lolling thing whose emptied veins were now filled with celestial fire—and scampered off as reality shivers—

—breaks, into:

Darkness.

REMEMBER

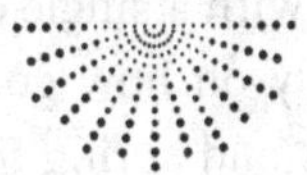

ELARAM WAS A VERY FORGIVING PERSON.

You had to be, if you wanted to achieve any measure of success as a Seeker. Seeking made you confront the very worst of people—yourself included—on a daily basis and if you didn't learn how to forgive shortcomings gracefully, all that resentment would pile up in your veins like the toxic sludge in an artificer's workshop and eventually it would eat you from the inside out.

The trick to forgiveness was to set aside your own feelings and submerge yourself in the other person's worldview. Think how they think, feel what they feel, and so on. That way, when you discovered their little acts of self-deception, you understood their reasons perfectly.

She ignored the knot of rage and grief inside.

She ignored the burning sky.

She ignored everything.

The distant scream. The tremors in the ground. The jagged cracks that raced her down the glassy stone steps. The way the entire caldera shuddered as it shed gravel and ash. The angular ebon slabs from the obelisks that smoked red with rage as they toppled into the crashing surf. The resultant shockwaves that tossed ships about like dice. The images of Ylaen and Jhobon and Rahelu and Ghardon—even Ghardon—turning away from her, all of them bent on going to some place they didn't want to go where she couldn't follow for reasons that she understood all too well even though she didn't agree with a single one.

She concentrated only on how good it felt to stretch her legs and swing her arms and spring from rock to rock as she flew down the mountain, going so fast that the wind of her passage made her eyes water. Altogether, she was spending more time airborne than not so it wasn't a lie to call what she was doing flying because she was, literally, flying the way some seabirds did: soaring out and over as she looked for a safe place to land, gather herself, and launch her body in an arcing glide towards the next stop.

It was nice to feel so weightless.

By the time Elaram got to the beach and the boat, she had decided to forgive Ana her manipulative posturing and everybody else their stupid decisions because she had concluded that if she were them, she wouldn't have done things any differently so their decisions were plenty justified (if remarkably flawed) according to their worldview which meant it was pointless for her to hold a grudge (since they would never agree they were in the wrong) even though she, the worst mage on the team who wasn't even an Evoker at all, seemed to be the only one who still remembered what House Issolm stood for—and it was *not* the extremely Ideth mentality of, '*look-at-me-aren't-I-such-a-wonderful-devoted-dutiful-paragon-of-selfless-self-sacrifice*'.

(An oxymoron, if there ever was one, and '*moronic*' was the perfect way to describe that kind of behavior because '*self-sacrifice*', by definition, was a selfish act—'*self*' was right there, in the very fucking term for it—because who was going to have to deal with the mess afterwards but all those people you supposedly sacrificed yourself for?)

By the time everybody else got in the boat and they got the boat out into the bay, Elaram had, more or less, caught up on what she had missed through several discreet indirect Seekings, and—hooooooooly fuck!

The sheer number of events that had to align for this particular set of outcomes to eventuate was staggering. No way that Ana had managed all that on her own.

(How many favors had she called in? How many promises had she made? I hope you're happy, Ana, because I don't think Mother will agree trading Ghardon away was worth it and she's not as forgiving as I am.)

By the time their boat got back to the *Stormbringer's Judgment* and the *Stormbringer's Judgment* got out of the harbor, Elaram had convinced herself that this particular set of outcomes was, all things considered, the best possible thing that could have eventuated.

Sure, they had suffered considerable setbacks.

The *Sooty Gull* had been sunk. The Free Territories warship was on fire. Xya had lost nearly two-thirds of her crew.

Nobody knew whether or not the grand Fortunement was a success since Anathwan had been repeatedly interrupted—first because Nheras hadn't been quick enough to stab Rahelu (just one of the many reversals of the natural order in this gods-forsaken place), then because Enjela had thrown a tantrum (you had to hand it to the dead archmage's shade: blasting the clouds with a column of rage at least three kual high had *style* and certainly made an impression), and finally, Dedicate Maketh and Ghardon had blown up the Endless Gate mid-working.

They also weren't entirely sure who, exactly, was currently resident in Rahelu's body, where the knife had gone (it had apparently *poofed!* itself out of existence after over-heating from resonance overload—and here Nheras had shown three forms of proof for her theory: the drip-like burn marks on her fingers and palms, an Evocation that cut abruptly between the ordinary sensation of gripping something solid and the agony of touching molten stone, and the ugly cauterized chest wound on Rahelu's body), or how that body kept breathing when there was no sign of a discernable pulse.

Elaram ignored all that shit.

Life was more fun when you concentrated on the good stuff.

Rahelu—and since Nheras had finally proven herself to be wholeheartedly Issolm, Elaram chose to believe her when she insisted it really was Rahelu—had, against all odds, made it out alive.

And though Ghardon might not currently be on speaking terms—or even seeing terms with her (he had actually volunteered for *physical labor*—something she hadn't volunteered for because she'd done plenty of it digging the boat out of the sand and dragging it to the high water mark; also because she wasn't going to forego the frontmost seat to the epic three-sided ship battle being waged all around them—simply because rowing the boat with Maketh meant he had to sit in it with his back to her), there would be plenty of time to rectify the situation. She hadn't meant to reveal his secret in front of everybody in quite so dramatic a fashion but she'd been a little upset and gotten carried away and who could blame her for that? (They had, after all, been discussing the notion of *killing their sister*; a subject that ought to have had everybody engaging in some so-called theatrics.) So she would let him sulk for a while, and then she would apologize —and he would listen!—after he calmed down, and then she could explain how he didn't have to go to the colossally stupid and unnecessary lengths of committing to his ill-thought-out consorting with Kyrosh anymore because she could now make a much better match that was both fun *and* the stuff of Mother's political ambitions.

Keep smiling, Elaram.

Ignore your shaking hands and the crumbling islet on the horizon and focus on the smoke and explosions. Doesn't it remind you of the New Year celebrations back home? You missed those because you were…elsewhere, but the next ones—if you ask, he'll take you down to the common-born celebrations in the harbor and Mother won't dare say no to a future Atriarch.

(There was the *slight* difficulty of the two renunciations to get around but it was a long way to Tsorek-fa and memories could be such tricky things and Elaram knew, from personal experience, that everybody would remember the same set of facts so long as she reminded them in the right way.)

Be *happy*, Elaram. This mission has been everything you could have hoped for. You've:

Seen stranger sights than most people dared dream; things that could've come straight out of the wildest fireside tales told in dockside taverns, like the rise of a long-dead shade out of legend!

Sailed to places that weren't even drawn on, let alone named in, most maps and—thanks to Ana's swift negotiations—joined the crew of an infamous pirate ship!

Discovered and enjoyed forbidden freedom. Stumbled into new magic. Found unexpected love—then lost it.

You'll find it again.

Remember: you are, after all, an excellent Seeker.

Therefore, while:

Maketh carried Anathwan off to confer with Captain Xya in her stateroom and do something about the Belruonian ship full of mage-priests chasing them—

Ghardon and Nheras took Rahelu two decks down to the healers in the overcrowded apothecary—

Elaram hummed to herself as she followed a beacon more tantalizing than any starsong to the stern to do something equally important. Passed the spot where Snuffles had died. Opened the door to the next cabin over and...

There he was.

Fast asleep, in a tangle of loose hair and bedsheets, fevered brow glistening with chill sweat.

His wounds had been washed and bound with astringent healing poultices—she smelled numbweed for the pain, bloodvine to encourage clotting, and knotweed to ward off infection. The bandages around his left shoulder and chest had been wound so tight that they thwarted his ribs in their efforts to expand to their fullest and forced him to breathe in rapid, shallow snatches of air. The crisp, bleached linen was already spotted with blood. A quick peek underneath confirmed it was only a superficial bleed—his restless tossing and turning had pulled some of the scabs loose—and that the largest, most concerning wound (the one Rahelu had given him at the cultist's behest; the one that marred the pattern of scars carved on his breast) was closed (also neatly cauterized, as Rahelu's wound had been).

She shut the door behind her with a firm *click*—barred it too, so nobody could intrude on their little sanctuary—then proceeded to do the same with the shutters. One by one, she snipped off the pale dawn rays, stuffed the cracks with her clothes until only the faintest suggestion of light seeped through to silver all the shadows, then slipped under the sheets with him.

He stirred. Instinctively coiled his arms around her as she wrapped her body around his and mumbled, "Who...?"

Her hopes rose at hearing his bewildered tone.

"Hello," she said, her heart fluttering in her chest.

He stiffened at the sound of her voice and the touch of her hand—and not in the way she had hoped. Very flatly, with none of the nuances she longed to hear: "Elaram."

But he didn't push her away.

So she stayed right where she was and left her hand resting where it was. She limited herself to wondering aloud, "Remember our first time?" and let the dark of his cabin, the warmth of her proximity, and the urgent press of her bare skin against his speak the rest: *Want to do it again?*

Please, Skymother, please let him remember.

If he put her on her knees, if he even so much as alluded to gravel in passing, she would get up and leave him forever.

He was silent for a very long time.

She had almost given up, had spent the intervening eternity debating whether she ought to provide him with a subtle hint or ten or maybe even reach out with her resonance senses and delve into a very, very, very light Evocation to win him over, when his fingers moved and glided down her side. Hesitant, but methodical in their exploration.

If he often paused in the midst of what they were doing; if there were moments when his movements faltered; if sometimes his resonance signature skipped beats, modulated its rhythm, or faded altogether, the lapse never lasted long. A soft murmur in his ear was all the reminder he needed to remember and resume where they had left off and if he needed her to be patient then she could be patient for she had learned the value of patience from him.

Finally, finally, he cried out, "Elaram, *Elaram*—" and his cry was exactly as she remembered: terrified wonder, tender affection, and trembling worry over a million details of how this was going to work.

Last time, she had giggled and teased and distracted him with a long list of all the *possible variables* and *limitations* and a ridiculously arbitrary rubric for evaluating whether or not he had, in fact, kept his promise to '*make the wait worth your while*'.

This time, she shushed him and said, "Later."

House politics, Guild ethics, quandaries both moralistic and philosophic—they could deal with all those '*–ics*' later.

Much later.

After they figured out—and fixed—the problem of *what* and *how much* Jhobon wanted to remember.

GHARDON GAGGED as they stepped inside the warship's apothecary—the place reeked like a crematorium—and immediately had to retreat to avoid being jabbed in the face by a scalpel.

"Out, out!" The healer in charge shoved past him and Nheras without sparing a glance for the unconscious body they carried. "Get that out of my surgery."

The normally mild-mannered fellow gesticulated ferociously with the bloodied instrument as he shouted to his apprentice for clean water.

"*That* is my sister." Somehow, Nheras managed to pitch her nasal tones to carry through the screams and cries and moans of the wounded and dying without shouting. "And she is no longer one of Zovresh's slaves, whom you can neglect, but one of the ship's mages, answerable only to the captain and critical to the ship's defense."

"Escaped slave or another pet mage makes no difference; I've no sickbeds to spare."

That was an understatement. Every surface large and flat enough to lie on was crowded with bodies, some doubled up in piles. Corpses, Ghardon had assumed, until he took a closer look and saw their mouths moving.

Here, take her weight, Nheras sent impatiently and made a fist.

The healer's patient stopped writhing beneath his scalpel as every bit of her pain flew into Nheras's grasp.

"She doesn't need a sickbed," Ghardon quickly said, before Nheras could turn the poor healer's insides out by redirecting his patient's pain at him.

Nheras bristled. *She needs him to fix her!*

How will we survive long enough to reach Tsorek-fa—let alone home—if all of Xya's crew perish?

No reply.

Out loud, Ghardon said, "We just need a diagnosis." Privately, he told Nheras, *Once we know what's wrong, we'll take her to your cabin. We'll take care of her, and we'll do whatever we need to do to find a way to fix her.*

The healer glanced at the steady rise and fall of Rahelu's chest. "She's in no danger of dying, so she can sleep it off," he snapped. "Now get out. I have lives to save."

With that, the healer returned his attention to the next waiting patient. He shook his head at the crushed leg and called out to his harried apprentice, who was still wrist deep in someone else's slit abdomen.

Nheras picked up the bone saw.

The preoccupied healer registered the movement and absentmindedly held out his hand.

Nheras, Ghardon cautioned her, *be nice.*

"Honorable master healer," Nheras said, sounding very respectful and looking anything but as she brandished the bone saw. "We require but a moment of your wisdom."

Threats are not nice.

This is nice, by their standards, she retorted and left it up to him to exercise diplomacy.

"In return for your wisdom, we both offer you a favor," Ghardon said.

Nheras's expression did not change, but her mental retort was scathing. *Wonderful. Now you've made us look desperate and weak.*

The healer sighed.

"I will look at her next," he said tiredly. "And perhaps you both might do me the favor of drawing away Aluud's pain, too, while I remove this leg."

They did him one better.

While Nheras replaced Aluud's pain with deep exhaustion, Ghardon delved into the man's mind and erected a few flimsier versions of the Obfuscation barriers Guardian Maketh had used to render Rahelu unconscious.

In less than five heartbeats, Aluud was asleep—and remained so, even as the healer sawed through his thighbone.

"Now," the healer said as he threaded his needle. "Describe what happened."

When they ran out of ridiculous-sounding things to say, the healer swept a jaundiced eye and cursory Seeking over Rahelu as he rinsed his hands.

The diagnosis he proceeded to reel off was a mostly incomprehensible spiel.

Ghardon memorized it anyway. Given that their original mission was over, and Ana and Xya had come to terms, he could try negotiating for limited access to the captain's long-distance relay node and consult the Healers' Guild.

"So what is her prognosis?" Nheras asked when the healer paused for breath.

"Lass, your sister should have bled out within a ten-count of that knife piercing her heart. But since her body was acting as a conduit for resonance transfer, the raw power passing through her veins kept it alive. When you lot destroyed the Endless Gate mid-working, that power had nowhere else to go. It turned back on itself—except that knife wasn't designed to accommodate that kind of reversal in the flow. As a byproduct of its combustion from the mounting pressure, it also cauterized the wound and sealed in the remaining resonance. You can thank the Starfather for that miracle—it's the only reason she's still breathing."

"How long will it last?" Nheras fretted. "She still doesn't have a pulse and her resonance signature is—"

"Gone," Ghardon finished the sentence when Nheras wouldn't. "We can't find her."

"A pulse requires the body to have blood in its veins and a heart to pump that blood around, and I'd wager she has neither." The healer shook his head. "You're fortunate to have recovered a body in the first place; that much raw power ought to have vaporized flesh and bone instead of leaving a viable vessel. I won't argue what's in front of my eyes, however. As for her resonance signature, if you say you felt her spirit return, then she's likely still in there—somewhere—thanks to her anchor."

The healer tapped the Ideth pendant that hung around Rahelu's neck. The silver chain and backing had blackened but the resonance crystal itself was untarnished. The inside of the stone, however, was perfectly clear—all traces of swirling mist gone from its depths—and marred by an ugly crack down its center.

"You won't be able to find her amidst the chaotic foreign frequencies still lingering in her body, though," the healer concluded.

He kept talking over them both before they could get further questions out.

"No, we cannot purge her body. This girl has undergone acute spiritual trauma, which led to forcible separation of her mind from her body, which was followed by spiritual recoil. Look at these severe distortions in her aura! She has already been subjected to a tremendous flow of power far beyond her body's natural capacity. Subjecting her to a battery of counter-frequencies or overwhelming her with Evocations or introducing more foreign influences through direct Seeking will only destabilize and aggravate her condition."

"What about Obfuscation?" Ghardon asked. "Couldn't I wall off some of the pressure and—"

"Skymother save the world from eager young fools and Dominion mages—not everything can be solved with resonance!" The healer took a deep breath. "What she needs is time and undisturbed rest. Her body and spirit must be allowed to heal on their own."

"So she will recover, then?" he pressed.

"In normal cases of biological resonance overload, patients with a hale body free of incompatible frequencies and a well-anchored, relatively intact spirit have a probability of successful reintegration of approximately fifty to eighty-seven percent, depending on the duration of separation. In severe cases, between twenty-two and thirty-six percent."

"And in this case?" Nheras asked as the three of them were ejected from the apothecary.

"Only the Starfather knows."

Ghardon tried one more time. "Is there anything else we can do to increase her chances of recovery, besides praying?"

"Talk to her," came the reply. "Help her remember who she is."

THEY RAN out of useful things to talk about long before their voices grew hoarse. The sky outside her open cabin window was beginning to lighten when Nheras was forced to confront the difficult truth.

None of the shit they were saying mattered.

Ghardon, being Ghardon, had approached their 'assignment' (such as it was) with Evoker-trained methodicalness, and began by introducing Rahelu to herself in the second person, as though she were a stranger just arrived and they were all sat around the rosewood table in the *Winged Arrow's* great cabin, filling the silence with polite small talk and chatter as they awaited the Elder's mission briefing:

"You are Rahelu of Issolm, formerly Rahelu of the Lowdocks in Aleznuaweite, a graduated mage of the Resonance Guild and a Supplicant of House Issolm in good standing," he told her. "Before that, you were Rahelu of Chanaz. You and your family left your fishing village by the Elumaje to live in Ennuost Yrg. We studied Evocation together, Petitioned together, swore our oaths of Supplication and served our House and the Dominion under Elder Anathwan Issolm together. Your father is a fisher contracted to the Isonn fleet. Your mother is a seafood hawker and she runs the best stall in Market Square."

Nheras rose from her seat to pace as Ghardon went on talking with his eyes closed, seemingly intent on recounting the events of every single span he had ever shared with Rahelu during their years at the Guild and the months since—taking great pains to describe them with an obnoxious level of detail, as though he could transmit the exact Evocation he held in his head to Rahelu with a surfeit of words.

But Jhobon had had the right of it. Words were an imprecise medium.

Rahelu of Elumaje.

Rahelu of Chanaz.

Rahelu of Aleznuaweite.

Rahelu of the Lowdocks.

Rahelu of Issolm.

Labels, all of them; just inference-laden labels. Shorthand conveyances that only meant something because they represented ideas you had formed through your own lived experiences, which were never the same as someone else's.

Take 'Elumaje'.

Nheras knew of the place in the abstract.

She'd seen it on her grandmother's maps; could describe its shape and placement on the Ngutoccai continent as the cartographers had drawn it: the smallest, roundest, and northernmost of Chanaz's three great lakes, with a forest to the west and grasslands to the east. Unremarkable, because it was known for producing an unremarkable quantity of unremarkable fish, and because it was located far from Anazvela. The local inhabitants led simple lives and slept in dirt-floored, reed-thatched mud huts and were so uneducated that they relied on folk songs and other oral traditions to pass on their knowledge.

Rahelu knew the Elumaje as home.

A beautiful place of sunlight and song, love and laughter, filled with fish and food and family, but also a place where blood-sucking insects and buzzing mud-flies would eat you alive in the sweltering summer heat so everyone would retreat to the lake to cool themselves in the crystal-clear waters and sleep beneath the stars until the Stormbringer sent a sudden squall that snatched you off your raft and it broke apart, because you were only nine and it was the first one you had made without Anenje to double check your lashings and there was a knot you still hadn't quite gotten the hang of but you wanted to prove that anything Anenje could do you could do so when your mother had worried and your father asked, you summoned the rudimentary Evocation you had relied on and told them you had copied Anenje exactly while you laid on the beginnings of a subliminal Projection to *believe me believe me I'm telling the truth* and they had, and now you were paying for it—they were paying for it—because you were drowning because you were too stupid and too proud to admit that you needed help.

Nheras took a shuddering breath.

How could they help Rahelu remember who she was when they themselves didn't truly know? The story of Rahelu's life couldn't be recounted by naming the people she had known, the places she had been, or the things she had done, because a person was more than their name, their biography, and a list of their personal attributes and achievements.

At last, Ghardon ran out of amusing anecdotes about all the ways Rahelu had driven their Evocation instructor mad with her unorthodox solutions to their assignments, so he unleashed an in-depth review and critique of every significant decision Rahelu had made since graduation.

When he ran out of those too, he got up from the bed to trade places with Nheras.

"Six years," he croaked as he slouched against the bulkhead. "Six years we've known each other, and you could sum up everything I've just said with, 'Rahelu, you aggravating, obstinate, ill-mannered, short-sighted, fish-brained fool; you're so committed to doing what you think needs to be done, for the sake of repaying a debt you don't believe you can ever repay, that you never stop to question what that dedication costs you, and I love you.'" He closed his eyes and muttered, "May the Skymother help you find yourself again, devoted sister mine."

Then Ghardon gave up on maintaining his vertical state altogether, sliding down the bulkhead's wood paneling until he, too, was another limp body lying in her cabin.

NHERAS SAT and stared at Rahelu, and said nothing for a very long time.

So long, in fact, that Ghardon had time to fall asleep, wake up spans later with a sore neck and stiff bones, fetch the three of them their water rations and breakfast, attend Guardian Maketh on deck when requested to assist with renewing the warship's barriers and wards, deliver a two-word report on Rahelu's condition to Elder Anathwan ("no change"), help Nheras feed and wash and change Rahelu after a non-existent dinner, tell them both the story of the Skymother's mirror—

(because Nheras didn't have a favorite story; because Rahelu needed to hear it; because Rahelu's favorite tale had been Enjela's Ballad, the way her father sung it, and Ghardon did *not* want to make a wager on which of the two spirits that had inhabited Rahelu's body might triumph if he asked her to remember how *that* story went)

—and fall asleep again.

When he next woke, he woke to dawn streaming in through the open shutters of Nheras's empty cabin.

HE FOUND them seated cross-legged in meditation at the warship's bow, surrounded by spare rope, fishing lines, and half a dozen gulls, with the sun sparkling off the droplets of sea spray that flew up from the warship's prow to settle in their unbound hair like jewels as the *Stormbringer's Judgment* sped south and west, running before the wind and the Belruonian ship in the distance.

Correction:

Rahelu seemed to be meditating. Her eyes were closed, her face relaxed and serene, and the corners of her mouth curled up in a tiny smile.

(When had she regained the ability to sit up? Yesterday, they had had to prop her head on his shoulder before they could brush out her matted hair.)

Her hands, though, weren't resting on her knees. Someone had spread a salt-crusted fishing net across her lap and her fingers had gotten tangled in—no; her fingers were methodically moving row by row, column by column, slowly probing at the twisted fibers and knots of the web.

Nheras was attempting to bait a fishhook and talking in a murmur so low that Ghardon had to strain his ears to hear what she said.

REMEMBER THE DAY WE MET?

We were twelve and it was a bright and sunny day in early summer—Petition Day—and I was so worried about failing the Guild's admittance test that I spent the whole time practicing in my grandmother's palanquin on the way there and you got caught up in my Projection.

Remember how, when the palanquin stopped at the intersection, you ran right up to the curtains and lifted them?

You told me your name, but you spoke in Chanazian and I didn't understand. When you said it again, in Aleznuawei-thish, so I would understand, I couldn't pronounce it right, but you laughed and told me it didn't matter; you couldn't pronounce anything right either, my name included, and then you noticed I was hungry, because I'd been too nervous to eat breakfast, and asked if I wanted any fish and I said—I said—

I said yes.

I said yes.

I said yes, remember?

You gave me your entire packet of dried fish—all ten pieces of it—and I didn't know how much it had cost you and

I didn't have any coin of my own so I gave you my bracelet instead.

And then the traffic ahead cleared so you waved at me and let the curtain fall and the palanquin started moving again, with me trapped inside, and I remember—

I remember.

I remember.

I remember you had said: "I...Rahelu. Guild. You?"

—so I made the palanquin stop and I got out and I found you, wandering down the middle of the Westroad, staring wide-eyed at the city, five heartbeats away from being trampled by the would-be Petitioners sprinting through the streets.

They knocked us over.

Remember how, when we picked ourselves off the ground and my grandmother's palanquin had caught up, we were covered in road dust and horse dung?

I—I had torn the sleeves on the new silk tunic my grandmother had made me wear, and I cried as we got in because I had disobeyed her, and in disobeying Grandmother, I disgraced her, and she was sure to punish me.

You—you held me until my sobs stopped; until the palanquin stopped, and we looked outside and found ourselves at the Guild.

Remember how you looked at me then?

Your face, which was just as scratched up and anxious as mine, twisted and you frantically started shouting "Coin! Coin!" as you began patting yourself down, digging through your trouser pockets and breastband, taking off your tunic to turn it inside out, but the silver kez your parents had given you for the Guild's registration fee was gone.

We got out.

Two sniffling messes, the both of us; all dirtied from rolling around in the gutters.

We dragged ourselves through the Guild gates and up the steps to the Guild Registrar's office, where we met Myreil, who sneered at you, and Kyrosh, who called me a "gilt-painted daughter of a third-rate mage so lacking potential her mother had had to hire a jumped-up songhouse stud to breed her" and you—

You walked right up to them, the heir to the Exalted Dominance's own House and her cousin, and told them:

"Nheras I friend. You problem?"

When Kyrosh insulted us again, you broke his nose.

When Myreil threatened to have us arrested and summoned fear to make us beg for mercy, I turned her Projection back and made her wet herself with terror.

You remember all that, don't you?

You remember what we chose.

You remember, I know you do.

Hey. Hey.

Wake up.

Wake up.

Wake up.

Tell me you remember who I am, and who you are.

EPILOGUE: RISEN

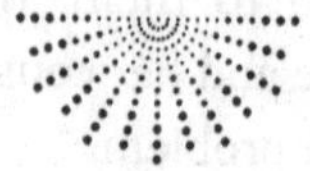

UVESHT-MO HAD LIVED HIS DEATH A THOUSAND times. You could not bend the lives of others without full knowledge of how your own began, all the choices that had altered your course, and the myriad ways it could end.

This is how I die.

For most of his youth, death had worn a singular guise regardless of the manner of its visitation: all met their end at the hands of the Divine Holiness who fed their blood to the sea, their bones to the earth, and their hearts to the void, so that their souls might return to the stars. Since his exile from the blessed shores of the Divine Kingdom, death had donned many guises. Disease was common: incurable hacking coughs and wasting fevers that chilled and racked the body with shivering. Danger, too, in all its permutations: inadvertent or intentional, sudden or slow, welcomed or unwelcomed.

But chief among death's new favorites was disaster.

The ambient resonance rang with ruination. Twisted harmonics rose in place of the tolling of the stars. A sour glassine drone permeating the silence left behind by the earth-shaking concussive blasts that had toppled the ancient anchors, sheared Enjela from her source of power, and would soon cast her broken throne into the sea.

Uvesht-mo looked upon destruction and was glad.

On the horizon, his once-brethren chased the heathens across the seas.

On the beach, the Tower dredged their sunken ship and rescued the fallen bones of the Endless Gate.

Perhaps the new Chosen might recover Enjela's sacred instruments; perhaps the heathen adepts would piece together fragments of Enjela's secrets. But as for Enjela herself, her undying reign was at an end.

They had succeeded.

In a century or two, all would be forgotten.

Uvesht-mo breathed deeply of the smoky air and reached out to touch the constellations, to pray and give thanks one last time before he, too, cast his soul into oblivion. He had no incense to burn, no more blood to spill, but the forms did not matter, for the transformative essence of every ritual lay in the intention, not the trappings of pageantry.

For this, devotion would be enough.

And yet, when he at last fell into the void, death still surprised him:

Come to me, my faithful, for I am risen.

Here ends Book Two of the
RESONANCE CRYSTAL LEGACY

A NOTE FROM THE AUTHOR

What happened in Ennuost Yrg
while Rahelu's been away? Find out in

DEDICATE
(Forthcoming)

And if you want to know what really happened when Rahelu
and Nheras first met, you can tap into that Evocation here:

https://www.delilahwaan.com/jointheguild

GLOSSARY

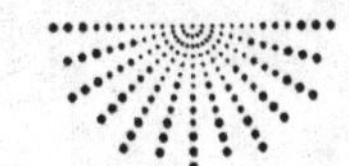

GLOSSARY

ABAN—Chanazian term of address from child to father.
  pronounced: AH-ban
ABMERDU—see Free Territories of Abmerdu.
  pronounced: ab-MER-du
ABMERDUAN SEA—sea surrounding the island archipelago known as the
Free Territories.
  pronounced: ab-MER-du-an SEA
ACHWA-TE—a ceremonial Free Speech phrase meaning "dance".
  pronounced: AH-chwa-TEY
ACHWA-TE-GISH-NO—a ship clan tradition.
  pronounced: AH-chwa-TEY-GISH-noh
A.E./A.F.—abbreviations for "After Exile/After Founding". Dominion
calendars use "A.F." while Chanazian calendars use "A.E." to designate
years in the present-day calendar.
AHEL—Chanazian word describing the airborne motion of aquatic creatures. See also ehel and ohel.
ALEITUAN—sea by the city of Ennuost Yrg in the Dominion of Aleznuaweite on the Ngutoccai continent.
  pronounced: ah-LEY-tu-an
ALEZNUA—a civilization that once spanned the Ngutoccai continent.
Fractured into the present day Chanazian Federation and the Dominion of
Aleznuaweite in an event known as "Exile" in Chanaz and "Founding" in
the Dominion.
  pronounced: ah-LEZ-nu-ah
ALEZNUAWEITE, DOMINION OF—a nation on the northeastern part of
the Ngutoccai continent commonly referred to as the "Dominion",
governed by the Houses.
  pronounced: ah-LEZ-nu-ah-weight
ALEZNUAWEITHISH—adjective form of Aleznuaweite; also the language
and culture of the Dominion of Aleznuaweite.
  pronounced: ah-LEZ-nu-ah-weith-ish
ALOZEI—a Dedicate of House Imrell.
  pronounced: ah-LOH-zey
ANATHWAN—a Harbinger and an Elder of House Issolm. Entrusted by
the Exalted Dominion to lead a secret mission of strategic importance to
the Dominion in 530 A.F./A.E.
  pronounced: ah-NAHTH-wan

ANAZ—Chanazian term of address, meaning "master and teacher".
  pronounced: AH-naz
ANAZVELA—capital city of the Chanazian Federation.
  pronounced: AH-naz-VEH-lah
ANENJE—Chanazian birth name for Tsenjhe Isca.
  pronounced: ah-NEN-jeh
ANMA—Chanazian term of address from child to mother.
  pronounced: AN-mah
ANMABANELAVELANAZ—Chanazian concept of legacy embodied by
interconnected generations of family.
  pronounced: AN-mah-ban-NEH-lah-veh-lah-NAZ
ANUVELOMAZ—the three great lakes of Chanaz.
  pronounced: ah-nu-VE-loh-maz
ARC—unit of measurement for time. A day is divided into four arcs, with
each arc divided into six spans.
  Eartharc: dawn to high sun
  Skyarc: high sun to dusk
  Stormarc: dusk to deepnight
  Stararc: deepnight to dawn
ATRIARCH—Aleznuaweithish term meaning "ruler"; both title and rank
for the head of a House of the Dominion.
  pronounced: AY-tree-arc
AUGUR—a mage specializing in Augury and Fortunement.
AUGURY—one of the six resonance disciplines taught by the Resonance
Guild; the art of soothsaying.
AVELA—an intimate Chanazian endearment for a lover or consort.
  pronounced: ah-VEH-lah
AZOSH-EK—an exile from the Divine Kingdom. Responsible for ritual
murders of various Ennuost Yrg citizens in an attempt to open the
Endless Gate.
  pronounced: ah-ZOH-sh-ek

BATTLE FOR THE DAWN—a battle during the War of the Five Dominions.
BELRUONIA—Aleznuaweithish name for the Divine Kingdom.
  pronounced: beh-LRUON-ya
BHAROST—a boar-like animal, native to the Ngutoccai continent.
  pronounced: bah-ROST
BHARYX—a large predatory feline, native to the mountainous regions of
the Ngutoccai continent.
  pronounced: BAH-rix
BHEMOL—an Ilyn-born applicant and cousin to Nheras Ilyn.
  pronounced: BEH-moll

BRONZE TURTLE—the workshop of the artificer Ruarem, located in Peshawar Yrg's Outermarket.

BZEL—son of the fishmonger, Hzin, and Tseiran. Missing, presumed sold into Suborned slavery by his father, Hzin.
  pronounced: beh-ZEL

CHANAZ, FEDERATION OF—a nation on the southwestern part of the Ngutoccai continent commonly known as "Chanaz", governed by the arch-mages of the Conclave.
  pronounced: CHA-naz

CHANAZIAN—adjective form of Chanaz; also the language and people of Chanaz. The Chanazian language is distinctive for its rounded syllables and flowing sounds. The "r" sound in Chanazian is pronounced with the tongue rolled back to the roof of the mouth. Native speakers of Aleznu-aweithish typically struggle to pronounce the Chanazian "r" correctly.
  pronounced: cha-NAH-zi-an

CHENYA—Atriarch of House Imrell, originally hailing from the Free Territories.
  pronounced: CHEN-yah

CHOSEN—title for a mage-priest of the Divine Kingdom.

COMMON-BORN—a child who is not House-born.

CONCLAVE—organization responsible for the training, accreditation, and licensing of mages in the resonance disciplines, and regulation and enforcement of laws in relation to the use of resonance in Chanaz; also the governing body of Chanaz, often referred to as the "Tower".

CONCORDANCE—a state of intense focus where two or more mages join minds to perform a blended working in concert.

CRIMSON STORM—a ship clan of the Free Territories. See also Zovresh.

CSERYL—an Ideth-born Supplicant; daughter of Atriarch Mere Ideth, younger sister to Keshwar Ideth, and cousin to Lhorne Ideth.
  pronounced: SEH-rill

CSINYRG—an Imrell-born Supplicant.
  pronounced: SIN-yirgh

CSONNYRG—Founder of House Isonn, famed for an Obfuscation barrier formation known as Csonnryg's Trap.
  pronounced: SOHN-yirgh

CSONNYRG'S HAMMER—flagship in House Isonn's warfleet.

CSOLIM—a member of the Jade Eye Company.
  pronounced: SOH-lim

CSORATH—a Seeker and a Dedicate of House Isonn. Also the captain of the Dominion's diplomatic flagship, *The Winged Arrow*.
  pronounced: SOH-rath

DEDICATE—middle rank within a House, third after Atriarch and Elder. Mages of this rank typically specialize in a particular resonance discipline.

DEEPNIGHT—time of night when the sun is at its farthest below the horizon and the sky is darkest.

DESOLATE ISLES—a collection of scattered islands in the remote North Ocean.

DETHIRAM—a legendary archmage; Founder of House Ideth, inventor of the Obfuscation barrier formation, Dethiram's Shield.
   pronounced: deh-THI-ram

DHARYAS—an Isca-born applicant; friend of Lhorne Ideth and protege of Tsenjhe Isca. Murdered by Azosh-ek and his accomplices.
   pronounced: DAR-ryuss

DHIRNE—a member of the Jade Eye Company.
   pronounced: DURN

DIVINE KINGDOM—the nation on a continent to the far east, governed by mage-priests who exclusively worship the Starfather.

DIVINE HEIR ASCENDANT—the successor to the Divine Holiness.

DIVINE HOLINESS—spiritual leader of the mage-priests.

DOMINION, THE—see Aleznuaweite.

DRAGON'S TEETH, DRAGON'S SPINE, DRAGON'S TAIL—a collection of coral atolls located east of the Free Territories.

EARTHGIVER—deity with dominion over the earth and land-based creatures, commonly depicted as a rounded figure with horns.
   associations: darkness, harvest, protection, shield, Obfuscation

EGISS-TE—an exile from the Divine Kingdom and accomplice of Azosh-ek. Responsible for ritual murders of various Ennuost Yrg citizens. Killed by Rahelu in the attempt to open the Endless Gate.
   pronounced: ee-GISS-tey

EHELI—Adverbial form of ehel, a Chanazian word describing the airborne motion of living creatures gifted with the ability to fly. See also ohel and ahel.
   pronounced: eh-HEE-lye

ELARAM—an Issolm-born Supplicant; daughter of Suurynn Issolm and younger sister to Ghardon Issolm.
   pronounced: eh-LAH-ram

ELDER—senior rank within a House, second only to Atriarch.

ELUMAJE—a lake in Chanaz; see also Anuvelomaz.
   pronounced: eh-lu-MAH-jeh

ENITH—an Isonn-born Supplicant.
   pronounced: EE-nith

ENJELA—a legendary archmage of old Aleznua.
   pronounced: en-JEH-lah

ENNUOST YRG—a city in the Dominion of Aleznuaweite.
  pronounced: EHN-nu-oh-st YIRGH
EVOCATION—one of the six resonance disciplines taught by the Resonance Guild; the art of remembrance.
EVOKER—a mage specializing in Evocation.
EXALTED DOMINANCE—the highest political office in the Dominion, chosen from amongst the Atriarchs of the Houses.

FISHGUTS—see Rahelu.
FORTUNEMENT—one of the six resonance disciplines taught by the Resonance Guild; the art of change.
  pronounced: for-TUNE-ment
FREE CITIES—cities in the Free Territories.
FREE TERRITORIES OF ABMERDU—an archipelago east of the Ngutoccai continent, renowned as a lawless haven for freebooters, smugglers, and exiles, and commonly referred to as the "Free Territories". Its inhabitants speak a creole of Aleznuaweithish, Belruonian, and Chanazian commonly known as the "Free Speech" and practice ritual scarring. See also ship clans.

GHARDON—an Issolm-born Supplicant; son of Suurynn Issolm and elder brother to Elaram Issolm.
  pronounced: GAR-don
GHELIK—Aleznuaweithish slur meaning "foreigner".
  pronounced: GEH-lick
GUARDIAN—a mage specializing in defensive applications of the resonance disciplines, particularly Obfuscation.
GUILD, THE—see Resonance Guild.

HARBINGER—a mage specializing in offensive applications of the resonance disciplines, particularly Projection.
HEMORU—a fisher; consort to Jenura and father of Rahelu.
  pronounced: heh-MOR-ru (with Chanazian "r")
HIGH SUN—the time of day when the sun is at its apex in the sky. See also arc.
HNAN—Atriarch of House Imos.
  pronounced: he-NAN (very short "he", where the "e" has an "er" sound)
HOUSE—an Aleznuaweithish designation, given in recognition for a body of Guild-accredited mages who collectively hold sufficient wealth, power, and influence over the affairs of the Dominion of Aleznuaweite. Each House is led by an Atriarch and named after its founder, whereby an "I–" prefix is added to the first syllable of the founder's name. The Dominion currently recognizes eight Houses.

 Major Houses: Ideth, Isilc, Isonn, and Imos.

 Minor Houses: Imrell, Issolm, Isca, and Ilyn.

HOUSE-BORN—a child born to (or adopted and raised by) at least one parent who has been accepted by and sworn oaths to a House.

HZIN—a fisher and seafood hawker of a stall in Market Square; consort to Tseiran and father of Bzel.

 pronounced: he-ZIN (very short "he", where the "e" has an "er" sound)

IDETH—a major House in the Dominion of Aleznuaweite, founded by the legendary archmage Dethiram.

 Present Atriarch: Mere Ideth

 colors: pale green and sky-blue

 pronounced: ih-DETH

ILYN—a minor House in the Dominion of Aleznuaweite founded by Lynath Ilyn; the newest and least of the eight Houses.

 Present Atriarch: Lynath Ilyn

 colors: red and cream

 pronounced: ih-LIN

IMBUEMENT—the art of infusing objects with resonance.

 pronounced: im-BUE-ment

IMOS—a major House in the Dominion of Aleznuaweite, by virtue of its vassal, House Imrell.

 Present Atriarch: Hnan Imos

 colors: yellow and white

 pronounced: ih-MOSS

IMRELL—a minor House in the Dominion of Aleznuaweite founded by Mrellos Imrell; vassal to House Imos.

 Present Atriarch: Chenya Imrell

 colors: orange and white

 pronounced: ihm-RELL

ISHTREL—a bird with very colorful and striking breeding plumage, known for its elaborate courtship displays during mating season.

 pronounced: ISH-trel

ISCA—a minor House in the Dominion of Aleznuaweite.

 colors: dark blue and copper

 pronounced: ih-SCA

ISILC—a major House in the Dominion of Aleznuaweite; its reigning Atriarch, Relk Isilc, is the current Exalted Dominance.

 Present Atriarch: Relk Isilc

 colors: purple and black

 pronounced: ih-SILK

ISONN—a major House in the Dominion of Aleznuaweite.

 colors: dark green and brown

pronounced: ih-SOHN
ISSOLM—a minor House in the Dominion of Aleznuaweite.
colors: white and black
pronounced: ih-SOLM
IWETH-NA—an exile from the Divine Kingdom.
pronounced: ih-WETH-nah

JADE EYE COMPANY—an independent company providing resonance-based security headquartered in Peshawar Yrg.
JHALYX—a large predatory feline, native to the forested regions of the Ngutoccai continent
pronounced: JAH-lix
JENURA—a fisher and seafood hawker; consort to Hemoru and mother of Rahelu.
pronounced: je-NU-rah (with Chanazian "r")
JHOBON—an Imrell-born Supplicant.
pronounced: JOH-bon

KERG—an Isonn deckhand and third mate serving under Csorath Isonn aboard the *Winged Arrow*.
KESHWAR—an Augur and a Dedicate of House Ideth who sponsored Rahelu's Petition; son and heir of Atriarch Mere Ideth and elder brother to Cseryl Ideth.
pronounced: KESH-waar
KEZ—Aleznuaweithish unit of currency, with denominations of copper, silver, and gold.
pronounced: KEZ
KIRAN—an Ilyn-born applicant; cousin to Nheras Ilyn.
pronounced: KIE-ren
KUAL—Aleznuaweithish unit of measurement for distance.
pronounced: cue-AHL (the syllables are often rolled together)
KUATH BAY—small bay of the port city of Ennuost Yrg.
pronounced: cue-ATH
KYROSH—an Isilc-born Supplicant, dubbed Whiplash by Rahelu for his primary weapon. Cousin to Myreil Isilc.
pronounced: KIH-rosh

LHORNE—an Ideth-born Supplicant; nephew of Atriarch Mere Ideth and cousin to Keshwar Ideth and Cseryl Ideth.
pronounced: LORN
Little Fishguts—name given by Nheras to a young gull. See also Nelavonezra.
LYNATH—Atriarch of House Ilyn; grandmother to Nheras Ilyn.

pronounced: lih-NATH

MAGE—a person who primarily earns their living through the use of resonance skills. This is a regulated profession in the Dominion of Aleznuaweite and Chanaz. Mages are required to undergo training with official bodies, complete licensing examinations, and maintain ongoing certifications in order to legally practice.

MAKETH—a Guardian and a Dedicate of House Imos.
  pronounced: ma-KETH

MAL-EK—Free Speech phrase meaning "mine".
  pronounced: MAH-lek

MERE—Atriarch of House Ideth, an archmage and a powerful Augur; mother of Keshwar Ideth and Cseryl Ideth.
  pronounced: MIR (as in "mirror")

MRELLOS—Founder of House Imrell.
  pronounced: m-RELL-os

MYREIL—a Supplicant of House Isilc; daughter and heir to Relk Isilc. Dubbed Precious by Rahelu.
  pronounced: MIHR-reil

NAL-EK—Free Speech phrase meaning "yours".
  pronounced: NAH-lek

NELA—intimate Chanazian term of address for a child, meaning "of my heart".
  pronounced: NEH-lah

NELAN—intimate Chanazian term for younger sibling/charge, meaning "of my heart".
  pronounced: NEH-lan

NELAVONEZRA—Chanazian name given by Rahelu to a young gull, affectionately meaning "little nuisance". See also Little Fishguts.
  pronounced: NEH-lah-voh-NEZ-rah

NGUTOCCAI—name of the continent shared by the Dominion of Aleznuaweite and the Chanazian Federation.
  pronounced: ngu-TOH-kai

NHERAS—an Ilyn-born Supplicant of House Issolm; granddaughter of Atriarch Lynath Ilyn, cousin to Bhemol Ilyn and Kiran Ilyn.
  pronounced: NEH-ras

NHESHWYR—a deadly, venomous snake-like animal.
  pronounced: NEH-shwir

NHORWEN—an Elder of House Imos.
  pronounced: NOR-wen

NIGHT OF SOLACE—a festival celebrating the summer solstice in ship clan tradition.

pronounced: rue-AH-rem
RYSERE—mother of Ylaen Imos.
pronounced: RIH-zeer

SABLE GULL—an inn in Ennuost Yrg's Lowdocks district; see also
Tlareth.
SCARFACE—see Ruan.
SEEKER—a mage specializing in Seeking.
SEEKING—one of the six resonance disciplines taught by the Resonance
Guild; also known as the art of truth-telling.
SHADE—a simulacrum of a person created with Evocation.
SHIP CLANS—mercenary fleets of varying sizes that control the Free
Territories of Abmerdu and the Abmerduan Sea.
SHUALM—a member of the Jade Eye Company.
pronounced: shu-AHLM
SILCAREZ—a legendary archmage and Founder of House Isilc famed for
his exploratory voyages.
pronounced: silk-CAH-rez
SKYMOTHER—deity with dominion over the known, commonly depicted
as a feminine visage in the sky
associations: light, day, harp, lamp, summer, skyarc, knowledge, past,
present, Seeking, Evocation
SNUFFLES—name given to a rat aboard the *Stormbringer's Judgment* by
Elaram.
SOLMORAM—a legendary archmage and Founder of House Issolm.
pronounced: sohl-MOH-ram
SOOTY GULL—a sloop under the command of Alozei Imrell.
SPIRIT ESSENCE—a specific set of know-how, instincts, and skills created
with Evocation.
STARFATHER—deity with dominion over the as-yet unknown
associations: night, chance, stars, stararc, Augury, Fortunement
STORMBANE—see Symezosh.
STORMBRINGER—deity with dominion over sea, lakes, rivers, and other
bodies of water.
associations: water, judgment, spring, storm, stormarc, spear, Projection
STORMBRINGER'S JUDGMENT—a warship belonging to Zovresh and
the flagship of the Crimson Storm.
SPAN—unit of measurement for time. Each arc of the day is divided into
six spans. Spans within an arc are typically numbered from the marker for
that arc, e.g. the first span after sunrise.
SUBORNED—a state of being where an individual's will and consciousness is made subservient to another's through the use of an Imbued

object, typically forged in the shape of a collar or a chain worn around the neck.

SUPPLICANT—a junior rank within the Houses, given to the newest recruits who have been granted permanent membership.

SUURYNN—mother of Elaram and Ghardon Issolm.
 pronounced: SUU-rynn

SUUSRADI—river located south of the city of Ennuost Yrg.
 pronounced: suu-SRAH-dee

SYMEZOSH—a legendary archmage of old Alezuna, also named "Stormbane".
 pronounced: sih-MEH-zosh

TATTERED QUILL—a scrivener's workshop in Ennuost Yrg's Blackforge district; see also Xyuth.

TALOG-TE—Free Speech phrase meaning "deed"
 pronounced: TAH-log-TEY

TILES—a game for four players played with 144 pieces divided into three types of tiles. One game consists of four seasons, with each season consisting of four hands. To win a hand, a player must collect fourteen tiles that typically consist of four melds (either three of a kind, known as a Concordance, or three in a numerical sequence, known as a relay) and a pair. Hands are ranked according to their composition and difficulty of achievement.

 Numbered house tiles (108 total): Four copies of each number from 1 to 9 in three variants of feathers, scales, and blossoms.

 Honor tiles (28 total): Four copies of each of the seven varieties, comprising of the four mages (Seeker, Evoker, Guardian, Harbinger) and three legacies (kez, crystal, blood).

 Blessings (8 total): Unique tiles comprising of the four celestials (sky, earth, storm, stars) and seasons (summer, harvest, spring, winter).

TLARETH—proprietor of the Sable Gull, an inn in Ennuost Yrg's Lowdocks district.
 pronounced: teh-LAH-reth

TOWER—see Conclave.

TSEIRAN—consort to Hzin and mother of Bzel.
 pronounced: SEY-ren

TSENJHE—a common-born Dedicate of House Isca and highly reputed artificer, who hails from the same fishing village as Rahelu. See also Anenje.
 pronounced: SEN-je

TSOJO—river located north of the city of Ennuost Yrg.
 pronounced: SOH-joh

TSOL-AN-MAK—a Free Speech phrase meaning "unbonded".

  pronounced: SOHL-an-MAHK

TSOL-EK—term of address in the Free Speech for the secondary partner in a tsol-bond.

  pronounced: SOHL-eck

TSOL-EK-NA—Free Speech phrase for the partners in a tsol-bond.

  pronounced: SOHL-eck-NAH

TSOL-MAL-EK—an intimate form of partnership practiced by the ship clans of the Free Territories.

  pronounced: SOHL-mah-LECK

TSOL-NA—term of address in the Free Speech for the primary partner in a tsol-bond.

  pronounced: SOHL-nah

TSOL-BOND—a ritual form of partnership practiced by the ship clans of the Free Territories.

  pronounced: SOHL-bond

TSOREK-FA—a city on the largest of the islands in the Abmerduan archipelago.

  pronounced: SOH-reck-FAH

UNNOMOBUNEZRA—Chanazian insult meaning "heartless one".
pronounced: OO-noh-MOH-bu-NEZ-rah

UVESHT-MO—an exile from the Divine Kingdom.

  pronounced: u-VESH-t-mo

VAAQIN—first mate serving under Xya aboard the *Stormbringer's Judgment*. Dubbed One-Ear by Rahelu for his missing left ear.

  pronounced: VAH-keen

VENAZ—intimate Chanazian term of address for elder sister, meaning "of my heart".

  pronounced: VEH-naz

VENORU—a Conclave mage.

  pronounced: veh-NOH-ru

WAR OF THE FIVE DOMINIONS—the period of conflict during which old Aleznua fractured into five regions, which ultimately ended in the establishment of the present-day nations of Aleznuaweite and Chanaz.

WELM—a grain factor in the city of Ennuost Yrg, murdered by Azosh-ek as part of a ritual to open the Endless Gate.

  pronounced: WELM

WHIPLASH—see Kyrosh.

WINGED ARROW—diplomatic flagship of the Dominion of Aleznuaweite, captained by Csorath Isonn.

WYRHOUND—a large breed of domesticated canine, prized for its intelligence, keen nose, and use of Seeking to track its prey.
  pronounced: WIHR-hound

XUUQOSHTALOG-TE—name of a rite sacred to the mage-priests of the Divine Kingdom.
  pronounced: ZUH-kosh-TAH-log-TEY
XYA—acting captain of the *Stormbringer's Judgment*, the flagship of the Crimson Storm, in Zovresh's absence.
  pronounced: ZAI-yah
XYUTH—a scrivener and proprietor of the Tattered Quill in Ennuost Yrg's Blackforge district. Murdered by Azosh-ek and his accomplices.
  pronounced: ZAI-youth

YLAEN—an Imos-born Supplicant, dubbed No-sleeves by Rahelu due to his penchant for cutting the sleeves off his shirts to display his ritual scarring.
  pronounced: ye-LANE (often mispronounced IH-len by Aleznuaweites)

ZOVRESH—the leader of the Crimson Storm.
  pronounced: ZOHV-resh

ACKNOWLEDGMENTS

"It's not your first time anymore," I said. "You've got the world; the characters; the story—it'll be easy as," I said.

Yeah, nah. Writing this sequel just about killed me.

I didn't know this story was gonna be a trilogy in one volume, or that it would take more than two years to wrangle into a form that I am proud to publish. The fact that this book exists and that my sanity remains (mostly) intact, is due to my indomitable writing group and alpha readers: JP Weaver, Ivy C. Kendall, Caitlin L. Strauss, AJ Lambert, Dan Harris, Machine Capybara, and Leon W-K.

Special thanks to my beta readers, especially to those who got this book piecemeal, months apart, because I was that behind on writing it: Rohan Bassett, Angela Boord, Will Greatwich, John Jones, Rebecca Lai, K. T. Lyn, Del Sefton, Tim T. Wong.

Eternal gratitude to my early champions who took a chance on *Petition* and loved it enough to tell the world: Łukasz Przywoski (u/barb4ry1), Jamedi (JamReads), Krystle Matar, Blaise Ancona (Under the Radar SFF Books), Dom McDermott (Dominish Books), Isabelle (The Shaggy Shepherd), Taylor (Maed Between the Pages), Kris Marchesi (The Fictional Escapist).

To my heroes, who give me strong examples to follow: Janny Wurts, Helen Lowe, Seth Dickinson, Sascha Stronach, Will Wight—I still can't believe you know I exist, and that you've repeatedly taken the time to give me advice, encouragement, and shout-outs.

To my infinitely patient family: I love you.

A word of apology: the most sailing I've ever done is catch a ferry or go for a leisurely cruise. Credit for any verisimilitude of nautical life goes to Tom Cunliffe, Sampson Boat Co, José Salvador Alvarenga for his story and Jonathan Franklin who wrote it down, *The Tall Ship Chronicles* documentary, and too many others to list here. All errors and inaccuracies are mine.

TO MY WONDERFUL KICKSTARTER BACKERS

The *Supplicant* Kickstarter project has succeeded beyond my wildest hopes and it would not have been possible without each and every single one of you: Adam Nemo, Alexandra Corrsin, Andrea Tolu, Angela Boord, Angus McLennan, Annarose Willhite, Arden Tse, Ashley Capes, B. Plaga, Betsy Hanes Perry, Blaise Ancona, Brett H, Brian Adler, Bryan K., Buddhima R, Carl Ferlay, Carl Spitzer, Chase McGlinchey, Cherelle H, Cheryl Ruckel, Claire J, Cora Nicole, Corbin Igoe, Cortney Babcock, Darragh Kelly, David Scoggins, Deborah A Torrance, Derrick Hill, Dylan Harney, Edgar D. Rodriguez, El McInerney, Elaine W, Elisha X. Eshoo, Emma Adams, Francesca Frezza, Gee Rothvoss, George Lundie, Graham Dauncey, Hampus Lind, Heiko Koenig, In loving memory of Basil Martin, J.C. Snow, James R McGinnis Jr, Jan B, Jared, Jeffrey E. Parker, Jennifer Osterman, Jesper D, Jessica A. McMinn, Josh & Ashley Bossie, Joshua Villines, K. Hegedus, Katherine Malloy, Katrina Gilles, Kirsten Johnson, Kris Marchesi, Kupo, Kyle Dawson, L.L. MacRae, Lead Out in Cuffs, Lindsay Popowski, Lisa Herrick, Lisa L., Madge Watson, Max G, Melissa St-Pierre, Melissa T, Michael H., Michael Kirschenman, Mike Urban, Mitchell Hogan, phoenix17, Pull_Out_Queen, Qavee, quail, Quinn Giguiere, Rari Rajesh, Raymond Giroux, rg9400, Ricardo Monascal,

Richard Ulmont Campbell, Rick Gagné, Rob Stacey, Rocco, Roderick Huizing, Rohan Bassett, Rosa Thill, Russ Isler, Ryan H., Ryan Kirk, Ryan Tucker, Samantha Newberry, Seihera Emiko Asao, Shane Boyce, Simon Emmerson, SKPM, Stephanie Suber, Stephen W. Buchanan, Syazana Amirulmokminin, Tatiana Obey, Tim Hardie, Toby G, Vehvis, Vid Lenarcic, Virginia McClain, Wilfredo J. Villafañe Ortiz, William Ryan, Yvonne Richardson, Zachary Karry, and Zeth.

Thank you for joining me on this incredible journey.

ABOUT DELILAH WAAN

I am a literal bookworm who alphabetically devours my way through the shelves at my local library.

My preferred diet is epic fantasy—full of complex intrigue, morally ambiguous characters, and tragic ends—though I do enjoy the occasional quippy, fast-paced action-adventure. (Sappy romances, however, give me indigestion.)

When I'm not binge-reading the next doorstopper on my TBR list or engaging in frantic theory crafting in between Brandon Sanderson and Will Wight book releases, I like to spit bars in my best Angelica Schuyler impression and walk my cat.

bsky.app/profile/delilahwaan.bsky.social

instagram.com/delilahwaan

youtube.com/@delilahwaan

facebook.com/delilahwaan

x.com/DelilahWaan

amazon.com/author/delilahwaan

goodreads.com/delilahwaan

bookbub.com/authors/delilah-waan